Shadow Assa

Cyndi Fr

Book Four: Fallen Star

When a devastating accident ends Jillian's dancing career, she thinks her life is over. Then a gorgeous man, claiming to be her alien protector, offers to heal her injuries. She has nothing to lose by trusting him and everything to gain. But trust doesn't come easy for Jillian.

Odintar has never met a woman as captivating as Jillian. He's lived life on the fringes, tolerated yet never truly accepted. Desire ignites between them with the first brush of his hands. He was sent to protect and heal her, but he wants so much more. Their enemies are closing in and Jillian is more deeply involved than either of them realize. Secrets loom and past mistakes twist current circumstances. And through it all the only constant is their consuming desire for each other.

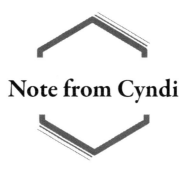

Note from Cyndi

This is book four in a six-book series, so I figured it was time to offer a quick review. Shadow Assassins are genetically enhanced super soldiers who were created at the height of the Ontarian Great Conflict. The war on Ontariese ends and the Shadow Assassins are forced to disband. Most of the men transition well into Ontarian society, but the hunters, powerful leaders who are used to making their own rules, find this new way of life intolerable. So they make an alliance with Sevrin Keire, a ruthless royal from the planet Rodymia.

Sevrin brings the hunters to Earth, promising them everything they had on Ontariese and more. However, they are merely pawns in her much larger plan. Sevrin is obsessed with the possibility of being able to manipulate magic and she believes Shadow Assassins are the key to her long-awaited success. Each Shadow Assassin triggers a metamorphosis in his female when he claims her as mate. Sevrin believes this change can also be used to transfer the Shadow Assassin's paranormal abilities to the female. If she can identify then reproduce the trigger mechanism, it will bring her one step closer to her ultimate goal of controlling magic.

A team called the Mystic Militia is sent from Ontariese to apprehend the Shadow Assassins. They soon network with a human taskforce, but Sevrin and her hunters remain one step ahead of the Ontarians and their human allies.

As *Fallen Star* begins, five of the Shadow Assassins have been captured and returned to Ontariese. The Mystic Militia has learned of the Rodyte involvement and a notebook filled with information about potential mates for the hunters has been recovered. Unfortunately, there are over two hundred women listed in the notebook so the Mystic Militia can't possibly protect them all.

The hunters are restless and frustrated by Sevrin's broken promises. They came to Earth in search of freedom and to preserve the only life they've ever known. Tension mounts within the alliance and the Mystic Militia draws closer every day.

I can't say more without revealing what happens in this book. I hope the mini-review helps and that you enjoy Odintar and Jillian's story. Happy reading!

Prologue

Sevrin Keire shifted her weight from one foot to the other and slid her hands down her thighs. Had she always been a voyeur or had the demands of her massive project created this hunger in her? The couple she observed sprawled on a rumpled bed in the shabby motel room adjacent to hers. Their wrestling match had finally ended and the man was enthusiastically claiming his prize. The woman was on her stomach, hips elevated by a stack of pillows. Her hands were bound by a velvet rope as the man thrust into her from behind. She looked dazed, flushed, utterly conquered, yet each of his strokes dragged a louder cry of pleasure from her throat.

Glancing at her companion, Sevrin felt a fresh wave of heat pass through her body. Nazerel watched the scene with stoic detachment. His tall muscular body remained tense and alert while his rugged features revealed nothing. As usual. She'd never encountered a more closely guarded person in her life.

"Did you install the observation window or was it here when you leased the complex?" His deep voice was as expressionless as his face. The "complex" was an aging motel in an unsavory part of downtown Las Vegas. But if things went as planned, she wouldn't be trapped in this hovel for much longer. She had better, much more comfortable accommodations lined up. They just weren't quite ready yet.

"We found the rooms just like this. You can see in from this side, but it looks like a large mirror from the other side." He only nodded, so she shifted her gaze back to the entwined couple as a different sort of question echoed through her mind. What would it feel like to be pinned beneath Nazerel, a willing captive to his aggressive desires? Her pulse quickened every time she thought about being the focus of Nazerel's need, his obsessive passion. He was the strongest, most powerful Shadow Assassin and she was project leader, not to mention a member of Rodymia's royal family. A match between them had seemed obvious, at least to her. Yet he'd made it clear from the start that he had no intention of sharing her bed. Even after two months, and several lovers, the rejection still stung.

Shrugging aside the tangent, she returned her focus to the couple in the adjacent room. It had taken four days of continual seduction for the Shadow Assassin to subdue his potential mate. He'd wooed her with a dizzying combination of forceful control and tenderness until she'd finally succumb to his will. He'd used every trick in the book and some Sevrin had never imagined, but one thing had been clear from the beginning. He would not stop until he attained his goal. It had just been a matter of time.

Shadow Assassins were predators, bred for, and conditioned with, ruthless focus to accomplish any given task. And Sevrin was responsible for the Shadow Assassins. Not for their existence or their remarkable abilities, but for their presence here on Earth.

After their underground hideout had been found and their secret society dismantled, the Shadow Assassins had grown restless and discontent on their home world of Ontariese. They wanted to live by their own rules and hunt for their mates as they had for generations. Sevrin simply brought a select few to a place where that was still possible. All she asked in return was that they allowed her to study their unique ability to trigger metamorphosis in their potential mates.

It had been her original hope to identify the various components of the physiological process then replicate it in a lab. Unfortunately, her scientists hadn't been able to duplicate the reaction, so she was stuck with live test subjects. At least for now. She'd had to contend with multiple setbacks, but she would never surrender her dream. One day she would possess paranormal abilities or she would die trying to attain them.

"When was she captured?" Nazerel looked at her, lust making his dark eyes shine. He wasn't as unaffected by this as he appeared. She started to answer then he made a strangled sound and staggered back a step. "What the—" He shook his head, eyes tightly shut as he muttered something under his breath.

She looked around, unsure what had caused the odd reaction. They were alone in the motel room and the scene they were observing was nothing they hadn't seen before, repeatedly. "Are you all right?"

Before Nazerel could answer, Lor dar Joon, leader of the Mystic Militia, and one of his men materialized right in front of them. Without warning, the unfamiliar Mystic launched an energy pulse directly into Nazerel's face. He screamed, frantically blinking and shaking his head. Lor lunged for Nazerel, but Nazerel anticipated the attack and twisted out of reach. Then Nazerel shoved the first Mystic out of his way and grabbed her so fast and hard that she cried out.

Reality exploded in a burst of acceleration. Her breath escaped in a useless whoosh as they materialized in the desert. She didn't even have time to inhale before Nazerel set them in motion again.

The second jump was longer, yet smoother, easier to tolerate. Images focused for an instant then stretched into distorted, shadowy shapes. It didn't matter where he was taking her. Without his quick reflexes and exceptional range, she would be a prisoner of Lor dar Joon and his Mystic Militia right now.

That had been close, way too close.

Trembling with excitement and fear, Sevrin clung to Nazerel. His arms felt strong, his body long and lean pressed against hers. Many nights in the past two months she'd imagined what it would feel like to be embraced by him, touched and tasted by him. He would be a fierce lover, no tender seduction for Nazerel. No, he would stalk his mate with obsessive intensity and then claim her with consuming heat. And she wanted to be his prey so badly it was driving her insane!

They materialized in the darkened corner of her warehouse headquarters. He'd effortlessly teleported through the shields, a feat of which she hadn't realized he was capable. How often had he let himself in and nosed around without her being aware of his presence? This breach should have set off alarms and brought guards running from all directions.

His face was red, especially around his eyes. "Are you all right?" Despite her annoyance, the question slipped out in a breathy whisper. Other than the mild discoloration, he seemed unharmed. "How did they find us?"

He released her so suddenly she stumbled back. "Angie was in my head," he growled out the statement, clearly agitated by the realization. His features were naturally strong, but he looked deadly right now. "How did she acquire such skill in so short a time?"

"How did you flash past my safeguards?" she countered, all thoughts of sex evaporating beneath the heat of her temper. "Have you done this before?" Having a reluctant ally was one thing. She would not tolerate betrayal of any kind.

"She was in my head." He stressed each word as if she hadn't heard him the first time. "How did a human develop Mystic abilities in a few short days?"

"She's only half human. You knew she had latent abilities; that's why you wanted her so badly. Why are you surprised?" She crossed her arms over her chest and glared up at him. "Now answer my—"

"*Latent* abilities. Abilities that should have taken months, even years, to cultivate." He began to pace, obviously having no intention of indulging her curiosity.

"We need to send backup for the others. There had to have been more than just the two we saw. Lor would never attack without his entire team. He's not that reckless."

"It's too late," Nazerel dismissed. "Anyone who didn't flash out by now is beyond our reach."

He was probably right, but she was annoyed by his callous attitude. "I'm going to send a car over just in case someone managed to hide and avoid—"

"Shadow Assassins don't hide. We don't retreat. We meet danger head-on."

Rather than argue with him, she tried to step past him. He blocked her path.

"This is the second time the Mystics have almost instantaneously turned a helpless human into a threat." He collared her throat with one long-fingered hand, exerting just enough pressure to restrain her without cutting off her air. "Tell me how they're doing it."

She grabbed his wrist with both hands and glared into his eyes. "I don't know any more than you do." It was unlikely he'd strangle her, but she had no doubt he would cause her pain. She couldn't decide if the realization intimidated or excited her.

"We're supposed to be partners, yet you've fed me nothing but lies and half-truths ever since I arrived on this planet."

"When have I lied?" She kept her voice even as she stubbornly met his gaze.

"You've twisted the truth and kept vital information from me. That's the same thing." His fingers tensed then relaxed without releasing her. "You didn't just locate these women once we'd agreed to work with you. I can't figure out how, but you were responsible for their... The information you've complied on each woman goes back long before the Shadow Maze was liberated. Why have the Rodytes been watching these females?"

Everything really would be easier if Nazerel became a true ally. Trusting him with certain details was dangerous, but keeping him in the dark had only led to frustration for both of them. "Can we go downstairs and discus this like civilized people or should we—"

He slammed her back against the wall and leaned in close. "I haven't decided if I'm going to let you live. Start talking."

Never one to respond well to threats, she clenched her teeth and stared past him mutinously. His fingers tightened again and still she remained silent. Flickers of light danced before her eyes. Panic sent frantic impulses skittering through her body. Before she could act on them, his fingers gradually loosened and she sucked air back into her lungs. He couldn't kill her and they both knew it. Like it or not he still needed her.

He grasped one of her wrists with his free hand and guided it between their bodies. "Is this what you want?" He pressed her fingers against the considerable bulge in the front of his jeans.

Her gaze snapped back to his and then narrowed. Her first instinct was to caress him, to encourage his unexpected strategy. She'd wanted him ever since she saw him and ached for him still. Even so, her pride wouldn't let her give in. "You'll be my whore if I tell you about the project? Is that what you're offering me?" He snarled and scrambled back just as she knew he would. "I don't barter with my body. I hadn't realized you did."

"I'm nobody's whore." He crossed his arms over his chest, feet planted far apart, the picture of indignant male. "Tell me about the project because I can't protect my people if I don't understand the situation. I've had enough of hints and innuendos. How long have Rodytes been on Earth and what are their plans for these women?"

He'd said Rodytes as if it were something toxic. She should be insulted; after all, her father once ruled the planet and her uncle ruled there still. Instead, she wrestled with the possibilities for another moment, then took a deep breath and told him how it all began.

Chapter One

The Bunker, Arizona
    Two weeks later

Odintar Voss shifted in his chair, too restless to contain his movements. Another briefing. How could these people waste so much time talking? His jaw clenched as he fought to maintain his calm expression. He sat between Lor and Blayne on one side of a large conference table. Elias faced them and Morgan presided over the meeting from the head of the table.

"Am I boring you?" Morgan's sharp question snapped his wandering mind back to the present. How a beautiful woman could sound so authoritative, Odintar hadn't quite figured out. But Morgan had a way about her. She was obviously comfortable with the power she wielded, yet she still managed to appear distractingly feminine. With flame-red hair and intense blue eyes, she drew attention without even trying, but being memorable could be a disadvantage for a Black Ops agent.

"No disrespect, Director," he muttered, "but we've been here over an hour and you've yet to say anything we didn't already know." The observation earned him a warning glare from Lor and a smirk from Blayne. His comrades had to be as impatient as he was. They were just better at playing the game.

"If you have important things to do, skip the next briefing and have one of the others fill you in on what we discussed." Her brows arched as she turned back to the diagram displayed on the massive monitor inset in the far wall. Then she went on as if his attitude hadn't disrupted her speech. "This is the section I'm proposing. It's secluded enough from the rest of the compound to offer privacy and it's not currently in use."

Networking with the human taskforce had given the Mystic Militia access to information and resources they badly needed. On the other hand, quadrupling the number of people involved in their mission increased the risk of discovery and inevitably slowed everything down. Odintar was still debating whether or not cooperation was a fair exchange. And now Lor was considering moving their operation into the humans' facility. Granted the Bunker offered amenities not available on their ship, but it left them at the mercy of the humans. And Odintar refused to be beholding to anyone.

"It will be nice to have private quarters again," Lor told her. "My men have been tripping over each other ever since we left Ontariese."

That much was certainly true. The cabins on the ship were tiny and most were shared, making the limited space even more confining. Still, how well did they know these humans? High Queen Charlotte had assured Lor that Morgan could be trusted and the human's actions thus far had reinforced the claim. Even so, Odintar remained wary.

He looked at the floor plan Morgan was referencing. The Bunker was much larger than he'd realized, or had been allowed to see. A small above-ground storage unit created the illusion of insignificance, while three subterranean levels spread out below. How many people did Morgan command? A compound this size could accommodate hundreds. There was so much about the human operation they simply didn't know.

"What will we do with the ship?" Blayne asked. "We can't leave her unattended even if she's shielded."

"I've emptied the largest of our hangers. It will be a tight fit, but I'm sure you can manage. The choice is entirely up to you. If you'd rather leave things as they are, I understand." She glanced at Odintar and a faint smile curved her lips. "Now Elias will explain the new developments."

Odintar hadn't been aware that there were new developments. He straightened and scooted closer to the table as his attention shifted to Morgan's lieutenant. With a muscular build, short dark hair, and sharp assessing gaze, everything about Elias Bartram screamed military. They had only interacted a couple of times, but Odintar found Elias surprisingly competent for an ungifted human.

"The new safe house is operational," Elias began. "It's designed to be used as a remote headquarter and we believe the shield generator is finally producing a field dense enough to prevent even Shadow Assassins from sensing what goes on inside."

"At the risk of sounding rude..." Odintar started.

"As if that's ever bothered you before." Blayne snickered, the humor in his silver eyes keeping the comment light.

"Where did humans get tech advanced enough to block Shadow Assassins. We have to reinforce our shields with Mystic energy or they can sense us."

Elias glanced at Morgan. She nodded and the soldier grinned. "How much do you know about Operation Hydra?"

Shocked by the question, Odintar looked at Lor. The events surrounding Operation Hydra had the highest security rating. How had humans in this era learned of events that took place nearly two centuries into their future? His commander looked as confused as he was, so Odintar turned back to Elias. "How the hell do *you* know about Operation Hydra?"

He'd been looking at Elias when he spoke, but Morgan answered the question. "When High Queen Charlotte first established an alliance with Earth's leaders, one of the terms was full disclosure. We needed to know how often Ontarians had been to Earth and what they were doing while they were here. Now tell us what you know. It will verify the information we were given."

If the knowing gleam in her eyes was justified, she knew more about the subject than he did. Still, he saw no reason to object. "Dr. Hydran was the human responsible for imprisoning and experimenting on Ontarians. Several of High Queen Charlotte's relatives were among his captives."

Elias nodded. "He was also responsible for the technology integrated into Saebin's body armor."

The technology he was referring to was incorporated into more than Saebin's body armor. Saebin, the Overlord's life mate, had munitions and sensory implants so integrated into her body that they couldn't be removed. "Those technologies are from Earth's future. Doesn't Earth have laws preventing their use?"

"Yes and no." Elias chuckled. "The attitude of the current administration is to fight fire with fire. We're allowed to utilize advanced technologies when we're battling those with similar technologies. I think you would agree that any and all technologies are necessary when dealing with the Shadow Assassins."

"What other toys does this safe house provide?" Lor's expression remained tense and watchful. "Could Shadow Assassins be incarcerated there? It would be a definite advantage if we didn't have to take each one back to Ontariese for interrogation."

"As it happens, there are four detention cells in the basement of the safe house. We believe they prevent teleportation, but for obvious reasons, we've been unable to test them," Morgan explained.

"You want one of us to test drive your detention cells?" Suspicion spiked through Odintar. Was this a clever ploy to...to what? Why was he so doubtful of these humans? They had done nothing to earn his mistrust. In fact, just the opposite was true. They had been helpful, honest and supportive every step of the way.

Obviously sensing his doubt, Morgan suggested, "Why don't two of you go over there with Elias. One can protect the other while he's helpless, at least we hope to make him helpless."

"That's not necessary," Blayne said. "I'll test the containment for you."

"Wonderful. If it works, we'll begin retrofitting the detention cells here. Shadow Assassins aren't the only ones who have been a challenge to contain." When no one had anything to add, she said, "Well then, I'll leave you to it. Despite what Odintar obviously thinks, I don't spend my days in meetings." She pushed back her chair and stood. "Let me know what you decide about moving in. There are a few more arrangements I need to make if you take me up on the offer."

Lor nodded and she left the conference room.

"What the hell is wrong with you?" Lor flared as soon as the door closed behind her. "I've never seen you be so disrespectful to anyone who didn't deserve it."

The qualification made Odintar smile. Respecting authority figures simply because they were in authority was definitely not his strong suit. "When something seems too good to be true, it usually is."

"We're not doing this out of the kindness of our hearts," Elias stressed. "We have the most to lose by letting the Shadow Assassins roam free. They came here to hunt our women. Do you honestly think we'll sit back and let others try to shut them down? They've invaded our space and endangered our females. It's our responsibility to neutralize the threat."

"You're right." Odintar didn't often make mistakes, but he was willing to admit when he did. "We're working toward the same goal. My mistrust is inappropriate."

"Suspicion can keep you sharp. Just don't let it take over."

Odintar nodded in agreement with Lor's point then added, "I'll apologize to Morgan."

"We're still waiting for the translation of the notebook. Are you finished with it yet?" Elias asked after a brief pause.

The notebook, just the thought of it made Odintar cringe. Like some ruthless madam, Sevrin Keire had composed detailed dossiers on potential mates for the Shadow Assassins. Elias found a copy of the notorious collection during the raid on Team North's house, one of four Shadow Assassin hideouts. "I'm finished with the translation, but it wasn't as helpful as we'd hoped. The first thirty-six entries were detailed, the information easily understood. The other entries are still encoded. Without some sort of key, the entries are basically meaningless."

"How many entries are there?" Blayne asked.

"Almost three hundred."

That seemed to shock Elias. "There are three hundred Ontarian hybrid females on Earth? How is that possible?"

"We don't know that they're all half Ontarian," Lor said. "It's possible that other factors landed them in the notebook."

Odintar hated to argue with his commander, but on this particular subject Odintar happened to be an expert. "It's equally possible that there are even more. There were twelve renegades on the loose for roughly three years and each was intentionally trying to impregnate human females. One pregnancy per week per renegade brings the total to 576 hybrid children. And that estimate is probably too conservative."

"Not if we factor in how many of the pregnancies would have been carried to term," Bryce added. "Few of the females would have welcomed the news once they realized they were carrying a child. Besides, that estimate calculates pregnancies not female offspring."

"Wait." Curiosity flared in Elias' gaze. "What are you talking about?" Apparently Odintar hadn't been the only one hesitant to divulge secrets to their human counterparts. "What renegades? This was done deliberately?"

"Not by us," Lor assured. "We're not sure when or why the renegades went out on their own, but they broke every rule in the program by doing so."

"What program? This is the first I've heard about any of this. Does Morgan know?"

Lor hesitated, likely debating how much to explain. "We've only just confirmed the connection, so I haven't shared the details with Morgan."

"I'll fill her in. Tell me what you were talking about."

It was an order and Odintar watched Lor closely, waiting for him to object. Master-level Mages didn't respond well to orders.

Rather than refuse, Lor tensed, paused for a moment then complied. It was obvious Lor intended to build a solid alliance with these humans. It was likely Odintar would have no choice but to do the same.

"As a result of the Great Conflict," Lor began, "the gender ratio on Ontariese is disproportionately male."

"I'm aware, but I thought the ratio had improved in recent years. The Great Conflict ended over a hundred years ago."

"We've made significant strides, but the problem lingers."

Frustrated by Lor's generalization, Odintar took over. If they were going to fill Elias in, then fill him in. This didn't need to be a two-hour conversation. "Thirty years ago the Ontarian Joint Council reluctantly agreed to let carefully screened Ontarian men recruit human females as life mates. Each man had to establish a connection with the female before he revealed anything about his origins."

"Were the females told once the 'connection' was made?" Elias narrowed his eyes, obviously uncomfortable with the implications.

"Of course they were told," Lor stressed.

"Full disclosure was supposed to take place before the relationship became intimate, but many of the men found it easier to convince their female to leave their homeworld after they were lovers," Odintar elaborated.

"The women were taken back to Ontariese?" Elias still looked annoyed.

Odintar nodded. "Risk of discovery was too great if the couple remained on Earth."

"What happened to the women who refused to leave but had already been told about Ontariese?" Annoyance hardened to disapproval as Elias waited for the answer.

Lor remained silent, so Odintar continued. "The men were careful not to leave anything that could substantiate the story. Even if the women told others that they had been dating an alien, who would believe them?"

Elias looked at him, a bit of the anger easing from his expression. "And these twelve renegades came to Earth as part of this program?"

After another nod, Odintar explained, "They called themselves the Dirty Dozen. At first their supervisor thought they'd found females who didn't want to leave Earth because they'd disabled their tracker chips and gone off the grid. It wasn't until stories about their antics began to circulate that he asked for help retrieving them."

"You said they were on their own for three years. How did they elude capture for so long?"

"The details aren't important," Odintar dismissed impatiently. He'd led the retrieval team and the entire mission had been a disaster. There was no reason to dredge up all that pain. "Numerous mistakes were made that allowed them to operate for much too long. It's history and it can't be undone. All that matters now is that we're dealing with the fallout of their misbehavior."

Elias accepted the statement with a stiff nod. "How do you know any of the females listed in the notebook are the result of the renegades?"

"A DNA test identified Tori and Angie's father as one of the renegades," Lor answered.

"They're the only two we've been able to confirm," Blayne added, "but it's a logical assumption that the majority of these females have latent abilities."

"What happened to the renegades?"

"They were rounded up and returned to Ontariese," Odintar obliged even though he'd tried to end the topic.

"Their leader is believed to be dead," Blayne countered. "But there is a small possibility he's still out there."

"Which brings us back to the present," Lor concluded. "Jillian is scheduled to be discharged from the hospital tomorrow. We need to decide what to do with her."

Jillian. Odintar sighed. He'd spent way too much time in the past two weeks thinking about the unfortunate human. He'd been sent to guard her after Angie's vision identified Jillian as Nazerel's next target. Not wanting to upset her or explain his presence in her room, Odintar had remained shielded from view during his twelve-day vigil. He'd watched her interact with visitors and medical personnel, putting on a brave façade for their benefit. Yet when she was alone, or thought she was alone, anguish and hopelessness pulsed from her in tangible waves. Her vulnerability incited his protectiveness. He wanted to comfort and heal her, help her rediscover her purpose in life.

"It's pretty obvious Nazerel is waiting for her to recover before he makes his move," Blayne pointed out. "Shouldn't we leave well enough alone?"

"There's another option," Odintar struggled to keep his tone light, yet his pulse thudded through his veins. "I could heal her and equip her for the battle to come. She doesn't need to remain helpless." Three sets of eyes focused squarely on him. Elias looked doubtful, Blayne amused, and Lor thoughtful. Their reactions were so in character that it made Odintar smile. "We know she's in Nazerel's sights, which means ignorance isn't an option. And if she knows about us, there's no reason to subject her to any more human healing." He let sarcasm emphasize the last word.

"Were you able to sense what her abilities are?" Lor asked, his brows still drawn together.

He shook his head. "She's very guarded. I was afraid she'd feel a scan powerful enough to penetrate her mental shields."

Lor rubbed his chin and stared past Odintar, obviously lost in thought. "If only you could restore her health without Nazerel realizing what you'd done." His turquoise gaze returned to Odintar's face as he added, "It would make one hell of a surprise if he came to collect a wounded kitten and found a lioness in her place."

"You could use the safe house," Elias suggested. "It would be a great trial run."

Lor shook his head, but the gears were obviously still turning inside his mind. "It would still look suspicious if she just disappeared."

"We could hire someone who could pass for Jillian," Blayne offered. "A leggy blonde shouldn't be too hard to find in a town full of showgirls."

"What if Nazerel snatches the double?" Elias looked less enthusiastic about the concept than the others.

"It would only take me a day or two to heal Jillian and another few to unleash her abilities. She would still need training, but if we leave her at the mercy of human medicine it will be months before she'll be able to walk again, much less defend herself."

Blayne nodded then reinforced Odintar's position. "The double will be safe as long as Nazerel thinks she's still helpless. Shadow Assassins have to take on a worthy opponent or there is no satisfaction in the victory."

"A double will only work from a distance," Lor mused without dismissing the idea entirely. "If Nazerel or one of his men scans the double, they'd easily detect the difference."

"Even if they discovered the switch, it would be unlikely they'd harm the double. An ungifted human isn't a worthy opponent and any action they take at this point risks us finding them."

Odintar had no idea why Blayne was helping him sell the idea, but he was grateful for the backup. Besides, the suggestions sounded less desperate coming from Blayne.

Lor went back to rubbing his chin as he mulled over the possibilities. "The Shadow Assassins have been laying low since our raid on the motel. It's almost as if they're hoping we'll forget about them."

"Or they're waiting for reinforcements." Elias shifted his gaze from one Mystic to the others, his hazel eyes narrowed and assessing. "Morgan is starting to wonder if they're preparing to leave Las Vegas."

"We need to draw them out," Lor concluded. "A miraculously restored Jillian could be the perfect ploy."

"Jillian will have to be told the truth if you intend to heal her, but what do we tell the double?" Elias asked. "She has to be aware that there's significant danger, yet we can't tell her the truth."

The tension in Odintar's chest increased as they moved closer to a viable plan. He wasn't sure why Jillian had affected him so deeply, but he couldn't shake the longing. He wanted to help her, no, he *needed* to help her, to see hope reignite within her eyes. "We tell the double that Jillian is being stalked by an obsessed fan. She's at a serious disadvantage because of her injury, so we're hiring a double to take her place. The double will only be pretending to be hurt, and she'll be heavily guarded, so she'll be in far less danger than Jillian."

"Simple, clean and close enough to the truth to be believable." Lor nodded. "I like it."

"We can have Tori drive the double to Jillian's apartment while Angie brings Jillian to you," Blayne suggested. "Jillian will accept the truth more easily from someone she knows."

"You'll need to teleport in with Jillian," Elias told Odintar. "Even with a decoy, we can't risk leading the Shadow Assassins to the safe house."

Odintar nodded, no longer able to conceal his smile. "Not a problem. I'll work out the details with Angie. Expect us tomorrow afternoon."

JILLIAN RESTED HER hand on the hinged brace confining her right leg and stared out the car window. "Are you sure you know where you're going? This is one screwy way to get to my apartment." She didn't want to sound ungrateful, but she was anxious to get home and drug herself into oblivion. She'd grown accustomed to the pain in the three weeks since her accident. The throbbing never went away completely, but most of the time she could simply ignore it. The pain meds gave her a few hours of peace from the gaping emptiness that had become her future.

"I have an errand to run first. Hope that's okay. It shouldn't take too long."

The tension in Angie's voice made Jillian turn her head. Angie stared straight ahead, both hands firmly gripping the steering wheel. "It's fine. I appreciate the ride. It would have cost half a week's salary to take a cab and who knows when I'll see another paycheck."

Angie glanced at her and smiled, but the smile didn't reach her eyes. "Isn't the show covering your expenses? It's the least they can do, if you ask me. They're damn lucky you don't sue them."

The thought had crossed her mind more than once, but everyone involved had followed safety procedures. It would have felt better if she had someone to blame, but the show hadn't been negligent. A rope snapped and a section of scenery toppled. She'd just been standing in the wrong place at the wrong time.

"Worker's Comp is coving the medical bills. I was told there will be some sort of stipend to compensate for lost wages, but it only runs the length of my existing contract and I was about to renew. So I have five weeks to find a new job and I won't even be off crutches that soon." Actually she had five weeks to find a new occupation and dancing was all she knew.

"This has to be so frustrating for you," Angie's voice turned soft and sad. "But I might be able to offer a glimmer of hope."

Unable to stomach another pitying look, Jillian turned back to the window. They were traveling southeast on I-95, heading out of town. Where the hell was this errand taking them? She shifted position as the discomfort in her leg became more persistent.

"I'm going to tell you a story," Angie began a few minutes later. "You'll probably think I'm nuts until Odintar heals your leg, but everything I'm about to say is true."

"Until who does what to my leg?" She turned back around. Was Angie trying to be funny? She was failing miserably.

"Blayne and Lor aren't from another country. They're from a planet called Ontariese."

Jillian laughed as their images popped into her mind. One blond, one dark-haired, each compelling in his own way. She'd been surprised when Tori strolled into her hospital room with Lor, then a few days later Angie showed up with a new boyfriend as well. Jillian had thought it odd, yet wished them well. The sisters had survived years of tragedy and uncertainty. It was time for a little happiness. "They're both attractive, I'll admit, but they looked pretty human to me."

"They've made adjustments to their appearances so they don't draw too much attention. Aren't you curious why they're here?"

Another chuckle escaped as Jillian looked at Angie. "Because Earth girls are easy?" Jillian spent more time with Tori than Angie. Still, she knew Angie well enough to anticipate outlandish behavior. This seemed bizarre, even for Angie.

"They're chasing a group of fugitives called Shadow Assassins."

"Wow. That sounds ominous. Hope they catch them soon."

"I know you don't believe me, but you will. So pay attention."

Semi-amused by Angie's strange attempt to cheer her up, Jillian pivoted toward her and said, "Go on. I'm listening."

"The leader of the Shadow Assassins is called Nazerel and he's targeted you. It's likely he would have captured you by now if it weren't for your accident. Shadow Assassins are all about the hunt. No prize is worth having if they don't have to work for it."

Rather than laugh off the twisting tale, Jillian just nodded. Angie's imagination was impressive.

"Still, Nazerel won't be put off forever. He wants you and he will come for you as soon as you're stronger."

"So it's in my best interest to take as long as I can to recover?"

Angie winced. That was obviously not the conclusion she'd wanted Jillian to draw. "That's one possible strategy. Another is to be ready for the confrontation."

A tingle slid down Jillian's spine and her pulse gave an erratic leap. She saw no hint of amusement in Angie's gaze. Had the men done something to her? She either honestly believed this nonsense or she deserved an Academy Award. "This isn't funny. My leg is really starting to hurt. I want you to take me home."

Angie pressed her lips together and remained silent for several minutes. Then she sighed and continued with renewed conviction. "You're never going to believe everything that's going on, so let's focus on you. What have the doctors told you about your leg?"

"You know what they said," Jillian snapped, no longer willing to indulge Angie's irrationality. "They were able to save my leg so they consider themselves successful. However, I have at least three more surgeries to look forward to and months, perhaps years, of physical therapy. I'll be lucky if I can walk without a cane and I will never dance again."

"What if you could change that diagnosis? What would you be willing to risk?"

"It can't be changed so what's the point of this conversation?" Angie rubbed her eyes and pressed back against the headrest as she tried in vain to find a more comfortable position. "I don't have the energy for the 'what if' game."

"This isn't a game. Odintar can heal you." She waited until Jillian looked at her then added, "I know his power is real. He healed me."

She sounded so sincere, so matter-of-fact. It was hard not to believe her. "What was wrong with you?" Her leg pulsed, echoing her agitated heartbeat.

"I was seriously injured during a fight with Nazerel. If it hadn't been for Odintar, I would have died."

Angie looked at Jillian so often it was making her nervous. And Angie's earnest expression was burrowing through Jillian's disbelief. "Watch the road. I'd rather not be in another accident." Angie obediently switched her gaze back to the highway and Jillian sighed. Healers didn't exist. Angie might think this was harmless fun, but this game was just plain mean.

"Your disbelief is understandable. I wouldn't believe me either, but you need to know that Odintar is a trusted friend and coworker. He won't hurt you and he will heal you. At least let him try. What do you have to lose?"

Hope flickered in the distance, mocking her. This was so unfair. "Where are we going? My apartment is way back there."

"I'm taking you to Odintar. He'll take you to a safe house equipped with shields that will prevent the Shadow Assassins from locating you."

The Shadow Assassins again. Jillian shook her head. Why was Angie persisting with this wild tale?

"Grab my phone." Angie motioned to the slim devise stuck in one of the cup holders. Jillian picked it up and Angie said, "There's a video clip called Tori. Play it."

Jillian found the video and activated the file. Tori's image came to life with a friendly smile. "Hey, Jill. By now Angie has probably told you some wild story about psychic healers and outlaw aliens. Hate to complicate your life, hun, but it's all true. I dragged Angie into this mess and unfortunately you're a target too. I don't want to say too much just in case baby sister loses her phone again, but you need to understand that she hasn't lost her mind. You know me. I would never lie to you and I'm telling you to believe what Angie tells you. This could be a really good thing, but you have to trust us. Hope to see you soon." The video ended and Jillian just stared at the phone, numb and uncertain.

"You okay?"

Jillian couldn't think past the roaring in her ears. "Where's Tori?"

"She left the hospital a few minutes before we did with your double. By now they should be in your apartment, convincing everyone that the double is you."

She powered off the phone and returned it to the cup holder. Focusing on each mundane task kept her from feeling so overwhelmed. "You hired a double for me?" She shivered. This was starting to feel real. "Doesn't that put her in danger?"

"Nazerel wants a mate worthy of him, not..."

"An invalid?" It might be a temporary label, but the description fit. She could barely dress herself and walking without assistance was a distant goal.

Angie nodded. "If you let Odintar heal you, you won't be an invalid. You'll be better than you've ever been before."

Her head was throbbing almost as powerfully as her leg. She rubbed her temples as she tried to compose a rational response. "If Odintar can do what you say, won't that encourage Nazerel to come get me?" Why was she encouraging this fantasy? *Because Tori would never lie to you.* They'd known each other for years and, unlike her free-spirited sister, Tori was practical, logical, honest. She would never be part of such a cruel prank.

"First things first, remember?" Angie said softly. "Let Odintar heal you and then we'll all work together to make you less vulnerable."

Before Jillian could react to that bit of nonsense, Angie pulled off the highway and into a rest stop. Jillian looked around. Were they still on I-95? This seemed too secluded. As the conversation had gotten more unbelievable, she'd stopped paying attention to their location. There were no other cars in the small parking lot and the nondescript building offered restrooms, tourist information and nothing else. She knew Angie wouldn't hurt her, but what about Odintar. Was he even real or simply a figment of Angie's overactive imagination?

As if to answer her question a tall, dark-haired man strode toward them from the far side of the building. Did he have a vehicle parked back there or had someone dropped him off? He hadn't come out of the building. It was more like he'd been waiting behind or beside it. How odd.

His clothing was unremarkable, jeans and a solid black T-shirt. Like the other two men Angie claimed were aliens, this man's features were sculpted to masculine perfection. With his strong jawline and high cheekbones he could make a fortune with his face.

"Are all the men on Atari good looking?" she muttered under her breath.

"Ontariese. Their planet is called Ontariese."

Jillian didn't look away from the approaching stranger. His hair was short on the sides and just long enough on top to reveal its tendency to curl. He inclined his head as he noticed her stare, but his steps didn't falter. He stopped beside the car and reached for the door handle. Paralyzed by the absurdity of the situation, she just watched him open the door.

"Jillian, that's Odintar. Odintar, Jillian."

Framed by thick brown lashes, he had the darkest eyes Jillian had ever seen. Black, yet incredibly reflective, his gaze seemed to capture and caress her. "How did you get here?" It was an irrelevant question, but she couldn't think of anything less absurd.

Odintar looked at Angie and displeasure creased his brow. "You didn't tell her what to expect?"

"She doesn't believe you can heal her. Telling her you can teleport would have been a waste of time."

"T-teleport?" Jillian scoffed. "A psychic healer who can teleport. Seriously?"

Without warning, Odintar reached across her lap and unfastened her seat belt. The straps retracted with a noisy clatter as he slipped one arm beneath her knees and the other behind her back. "Grab my neck."

"Why?" She tried to move away from him, but she had nowhere to go. And her useless leg made escape impossible. "Don't touch me! What do you think you're doing?"

He lifted her out of the car, carefully angling her body until her injured leg was free. Then he straightened and looked into her eyes. "Hold on. I don't want to lose you in the vortex."

Vortex? Determined not to sound like a parrot, she let the word echo through her mind. What if it wasn't all nonsense? Was it possible he could fix her leg? Hope surged through her uncertainty, though the uncertainty remained. She trusted Tori and Tori trusted this man. Like Angie said, what did she have to lose? Reluctantly, she rested one arm across his shoulders and left the other in her lap.

He chuckled. "Are all Earth women this stubborn?"

His arms tightened and reality blurred. Jillian cried out and rolled toward him, wrapping both arms securely around his neck.

Odintar smiled as his passenger clung to him. He'd imagined Jillian in his arms ever since he saw her in the hospital, so helpless and miserable. She had classically beautiful features, delicate yet distinct. With pale blonde hair and bright blue eyes, she was captivating.

He materialized in the living room of the safe house and waited for her to notice that they were again on solid ground. Her face was pressed against the side of his neck and her body trembled.

"You're safe, *genarri*. There's nothing to fear." Rather than pry her away from him, he moved to the sofa and sat down with her still cradled in his arms.

The safe house wasn't large, two bedrooms, each with a private bathroom, the living room, and an eat-in kitchen were all on the main floor. The command center and detention cells were tucked away in the basement. He knew Elias was monitoring the situation from somewhere nearby, but he'd insisted on privacy for the next few days. At least the illusion of privacy.

Jillian relaxed enough to settle on his lap then slowly raised her head. "You're really from another planet?" She whispered the question as her gaze locked with his. The color drained from her cheeks, making her eyes appear massive and luminous.

"I am, but you have nothing to fear from me. I'm here to help you." Wiggling backward, she scooted off his lap and tried to swing her legs to the floor. He gently caught her uninjured calf and held her in place. "I didn't grab your crutches. You can't walk without them. Just relax."

"Relax?" She laughed, looking anything but amused. "Where are we? How long have you been on Earth? Does my government know you're here?"

"It's better if you don't know exactly; not quite two months; and certain government officials if not the government as a whole."

Her arching brows drew together as she matched his answers to her questions. "Did you teleport all the way from Ontariese or do you have some sort of ship?"

"Is that really what you want to know?" He moved his arm to the back of the sofa, resisting the urge to touch her. She wasn't ready for his touch and he wasn't here to seduce her, a fact his body hadn't quite registered. "Didn't Angie tell you why I brought you here?"

"She said you could heal my leg." Her lips pressed together then her voice tensed as she asked, "Can you?"

"I can and I will, but not until you're ready to let me."

She averted her gaze and fell silent. He didn't need to scan her mind to understand the conflict raging in her gaze. Things like this didn't happen on Earth. She was scrambling for an explanation that remained within the confines of her reality.

"I have to be dreaming," she whispered. "This can't be real."

"This is real and it's important." He allowed an authoritative edge to sharpen his tone. Unless he took control of the situation she might slip into hysteria and he didn't have the time to waste or the patience to deal with that. "You can't return to your life until you're strong enough to protect yourself. It's as simple as that."

Her gaze snapped back to his and she slowly licked her lips. "How do I know anything you tell me is true? For all I know, Angie and Tori could be brainwashed or under the influence of some psychotropic drug."

He couldn't help but smile. Her determination to cling to the familiar was understandable, but he couldn't allow it to go on indefinitely. If she continued with these pointless denials, he would have to find a more direct path past her reservations. "That's easier to believe than the possibility that I just want to help you?"

"What do you expect in return?"

Her bitterness surprised him. She'd seemed dejected and frustrated when he'd observed her in the hospital. The anger was new. "Why would I expect anything?"

"Everything comes with a price. I want to know yours up front."

Annoyed by her presumption, he muttered, "I'm a man. Surely I could only want one thing from a beautiful woman." Her suspicion wasn't completely unfounded. He did find her incredibly desirable. Still, he would never extort sexual favors from someone who needed his help.

Her nostrils flared and her lips trembled. "Are we talking one night or—"

He caught her chin and gazed deep into her eyes. "I will heal you because I can. I expect nothing in return."

"I don't believe you." Her voice was barely a whisper and she twisted out of his light grasp.

"You don't believe I'll heal you or you don't believe my assistance comes without a price?"

"Both." She looked at him then away as tears gathered behind her long lashes. "There's always a price and it's always devastating."

Determined to shift her focus and lighten her mood, he guided her gaze back to his. "I've had many adjectives attached to my lovemaking, but devastating is not one of them."

"Then you don't want sex?"

Her attitude was a reflection of the men in her life, not his behavior, but her persistence was starting to chafe. "When, and if, you share my bed, it will have nothing to do with obligation. Do you want me to heal your leg or not? I offer my abilities freely. All you have to do is agree."

Chapter Two

Faint blue rings ignited in the depths of Odintar's gaze and Jillian gasped. The color receded as fast as it appeared, but she hadn't imagined the unearthly gleam. He wasn't human. He'd teleported with her in his arms and claimed that he could heal her. All she had to do was trust him enough to let him try. The problem was, she didn't trust him. She didn't even know him.

But she knew Tori and—if the video message could be believed—Tori trusted Odintar.

Jillian took a deep breath and then another, carefully keeping her eyes averted from his handsome face. When she looked at him, his gaze surrounded her, muddled her thinking. He exuded power and menace, yet the danger didn't seem to be directed at her. He would make a fierce adversary and a welcome champion. She'd never had someone to defend her, to protect her from—he was a healer, not a knight in shining armor. She had to pull her head out of the clouds, even if the situation felt like something out of a fairy tale. *Helpless maiden thinks her life is over, her dreams obliterated, then handsome prince rushes in and sets her world to rights.* No wonder her head was spinning.

"If I let you do this..." She glanced at him then looked away. His gaze hadn't lost its power. Despite his casual clothes and calm manner, he didn't seem quite civilized. "How long will it take to fix the damage? Can you really restore my leg completely?" *Will I be able to dance again?* She couldn't bring herself to ask the last question. It was too painful to even consider.

"I won't make specific promises, but I can certainly produce a better result than your human doctors."

The other elements of Angie's "crazy story" returned with a vengeance. If Odintar was actually a healer, did that mean the rest was true? "Is someone really after me?" Fear penetrated her shock and brought the present into sharper focus.

"Let's concentrate on your leg right now. Once your physical limitations are resolved, I'll answer all of your questions."

It was hard to argue with his logic. As it was right now, she couldn't move off the couch without his help. She'd be a fool not to make herself less vulnerable. Empowered by a renewed purpose, she finally met his gaze. "What do you need me to do?"

"Any barrier between your skin and mine will disrupt the concentration of energy. We can use a blanket to cover your other leg if you're self-conscious, but I need access to your injury."

She chuckled. Didn't he know how she made her living? She'd always refused to go topless, but she frequently danced in a thong. Her legs were her best asset. She was certainly not self-conscious about them. "You'll need to help me. If we take off the brace, it's really painful for me to move at all."

He carefully lifted her feet off his lap and stood. Then he steadied her leg while she released the Velcro straps. His touch was surprisingly gentle for such a large man. But then he looked more like a football player than a healer. No, an Army Ranger. He definitely put off military vibes. He supported her leg with one hand and gingerly removed the brace with the other, faultlessly anticipating where she needed his help.

She sighed. It always felt wonderful to have the pressure gone. Until the slightest movement shot ribbons of pain up and down her leg. Leaning back against the arm of the sofa, she unzipped her jeans and tried to wiggle out of them. Discomfort spiked to her hip and she gasped.

His hands brushed hers aside and he grasped the sides of her jeans. "Lift your hips and let me do the rest."

Awareness crackled around them as he bent over her. His scent, clean yet faintly spicy, teased her nose. Unable to resist the temptation, she inhaled deeply, imprinting the unique smell on her memory. The T-shirt hugged his broad shoulders then skimmed over his chest and abdomen, hinting at muscular definition she couldn't actually see. His hips were lean, legs long. And those night-black eyes hypnotized her. She couldn't remember ever having been this intrigued by a man she'd just met. It usually took her forever to develop a connection with anyone, male or female.

He slowly peeled her jeans down, supporting her injured leg as he drew the pant leg off. His fingertips brushed her inner thigh, her calf, and then her ankle. She tried not to squirm as heat rolled through her abdomen and settled between her thighs with unmistakable intent.

"You okay?" He straightened and set the jeans aside.

The red-and-white-striped thong she'd slipped on that morning left not only her legs bare, but her hips and a good deal of her abdomen. "I'm fine." The words sounded thin and uncertain and heat burst across her cheekbones. Good God, was she actually blushing? If he was a healer, he had to be used to seeing naked body parts.

"Relax for a moment. I need to find a pair of scissors." He turned and crossed the room, disappearing into the adjoining kitchen.

She pulled her shirt down, covering her belly and most of her hips. This was ridiculous. Teleporting must have addled her brain. He was a healer, not a potential date.

He returned with a pair of scissors and slowly removed the bandages covering her leg. There was a large incision on her thigh and a smaller one three inches below her knee. From upper thigh to ankle, her flesh was a mass of purple bruises. She needn't have worried about him being aroused by her legs. Who would find this attractive?

"Have they put pins or plates in your leg, anything artificial?"

She shook her head. "So many of the blood vessels were damaged, they weren't sure they were going to be able to save my leg. The focus of the first surgery was restoring blood flow while keeping me from bleeding to death. They wanted to make sure my leg was capable of healing before they bothered with any sort of reconstruction."

"That will work to our advantage. Anything metallic would have hindered my abilities." He knelt beside the sofa and rolled his shoulders. "Make sure you're in a comfortable position, this will take some time."

Relaxing back against the padded armrest, she watched him closely, waiting for him to begin. His chest expanded as he drew in a deep breath.

He closed his eyes for a moment then opened them and focused on her leg. She didn't ask the questions buzzing in her mind, didn't want to distract him in any way.

Tension banded her chest and she fought to remain still. Was this really happening? Her mind refused to register the possibility that she could be made whole again, that the shattered pieces of her dreams could be reassembled.

He extended one hand and then the other, his palms hovering over her skin. A faint tingle rippled along her shin then spiraled through her thigh. She closed her eyes, trying to soothe her anxiety with pleasant thoughts and deep breaths, but his scent lingered in her nose, prolonging her restlessness. His fingers brushed her knee and she tensed.

"There will be sensations, but this shouldn't hurt. If you feel pain, let me know immediately."

She opened her eyes as she nodded, but he'd closed his eyes, so she said, "I will."

He slipped one hand under the bend of her knee and carefully pressed the other over the smaller incision. Heat passed between his hands in rhythmic pulses. Her calf muscle tensed and released over and over, the intensity not quite painful.

By the time he moved on, she felt flushed and dizzy. Was this a side effect of the healing or was she hyperventilating? She tried to relax by counting her breaths. *One in, out. Two in, out. Three...*

It was no use. An alien was healing her leg. The realization echoed through her mind, compounding her agitation. Aliens were on Earth, hunting mates, endangering her friends. Even in her mind it sounded ridiculous, yet how could she disregard the facts. Odintar could teleport and she'd yet to assess the result, but it sure as hell felt like he was healing her.

He paused, his hand resting just above her knee. "You're starting to resist me. Do we need to talk this out before I go on?"

"It's just surreal. I can't stop thinking about all the things someone like you must be capable of doing." The nonspecific fear hovered in the back of her mind, intensifying her anxiety.

He moved his hand off her leg. "I will not harm you. Do you believe that much at least?"

"I do." She sighed. "But I can't help wondering why you're willing to help, not just me but humans in general."

"I understand your doubt and I will explain, but I need to finish stabilizing the fractures. Once the bones are solid again, I'll stop and we can talk. All right?"

"All right."

Moving closer to the sofa, he placed one hand on the outside of her leg and the other on her inner thigh. His long fingers splayed against her flesh and the warm pulsing resumed. She bent her uninjured knee and rotated her leg outward, giving him more room between her thighs. There was nothing sexual about his touch, but each time his hands shifted heat curled through her abdomen.

She stared at the ceiling and fought the urge to wiggle. His hands were warm and each anxious breath drew his scent deeper into her lungs. Maybe there was something in his scent that was making her antsy. There had to be a reason she was reacting this way.

He worked his way up from her knee and then back down. The sweeping motion spread tingling heat through her muscles and joints. As he'd promised, it didn't hurt. Still, her body registered an intimacy she knew he didn't intend. Was she just so starved for human contact that she...but he wasn't human!

"It's probably best if you don't try to walk on it yet. The damage is extensive. Mobility should be better, though. See if you can bend your knee."

Desperate for a distraction from her convoluted thoughts, she happily complied. She slowly bent her knee and then straitened her leg again. Her muscles protested and her joints burned, but the sensations were uncomfortable not excruciating. She repeated the motion, faster this time and the pain was even less intrusive. "Wow. It really is better."

"Good." He raked one hand through his hair and rolled his shoulders. "I need to eat something and rest for an hour or so, then we'll get back to work. Are you hungry?"

"Actually, I am." The realization surprised her. Her appetite had been basically nonexistent since the accident. "Could you hand me my jeans." She was no longer worried about him doing something inappropriate. It was her body bent on misbehavior.

"I have a better idea." Without explaining what he meant, he headed down the hallway toward the back of the house. He returned a few minutes later with a pair of pull-on shorts. "Tori gathered some of your things for you. They're in the first bedroom."

"How long have you guys been planning my disappearance?" She took the shorts from his outstretched hand and scooted to the edge of the sofa so she could dress.

"Not long. We knew something had to be done when we found out you were being discharged from the hospital." She slipped the shorts on then stood so she could pull them up. Odintar was beside her in an instant, steadying her and making sure her weight remained centered on her uninjured leg. "Shall I carry you into the kitchen or bring the food out here?"

His gaze moved over her features with caressing intensity and the blue rings flickered within the pools of black. "Why do they do that?" she whispered.

"Why does who do what?"

The jumbled question made her smile. "Your eyes. At times I see rings of blue inside your eyes. Is something causing the flash of color or is it spontaneous?"

His features relaxed and the rings reformed, bright, solid circles separating his pupils from his equally dark irises. "I'm able to make subtle changes to my appearance. It helps me blend in with humans. Sometimes, when I'm particularly distracted, I lose control of the shift."

Heat crept up her neck as she absorbed the inference. He found her as distracting as she found him. Tension arced between them, pulling them closer like a gravitational field. She swayed toward him, tilting her face up in the process. He leaned down and her lips parted, but he didn't kiss her. Instead he swept her up in his arms and carried her into the kitchen.

Without her jeans she was inescapably aware of his arms, his hands, and the fluid strength with which he moved. He was staring straight ahead, so she took advantage of the opportunity and examined his features up close. Whiskers shadowed his jaw as if he hadn't shaved for a day or two. Rather than make him look slovenly, the bristles accented the angle of his jaw and his prominent cheekbones. Were his eyes the only feature he altered or was his natural appearance even more alien? The question seemed rude, so she kept her speculation to herself.

He pulled out a chair with his foot and set her down. "Are you warm enough or should I find a blanket."

"I'm fine," she assured, warmed by his ongoing concern.

"All right." He crossed to the refrigerator and pulled it open. "Unfortunately, I'm not much of a cook. How about a sandwich."

"Beggars can't be choosers. Whatever you're having is fine with me."

He gathered what he needed for their makeshift meal and brought the supplies to the table. "So how much did Angie tell you? I don't want to be repetitive."

He'd brought a bottle of beer and a can of cola. She picked up the cola and left him the beer. "You probably better start over. I didn't take her seriously." She opened packages and handed him utensils, not wanting to feel completely useless.

"Shadow Assassins were created during the Great Conflict on Ontariese."

"Created? Don't you mean their organization formed during the Great Conflict?"

"Yes and no. Their society formed because of the war, but the current generation of Shadow Assassins is equipped with nanotechnology that heightens their natural abilities."

She had no doubt they could spend days discussing history, but she was far more interested in the current conflict. "What brought them to Earth?"

"Their hideout was discovered and their society disbanded. They were taken to the City of Tears, our largest military compound. Most of the soldiers transitioned well and welcomed the changes, but the hunters—"

"Hunters?" She shivered. "Do I even want to know what they hunt?"

"I suspect from your reaction that Angie told you." He paused long enough to set a sandwich on a plate and hand it to her. "They hunt potential mates. On Ontariese the females were kidnapped and held against their wills until they produced offspring. If the child was male, the mother was released while the son remained with his father. Any memory she had of her captivity was scrubbed from her mind."

These people could teleport and heal. Was it really surprising that they could manipulate memories? The disconcerting thought was rapidly eroding her appetite, so took a couple of bites before asking, "What if she had a girl?"

"The Shadow Assassin would try again." He raised his sandwich to his mouth and took a bite.

"Their operation was shut down on Ontariese, so they came to Earth to start over?"

"Not exactly." The subject had no effect on his appetite. He devoured one sandwich and started on the other before he explained, "Their objective now is different than it was on Ontariese. Their primary concern before was maintaining their population. Now they hope to find females worthy of joining their society so they can create traditional family units."

"What can they offer human females that would make them do anything other than run screaming in the other direction? Or do they intend to hold them prisoner as they did before?"

"They're frantically working on a procedure that will allow them to transfer their abilities to their mates. Would human females be tempted by the possibility of attaining paranormal abilities?"

She set down her half-eaten sandwich and reached for a napkin. As long as she thought about the concepts in the abstract, the subject was interesting. But she couldn't quite suppress the fact that she was the target of one of the Shadow Assassins. These weren't meaningless facts. Odintar was explaining what Nazerel had in mind for her. "You made them sound like mercenaries. Do these men have the scientific background to accomplish the transfer?"

"They don't, but they're being sponsored by someone who does. Her name is Sevrin Keire and she's from a planet called Rodymia."

"Oh we don't just have Ontarians on Earth. We have Rodymians too?"

"They're called Rodytes, but yes. There are two kinds of 'aliens' on Earth." A smile turned up one corner of his mouth as he said, "My mother was from Bilarri, so I guess that make three kinds of aliens."

"Ontariese, Rodymia and Bilarri? How many of the planets in your star system are inhabited?"

"Just those three in my star system, but we interact with many outside our star system."

"Of course you do. You can will yourself from one side of the cosmos to the other in the blink of an eye. How foolish of me." She set her napkin down on top of her plate, no longer interested in the sandwich. She must seem so simplistic, so useless to him.

"It's a bit more complicated than that, but we do travel extensively."

"How many Shadow Assassins are there and how many people have been sent to... Are you trying to apprehend them or kill them? I have no idea how this works on your world."

"The Mystic Militia consists of six men. Three are Master-level Mages. The other three are highly trained soldiers."

"You're one of the mages?"

"I am. Lor is our leader and Blayne is also able to manipulate magic. I believe you've met them."

She nodded. She'd been introduced to Lor by Tori and apparently Angie had hooked up with Blayne, but Jillian didn't really know either man. "They're involved with friends of mine. Are you sure it's only the Shadow Assassins who came to Earth to find mates?"

He had the audacity to grin. "Finding mates is not our primary objective, but being on a planet where females are plentiful is a rare treat for us."

His gaze took on that warm, caressing quality again and she picked up her cola, needing something to do with her hands. "What happened to the females on Ontariese?"

"A biological weapon annihilated millions during our last war."

She cringed then shook her head. The outcome of most wars didn't justify the sacrifice, in her estimation, but she kept the opinion to herself. "Were women intentionally targeted?"

"Yes. Our society has been matriarchal for several millennia. One side of the Great Conflict wanted to continue the sacred traditions while the other wanted to explore other power structures. The leader of the Reformation Sect launched the biological weapon, expecting it to kill off the majority of Traditionalist Sect females. Unfortunately, the inoculation that was supposed to protect Reformation Sect females didn't work, so his need for power nearly obliterated our entire species." He released a long, shuddering sigh before he added, "The ratio is better now, but there are still many more men than women."

She had a million questions about the Great Conflict, but there was too much she needed to understand about the present situation for her to explore the past. "How many Shadow Assassins are here on Earth?"

"They started with twenty, but they're down to fourteen or fifteen. There is one we're not sure about. He ran from a fight, so it's unlikely his companions allowed him to live."

In an instant the warmth in his eyes was gone and she caught a glimpse of the ruthless soldier. She shivered, suddenly glad they were on the same side. "What happened to the other five?"

"We took them home for interrogation and punishment. Our system of justice is more streamlined than yours, but those accused of a crime still have their day in court."

"I'm glad. It sounds like these guys deserve punishment, but assassination on the spot seems a little extreme."

"It would also be foolish." His smile was nearly as cold as his gaze. "Each hunter we catch has information about the others. Shooting them where they stand would prevent us from accessing that information. This retrieval mission has already dragged on longer than we'd hoped. We want this mess cleaned up as quickly as possible."

"And that's where I come in?" She scooted back in her chair and crossed her arms over her chest. "Have I finally uncovered the reason you agreed to heal me?"

He shook his head, clearly frustrated by her conclusion. "You are in a position to assist us, but your participation will be strictly voluntary. I will heal you either way."

"All right, so it's not strictly quid pro quo. Your motivation is still hoping that I'll help you."

"Helping us is in your best interest. Nazerel will come after you with or without our support. The real question is, do you want to take him on by yourself?" He pushed back from the table and stood. "I'm going to meditate before we begin again. Would you rather remain here or go back to the living room."

Tension made his voice sound brittle and his fingers gripped the back of his chair much harder than necessary. "Here is fine." She wasn't sure how she kept pissing him off, but he was obviously angry. He'd taken two steps toward the hallway when she added, "Thank you."

He muttered something she didn't understand and kept right on walking.

"MUST YOU BE SO DAMN mysterious?"

Sevrin smiled at the impatience in Nazerel's tone. She still hoped to seduce him at some point, but annoying him was nearly as much fun. "I'm not being mysterious. I just don't see the point in explaining my every action when everything will become clear as we go along."

He snarled, a sound that never failed to curl her toes. The less civilized he acted, the more excited she became. She couldn't explain the phenomenon, but it was consistent and powerful.

"If you'd simply explain where we're going, I could flash us there. I despise these primitive vehicles." He motioned toward the car surrounding them.

"Your motorcycle is a primitive vehicle. How is it any different than riding in this car?"

"I'm in control of the motorcycle. You are driving this car."

"Ah," she chuckled. "Then it's your lack of control that frightens you and not the car."

"I'm not frightened," he snapped. "Merely impatient. If you'd let me teleport, we could have been there long before now."

"And what happens if someone sees you as you materialize. Didn't your fight with Blayne teach you anything?" The incident had been caught by a surveillance camera and ended up on the internet. If the Mystic Militia hadn't managed to convince everyone that it had been a publicity stunt by a fledgling film crew, Nazerel might have found out how much fun it was to be a celebrity in America.

"I never repeat a mistake." His jaw clenched as he stared out the windshield.

"How can you be certain if you insist on teleporting everywhere?"

"I am able to scan ahead. If there is anyone nearby, I manifest an invisibility shield as I materialize. No one will catch me unaware again."

"What about the others? Can everyone maintain that level of control?"

He glared at her, his impatience obvious. "Those who can't shield themselves as they arrive have been instructed not to teleport. I understand the need for discretion."

"Good. I'm not sure when it happened, but the Mystic Militia has definitely networked with some sort of human taskforce. Either that or they've received reinforcements from home."

She had his undivided attention now. He pivoted slightly in his seat, staring intently at her. "Wouldn't your ship's sensors have detected another team's arrival?"

"Yes, which is why my money is on human intervention."

Curiosity overtook his annoyance, smoothing his expression. "What makes you think they have help?"

"According to my informant back on Ontariese, there are currently six members assigned to the Mystic Militia and that includes Lor. Three are Mystics, the other three are soldiers. Yet reports of investigators are coming in from all over the city. It made me curious, so I mapped out the sightings last night and there were fourteen separate locations reported at about the same time. Teleportation could account for some of the overlap, but I think it's more likely that they've teamed up with someone here on Earth."

Nazerel accepted the information with a nod though he didn't offer a comment.

She pulled into the parking lot at one end of a large public park and turned off the car. She always met Gerrod in a different public place. His participation was more or less coerced and he never let her forget it. Gerrod had been her father's lackey, faithfully serving the crown for decades. But after her father's death, Gerrod had insisted that his obligation to Rodymia was met. For the most part she left him alone to wallow in anonymity. Still, Gerrod had been on Earth longer than she'd been alive and his network of contacts was invaluable. It was the only reason he was still alive.

"Are we going to have a picnic?" Nazerel grumbled as he swung his door open.

Without responding to his sarcasm, she got out of the car and triggered the door locks with her remote. She headed toward the benches surrounding the playground without pausing to see if Nazerel followed. There was much he could learn if he listened closely. If he chose to sulk, then he'd miss out on the opportunity. She didn't particularly care one way or the other.

Gerrod stood behind one of the benches, hands lightly clasping the back support rail. The late-afternoon breeze ruffled his longish blond hair, occasionally sweeping a lock across his piercing blue eyes. He ignored the irritant and focused entirely on her.

"You summoned. I'm here." Resentment rang through each syllable. "Make it quick. I have things to do."

She laughed. "Am I keeping you from your game shows or is it late enough for Judge Judy?" His gaze shifted to somewhere behind her and her smile turned calculating. She hadn't heard Nazerel approach, but Gerrod's shocked expression made it obvious he was looking at the Shadow Assassin. "You look like you've seen a ghost."

"He can't be..." He came around the bench but didn't approach the other man. "Who are you?"

"Nazerel of—Nazerel Southmor."

Her smile broadened. It had taken months of prompting for Nazerel to drop his tribe affiliation in favor of a last name. This was the first time he'd done so without a reminder.

"Gerrod Reynolds." The two shook hands, likely using the physical contact to disguise their light scans. "You look very much like someone I used to know."

"He's the spitting image of his father," Sevrin told Gerrod with a secretive smile. "That's why I asked him to tag along today. Thought you might enjoy meeting him."

"This is the first son of South?"

Gerrod sounded suitably star struck, but Nazerel just looked annoyed.

"You were not part of the world below. How could you have known my father?" Nazerel stood statue still, hands clenched at his sides.

Severn laid her hand on his tense forearm and waited until he looked at her. "Unlike most of his men, your father wasn't held captive within the Shadow Maze. South came and went as he pleased and interacted with whomever he chose. My father arranged for Gerrod to be trained by South in exchange for his participation in our program."

"He is one of the Dirty Dozen?"

Gerrod chuckled. "Wow. It's been a long time since I heard that name."

"I thought you came up with it," she countered.

"I did, but that seems like another lifetime or even someone else's life."

Nazerel snapped his head around and looked into her eyes. "Is it possible that this man is Jillian's father?"

"There's a one in twelve chance," she explained. "I only have DNA samples of four of the men and about half of the daughters. I haven't tried to match any of them with Gerrod because he keeps refusing to give me a sample. So far Jillian hasn't been a positive match with anyone, so now her chances are more like one in eight."

"If that's why you summoned me here," Gerrod warned, "you're wasting your time. I don't want to know how many times I succeeded. Those years are the biggest regret of my life."

"You don't need to know, but I do." She sighed. "Give me a sample of your DNA or I'll have no choice but to take it from you."

Gerrod laughed, head tilting to an arrogant angle. "Go for it, princess. This should be amusing."

Rather than attack him herself, she turned to Nazerel and said, "Break his nose."

For once in his life, Nazerel didn't argue or hesitate. He closed the distance between him and Gerrod with one long stride and punched him squarely in the face.

Gerrod's shocked cry ended in a vile curse as he raised his hand to his gushing nose.

Sevrin was half a step behind Nazerel. She shoved Gerrod's hand out of the way and pressed a cloth to his nose, soaking up some of the blood. Then she turned back to Nazerel and said, "Flash us out of here now!"

Nazerel swept her into his arms and teleported away from the park. She enjoyed the strength of his embrace for only a moment before they materialized in a vacant lot on the outskirts of Las Vegas. His smirk made her shove off his chest and step back despite how much she was enjoying the embrace.

"Are you sure no one saw us flash out of sight?" he challenged.

"We were the only ones in the park." Her heart lurched in her chest as she realized she hadn't even bothered to check.

"Are you sure."

She tensed. Was he just jerking her around or had she overlooked a spectator? "You're aware of everything that goes on around you. Was someone there?"

"No, but you didn't assess the situation before you told me to go."

"This was important." She carefully folded the cloth, securing the blood sample on the inside of the wad. "If it's safe to do so, take me back to my ship and arrange for someone to go pick up my car."

"All of this would have been much simpler if you'd just told me where we were headed in the first place."

"If I'd told you what I intended to do, Gerrod would have sensed it when you shook hands. I wasn't being mysterious just to piss you off. Anything you knew, he would have found out."

He accepted the point after a moment of contemplative silence. "I'll forgive you if you tell me why my father would have agreed to help a Rodyte."

She smiled. Working with Nazerel was definitely easier than struggling against him. "Let me get the DNA sequencer running and I'll explain it all over dinner."

Chapter Three

Jillian squirmed on the kitchen chair, wishing she had her cell phone so she could call Tori. Even Angie, with her unusual take on life in general, would be better than trying to sort through these chaotic thoughts and feelings alone. Jillian pulled out another chair and propped her leg on it, but her thigh started throbbing again. That she could move it at all was a miracle undeniably attributable to Odintar.

Her mind was still reeling from all the things Odintar had told her. It was hard to believe that half of what he'd said was true, yet everything she'd experienced since meeting him pointed toward fact not fiction. Aliens had come to Earth and she, along with two of her closest friends, were caught in the middle of their conflict.

She thought back to the first time she'd seen Lor. Tori had spotted him in a casino and their attraction had been immediate, but no one would deny he was physically striking. Then later in the hotel bar, he'd performed a "magic trick", causing a flame to jump from candle to candle. Now she suspected the trick hadn't been a trick at all but legitimate magic. Legitimate magic? The phrase made her shake her head. Until today she would have considered it an oxymoron.

Unable to sit idly by while Odintar meditated, she carefully stood and turned her chair around so she could use it like a makeshift walker. Her leg felt solid as she positioned it, yet as soon as she put weight on it, pain radiated from ankle to hip. Ignoring the discomfort, she hobbled to the window over the sink. All she could see was an average-sized backyard with a wooden privacy fence. She could be almost anywhere.

The back door was locked and she couldn't figure out how to unlock it. There was no deadbolt to rotate or lever to shift. The door handle just refused to move. Even though she suspected she would find the same in the front room, she slowly made her way to the main entrance. It was also locked with no obvious way to release it. It didn't really matter. Her mobility was still so limited, escape wasn't really an option.

She parted the drapes obscuring the front window and looked out at a residential street like any other. The house wasn't large or luxurious. The neighborhood, what little she could see of it, seemed well maintained, yet somewhat mature. Were they even in Nevada any longer? They could be on a different planet for all she knew. She had no idea the scope of Odintar's abilities.

Her leg protested each movement, so she limped over to the couch and reclined, stretching out her legs across the seat cushions. It was pretty obvious the Ontarians hoped to use her as bait once her injury was mended. Was Odintar right? Would Nazerel come after her even if she refused to align with his enemies? Angie frequently followed her heart into danger, but Tori was logical. If Tori allowed herself to become involved in this cause, it had to be important. At the very least, Jillian needed to find out more about the Mystic Militia in general and Odintar in particular.

As if sensing her thoughts, Odintar strolled into the living room. She was struck again by the graceful strength that defined his every movement. He had the fluidity of a dancer, yet the overt purpose of a Navy Seal. The contrast was fascinating.

"Feel better?" she asked with a tentative smile.

"I've recovered enough to continue."

He sounded so stiff and formal that she cringed. "Are you still angry with me?"

"I was frustrated not angry, but either way it wasn't your fault. I keep forgetting Mystic abilities are basically nonexistent on Earth. With all that you've endured, you're skepticism is understandable. I'll try to be more patient."

She propped herself up against the armrest, making room for him at the other end of the couch. "How many sessions will it take to heal my leg?"

"That depends on you." He sat and pivoted slightly toward her. "If you relax and allow me to work unhindered, we'll progress much faster than if we wrestle the entire time."

Wrestling with Odintar held a certain appeal, but restoring her leg was her top priority. "I'm not intentionally fighting you. Everything about this feels strange and threatening."

He placed his hand on her ankle, his touch light and casual. "I would never hurt you and I would attack anyone who attempted to harm you. There's no reason for your fear."

"Consciously I know you're trying to help me, but something inside me resists the intrusion."

For a long moment he just looked at her, his eyes narrowed, lips compressed. "I'd intended to assess your latent abilities after your leg had been restored. Maybe you'll feel less vulnerable if they're active."

Here was another piece of the puzzle, another clue to his true motivation. She knew his agenda wasn't self-serving, but neither was it as selfless as he pretended. "What makes you think I have latent abilities?"

"Nazerel wouldn't have targeted you unless your potential was extraordinary."

"I thought my connection to Tori and Angie was why he targeted me." She lowered her gaze, breaking the mesmerizing pull of his dark eyes. He wasn't coming on to her, so why did she long to crawl onto his lap and bury her face against his neck?

"Your friendship with the Logan sisters brought you to Nazerel's attention, but your potential is what motivated him to act."

Challenge calmed her enough to lift her gaze. Ever since the accident she'd felt devastated, her life so disrupted she barely recognized her own reality. If Odintar could heal her—and it was looking more and more like he could—she would be able to shape her future into whatever she wanted it to be. But first they had to deal with Nazerel. "What does he look like? Maybe I've seen him hanging around backstage or something?"

"Close your eyes."

No sooner had her lids drifted shut than an image formed within her mind. Nazerel had short dark hair and piercing eyes. His features were rugged, very masculine. He looked hard, even brutal, with a body easily capable of enacting every ruthless impulse. She shivered, very glad she was no longer alone.

"He might have made subtle changes, but that's his basic appearance."

She opened her eyes, glad to be rid of that penetrating stare. "I've never seen him before. I would have remembered those eyes. Still, he hasn't actually done anything yet. Why are you so sure he will?"

"When we raided one of their hideouts, we discovered a binder, a collection of dossiers with detailed information about human females. You're one of the women featured in the notebook."

Her recent surge of confidence shuddered as she absorbed the implications. For there to be detailed information about her in the notebook, she had to have been watched, followed, *investigated*. "Who collected the information? How long have I been under surveillance?"

"The notebook was likely compiled by the Rodytes. The hunters haven't been here long enough to have done it themselves."

"And what brought me to the attention of the Rodytes?"

"It's quite likely your father was Ontarian."

She just stared at him in disbelief. It made perfect sense that her connection to all this drama hadn't been random. Still, there was only so much one shell-shocked brain could absorb. She was being hunted by an alien who wanted to make her his mate because her father had been an alien. Yeah, that happened every day.

She didn't know enough about her father to confirm or disprove Odintar's claim. Her mother seldom spoke of him and when she did it was to warn Jillian away from "men like that".

Odintar sighed and carefully lifted her legs, sliding under them until her knees arched over his lap. "Let's focus on your injury. We can sort through the rest when you're feeling stronger."

And I can run the hell away from you! The rebellious thought calmed her, allowed her to think beyond the newest revelation. "I'd rather you figured out if I have abilities first."

"You definitely have abilities. I'm just not sure what they are." He rested both hands on her uninjured leg, one above her knee, the other below.

Awareness expanded, sweeping through her body in slow, tingling waves. His touch wasn't seductive, yet the restlessness returned with a vengeance. "How do you determine what my abilities are?"

"If I infuse them with energy, they will likely activate." He shifted his left hand to her injured knee. "I hesitate to do so until your healing is complete. I don't want to empty my tank before we reach our destination, yet the loss might be worth it if doing so allows me to heal you faster. Does that make sense?"

"I think so. You're saying it's a gamble either way."

"Exactly."

"Then let's stick with my leg."

He nodded then asked, "Can you put your left leg behind me?" He scooted slightly forward, making room for her to complete the maneuver. She drew her knee toward her chest and eased her leg between his broad back and the sofa's cushions. Even though he was between her legs now, the position wasn't really sexual. At least it shouldn't have felt that way. So why had her pulse kicked into double time and her core clenched so hard she fought back a moan. "Try to relax."

The suggestion was absurd. She pressed back into the armrest and closed her eyes. His hands swept from her upper thigh to ankle, rotating and repositioning in a pattern only he understood. Energy flowed between his palms, pulsing through her damaged flesh, creating heat and tension.

She emptied her mind and floated in the darkness, but the rhythmic surge of his healing waves electrified her senses. A particularly sharp throb made her gasp and the deep inhalation drew his spicy scent inward. The tantalizing smell filled her nose and lungs then spread through her entire body with every beat of her heart. Her back arched and her nipples drew tight, yet the swirling caress of his hands didn't falter.

Stubbornly battling the urge to writhe, she released the tension in her back and ignored her tingling nipples. It wasn't intentional. He wasn't trying to turn her on.

Or was he?

She opened her eyes and assessed his expression. His eyes were closed, features tense with concentration. His fingertips occasionally skimmed over her inner thigh, but he touched nothing except her injured leg.

It was all her. Guilt managed to cool her ardor for a few minutes, but the surging heat couldn't be contained for long. The fingers of one hand splayed across her outer thigh as he worked a particularly stubborn spot high on her inner thigh. He circled the spot with three fingertips, driving energy deep into the muscle.

"Stop," she gasped, trembling on the verge of orgasm.

"What's wrong?" His fingers remained against her thigh, but the energy pulses halted.

"I can't…" She sat up, panting harshly. "I just need a break."

He steadied her with one hand, but moved the other away from her inner thigh. "Was I hurting you?"

"No." Too embarrassed to face the truth, she looked away from his expressive eyes.

His warm fingers cupped her chin and turned her face back around. "Did it feel a little too good?"

"Yes," she admitted with a nervous laugh.

"It's not unusual and it's nothing to be ashamed of. I'm flooding your body with energy and your nervous system doesn't know what to do with it. I've had patients break down in tears and others can't stop laughing. Your body is just trying to vent the excess energy."

She was his patient, not a potential lover. She couldn't let herself forget. "I'll be fine. I just need to catch my breath."

"It's better if you don't fight it and I won't take it personally. I'm aware that the reaction is beyond your control." He punctuated the claim with a gentle smile that made her feel even more self-conscious. Having his patients come while he healed them might be commonplace for him, but orgasms were intensely personal for her.

She lay back and closed her eyes, determined to ignore the arousing sensations. From an early age, her mother had warned her that men were only after one thing.

They'll say anything and do anything to get inside your pants, then they'll forget you as soon as they've had you. Her mother's embittered warning echoed through her memory. *Women have needs too. They're natural and you don't need to be ashamed of them. But we're perfectly capable of taking care of them without the complication of a selfish man.*

Jillian's first lover had been a high school crush. Every teenage boy thought of nothing but sex, so she hadn't held it against him. Her second lover hadn't come along until college. Physical attraction had been the primary draw, but he hadn't been the sex-crazed monster her mother described.

After graduation, Jillian dedicated herself body and soul to her career, leaving little time or energy for romance. There had been one final affair, but that's all it had been, a quick, hot flirtation. Sex had been the driving force behind each of Jillian's relationships and each relationship had failed. She didn't blame it all on the men. She had been an active participant. Still, it saddened her that she'd been unable to prove her mother wrong.

Odintar returned to the spot high on her inner thigh. The pulses seemed more concentrated this time. Was he trying to minimize the side effect for her?

Though she appreciated his effort, it didn't help. Heat spread through her abdomen and her core contracted in rippling spasms, each slow clench pushing her closer to the inevitable end. She resisted, breathing deeply and relaxing muscles as quickly as she felt the urge to tighten them.

She held perfectly still, staring into the blackness created by her lowered lids. Then images formed within the darkness, sensual glimpses of what her body craved. She saw Odintar crawl onto the couch and kneel between her spread thighs. He arched over her and kissed her. His chest brushed her sensitive nipples while his mouth caressed hers.

Fighting back a helpless moan, she surrendered to the fantasy. Their clothes dissolved, first hers then his. His body felt warm and solid as it rocked against hers. Skin against skin, they pressed and slid. His kiss turned hungry, consuming, and his touch became more focused. He cupped her breast, his thumb teasing the nipple. She wanted his mouth there, sucking, nibbling, but she needed his kiss more.

In her mind, she wrapped her legs around his hips and felt his cock press against her aching mound. He was incredibly hard, more than ready to fill her. The emptiness intensified. She needed him inside her, moving over and into her. She needed him now!

She cried out softly and her eyes flew open as her orgasm suddenly crested. Her gaze locked with his and she trembled. His objective calm was gone, replaced by predatory fire. The blue rings in his eyes burned brightly and his features had sharpened.

He turned toward her, bracing his hand on the armrest beside her. His head descended slowly and she ducked beneath his arm, scrambling off the sofa and out of reach. She was halfway across the room when her panicked mind registered that she was walking.

Her steps faltered then she stopped and took stock of her body. "There's hardly any pain," she whispered without turning around. "You did it."

"Sex makes a damn good distraction."

The growl in his voice made her tense then slowly turn around. "You said you wouldn't take it personally." He was sitting now and the rings had disappeared. Still, his features looked more angular and hunger simmered in his gaze.

"It would have been easier to keep my promise if you hadn't filled my mind with sexual images."

She gasped. "I didn't mean to."

"I know." A smile parted his lips and he shook his head. "I'm not blaming you. I'm trying to explain my less than professional reaction." He raised his hand then motioned with his fingers. "Come back here, but take it slowly. Without the rush of adrenaline, things might feel different."

She returned to the couch with measured steps, focusing on the flex of her muscles and the movement of her joints. "There's no pain." She looked down as wonder unfurled within her soul. "Even the bruises are fading." She looked at him and smiled as tears blurred her vision. "This is amazing. *You're* amazing."

Her praise pleased Odintar more than it should have. Everything about her affected him more powerfully than it should have. When her resistance melted away, he knew how she was distracting herself. Still, he hadn't allowed himself to be drawn into the sensuality crackling around them. He had a job to do and the sooner he did it the sooner they could move on to the next challenge. Then her mind inadvertently reached for his and shared the images rolling through her imagination. His body was still hard and achy thanks to those images.

It wasn't just her beauty, though he found her appearance more than pleasing. He sensed an intriguing combination of strength and vulnerability in his little dancer that... He pulled back from the thought. She wasn't *his* little anything. They barely knew each other.

"You should still take it easy for a while," he told her. "I'm confident your recovery will be complete, but the regeneration is ongoing." He'd used her distraction to explain why he'd been able to heal her so quickly. Unfortunately, the truth was more complicated. Ever since he was injected with nanites, his abilities had been amplified. He was able to do more and do it faster than before the controversial procedure. There was another possibility, of course. She could be a potential mate. He dismissed the notion before it took root in his mind. He didn't want to think about the fallout from such a development. They were here to protect human females from aggressive predators not join the hunt.

"I understand." She sat down beside him and squeezed his forearm. "Thank you. You have no idea what this means to me."

The simple contact sent heat curling up his arm while restless need cascaded through his body. Discipline alone kept him from pressing her back into the sofa and exploring her entire body with his hands and his mouth. It had been far too long since he sought the comfort of a willing female and this particular female tempted him more than any he'd encountered before. He cleared his throat and focused on the subject at hand. "It means you have decisions to make. I hate to put more pressure on you, but we can't stay here indefinitely."

She shifted her hand to her lap with a sigh. "Are we still in Nevada?"

"We are, but I won't be more specific. We can't risk Nazerel finding this place." He pivoted toward her and she did the same, only she also scooted back against the armrest, putting distance between them. Was she still grappling with the surreal situation or could she sense the hunger smoldering just below the surface? He didn't react outwardly to her retreat, but determination surged, compounding his restlessness.

"Will you finally admit you want to use me as bait for Nazerel?" Her brows arched and challenge ignited inside her eyes.

"I never denied it. But you won't be forced to do anything." He wasn't sure why she insisted on giving him an ulterior motive. Apparently events in her past had taught her to be wary. Instead of allowing her attitude to frustrate him, again, he presented her with choices. "If you want me to take you off world until this thing is over, I will. However, every female in the notebook remains in danger until all of the Shadow Assassins are apprehended."

"I've already decided to help you, so you don't need to sound so defensive."

He started to object then realized his response would prove her point. Instead, he inclined his head and said, "Welcome to the team."

Her smile didn't quite reach her eyes, but some of the tension eased from her shoulders. "What's our next move?"

"I hate to admit it, but I'm exhausted." He raked his sweat-dampened hair with his fingers. "I think we should both get some sleep and we'll start on your abilities in the morning."

"Do you have a phone? I'd like to call Tori."

"Cell signals can't penetrate the shields and telepathic communication is risky." The hope in her gaze made him cringe. She had to feel isolated and overwhelmed, yet she'd remained remarkably calm and cooperative. A candid conversation with her best friend really wasn't too much to ask. "There's another way, but it requires a mind-to-mind connection."

"You say that like it's painful or dangerous." She drew her uninjured leg up toward her chest then wrapped her arms around her knee. Another subtle barrier between them.

"It shouldn't be either, but you've fought against even the lightest mental touch. Your resistance could prove challenging."

"I'm not trying to resist you." There was an almost defiant cry in her voice. "Humans are programmed for fight or flight. Some part of me must still perceive you as a threat."

"The connection will help with that, but first we have to form the link."

He no longer needed a physical touch to initiate this sort of link. Still, it often soothed the person with whom he was connecting. Making each movement slow and obvious, he lifted her injured leg and draped it across his thighs as he scooted closer. She released her uninjured knee and angled her leg, making room between her thighs.

She watched him closely. Obviously aware of the intimate position, yet unsure if she should protest. "Now what?" Her tone became husky and soft.

Slowly pushing his fingers into her loose hair, he pressed his thumb against her temple. "Close your eyes and try not to fight me. I'll go as slowly as I can."

Her mental shields were amazingly strong, considering that they were instinctive. He spread his energy across the surface of her shields, absorbing the rhythm, trying to emulate the pattern. His energy melded with hers and for just a moment their patterns were in sync. Then her shields adjusted and her rhythm changed. Remarkable. The modulation might not have been conscious, but it was undeniably effective.

All right, if stealth wouldn't defeat her defenses, he'd have to try distraction.

He eased his fingers from her hair and slid his hand downward. His thumb pushed across the crest of her cheek then traced her petal-soft lips. She made a nervous sound and her eyelashes fluttered, yet her lids remained lowered.

Warning her of his intention would compromise the distraction, so he wrapped his hand around the back of her neck and covered her mouth with his. She gasped as his tongue parted her lips and shivered when he ventured deeper. She tasted sweet and her breath made his lips tingle. He wanted to revel in the kiss, to enjoy the sensual slide of their lips and tongues, but her surprise wouldn't last long. So he found a subtle weakness in her shields and drove into her mind.

She arched beneath him, smacking his chest with her fists and kicking out with her legs. His position between her thighs saved him from her feet, but he grasped her wrists and pinned them to the sofa's armrest. *I'm almost finished. Calm down.*

He wasn't really kissing her now, though he'd yet to separate their mouths. She remained tense and unresponsive as he firmly anchored the link. Fear and resentment shoved into his mind, blocking his access to any other emotion. He was inside her shields, but she remained guarded. Finally, he pushed up, his face hovering over hers.

"It's done," he assured her.

"Why did you kiss me?" She sounded indignant, but her cheeks were deeply flushed.

"Would you rather I slapped you?"

Her brows drew together. "Those were the only two options?"

"I needed to distract you." He couldn't stand the hypocrisy of his own words, so he admitted, "And I've wanted to do that ever since I first saw you in your hospital room two weeks ago."

She pulled her hands free from his light grasp, but remained against the armrest, more or less pinned beneath him. "What were you doing in my hospital room?"

"Guarding you without terrifying you. There was no reason for you to know about us if Nazerel targeted someone else."

"But he didn't."

It wasn't a question. Still, he felt compelled to clarify. "All indications point to you still being his primary target."

She stared up at him with impossibly blue eyes. "And how does this help me talk to Tori?"

A guilty smile crept across his lips. He'd nearly forgotten why he formed the link. Apparently, she wasn't the only one who'd been distracted by the kiss. "Mystic energy emanates from and is most easily controlled in a place called the metaphysical plane. The connection I formed will allow me to take you there and we'll see if Tori is available to join us."

"You're going to take me to another dimension?" Fear sparked across their link even though she maintained a calm expression.

He should probably warn her about the empathic nature of their connection. "It's not a physical dimension, though it can be manipulated so it seems that way. For our purpose, a simple visualization should suffice."

"And this is less dangerous than stepping outside and using a cell phone?"

He chuckled. "I can create extremely dense shields on the metaphysical plane. It also gives me direct access to Mystic energy which I desperately need right now."

"I'm not sure what that means, but I'll take your word for it. If Tori doesn't respond, can we try Angie? I'd really like to chat with someone I knew before this all began."

"Of course." He started to warn her that he could sense her emotions, then decided to compress his end of the link instead. If her emotions spiked for some reason, he needed to know about it. Otherwise, she should be protected from casual curiosity, namely his. He sat up, so he wasn't arched over her, but remained between her legs. "Give me your hands." Again the suggestion was for her benefit rather than his need for physical contact. "Now close your eyes again."

He activated their link, ensuring that her consciousness followed him. Then he launched them toward the metaphysical plane. Quickly scanning her mind, he found an image that seemed familiar and nonthreatening. The building was easily recognizable as a neighborhood coffee shop. Rather than return to her mind for details, he added the rich aroma and cozy ambiance shared by such establishments then drew her into the visualization.

She grasped his arm and swayed, clearly unaccustomed to the slightly unfocused sensations. "It feels way more real than I expected. It even smells right."

He smiled. "It takes decades of practice to achieve this level of control, but basic access is a simple skill."

"Decades." She looked him over with bold assessment. "You must be older than you look."

He laughed. "How old do I look?"

"Thirty, maybe thirty-five."

Why would she care about his age if her interest were purely professional? His pulse leapt and the possessive hunger he'd been battling all afternoon pushed even closer to the surface. "I'm older than I look." He didn't offer any more information and thankfully she moved on.

"So how do we reach Tori?"

He motioned toward one of the round tables. "Have a seat and I'll see if she'll respond to a telepathic ping."

The subtle signal had barely left his brain when Tori flashed into view. Lor appeared half a second behind her. Jillian stood and the women embraced. Odintar motioned Lor away from the table. "They need to catch up."

Lor followed him to the other side of the coffee house. The move was a courtesy. Either Mystic could amplify their hearing at will and make out what the women were saying. Rather than sit, both men chose to stand with their backs to the wall so they could anticipate any danger.

"How is Jillian reacting to—well, to everything?" Lor wanted to know.

Odintar felt Lor's energy reinforce his, doubling the strength of the shield surrounding them. He hadn't needed to request the support. They'd worked together often enough to anticipate each other's actions. Their relationship was comfortable, almost effortless. "I've managed to repair the worst of her injuries, though regeneration will continue for several days, perhaps weeks. I'll assess her abilities, if she has any, in the morning."

Lor shot him a speculative glance. "Isn't that fast, even for you?"

"It is. I'm not sure if my nanites are becoming more effective each time they repeat something they've done before or..." He wasn't ready to vocalize the other possibility.

"Or?" Lor prompted, but Odintar just shrugged.

"There might be another possibility, but it's too soon to tell one way or the other."

"These women were basically bred to be compatible with our species. We shouldn't be surprised that we find them appealing."

He didn't agree with or pose an argument against the conclusion. He needed more information before he formed an opinion.

Lor's expression turned thoughtful. "If the healing is basically complete, we can move her to the Bunker tonight. She might be more comfortable—"

"The original schedule makes more sense." Odintar's insistence inadvertently tipped his hand. Not that Lor needed help seeing through him. They knew each other too well. "We still have a lot to accomplish."

"All right." Lor flashed a knowing smile as amusement gleamed in his turquoise eyes. "I'll give you a few more days alone with her, but you can't keep her isolated forever."

"That's not my intention," Odintar grumbled, yet forever had never sounded so tempting before.

Jillian reached across the table and squeezed Tori's hand. "If this is all in our minds, how can it feel so real?"

"Odintar is controlling the visualization and he's extremely skilled. Speaking of which," she motioned toward Jillian's unencumbered leg. "How are you feeling?"

"Apparently, my leg is the least of my worries." She shook her head, struggling even to find a place to start. "The whole time I was lying in that hospital bed, all I could think about was how empty my life would be if I could never dance again. Suddenly I'm on my feet again, but my life is still a disaster. Are you sure we can trust these guys?"

"Absolutely." The sincerity in Tori's eyes left no room for doubt. "I was suspicious too, but everything they do supports their story. Lor threw himself in front of a pulse pistol for me. How do you argue with that sort of loyalty? Besides, my gift allows me to sense deception. They're really here to protect us and stop the Shadow Assassins."

"Your gift? Yesterday that would have made me laugh. Right now, I'm not even surprised." She rubbed her forehead, elbows lightly resting on the tabletop. "How can this be happening? It's all so...unbelievable."

"Actually this isn't the first time you've met an alien." Tori's smile was warm and patient. "The clues have been there for years. It was just more comfortable to ignore them."

Intrigued by the semi-cryptic comment, Jillian said, "All right. I'll bite. When was the first time I met an alien?"

"Angie ran into Aria Myer on a planet called Bilarri. Aria wasn't murdered like so many people thought. She's alive and well and happily married to a Bilarrian nobleman."

Jillian felt her eyes round. "Angie has been to another planet?"

Tori laughed, obviously pleased by Jillian's easy acceptance of her claim. "That's not what was supposed to surprise you, but yes. So have I, if you're wondering."

"I was Aria's understudy, so I spent more time with her than most. I wasn't sure what she was, but I was pretty sure she wasn't human. I'm glad she's okay. She was, or is, a sweetheart." Jillian couldn't drag her mind away from Tori's other revelation. "Where did you go when you left Earth? How did you get there?"

"Lor took me to Ontariese shortly after we met. The original leader of the Mystic Militia switched sides, so Lor needed to know what his supervisors wanted him to do about it."

"What was it like? Are sci-fi movies even close to how it really is? How long were you there?" She suddenly wished Odintar had built a bar instead of a coffee shop.

"It was similar to Earth, yet totally different too. It's hard to explain. They have two moons. One is dead, like ours. But the other is like a little planet. There are still trees and flowers, rivers, lakes and oceans, but they're all uniquely Ontarian. I met Lor's mentor and Odintar's boss. They were both extremely impressive."

"It's hard to picture these guys with supervisors." Authority generally came with power and Jillian wasn't ready to picture a being more powerful than Odintar. Instead of tying herself in knots, she focused on mundane details. "And how did you get there?"

Tori paused and her gaze shifted to something in the distance. Jillian followed the direction of Tori's stare and found Lor looking at Tori intently. Were they speaking telepathically? "Are you telling secrets?"

"Just asking permission to reveal some of their secrets," Tori assured. Lor must have agreed because Tori said, "They can open a portal that allows them to move from one dimension to another. That's how Lor took me to Ontariese. On the way back we came in a spaceship."

"If they can create transportation portals, why do they need spaceships?"

"Not all Ontarians can Summon the Storm. That's what they call it when they open an interdimensional portal. And trust me, the phenomenon is well named. When we returned, we had soldiers and all sorts of equipment with us, so the portal wasn't an option."

"Wow." Jillian slumped back in her chair, feeling rather stunned. "Let me soak all that in for a minute."

Tori looked around as she said, "Take all the time you need, but the smell of this place is driving me crazy." Two tall mugs of steaming coffee materialized on the table. Tori chuckled then raised her mug toward the men. "Thank you."

Jillian picked up the other mug and inhaled the steam. It not only smelled like coffee, it smelled like a cinnamon latte. She tensed. There was only one way Odintar could have known her drink of choice. He had to be reading her mind. Despite the disconcerting thought, she took a sip and sighed. The rich, spicy flavor rolled across her tongue and warmed her belly. Even so, knowing how he'd created the scene made her feel vulnerable.

With the mug pressed between her palms, she leaned slightly forward. "Odintar formed a mind link so he could bring me here. What will it allow him to do?"

Tori started to speak then hesitated. Indecision spread across her features as her expression turned grim. "I know you're confused, but I've never been good at blowing smoke. I'm a realist and I think honest information will do more good than hollow reassurance. You're safe with Odintar because he chooses not to harm you. He's honorable and dedicated to the mission. The mission at the moment is keeping you safe and equipping you for the realities of your new life."

"My new life." She set down the mug and tucked a stray lock of hair behind her ear. "I guess I need to look at it like that. Don't I? The life I knew before is over and I need to adapt."

"It doesn't need to seem so ominous. You have access to possibilities now that you never would have dreamed of before. This can be really exciting if you let yourself embrace the possibilities."

"And if I don't want to 'embrace the possibilities'? What if I just want to dance?"

"Then you'll dance." Tori reached across the table and squeezed Jillian's hand. "As soon as the danger is over, your life can be anything you want it to be."

"Yeah, there's just that tiny little obstacle." She blew out a shaky breath then finished her latte, or the magical representation of the latte. The distinction made her smile. "So tell me about your powers. Are you like a super hero now?"

Tori snickered. "More like a human lie detector. I'm what's called a sensitive. I can sense deception and Mystic abilities. I'm still learning to control it, so the impressions can be pretty confusing."

"What do you sense about me? Odintar said I probably have latent abilities." Tori closed her eyes and Jillian felt an itchy sort of tingle deep inside her mind.

"There's definitely something there, but I'm not sure what it is. That's odd. My impressions are usually more specific."

"That's basically what Odintar said." Jillian tapped her thumb against the side of her empty mug. "How serious have things gotten with you and Lor?"

"I know I've only known him for a couple of months, but—"

"Six weeks," Jillian corrected. "It hasn't even been two months."

"You said Odintar linked your minds when he brought you here. Has he allowed you to see beyond his shields?"

"No. He's been focused on healing me. What does that have to do with you and Lor?"

"Mind-to-mind links allow Mystics to share thoughts, emotions, even memories. Humans can spend years, even decades, together and never know each other as well as I know Lor. I've seen into his mind, shared his feelings and experienced the forces that formed his personality. It's an intimacy most humans will never know."

"Odintar is just my doctor. There's no reason for us to exchange those sorts of things."

Tori chuckled, clearly not convinced. "You don't find him attractive?"

"He's easy on the eyes, but that doesn't mean I want to have his babies."

"If you manage to keep it professional, you're a stronger woman than I am. Not only are these men physically attractive, they're smart, protective, and they come from a planet where men greatly outnumber women. Being treated like you're the most precious person in the entire universe is a little hard to resist. If Odintar decides to pursue you—"

"He won't." Her response was a bit too emphatic to be believable. "He knows my life is too chaotic right now for even a casual fling."

"These men don't do casual flings."

"One night in his bed and I'll believe in true love?" she scoffed. Tori's attitude was so out of character, it was starting to irritate Jillian. Tori had always been the cautious, logical one, talking others out of rash decisions. "Maybe I'll sleep with him just to prove you wrong."

Tori shook her head, her expression suddenly serious. "Don't even consider sleeping with him unless you're ready for a serious entanglement. Like I said, Ontarians don't think about sex the way humans do. They become possessive fast once intimacies are exchanged."

Tantalizing images teased Jillian's memory for just a moment before she forced them away. Odintar holding himself above her as his tongue explored her mouth. The kiss had been strategic, but she couldn't seem to rid her mind of the sensations, the heat. "Enough about sex." She waved away the topic, though the slow, simmering warmth lingered in her core. "Is Lor staying with you or are you staying on his spaceship?"

Tori chuckled. "Give Odintar a couple more days to bring you up to speed and then we'll give you the grand tour."

She pushed her fingers through her hair, brushing the wavy mass back from her face. "I can't help noticing that each woman they've 'rescued' so far has ended up with one of the Mystics. Are you sure the Shadow Assassins are the only ones hunting for mates?"

"It's a valid point, but there's one significant difference. The Mystics might be taking advantage of an unusual opportunity, but their women are willing. The Shadow Assassins aren't giving their victims a choice."

They lapsed into silence as Jillian mulled over her options. Unless she'd had some sort of psychotic break from reality, this was really happening. The dangers she faced might be beyond her control, but her responses to them weren't. She'd always been self-reliant and she didn't intend to sacrifice her independence now. If Odintar could make her strong and capable of protecting herself, then she'd focus on the process with the resolve and discipline that had driven her dance career.

Still, trust was hard. Especially when she was feeling pressured to connect with a stranger. "How well do you know him?"

"Odintar?"

"Yeah. Have you 'seen beyond his shields'?" Jillian softened her sarcastic tone with a smile.

"No, but he's worked tirelessly and risked his life over and over." She glanced at the men and smiled, then her gaze turned intense and compelling as she looked into Jillian's eyes. "He saved Angie's life when no one else could have. He's one of the good guys, Jillian. I promise, you can trust him."

Chapter Four

Odintar could go without sleep for days at a time as long as he replenished his energy in other ways. His visit to the metaphysical plane had allowed him to feed, but his thoughts were still scattered, his spirit unusually restless. After a quick shower and shave, he changed his clothes and attempted to meditate. Every time he cleared his mind images of Jillian crept in, titillating images of her long legs and supple curves, her expressive eyes and soft lips. He'd never struggled so hard to suppress his lust for a female.

Unlike his Ontarian companions, he'd never lacked for female companionship. But women had always been amusing diversions from the things that were important in his life. His job frequently required that he travel, which made long-term relationships hard. So what was it about Jillian that made him want to linger, to spend time with her in and out of the bedroom? Their time together had only been interactive for less than a day, but she'd dominated his thinking—and his fantasies—ever since he saw her. He didn't understand the impulses she drew to the surface. Still, their connection was undeniable.

A ripple of emotion drew him toward her bedroom door several hours after dawn. Fear, defused and distant, had him reaching for the door handle. Then a conflicted jumble of excitement, wonder and hope pushed through the anxiety. He heard her stir so he renewed the constriction on his end of their link. Until she knew he could sense her emotions, it was rude to intrude on her privacy.

She'd been quiet and distracted after they returned from her conversation with Tori. Knowing Jillian needed to sort through her feelings and reconcile her new reality with the one she'd been forced to leave behind, he'd allowed her reticence. If her withdrawn mood continued, however, he'd have to find a way to draw her out.

Caffeine wasn't a stimulant to Rodytes, but he'd learned to enjoy coffee's taste. He went to the kitchen and made a pot of the fragrant brew as he waited for Jillian to appear. She took a shower and changed clothes before venturing out of her bedroom. She'd chosen jeans and a clingy T-shirt that showcased her trim torso and full, round breasts. The outfit wasn't particularly daring, but it sure as hell wasn't helping his concentration.

"Did you sleep well?" he asked as she joined him in the sun-drenched kitchen.

"I did, but I still feel sort of weak and shaky. Do I smell coffee?"

"You do." He filled two mugs and handed her one before crossing to the table. "And as for the weakness, it's to be expected. Your body is still healing." They sat and he paused for several sips before he went on. "If you want to wait until you're feeling stronger to explore your abilities, I'll understand. We've expected you to deal with an awful lot all at one time."

"Other than not overwhelming me, are there advantages to waiting?"

"It might help with the side effect of processing so much energy." She'd seemed troubled by her sexual reaction, so he was purposefully vague.

She pushed back from the table and stood, the mug still in her hand. "Are there eggs or something? I don't think a liquid breakfast is going to cut it for me this morning." Before he could answer she crossed to the refrigerator and opened the door. Now that she had something to do, she became less self-conscious. "You blast me with energy and I get turned on. You said it wasn't unusual."

"Reacting to the excess energy is inevitable. Having your body channel the overflow into a sexual outlet is a bit more unique." The distinction was counterproductive to her calm, but he wanted to be completely honest.

"So I'm an oversexed freak?" She began cracking eggs into a bowl, carefully keeping her face averted.

He moved to the counter and stood beside her, yet she remained focused on her breakfast preparations. "You're not a freak." He touched her shoulder and she paused but still wouldn't look at him. "We're attracted to each other and the energy amplified the attraction. That's all there was to it."

She finally glanced at him. "What if it happens again?"

"That's up to you. I'll remain completely professional." He moved closer and felt the familiar sting of transformation in his eyes. "Or I can help you through it."

"Tori warned me about this." She put the eggs back in the carton and faced him. "If we end up in bed together, you'll consider it a marriage proposal."

He stubbornly fought back a smile, knowing it would rile her. "I think Tori's forgetting a pivotal fact. I'm not Ontarian."

Her brows scrunched together and she tilted her head a bit to the side. "Then what's your connection to this mission?"

"Finish your breakfast and I'll explain." Few people knew his history. He wasn't ashamed of his past. He just didn't see the value in dwelling on events that couldn't be changed. He needed Jillian to trust him and this seemed like a good way to start building that trust. "Most people know my father is Rodyte and most assume my mother was Ontarian."

Jillian returned to her preparations as she asked, "Why do people presume she was Ontarian?"

"Because I'm a Master-level Mage. It's highly unusual for the Conservatory to accept an outsider, much less one with no Ontarian blood."

"What's the Conservatory?" She glanced at him, eyes bright with curiosity.

"It's the elite training facility for Mystics on Ontariese."

"You said '*the* elite training facility'. Is there only one?"

He smiled. She didn't miss much, but her attention to details could be counterproductive when they had so much to accomplish. "There are many training facilities, but only at the Conservatory can one become a Master-level Mage. Still, it's not important to this story."

"Sorry." She returned his smile. "I'll try and hold my questions until the end." She motioned toward the eggs. "Do you want some?"

He shook his head. "I've already eaten." It wasn't an outright lie. He just didn't want the means by which he'd replenished his energy to launch another tangent. "My mother was my father's captive for three years before she escaped. She knew I'd be taken away from her as soon as I was weaned, so she started planning for our escape as soon as she realized she was pregnant."

"He was a Shadow Assassin?"

"No. The Shadow Assassins were established by a Rodyte named Vade. He built upon traditions that have been observed by Rodyte warriors for centuries."

"Is there a shortage of women on Rodymia?"

"Not at all. It has to do with magic. The war between Bilarri and Rodymia surrounds the ability to manipulate magic. Basically—and this is extremely simplified—Bilarrians can do magic and Rodytes can't."

"So Rodytes capture Bilarrian women hoping their offspring will be able to do magic?"

Again he was impressed by her perceptiveness. "Primarily. It's also an act of rebellion. They consider the captive females prisoners of war. In fact, they're called war brides."

"Wow. That's twisted, but I understand the concept."

"My mother barely escaped, but she expended so much energy in doing so that she never recovered. She had friends on Ontariese and they raised me as their own. My name was changed and everyone was told that I was the orphan of an Ontarian slave and a Rodyte warrior."

She turned off the burner and carried her plate of scrambled eggs to the table. He refilled their mugs then joined her.

"It's easy to understand why you'd be interested in stopping the Shadow Assassins." She paused for a forkful of eggs. "Were you assigned to the team or did you volunteer?"

"Lor asked if I was interested, so I guess I volunteered. We've worked together many times in the past and my connection to this mess is even more twisted than just my personal history."

"Really?" She waited for him to elaborate and when he didn't, she said, "You can't just leave me hanging. How are you connected to the Shadow Assassins?"

"I'm not. I'm connected to the women in the notebook."

She set down her fork and swallowed hard. "Please tell me we're not related."

He chuckled, thrilled by the dread in her eyes. "Not even remotely. I led the team that was sent to hunt down the renegades."

"Renegades? What renegades?"

He thought back on everything he'd told her and realized they'd not discussed the Dirty Dozen. He sighed. Not only was the topic distasteful, it also highlighted the biggest failure of his career. "Ontarians have tried multiple strategies for improving the ratio of men to women on their planet. Many humans are genetically compatible with Ontarians. So about thirty years ago, they worked with the US Government to recruit unattached females who were willing to relocate to Ontariese."

"Sort of like mail order brides?"

"I'm not familiar with that term."

She shrugged. "What you described sounds similar. Anyway, go on."

He paused, trying to encapsulate the information so they didn't spend the next hour talking about the unpleasant subject. "We're not sure why, but twelve of the participants in the program broke off and completely disregarded the rules. They targeted college campuses and seduced countless females. Rather than courting a potential life mate, they lured them into bed, did their best to impregnate them, and then moved on to their next conquest. They called themselves the Dirty Dozen."

"There are so many disgusting elements to that story. I'm not sure what to say."

"The Ontarians were equally disgusted. I led a team that was tasked with finding the Dirty Dozen and returning them to Ontariese to pay for their crimes. The mission didn't go well. It took much longer than it should have to complete and one of my people was killed in an ambush I should have seen coming. Their leader, the most ruthless of the lot, might have escaped. We never found his body."

"This was thirty years ago?"

"Just under."

"You think these assholes are responsible for all the women in the notebook?" Her revulsion was understandable. The renegade's behavior had been reprehensible.

"It's likely."

She stared into the distance, her gaze troubled. "Tori's the right age. Even Angie barely fits into the criteria, but I'm only twenty-six. I couldn't have been fathered by one of the renegades."

"You could have if the leader is still alive."

Pushing her plate away, she stood and crossed to the coffee pot. Odintar spotted her mug still on the table and brought it to her. "Thanks," she muttered as she filled the mug. "This is the gift that keeps on giving."

"No more surprises." He took the coffee pot from her and returned it to the burner. "There are still countless details you need to understand eventually, but you know the important things now."

She drank most of the coffee faster than he'd thought possible then set the mug in the sink. "Let's get started. I want to know who I really am."

"And I'm hoping to help you learn. But you have to understand that it won't happen instantaneously. Even if I succeed in releasing your gift, or gifts, it could take you years to explore their full potential."

"I get it." She smoothed her hair back from her face and squared her shoulders. "This is only the beginning."

"And how shall we handle it if my energy has the same effect on you that it did last night?"

She shrugged again and her lips twitched with the hint of a smile. "As long as we're clear that it's just for fun, I'm not opposed to letting you 'help me through it.'"

As if of their own volition, his arms pulled her against his chest and his mouth angled over hers. She gasped, tensed, then melted into his embrace. It took a moment longer for her to respond, but her arms wrapped around his neck and her lips parted beneath the gentle probing of his tongue.

He pushed his fingers into the back of her hair and made a loose fist. She tasted faintly of coffee and her scent fueled his desire. He tilted his head, fitting his mouth more firmly to hers. This was what he'd wanted all morning, what he couldn't stop wanting. His tongue moved with slow, thorough stokes, memorizing every hollow and surface of her mouth.

His other hand found the hem of her T-shirt and slipped beneath. Her skin was so soft and warm that he moaned. He wanted her naked and spread beneath him as he slowly tasted every inch of her amazing skin.

"I don't want a relationship," she whispered when his mouth freed hers and trailed along the underside of her jaw. "You have to accept that."

"I know." Which didn't mean he agreed; it just meant he'd go slowly until he convinced her that she had nothing to fear. He nipped her chin then continued down the side of her neck.

She eased her hands between them and pushed against his chest. "I thought you were going to explore my mind, not my body."

He loosened his hold without letting go. "Can't I do both?"

Jillian trembled in his embrace, but it wasn't fear that made her shake. If any other man had pounced on her the way Odintar had, she would have shoved him away. So why had Odintar's aggression made her melt? The man knew how to kiss. There was no denying that. Still, the overt hunger in his gaze should have been enough to warn her away. And still she stood there staring into his blue-ringed eyes.

"We're here for a reason and it's not this." Her body clenched as if in protest of her sensibility.

He closed his eyes and slowly released her. When he raised his lids again, the blue rings were gone. "I apologize."

"Why?" She smiled, hoping to ease the tension arcing between them. "I enjoyed it. Didn't you?" His eyes narrowed and he reached for her again, but she twisted sharply to the side. "Work before play, you naughty boy." He chuckled and for an instant ruby-red rings appeared in the depths of his gaze. "What the..." She moved closer and touched his face just below his left eye. "Now the rings are red."

He laughed and the rings burned brighter. "That doesn't happen very often. Rodytes have blue rings in their eyes while Bilarrians have red. Mine are triggered by emotion. Primal emotions like anger and passion bring out the Rodyte blue. Lighter emotions like amusement and joy turn the rings red."

The color scheme seemed backward to her, but she couldn't argue with the facts. Each time she'd seen the blue rings he'd been aroused or annoyed. It was only his laughter that turned them red. "I'll do my best to keep them red." She took another step backward and motioned to the wide opening leading to the rest of the house. "Should we go back to the living room?"

"Wherever you're most comfortable."

She snickered. "I'd be most comfortable in my apartment."

"For the time being, you're stuck here with me."

Rather than belabor the point, she walked into the living room and sat in the chair facing the sofa. She expected Odintar to move to the sofa, but he pulled the ottoman slightly back from her legs, then sat down. He held out his hands and she slowly took them, dreading the helplessness that surged through her whenever he touched her mind. Powers like his were supposed to be fiction, yet he moved through her mind as easily as she could cross a room. He didn't need to tell her to close her eyes. With the first brush of his energy, she lowered her lids and braced for impact.

"Jillian." When she didn't open her eyes, he squeezed her hands. "Look at me."

She opened one eye and then the other, feeling rather foolish.

"We don't have to do this. Now or ever. I thought you wanted to learn your true potential."

"I do."

"Then why are you preparing for battle?"

With a sigh, she drew her hands out of his and scooted back in the chair. "I've always had a thing about personal space. Unless I'm onstage, I don't like anyone getting too close to me. When you enter my mind, it feels like the worst sort of invasion."

"Is there a reason you're this distrustful? Were you traumatized in some way?"

Her gaze narrowed and she folded her hands in her lap. "Do you know about Angie's attack?"

"Yes. Were you—"

"No. It's not physical with me." She sighed. It was hard to explain without sounding petty and she fought daily not to be defined by her mother's attitudes. "I spent my childhood listening to my mother rail about how I couldn't trust anyone. According to her, friends would always disappoint me and men would use me then throw me away. I didn't want to believe her, tried not to let her attitude shape my personality, but too many of my own experiences reinforced her position." She shrugged with an indifference she didn't feel. "Even after years away from her influence, I find myself pushing people away."

"What about Tori and Angie? Have they disappointed you?"

"No, but that doesn't keep me from being cautious. It's really hard for me to let anyone get close."

"All right. How about if you get close to me?"

She stared at him, unsure what he expected. God, the man was gorgeous. He wasn't classically handsome. His features were too bold, his manner too assertive. But he appealed in that rugged, outdoorsy way that always weakened her knees. She licked her lips and opened her hands against her thighs. "What do you want me to do?"

"Whatever you want to do." His gaze narrowed for a moment and a tingly itch erupted in her mind. "Can you feel that?"

"Yes." It was a little hard to miss.

"It's the link I anchored last night. Close your eyes and follow it into my mind."

Shocked by the offer, she closed her eyes. Was this what Tori meant when she'd asked if Jillian had seen beyond his shields? Tori made it sound incredibly intimate. This must be something else. Rather than ask for clarification, she focused on the sensation and found the link. It looked like a shimmery thread stretching out into the distance. This delicate fiber had allowed him to pull her onto the metaphysical plane? It must be a hell of a lot stronger than it looked. Instinctively, she reached out and touched the cord. The image inside her mind was incredibly clear. It was like watching herself on video. She gently plucked the link, like an instrument string, and vibrations reverberated through her entire body.

"That's right," Odintar encouraged. "Now follow the strand."

"I don't know how." She didn't know how to do any of this and yet she'd managed to find the link.

He gently took her wrist and guided her hand to his face. His skin was warm and smooth. He must have shaved while she was sleeping. The image inside her mind focused as well and the sensations intensified. She scooted forward, easing her knees in between his. Yet in her mind, she stood beside the thread, her face lit by the fiber's silvery glow.

"Can you see where the link goes?" His tone was hushed and his fingers remained around her wrist.

"Yes."

"Picture yourself walking along beside it. Come closer."

She reached for the cord again, but her fingers sank into the strands this time. Energy rippled around and cascaded through her. She shivered, using the resulting restlessness to propel her forward, along the flickering thread.

She could sense him more clearly with each step, feel his strength and the astonishing scope of his power. Emotions pulsed from him and images flowed, detailed yet disordered. Like a high-speed montage, events inundated her mind. She saw a boy with curly dark hair and sad, watchful eyes; then a petulant youth sneaking down a shadowed corridor; followed by a young man locked in a passionate embrace with a blue-haired woman. Emotions accompanied each scene, yet they seemed random. These were not pivotal events in his life, just snapshots in time.

Too often he stood apart, an observer to the happenings around him. At first she couldn't tell if the separation was by choice or if the others wanted no part of him. Then bursts of anger and determination wove through the loneliness. He might appear indifferent, but his heart ached to belong.

Compelled by the memories, Jillian pushed deeper into Odintar's mind. She knew what it was like to be an outsider, to hunger for acceptance. The only time she felt truly at peace was when she was utterly lost in a dance.

Jillian saw the woman again. She was older now, her black hair only streaked with blue. Odintar stood beside a rumpled bed wearing only a pair of pants. Trying not to be distracted by the sculpted perfection of his body, Jillian assessed his expression. He clenched his jaw and his nostrils flared, but she saw only pain in his eyes. The woman hurriedly dressed as she shouted her frustration and disappointment at her soon-to-be-ex-lover. She stormed from the room and Odintar cursed then his image morphed into the sad-eyed little boy.

Compassion squeezed Jillian's heart and she blindly reached out of Odintar.

He caught her wrist and guided her hand back to her lap. *Don't pity me,* gennari. *That lonely boy is long gone.*

Gennari? Why did that sound familiar? Had he called her that... She'd heard his voice inside her head! Her eyes flew open and she gasped. "I knew it! You're telepathic."

As are you. His lips only moved to form a lazy smile.

"Really? Then why is your voice the only one I've ever heard?"

Your mind is heavily shielded. Push a thought across our link. The connection makes it easy. It's a good way to practice.

Can you hear me now? She felt foolish echoing the familiar commercial, until he responded.

Loud and clear.

She stared at him in stunned wonder for a moment, unable to believe it was really happening. Being told that her father was likely an alien and actually finding a resulting anomaly were two very different things. *Can I do this with anyone or just you?*

His smile turned predatory and he scooted closer, placing his hands on the armrests of her chair. He still wasn't touching her, but she was basically caged by his body. *Depends what you mean by 'this'.* Before she could respond he chuckled and waved away her answer. "Work before play. I keep forgetting. If you're finished looking around, draw me into your mind."

Like a child with a new toy, she wanted to explore. *Can I look around a little longer? Please.*

He leaned in and brushed his lips over hers. It wasn't really a kiss, just a tantalizing caress of skin against skin. *I have nothing to hide. Take as long as you like.*

She raised her other hand and framed his face, then reluctantly closed her eyes. Looking at him was a constant temptation. Still, she couldn't afford to squander this opportunity.

Easing back into the churning energy stream, she took a moment to familiarize herself with the sensations. Her senses felt overstimulated, making each impulse slightly painful. *This must be what it's like when a baby learns to walk, exhilarating yet terrifying.*

She drew his energy inward, mixing it with her own until she couldn't distinguish between the two. Rather than searching out his memories, she opened herself to the information and the images began to flow naturally. His youth and teenage years had been shaped by routine and discipline. Apparently a magical "conservatory" wasn't all that different from a school for the performing arts. Any talent, be it physical or metaphysical, was made better through hard work and endless practice. Jillian's favorite instructor liked to say, "Practice does not make perfect; *perfect* practice makes perfect. Imperfect practice only reinforces bad habits." Their talents might be vastly different, but their adolescent years had been remarkably similar.

You're about to witness my first sexual experience, he warned. *Are you sure that's what you want to watch?*

She pulled back as heat spread across her cheeks. "Thanks for the warning." There was only one person she wanted to picture Odintar having sex with and he couldn't remember something that hadn't happened yet.

"What else do you want to know?" He shifted on the ottoman, clearly restless. "This will be faster if I guide you."

Suspicion tingled down her spine and she lowered her hands to his shoulders. "Can you manipulate what I see?"

"I can if I send the images to you, but you're inside my shields. What you see is what you get."

She wasn't sure what she wanted to know. And she was starting to feel guilty about the exchange. If she didn't want him digging around in her mind, why should he allow her to rummage through his? "Show me your best friend." That seemed like a neutral enough topic.

"I don't have a best friend. I have several close friends who have moved in and out of my life for decades. Lor is one of them, but the others are just as important to me."

"Are any of them female?" She glanced away from his intense stare, refusing to consider what prompted the question. Why should she care if one or more of the important people in his life were female?

He chuckled. "If you really want, I'll show you every woman I've ever bedded. I'm not ashamed of my sexual needs."

"Neither am I," she insisted, but the claim sounded defensive and unconvincing. "I'm just not used to having a man I just met watch me c-come." She stumbled over the last word, compounding her humiliation.

He traced a path from her temple to her chin, his fingertip barely touching her skin. "I think we should move on or I'll forget we're supposed to be working. You already know more about me than anyone else on Earth. The rest is endless missions and finding creative ways to combat boredom."

She was ready to do as he asked, or nearly ready. One image lingered in the back of her mind, imprinted there because it had appeared so often in his memories. "Who was she? Is she still part of your life?"

He didn't bother with denials or deflections. They both knew who she meant. "Her name was Cizarro and no, she's not part of my life any longer."

"Was she more than just your lover? The connection seemed...complex."

His dark brows arched, accenting the challenge in his even darker eyes. "I'll tell you about Cizarro, but you'll have to tell me about the men in your past. I suspect there haven't been that many."

She wasn't sure if she was flattered or insulted by his conclusion. Had her kisses been that awkward? No longer comfortable touching him, she drew her hands back into her lap. All he had to do was look at her with desire in his gaze and she blushed like a schoolgirl. Of course he thought she was a sexual novice. Which wasn't too far from the truth.

"There have been three," she admitted. "And it's a deal."

He acknowledged the bargain with a nod before he began his tale. "Cizarro was brought in from Bilarri for the last phase of my training. Head Master Tal knew my true history and wanted me to explore Bilarrian techniques as well as Ontarian."

He'd slept with his teacher. She fought back a smile. He really was a naughty boy. "Was the attraction mutual or did she seduce you?"

His laugh was deep and dark, filled with sensual promise. "You clearly know little about Bilarrian males. I was the aggressor. She stubbornly resisted my advances for almost a year before I stopped listening to her excuses."

Dread washed over her, cooling her smoldering desire. Surely he didn't mean he'd forced her. There had been nothing in his memories that hinted at such cruelty. "On Earth that's called date rape." She watched his reaction closely, hoping for outrage and disgust. He didn't disappoint.

He shoved back from her chair and stood. "I have never forced my attentions on a woman. And after all you have seen, I find the insinuation insulting."

She was relieved by his outrage. It felt completely believable. "Then what did you mean by you stopped listening to her excuses?"

"They were just that, excuses. She wanted me every bit as badly as I wanted her. We were consenting adults and I was no longer willing to allow pointless rules to keep us apart." His indignation gradually receded, but he remained on his feet. "We were together until I finished my training. We tried to be discreet, but most knew we were lovers. When she was ready to return to Bilarri, she expected me to go with her. I genuinely cared for her, but my life was on Ontariese. I suggested a compromise, but she wasn't interested in a long-distance relationship."

"But you can teleport from planet to planet. Why did she reject the compromise?"

"Because it was a compromise. She said I loved my job more than I loved her and she deserved better." He slid the ottoman out of the way and knelt on the floor in front of her, hands resting lightly on her knees.

"She was right. I enjoyed her company, and the sex was great, but she wasn't my true mate."

Just the pressure of his fingers against her legs had her squirming in the chair. What would it feel like to be naked and at his mercy? At his mercy? Why would she want to be at any man's mercy? "You honestly believe there's just one woman in the entire universe predestined to be your mate?"

"Of course not." He slid his hands a bit higher on her legs, his gaze boring into hers. "There are any number of women who are physically and emotionally compatible with me. My body lets me know when I encounter a potential match so I can pay more attention to the possibilities."

She licked her lips and relaxed her leg muscles, not wanting him to realize how deeply his simple touch was affecting her. "And how often do you encounter such women?"

"It has never happened—before." His slight hesitation changed the meaning of the sentence. He slid his hands up her legs and grasped her hips as he eased between her knees. "Your turn," he whispered. "Tell me about the three fools who let you get away."

If she wrapped her arms around his neck and her legs around his waist, he could carry her into the bedroom. She already felt breathless and anxious and he hadn't touched anything more intimate than her hips.

"Number one," he prompted. "How old were you?"

"Sixteen. Typical first time. Awkward, utterly forgettable."

He chuckled, apparently pleased by the confession. "Number two?"

"I met him during my sophomore year in college. We were much more serious. We even lived together for a while. But sort of like you, I knew he wasn't the one and I was more interested in my career."

"And number three?" He pulled her closer, spreading her legs in the process.

"Most entertaining mistake of my life."

He tilted his head and slid his hands up to her waist. "Explain."

She didn't want to talk. She wanted to wrap her legs around his hips and rub against his chest. Her core ached and her nipples tingled, but she'd promised a full accounting. "I knew he was a womanizer, that he'd quickly lose interest if I gave in, but I'd never had a man pursue me like that before."

"You like being pursued?" It was impossible to miss the underlying question. Would she like being pursued by him?

She swallowed hard, barely able to remember what they were talking about. "We—Tori, Angie and I—readily admit we're drawn to bad boys. But the qualities that attract us are also the qualities that keep long-term relationships from working out."

"Which qualities are you talking about?" His hands inched higher, his thumbs teasing her midriff through her T-shirt. "What makes a man a bad boy in your eyes?"

"Arrogance, not giving a damn about what anyone else thinks of him, and an affinity with danger."

His lips curved without parting, his smile speculative. "Do you consider me a bad boy?"

God yes! He could be the poster model for bad boys, but her throat was so tight she could only nod.

"Were you right? Did Three lose interest after you'd shared his bed?"

Just when she was ready for him to cup her breast and end the teasing game of almost touches, he pulled his hands away. It was all she could do not to grab his wrist and press her breast into his palm. "He strung me along until he had his next conquest in sight. I'm not sure if he actually cheated on me or not, but he was definitely more interested in the other woman."

"Who broke it off?"

"I did. That's the only part of the relationship I don't regret." Unable to bear the smoldering heat of his eyes, she looked down. He was still too close, but she felt the absence of his touch even more powerfully than she'd felt the tantalizing caress. "He was everything my mother warned me about and more. In fact, they all were in one way or another."

He curved his index finger beneath her chin and raised her face until she looked at him again. "All men aren't like that. Even bad boys."

"I know." She sighed. Their trip down memory lane had only shined a glaring light on how empty her relationships had been. She'd always dreamed of a man who could prove her mother wrong, someone so utterly committed to her that he'd never leave her side. Or at least never want to.

His fingers brushed the side of her neck then lightly cupped her shoulder. "You all right? You seem really sad."

"Where is all this leading? Why did you let me see into your mind?" He wanted her and she wanted him. That much was obvious to both. So why did he keep toying with her? Maybe if they had sex, she'd be able to concentrate on something other than Odintar.

"I need your trust and I don't have time to earn it in a more conventional way."

"So distract me again." Had that breathy, needful tone actually come out of her?

He accepted the offer with actions rather than words. In a flash, he lifted her and reversed their positions. He sat in the chair and brought her down straddling his lap. His strong fingers wrapped around the back of her neck and pulled her face toward his. Her lips parted, encouraging the bold thrust of his tongue, but that only incited his aggression.

Catching both wrists, he drew her arms to the small of her back and secured them there with one of his long-fingered hands. His free hand returned to her neck, holding her still as his mouth plundered hers. She wasn't resisting, but his hold remained firm, a warning she didn't quite understand.

His energy barreled across their link and pushed through her shields. She shivered then moaned, shocked yet intrigued by the emotions flowing in the wake of his thrust. Desire blazed, easily recognizable, while fascination, resolve and anxiety twisted around each other and threaded through the blatant lust.

Before she could sort through the tangled mess and figure out what caused each reaction, she felt a sharp tear. She tried to turn away from the pain, but he held her securely. Energy gushed from the opening, rushing through her body and pouring back across their link. She felt as if she were drowning from the inside. Panic drove rational thoughts from her mind. She writhed within the surging current, tossed about like a boat on a raging sea.

Don't fight it. It won't harm you. He released her arms and pulled her snugly against his chest. *Don't be afraid.* His mouth still moved over and against hers, but the distraction was insufficient now. *Absorb as much of the energy as you can.*

As if understanding his words, her body obeyed his directive. She felt the energy being soaked up by her muscles, organs and tissues. Every molecule inside her suddenly acted like a thirsty sponge.

Very good. He pushed his fingers into her hair as he separated their mouths and waited for her eyes to focus. "Can you feel what changed?"

"Yes." It was a little hard to miss. Every cell in her body felt as if it were vibrating, ready to burst through her skin and fly away. Her muscles twitched, her skin tingled, and she couldn't seem to catch her breath. "But I don't understand it. What did you do?"

"I just created an opening and let your true self out. Can you channel some of the energy across our link or should I distract you again?"

Even though they'd both enjoyed the kiss, determining the nature of her abilities was more important. She gathered a particularly restless wave and used it to saturate their link. "Is that enough?"

He nodded. "I have a clear reading, but what I'm sensing is confusing."

"Confusing how." She shivered and her hair blew out around her as if she were standing in front of a fan. "Did I do that?"

"You did."

"What does it mean?"

He started to speak then paused. "Remember the sensation and see if you can recreate it."

She closed her eyes, tried to feel the burst of air upon her face and her hair rippling around her again. A cool current of air swirled around her and she gasped. Her hair danced in a breeze strong enough to ruffle his hair as well.

"I did it." She gave him an excited hug, but he looked concerned not pleased. "What's wrong?"

"Nothing is wrong. We were just mistaken. Your father wasn't Ontarian." He smoothed her hair back from her face as he looked into her eyes. "What I'm sensing is elemental magic, which means your father was either from Rodymia or Bilarri."

Chapter Five

The door chime announced a visitor and Roxie Latimer hurried to the front of her shop. She'd opened Unique Ink three years ago after her appearance on a popular television show had quadrupled her following overnight. Tattoo artists were a dime a dozen in Las Vegas, so she was grateful for the exposure. Her two best friends, and fellow tattoo artists, had gone to lunch together, leaving Roxie to hold down the fort.

"What can I..." Her visitor turned around and Roxie's throat refused to function. Sevrin Keire was always polite and ridiculously generous, but there was something about her that terrified Roxie. Perhaps it was the fact that she only appeared when Roxie was alone. She cleared her throat and tried again. "It's good to see you again, Ms. Keire. What can I do for you?"

Sevrin crossed the room, her stride rolling yet graceful. Her style of choice was always leather despite the desert heat. But never biker black or cowboy brown, Sevrin loved unusual colors. Today's selection was powder blue with sapphire stitching and two-tone ankle boots. The skirt skimmed her hips and accented her narrow waist, while the bolero jacket framed a set of breasts any stripper would covet. How could she tolerate a leather jacket when it was at least eighty outside?

"Are my boys keeping you busy?" There was a salacious undertone to the question, but Sevrin's sculpted features revealed nothing.

"Always. I've had to refer some of my regulars to the other artists to make time for your men, but I've stuck to our agreement." Roxie had encountered Sevrin for the first time nine weeks before. The enigmatic woman strolled into the shop and offered Roxie a small fortune if she would make herself available exclusively to Sevrin's "boys". Instead, Roxie had agreed to make them top priority if she was allowed to work her other clients in as time permitted. Sevrin had decreased the amount of the retainer—which was still more than Roxie usually made in a quarter—and the deal was struck. Then came the parade of musclebound men. Sevrin either trained bodybuilders or she ran some sort of private army. Roxie's money was on the latter. To be more specific, she was convinced Sevrin's boys were foreign mercenaries and she'd been tempted more than once to notify Homeland Security.

"I'd like to renegotiate our deal."

Dread dropped like a brick into the pit of Roxie's stomach. Despite the strangeness of it all, her deal with Sevrin had been the best thing to happen to her since the TV competition. "Have I disappointed you in some way?" She cringed. That made her sound like a mealy-mouthed servant. "Your men have never waited on another client and they have each seemed pleased with my work."

"You were a novelty. They were thrilled just to be alone with an attractive female, but the novelty has worn off."

What the hell was she talking about? Why would full-grown, extremely well-developed, men find being alone with a woman novel? Rather than admit her confusion, she remained silent and waited for Sevrin to elaborate.

"I expected this obsession with tattoos to wear off as well, but some of them seem determined to cover their entire bodies in ink."

They need the pain. Roxie kept the observation to herself as well. Most people experienced a rush of endorphins when they went under the needle. It could be oddly relaxing, exhilarating, even arousing. With Sevrin's men it was like a drug. They felt it faster and more intensely than anyone Roxie had ever seen before. It was as if they were wired, or had been conditioned, to process pain as pleasure. And it happened with each and every one of them.

"If they're interest is still strong, I'm not sure I understand the problem." She chose her words carefully. She'd yet to see it happen, but she suspected that Sevrin could strike like a riled cobra, fast and deadly.

Sevrin stared at her silently for a tense moment. Roxie held her gaze, refusing to cower, yet trying to appear respectful. She needed this arrangement. Sevrin had provided a more lucrative revenue stream than Roxie ever dreamed and she intended to enjoy the windfall as long as possible. Commercial space anywhere on the Strip was far beyond her means, which limited her clientele to locals and the rare tourist who cared enough to seek her out.

"Who said there was a problem?" Sevrin smiled, but her brown eyes remained flat and lifeless.

This wasn't the first time Roxie had wondered if Sevrin was wearing colored contacts. Even the most realistic ones muted a person's ability to emote. But if she was wearing contacts, why choose such an ordinary shade of brown?

Shaking away the useless speculation, Roxie allowed herself to relax. "If there isn't a problem, why does our agreement need to be changed?"

"There are other *services* I wish to arrange."

Roxi glared, no longer caring if she lost her most important client. "I don't turn tricks for anyone. Never have. Never will."

Another cold, calculating smile parted Sevrin's lips. "And I wasn't asking you to spread your thighs. Relax. This is simple and it pays extremely well."

She moved behind the counter, needing some sort of barrier between her and her unsettling guest. "I'm listening."

"You're like a bartender. People trust you, like you. Talk to you."

"I'd love to take your money, but none of your men have said anything important to or in front of me."

"How do you know?" She paused, allowing the question to resonate. "Do you speak our language?"

She wasn't even sure what their language was. It had fascinated her ever since the first man switched to the guttural dialect. She'd listened to language samples on the internet, determined to identify theirs and failed. She'd never heard anything like it. "You know I don't."

"And so do they, which is why they speak freely in front of you."

"I tried to learn Spanish a few years ago." She shook her head, remembering the frustration and her utter lack of aptitude. "I suck at it."

"My country has pioneered learning technology that isn't as yet approved by your government." She smoothed down her narrow skirt then moved closer to the counter. "That's one of the reasons I'm here."

If she were in negotiations with the US government, wouldn't she be in Washington, DC? Suspicion urged Roxie back, but curiosity held her steady.

"I know what you're thinking. National negotiations don't take place in Las Vegas. But you're wrong. Influential government officials agreed to meet me here because we don't want the media finding out about the technology until we're ready for an official announcement."

That more or less made sense, but it also flooded Roxie's mind with questions. "Where are you from? Every time I've asked, you or your men, you dodge the question."

"Korzakistan. It's a tiny country in Eastern Europe, doesn't even appear on most maps. But it has always been politically neutral, which is why so many scientists sought asylum there."

"Then you speak Russian?" Roxie was by no means a linguist, but their language hadn't sounded like Russian to her.

"We do, but that's not what they have been speaking in front of you. When my men become secretive, they revert to an ancient dialect known only to a select few. It amuses them to exclude others from their conversation."

"And you have technology that can teach me this ancient dialect?"

Sevrin nodded and the overhead lights accented the subtle blue streaks in her dark hair. "You would be required to sign a nondisclosure agreement, of course. I can't have something you say in passing compromise the negotiations."

"If the technology works as well as you claim and I can miraculously understand them, what then?"

"You report back to me daily with a summation of everything you've heard. Obviously, if they realize you can understand them both our agreements will be terminated."

"Obviously," Roxie grumbled. "Is continuing our original agreement still an option if I turn you down?"

"Sorry. I need more from you."

All or nothing. She wasn't surprised, but she sure as hell didn't like it. "How do I know this mysterious technology won't scramble my brain? There could be a very good reason it's not available in the US."

"How do you think I learned English? The technology is perfectly safe."

Roxi hated being backed into a corner, but her only option was to walk away. Her first instinct was to tell Sevrin to go to hell, but she had more than just herself to think about. Sevrin's generosity had allowed her to update equipment, triple the marketing budget, and fund renovations that had only begun. Her friends were busier than ever, which allowed them to charge more for their time. All of that would disappear in an instant if she said no.

"I need to think about it."

"I'd allow you time if I could. Nazerel is scheduled this evening and he's my primary concern."

Now that made perfect sense. Nazerel emanated belligerent authority and subtle menace. A clash between Nazerel and Sevrin would be inevitable. "He comes in all the time. I'll just—"

"He's recently been made aware of some delicate information. I need to know if I can trust him with what he's learned."

Information might be powerful, but it was also dangerous. Roxie had watched enough crime dramas to know what happened to the informant once she knew too much. "I'm really not comfortable with any of this."

"Then I'll take my business elsewhere." Sevrin rested her fingertips on the countertop and slowly leaned in. "You already know more than I'd intended to tell you. You're only safe because you're useful."

Roxi's pulse thudded wildly and her ears began to ring. How had she gotten herself caught up in this mess? It didn't matter. As the boss lady said, she was already in too deep. "All right," she whispered. "I'll do it."

WITH OBVIOUS RELUCTANCE, Odintar lifted Jillian off his lap and set her on the ottoman. It was probably a wise precaution. If they remained within touching distance, they were sure to touch and likely a whole lot more. She'd never been this attracted to a man she'd just met and couldn't explain the fascination now. All she knew was she couldn't seem to get enough of Odintar.

"I need to let Lor know what's going on." He sounded hoarse yet breathless.

Her cheeks were hot and her lips tender, but she'd never felt more desirable. "Cell phones are still not an option?"

He nodded. "I'll just be a minute."

"Go on." She waved him away. "I could use a minute to catch my breath anyway."

He rested back in the chair and closed his eyes, then his features went lax. Before she had time to miss him, their mental connection buzzed to life. Had he intentionally activated their link so she could hear the conversation or was it a side effect of her newly released power? The specifics didn't matter, as long as he knew she wasn't intentionally spying on him.

She felt Odintar's telepathic ping requesting Lor's presence on the metaphysical plane. Rather than waste energy on visualizations, they increased the strength of their shields and communicated spirit to spirit. She found it all interesting yet daunting. Could she really learn how to do all these things?

How's your patient this morning? My mate is concerned that we're expecting too much from her after the trauma of her accident.

Mate? Lor had to mean Tori? Did Tori consider Lor her "mate"?

Odintar was amused by Lor's ambiguity. Not knowing their enemy's exact capabilities was making them all paranoid. *Tell your mate not to worry. My patient is remarkably resilient.*

Do you have something specific to report or are you just checking in?

Translation: cut to the chase, buddy. I'm a busy man.

Odintar didn't seem insulted by Lor's impatience. *We've never been able to pin down the motivation of the Dirty Dozen.*

Beyond flagrant disobedience and lust?

Rebellion might have launched their campaign, but what kept it going for so long?

Outsmarting the people sent to capture them.

She didn't think Lor was being intentionally cruel, but even after all these years the failure still stung Odintar. Odintar didn't like to lose and his showdown with the Dirty Dozen had been a disaster. *I'm sure that was part of it, but I now have evidence of Rodyte involvement.*

Rodytes, Lor sneered. *Always the gods damn Rodytes.* His tone was calmer as he asked, *What evidence?*

My patient is filled with elemental magic. There is no way her father was Ontarian.

How does that implicate Rodymia? Most elemental magic flows from Bilarri.

True, but Lord Drakkin discovered a segment of the Rodyte population that retained the ability to manipulate magic.

Who the hell was Lord Drakkin? Damn it. She still had so much to learn.

That's right. He defused the conflict so quickly, I'd almost forgotten about it.

I have more reason to keep up with Bilarrian developments than you do.

Can't argue with that. Lor's amused chuckle rippled into Odintar's mind then slid across their connection. It was all so strange. *Still, the odds point to Bilarri not Rodymia.*

We both know Rodymia had far more to gain by involving themselves with the Dirty Dozen than anyone on Bilarri. We know for a fact Rodymia is sponsoring the Shadow Assassins and we have strong indications that the two situations are linked.

Get me a sample of your patient's DNA and I'll prove or disprove your hypothesis.

Soon.

A burst of possessiveness propelled Jillian back into the present. There was no denying that Odintar thought of her as his, but the impulse felt protective rather than malicious. She'd have to rid him of the idea sooner or later. But first she had to decide what she wanted out of their relationship. Relationship? She fought back a laugh. When had they entered into a relationship? He was her doctor turned teacher and they had the hots for each other. No one would define that as a relationship.

He pinched off the connection and took a deep breath. She couldn't sense him anymore.

"That was fast." Jillian quickly formed a smile as he opened his eyes. Should she tell him she'd heard his exchange with Lor and that she'd been able to sense his emotions? He already had all sorts of advantages over her. She decided to hold on to this one for a while. Not that it was much of an advantage unless the link spontaneously activated again.

"Didn't want to give you time to cause trouble."

"Me?" She chuckled. "Never. Angie's the one who runs headfirst into danger."

"So we noticed. Blayne will have his hands full just protecting her from herself."

Jillian stood and moved away, but her gaze lingered on him. "What now? Is Bilarrian magic controlled differently than Ontarian?"

"Ontarian magic requires discipline and focus. Bilarrian magic accesses the powers of nature. It's raw, instinctual. It's about releasing control and letting your elemental nature take over. Generally a Bilarrian is more attune to the element of his or her ancestral region. Your abilities appear to flow from Air, so your father's people once lived somewhere in the San Adrin deserts."

"Unless he was from the other planet. How does Rodyte magic work?" Needing something to do with her hands, she slipped them into her back pockets. His gaze started to descend and she realized the position thrust her breasts forward. She immediately crossed her arms instead.

"The vast majority of Rodytes can't control magic," he reminded as his gaze settled again on her face.

"That's right. They're at war because of it." She raised her fingertips to her temples and rubbed in tight, slow circles, hoping to head off the pressure building there. The day had just begun. The last thing she needed was a migraine. "Then what made you think my father could be Rodymian or Rodyte or whatever the hell they're called."

"Rodyte, and if magic were the only factor, I'd say your father was Bilarrian. However, it's far more likely that a Rodyte would be in league with reprobates like the Dirty Dozen than a Bilarrian."

"Wow. That's a sweeping generalization. You basically said all Bilarrians are good and all Rodytes are evil."

"That's not what I said." He pushed to his feet and sidestepped the ottoman. "Rodytes, like Sevrin Keire, are trying to find a technological way of attaining magical abilities. Most Bilarrians don't need such technology because they can already manipulate magic."

"That aligns them with the Shadow Assassins not the Dirty Dozen." She wasn't intentionally provoking him, but she was annoyed by his narrow-minded views. "You're not even sure those two are related."

"I might not have empirical evidence proving the connection, but I am more than sure it's there."

"Okay, for the sake of argument, let's say you're right."

"You'll only allow me to be right for the sake of argument?" He laughed as something dark and dangerous shadowed his gaze. No blue rings yet, so she hadn't totally pissed him off, but she was definitely headed in that direction.

"Isn't it just as possible that this Sevrin person found out about the Dirty Dozen and decided to capitalize on a coincidental opportunity?"

"I don't believe in coincidence."

It was her turn to laugh and hers was as humorless as his had been. "And that makes it a fact?"

He stalked toward her. She held her ground. "I'm glad you're feeling stronger, but I know the situation better than you do. I have extensive history and context for my opinions. I'm not the bigot you're trying to paint me."

She softened her tone without looking away from his penetrating stare. "I never said you were a bigot. I was just asking you to consider other options."

"I've considered every option imaginable. For the past thirty years, options and possibilities have haunted my dreams and complicated my thinking." He grabbed her upper arms and yanked her toward him. "Don't you get it? I'm responsible for their suffering. If I'd been a better leader, if my team had performed to their potential, far fewer lives would have been shattered."

"How can it be your fault? They came here as part of a program sponsored by both the Ontarian and US governments."

"The program might have created the opportunity, but no one could have anticipated such dishonorable behavior."

"I agree." She moved even closer and raised her hands to his chest. "They were sexual predators. Unless the people running the program had warning signs they ignored, no one is to blame but the men themselves."

"That would be true *if* I'd done my job. I was my first off-world mission as Team Leader and I failed utterly. I was so arrogant, so inflexible that I compromised the objective." His forehead creased and regret ignited the blue rings in his eyes.

She slipped her arms around his neck and pressed against his body. "You keep saying that, but I don't understand *why* you think it's true."

"Their behavior escalated once they realized they were being pursued. They dared us, provoked us at every turn. And each of their 'lessons' was taught at the expense of human females. It dragged on for three years."

As if his gaze wasn't tragic enough, emotions trickled across their link. Guilt, shame and sorrow heaved and twisted, blending into one indistinguishable pain. She knew he was blocking the emotions, so the intensity of each must have been one hundred times stronger than what she was feeling.

"I don't know about the other women, but my mother's life wasn't 'shattered' by my birth. Yes, it made her bitter and shifted her priorities, but she loved me, still loves me. And for the most part her life has been happy." Her words were as much a reminder to herself as a statement to him. Her mother was more than her mistrust of men and Jillian sometime forgot all the good. Her mother had built a satisfying, if a bit unconventional life for herself and she had provided well for her daughter. "If your mission had gone as planned, I might never have existed."

The blue faded from his gaze and he released a weary sigh. "It's hard to argue with that."

"Then don't." She rolled to the balls of her feet and pressed a quick kiss on his lips. "Besides, I think you're forgetting one uncomfortable fact. Even thirty years ago, women had options. If the pregnancies had been completely unwanted, many would have terminated."

"I am well aware." He shuddered and shook his head. "Each termination created another victim of my—"

"Don't." She pressed her fingers to his lips. "I'm not going to debate the morality of abortion with you. No more blame. The present is screwed up enough. We don't need to borrow problems from the past."

He nipped her finger then sighed. "You're right. Each life is a celebration regardless of the circumstances of their birth. I won't allow myself to forget again."

"As an official representative of your past mistakes, thank you." She lowered her arms and stepped back. Their desire for each other was a continual temptation, but they really did have things to do.

As if to echo her thought, he asked, "How does your leg feel this morning? Do I need to relax your muscles before we begin?"

"I'm a little tight, but I think I can stretch it out on my own. I'm still amazed. There's no real pain."

"Excellent." He pushed the coffee table toward the wall, clearing more space in the center of the room. "How about your head? I saw you rubbing your temples."

She waved away his concern. "A minor annoyance. If it gets worse, I'll let you know."

"All right. Then we'll start with some simple concentration exercises and see how quickly you progress." He motioned her toward him until they stood about three feet apart. It didn't give them a lot of room to maneuver, but it was their only option. Unless they went outside and his insistence that she stay inside told her the entire property wasn't shielded. "You're a dancer, so I presume you understand the concept of muscle memory."

"Of course. Repetition allowed me to perform common motions without having to think about them."

"This works along the same lines, but the exercises are mental."

"Other than blowing my hair dry, what use is being able to manipulate Air?"

"There are many ways to approach most tasks. If I wanted that remote in my hand." He pointed to the television remote perched on the lampstand across the room. "I would dematerialize the object and reform it in my hand. Someone who was telekinetic would simply command it to move. You can lift it on a current of Air and sail it across the room into your hand. Each accomplishes the same thing, but each requires a different skill set."

Curious, yet skeptical, she stared at the remote, waiting for it to move.

"Think about the gust of wind you created earlier. Remember how it felt and push the sensation toward the remote."

He made it sound so simple, so possible. But she had created a gust of wind. Could she do this too? She kept her eyes open yet focused inward, searching for the sensation, the outward rush. It built gradually, rising from deep inside her. At first she thought she was only remembering what had happened before, but then her skin tingled and the hair around her face rippled. The tension continued to build, so she pictured a straw stretching between her and the lampstand. When the sensation became uncomfortable, she pushed the energy through the imaginary straw and the remote slid off the far side of the table.

"Very good." He clasped his hands behind his back. "Now put it back."

She shot him a sidelong look, but he was watching the remote, apparently waiting for her to comply. "Just like that?"

"Just like that."

Before she had time to think about all the reasons the task was impossible, she pictured a miniature tornado, swirling around the remote, lifting and spinning it from the floor to the lampstand. The remote rotated clumsily several times then flew into the air, completely missing the desired landing pad.

"Again." He remained calm and assured. "Slow it down so you can control the trajectory."

His confidence made it easier for her to believe that she could actually do it. Her second effort was smoother, but she still missed her target. The third try, however, returned the remote to its original location. "I can't believe I just did that." Relief pushed a soft laugh from her throat.

He finally looked at her and smiled. "You're a natural. Air is the hardest element to control, but it offers the widest range of abilities. At some point I should have a guild master assess your potential, so we can focus on the areas for which you have the strongest aptitude."

"What sort of guild master?" Would they have to go to Bilarri for the screening? Unlike Tori, she wasn't sure she wanted to go hustling across the cosmos. There were plenty of things to terrify her right here on Earth.

"Bilarri is separated into four regions. Each region honors one of the four elements. You need to be assessed by one of the masters from Guild Air."

"What guild was Cizarro from?" Not that she wanted Odintar's old lover to assess her!

His lazy smiled warned her that he knew jealousy played a part in her curiosity. "I didn't know which region my mother's people came from, so Tal asked for a mentor who moved in multiple elements. Cizarro was strongest in Fire, but she'd also trained with members of Guilds Air and Water. My natural element turned out to be Water, but her parting gift was a Bilarrian sigil."

"I don't know what that is."

"It's an image or symbol empowered with the giver's abilities. Mine is in the shape of a dragon."

"Really?" She felt her eyes round and smoothed her expression. "Do you have it with you? I love dragons."

He chuckled. "It's a little hard to leave behind." He raised his T-shirt, bunching the material around his neck as he turned around. Even the spectacular expanse of his naked back couldn't distract from the intricate dragon emblazoned on his skin. The wings spread from shoulder to shoulder and the long, muscular body undulated down along his spine. Primarily black and gray, the image was unlike any tattoo Jillian had seen before. It was three dimensional, raised and etched as if it had been carved—or burned—into his flesh.

"How did she... Is it a brand?"

He righted his shirt as he faced her again. "In a way. Cizarro possesses the same artistic flare as the best tattoo artists. Only she works with fire rather than needles and ink."

"She burned that into your back." She shuddered and shook her head. "How did you deal with the pain?"

"It was a rite of passage, a ceremony in honor of my achievements. Like birth, pain was a natural part of the celebration."

If she dwelled on the process, she'd probably throw up, so she switched to the other element of the gift. "You said it was empowered. What does it allow you to do?"

"I can catch things on fire or absorb the heat of something that's already on fire. But it only works once, then she has to recharge it."

"Have you ever used it?"

"Twice. It's unpredictable, so I have to be really careful. Luckily my Water affinity allows me to minimize the damage if things get out of control."

"It's beautiful, but I still can't imagine allowing someone to burn my back for hours and hours."

He ran his index finger down the side of her face and smiled. "It's not a tattoo, sweetheart. It only took a few minutes and then we both got good and drunk."

It was too easy to imagine where that led, so she asked, "What should we do now?"

"More of the same, I'm afraid. You can feel the Air within you, which is an important first step, but you must learn to channel the power without stifling it."

For the next three days they worked continually, stopping only long enough to eat and sleep. At least Jillian presumed Odintar slept. He was always awake when she emerged from her bedroom in the morning and awake when she tumbled into bed exhausted each night. She suspected part of the reason he worked her so hard was to keep them from acting on their attraction. But each time they touched, each lingering look, kept the heat simmering.

Day one focused on moving objects. She repeated the simple exercise with progressively heavier items until the action became effortless. Then she experimented with using Air to increase her strength and speed. More than once she ended up sprawled on the floor as her feet failed to keep up with the Air-infused pace. Still, by the end of the second day, she felt comfortable with her invisible assistant.

After lunch on the third day, Odintar taught her how to create resistance. Each time he advanced, she blew him back with a powerful gust of Air. She even managed to create a spinning current that prevented him from moving at all.

"Can you really not move or are you indulging me?" She let the miniature tornado dissipate as she waited for his answer.

His lips curved into a guilty smile. "A human wouldn't be able to force their way through the barrier."

She tensed. His tone had stopped just short of condescension. Even so, she refused to be coddled. "You're not human and neither are the Shadow Assassins. What am I doing wrong?"

"You're not doing anything wrong. You've made remarkable progress in so short a time."

"But," she prompted. Superficial praise was always followed by a but.

"Pausing to picture what you're trying to accomplish is slowing you down. Air needs to flow freely. You're still trying to control it. The harder you try to wrestle it into submission, the less effective you'll become. Air must be guided along a helpful path, not forced to do our will. Do you understand the distinction?"

"I understand what you're saying." She sighed. She'd thought she was doing so well, yet he seemed disappointed. "I'm not sure my mind works that way."

"That's part of the problem. This can't come from your mind. It has to be instinctive. You have to *feel* it."

Her emotions generally ran so close to the surface that she struggled to remain focused. She'd spent years controlling her emotional impulses and only "emoting" enough to sell a routine. "But how can I concentrate on the outcome if I allow myself to become emotional?"

"Concentration isn't your problem. In this case, your laser focus is holding you back. You need to relax and let it flow naturally."

Another sigh escaped as she rubbed her eyelids with her fingertips. "That seems backward from how I've always done things."

"Are you questioning my judgment?" His voice snapped with autocratic intensity.

Her eyes opened and she lowered her hand. All emotion vanished from his face and his posture tensed. What had him so wound up? "I'm not questioning anything. I'm expressing an opinion."

"You don't know enough about this to have an opinion." He sneered and raised his chin. "Humans are so frustrating."

Her jaw dropped and indignation shoved through her shock. "Are you serious? I've worked my ass of for the past three days—"

"Three days." He scoffed then took a menacing step toward her. "I've spent more years in training than you've been alive. You aren't qualified to question anything I say. Now get back to work!"

"Screw you!" She punctuated the curse with a blast of Air strong enough to slam him against the wall.

"Yes!" He laughed. "Do it again."

Before her temper cooled, she harnessed the power and shot it at him like a fire hose. He spread his arms for balance and fought through the blast, so she poured more energy into the stream and gradually immobilized him.

Odintar finally teleported to her side, a pleased smile softening his expression. "Do you understand now? Elemental magic feels very similar to emotion. All the logic in the word won't help you use it."

"Are we really accomplishing anything? All you had to do was flash out of the way. Won't Nazerel be able to do the same thing?"

He pushed his hand through his hair and his gaze turned smoky. They weren't touching, but they stood close, easily within reach of each other. "The best move isn't always offensive. If you can immobilize him, even for a moment, it will give you time to flash to safety."

"Are you saying I can teleport?"

"Those empowered by Air can move effortlessly through space. The most powerful can even manipulate time. Once your training is complete, you'll easily outdistance me."

"And how long will that take? Have you really spent more years in training than I've been alive?"

"I was at the Conservatory for twenty-five years and spent another three decades learning from the guild masters on Bilarri. You can't expect this to happen overnight."

"I'm not." She grinned. "It's been three whole days."

He chuckled "And you're doing incredibly well."

"For a human?" She sounded playful, but even knowing why he'd turned into a world-class dick, didn't keep his comments from stinging. "If you spent almost sixty years in training, you have to be pushing one hundred. How long do Bilarrians live?"

"I'm one hundred forty-eight, if you must know. And it depends on the Bilarrian. Certain abilities can drastically increase a Bilarrian's lifespan."

"How long will I live?"

"That's a great question for the guild master."

She sighed and stepped back. "Does that mean you're taking me to Bilarri? I'm not sure I'm ready for interdimensional travel."

"I had to pull a few strings and call in a long overdue favor, but a representative of Guild Air is meeting us at the Bunker tomorrow afternoon."

Chapter Six

Roxie sprayed glass cleaner on top of the display case and wiped it down with a paper towel.

"I think you got it clean the first time you did that." Tess snatched the spray bottle from Roxie's hand and scowled. "What's wrong with you today?"

Before Roxie could summon a believable excuse, Jett joined Tess on the other side of the counter. Two against one? That wasn't fare.

"Today?" he scoffed. "She's been stumbling around on autopilot for more like three days." He fixed his dramatically lined gaze on Roxie and asked, "Hasn't there been enough beefcake in your diet lately?" His brows arched while playful mockery shimmered in his dark eyes. "You always get mopey when Nazerel misses an appointment."

Jett had the source of her distraction right, but his conclusion was so far wrong it was almost laughable. Nazerel's failure to appear for his past two appointments was responsible for her concern. A secret crush, however, had nothing to do with her anxiety. Unfortunately, she couldn't correct Jett's misconception. Part of her deal with Sevrin was absolute discretion. "Nazerel has an amazing body. We're all in agreement on that." The other two supported the claim with enthusiastic nods. "He's also an arrogant jerk. There's only so long you can enjoy running your hands over a sculpted torso. Eventually, it's nice to engage in conversation."

"I don't need to talk." Tess closed her eyes in apparent rapture. "Just let me get my hands on him!"

Jett laughed and even Roxie smiled. "Sorry. No substitutions. Their benefactor is sort of twitchy."

"Benefactor," Tess muttered. "Why do full-grown, obviously capable, men need a benefactor? Have you decided what they are? Stunt men? Professional athletes? Fitness models?"

"Mercenaries?" All amusement suddenly vanished from Jett's expression. He crossed his arms over his chest, prominently displaying the colorful tattoos covering his forearms. "I know Sevrin is paying you a fortune to indulge her crew, but those men are dangerous. You should never be alone with any of them."

It was always nice to have a defender, even though any of Sevrin's boys could snap Jett like a twig. Besides, his concern was misplaced. "The only one that really scares me is Sevrin."

"The phantom benefactor." Tess wiggled her eyebrows in mock drama. "Maybe she's on the run from a foreign government or—"

"It's nothing like that. She's in private negotiations with our government for some newfangled technology. Don't ask me to be more specific. You know I can't."

Jett didn't look convinced. His overly long bangs angled across his face, shadowing one of his eyes. "The men in her entourage don't look like techies to me."

"I don't care what they look like," Roxie insisted, "as long as their boss keeps paying the bills."

The main door opened, postponing the rest of their conversation. One of Jett's regulars walked in and Jett turned to greet his customer. Jett was the sort of man most people expected to find in a tattoo shop. His asymmetrical hair had been dyed black to match his moniker and he had eleven piercings, only half of which were fit for public display. He was friendly, ridiculously talented, yet temperamental. Typical artist.

Tess, on the other hand, concealed her talent behind conservative clothing and a nonthreatening smile. She appealed to casual shoppers, to coeds and housewives who wanted hearts and teddy bears tattooed on their ankles. Roxie valued them both and they worked well together because their clienteles were so different.

And Roxie fell right in the middle of her two employee/friends. With dark brown hair and ice-blue eyes, she wasn't as intimidating as Jett, nor as mainstream as Tess. She didn't wear enough makeup to be considered Goth, yet her formfitting clothes and colorful tattoos drew scornful looks from soccer moms.

"Jett's right, you know." Tess waited until the customer was out of earshot before she spoke again. "They might be fun to look at, but there's something about those men that has me reaching for the pepper spray."

"What do you want me to do?" She moved closer to the display case and lowered her voice. Each artist had their own station in the back, but they were only separated by pull-around curtains. "They haven't done anything wrong and we've all benefited from their business. Should I tell them to go somewhere else because you and Jett don't trust them?"

"Just be careful and don't schedule sessions with them unless someone else is going to be here too."

"Yes, *Mother*." Sevrin was the only one who liked to drop by unannounced, so the promise should be easy to keep.

"Do you know where they're from? I've never heard an accent like theirs and their language is even stranger."

"Sevrin told me the name of the country, but it didn't mean anything to me. I think it's one of the countries that formed after the breakup of the Soviet Union."

"That makes sense. I can picture them working for the KGB."

Roxie laughed and shook her head. "Their grandfathers might have worked for the KGB. All of these guys are way too young to have had anything to do with the Cold War."

The front door opened again and Nazerel walked in followed by a man Roxie had never seen before. Usually the sight of Nazerel filled Roxie with a combination of trepidation and appreciation. The artist in her appreciated the savage beauty of his physical form while the woman in her retreated from the obvious brutality of his nature. Today, however, all she could think about was the disorientation and pain she'd endured in order to spy on a meeting that had never taken place.

Sevrin had made it sound like the mysterious infuser would painlessly implant their language in Roxie's mind and she would magically understand every word they spoke in her presence. Instead she'd been taken to an upscale hotel room where she'd been subjected to hours of mind-twisting...she couldn't even define the sensations the infuser had triggered. Not so much physical pain as mental trauma, the infuser stretched and twisted her thinking in ways that felt unnatural and dangerous. When it was finally over, Roxie had been able to understand the other language, but her thoughts had been jumbled and sluggish for days.

"Good afternoon," Nazerel greeted in accented English.

Roxie manufactured a smile. "I don't have you on my schedule. Did I miss something?"

He looked meaningfully at Tess and she offered him a nervous smile. "Mico has a four-hour appointment this afternoon. He's otherwise occupied, so Flynn will take his place."

Sevrin's boys never asked; they informed. Roxie acknowledged the statement with a stiff nod then motioned toward the back of the shop.

Nazerel skirted the display case and headed for Roxie's station with Flynn half a step behind. Roxie took a deep breath and cleared her mind of everything but what was going on in that moment. She had a new customer. That meant a consultation, putting him at ease and helping him express what he wanted. This was something she'd done hundreds of times before.

She moved into the back of the shop and hooked her foot around the bottom rail of her wheeled stool. Drawing the stool closer to the dentist-style chair on which Flynn lounged, she sat. "So, what would you like and where would you like it?"

Flynn glanced at Nazerel and muttered in their native language, "I'd like her naked and wet as she straddles my lap so I can bury my cock deep inside her."

"She's off-limits and you know it." Absolute finality snapped through Nazerel's tone.

Flynn shrugged. "Doesn't mean I can't imagine her right here, bouncing up and down." He positioned his hands above his lap, fingers curved as if he grasped her hips.

Roxi tensed and heat spread across her face, yet she tried hard to conceal her anger. She'd suspected they frequently made rude comments about her. Now she knew for sure. "If you're going to tell secrets, I'll come back."

"Sit on my face and you can come right now." Flynn continued his offensive behavior.

"Flynn speaks no English." Nazerel's dark gaze gleamed and one corner of his mouth lifted into a secretive smile. "He was explaining what he wanted from you."

His second statement was certainly true, but she seriously doubted the first. "Will you please translate so we can get started. I have another appointment after this."

"Cancel it." Nazerel crossed behind Flynn and stalked toward her. "Serving us is your top priority."

Her independent heart rebelled against his words, but technically he was right. She had basically indentured herself to Sevrin for the foreseeable future.

"She should offer me her mouth while you pound her from behind." Laughter made Flynn's chest rumble. "Or better yet, I'll shove it down her throat while you pound *into* her behind."

Roxie fisted her hands, squeezing until her nails bit into her palms. If Flynn didn't shut the hell up, there was no way she'd maintain her cool. She stood so fast her stool flew into the privacy curtain. "I forgot my water bottle."

Nazerel caught her upper arm as she tried to brush past him. "Why are you angry?" His gaze drilled into hers. His long fingers easily prevented her retreat, yet the force stopped just short of pain.

"I'm not a fool." She met his stare with calm annoyance. "I don't need to understand his words to read his expression. He's being crude and I don't like it."

After acknowledging her complaint with a single nod, he looked at Flynn and switched to their language. "Enough. It's not wise to upset a woman then give her a sharp object to use on you."

Flynn chuckled, but his demeanor changed, becoming more respectful. "Tell her I'm sorry, even though I'm not. If she were willing, I would—"

"She's not, so your desires are irrelevant." Nazerel turned back to her and switched back to English. "Flynn apologizes for his rudeness. He finds your beauty distracting, but that is no excuse for his behavior."

She eased her arm out of Nazerel's grasp and retrieved her stool from the curtain. Then she grabbed her sketch pad off a nearby counter and returned to her seat. "What sort of tattoo would Flynn like?"

The specificity in the question made Nazerel smile. "He would like a sleeve similar to the one you did for Micorian."

"Micorian?" What an odd name.

"Sorry. Mico. We have been encouraged to shorten our names so they sound more American. I find myself resisting the concept."

"Is that why you're Nazerel rather than Naz?"

"Exactly." His smile was almost playful. On the rare occasions when he wasn't scowling, he actually had a certain charm.

"Speaking of Mico, he skipped his last appointment as well. Do you know when he'll return so I can finish his sleeve?"

"Recent developments are keeping my men busier than usual."

"*Your* men?" She allowed a touch of challenge to shape her words. "I thought you guys work for Sevrin."

"The others work for me. I work for Sevrin. And you were hired for your talent not your curiosity."

The leer returned to Flynn's gaze. "Maybe if we indulge her curiosity, Sevrin will let us take her with us."

Nazerel shot him a warning glare. "You aren't supposed to understand English."

"She has no idea what I'm saying."

Take her with them? Where were they going? And how long before they left? She wasn't even sure if this was good news or bad.

Despite the questions spinning through her head, she opened her sketch pad and drew the outline of an arm, then continued as if they hadn't spoken. "Mico's sleeve is pretty abstract. Random images surrounded by a tribal influenced background. Is that what Flynn has in mind?"

"Actually there was one particular image he wants to build upon," Nazerel told her.

"Which one?"

"Near Mico's shoulder there was a section that looked as if his arm was mechanized."

She nodded. Peel-backs were a favorite of hers. "Is there anything else he'd like included?"

"No. He wants his entire arm to appear mechanized."

That was completely different than what she'd done for Mico, but she wasn't about to argue. "What you've described looks best in black and gray. Make sure he isn't expecting color."

Nazerel muttered something she didn't catch and Flynn chuckled. Then Nazerel looked at her and said, "Black and gray is fine with Flynn."

"It'll take me awhile to complete the sketch. Do you want to come back or wait around?"

"We'll wait," Nazerel decided without asking Flynn.

Wonderful. She sketched faster and better when she wasn't being watched, but this wasn't really about Flynn's tattoo. This was an opportunity to gather information and Sevrin expected her to take full advantage of it. "At least have a seat," she motioned toward the chair against the wall. "You're making me nervous looming over me like that."

He strolled around the client chair, his gaze lingering on her. She waited until he sat in the chair she'd indicated before she started drawing. The sketch pad was rigid enough to allow her to work on her lap. Still, she would have been much more comfortable at her desk. She tilted her head, causing her hair to swish forward. It wasn't exactly privacy, but it was better than nothing.

"So where did Sevrin take you the other day?" Flynn asked a few minutes later. It hadn't taken him long to forget she was there. Of course, they would only speak freely as long as they thought she couldn't understand them, so she kept her pencil moving and her head down.

"She had a meeting with a former colleague and she wasn't sure what to expect."

"She has guards to protect her. Why take you?" Suspicion or maybe envy sharpened Flynn's tone. That was interesting. Were the soldier bees fighting over their queen?

"Who knows why that bitch does anything?" Nazerel crossed his legs at the ankle, taking up most of the limited floor space. He was built like a linebacker and had the predatory stare of a career criminal. He never failed to unnerve her. "She said let's go, so I went."

"What did she want from her 'former colleague'?"

Tension rippled through the room and Roxie risked a glance at Nazerel. He was glaring at Flynn. "Why all the questions? Did she tell you to test me?"

Flynn laughed. "This planet is making everyone paranoid. I'm just making conversation."

This planet? A shiver dropped down her spine. Not this country or this place. This *planet*. Maybe it was just a glitch in her language transfusion. Words could have multiple meanings. She bowed her head again, hiding behind her hair.

"Every time I think I've untangled Sevrin's motivation, I discover a new lie." Nazerel sounded frustrated now. "She'd have us believe she's the selfless champion of our brotherhood. In reality we're simply a vehicle on which she's moving her ambitions forward. We're useful to her. If that changes, she won't hesitate to kill us all."

Roxie lifted her pencil. Her hand was trembling so badly she couldn't even pretend to draw. Nazerel's words sounded more than familiar. She'd come to exactly the same conclusion about herself. She was safe as long as she remained useful, which meant she had no choice but to betray Nazerel. Unless... Could they help each other evade the danger? Was she safer with Sevrin or her boys?

"If we became more *proactive*," Flynn emphasized the word, making it sound threatening. "How long do you think it would take her uncle to realize she was gone?"

Her uncle? Damn it. Why hadn't he used a name? Even with a language barrier to protect them, these men were frustratingly careful.

"Her uncle is the least of our concerns. Without her contacts, we're at the mercy of humans. We've learned a lot since our arrival, but I still like my chances better with Sevrin. We just need to figure out a way to control her."

Unable to conceal her emotions any longer, Roxie pushed to her feet. "I'll be right back."

"Where are you going?" Nazerel stood as well.

She blew out a calming breath then looked into his eyes. "I need a potty break. Too much coffee this morning."

His eyes narrowed to glistening slits. "Very well."

Had he just granted her permission to pee? Seriously? Rather than play into his surliness, she smiled. "Thank you, kind sir. I'll return momentarily."

He returned to his chair and she made a beeline for the bathroom. She flipped on the light and locked herself inside the tiny room. This "planet" was making them paranoid and Nazerel didn't want to be "at the mercy of humans". The implication was obvious, so why wouldn't her mind accept what had been revealed? They couldn't be aliens. This was an elaborate hoax set up for their amusement.

But the language infuser had been real. In the span of a few hours, she had learned a foreign language. No, in the span of a few hours, she had learned an *alien* language.

Her ears began to ring and the frantic beating of her heart made it hard to breathe. She moved to the sink and splashed water on her face, not caring if it ruined her makeup. What should she do now? What could she do? It wouldn't take Sevrin long to learn about this visit. The woman seemed to know everything that took place moments after it happened. She'd appear at Roxie's front door and demand a full accounting.

So what did she really know? Nazerel didn't trust Sevrin, didn't feel safe around her. Sevrin obviously knew that much already or she wouldn't have recruited Roxie to spy on him. He hadn't revealed any secret plans, at least he hadn't yet. Complete denial was pointless, but could she twist the truth just enough to protect Nazerel from Sevrin's wrath? Roxie shook her head. It was hard to imagine Nazerel needing protection from anyone.

Someone knocked on the door, so Roxie turned off the water.

"You all right in there?" Tess called.

Relieved to hear a familiar voice, Roxie smoothed her hair back from her face and sighed. "I'm fine. Almost done." She reached over and flushed the toilet, still feeling shaky and unsure.

The worst part was she couldn't confide in anyone without endangering them. She'd never felt so isolated or vulnerable.

One step at a time. That was the only strategy that made sense. She'd get through this session with Nazerel and Flynn, then deal with Sevrin. Roxie wasn't sure what she'd say. She'd keep it vague yet truthful and hope that Sevrin would be pleased enough to give Roxie more time.

"THAT WAS EXCELLENT." Odintar watched Jillian closely, unsure how to interpret the ripples of emotion surging across their psychic link. Her stance was solid, her expression calm, yet spikes of random emotions kept stabbing into his mind. "I think we've accomplished enough for one day. Why don't you take a bath?"

She bent her head and playfully sniffed her armpit. "Am I that ripe?"

"Not at all. I only thought it would help you relax before you go to bed."

Desire swelled then receded as quickly as it had formed. She was still fighting her emotions. She would never experience the full strength of her power until she learned to let go. Still, he'd pushed her hard today, expecting more than he would have from an ordinary apprentice. But then there was nothing ordinary about Jillian. She was the most fascinating combination of strength and vulnerability. Her potential seemed nearly limitless, yet she had serious obstacles to overcome if she hoped to tap that potential.

"A bath sounds nice." Her gaze lingered for another moment before she turned and headed off down the hall.

It was for the best. Spending the night in her bed was more than tempting. He'd fought his need to touch her all day. She must trust her emotions, learn to use them as fuel for her abilities. Lust was a powerful emotion. If he aroused her, he could teach her how to... It was an excuse. His desire for her had nothing to do with training and he wasn't willing to blur the lines.

After indulging in a frustrated sigh, he went to the kitchen and opened the pantry door. The back wall of the small walk-in pantry slid to the right, revealing another door. He triggered the door with a facial scan, then descended the simple wooden stairs.

The basement was stark and utilitarian, windowless walls and exposed support beams. He glanced at the detention cells. Without the containment field active, they looked like concrete cubicles. In the back corner of the basement nestled the control hub. Not only could Elias, or whichever of his men was on duty, observe every room in the safe house, they could contact the Bunker and access the program's expansive database. A row of bulletproof windows kept the room from feeling claustrophobic.

Elias noticed his approach and waved him in. The door hummed then popped and Odintar pulled it open. "Why aren't you climbing the walls? You've been down here for hours."

"I've had plenty to keep me busy." He gestured toward the multi-screen display that spread the length of his workstation. Three of the six screens featured interior views of the safe house, while the other three displayed search engine results and various forms of data. Elias turned his chair around without standing up. "In fact, if you hadn't come down here, I was about to go get you."

Odintar had spent more time with Morgan than Elias. But Morgan trusted her lieutenant implicitly, so Odintar was willing to give him a chance. "What's up?"

"We have a lead that we need explored and Jillian is uniquely qualified to do the exploring."

Odintar crossed his arms over his chest, immediately leery. Jillian had barely begun to test her limits and utilize her gifts. She was weeks, perhaps months away from a field test. "Explain."

"We have substantiated reports that various Shadow Assassins are visiting a tattoo shop called Unique Ink. We'd hoped to follow one of them back to their team house, but they always walk a few blocks from the shop and then teleport to God knows where."

"And how can Jillian help?"

"The owner," he glanced at one of the screens, "Roxie Latimer, is trying to hire a receptionist, someone to greet customers and answer the phone. We wouldn't have to invent a backstory for Jillian. She's lived here for years and has verifiable references."

Odintar nodded with reluctant understanding. "And she has a reason for seeking another line of work."

"All she'd have to do is limp or maybe go back into the brace for a bit."

"What about her double?"

Elias shrugged. "This is the perfect opportunity for her to retire. There's a coffee shop three doors down from Unique Ink. The double could drive Jillian's car to the tattoo shop then decide she needs a cup of coffee. We'll have Jillian waiting in the coffee shop and the double can sneak out through the back. We'll drive the double home and the real Jillian can return to her old life, more or less."

The plan should work as long as no one was watching too closely. And as long as the tattoo shop was under surveillance, Jillian should be relatively safe. "They'll have to wear identical clothing and...the details aren't important until we know if she's willing."

Elias spun back around and typed a command into the wide console. Images scrolled across the six monitors, more interior shots replacing the data. Jillian's bedroom appeared directly in front of Elias and Odintar tensed. He'd known they were under surveillance, but seeing the actual image made him much more uncomfortable than the knowledge that they were being watched.

Jillian sat on the side of her bed, back to the camera. She was dressed in a bathrobe and she was working the tangles out of her damp hair. She must have opted for a shower rather than the bath he'd suggested. The first sob was so soft, Odintar wasn't sure what he'd heard. The second shook her shoulders. She set the comb aside and covered her face with her hands.

"Turn it off," he commanded as he headed for the door. "And leave it off!"

Elias' only response was a knowing chuckle.

EMOTIONS PELTED JILLIAN like sensory hail. Burning anger urged her to pummel the walls while loss leeched the strength from her body and made it hard to breathe. She wasn't even sure why she was so upset. The feelings had overcome her without warning as she stepped out of the shower. She crossed her arms over her stomach and rocked back and forth, tears flowing freely down her cheeks.

Odintar knocked on the door, but she ignored him. She'd had enough of his detachment and pointless rationalizations. Life as she'd known it was over, whether she liked it or not. The things she'd thought were important, the things she'd worked so hard to achieve, seemed meaningless now, as if they belonged to someone else.

He knocked again, calling her name, and loneliness consumed her anger, leaving only aching isolation. She covered her mouth with one hand and clutched her waist with the other. How could emotions be so painful?

"Answer me or I'm coming in."

She lowered her hand and tried to shout at him to leave her alone, but she was sobbing too hard to speak.

He flashed into view and rushed to her, kneeling on the floor in front of her. Placing his hands on her knees, he spoke in a calm, clear voice. "You've strangled your emotions for days while your power keeps making them stronger. You must let them out."

As if she had a choice. An especially violent sob tore through her chest and she covered her face with her hand. Staring into his compassionate face was only making it worse. "Go." She sobbed. "Away!"

"Hit me." He lightly grasped her wrist and pulled her hand away from her face.

She glared at him, unamused by the ridiculous suggestion.

"Your abilities are amplifying your emotions. It's going to take more than tears to defuse this storm." He stood, pulling her to her feet right along with him. "Now hit me."

Suddenly thrilled to oblige, she balled up her fist and swung. Her knuckles connected with his jaw and she cried out, shocked by the pain shooting up her arm. "That hurt!" The realization made her furious, so she swung with her other hand. He absorbed the force with a barely audible grunt that snapped what remained of her control. She swung and kicked at him wildly, lost in a haze of fury and sorrow.

For a while he just let her hit him, apparently hoping she'd wear herself out. Then he began deflecting her blows and blocking her kicks, controlling her movements as her tantrum continued.

Finally, when it was obvious that violence alone wouldn't drain her overload, he urged her back against the wall. He pinned her hands above her head and sealed his mouth over hers. She arched and twisted, tugging against his hold, but he easily restrained her as his lips explored. He was exasperatingly patient as his mouth slid and pressed, his tongue gently teasing.

She'd wanted to kiss him for days, imagined them sharing all sorts of intimacies, but not because she'd momentarily lost her mind. She didn't need his pity and she refused to be indulged. Her fists clenched and her chest burned. His tenderness only made the ache worse. She wanted him wild and out of control, consumed with passion. Did he feel nothing but obligation when he touched her?

Jerking her face to the side, she panted harshly as his mouth brushed the underside of her jaw. "Stop it." She tugged against his hands. "That's enough. I'm better now."

He laughed, his warm breath fanning her skin. "Why do you think I waited so long to kiss you again?" He shifted her wrists into one hand and collared her throat with the other. "There's no way in hell I'm stopping now." Their gazes locked, hers wide and uncertain, his glowing with passionate promise. He tensed and frustration hardened his expression. "Unless this really isn't what you want."

"It is." The admission sent carnal hunger twisting through her abdomen. "But why'd you change your mind?"

"I didn't. I've known this would happen since we first met. I was just waiting until you were ready." Before she could argue further, his mouth covered hers again. This time all hesitation was gone. He tilted her head to a better angle and deepened the kiss.

Parting for him, she greeted his tongue with the warmth of hers. She inhaled his breath, intoxicated by his spicy-fresh scent. She'd dreamed of this, imagined it over and over as they trained. They weren't harming anyone with this indulgence and she refused to feel regret.

He tore his shirt off over his head, separating their mouths for just a moment. The kiss was even more intense when their lips found each other again. She wanted to touch him, needed to feel the bunch and flex of his muscles beneath her eager fingers, but he refused to release her hands. She pulled against his hold, making a disapproving sound in her throat as his tongue moved in her mouth.

If you touch me right now, gennari, *this will be over before it's begun.*

There was that word again. It was obviously an endearment, but she'd have to ask him if it had an exact translation. Later. Much, much later.

If you lose control, we'll just start over. She kept tugging and he finally let go. Rather than going straight for his jeans, she stoked her way along his neck, across his shoulders and down his arms. Every inch of his body was honed to perfection, yet his skin was incredibly soft. She squeezed his rock-hard biceps and shivered, immediately imagining another body part that was equally hard.

With frantic urgency, he disentangled her belt and tore open the front of her robe. Then he bent to her breasts and closed his lips around one nipple as he worked the other with his fingertips. She arched, savoring the firm suction of his mouth, feeling it all the way to her clit. They'd barely begun and already her body was thrumming, threatening to combust.

His mouth switched to the other side as his hands explored her straining body. She wanted his touch everywhere all at the same time and she couldn't stop touching him. It was as if they fed off each other, as if they'd been starving for years. He grasped her hips and rocked against her, showing her just how right her imagination had been. He was long and hard, more than ready to fill her emptiness.

He lifted his head and looked at her, his breathing as ragged as hers. "Gods, I need inside you."

She was too keyed up for subtleties. With nearly violent motions, she unfastened his jeans and freed his erection, stroking the shaft boldly from base to tip. "Now. Put it in me now!"

Firmly grasping her waist, he slid her up the wall. She braced herself against his shoulders and wrapped her legs around his hips. His tip found her slick entrance and then he paused and looked into her eyes. He didn't say anything, but sapphire rings warned of his consuming passion, his need to possess.

She groaned, trembling as anticipation coiled through her, amplifying the emptiness. Her body was a reflection of her life. Her old world had been hollowed out, ruthlessly emptied by forces beyond her control. Now she was ready for new experiences, new challenges and new companions. Slowly, oh so slowly, he lowered her onto his cock, filling her inch by incredible inch. She stared into his eyes as he pushed deeper and deeper into her body. This was just sex, a much needed release of pent-up emotions. So why did it feel so different, so important?

A knowing smile curved his lips as his pelvis pressed against hers. He didn't move, didn't thrust wildly as she'd expected. Instead he widened his stance and eased his hand between their bodies. He pressed against her belly, accenting the fullness inside her. She wasn't sure what he was doing until his thumb found her clit. She gasped then shivered as he caressed the sensitive nub.

"Squeeze me." He whispered the command against her parted lips.

She tightened her inner muscles and he echoed her groan. His thumb circled her clit, sending mini-tremors vibrating through her core. It all felt wonderful, yet she wanted more, needed the strong slide of him in and out and against her. "Please," she cried. "I need you to move."

"Then let go. I'm not moving until you come."

With a frustrated hiss, she pressed her head against the wall and closed her eyes.

"No. Look at me. Offer me your pleasure."

She'd never responded well to sexual commands, but her body didn't seem to care. Her core tensed, rippling with the start of an unexpected orgasm. She opened her eyes and his finger joined his thumb, applying pressure with a careful pinch.

The pleasure burst deep inside her, flowing along her inner muscles in a series of rhythmic clenches. She rode the wave gladly, instinctively reaching for his mind.

That's right. She felt his excitement responding to hers. *Share it with me, love. Let go.*

Before the last spasm eased, he pulled his hips back and drove his shaft deep into her. She gasped and clutched his shoulders, riding the pleasure to an even high peak. He caught the back of one knee and spread her legs so he could move fast and hard between her thighs.

She felt off balance and out of control, so she wrapped her arms around his neck, clinging to him helplessly. Their faces were side by side now as he drove into her again and again. He took her with hard, deep thrusts, filling her completely with each stroke.

Her body responded to his skill and the demand with which he moved, but her mind resisted the penetrating intimacy of their link. She wasn't afraid of him, knew he would never harm her, but she wasn't ready to share herself so completely with someone else.

His hands shifted to her ass and he thrust his entire length into her pulsing core. For just a moment his energy blazed into her mind, consuming and possessive, yet...beautiful. Then he withdrew from her mind and pulled out of her body, spilling his seed against her belly.

She gasped and bit back a disappointed cry. "You didn't have to do that," she whispered. "I'm protected." Against pregnancy sure, but what about STDs? Safe sex practices had been the furthest thing from her mind as she ripped open his jeans and begged for him to put it inside her.

Shame chased a shiver down her spine. Was this how it happened with her mother? One moment of booze-induced weakness and her life changed forever?

"The concerns of humans don't apply to us. We both have Bilarrian blood. Each time we join, our link will expand, even if I don't come inside you. If I do, the expansion will happen that much faster." He wrapped his arms around her as he pulled her away from the wall. "Judging from your reaction just now, I didn't think you'd welcome a deeper bond."

Clinging to him more to hide her face than out of any fear that he'd drop her, she tried to figure out why his statement stung. She *had* retreated from their connection and he didn't sound angry, just disappointed. Still, the observation made her feel like a coward. She'd freely offered her body, yet blocked his access to her emotions. It was a strange dynamic, nearly backward from what she'd experienced in the past. And the past dynamic had been incredibly hurtful. He was the one who should be upset.

He set her down on the bed and hurried to the bathroom. She was looking around for a box of tissues when he returned with a wet cloth. Rather than hand it to her, he wiped his seed off her skin with obvious disappointment. With each gentle swipe of the cloth, her heart broke a little more.

"I'm sorry." The word slipped past her lips before she could stop them. A few minutes ago they'd both been breathless with pleasure. How had the mood turned so dark so quickly?

He tossed the washcloth in the general direction of the bathroom and crawled onto the bed. Without looking at her, he lay on his back and folded his hands behind his head. "You have no reason to apologize. If anything, the fault is mine. My lack of control made you feel guilty and that was not my intention."

The formality with which he spoke revealed more than his words. His Mystic mask was firmly in place, but he was obviously pissed. Well, maybe not pissed but upset.

Wishing he'd pulled down the covers before making himself comfortable, she lay on her side and propped her head against her hand. "Pretending you don't feel anything is just as dishonest as pretending you do. I don't want that sort of relationship for us."

He pulled her toward him until she rested half on and half off his chest. Their faces were only inches apart. "Is this a relationship or were you just caught up in the moment?"

Unless she wanted to push him away, she better find the courage to be brutally honest. "I know this was more than just sex. Even as emotion-drunk as I was, I felt the difference."

"That's too bad," he whispered, his lips brushing over hers.

Her brow creased and she searched his gaze for an explanation. "Why is that too bad?"

A slow, sexy smile parted his lips and desire ignited within his eyes. "I was hoping you'd require a more elaborate demonstration." He suddenly rolled, sweeping her beneath him as he went.

She laughed then sighed as he parted her thighs with his knees and settled between her legs. "I welcome your most elaborate demonstration if you answer a question first."

"All right." He bent and nipped her earlobe, obviously not willing to indulge her for long.

"You keep calling me gen-nau-ry or something like that. What does it mean?"

"*Gennari* is the old Bilarrian word for sweetheart." Secrets swam in the depths of his dark eyes. A hint of red flashed for an instant and then was gone.

"Does it have an alternate meaning?"

"It might." He chuckled then claimed her mouth and drove all speculation from her mind.

Chapter Seven

The following morning Odintar woke up slowly. He felt contented and lazy for the first time in months, perhaps years. Jillian cuddled against his side, her head resting on his shoulder. Their second bout of lovemaking had been nearly as frantic as their first. He wanted to slow down, to savor every touch and tingle, but their need seemed to explode as soon as skin met skin.

Determined to awaken her tenderly, he stroked his hand down her bare back as he rolled to his side. She wiggled against him, her leg insinuating itself in between his. Desire hardened his cock and sizzled through his blood. She was so soft and warm, inviting his touch with breathless sighs and sensual arches. How could any mortal man resist?

He'd known touching her would be amazing, but he hadn't expected the soul-deep ache to join with her completely. Although he probably should have. He'd called her *gennari* the first time he held her in his arms. What he'd told her last night was true. Over the centuries *gennari* had become a generic endearment, like sweetheart or dear, but it also had a deeper meaning, one most had forgotten.

When a Bilarrian male encountered his soul's mate he declared his intention to claim her by calling her *gennari* in front of her family. Then he pursued her, seduced her, did everything in his power to convince her to accept him as mate.

Is that what he wanted from Jillian?

He smiled into her soft hair. Could there really be a doubt when every molecule of his being ached for her?

Brushing her hair back from her face, he kissed his way to her mouth. Her lips parted with the first touch of his. She whispered his name and passion spiraled through his body, igniting his senses and stimulating his energy.

No! He would not be swept away by his desire. She didn't trust his words, so he would show her how important she was to him and how wonderful the rest of their lives could be.

His mouth moved over and against hers, his tongue gently tracing the space between. She allowed the teasing dance for a few moments then touched her tongue to his. He sucked, drawing her tongue into his mouth. She gasped and her fingernails dug into his back.

He rolled, wanting her beneath him, needing to feel her arch and wiggle for more of him. Her legs parted automatically and she tangled her fingers in the back of his hair as he like to do with her. His tongue slid against hers and curled around hers, finally slipping between her lips.

Their link vibrated as emotions pulsed from their minds. He sent a scorching wave of carnal hunger across the connection and felt her shudder in response. Her body accepted the exchange without question or reserve, but her mind soon registered the source of the sudden heat and blocked his access to her emotions.

Refusing to be deterred by her instinctual reaction, he concentrated on physical sensations. She needed time to learn to trust him. If he rushed her, he would likely destroy the progress they'd made so far.

He made love to her mouth, sharing his breath and filing her with his tongue. She rubbed against him, her nipples distinct peaks abrading his chest. Her hands were just as greedy as his, moving over his back and squeezing his ass.

He shifted his weight to his knees and reluctantly released her mouth. Their gazes locked and he smiled. "Good morning, *gennari*," he whispered then kissed his way down her throat.

Her breasts were perfect, wonderfully round with dark pink nipples. He cupped the fullness of one while he explored the other with his mouth. Her skin was silky against his lips, her nipple already puckered. He closed his teeth on the very tip and heard her gasp. "Too hard?"

She shook her head, her fingers combing through his hair. "Don't stop."

"Never." He sucked firmly on one nipple and then the other, loving the way she twisted, increasing the pressure.

The scent of her arousal reached his nose, stirring the dark, primitive side of his nature. He released her nipple, leaving it wet and tightly peaked. Scooting down, he paused to enjoy the sight of her spread before him, arms raised, legs open, skin deeply flushed. She watched him through passion-muddled eyes, surrendered and waiting.

He caught the backs of her knees and pushed her legs wider. She gasped then caught her lower lip between her teeth. She obviously knew what he meant to do and had no objection. Bending slowly, he inhaled deeply then traced her slit with his tongue. She was already slick and soft, ready for their joining.

Needing to be inside her too badly to deny himself completely, he pushed his middle finger into her core. Hot, wet flesh tightened around him, dragging a moan from his throat. He watched her face as he slid his finger in and out, teasing himself as much as her.

"Please." She squeezed him tightly. "I need more than a finger."

He chuckled and eased a second finger in beside the first.

"No." She caught his wrist, trapping his fingers deep inside her. "I need you, all of you, inside here." She squeezed him again then released his wrist.

He should make her wait, lick her until she was screaming, but his desire was just as demanding as hers. Withdrawing his fingers, he bent for another taste, then thrust his aching cock into her body. She cried out, clutching him so tightly he felt himself start to come. Discipline alone allowed him to pull back from the brink.

This was not what he'd imagined when he kissed her awake. He rocked between her thighs, shuttling in and out of her snug passage. He threw his head back, reveling in the heat and motion. His skin felt electric and his blood seemed to race through his veins.

She cried out and trembled beneath him and sparks of her pleasure skittered across their connection. His hoarse cry echoed hers, but he miraculously held back his release. He would not allow this to end so quickly. He was stronger than that.

Pulling out was painful, but he wasn't without her for long. He flipped her over and drew up her hips. Easily finding her entrance, he thrust back in and they groaned in unison. He pulled back his hips and slid in slowly, determined to prolong their enjoyment. Her energy surrounded his shaft, caressing him just as tangibly as her body. He shuddered, knowing he wouldn't last long if he continued to move.

Instead he drew her up, pressing her back against his chest. She turned her head sharply, offering her mouth. The position thrust her breasts forward and he took full advantage of both offerings. He caressed her breasts with one hand as his tongue moved in and out of her mouth.

Soon caresses weren't enough. He wanted to feel her come around his cock, know she needed him as desperately as he needed her. With their mouths still clinging, he held her close with one arm as his other hand moved between her thighs. He caressed her folds, accenting how tightly she stretched to accommodate his thickness.

She grew restless beneath his touch, but he didn't release her. His middle finger found her clit and her entire body tensed. *Come for me, gennari.* He pushed the directive into her mind with a hint of his consuming need.

Her breasts quivered against his forearm and her core tightened on his shaft. His finger circled and stroked her clit until pleasure radiated across their link. He didn't analyze the development, just accepted her momentary surrender. With his finger still covering her clit, he bent her forward, supporting her until she pressed her hands against the bed. Then he pulled back and drove deep, pairing each thrust with a pass of his finger.

She tossed back her hair and arched, taking him deeper into her body. Her energy swirled again, stealing his breath for a moment. He wasn't sure if she was doing it intentionally and he really didn't care. Nothing had ever felt more amazing than her essence caressing his cock.

Finally lost in the storm, he moved both hands to her hips and increased his speed. She went down to her elbows, creating a better angle for his forceful strokes. Hard and deep, he claimed her body, all the while aware that something was missing.

Her body couldn't have been more perfect or the pleasure more intense. Still, he would always hunger for more than these physical sensations.

Looking down, he watched his wet cock moving in and out of her willing body. Lust surged, burning away regret. Energy gathered at the base of his spine, making his balls constrict in preparation for an explosive release. The pleasure was so overwhelming he nearly forgot that she wasn't ready for his seed.

His fingers dug into her hips and he gritted his teeth as he forced himself to pull out. He squeezed his painfully engorged shaft then frantically stroked until his seed jetted onto her back.

She collapsed onto the bed with a frustrated hiss. "I hate it when you do that."

Her voice was muffled by the covers, but he understood every word. "I'm protecting you."

"I know." She looked back at him, her gaze sad. "And I appreciate it."

Unable to conceal his disappointment, he crawled off the bed and went to the bathroom for a washcloth. He couldn't force this. She would open up when she was ready and not before.

Her arms wrapped around him and she pressed against his back. "Are you mad at me?"

He turned around and drew her tightly against him. "I'm not angry." He wiped up the mess he'd left on her skin then tossed the washcloth into the sink. "This is hard for you. I understand that and I'm trying to be patient."

She ran her hands up his chest and locked them behind his neck. "You're the most amazing man I've ever met and I'm so glad you're in my life. My reluctance has nothing to do with you."

He bent and kissed her as his fingers combed through her hair. "I'll wait as long as you need and we'll move forward as slowly as you like. Just don't push me away."

"It's a deal." She pushed up to the balls of her feet and kissed him with tender affection. "Now tell me what *gennari* really means."

He chuckled as she nibbled at his earlobe. "It's a declaration of intent."

She pulled back, her expression quizzical. "You're intent to do what?"

He laughed then lightly slapped her luscious behind. "I would think that was obvious." She obviously needed to hear it and he needed to say it. "I feel a connection with you that I've never felt with anyone else. I want you as my mate."

Much to his relief she didn't tense nor did she pull away. "You're much too tempting when you're naked. This isn't fair." She pushed him toward the shower. "And we both smell like sex!"

JILLIAN RAISED THE coffee mug toward her face and inhaled. The coffee shop might be new to her, but the rich aroma was soothingly familiar. "If we're finished with the double, does that mean I can go home?"

"That's not my call," Elias told her. "You'll have to ask your handler." His smirk told her he knew just how well Odintar had "handled" her lately. It didn't bother her. She'd handled Odintar just as thoroughly by the time they'd fallen into an exhausted sleep. And this morning had been even better, an overwhelming combination of intensity and tenderness.

I feel a connection with you that I've never felt with anyone else. I want you as my mate. As proposals went it was rather oddly worded. Still, the possibility of spending the rest of her life with Odintar was much more tempting than she expected it would be.

Distracted by the development, she'd lingered in the shower after they'd finished washing each other. She hadn't come to a definitive conclusion, but she hadn't talked herself out of it either.

When she finally emerged from her bedroom, she found Elias and Odintar at the kitchen table deep in conversation. Odintar made the introductions, explaining that Elias was part of the human taskforce that was assisting the Mystic Militia. Elias seemed annoyed by the description, but he hadn't argued the point. Instead he told her about a tattoo shop the Shadow Assassins had been patronizing on a regular basis. They needed her to apply for the receptionist position and gather as much intel as she could.

"Say I get the job. What happens if Nazerel strolls through the door?"

"You treat him like any other customer," Odintar said. "The only way you would know he's after you is if you'd had contact with us."

"And the whole point of the double was to keep him from realizing where you've been," Elias reminded.

"We're not sending you in alone," Odintar assured. "We'll be with you every step of the way."

So here she sat, waiting for her double to arrive. As soon as Elias' men spotted Jillian's car, Jillian would go into the bathroom. Her double would go into the bathroom as well and wait until Jillian was long gone before she snuck out through the back.

It was a simple plan, but there were still so many things that could go wrong. First and foremost, the shop's owner might not want to hire an ex-showgirl with a bum leg. Even if the bum leg was being greatly exaggerated. She'd refused to wear the god-awful brace, but agreed to affect a limp, so they'd instructed her double to do likewise.

"The car just turned the corner." Elias motioned toward the bathroom. "You're on."

Swallowing past the lump in her throat, Jillian pushed to her feet and hobbled over to the bathroom. A strange sort of dread spread through her. If it hadn't been for Odintar, this might well have been her life for the next few years. Surgeries and physical therapy, frustration and pain. She whispered a prayer, thanking whatever god had sent him into her life for their generosity.

She stood awkwardly in the bathroom and waited for her double to arrive. If the other woman hadn't been dressed in an outfit identical to Jillian's, she might not have realized who she was supposed to be. They were both tall and athletic, but her "double" was at least twenty years older than she was and much more...weathered. She couldn't think of a less insulting adjective.

"Hi," she greeted with an awkward wave.

"Hi, yourself." She fished through her shoulder bag and found a cigarette. "Oh God how I missed these." She lit the cigarette and inhaled deeply, a blissful expression spreading across her face. "Loved your apartment. It's way nicer than mine. But the confinement was getting to me. Glad it's over. Keys are behind the visor. Cheers." She walked into one of the stalls and closed the door, dismissing Jillian.

Jillian smiled at the odd exchange and rushed from the bathroom before the cloud of cigarette smoke found her clothes.

Elias was nowhere in sight when she returned to the small seating area. Odintar was here somewhere as well, but he'd warned her that the level of shielding needed to hide from the Shadow Assassins would make him undetectable to her as well.

Feeling a little abandoned, she headed for the door. This plan still seemed overly risky to her. Nazerel might not be the only Shadow Assassin who had looked through the notebook. What if one of the others chose her as their prospective mate? The thought was even more upsetting after the amazing night she'd just spent in Odintar's arms.

She couldn't think like that or the Shadow Assassins might sense her fear. They didn't realize she knew about them. That was her main advantage. As long as they didn't suspect she knew their secrets, and as long as they thought she was still physically impaired, she should be relatively safe. It was imperative that she seem intrigued and a little intimidated by them, but nothing more.

Her real goal was to see if she could get the employees gossiping about their unusual clientele. They might know more than they realized they knew. But first she had to earn their trust.

No. First you have to get the job. She accepted the reminder and smoothed down her hair before she opened the front door. The shop was in a newly renovated strip mall in one of the older parts of town. Not fancy by any means, but she'd seen far worse.

The door chimed as she pulled it open. The interior was light and open, arranged to maximize limited space.

"Have a seat. I'll be right out," someone called from the behind the curtain obscuring the back of the shop.

She moved to the couch situated perpendicular to the long case displaying jewelry and various forms of body art. Did they do piercings and implants or just tattoos? As tattoos became more mainstream, the popularity of body modification had begun to rise.

There were three photo albums on the coffee table directly in front of the couch. Each cover featured a name in bold, block letters. Tess, Roxie and Jett. The owner's name was Roxie, so Jillian picked up Roxie's book. From the first page on it was obvious that Roxie was a genuine talent. Her designs were original and distinct, bold, yet elegant.

"What do you think? And don't tell me they're nice." An attractive woman in her late twenties or early thirties skirted the display case and approached Jillian.

Jillian smiled. Apparently her interview had just begun. She didn't know for sure that this was Roxie, but she suspected she was. With dark brown hair and pale blue eyes, her face was as stunning as her artwork. "You like to over complicate your designs, like you're never sure when it's finished."

The young woman smiled, apparently pleased by the observation. "Go on."

"You've spent a lot of time playing—or watching others play—video games. I see the influence of several well-known gaming studios."

"Guilty. But what made you think I watched rather than played?"

So this was Roxie. "I can't picture you setting down your sketch pad long enough to get good at a video game."

"You're very perceptive." She crossed to the coffee table and held out her hand. "Roxie Latimer and please tell me you're Jillian Taylor."

Jillian set the photo album back on the coffee table and stood before she shook Roxie's hand. "I am. It's nice to meet you. I don't want to misrepresent myself. I'm an art fan, but I'm not an artist. Do you only need a receptionist or were you hoping to recruit a fledgling artist?"

"The stations are full. We need a receptionist." She motioned toward the couch as she rounded the table and sat as well.

Jillian pivoted toward her, carefully positioning her formerly wounded leg.

Roxie noticed the motion, but didn't mention it. At least not directly. "So tell me about your work history. Are you currently employed?"

"I was a dancer until a recent accident forced me to reassess my career plans." She didn't need to fake the pang of sadness in her voice.

"Oh my God! I knew you looked familiar. You're *the* Jillian Taylor. I saw *Star-Crossed* three times. Jett said you'd landed a headline gig. What are you doing here?"

"I'd performed sixteen shows when the accident happened." She motioned toward her leg. "It's damaged beyond repair. Dancing is no longer an option."

Roxie reached over and squeezed her arm. "I am so sorry. You were brilliant in *Star-Crossed*."

"Thanks." Her throat felt tight and tears stung her eyes. Stubbornness alone held them back.

"I'm sorry. I'm being really insensitive. The job is yours if you want it. The pay sucks, but you can have all the free ink you want."

"I'm not sure you want to make that offer. I'm still a virgin."

"I'd be happy to help with that," the smoky male voice drew her gaze to the opening leading to the back of the shop. A lanky young man stood there, his asymmetrical hair and heavily lined eyes broadcasting his profession. Not to mention the tattoos that covered both arms and one side of his neck.

"Jett, this is—"

"Jillian Taylor requires no introduction. Not in this town."

It was torture. Every word they uttered shined a glaring light on the life she was leaving behind. She'd been a star. Well, more like an aspiring star, but she'd just started to build momentum when it all came crashing down. Now she was a fallen star trying to redefine herself in a reality she didn't quite understand.

"And I'm pretty sure she was referring to her lily-white skin not her sex life," Roxie pointed out playfully.

"I'd love to take my needles to her almost as much as—"

"Only you would call it a needle," a female pushed past him and smiled at Jillian. "At least he's honest. Most men exaggerate, or worse, compensate."

"That's Tess," Roxie told her.

Tess looked more like a librarian than a tattoo artist, but Jillian returned her smile. "Nice to meet you, Tess."

"Likewise. And I specialize in tattoo virgins, so ignore him. Jett would be drooling all over you the entire time anyway."

"What, you don't think she's gorgeous? You don't have to like girls to appreciate a bod-face like hers."

The slip had been so obvious all three females laughed.

"Yes, she's gorgeous, face and body," Tess volleyed, "but so is Roxie."

"I've worn out all my fantasies about Roxie. I was about to start fantasizing about you."

"Naughty nanny or hot for teacher?" Tess waved away both ideas. "You're so predictable."

"They never stop," Roxie warned. "It's better to just ignore them."

The door chimed and everyone looked at the newcomer. Even dressed in jeans and a T-shirt, the man looked intimidating. With sharp features and a dramatically sculpted physique, he was either a Shadow Assassin or a world-class body builder.

"Flynn," Roxie greeted as she stood and walked out from behind the coffee table. "I don't think you're on my schedule. Are you taking someone else's slot again?"

"Nazerel said you make time." His accent was so heavy his words were hard to understand.

"Go on back. I'll be just a minute longer."

He nodded and headed for the doorway leading to the work area.

Roxie turned back to Jillian with an apologetic smile. "I don't know why they're suddenly in such a hurry. You'd think they were leaving town or something." She sighed and smoothed down her black leather pants. "Anyway, when can you start? We can work out a schedule that makes sense to both of us when I don't have one of my boys breathing down my neck."

"How about Friday afternoon. That will give me a day and a half to tie up loose ends."

"Perfect. Come in around two."

"I'll be here."

She waited until Roxie disappeared through the doorway before she turned to Tess and asked, "Did she actually refer to that mass of muscle as a boy?"

Tess laughed. "Their boss refers to them as her boys and Rox has picked up the habit."

"Their boss?" Jillian shook her head. "Do I even want to know?"

"Oh we all want to know," Jett interjected. "But Roxie is keeping this mystery all to herself."

"Not to mention a bunch more like Flynn. No one else is allowed to work on 'the boys'. It's ridiculous." Tess crossed her arms over her chest and glared at the doorway through which they'd passed.

"Well, I better get going." Jillian stood, reminding herself to favor her leg. "My numbers are on my application. If anything changes, call. If not, I'll see you Friday."

The sun stabbed into Jillian's eyes as she stepped out onto the sidewalk. She quickly found her sunglasses and put them on, then looked for her car. She'd been so distracted when she walked into Unique Ink, she'd forgotten to see where her double had parked.

Carefully maintaining her role until she was seated behind the wheel, she flipped down the visor and the keys to her car, mailbox and apartment dropped into her lap. "I'm a person again," she muttered under her breath as she slipped the car key into the ignition.

"No you'll need a cell phone for that."

She gasped. Odintar's voice had been audible, but he was still not visible.

"Where are you?"

"Backseat. There's too many curious eyes right here for me to lower my shields."

"Got it." She started the engine and drove away from the strip mall. She found a secluded parking lot, checked to make sure there were no surveillance cameras, then pulled to the back corner of the lot.

"That went incredibly well." Odintar finally lowered his shields. "Seemed like a fun place to work."

"Until the Shadow Assassin walk in."

"You've already been more successful than you realize. Think about what Roxie said. All of her clients are rushing to finish their tattoos. Like they're leaving town or something."

"Does that mean something specific to you?"

"We've known for some time that they intend to relocate to different cities. Team East was the first to leave. Teams West and South have basically combined and we think they'll be the next to go. Flynn was on Team West."

"All that means is we're running out of time to find them. We already knew that."

"An operation like theirs takes serious planning to relocate. There are signs, if you know what to watch. This is encouraging."

She didn't feel encouraged. She felt exposed and...used. This wasn't even her fight. Why did she have to be the one on the front line?

With a frustrated sigh, she contained her pessimistic thoughts. It was her fight, whether she wanted to be part of it or not. If they didn't protect Roxie, it was more than likely she'd disappear. And she'd die never knowing what she'd stumbled into. Now that would be tragic.

"Care to share your thoughts. Your mind is locked up tight."

She met his gaze in the rearview mirror then shook her head. "They're not worth sharing. I'm just being morose."

He shifted into the front seat. He never really disappeared completely. His body just sort of flowed from one seat to the other. "I can handle morose. Did all the adulation make you homesick for your old life?"

Adulation? Had it really seemed like worship to him? Probably. Jett had been especially gushy. "I know I can't go back and Tori would argue that I've gained more than I've lost. But I miss it."

"That's understandable. Your life was utterly focused for a very long time. Now your focus has expanded. That's all. It doesn't mean dance can't be part of your life. You just have more options now."

She chuckled and playfully shoved his arm. "Way to sell it, Mr. Mystic. Did they teach you that crap at the Conservatory?"

"No. The Conservatory was all about self-denial and serving the greater good. Might be why I headed to Bilarri as soon as I finished my training."

"Did Bilarri feel like home?"

He glanced out the window and took a moment before he answered, "I've yet to find a place where I feel completely at home. That's probably why I've traveled extensively. I'm still searching."

"I'm sorry. That must be hard."

His lips quirked and he shot her a sidelong stare. "Not nearly as hard as it could be."

It took her a moment to realize he wasn't talking about home anymore. Men! They never changed. "You might not know where your home is yet, but I know where to find mine. Can I please go there now?"

"Soon. We have one more stop to make, then I promise I'll take you home."

"I'll sleep in my own bed tonight? Honestly?"

"You have my word. You will sleep in your own bed tonight."

NAZEREL LOOKED AT THE progress Roxie had made on Flynn's tattoo and then glared at Flynn. "It's amazing, as always, but you were supposed to be home all afternoon. Just like the rest of us."

"I want this thing finished before we leave." Flynn lifted his chin and glared right back at Nazerel. "Unless we take Roxie with us."

Flynn was the only member of Team West Nazerel trusted. They'd known each other before they came to Earth, even before they were forced to leave the Shadow Maze. Flynn's half-brother was a sweeper who'd been assigned to Team South, despite the loud protestations of his father. Flynn thought he should have been chosen as alpha hunter rather than Zacharous and most of the hunters here agreed with him. Nazerel wanted someone strong at his back, yet needed someone uncertain enough to follow his lead without question. Flynn fit the bill perfectly.

"If Roxie were in the notebook, someone could claim her and Sevrin couldn't argue with our choice. But Roxie isn't. I already checked." The stubborn look on Flynn's face made Nazerel smile. He wasn't the first to suggest they take Roxie with them. She'd developed a loyal following. There was something about being hurt by a beautiful woman that they all found addictive. The art she created was just a bonus.

"So we do it anyway. Like you're always saying, it's easier to beg forgiveness than ask permission."

"Not with Sevrin. She'd slit Roxie's throat and make us watch her bleed out. And I mean that literally."

Flynn huffed out a sigh then shrugged. "Well, I'm here now. What still needs to be done?"

Nazerel looked around the spacious house. Boxes were stacked in every corner and still much remained unpacked. It amazed Nazerel how much they'd managed to accumulate in two short months. "Find a box and put your shit in it. It's not complicated, just time-consuming. The trucks arrive Friday morning. Anything not boxed up and ready to go will be left behind."

"So I just need to find a box big enough for Roxie," Flynn laughed as he headed for the front stairs.

"Give it up!" Nazerel returned to his own packing as Flynn disappeared down a hallway. The house was currently home to nine men when it was designed to accommodate five. Hopefully the new house would be more manageable. If not, he was going to harass Sevrin until she hired a housekeeper.

As if summoned by his thoughts, Sevrin let herself in and crossed the foyer, heels clicking rhythmically against the stone tiles. "Are you having fun yet?" Her voice echoed off the vaulted ceilings until she stepped down into the living room.

He allowed himself to acknowledge her physical beauty. She looked particularly attractive in a snug skirt of buttery leather. The matching vest was doubtlessly meant to be worn over a shirt, but she let it showcase her round breasts and sleek arms. Regardless of her appeal, he was too smart to mix business with pleasure. Besides, Sevrin's loyalty shifted without warning. There was no way he'd make himself vulnerable to her whims.

Ignoring her facetious question, he asked, "What can I do for you?"

She smiled, yet her unringed eyes remained cold and calculating. She was pureblood Rodyte. There had to be some sort of film covering her eyes. "Are you finally ready to take my order?"

"Depends on the order. You respect my boundaries and I'll respect yours."

"Is Flynn around?" Challenge warmed her gaze while her smile turned brittle.

If she'd set her sights on Flynn, Nazerel would be thrilled. Flynn was vain enough to think he'd caught her attention all by himself, yet resentful enough to tell Nazerel everything that happened behind closed doors. Still, the timing couldn't be worse for her to break in a new plaything. He needed every set of hands if they were going to be ready by Friday morning.

"We're all really busy. Can this wait?"

She scowled at him and moved two steps closer. "Would I be here if it weren't important?" Even in sky-high heels, her head only reached his chin. Did she really think she could intimidate him?

Without shifting his gaze from her angry face, he called out, "Flynn! Get your ass down here!"

Flynn rushed into view a few seconds later, followed by two other members of Team West. "What's the prob—" He spotted Sevrin and immediately schooled his expression. "Mistress."

Sevrin waited until he reached the main floor before she spoke to him, but her tone was clipped and cold. "Did you visit Unique Ink this afternoon without an appointment?"

After glaring at Nazerel, he returned his gaze to Sevrin. "Roxie assured me that I wasn't bumping anyone else. If she'd had a customer, I would have left."

"That's not what I asked."

"Yes, mistress. It was selfish and disobedient. I apologize."

Much to Nazerel's surprise she rolled her eyes. "You're not in trouble, silly boy. Stop groveling." Flynn snapped to attention and clasped his hands behind his back. The pose stretched his T-shirt across his chest and showcased his biceps. Sevrin took full advantage of the display. "Was anyone else there when you arrived?" She circled him slowly as she waited for his answer, her gaze moving up and down his body.

If any of them looked at her like that, she'd have them beaten or worse. She was such a hypocritical bitch.

"There was a customer on the couch looking through the design books. But both Jett and Tess were available to help her."

"Male or female?" She completed her orbit and studied his face.

"Female. Blonde. Sorry. I didn't pay much attention to her."

"Damn." She waved Flynn away. "Go back to whatever you were doing."

After a momentary pause, Flynn obeyed.

"Is there a problem?" Nazerel asked as Sevrin turned to leave.

"I'm not sure yet. Roxie decided she needs a receptionist and it's the perfect opportunity for one of our enemies to insert a spy."

One of their enemies? Was she referring to the human taskforce or were there even more threats than she'd revealed? He started to ask her, but changed his mind. She enjoyed making him beg for information. She enjoyed making him beg, period. Well, he was sick of begging. In fact, he was sick of Sevrin's games.

"Does it even matter? We'll be out of here in a few days."

"Depends how talkative your people became while Roxie worked on them."

Nazerel tensed. As usual, she was diverting anything resembling accountability away from herself. She had handpicked Roxie, insisted they use only her. "'My people' were instructed to speak Rodyte as much as possible. Even if they ran their mouths in front of Roxie, she wouldn't have understood what they said. The receptionist is irrelevant."

Sevrin narrowed her eyes and stared past him for a moment, obviously lost in thought. "You're probably right, but you know I hate loose ends. No more visits. As of right now, Unique Ink is off limits."

"I'll make sure everyone knows."

"Besides, it looks like you still have plenty to do around here." Without another word Sevrin departed.

Roxie's image formed in Nazerel's mind, her silky dark hair and kind eyes. She was an irresistible combination of sweet and feisty. Little wonder every hunter who spent time in her chair wanted to take her home with him. Similar thoughts had flitted through his mind as she bent over him. Only grander aspirations had kept him from acting on the impulse.

For the moment, Sevrin was fixated on the receptionist. But it wouldn't take long for her to realize the real problem was Roxie. The receptionist could only learn what Roxie knew. Roxie was the loose end. And Sevrin didn't tolerate loose ends.

He had to warn Roxie. The realization fisted his gut and wouldn't let go. He had a stash of money he'd squired away because of Sevrin's miserly habits. If he gave her the money, would she run? Could he convince her that the danger was real? And could he convince all of the hunters not to help Sevrin find her? Unlikely. He fisted his hands and blew out a frustrated breath. She needed a protector, someone who knew how to hide and owed no allegiance to Sevrin.

The Mystic Militia was an obvious choice, but Nazerel suspected that Roxie had a value he'd not yet discovered. Las Vegas was filled with tattoo artists, yet something specific had drawn Sevrin to Unique Ink. He didn't believe in coincidences, which meant there was something special about Roxie. He wanted to keep Roxie safe, but he'd rather not turn a possible advantage over to the enemy.

Other than the Mystic Militia, there was only one person on Earth who met the qualifications. Gerrod Reynolds. At least he came closer than anyone else.

Despite Sevrin's promise to explain the connection between his father and Gerrod Reynolds, all she'd offered were vague half-truths and outright lies. It had taken him four days and several bribes, but he now possessed a current address for the mysterious Ontarian.

A calculative smile spread across his lips. As Flynn pointed out, Nazerel generally found it easier to beg forgiveness than ask permission, so he'd snatch the girl and take her to Gerrod. It would be harder for Gerrod to refuse Roxie protection once he'd seen her tear-streaked face.

Knowing he'd need an alibi, once Roxie's disappearance was realized, he moved into the foyer and called up to the second level. "Flynn, toss me down a roll of tape. I'm going to get started in the basement." He'd already cleared out most of the basement, but Flynn didn't know that.

A roll of tape came flying in an indiscriminate arc. Nazerel snatched it out of the air before it shattered the mirror toward which it was headed. "Thanks. Asshole." He whispered the last under his breath as he stashed the tape in a half-full box. This would only buy him an hour at most, so he had to get moving.

He looked out the front window to make sure Sevrin was really gone. It wouldn't have been the first time she sat in her car and watched what went on inside the house after they thought she'd left. She was sneaky to the marrow of her bones.

Satisfied that the queen bee had flown back to her hive, he closed the blinds and stepped away from the window. Roxie was in for a shock, because he didn't have time for explanations. He flashed to her shop without lowering his shields then waited until she was alone. As soon as Tess walked into the storeroom, Nazerel clasped his hand over Roxie's mouth as he wrapped his other arm around her waist and flashed them toward the suburbs.

She fought wildly, her efforts surprisingly strong. He had more control when he wasn't struggling with a passenger, so he sent a pulse into her mind and commanded her to sleep. His compulsions weren't always effective, but she went limp in his arms. Thank the gods.

Gerrod lived in a modest two-story, surrounded by a sea of similar houses. Nazerel scanned ahead and found a dark corner of the backyard in which to materialize. Roxie was still unresponsive, so he lifted her into his arms and approached the back door slowly. Many humans were fond of weapons and he wasn't in a position to defend himself at the moment.

He kicked the screen door several times then stepped back so Gerrod could see the helpless female in his arms. "I mean you no harm, but this woman needs your assistance."

The porch light flashed on then off and Gerrod slowly opened the main door while leaving the screen door closed. "What the hell do you want?" Then more gravely, he asked, "How did you find me?"

"This isn't about me. It's about her." He raised Roxie slightly, drawing Gerrod's attention to her pale face.

"What did Sevrin do to her? I'm no doctor."

"She's not harmed, just frightened. May I please bring her inside?"

He looked around, obviously concerned that it was some sort of trap. Then he sighed and unlocked the door, pushing it open so Nazerel could enter.

Nazerel found the living room and placed Roxie on the sofa. She made a distressed sound, but didn't awaken. That was probably best for now.

"Do you even know who that is?" Gerrod snapped from across the room. "Sevrin will kill us both if she thinks we've harmed her."

That froze Nazerel in his tracks. What the hell was he talking about? "I brought her here because I was afraid Sevrin would kill her. Were my fears unjustified? Who is she?"

"What a cluster." Gerrod crossed the room and looked at Roxie more closely. "Did she faint or did you flip her switch?"

"I used a compulsion. She should wake up shortly."

"You better hope she does." Gerrod sounded almost amused and Nazerel definitely didn't understand the joke.

"Who is she?" He tried again, allowing his impatience to show.

"Why did you think Sevrin meant to kill her?" Gerrod evaded.

"Roxie's a tattoo artist and she's been working on my men. Sevrin is afraid she's overheard things she shouldn't and Sevrin always ties up loose ends."

Gerrod chuckled and turned around. "Want a beer."

After one concerned glance at Roxie's still form, Nazerel followed Gerrod into the kitchen. "Sevrin has obviously been screwing with me, which I'm sure doesn't surprise you. Who the hell is the girl?"

"That, my foolish friend, is the ace up my sleeve. If Sevrin tries to screw with me again, the Mystic Militia will learn all of Roxie's secrets."

"Meaning you have no intention of telling me anything."

Gerrod pulled two beers out of the refrigerator and handed one to Nazerel. "I will tell you that Sevrin needs Roxie much more than she needs you. Take Roxie back before she wakes up and pray to every god you know that she thinks she imagined the entire thing."

Nazerel twisted off the top and took a long swig of beer. It did nothing to calm the anger seething inside him. Sevrin obviously thought he was a fool, managed to make him look like a fool at every turn. "How do you know my father?"

"What Sevrin told you was basically true. I worked for Pern Keire and so did your father. Pern arranged for South to train me and—"

"You founded the Dirty Dozen," Nazerel cut in, already confused. "Aren't you Ontarian? My father trained Rodytes."

"Your father trained hybrids of many varieties using Rodyte techniques."

"You're an Ontarian hybrid?"

Gerrod's brows arched as he took a swig. "Something like that."

"Why are you still on Earth?"

Gerrod laughed. "Hasn't anyone told you what happened to the others? I wasn't going to let some prissy Mystic rearrange my mind. I was ready to die fighting, and when the team chasing me thought that's what I'd done. I stepped back and let them believe it."

"Which stranded you on Earth, living as a human."

Unaffected by the distain in Nazerel's tone, Gerrod shrugged. "At least I'm living." He set down the bottle and motioned toward the other room. "Go put her back before she wakes up. Sevrin is not going to kill her."

Chapter Eight

"This looks like the ultra-secret army base they create for movies. I just didn't realize places like this actually exist." Jillian walked beside Odintar, feeling like a rescue puppy exploring a real house for the first time. "Why do they call it the Bunker?"

"This is the only level that's above ground. The rest of the complex is subterranean."

"Of course it is." She laughed. "Aren't all the best Top Secret installations buried underground."

She'd driven to a rest stop just off the highway that allowed overnight parking. Odintar still insisted she'd sleep in her own bed tonight, but he was making allowances for the unexpected. Probably wise, being that the unexpected seemed to be his stock and trade.

"Morgan Hoyt, that's Elias' boss, runs this place and she's been gracious enough to sublet a portion of the complex to the Mystic Militia. We were going stir-crazy on our ship."

"Wait, did you say 'she's been gracious enough'? Morgan is female?"

"I've never seen her naked, but I have no reason to doubt her claim."

She slapped his arm. "I bet you've pictured her naked, you pervert."

He was obviously unmoved by her annoyance. "I suspect every man on this base has pictured Morgan naked, or at least the ones partial to curvy females."

If he was trying to make her jealous, he was succeeding.

They turned right at the end of a long corridor and found Elias waiting for them. Well, two could play at this game. Elias was certainly fantasy worthy. "Hi there, handsome." She looped her arm through his and flashed a flirtatious smile.

Elias looked at Odintar and raised both brows. "What did you do to piss her off?"

"Told her about Morgan."

"I see." He patted Jillian's hand. "Morgan is a bona-fide workaholic. She keeps herself much too busy for any sort of social life. There's not a man around who can turn her head. And believe me many have tried. You have nothing to fear from Morgan."

"So the only reason I don't need to worry is because Morgan's not interested in men?"

Odintar laughed while Elias looked confused. "That's not what I said at all. Morgan is interested in men. She's just more interested in the work we do here."

She took pity on him and smiled. "We're just having fun while we can. I'm not looking forward to this meeting."

Elias reached over and activated the elevator before he spoke again. "I just met King Indric, but from what I've been told—"

"King Indric?" Odintar and Jillian chorused. Then they each clarified the reason for their outburst.

"I requested a representative from Guild Air," Odintar said. "Not the region's king. Is Lor responsible for this?"

"I'm going to be assessed by a king?" Panic sped Jillian's pulse and urged her to run in the opposite direction. "Why would a king, any king, bother with me?"

"King Indric wouldn't be here without a good reason. I just don't know what it is." The elevator door slid open and Elias motioned them inside.

"Am I allowed to refuse?" She hated feeling like a coward, but she couldn't seem to slow her breathing or calm her racing heart.

"No one is going to hurt you, *gennari*." Odintar took her by the shoulders and turned her to face him. "We are sworn to your protection."

"He's right." Elias moved into her peripheral vision. "None of us will let King Indric harm you. Even if that were his intention, which I'm certain it's not."

"What if he wants to take me to Bilarri for training or whatever? Earth is my home. I don't want to leave here."

Elias held the door with his outstretched arm. "You won't be forced to do anything."

She scoffed. "You're going to say no to a king?"

Her doubt didn't change his determined expression. "Not just me. You're part of our team and we protect our own. If King Indric steps out of line, we'll all be there to pull him back. Now get on the damn elevator. Your doubt is insulting."

Odintar chuckled, clearly agreeing with Elias' strategy.

The slap had been verbal not physical, but the result was the same. Her panic eased and she was able to process his words. Okay fine, so she was about to go before alien royalty. Why should that rattle her after everything else she'd been through?

She moved to the back corner of the elevator and scrubbed her hand over her face. She had to stop thinking with human perspectives. The rules had obviously changed. She wasn't a showgirl anymore. Hadn't Tori said Lor was the head of some Great House? Aria had married a Bilarrian nobleman. And now Jillian was about to go before a king.

Rather than bombard her companions with questions, she took a deep breath and tried to calm down. Focus on one thing at a time. "How should I greet him? Do I bow or curtsy or something?"

"Royal protocol is only observed at formal events and official court functions," Elias told her. "A simple handshake will do."

"And rumor has it King Indric is a terrible flirt, so don't take it personally," Odintar added.

"I won't if you won't," she countered, unable to even imagine what a Bilarrian king looked like.

Elias led them to a large open area. It looked sort of like a gymnasium crossed with a martial arts dojo. Familiar, and some not so familiar, workout equipment was situated at one end, while the other was surrounded by mirrors. Large padded mats carpeted the floor.

She hadn't been sure what to expect, but this was definitely not it. Three men stood in the middle of the padded area. All three turned as she entered the room. She recognized Lor, but the other two were unfamiliar. One stayed slightly back and only glanced at her, while the remaining man met her gaze directly. From his square stance to the confidant tilt of his head, everything about him projected authority. His gold-streaked black hair had been pulled back and bound into a wrist-thick mass. His black-and-gold coloring was echoed in his rich garments. The outfit looked part business suit and part uniform. As she approached, she realized the rings separating his pupils from his irises were gold rather than red or blue. She'd never seen anything so beautiful.

Despite Elias' advice, she dipped into an automatic curtsy. "Your Majesty."

Indric caught both her hands and raised her knuckles to his lips for a light kiss. Then his gaze locked with hers and the golden rings shimmered. "May I enter?"

She felt the brush of his energy against her mind and tried not to panic. This was common for these people. They exchanged images, thoughts and energy as easily as humans sent text messages. Unsure of her voice, she nodded and quickly closed her eyes.

With a deep chuckle, he released her hands and stepped back. "You can open your eyes now. I've seen all I need to see."

But she hadn't felt anything yet.

Realization unfurled and Jillian shivered. He'd only asked permission out of courtesy. He could have scanned her mind without her knowing it; scanned it and probably a whole lot more.

"What did you see?" Her voice sounded calmer than she felt. Hopefully her expression was equally convincing. She might be quaking on the inside, but she didn't want this powerful stranger to think she was a spineless fool.

"It's a rather long story. Shall we find a more comfortable setting?" Without waiting for her preference, he waved his hand and the scene around them morphed.

Jillian gasped and wobbled before her mind accepted the new input. She stood beside an ornate loveseat in a stylish salon. Complete with massive marble fireplace and oversized oil paintings, the room created an old-world ambiance. Odintar stood at her side, but Indric hadn't allowed the others to...transport with them? "Did we teleport or is this some sort of mind trick?"

Amusement softened Indric's gaze as he explained, "We're on the metaphysical plane and I've paused our time stream. As soon as I release the visualization, we'll return to reality and everything will continue on as if we never left."

"Nifty trick." She was pretty sure even Odintar couldn't pause a time stream. This was another indication of Indric's power.

"Have a seat." He looked at Odintar and added, "Both of you."

"Is Lor not allowed to know what you discovered?" Odintar sat and held out his hand, encouraging Jillian to join him on the loveseat. She sat and he stretched his arm along the back, barely touching her shoulders.

"It's up to Jillian whom she informs." Indric sat facing them and the padded armchair suddenly seemed like a throne.

"And yet I am here."

Indric's smile made him look younger and less intimidating. "I just looked into her mind. Mates should have no secrets from each other."

Odintar cringed and Jillian felt obliged to point out, "We're lovers, not mates."

"If you say so."

Rather than argue about something that was really none of Indric's business, Jillian asked, "What have you learned?"

"You are not merely a child of my region; you are a direct decedent of my bloodline."

She kept herself from laughing, but just barely. Her mind was so saturated with unexpected developments she couldn't even find the strength to feel surprised. Less than a week ago she'd been lying in a hospital bed, barely able to walk, and now she was moving things with her mind and an alien king had just claimed her as kin.

Was this where he insisted that Bilarrian royalty, no matter how distant, belonged on Bilarri? If that was where this conversation was headed, he was in for disappointment.

"How is that possible?" Odintar asked. "She isn't a foundling. She was raised by her human mother." His arm shifted from the loveseat to her shoulders.

"My sister was a war bride." Indric paused. "You're Ontarian. Do you know what that term means?"

Tension rolled up Odintar's side and hardened his expression. "Most believe I'm half Ontarian. In truth, my mother was a war bride. She hid me with friends on Ontariese when she was lucky enough to escape her captor."

Indric shifted his gaze back to Jillian. "And do you understand the complexities of this subject?"

She nodded. "Rodyte warriors captured Bilarrian females, claiming they were spoils of war. That's where the Shadow Assassins got the idea to capture their mates."

"Shadow Assassins were simply replenishing their ranks," Indric pointed out. "With war brides, the intent was more convoluted. Rodytes were trying to restore magic powers to their offspring, but it also became a battle of wits. They prided themselves in besting our security measures. The harder we tried to protect our women, the bolder the Rodytes became."

"Can I ask a rude question?"

"I doubt I'll find it rude, but please continue."

Each time Indric spoke Jillian felt warmth melt the tension from her muscles. Was he doing it intentionally or was it a side effect of the metaphysical plane? "Rodytes can't manipulate magic, correct?"

"Most can't, though they have technologies that replicate many of our abilities."

That was new information. When Odintar explained the conflict, she'd pictured Rodyte hostilities growing out of a sense of inferiority or at least having been treated as inferiors. As with most conflicts, it was obviously more complicated than she'd first thought. "If your sister had abilities similar to yours, how was a Rodyte able to imprison her?"

"They developed a collar that suppresses our access to elemental energy. Without such energy, we are powerless. We have since engineered a device that disables the collar, but it was still in use when Lierra was captured."

She shuddered. It was so easy to imagine the terror and hopelessness Lierra must have endured. "Is it still going on?"

"We're enjoying a prolonged lull in hostilities. I'm not sure the war will ever be over. Resentment on both sides runs too deep."

"I'm sorry about what your sister suffered, but she couldn't be my mother. My mother has photographs of me in her arms shortly after I was born."

"You misunderstand." Indric crossed his legs and offered her a patient smile. "You're too young to have been battle born."

"Battle born?"

"The offspring of war brides are referred to as battle born. My sister was returned to us forty-three years ago. As is the custom, she was released from captivity without her battle-born son."

Another shiver raced down Jillian's spine as the subject became more personal. "You think your nephew is my father?"

He chuckled and shook his head. "There's no speculation involved. The rhythm of your energy is so similar to mine, you can only be a blood relation."

"What made you suspect a connection?" Odintar asked.

Damn good question. What made the King of Bilarri drop everything and flash to another planet?

"It took many years, but I was able to confirm the identity of my nephew. I have attempted to make contact with him, but he considers himself Rodyte and wants nothing to do with his Bilarrian heritage."

"Who is he?"

Jillian appreciated Odintar's directness. Her thoughts were too chaotic for such clarity.

"Gerrod Reynolds. He organized the despicable group of rebels known as the Dirty Dozen. When Drakkin told me about the notebook, I knew it was only a matter of time before one or more of Gerrod's offspring was located."

"It's possible I have half-brothers and sisters?" Her heart did a little flip. She'd always longed for siblings, had always envied the closeness Tori and Angie enjoyed. Despite the numerous conflicts the sisters had endured, they each knew the other would be there to support them if the need arose.

"It's not just possible, it's likely. The goal of the Dirty Dozen was to create as many offspring as they could."

"Wait a minute." She paused, hoping to organize her thoughts. "Weren't the Dirty Dozen from Ontariese? I thought the Ontarian government sanctioned the program, even brought them to Earth."

"The facts are sketchy at best," Odintar admitted. "Nine of the twelve were taken back to Ontariese. Two were killed during the manhunt and their leader was presumed dead. The nine we had in custody were interrogated at length, but their stories varied greatly."

"Why didn't someone just read their minds and learn the truth."

The knowing smile Odintar and Indric exchanged made her feel naive. So many of their explanations began with "it's not that simple".

"Truth is greatly influenced by perspective," Odintar began. "If a person is told an untruth, but they have no reason to doubt it. The falsehood becomes true to them."

When she didn't respond to Odintar's comment, Indric elaborated. "From what I've been able to piece together, Gerrod was working for Pern Keire, the ruler of Rodymia at the time. Gerrod recruited the others then dispatched them to different locations so they had minimal contact with each other. It's likely the others didn't realize they were being manipulated by a Rodyte."

And this delightful Rodyte spy was her father.

"What did the Rodyte gain by...never mind. I don't think I want to know." She folded her hands in her lap and interlaced her fingers. "What do you expect from me?"

"I expect nothing," Indric insisted. "Lierra passed beyond years ago, but you have a variety of other relations who will be anxious to meet you."

"I'm not ready to leave Earth. Is that a problem?" A touch of rebellion sharpened the question.

Indric chuckled, unaffected by her attitude. "I'm not going to throw you over my shoulder and zap you to Bilarri. That's not why I came. All of Lierra's wealth and property were held in trust for her son. When I located Gerrod, he stubbornly relinquished all rights to his inheritance. There were no specific provisions for grandchildren in Lierra's will, but Bilarrian law requires a ten-year waiting period in which offspring can register a claim. Gerrod renounced his inheritance six years ago, so you have four years to decide what you want out of the rest of your life."

"What happens if I don't register a claim?"

"I'm the clan patriarch, so everything reverts back to me." Again the tingling lethargy accompanied each word.

"All you had to do was stay quiet and Lierra's wealth would have been yours?"

He scooted to the edge of his chair and rested his forearms on his knees. "This isn't about money. It's about family. You are a member of my family. None of us will force our way into your life, but I hope, at some point, you'll be curious enough to explore the possibilities."

Standing suddenly, she walked around behind the loveseat. She wasn't afraid of Indric. She just felt the need for a little more separation. "If you're drugging me intentionally, stop it! I'm not hysterical."

"I apologize." The words came out of his mouth, but there was no remorse in his expression.

"Then you were doing it intentionally?"

"Some find my voice soothing. I won't do it again."

Those mysterious eyes hinted at a lot more than the ability to soothe. He could pause time, for God's sake. Was it really surprising that he could control emotions with his voice?

"May I ask a question, sire?" Odintar had remained silently supportive through the entire exchange.

"Of course."

"Do you know his current location?"

"Gerrod's?" The king seemed genuinely surprised by the question.

"Yes. He's a fugitive who has escaped justice for a very long time."

Indric's tense nod made Jillian think he wouldn't answer. "I'll give Lor his last known address, but I seriously doubt he's still there. He obviously knows how to evade capture. Even my network of spies had a hard time locating him."

"And yet you allowed him to disappear." Odintar pushed to his feet, momentarily blocking her view of Indric. "Why didn't you notify the authorities when you found him the first time?"

She took a step to the side so she could gauge Indric's reaction.

His chin came up a notch and the rings in his eyes gleamed. He was clearly not used to having his actions questioned. "His behavior is amoral and utterly objectionable, but he has not broken any laws. As long as the females were willing, which it's my understanding that they were, I have no reason to pursue the matter further."

"Would your attitude be the same if he weren't your nephew?"

Stop it. She rushed around the loveseat and grasped his upper arm, half afraid Odintar would charge Indric.

"This is an Ontarian conflict." Indric stood as well, though he appeared calm. "I have neither assisted nor hindered any attempts to capture him. If High Queen Charlotte is dissatisfied with my approach, she is free to contact me."

His arm flexed beneath her hand then gradually relaxed. He took a deep breath and then inclined his head. "I apologize for my attitude. I have expended too much time and energy trying to bring Gerrod Reynolds to justice. The ongoing effort sometimes overshadows my reasoning."

"I'll give Lor all the information I have on Gerrod, but don't expect much. The last time I had contact with him was six years ago."

"I appreciate the compromise."

Indric acknowledged the statement with another regal nod, then turned back to Jillian. "I'll stress this again. Nothing will be forced upon you. But you have opportunities open to you now that weren't there before. First and foremost, you would be much safer on Bilarri. I encourage you to seriously consider coming home."

"Home." She laughed. "I've been trying to go home ever since this *adventure* began." Odintar looked at her, obviously catching the sarcasm in her tone. She glanced at him then continued her standoff with the king. "I'm not leaving Earth until the Shadow Assassins are apprehended. I won't make myself safe by making someone else a target."

Though Indric didn't seem pleased, he didn't argue. "Security within the Bunker is acceptable, but Lor mentioned some sort of undercover operation. Tell me more about that."

Odintar slipped his arm around her waist as he explained, "We've identified a tattoo shop frequented by the Shadow Assassins. Jillian was just hired as their receptionist. She'll be accompanied by a human surveillance team as well as me or one of the other Mystics."

Indric narrowed his gaze, clearly unsatisfied with the description. "I'll dispatch a security team to augment the Mystic Militia. Three empowered players is not nearly enough."

"Two weeks ago I would have argued with you, but we're no longer limited by the confines of our ship. I suspect Lor will welcome reinforcements. However, the final say is his."

"Jillian will have a security contingent," Indric asserted. "Whether or not Lor chooses to incorporate them into current missions is up to him."

"And if I don't want bodyguards?" She knew the answer. She just couldn't believe her freedom had been compromised by a father she'd never met.

"I'm trying to be patient. I know this is overwhelming for you. But it's my responsibility to keep you safe." The friendly openness she'd sensed evaporated. She was no longer speaking with a member of her family. This was *King* Indric. "Don't fight me on this. I will not relent."

She stared back at him, neither accepting nor objecting to his decision.

He turned to Odintar and added, "I'll arrange for a mentor from Guild Air. Your intimate relationship disqualifies you to train her properly."

Much to her surprise, Odintar nodded. Just like that he handed her over to someone else?

"Don't I get a say in any of this?" She looked from Indric to Odintar and back. "I happen to like training with Odintar. I trust him and I—"

"He's right," Odintar insisted. "You'll progress faster with someone who's able to remain objective. I lost that ability the first time I kissed you."

She was about to voice her annoyance when Indric changed the subject. "Is your mother still alive?"

"Why?" The question was so unexpected, she finally felt surprised.

His easy smile returned. "She suffered at the hands of one of my progeny. I would like the opportunity to make amends."

Jillian crossed her arms over her chest, not sure what to make of the offer. "What did you have in mind?"

He shrugged. "I can take her to Bilarri where she will live in the lap of luxury or I can arrange for her to receive an inheritance from a previously unknown relation. I can provide for her needs without her ever knowing the source of her good fortune. It's up to you."

"Let me think about it. I'm not sure which makes more sense for her."

"All right." He clasped his hands behind his back and squared his shoulders. "I've taken up enough of your time. Prepare yourself for the rush. I'm going to release the visualization."

The salon blurred for a fraction of a second and then they were back in the training hall.

"I suppose my office is more comfortable," Elias was saying. "Will that be satisfactory, sire?"

Lor flashed a knowing smile. Even with the time strand paused, he must have sensed their absence. "I don't think that's necessary any longer."

"I had an investigator locate Gerrod Reynolds six years ago. I don't know if any of the information will be useful now, but I'll send over a report." Before Lor could respond to the offer, Indric turned to Elias. "I appreciate your hospitality." Then to Odintar he said, "It will take me a day or two to make the arrangements. I'm trusting you to protect her until then."

Odintar bowed and, without further ado, Indric flashed out of sight.

"All right," Elias grumbled. "What the hell just happened?"

Lor laughed and patted him on the back. "I think we're looking at the newest member of Indric's family." He moved toward Jillian as he asked, "Am I right?"

She sighed. "So he tells me."

"Then why aren't you excited?" Lor glanced at Odintar as he waited for her answer. "You just found out you're royalty."

"I just found out I'm an obscure member of a royal family on a planet I'd never heard of until a few days ago. Meanwhile, I'm being hunted by another group of aliens who want to use females like human incubators."

"Well, when you put it like that..." Elias maintained a straight face as the other three laughed.

Lor carefully placed his hand on her upper arm. "We know this has been hard on you and Odintar told me that what you'd really like is to go home for a night or two."

Jillian tensed. Was this where he refused because it was too dangerous? Sleeping in her own bed, surrounded by her own things was such a simple request, or it would have been without the Shadow Assassins.

"Blayne and I spent the last three hours warding your apartment," Lor explained. "The shields won't last forever, but you should be safe for a night or two."

She wasn't sure what "warding" entailed. "Did you create an actual barrier or just some sort of shield?"

"It's an extremely sensitive alarm. You'll be warned if anyone approaches, even if they try to teleport in. It will give Odintar time to flash you to safety."

Which meant Odintar was coming with her. Her stomach tightened while her pulse leapt. Why did she still feel so conflicted? Their romance was exciting, exhilarating, but one night of peace and quiet had its own appeal. Whether Odintar meant to or not, he'd influenced each decision she'd made since he barreled into her life. Still, they were trying to accommodate her needs and she didn't want to seem ungrateful.

"Thank you," she said to the three at large.

"Tori's in the lounge," Lor told her. "Why don't you go visit with her while Odintar briefs us on the last few days."

Despite the polite wording, Jillian knew an order when she heard one. She'd been dismissed, pushed aside so the adults could talk without upsetting the child. "I'd be happy to, if I knew where the lounge was."

"Take a left, then a right, then another left. Then it's the second door on your right." Elias used an angled hand gesture to illustrate each turn.

"Left, right, left. Got it." Suddenly anxious to be away from the bossy men, she spun on the ball of her foot and hurried down the hallway.

Warmth and encouragement seeped into her mind, making her link with Odintar tingle. At any other time she would have welcomed the affection. Right now, it felt too much like what Indric had done. She found her end of the link and squeezed it shut, blocking Odintar's access to her mind.

She darted around a corner and collided with someone. Stumbling back as the other person reached out and steadied her. "Sorry."

"No problem." The hand grasping her upper arm released. "You must be Jillian."

Jillian looked up and fought for a reply. Tall and curvaceous, the red-haired woman emanated authority while still maintaining her femininity. Not an easy balance to achieve. "Are you Morgan?"

The woman smiled and went from pretty to stunning. "I am. Can I help you find something?"

"I was headed to the lounge. At least I hope I was."

"You're almost there. Turn left at the next corner and you'll find the lounge a little ways down on your right."

Beauty was generally an advantage, but a woman in Morgan's position would be seriously hampered by physical appeal. Jillian didn't envy Morgan her challenges. "Thanks."

"Will you be staying here now or were they able to work out the logistics of your apartment?"

"I'm going home for a day or two. We'll see what happens after that." She tried to sound as assertive as possible. Too many forces already had influence on her decisions.

Morgan's sky-blue eyes narrowed as if she'd object, then she nodded. "Very good. It was nice to meet you."

"Likewise." Jillian lingered in the hallway as Morgan continued on her way. There was a fine line between protective custody and captivity. Jillian would not allow these people to make her a prisoner in her own life. She wouldn't put herself in unnecessary danger, but neither would she cower in the corner like a frightened child.

She found the lounge and was relieved to see that Tori was the only other person in the medium-sized room. Tori sat at a square table working on a sleek laptop. She glanced up from the screen and smiled. "Hey there, stranger."

Jillian slipped into the chair across from her. "Hey yourself." The back wall was lined with vending machines and couches had been arranged to one side, leaving room for the tables on the other. "Did Lor put you to work or are you researching a new design project?"

Tori closed the laptop and looked at Jillian. "I think my set design days are part of my past. As soon as this crisis is neutralized, Lor and I will probably go back to Ontariese."

This didn't surprise Jillian. Lor was some sort of hotshot on his planet, so Tori's life would have to conform to his. Still, it bothered her that Tori was willing to abandon her entire life without a backward glance. "What about Angie?"

"Angie will likely come too. Blayne wants—"

"What about what Angie wants? Or what you want? Why are you rearranging your lives to fit the needs of these men?" Tori opened her mouth, obviously ready to defend her choices, so Jillian rushed on. "Angie has always been part Gypsy, but you have a life here, an occupation and—"

"And what? An occupation was all I had before I met Lor."

"Thanks a lot. We've been friends for years. That means nothing to you?"

Tori paused, her expression tense yet compassionate. "You've never questioned my decisions, even when you didn't agree with them. What is this really about?"

"He promised there wouldn't be any more surprises and then—Bam! I get sucker punched."

"Who made the promise and who threw the sucker punch?"

Jillian tried not to sound melodramatic, but the past week had been surreal. "After rearranging reality as I had known it, Odintar promised he was finished screwing with me."

Tori laughed. "I wasn't aware that he'd started screwing with you."

"You know what I mean."

"I do, but I'd like you to answer the question. Has there been literal screwing?"

Jillian rubbed her eyes. She was so not in the mood for Tori's sense of humor. "Yes, we're lovers. Now can we return to the important subject?"

"Do you mean the part where you're Bilarrian royalty?" Tori grinned at her.

"Lor warned you?"

She nodded, clearly unwilling to let Jillian's grumpiness rub off on her. "I've heard that King Indric is even better looking than Lord Drakkin. Is it true?"

"Why would you care and who the hell is Lord Drakkin?"

"Aria's mate. Remember, she's on Bilarri. Drakkin once ruled the mountain region of Hautell. I think one of his sons is king there now."

"There's more than one king on Bilarri? Or is Indric Drakkin's son?"

"No relation, but Lor said they've been best friends for centuries. Bilarri has four regions and each region has its own monarch. Indric rules the deserts of San Adrin."

That's right. Odintar had mentioned the four regions. The people from each region were empowered by a different element. It made sense that they'd have separate rulers. Jillian tucked away the facts, not sure when, or if, she'd need to know more about her homeworld. No, Earth was and would always be her homeworld. Bilarri was simply the planet that had produced her paternal grandmother.

"Is there any chance I can make a phone call? I really need to talk to my Mom."

"Does she do internet calls? I could text her phone and tell her to go online. Internet access is scrambled or encrypted or whatever. I had to register my facial scan before they issued me a logon."

"You can try. She has a smart phone, but she's bad about letting the battery run down." She told Tori the number.

Tori opened her laptop and sent the text. "And you never answered the question. Is Indric hot? I'm asking strictly as an artist, you understand."

"Sure you are." Jillian chuckled. Just because Tori was married didn't mean she'd gone blind. Artists were notoriously visual and Tori was no exception. Besides, without her work as a set designer, she would need a new artistic outlet. "King Indric was arguably the best-looking man I've ever seen." Indric had been more classically handsome than Odintar, yet it was the subtle savagery in Odintar that fascinated her.

"Form his image in your mind so I can see him. I'm starting a sketch book of the different...species sounds so strange, but I guess that's what we're encountering, different humanoid species."

Jillian thought about Indric, letting his image form with as much detail as she could. She felt the brush of Tori's presence then her friend sucked in a breath.

"Okay, wow. I thought Drakkin was a challenge. I'm not sure I can do justice to Indric."

"Lor doesn't mind you drawing all these other men?"

Tori shrugged. "I've drawn just as many women. Have you seen Morgan? OMG That woman is disgusting."

Before Jillian could respond a musical pinging drew Tori's attention to her computer screen. "We're in luck. Your mom is logging on. Do you want video?"

"No. I don't want to explain why I'm not at home."

Tori established the connection then slid the laptop toward Jillian. "I'll be back in a few."

Jillian wasn't sure the gesture was necessary. Tori knew everything she knew and more.

"Hello? Are you there? Jillian?"

The anxiety in her mother's tone drew Jillian closer to the screen. "I'm here, Mom. Are you okay?"

"That's my question? Where the hell have you been for the past week? Why haven't you returned my calls?"

Damn it. She should have rehearsed an excuse for her thoughtlessness. In truth she'd been so busy and so overwhelmed by all the changes that the complication hadn't crossed her mind. "I dropped my phone and can't afford to replace it right now. I'm sorry if I worried you."

"Worried? I was worried the first two days, then I was frantic. Yesterday I got mad. Today," she sighed loud enough for the microphone to pick up the whoosh of air. "I'm thrilled to hear your voice, but I'm still angry."

"I'm really sorry. I don't know what else I can say."

"I was going to come see you, but the hospital said you'd been discharged. How are you feeling?"

She hated lies. Honesty might hurt more in the short term, but it seldom sneaked around to bite one in the butt. That was deception's favorite game. Besides, she didn't see an alternative. At least not right now. "I'm doing as well as can be expected. Getting around sucks, but I was able to sleep through the night for the first time since this happened."

"Are you at your apartment or are you staying with someone?"

"I'm at home, but Tori and Angie are helping out." That wasn't too far from the truth. "They've been wonderful."

"True friends are hard to find. You need to hang on to those two."

"I intend to." Tension built as the conversation lagged. "Mom, I understand why you don't like to talk about him, but I need to know more about my father." Or at least her perception of who he had been.

"He was a mistake, a youthful indiscretion. That's all you need to know."

"Unfortunately, it's not." Now it was time for some creative embellishment. If her mother honestly had no idea her father had been anything other than a collage Romeo, she'd make sure her mother never found out about...reality? Could she really keep the truth from someone she loved? "Some of the blood tests they ran while I was injured revealed something odd in my blood. I was able to give them your medical history, but they really need his too."

A long pause followed. Jillian could picture her mother's tormented expression, had seen it often enough while she was growing up to remember every detail. Questions about her father always drew that reaction from her mother.

"Do you at least know his name?" Jillian persisted.

"His first name was Jerry, but I know that's not what you're asking." Another long silence followed and Jillian wished she'd done this in person. It would have been worth the four-hour drive. "How 'odd' was what they found in your blood? You're not being harmed by it, are you?"

She knew. Those few questions made it obvious. Her mother either knew or suspected. "The anomaly isn't harming me. They've just never seen anything like it before."

"Oh, baby, you have to be careful. Or better yet, drop it completely. Get a new phone number not just a new phone. Move to another apartment. No, another city. If the wrong people get ahold of your blood, they could..."

Soft sobbing came over the speakers and Jillian wrapped her arms around herself. The past was fracturing, bleeding, spilling over into the present. Would they be liberated by the truth or consumed by the destruction. "It'll be all right, Mom. People are protecting me. I'm safe and so are you."

"You can't trust *anyone*. Jillian, you have to listen to me." Her voice was suddenly stronger, filled with purpose. "This is so much bigger than you ever imagined."

The last thing she wanted was to cause her mother more pain. Her mother had already endured a lifetime of isolation and fear. Much of it had been self-imposed, but that didn't matter now. "I'll come get you. Pack a bag and be ready in an hour. Don't tell anyone you're leaving."

"In an hour?" A thin laugh followed the question. "You can make it from Vegas to LA in an hour?"

"Just be ready."

"All right. I'll be ready."

Jillian ended the call and powered down the computer. She pushed back from the table and Tori walked back into the room. "Sorry. I overheard most of that. What are you planning to do with her?"

"King Indric offered her a home on Bilarri and I intend to take him up on the offer."

Tori nodded as Jillian handed her the laptop. "You should go with her. Lor's convinced the Shadow Assassins are on the move. The receptionist gig is probably a waste of time."

"I'm not leaving until I have one last conversation with Roxie. She might not realize what she knows, but she could have seen all sorts of things that could be helpful. I'm not going to squander the opportunity."

"Fair enough. Let's round up our men so you can go get your mother." Tori tucked the laptop under her arm and headed for the door.

Chapter Nine

Sevrin paused outside the holding cell and adjusted her midnight-blue bustier. She'd taken off the matching jacket, leaving her in a short, tight skirt and high-heeled ankle boots. The outfit was one of her favorites because it perfectly showcased her figure, and she needed every advantage for this negotiation. Satisfied that she looked her best, she triggered the door and stepped inside the small room.

Flynn charged the energy barrier separating them. His hands touched the shimmering field and he shook with what had to be agonizing pain. His dark gaze remained locked with hers and his murderous expression didn't change, but he didn't make a sound. Stubborn fool.

"Cut it out. You'll only damage yourself."

He slowly lowered his arms, yet remained half a step from the barrier. "I should have listened to Nazerel. You're a deceitful bitch!"

"But I don't have to be. I don't even like being bitchy. You drove me to it." She dragged one of the two chairs in the observation area closer to the barrier then sat. With her legs crossed, her skirt crawled well up on her thighs. The fact wasn't lost on her prisoner. "You can either be my reluctant messenger or my willing partner. I'd much rather work with you than force you to do my bidding, but I am able to accomplish either goal."

He tugged on the metal collar circling his neck. "Take this off me *now*."

"After I've gone to all this trouble?" She snickered. "You really must think I'm a fool."

"I told you what I think you are. This is a waste of time."

She lifted one bare shoulder in a careless shrug that drew his attention to the swell of her breasts. "The precautions are necessary. You and your brothers have significant advantages. The collar simply ensures your obedience while you're here."

"Where the hell is here? I can't believe I let you drug me." He turned his back on her and tried to rip open the collar for what had to be the hundredth time.

"This is my new headquarters. None of you will ever know its actual location. It has been under construction for the past two years and houses state-of-the-art technology. You would not be better served if you were taken to the Rodyte capital." She paused, allowing her words to sink in. "For obvious reasons, I must be careful. You and your brothers have disregarded many of my fundamental rules and you've ignored my warnings. That's about to change."

"Fuck." He turned back around. "You."

"We'll get to that in a moment." She stood and slid the chair out of her way. "You need to pay attention. You will be required to explain my expectations to the others. Now that we have the staff and the technology required for success, there will be no more self-directed hunts. I will sanction one hunter at a time. Anyone who disregards this rule will be shot on sight. There will be no second chances. Do you understand?"

"I understand that you're insane. How do you intend to stop us from hunting? Are you going to kill us all?"

"If need be," she replied without pause. "You seem to have forgotten that there are thousands of Shadow Assassins back on Ontariese. Everyone is expendable."

"We're the strongest. The best." He planted his fists on his hips and dared her to argue with his belligerent expression. "Are you ready to settle for second best?"

"I'm ready for success. If that requires a massive purge in personnel, I'm prepared for the sacrifice. Are you?"

He just glared at her.

She held up her index finger. "No unsanctioned hunts." Adding her middle finger to the gesture, she went on. "The sanctioned hunter will bring his mate to the old warehouse. He will be collared. He and his mate will be drugged then they will be transported to this location. I am the only female allowed in the team houses."

"The others will never agree."

She shrugged. "They have no choice."

"They'll run."

She smiled, anticipation making her giddy. She'd tried to play nicely with these men and they'd taken advantage of her generosity. Well, they were about to find out why people whispered her father's name with fear and reverence. And everyone that knew her said she was just like her father.

"Your nanites were manufactured on Rodymia. I now have the means to track them. And unlike an Ontarian tracking chip, your nanites cannot be removed."

He stared at her silently, nostrils flaring, eyes narrowed and hostile. "This is intolerable."

Again she shrugged. "Only if you make it so. The rules are flexible. You've lost my trust. Regain it and I'll grant you more freedom."

"How do we regain your trust?"

"By following the rules."

His hands folded into tight fists. "We had it better on Ontariese."

"Oh now that's just nonsense. You will each be granted the opportunity to hunt and I will enable you to transfer your abilities to your mate. Can Overlord Lyrik say the same?"

"None of your attempts have been successful. Why should we believe you now?"

"I have staff and equipment now that I didn't have before. Dr. Porffer, bless her soul, tried as hard as she could, but even she admitted that she was in over her head. Her teacher's teacher and his hand-selected team are now at my disposal. The next time we attempt a transfer, it will succeed."

The fury in his gaze gradually became something more calculative. He licked his lips and gazed into the distance. "What do I have to do to be the one you choose?"

Now that was more like it. "This is rule number three. Each hunter must pay for his sanction with sexual tribute. I've decided it's too great an honor for any hunter to know that he fathered my child. I will enjoy the talents of each hunter before he begins searching for his mate."

"If you're hoping to absorb our abilities; it doesn't work that way."

"Let me worry about how it works. All any of you need to worry about is pleasing me."

He tore his shirt off over his head, chest heaving. "I'd like to pay for my sanction. Please."

He added the last word with such rancor it made Sevrin smile. This was going to be even more fun than she'd imagined. "Tribute must be offered willingly."

"Oh I'm more than willing. I've been imagining this since I first saw you."

She chuckled. No doubt he'd been imagining all sorts of cruel things, but this was about her pleasure and his surrender. These men were impossibly arrogant and in desperate need of a lesson in humility. "Take off your pants. Let me see what you're offering."

It took a moment for him to unclench his hands enough to use them. He ripped open the front of his jeans and shoved them down his thighs. He wore nothing underneath. All the while he glared at her, rebellion evident in every movement. He had a fabulous body, but then they all did. The current generation of Shadow Assassins had been genetically engineered for height and muscle mass then sculpted to perfection by exercise and discipline. Flynn also had a pleasant face. Symmetrical features and light brown hair.

She took her time, enjoying every aspect of his masculine form. Strength and tension were evident in every limb, every bulge and ripple. Except his cock. Though well shaped and full of potential, the shaft wasn't even hard.

"You don't look very willing to me." She motioned toward his crotch.

"Let me touch you, mistress. I promise you won't be disappointed."

"No. I'd be dead. It's obvious you're still angry." She moved to the control panel on the wall and activated a compartment at the head of his bunk. The compartment slid open and restraints spilled onto the thin mattress. "Lie on your back and cuff your wrists."

"I can't perform in such a demeaning manor," he snapped. "Shadow Assassins are always in control."

"Not anymore." She kept her tone light and tried to look bored. "Restrain yourself or I'll find another messenger. It really makes no difference to me."

He stomped to the bunk and spread out on his back. Each movement radiated resentment, which made his surrender even sweeter. He closed his eyes and blew out a harsh breath. "You have my word I will not harm you. Please leave my hands free."

Did he really think she was that stupid? "Not a chance. Stop stalling."

With obvious reluctance, he raised his arms over his head and fastened the alloy cuffs. Then he turned his head and glared at her. "Let's get this over with." Anger intensified the green of his eyes. They were really quite beautiful.

She deactivated the energy barrier and moved two steps closer. "It doesn't work like that." Angling her body so he could see her cleavage and her ass, she bent from the waist and unlaced her ankle boots. "I haven't had a man since Zacharous was captured. I intend to savor every moment of this."

After kicking off her boots, she reached beneath her skirt and removed her panties. She looked at him, pleased to find his eyes had followed each move. A zipper secured the front of the bustier, the laces on the back largely ornamental. She lowered the zipper several inches, allowing most of her breasts to spring free. The semi-ridged cups skimmed over her nipples, revealing a hint of areola with each breath.

She looked at his cock and smiled. That was better. "If you hurt me, I'll slit your throat."

He said nothing, just waited for her next move.

Tired of the perpetual ache between her thighs, she was tempted to just climb on and ride him fast and hard. But it had been weeks since a man last touched her. She really wanted to play. Besides, the longer she made him wait, the wilder he'd be when she finally took him.

She moved closer to the bunk, pulling up her skirt as she went.

His eyes drooped, nearly closing, and he inhaled deeply. "Are you as wet as you smell?"

"Why don't you find out?" She straddled his hand and closed her eyes, trembling with anticipation. He shoved his fingers into her wet passage without warning or preparation. Was that two or three? Gods she felt full. Her inner muscles rippled with near orgasm and she groaned. "Watch it. That almost hurt."

He rotated his hand and found her clit with his thumb. "Is this what you want? Or this?" He shuttled his fingers in and out.

She caught his wrist and pushed his fingers deep. "Now *gently* touch my clit and make me come."

His touch obeyed, but his words were another story. "You might think you want it gentle, but we both know you don't. You want me on top of you, pounding into you, while you fight against the cuffs." He spread his fingers, stretching her as his thumb carefully circled her clit. "Or better yet, let me hold you down so you feel my fingers biting into your flesh as my cock thrusts deep again and again."

An orgasm burst with shocking intensity, dragging a startled cry from her throat. Her inner walls caressed his fingers while his thumb prolonged the spasms with undeniable skill.

"Straddle my face so I can lick you."

She'd been just about to do just that, but his command made her change her mind. She unzipped the bustier and tossed it aside then climbed on top of him. Rubbing her breasts against his chest and her mound against his shaft, she ignored his frustrated thrashing and concentrated on pleasing herself.

Unfortunately, he was right. She enjoyed sex much more when she was being taken, overpowered and overwhelmed by a masterful lover. His body slid against hers, arching with obvious frustration. It was fun to deny him, but she was also denying herself what she really needed.

"Your scent is making me crazy." He panted. "I want you to ride my tongue."

"This isn't about what you want." She bunched the skirt up around her waist so she could straddle his hips. Then she reached between them and found his cock. "It's about what I want." She used his cock like a toy, rubbing it up and down her crease and around her clit, anywhere but into her core.

"Put me in. Gods! Put me in." He forced the plea out between clenched teeth.

Again she'd been about to do so. Why wouldn't he shut his damn mouth and enjoy the ride? "Each time you make demands, you postpone the pleasure." She slid back onto his thighs and waited until he looked into her eyes. "You do not have permission to come."

His exasperated growl made her grin, then she bent and sucked him into her mouth. He felt enormous as he slid between her lips, incredibly hard, yet also soft. She caressed his base with her hand as she worked his tip with her lips and tongue. Each of his shudders and groans made her bolder, more determined to hear him beg.

"I can't... Stop or I'll..." She pulled back just in time to watch his seed burst from his tip and splattered across his flat belly.

"Now look what a mess you've made." Careful to avoid the splatters, she crawled upward and positioned herself directly above his mouth. "You didn't have permission to do that, so this is your punishment. You will lick me until *I've* had enough, regardless of how long it takes or how many times I come. You'll keep right on licking."

"Yes, mistress," he muttered as she lowered her sex toward his mouth.

JILLIAN HAD NEVER SEEN her mother at a loss for words. Estelle Taylor was known for her strong opinions and her willingness to defend them, yet she'd barely spoken since Lor teleported her to the Bunker.

The men had made themselves scarce after facilitating the transportation. Jillian, Tori and Estelle sat around a small table in someone's office. The office likely belonged to Elias. Jillian just didn't know for sure.

"Do you want something to drink?" Tori asked.

Why did people always try to feed someone who was upset? It seemed like a good way to make them throw up. "What made you suspect he was an alien? And why didn't you ever mention it to me?"

"Would you have believed me?" A bit of the color crept back into Estelle's cheeks. "I trusted three people with what I'd seen and all three of them treated me like I'd gone crazy."

"What did you see?"

Estelle looked at her and sighed. "Do you really want to hear all the gory details of your mother's fall from grace?"

Jillian hesitated. No one wanted to think about their parent having sex, but she might have seen something crucial and not know its true importance. "Be as vague as you can, but tell me what you saw."

"The party was in a frat house and it was really crowded. My best friend, Pam, and I went into one of the bedrooms. We'd just met Jerry and Bill, so we didn't expect things to go as far as they went."

Jillian's chest tightened and she had to ask, "They didn't force you, did they?"

"No. It wasn't like that."

"You were with Jerry and Pam was with Bill?" Tori asked.

Estelle nodded. "Pam had been with a man before, but I'd just turned eighteen. I wasn't used to sexually aggressive men. The boys I'd dated were perfect gentlemen."

"Which is why you were still a virgin," Tori said with a gentle smile.

"Innocence wasn't something to be ashamed of back then," Estelle pointed out. "Anyway, I wanted to leave, but I didn't feel right walking out on Pam. It was obvious she was willing, but things can turn ugly fast."

"Go on," Tori prompted, but Jillian wasn't sure she wanted to hear more. Her mom wasn't doing a very good job of remaining vague.

"Pam and Bill were on the bed and me and Jerry were on a small couch. Jerry noticed I was more interested in what was happening to Pam than what we were doing, so he held me in front of him and told me to watch. He said I'd stop resisting if I saw there was no reason to be afraid."

There had to be a point to all this. Her mother wasn't one to enjoy airing her dirty laundry.

"As Bill grew more amorous, his eyes began to spin." Estelle paused looking at the other two as if to see if they believed what she was saying. "The first time I saw it, I thought I'd had too much to drink. But he looked right at me more than once and it was... It wasn't natural."

"He was Ontarian," Tori told her. "Most of the people on Ontariese have eyes that gently rotate."

"I was terrified, but Jerry wouldn't let go of me until Bill finished with Pam. I asked her if she saw what happened with his eyes and she said what I'd thought."

"That you were drunk?" It must have been so isolating to have no one believe her.

Her mother just nodded.

"If you didn't have sex with Jerry that night," Tori prompted, "when did it happen?"

"I don't think anyone had ever refused him before. He showed up in all sorts of unexpected places, determined to seduce me. The more I resisted him, the more attentive he became. His overt seduction became a tender courtship until I finally gave in." She licked her lips and stared down at her folded hands, obviously upset by what came next. "I thought I'd reformed a playboy. He told me he loved me and I believed him. But I looked into his eyes while he, you know, and I saw rings of blue glowing like...not like anything I'd ever seen before or since. I even asked him what happened and he pretended not to know what I meant. He said he'd pick me up the following morning, but I never saw him again."

Which was why she'd always been so over-cautious of men, so convinced they only wanted sex from any woman. Jillian had always understood the cause of her mother's bitterness. Knowing the details just made it even sadder.

"Did Pam become pregnant too?"

Good thing Tori was here to keep the conversation on track. Jillian wanted to pull her mother into her arms and have a mutual cry.

"No. We were roommates until I left collage. She wouldn't have been able to hide it from me."

"Jerry's real name is Gerrod Reynolds and he's from a planet called Rodymia. Odintar, Jillian's lover, is from the same planet. His eyes have the blue rings you described."

"Well, sometimes the rings are red," Jillian corrected.

"Really?" Tori turned from Estelle and looked at Jillian.

"Emotions determine which color appears."

"I did not know that." Tori sounded almost amused.

"I knew I wasn't crazy. I just didn't know how right I was."

Unable to bear the uncertainty in her mother's tone, Jillian knelt beside her and gave her a firm hug.

A light tapping drew her attention to the doorway. Elias stood there, a hesitant smile on his handsome face. "The Bilarrian envoy is here. Is she ready to go?"

"Go?" Estelle echoed. "Where are we going?"

Now came the tricky part, the painful part. "Do you remember Aria? She played Juliette in *Star-Crossed*."

"You were her understudy."

Jillian's throat was so tight she could only nod.

"What about her?"

"The envoy is here to take you to Bilarri," Tori took up the explanation, obviously sensing Jillian's distress. "Aria will be there when you arrive and she'll explain everything that has happened and why it's no longer safe for you to be on Earth."

"I'm going to another planet?" For just a moment excitement shimmered in her clear blue eyes. Then she looked at her daughter and the light faded to dread. "You're not coming with me?"

"I can't. Not yet."

"This is just a temporary separation," Tori stressed. "You will be together again very soon."

"I don't understand. If it's safe enough for Jillian to be here, then I'm willing to risk—"

"I'll be safer if I'm not worried about you." Jillian found her voice again as she pushed to her feet. "Aria will answer all your questions and I'll join you as soon as I can. You have some really interesting surprises waiting for you on Bilarri. I want you to revel in each one."

Estelle stood as well. "What sort of surprises?"

Curiosity worked every time. No one enjoyed a good surprise as much as her mother. "It wouldn't be a surprise if I told you, now would it?"

Tori rounded the table and took Estelle by the hand. "It will be easier for both of you if you say your goodbyes now."

Jillian gave her mom another lingering hug then kissed her on the cheek. "I'll see you soon."

"Not soon enough." Estelle returned the kiss then composed her expression as she turned to Tori and said, "Lead the way."

"YOU HAVE A SPECIAL request, Roxie," Jett called from the front of the store. "Can you talk or do you need her to come back?"

Roxie heard an angry voice respond to the suggestion though she couldn't make out the exact words. Lenna, one of Roxie's regulars had been squirming and cringing for the past few minutes. She could probably use a break. "Do you mind if I go see what this is about?"

"Please." Lenna laughed. "I think I've had about all I can take anyway."

"Another two-hour session should finish this up. When would you like to come back?"

"I'll have to call you. My schedule is crazy right now." She motioned Roxie toward the front of the store. "Go see about the 'special request.'"

"Thanks, Lenna. I'll have Jett bandage you up."

"Cool."

Roxie pulled off her latex gloves and tossed them in the trash as she left her station. She pushed the privacy curtain aside and froze. Sevrin stood on the other side of the display case, looking anything but amused. Roxie hurried forward. "Can you bandage Lenna for me? I've got this."

"You sure?" Jett was obviously reluctant to leave her.

"Hurry along, little boy. This conversation isn't for the likes of you."

Jett started to object, likely in very profane terms, so Roxie squeezed his arm and said, "Go."

"Touch her and I call the cops."

The warning made Sevrin laugh. "She'd still be dead long before they got here if that's the best you can do."

"She's not going to hurt me." *God please let that be true.* "Now stop antagonizing her."

Jett snarled, but obeyed.

"Oh, he's an adorable little pet. Not very well trained, but adorable."

Determined to prove that she wasn't as frightened as she was, Roxie moved around the display case and faced her tormentor. "What do you want?"

"You know damn well what I want. What have you learned?"

Roxie motioned toward the couch, but Sevrin ignored her. "Nazerel doesn't trust you. Didn't sound like he likes you very much either."

Sevrin rolled her eyes. "Damn you're observant. I never could have figured that out by myself."

Emboldened by her sarcasm, Roxie took a deep breath and looked into her eyes. "Flynn said this *planet* was making everyone paranoid and Nazerel complained that he was at the mercy of *humans,* not Americans or foreigners, humans. Don't suppose you want to explain that to me."

Sevrin tilted her head to a mocking angle, a favorite of hers. "Sounds like you have a theory already. Why don't you explain it to me?"

"I think you're from much farther away than Eastern Europe." Roxie searched Sevrin's gaze, hoping to spot the contact lenses she knew the other woman was wearing.

"You're a silly little girl." She averted her gaze as she asked, "What else did they say?"

"A bunch of crude nonsense about what they'd like to do to me and you. Honestly, it was about as helpful as stashing a tape recorder in a locker room. Fart jokes and bedroom bragging is all you'll ever hear."

Sevrin's gaze snapped back to Roxie and a cold, calculative smile parted her lips. "You're one lucky little *human.* Their locker room humor helped you dodge a bullet."

Sevrin walked out and Roxie stumbled to the couch, barely making it before her legs collapsed. "Thank God. Oh thank you God."

"Do you think she's gone for good?" Jett stepped out from behind the privacy curtain. His face was so pale Roxie didn't have to ask if he'd heard the entire conversation.

"Several of the men told me they were moving. I don't think we'll see her again."

"But you do think they're... What exactly do you think?" He sat down beside her, looking as shell-shocked as she felt.

"It doesn't matter anymore. They're gone and I'm still alive." She reached over and hugged him. He returned the hug so hard it hurt.

"Is everything okay?" Lenna asked from the doorway leading to the back.

A pang of guilt cleared away the rest of Roxie's fear. She'd completely forgotten about her loyal customer. "Everything's fine. In fact..." She stood. "Everything is wonderful!"

Chapter Ten

Jillian hugged the ratty accent pillow to her chest as if it were a priceless treasure. She didn't care if it was threadbare and out of style. It was hers! She was surrounded by her things, her smells, her memories. Home. She was finally home, even if it was only for a night or two.

"So do you feel different now that you know you're royalty?" Odintar softened the question with a lazy smile, but it brought tears to Jillian's eyes.

"I've never felt less like royalty in my entire life."

He took the pillow from her and tossed it to the sofa where she'd found it. "Come here." He pulled her into his arms and pressed her against his chest. "I'd say no more surprises, but that didn't work out so well last time."

She smiled against his throat, comforted by his warmth and nearness. "I sent my mother to a planet I've never seen and entrusted her to a man I'd only met once. I'm a horrible person."

"You acted swiftly and decisively to ensure her safety and comfort." He eased her away until she looked at him. "You are a loving daughter. Any parent would be proud to call you theirs."

He'd meant the words as encouragement, no doubt, but she couldn't help thinking about him. At least she'd had a mother's love as she was growing up. Odintar had never really known either of his parents.

"I know what you're thinking," he cautioned.

She quickly checked their link and found her side still compressed. So how had he known?

He chuckled. "Your eyes tell me everything I need to know, sweetheart. You were feeling sorry for me and now you're wondering how I figured it out."

"Is everyone that transparent to you or is it just me?" She wiggled out of his embrace and headed for the kitchen.

"Life has taught me to be observant, but I am unusually aware of your moods." He followed her into the kitchen and watched as she rummaged through the drawers. "What are you looking for?"

"A corkscrew. I really need a glass of wine. I don't even care if it's red or white." He joined the search and quickly produced the elusive utensil. "Thank you." She took it from his hand and opened the cupboard that served as her wine cellar. "Here we go." Always willing to compromise, she selected a light, refreshing rosé. She snatched two glasses off the bottom shelf. Odintar closed the cupboard door as she set the glasses on the counter.

"Allow me."

Handing him the bottle, she was curious to see if he'd use the corkscrew or pop it open with his mind. She was almost disappointed when he deftly used the corkscrew. "You've done this before."

"A time or two." She handed him the glasses and he poured a generous amount into each. "You should probably make a sandwich or something. You hardly ate anything at dinner."

"I'm not usually this hard to feed. Trauma has always played havoc with my stomach. I promise I'll have a big breakfast." She paused to savor the wine then took his hand and led him into the adjacent living room. They sat on the sofa and he pulled her feet into his lap, spinning her sideways in the process. "What are you doing?"

"Helping you relax." He took a drink of wine then set the glass aside and slipped off her shoes.

He was going to rub her feet, without having to be asked first? She didn't think it was humanly possible for...but then Odintar wasn't human. And neither was she. How long would it take her to absorb those basic facts? She wasn't resisting the truth anymore. Denial was utterly pointless. Still, her mind kept slipping back into her old way of thinking.

Of course, she'd spent twenty-six years as a human and only a week as a Bilarrian/Rodyte/human hybrid. She just needed time.

After tugging off her socks, he caught one foot between his hands and warmed her skin. "It was warm all day. How can your feet be this cold?"

He sounded amused not repulsed so she chuckled. "You should feel them in the winter."

"I intend to."

She looked at his face, but he was looking at her feet. "There was something about my mother's story that doesn't make sense."

He looked at her, but kept on rubbing. "What'd she say?"

"There was an Ontarian using the name Bill with Gerrod the first night she met him. Her roommate hooked up with him."

"Why did that surprise you?"

"It would have been twenty-seven years ago. Weren't the Dirty Dozen in custody by then?"

He paused and speculation clouded his gaze. "If Pern Keir was calling the shots..." Staring into the distance, he couldn't seem to organize his thoughts. "We presumed it ended when we rounded up the Dirty Dozen. Maybe they just became more careful, more secretive."

"I can't help feeling like we've just scratched the surface of this mess."

His gaze moved back to hers, but the shadows remained. "We originally thought the Shadow Assassins contacted the Rodytes. Now it seems more likely that it was the other way around. I think the Shadow Assassins have been pulled into a much larger Rodyte scheme."

"But what are the Rodytes really after?" She didn't feel qualified to draw conclusions. So much of this was new to her. "They created a hybrid gene pool. So what can be done with that?"

"I think they're after what they've always been after."

"Magic?"

He nodded. "Pern passed his obsession with magic on to his daughter and she's pursued it with a vengeance."

She sighed and let the unanswered questions slip to the back of her mind. "I guess we always want what we can't have." The observation sent a pang of longing through her soul. They'd had sex three times since her emotional overload, twice that night and again the following morning. Each time had been physically satisfying, yet emotionally hollow. He refused to spill his seed where it belonged and she refused to open her mind. Maybe they better talk about this before they went any further. Unsure how to politely introduce the topic, she just dove in. "I don't want you to, you know, pull out at the end."

His hands paused mid-squeeze and he looked into her eyes. "I told you what will happen if I don't."

"I'm willing to risk it."

"There's no risk involved. If I come inside you, our link will expand. Are you ready to accept me into your mind?"

This was bassackwards from how her love life usually worked. Always before, she had been the one wanting more of an emotional connection. "I'm ready for more." He smiled and leaned toward her. She laughed and pressed her fingers to his lips, "But not until you finish my foot rub. That feels *so* good." He returned to his task as she relaxed against the arm of the sofa. "So what did you guys talk about while I was chatting with Tori? Did you learn anything new?"

"I did most of the talking, but Elias said they've figured out that the power spikes they've been tracking are caused by teleportation. Unfortunately, they can't tell if the person is arriving or departing, so it's not as useful as they'd hoped."

"That's too bad. We can use any advantage at this point." He switched to her other foot. "I ran into Morgan in the hallway. She really is gorgeous. She's never been married?"

"I don't know. She's unattached now and seems to prefer it that way. Shall I ask if she'll be our third?"

She slapped his leg. "Pervert."

He just chuckled and kept on rubbing. "I have a present for you. Would you like it now or shall we wait until tomorrow?"

"Seriously? You can't tell me about a present and then expect me to wait for it."

He lowered her feet to the floor then stood and offered his hands. "Anticipation can be exhilarating, but that's a lesson for another night."

"Glad to hear it." She let him pull her to her feet then looped her arms around his neck and whispered, "I think part of the problem is I'm still struggling to believe anyone as amazing as you can be real."

He smiled. "I'm real and I'm glad you think I'm amazing." He brushed his lips over hers, but it was more of a promise than a kiss. "Come on." He headed straight for her bedroom.

"Don't I get my present before we—hold on." She dug in her heels and halted their progress. "Why do you suddenly know your way around my apartment?" There were three identical doors off the main hallway. How had he known which one led to her bedroom?

"I stopped by earlier and dropped off your surprise. Now do you want it or not?"

"Oh I want all sorts of things."

He laughed and pushed open her bedroom door.

She stumbled to a stop just inside the doorway. Spread across her bed was the most beautiful ball gown she'd ever seen. Strapless, with a billowy skirt, the dress was constructed of an extraordinary fabric that looked silver from one angle and smoky gray from another. The bottom half of the skirt had been lavishly embellished with embroidery and beads that shimmered like tiny raindrops.

"It's stunning. Where did you get this?"

Another warm chuckle made her look at him. "I had it delivered."

"From?"

He succumbed to a guilty smile. "I told Aria what I wanted and she did the rest."

Pressing her hand over her pounding heart, Jillian stared at her gift in wide-eyed wonder. "This came from Bilarri?" She was almost afraid to touch it.

"Try it on. We had to guess on your measurements. Let's see how we did."

"I can't wear this. It looks like something off the red carpet in Hollywood, or..."

"It's fit for royalty?" He grinned. "That's the point. You need to accept who you are and the sort of life you'll have once this crisis is over."

The sort of life she'd have? Was he giving her a soft place to fall as he pulled away?

In an instant he was there in front of her, his hands framing her face. "You are my mate. All you have to do is accept the fact and I will never leave your side."

Her lips trembled as she rapidly blinked back tears. "I want to believe that, but—"

"Then believe it. If you doubt it, look into my mind, my heart. I want you there, need you there. You're the one holding back."

"I want to try on the dress." She waited for disappointment to shadow his gaze and then added, "After you make love to me."

For a fraction of a second, she thought he'd agree then he solemnly shook his head. "Put it on. You can't accept the reality of my love until you accept your new reality."

She knew he loved her. His devotion was there in every touch, every smile. Still, she'd never heard him say it before. He watched her expectantly, obviously waiting for her to obey his directive. "If it means that much to you."

"It does."

"Then leave the room. I want to enjoy the big reveal."

"Fine," he muttered. "Call if you need help with the zipper."

She waited until he left then quickly undressed. Her bra would have to go, but the skirt was full, so she could keep her panties. After pausing to admire the fabric, she picked up the dress and stepped into the middle of the billowing skirt. She smoothed the stiff bodice into place and smiled as she discovered the discreet side zipper. The dress fit as if it had been made for her, probably because it had.

Standing well back from the dresser, she could see the entire effect. The bodice was simple, unadorned, designed to showcase the woman who wore it, while the skirt was lavish yet elegant. Was this really a glimpse at the rest of her life? Without wasting time on the question, she smoothed her hair back from her face and left the bedroom.

Odintar turned as the door opened and a slow smile spread across his lips. "It's a beautiful dress and you look wonderful in it."

She smiled, ridiculously pleased by his praise. She'd danced before hundreds of people and all of their applause hadn't warmed her as well as Odintar's smile.

"Come here." He held out his hand.

The skirt dragged a bit as she crossed to him. Apparently the gown had been meant to be worn with heels. He pulled her into his arms, not the passionate bear hug she'd been expecting, but the proper stance for a ballroom dance. The room around her skewed, blurring with the now familiar rush of sensation. A moment of darkness and then she found herself in a massive candlelit ballroom.

Her feet were suddenly adorned in snug, high-heeled sandals and his appearance had morphed as well. He wore a more elaborate version of Indric's uniform. The black and gold suited him perfectly. He had never looked more appealing.

The soft strains of a lilting waltz drifted in on a warm breeze. The candlelight flickered and Odintar began to dance her around the room. He was always light on his feet, but she hadn't expected his obvious skill.

"Why did you learn how to dance?"

He grinned. "I frequently work undercover. It requires a wide range of skills."

"Is this room real or entirely of your own making?" With dramatically vaulted ceilings and a highly polished parquet floor, it was hard to believe he'd imagined every detail. Four massive chandeliers bathed the entire room in warm, golden light that perfectly matched the cream-and-gilt walls.

"This is Indric's palace, or actually one of them. Hautell is the largest region on Bilarri, but San Adrin is the richest."

She stepped back out of his arms. Why was he doing this? "This will never be my home. I'm an American. I live in Las Vegas."

He sighed and held out his hand. "I don't want to argue. That's not why I showed you this."

"Why did you show me this?" She crossed her arms, rubbing her suddenly chilly skin.

"You're a professional dancer, a minor celebrity. I know that part of you craves the excitement, the notoriety."

She didn't deny it. Creating art with movements was its own reward, but she was honest enough to admit she enjoyed the attention.

"On Bilarri you will have that and more." He closed the space between them and resumed the proper hold. The music swelled as he guided her through several gliding steps. She enjoyed the swaying motion of their bodies and the romantic absurdity of it all. He spun her around then bent close and whispered, "I doubt you'll miss the stage once you learn to fly."

She looked down and gasped. They were three feet off the floor, swirling through the air as if they belonged there. "But you're doing this. It's not real."

"You're empowered by Air." They slowly floated down as he took her face between his hands. "Reality will become whatever you choose to make it."

"Twenty years from now," she grumbled.

He smiled. "Sorry, I can't help with that. It will take time and hard work, but Indric sensed immense potential in you."

"I don't want to think about Indric or Bilarri. Tonight was supposed to be a reprieve from all of that."

"You're right." He lifted her hands to his lips and kissed her fingers.

The ballroom blurred and she swayed toward him, not prepared for the sudden rush. "I didn't want you to shut it down." Her living room felt tiny and shabby after the grandeur of the ballroom.

He chuckled. "Do you want to go back?"

"No." She'd enjoyed seeing him all dressed up, but what she really wanted was to see him naked. "I want to go into the bedroom and let go of my past and everything else that's holding me back. Help me embrace the future."

"I thought you'd never ask."

Taking him by the hand, she led him back into the bedroom. "I want it all tonight. I want to join as we were meant to join." He swept her into his arms and kissed her passionately. By the time he released her mouth she was breathless and dizzy. "I need to touch you."

She tugged his T-shirt off over his head and reached for his jeans, but her hands were trembling too badly to function properly.

He kissed the tip of her nose then unzipped his pants, leaving them to sag around his lean hips as he dealt with the rest of his clothing. He kicked off his shoes, peeled back his socks, then quickly shed his jeans. After a quick pause, he held his arms out to the side. "Touch me, *gennari*." There was a hint of challenge in his tone. "If that's what you need. Take as long as you like."

Her skirt swished as she stepped closer and placed one hand on his chest, the other on his hip. She slid her hands up to his shoulder and then down, exploring the shape and texture of his impressive arms. So strong, so dependable, these arms would protect and support her as they faced each new challenge.

"I take that back." Already his voice sounded hoarse and harsh. "Take off the dress and I'll let you touch me."

She should argue that he couldn't "let" her do anything, but the chauvinistic phrase was doing unexpected things to her insides. He came from a culture where men didn't worry about seeming overbearing or crass. He was like a medieval knight or a highlander from the historical romances she devoured like candy. Getting naked was a small price to pay for an all-access pass.

"I'll indulge you," she said with a playful smile. "But you have to keep your promise. You're mine to do with as I will until I'm ready to release you."

He laughed. "I think you embellished on my promise, but I threw in a condition, so I guess fair is fair."

"I need to hear you say it." She reached beneath her arm and grasped the zipper, but didn't lower it. "Promise you'll let me play until I'm ready to stop."

"I promise I will not restrain your movements until you say I can."

That wasn't exactly what she'd asked for, but close enough. She slowly lowered the zipper and felt the front of the dress sag. His gaze followed the descent until her nipples were exposed, then he lost interest in the garment. He licked his lips, obviously anxious to do more than look.

Power sizzled around her and spiraled through her. She knew men found her attractive, but the huger in Odintar's eyes went far beyond male appreciation. He made her feel as if she had been specifically crafted for his enjoyment and still exceeded his expectations.

She undulated her hips as the gown sank lower and lower.

"You're trying to kill me, aren't you?" His hands clenched and released then clenched again.

Emboldened by his obvious discomfort, she stepped out of the dress then slowly bent over so she could pick it up. As usual, she was wearing a thong so he could see her bare behind. After carefully draping the gown over a nearby chair, she hooked her thumbs through the sides of her panties. "Are you sure you want these off? Seems like a cruel temptation."

"Like the rest of you isn't?"

His question filled her with warmth and hurried her toward the next phase of their game. "It's your call. On or off?"

"Off."

She watched his eyes as she pulled the panties down then kicked them aside. Blue rings burned through the black and she heard him inhale deeply. Was he scenting her? The possibility sent an elemental thrill through her entire body. It was so animalistic, so primal. So very Odintar.

"Touch me now, or I'll lose control. I don't want to break my promise."

He'd been hard when he took off his pants, but his shaft was so rigid now it curved out away from his body. She ran her hands up his sides, trying to ignore the column of flesh arching toward her. It was impossible. Her core ached and her hand gravitated there of its own volition.

Curving her fingers around his shaft, she let his needful groan wash over her. He wanted this as badly as she did. The realization only fueled her desire, making it difficult to savor the freedom he'd granted her.

With one hand absently stroking his shaft, she continued her exploration. His chest was a work of art, strength and discipline evident in every curve. Forcing herself to relinquish her prize, she opened her fingers and slipped around behind him. Maybe if she couldn't see his cock straining toward her, she'd be able to enjoy the rest of him.

His back tapered dramatically from broad shoulders to narrow hips. She traced the angle with her hands and then her lips. His skin was warm and faintly salty and she found herself inhaling his scent, needing to imprint his unique smell on her brain. Just like he'd done with her.

The dragon burned into his flesh was even more impressive up close. Detailed and intricate, it seemed almost alive. She traced the angle of one wing and then kissed a path down the middle of the creature's back. Odintar grew restless beneath her touch, so she shifted to his spine and repeated the teasing process.

Unable to resist temptation any longer, she moved back in front of him and knelt.

"Don't." The one word was part warning, part plea.

She pressed her teeth into her lower lip, tempted to take pity on him. Then feminine power surged, eroding the possibility. She wanted to feel him tremble, to watch him fight for control and know she had been the one to drive him to the brink—and beyond.

His cock jerked against her palm as she wrapped him in her fingers. "You promised to let me play." She let her wicked chuckle say the rest. There would be no pity for him tonight.

Leaning in with slow and obvious intention, she circled his tip with her tongue. His hands shot into her hair and formed loose fists, but he didn't stop her, didn't hinder her in any way. Thrilled by his continued cooperation, she closed her lips around him and let his taste spread through her mouth. Earthy, yet somehow fresh, his skin tasted of power and magic.

"I'll show you the same mercy you're showing me." His voice was barely a whisper, but she heard the warning loud and clear.

She moved her mouth up and down his length, savoring the slick slide and contrasting textures. Soon he rocked into each rotation, pushing deeper than she'd allowed him to go.

Heat and incandescent urgency streamed into her mind. His body told her how much he enjoyed this, but actually feeling his desire pushed the intensity even higher. She opened for him, showing him how much she enjoyed pleasing him and how exciting she found his passion.

He cried out suddenly and tried to pull out of her mouth.

None of that. She grasped his hips and held on tight. *You're mine tonight.*

Pushing to the back of her mouth, he shuddered and shuddered as release tore through him. His seed slid down her throat as his pleasure saturated her mind. She swirled her tongue and sucked greedily until he released her hair and stumbled back, dragging his cock from between her lips in the process.

"Are you. Finished. Playing with me?" he asked in between pants.

"For now."

Odintar's orgasm did little to ease the need raging through his body and mind. He couldn't remember the last time he'd trusted a female enough to let her command his release. But Jillian wasn't just a woman. She was his mate, the other half of his soul. He'd always thought the concept of soul mates was romantic nonsense, until he experienced it for himself. She was his match, his equal, his opposite. And he treasured every contrast and contradiction. Apart they were incomplete. Together they were unstoppable.

He scooped her up in his arms and placed her on the bed. Catching the back of her knees he pulled her toward him so suddenly it toppled her backward. She gasped then grinned as he parted her thighs. She resisted for half a second, then spread her legs wide and scooted even closer to the edge of the mattress.

Her skin was already flushed, her nipples tightly beaded. She'd honestly enjoyed giving him pleasure. He wasn't sure why it surprised him. He loved watching her come apart as he filled her with his fingers or caressed her with his mouth. He'd only gone down on her once before and she had been so anxious for his cock that he'd let her rush him. Well, there would be no rushing tonight. He intended to explore every inch of her trembling body and bring her to climax again and again before he surrendered to the final joining.

He brushed her folds with his fingertips, thrilled to feel how wet she was already. Gently parting her with his thumbs, he dragged his tongue tip from her core to her clit. She arched into the caress, tensing as he flicked the sensitive nub. Gods, she was responsive. And her taste was addictive.

Repeating the leisurely circle, he caressed her from core to clit and back over and over. She pushed up with her heels, trying to guide his tongue back to her clit.

"Please." Rather than give her what he knew she wanted, he slowly pushed his middle finger into her core. She whimpered. "That's just mean."

"Is it?" He carefully worked her with his finger while his mouth settled over her clit. He licked and sucked on the tender bud until her inner muscles rippled around his finger.

Her pleasure poured into his mind, unhindered and unashamed. He added another finger and went right on licking. Her second orgasm took longer to build, but he didn't mind. Her softness captivated him. Each of her gasps and wiggles sang his praises and communicated her thanks.

Possessiveness twisted through him as desire erupted again. He draped her legs over his shoulders and moved both hands to her hips. He pushed his tongue into her core, savoring her taste. She twisted and arched. Her body was open and, more importantly, her mind was open, utterly yielded to him.

Humbled by her trust, he tried to slow down, to be less aggressive. There was no hope for gentleness while her scent filled his nose and her taste filled his mouth. He dragged his mouth away from her sex and kissed his way up her body.

Her legs slid off his shoulders, catching on the bend of his elbows. He hovered over her perfect breasts, adoring the nipples with his lips and tongue. Everything about her pleased and excited him. He wanted to spend the rest of his life learning what made her gasp and giggle. What made her sigh.

Reluctantly releasing her nipple, he cupped both her breasts with his hands as he kissed his way up her neck. His taste still lingered in her mouth when he pushed his tongue between her parted lips. The combination of his taste and hers was nearly his undoing. He deepened the kiss, sliding his tongue over hers, mixing their tastes so completely he could no longer identify the separate components.

She drew her legs up along his sides, opening herself for his penetration. Rather than resorting to words, she pushed her hunger into his mind, intensifying his need in an instant. He angled his hips and found her entrance without moving his hands from her breasts.

You are mine as I am yours. The words tore from his soul as he drove into her clenching passage. Her snug walls caressed him like a rhythmic fist, yet her wetness allowed him to sink even deeper.

I am yours as you are mine. He wasn't sure how she'd known the ancient reply, but the thought thrilled him to the marrow of his bones.

Their link swelled, expanding as emotions flowed freely from one being into the other. Unable to pace himself in the face of the emotional deluge, he drew his hips back then slammed his full length back in. She came around him, her inner muscles squeezing so tight he moaned. So damn good!

He drew breath from her lips and shared his energy without reservation. Their bodies rocked against each other, over and into one another, perfectly synchronized. It felt as if they'd been born for this moment, this joining.

She wrapped her arms around his neck and returned his kiss with equal fervor, utterly lost in the sharing. Release raced up the back of his legs and drew up his balls. He stubbornly fought it back, not yet ready for it to end.

It won't end, my love. We have forever. If that's what we want.

Her thought shocked and thrilled him. Was she ready for forever? Just the possibility pushed him over the edge. He clasped her to him, shaking as he came deep inside her. Their link expanded again. The emotions carried across the connection focused with crystal-clear sharpness.

She wanted the same things he wanted, a permanent relationship, the ultimate intimacy of a soul-bonded mate. Her hesitation didn't come from indecision; it came from the fear that no one could love her the way she loved him. And she did love him, completely and without reservation.

He framed her face with his hands, still buried deep inside her body. "Search my mind, *gennari*. My devotion is true. I love you more with every beat of my heart. I will always love you."

Tears filled her eyes but happiness rippled across their link. "I can feel it now."

"If you ever doubt it again, do the same. My heart and my mind will remain open to you. Always."

"It still feels strange to have you there, but I'm not afraid."

"To have me here?" He contracted his abdomen and made his cock buck inside her. "Or here?" He pushed a wave of sweet contentment into her mind.

She smiled up at him as she whispered, "I'm rather fond of both."

"Glad to hear it, because I'm not going anywhere for a long, long time." He pulled back his hips and showed her what he meant.

LOOSE ENDS. SEVRIN worked hard not to create them, but once formed they had to be addressed. This particular loose end had been evading retribution for longer than she could remember. With the new lab fully functional, she could no longer tolerate the possibility of exposure. She was too close to her goals to watch it fall apart now. Which meant Gerrod Reynolds must die.

"Get dressed." She tossed Flynn his jeans, startling him awake as the garment smacked against his bare shoulder.

It had taken all night and part of the morning for her to break Flynn, but he'd been infinitely cooperative during their last encounter. She hadn't removed his collar, so there was a slim possibility he was toying with her. It was more likely, however, that he'd seen the advantages to playing the game by her rules and reluctantly swallowed his pride.

"Are you sure?" A cocky smile lifted one corner of his mouth. "I thought you wanted me naked and accessible whenever we're alone."

"We're not going to be alone for long, so get dressed."

After he'd surrendered the first time, she'd taken him out of restraints. When he physically dominated her without harming her the second time, she'd moved him to a standard employee apartment. Their third time had been wild and aggressive on both sides. They'd both been so sated when they finally finished, that they'd fallen into an exhausted sleep.

She'd awakened before him a short time ago and slipped from his room. After a quick shower and a large cup of coffee, she'd dressed and begun to plan the day. Rather than her usual chic leather outfit, she wore jeans and a black T-shirt. Once she made up her mind about something, she never hesitated.

"Where are we going?" Flynn asked after using the utility room.

"To clean up one of my father's messes."

Flynn paused with a clean shirt in hand, obviously confused by her statement. "You better not mean Roxie. You'll have a mutiny on your hands."

Sevrin threw her hands in the air and shook her head. "What is it about Roxie that turned trained killers into mother hens? I think I could strip her naked and lock her in a room with ten of you and no one would lay a finger on her."

"I wouldn't go that far." Flynn pulled on his shirt and tucked it into his jeans before zipping them up. "More like nine would end up dead and lucky number ten would claim her."

"Well, lucky for me this particular mess is middle-aged and male."

He sat on the edge of his bed and pulled on is boots. "Capture or kill?"

"Kill. Fast and clean, but there are complications."

His scoff sounded almost strangled as if he'd tried to suppress the sound. "Aren't there always."

"His range is extremely limited, but he can teleport."

"So give him one of these." Flynn tugged on his collar with obvious distaste.

"I was going to give him yours unless you've grown attached to it."

He stilled, gaze boring into hers. "A few orgasms and we're friends again? Am I supposed to believe that?"

She sauntered toward the bed, knowing the snug denim accented the sway of her hips. "I need a partner not a pet. Which would you rather be?"

"Partners have to trust each other. Pets only have to obey."

And he had obeyed every command she'd given him as if he were born to the role. "So let's start with obedience and work our way around to trust."

He parted his legs and pulled her between them. "I'm listening."

She ran her hands up his chest and along the collar. "I need your word that you won't desert me if I take this off."

His brows drew together and his eye narrowed to glistening slits. "I thought you'd want my promise not to hurt you."

"You don't need access to your powers to hurt me. You're much stronger than I am. If you'd wanted to hurt me, you would have last night."

He clasped his hand around her throat and squeezed just hard enough for her to feel the pressure of his long fingers. "I'm so glad you realize that fact."

"I need an assassin. Are you available and are you willing?"

His fingers released, trailing down over her chest as he lowered his arm. "How do you intend to pay me?"

Excitement tingled through her, but she didn't let it distract from the task at hand. "What's your price?"

"Your submission for one night."

She paused as if she were considering it, but already her insides were melting, softening, anticipating the things he would do to her. "*After* you've successfully ended Gerrod Reynolds' life, I will submit my body to you for one night."

He stood, forcing her to step back. "What are the logistics? Where is he?"

"He lives alone in a small suburban house. I'll drive you to the neighborhood and you can flash inside. It shouldn't take long. Slap him in the collar so he can't get away, then do what it is you do."

"Can I operate the collar? I thought it was DNA sensitive."

"Anyone can push it closed. It takes a DNA scan to open it." As if to prove her point, she reached up and scanned open the collar, disentangling the flexible band from around his neck.

She watched him for a moment, half afraid he'd leave.

"It will work much better if you go with me. You collar him while I do my thing."

"If I have to participate, you only get two hours."

"At the end of two hours, we'll renegotiate." When she didn't object, he asked, "Not that it matters, but why have you waited so long to take out the trash?"

"He served my father faithfully, so Father assured him that he'd be safe on Earth. It took me a long time to justify why I'd go back on my father's word, but there is no help for it. Gerrod knows too much. He needs to die."

"Then take me to his house. I'm anxious to enjoy my payment."

Chapter Eleven

"Are you sure you want to go through with this? Lor is convinced the Shadow Assassins are on their way out of Las Vegas."

Talking with a disembodied voice shouldn't have seemed odd. People talked on speaker phones all the time. Even so, it still felt strange to hold a conversation with someone Jillian couldn't see. She glanced in the rearview mirror, but the backseat appeared empty.

"If they're really on the move, then this opportunity is more important than before." She pulled her car into a parking space near the front door of Unique Ink and turned off the engine. "What do we have to lose? My new tutor doesn't arrive until tomorrow. I've got time to kill."

She opened the door and stretched, giving Odintar a moment to float out of the car. He could push his energy through the door if he needed to, but this was less exhausting.

With her purse slung over her shoulder and her sunglasses holding back the front of her hair, she walked into the shop.

"Hey there, beautiful," Jett greeted. "I thought you weren't coming in until tomorrow."

"I'm not official until tomorrow, but I was in the area. Figured I'd stop by and see how things were going."

Roxie snatched the privacy curtain open and rounded the display case, welcome shining in her pale blue eyes. "I thought I recognized that voice."

Before Jillian could do more than return her smile, Nazerel stepped into the opening. "Well, isn't this awkward?"

Her mouth dried up as her heart thundered in her chest. What was he doing here?

You shouldn't know who he is. Odintar cautioned, his signal reed thin and heavily shielded.

"Excuse me?" She recovered enough to reestablish her role. "Do I know you?"

"Oh I think you do." He brushed past Roxie and stalked toward Jillian, menace emanating off him in waves.

In a flash Odintar, Lor and Blayne surrounded Nazerel and the two humans crumpled to the floor. Jillian summoned Air, creating a swirling vortex around Nazerel. His eyes widened as he struggled against the confinement. Then he looked at her and smiled. "Very good." His dark gaze shifted to Lor and his smile evaporated. "Someday you'll have to tell me how you turn latent females into Mystics overnight."

Lor's arms were extended and fire swirled around his fingers. He ignored Nazerel's jibe and motioned Blayne forward. "Grab him. Let's go."

Nazerel drove Blayne back with a wave of his hand, but his gaze remained on Lor. "I am *not* looking for a fight. I came to warn Roxie."

Odintar crept forward. Nazerel pushed him back as well, though it took considerably more effort. "This is neither the time nor the place for a battle." Nazerel forced the words out between clenched teeth as Blayne and Odintar combined their energy. "She must be warned!"

Jillian poured energy into the vortex, but the struggling men barely noticed. Forget the invisible tug-of-war; they needed to get Nazerel out of here before Jett or Roxie woke up.

"Warn her about what?" Lor asked without relaxing his stance, then to his men he added, *Let him speak.*

Maintaining his hold on Nazerel, Odintar neither forced his way forward nor allowed himself to be driven back.

Nazerel panted, sweat now beading his brow. "Gerrod wouldn't tell me why, but Roxi is important to Sevrin. That bitch has a use for Roxi and I don't think it's good. She needs to disappear and disappear now!" As if following his own advice, he flashed out of sight, Lor and Blayne half an instant behind him.

"Damn that man is strong." Odintar rested his hands on his knees, panting harshly.

"What the hell just happened?" Jillian rushed over to where Roxie lay. She didn't seem to be harmed, just unconscious. "Can you wake them up?"

Odintar stumbled to the couch and collapsed. "It's better if the compulsion wears off naturally. They're still going to feel like shit. There wasn't time to be gentle."

So Odintar had been responsible for their sudden collapse. She'd known it was one of the Mystics. She just hadn't known which one. She checked Jett as well, straightening one of his legs so he lay more comfortably. "How long will it take to wear off?"

"Not long." Gradually his breathing returned to normal, but his face remained flushed, his hairline damp. "He resisted us, but why didn't he attack? He could have done some serious damage. Why'd he just stand there?"

"Trouble in paradise?" She crossed to the couch and sat beside him. "If Sevrin's hold over the men is slipping, it could be a very good thing for us."

He looked at her and smiled. "I like the way you said us."

She nudged his shoulder. "I might not have your mad skills, but I'm a member of the team."

"I consider you one. I'd just never heard you place yourself among us."

The door flew open and Elias rushed in, followed by two of his men. "There are definite advantages to the way you guys get around." He waited until his team confirmed that the scene was secure before leaving his position by the door. "Do they need a medical team?" He nodded toward the two lying on the floor.

"They'll be fine," Odintar assured. "But we better figure out what to tell them. They're going to be more than curious."

"Gas leak?" Elias offered with a sardonic smile. Then his gaze returned to Roxie and lingered. "Damn," he muttered under his breath as he went and knelt by her side. He pressed his fingers to the pulse point at the side of her throat then slid his knuckles along her jaw.

Jillian couldn't help but smile. Checking her pulse was probably procedure, but that caress had been interested male.

"Is this Roxie?" He glanced over his shoulder then carefully lifted her in his arms.

"Yeah." Odintar rubbed his temples, eyes tightly closed.

He was obviously distracted by his massive loss of energy. Still, Jillian was fascinated by this softer side of Elias.

Elias crossed to the large easy chair and arranged Roxie as comfortably as he could. "Her pictures don't do her justice and that's saying a lot."

Jett stirred, groaning loudly before his eyes flew open. "What the..." He sat up then pressed his hands to each side of his head. "Why do I feel like I just came off a three-day binge?"

Not trusting the men to invent a story that would satisfy the curious artist, Jillian hurried across the room and helped Jett to his feet. "Nazerel was right. I not only know him, he's the real reason I applied for the job."

"They're criminals. I knew it." Jett's usual enthusiasm was muted by his pain, but he hung on her every word. "What sort of technology are they into?"

She wasn't sure what he meant, but it set up her story perfectly. "Can't you guess? You just experienced the effects of one of their toys."

"They're arms dealers?"

"They're many things. Inventing new weapons is just one of their businesses."

Apparently Elias didn't want her tall tale to grow any taller. He moved up beside her and stuck out his hand. "Special Agent Elias Bertram." Jett shook his hand. "We're sorry about all this, but the less you know the safer you'll be. Suffice it to say that Nazerel and his companions are extremely dangerous. We believe they're headed out of Las Vegas, but we want you to lock up the shop and head out the back if you ever see them again." He handed Jett a very official-looking business card. "And then contact me immediately."

Jett nodded and put the business card in his wallet.

Jillian tapped Elias on the shoulder and pointed to Roxie, who was just beginning to stir.

Elias moved to the chair and waited until she opened her eyes. "Hello. How are you feeling?"

"Like someone kicked me in the head." She pushed her hair back from her face, her light blue eyes finally focusing on Elias. "Who are you?"

"Special Agent Elias Bertram." He held out his hand, but she ignored it in favor of rubbing her temples.

"Holy mother of God, my head hurts."

Odintar stood and moved behind her. "If you'll allow me to touch you, I can ease the pressure."

He could barely stand. Did he have enough energy to heal her?

I can do this in my sleep, gennari. *But your concern is sweet.*

Roxi sat quietly as Odintar pressed his fingertips against her temples. Elias, on the other hand, looked ready to dive over the chair and tackle Odintar to the ground.

"Wow." Roxie blinked several times and then opened her eyes. "What did you just do? The pain is just—gone."

"Pressure points," Odintar told her. "Western doctors scoff at the concept, but they really do work."

Roxie didn't argue, but she wasn't totally convinced. She stood, swaying a bit as she walked over to Jett. "Go cancel the rest of the appointments for today. I don't think either of us is fit to work."

"You got it."

He disappeared into the back and she turned on Odintar, gaze flashing. "What the hell are you?"

"*What* am I?" He laughed, genuinely caught off guard by her hostility. "I'm a human. What are you?"

"Humans can't materialize out of thin air or heal with a touch. And it wasn't just you. I saw the others. Don't bother denying it. I know what I saw."

"The weapon Nazerel used on you can cause hallucinations," Odintar told her.

"All right. Let's talk about whatever kicked in my head. Why didn't it work on you?" When he had no ready reply, she shifted her gaze to Elias. "I've had it with this bullshit. Who are you people and what are you doing on my planet!"

Lor flashed into view behind her, wrapped both arms around her, and flashed out before she could do more than gasp.

Jillian looked at Odintar. "Did you tell him to do that?"

"She has to be debriefed and likely kept in protective custody until we figure out what the hell Nazerel was talking about."

Elias nodded, obviously in complete agreement. "Tell Jett she left with me." He motioned his men from the room, leaving Jillian and Odintar alone in the reception area.

"That was not cool. She was terrified and now—"

"It couldn't be helped." Odintar placed his hands on her shoulders and kissed the tip of her nose. "I don't think Jett saw anything, but Roxie obviously did. The situation had to be contained before she made things worse."

Jett returned a few minutes later, his concerned gaze sweeping the room. "Where'd everyone go? Where's Roxie?"

"Her headache got worse," Jillian told him. "They have a medication that reverses the effects. She'll be released as soon as she's feeling better."

"Where'd they take her? I want to make sure she's okay."

"We'll have her call you as soon as she's able," Odintar told him.

"No way, man. I want to go there."

"I understand, but it's a private facility. No visitors allowed."

"This is bullshit!" He stomped right up to Odintar and glared into his eyes. "You're going to take me there or I'm calling the media."

"Roxi will call you in two hours or less. There is no reason for your hostility."

The pissing contest was getting them nowhere. She touched Jett's arm and waited until her looked at her. "Jett, you know me. I'm not a stranger. I have a history with this town. Roxi is going to be fine."

Gradually a bit of the fight melted from his posture. "Do you know where they took her?"

"I know you're worried about her, but I won't let anyone harm her." She looked right into his eyes, meaning every word. "I'll make sure she calls you and you can hear it from Roxie herself."

"It has to be a video call. Voices are too easy to fake."

She looked at Odintar and he nodded. "A video call in two hours or less. It's a deal."

"I really will call the media." He crossed his arms over his chest and glared at Odintar.

"There will not be a need."

She took Odintar by the hand and hurried him from the shop before the situation could escalate. "And what are we going to do when Roxie tells us to go screw ourselves?"

He finally smiled. "We'll cross that bridge when we come to it."

Jillian triggered the locks on her car then slipped in behind the wheel. Odintar joined her, in the front this time. "Do you know how to drive?"

"I do, but I don't mind. I gave myself a headache too."

After carefully backing out of the parking space, she headed off down the street. She couldn't forget the image of Roxie's terrified face as Lor appeared out of nowhere and grabbed her. At least when Odintar first teleported with Jillian, she'd had some sort of warning.

She was just about to turn onto Tropicana Blvd when something or someone pulled at her mind. "Did you feel that?"

"Only because our link is wide open. He's trying to reach you."

The driver behind her laid on his horn, so she pulled into a small parking lot on the right instead of entering the busy flow of traffic. "He? How could you tell that was a man?"

"Much can be learned from energy patterns. I've been deciphering them for years."

She searched inward, trying to understand what she'd felt. "It's gone. Whatever it was is—" Fear and pain stabbed into her brain and she saw the lighted canopy of Fremont Street. "He's downtown. What should we do? Can you tell who he is or what he wants? All I sense is desperation."

"Lor and Blayne will meet us there. We're to approach with extreme caution."

Yeah, no shit. No one needed to tell her to be careful. The real question was should she approach at all. Was this one of the Shadow Assassins? "Are all of our people accounted for? Who else could send that signal?"

"His energy feels similar to my mother's." Odintar looked at her meaningfully. "I think he's battle born."

To her knowledge there was only one battle born hybrid left on Earth—her father. "Why would he reach out to me?"

"It feels like he has no choice."

Even with the recent restoration efforts, downtown Las Vegas was a pretty scary place. "All right." She turned off the car, put the keys in her pocket and stuffed her purse under her seat. Then she held out her hand and braced for the sickening rush of acceleration. "Let's go."

The quick jump across town felt like nothing now that she knew what to expect. They materialized in an alley and she quickly unbent her knees.

"His signal is weak, but it's still there," Odintar told her. "Can you feel it?"

She closed her eyes and let her emotions surge, a lifetime of resentment combined with the fundamental desire to assist those in need. Air swirled up through her, bringing the sensation closer to the surface. "He's over there."

Checking the street for cross traffic, she hurried toward the area from which she sensed the signal. A three-story parking garage formed one side of the alley while the back side of narrow businesses lined the other. Late-afternoon shadows had given way to twilight, so she hurried. If they lost the light completely, they might never find him.

"Trust your abilities," Odintar urged. "Focus only on the signal. Tune everything else out."

Easier said than done. The pavement was slimy and the scent of rotting garbage and bodily fluids hung heavy in the air. She had to do this or her father could die. Did she care? The one and only contribution to her life had been seducing her mother. Why should she care if his life ended? Shame gave her a stubborn shake. Every life was precious. She had to help him if she could.

She paused, tuning out the rank smells and the distant pulse of muffled music. Air swirled around her, driving away the stench. She inhaled deeply and let the energy wash over her. Asshole or not, she needed to find her father.

"There!" She locked on to the signal and didn't let go.

Gerrod crouched in a corner created by a stairwell inside the parking garage. His legs were drawn up to his chest and one of his feet was bare. The front of his shirt and one side of his pants were soaked in blood, but the cause of the bleeding wasn't obvious.

"You came." He forced a weak smile. "I wasn't sure you would." His head dropped back against the brick wall and the signal blinked out.

With a worried cry, she fell to her knees, amazed by the fear and sorrow surging within her. "Is he dead?"

Odintar quickly scanned him then shook his head. "Unconscious. He's extremely weak."

Suddenly Blayne and Lor stood behind them. Their big bodies blocked most of the light in the narrow alley. "Can we move him? We're too exposed here?"

Odintar examined him more closely, searching for the cause of the blood. An alloy band encircled his neck. Odintar gingerly pushed the band upward and blood gushed from a long nearly surgical incision concealed beneath the band. "Shit! Someone slit his throat."

Someone handed him a wad of cloth. Jillian glanced back and found Lor had taken off his shirt.

Using the shirt as a pressure bandage, Odintar attempted to stop the bleeding. "This is pointless. Let's get him out of here."

Blayne pushed past her and scooped up her father as if he were a child. Odintar kept the shirt pressed tightly against his throat, but blood was already seeping through.

Odintar motioned toward her with his chin. "Will you—

"Go," Lor urged. "I've got her."

She rushed to Lor's side and he wrapped his arm around her waist, teleporting with staggering speed. She had time for one startled gasp and then they arrived inside the Bunker.

Blayne had carried her father into the clinic. Uniformed medics rushed around the bed, fighting the Mystics for much-needed space.

Suddenly Odintar ripped off his T-shirt and spread his arms. Fire ignited deep inside his dragon sigil, making the entire mark glow vivid red. Tension rippled up his back then rolled across his shoulders. Then he shouted, "Get back!"

The medics scrambled out of the way as a thin stream of Fire arced from Odintar's fingertip and cauterized the wound in Gerrod's throat. The stench of burning flesh filled the air, but the wound stopped bleeding. Unfortunately the pillow beside his neck burst into flames. Someone ran for a fire extinguisher. Odintar switched gears with practiced fluidity, showering the pillow with Water before the flames could really get going.

"That's one way to do it," one of the medics muttered with a dry laugh.

"It worked. His blood pressure has stabilized," another pointed out as she waved her hand in front of her face in an effort to dissipate the smell.

"I think we can take it from here," the first medic asserted. He was probably a doctor not just a medic. He seemed personally affronted by Odintar's actions and the intrusion into his domain.

"He needs blood and I'm your best bet for a match. He's a Rodyte/Bilarrian hybrid."

The female medic mouthed the words "A what?" But the doctor didn't seem surprised by the revelation.

"Kim type his blood. Let's hope we get lucky."

Kim, the female medic, gathered the supplies and drew a small sample of Odintar's blood. Jillian hurried to his side as Kim went into the adjoining lab. "How's your back? Does it hurt to activate the sigil?"

He chuckled. "Burns almost as badly as when she put it there."

"Well, thank you. I can't help feeling that this is important. The Shadow Assassins leave town and he ends up nearly dead. That can't be a coincidence."

"I don't believe in coincidences. Someone tried to kill him. We need to know who and why."

"And how he got away," she added with a helpless shudder.

Kim returned with some sort of vacuum-sealed kit clutched in her hand. "Doctor Reyes said you'll have to do." She smiled at Odintar. "That's a direct quote."

"No doubt it is."

"Could you move your chair over here by the bed. Some of these tubes aren't very long." She pulled a wheeled silver tray to the foot of the bed and opened the packages without removing what was inside. "According to Doctor Reyes, your blood isn't a perfect match, but your blood type is tolerated well by people with the other types."

"Like a human with O negative blood?" Jillian crept closer to the bed without getting in Kim's way.

"Exactly." She looked at Jillian and then Gerrod. "You should probably wait in the lounge. This will take at least an hour."

"You're transferring blood from my husband to my father. I'm not going anywhere."

Her claim made Odintar smile and Jillian realized it was the first time she'd referred to him as anything other than lover.

"If Blayne or Lor can give him energy, that will help as much as the blood," Odintar said. "I could use some too. It's been one hell of a day."

"I'll go find one or the other, or both."

Kim tried to conceal her curiosity and failed.

"First time you've worked with Mystics?" Jillian asked, suddenly feeling quite superior.

Kim nodded. "The orientation doesn't even begin to explain what just happened."

Jillian leaned over and gave Odintar a kiss. "I'll be right back."

"You know where to find me."

She was nearly out the door when she heard Kim ask, "Is the image on your back some sort of tattoo?"

Again Jillian smiled. She had learned so much in just a week and her education had just begun. Soon she'd have a Bilarrian mentor and access to something called the Wisdom of the Ages. It sounded like a truly interactive version of the internet.

Blayne and several soldiers were clustered in the corridor outside Elias' office.

Blayne saw her approaching and broke away from the others. "Lor is catching everyone up. Were they able to save him?"

"The bleeding has stopped and Odintar is about to give him more. He asked if someone could feed him energy."

"Odintar needs energy or Gerrod needs energy?"

"Actually both."

"Not a problem. I can at least get things started."

She turned around and headed back toward the clinic, Blayne at her side.

"Wait." She skid to a stop. "Roxie needs to call Jett. If he doesn't hear from her in under two hours he's going to notify the media."

Blayne chuckled. "And tell them what? He doesn't know anything and can prove even less. They'll think he's a nutcase."

She crossed her arms over her chest and glared at him. "I promised him I'd make this happen. Where's Roxie? I'll tell her myself."

"I never argue with that look. Give me a minute. I'll have Elias arrange the call."

"It's supposed to be a video call."

He shook his head with a muffled laugh. "Anything else?" he tossed the question over his shoulder as he headed off down the hall.

"That will be all—for now."

He waved without turning around.

She wasn't even sure what time it was. Hopefully they were still within the two-hour window.

Blayne returned a few minutes later, but all playfulness had evaporated from his demeanor. "Elias was not amused by your assignment. Apparently, Roxie has been giving him hell ever since she arrived."

"Go Roxie," she whispered under her breath, earning a startled look from Blayne.

Kim was back in the lab when they reached the clinic. Odintar sat beside the bed, his head resting back against the wall. A blood-filled tube ran from the bend of his elbow into a small device. The device hummed and a small divided screen displayed several sets of numbers that meant nothing to Jillian. Another tube ran from the opposite side of the device and into Gerrod's arm.

"What's the gizmo do?" She moved to Odintar's side and stroked his hair back from his brow. He was still shirtless, a state of affairs the female medics were enjoying no doubt.

"Not a clue," he muttered sleepily.

"Has Gerrod stirred at all?" Blayne asked as he moved to the far side of the bed where it was less crowded.

Odintar shook his head. "I've sensed several spikes of awareness, but he hasn't made a sound."

Without another word, Blayne pressed his hand against Gerrod's forearm and sent him wave after wave of energy. It didn't take long for Gerrod's color to improve and his breathing seemed less labored. Blayne looked up and smiled at her. "Next."

She stepped away from Odintar long enough for Blayne to feed him. "If he needs more, I can come back later. They both seem pretty peaceful."

She looked at Odintar and found his eyes closed, his body relaxed. "Thank you."

"Anytime." Blayne winked at her then left the clinic.

She moved to the far side of the bed so she could see Gerrod and Odintar. Her father and her mate. She wasn't sure which was more surprising. She studied Gerrod's face, searching for something of herself in his features. This was her father. The man who had captured her mother's heart then stomped it into the dirt. Did knowing he had an in-depth ulterior motive make it better or worse?

Gerrod moaned and his eyelids fluttered.

Odintar jerked awake, coming up out of the chair before he remembered where he was and sat back down. "Where's Kim? I'm feeling pretty woozy?"

"I'll go get her." There was a large window in the door leading to the lab and Kim saw her approaching.

"Is everything all right?"

"Odintar is feeling weak. Can you make sure he's not giving too much?"

Kim moved to the bed and checked the readout on the device. "If blood volumes in Rodyte/Bilarrian hybrids is similar to humans, we better call this good." She powered down the device then quickly gathered what she'd need to disconnect Odintar.

"Shoe." Gerrod said without opening his eyes. His voice was rough and raspy. Had the blade damaged his vocal cords? Or had the damage been done by the fire Odintar used to cauterize the wound? It didn't matter. He was alive.

After clearing his throat, Gerrod tried again. "Where is my shoe?"

He'd nearly bled to death in an ally and he was worried about losing his shoes? Both of his feet were bare now, so she looked at Kim.

"It's in a bag in the closet."

Jillian retrieved the bag and pulled out the shoe. "Safe and sound." She held it up so he could see it.

He made a hand motion, but it made no sense to her. She quickly filled a glass with water and took it to him. He shook his head and motioned toward the shoe that she'd left on the counter near the sink. Curious now, she brought the shoe to him and held it steady as he pulled a foam lining out of the bottom.

"For you." He handed the linerless shoe back to her.

"Is there something in there?" Odintar asked, obviously having watched the entire exchange.

She angled the shoe toward the light, so she could see inside. A small trench had been dug out of the bottom of the shoe and a thumb drive was nestled in the opening. She dug the thumb drive out of its hiding place and looked at Gerrod.

"What's on it?" she asked.

All he said was, "Insurance."

Chapter Twelve

"How do we know this isn't a setup?" Morgan asked from the head of the conference table.

Odintar understood her suspicion. The thought had crossed his mind more than once during the past two days. Gerrod's thumb drive was filled with dates, times, and specific locations, but all of the events had already happened. Gerrod had compiled a detailed log of Sevrin Keire's activities since her arrival on Earth. The log frequently mentioned interaction with "muscle-bound mercs", but it was obvious Gerrod didn't understand the importance of those meetings. The log would help them convict her of numerous crimes, but it couldn't help them catch her.

"You weren't there." Jillian leaned forward so she could see around him. "Whoever slit his throat meant business."

"She's right." Elias sat at Morgan's left and their opinions usually aligned. However, Elias wasn't a mindless yes man. He was always respectful while he formed his own conclusions. "Even Doctor Reyes agrees; it's a miracle Gerrod survived."

Morgan shook her head, still unconvinced. "It was Odintar's fast thinking and a well-known Bilarrian ability that saved Gerrod's life. I'm not saying he was in on it. It's more likely Sevrin used him as a sort of parting shot. Even if he had died, it's probable that we would have found the drive. I can almost guarantee there's a nasty surprise waiting for us at one of those locations."

"So we ignore the info and wait for them to strike in another city?" Frustration tightened Lor's voice, yet his face revealed no emotion. It was a game they all played. Contain. Compartmentalize. Remain composed, while inside everyone was punching through walls and screaming obscenities.

"Of course not. I want a munitions expert to clear each location before anyone else goes in."

"Understood," Elias replied.

"So what's this about a code?" Morgan tapped her thumb against the table top, illustrating her agitation.

"There's a section on the drive that's encoded and the code looks very much like what's used in the last two-thirds of the notebook," Odintar told her. "It's possible Gerrod can decode the rest of the notebook for us."

She scoffed. "If we can trust his results."

Lor shrugged. "The information is useless as it is. In my opinion, it's worth a try."

After nodding in response to Lor's conclusion, Morgan looked at Jillian and asked, "Is Gerrod strong enough for questioning. The information on that drive isn't nearly as valuable as his memories and observations."

"He was sedated yesterday so they could remove the collar. He should be more lucid today."

"Speaking of his collar..." Morgan looked at Lor. "Were you able to determine if it's functional? Have the Rodytes reengineered the suppression collar?"

"Yes and yes. There is no good news today."

The revelation was upsetting enough to bring Blayne out of silent observation mode. "That bitch can suppress our abilities and there's not a damn thing we can do about it?"

Finally looking as frustrated as he sounded, Lor nodded. "I tried all three of the neutralizers. None of them disrupted the collar's effect. If she gets one of those things around our necks, we're powerless."

"Then how did Gerrod send his telepathic SOS?" Morgan wanted to know.

"They're family. Nothing is powerful enough to silence that connection."

Odintar glanced at Jillian to see if Lor's words upset her.

I'm fine. She reinforced the claim with a gentle smile.

He nodded then returned his attention to the subject at hand. "It doesn't make sense." He crossed his arms over his chest and shook his head. "Why wait so long to use such an advantage?"

"There was a massive energy pulse four days ago," Morgan told them. "We weren't sure what it was, but subsequent developments have led me to believe it was the arrival of some sort of ship."

Lor's hands slapped the tabletop as he came up out of his chair. "And you're telling us now? Does alliance mean the same thing to humans as it does to Ontarians?"

"We weren't sure what it was, didn't know if it was important enough to mention."

"Bullshit." Odintar managed to remain seated, but he was every bit as incensed as his commander.

Morgan's brows arched as challenge filled her gaze. "When were you going to tell me about the twelve Bilarrian soldiers in my holding cell?"

Lor rubbed his forehead and sighed. "They weren't scheduled to arrive until tomorrow."

"They flashed in unannounced, setting off alarms all over the base. You're damn lucky they're alive. My guards are authorized to shoot intruders. Some sort of Mystic is with them. Claims to be Jillian's tutor." Morgan looked around the table, her eyes slightly narrowed. "Someone want to explain why Jillian needs a Bilarrian tutor?"

"That one's on me," Elias admitted. "I was on my way to brief you when they arrived with Gerrod."

Morgan eased back in her chair. "It appears communication can improve all the way around." Lor had returned to his seat and she looked at him as she said, "I'm not intentionally keeping things from you. We've all been unusually busy the past few days."

"I apologize for my outburst."

"Don't let it happen again." Authority snapped through her tone and then she smiled. "So what's with the Bilarrians?" They quickly told her about Jillian's ancestry and how it had been discovered. "King Indric was here?" She glared at Elias, but Odintar didn't know her well enough to determine if her ire was real. "You are in so much trouble."

"I figured as much," Elias grumbled.

When neither of them said anything else, Lor brought the conversation back around to the present. "We've prioritized the list of possible cities. Hopefully, Gerrod can help us narrow the list even further."

"I think I can do even better than that." Morgan folded her hands on the tabletop, appearing more relaxed than before. "The energy spikes didn't lead us to the team houses as we'd hoped. It's likely the houses are shielded, so the spikes don't register when they flash into or out of those locations. However, the phenomenon could prove useful now. There have been no spikes at all in Las Vegas the past few days."

"So as soon as the spikes resume, we'll know which city or cities they've targeted." Lor nodded, obviously pleased by the possibility.

"That's the hope anyway." She offered him one last smile. "Is there anything else I need to know?"

"Not at present." Lor returned her smile. "I'll go talk to the Bilarrians."

"I'll come with you, unless you object."

"Not at all." They walked out of the conference room together.

Odintar shook his head as he pushed back his chair and turned to Jillian. "It's always entertaining to watch two alphas attempting to play nicely with each other."

"I think they're doing a wonderful job, considering all of the challenges." She stood and stretched. "I'm going to go check on Gerrod."

"Want some company?"

"Always, but I'm sure you have better things to do than shadow me."

"Actually, I'm in desperate need of a good workout and Blayne has agreed to let me kick his ass."

"I've agreed to let him try," Blayne countered from the other side of the table.

"Go on." She rocked to the balls of her feet and kissed Odintar on the cheek. "I'll catch up with you in the gym."

"Don't I get a kiss?" Blayne pursed his lips and closed his eyes.

"Go find your mate." She waved away his silliness and kept on walking.

Jillian released a sigh as she hurried toward the clinic. She appreciated Odintar's concern, but she wanted a few minutes alone with Gerrod. She couldn't bring herself to call him Dad, even in her mind. He was a sperm donor, nothing more.

No, there was more to it than that. She just hadn't shared her discovery with anyone else.

Gerrod was alone in his curtained-off section of the clinic. He was also sitting up in bed and wide awake. "You look better." It wasn't much of a greeting, but it was the best she could do. Her emotions were so conflicted; she couldn't begin to untangle them.

"Thank you." His voice still sounded raspy.

"You need to thank Odintar. Without his help, I wouldn't have found you and you would have bled to death."

He nodded, but didn't speak.

"I've seen you before, more than once. In fact, you showed up in so many places I was afraid I had a stalker. But you never approached me, never tried to make contact."

"I couldn't stay away."

Indignation warmed her cheeks and pulled her hands into fists. "We both know that's ridiculous. It only took a murder attempt to make you break your silence."

"Hate me if you must, but there is so much I need to tell you."

She tensed, tempted to turn around, walk away and never look back. "I doubt anything you have to say would interest me."

"Indric came to see you, so you know I'm battle born. What he doesn't know—what Lierra never told him—was the identity of her captor." He pressed his hand over his scorched throat. Each time he swallowed appeared excruciating. Good. He deserved pain and a whole lot more.

"The details are irrelevant." Even in her ears the claim didn't sound convincing.

"They won't be if Sevrin figures it out."

Her hands clenched even tighter. This had been a mistake. The last thing she needed was another surprise. Despite her determination not to give a damn, curiosity won out in the end. "Figures out what?"

"That I'm her half-brother. Lierra's captor was Pern Keire, Crown Stirate of Rodymia."

If Lierra had confessed the identity of her captor, it would have exploded hostilities between Bilarri and Rodymia. No wonder she'd kept silent. Jillian would have done the same. Unless... There was another possibility. Had Lierra developed feelings for her captor? Had she loved Pern enough to protect him even as he tore her son from her arms?

"It's an interesting bit of trivia, but I'm not sure why Sevrin would care. Lierra and Pern are both dead. The Rodyte throne has passed on to another."

"Which is exactly why Sevrin will care. Once she completes her mission on Earth, she intends to return to Rodymia and claim her rightful place on the throne. Don't underestimate her ambition or her ruthlessness."

"What do Sevrin's grand ambitions have to do with me?"

"Are you really that naive? *Everyone* with Pern's blood flowing through their veins is a potential rival. Why do you think she tried to kill me?"

"Sevrin did this to you?" Then the inconsistency in his story slammed home. "Wait a minute. You said she didn't know. You said this would become a problem *if* she figured out who you are."

"Who *we* are." He paused as if to ensure that she absorbed the implication. "You are just as much a danger to Sevrin as am I."

"Could there be another reason she tried to kill you? For that matter, why are you so sure it was Sevrin?"

"I'm not sure if she pieced it together or if she just thought I knew too many of her secrets. All I know for certain is one of her pet mercenaries wielded the blade while Sevrin locked the collar around my throat."

"How did you get away?"

"It all happened in an instant. I had already started to teleport when they attacked. The collar cut short my jump and I ended up in that alley."

"Then she likely knows you're still alive."

He nodded his eyelids starting to droop. "It's more than likely." Fatigue and pain meds finished closing his eyes.

"Wait." She moved closer to the bed and he forced his eyes open. "Nazerel went to warn Roxie. He said you told him that she was in danger, that Sevrin had some horrible use for her. What was he talking about? What does Sevrin want with Roxie?"

He laughed, the sound distorted by his injuries. "Not a chance. Roxie's my ticket out of here."

"What do you mean? What do you know?"

"When I'm safe on some obscure planet where Sevrin can never find me, then and only then will I explain." His eyes began to droop again.

She reached out and grasped his hand, giving it a light squeeze. His lashes fluttered, but his eyes remained open. "Many of the entries on your thumb drive are coded. You will decode them before we agree to any further provisions."

"Fine." He coughed, turning his head sharply to one side.

"And we have a notebook full of information on human females. Many of those pages are secured by the same or a similar code. Can you decode those as well?"

"I'll need to see them to know for sure, but it's probable."

"Then the value of the information you provide us will determine how far we're willing to go on your behalf."

"Agreed. But nothing about Roxie until after I'm relocated." He closed his eyes again and slipped into sleep with a peaceful sigh.

"Shit." Jillian fought back the urge to stomp her foot like a child. As far as she knew, Roxie was still here, somewhere, so she was relatively safe. Even so, the question had nagged away in the back of her mind ever since she ran in to Nazerel. Why was a coldblooded killer risking capture to warn a human that she was in danger? It didn't make sense.

The disquieting question set Jillian in motion. She needed to talk to Odintar. Finding out she had royal blood had been much more fun with Indric. Having any connection to Sevrin Keire held no appeal at all.

She found Elias working out with a punching bag, but Odintar was nowhere in sight. Elias spotted her and paused. "He's in the locker room."

"Is he alone?"

"Doubtful. I'll go get him."

"In a minute. Is Roxie still here?"

Elias laughed. "Why do you think I'm pummeling this bag?"

"She's still being stubborn?"

"Roxie Latimer might well be the most stubborn female on planet Earth and Morgan won't 'trust' her wellbeing to anyone but me."

"Lucky you." She chuckled. "Can I see her?"

"I'll have to ask Morgan. So far she hasn't been allowed visitors."

"Why? Roxie's a victim, not a criminal."

He shrugged. "She's refused to cooperate with our investigation. That's called obstruction of justice, so technically she is a criminal."

"Oh my God, no wonder she shut down. Tell Morgan I need to see her ASAP."

A slow, humorless smile bowed his lips. He obviously didn't appreciate being ordered around. "Before or after I go get Odintar?"

"After." She refused to soften her expression. Roxie had been terrified the last time Jillian saw her and it sounded like their treatment of her had only compounded that fear. There was no way she was going to stand by and let these idiots abuse her friend. Even if Roxie no longer considered her a friend.

When Odintar emerged from the locker room, he had Blayne with him. They both looked freshly showered and invigorated. "Where's Elias?"

"Said he needed to talk to Morgan," Blayne told her. "Something about you being all fired up."

Fired up didn't begin to describe it, but her fight was with Morgan and Elias, so she tried to relax her frown. "Who won?" She motioned toward the mats.

"Depends who you ask," Odintar replied.

Too wound up for small talk, she dove right to the heart of the matter. "I just had a fascinating conversation with Gerrod. It was much more interesting than anything on that thumb drive."

"Do tell, my lovely." Blayne wiggled his eyebrows with playful drama.

"She's not *your* anything." Odintar's reminder lacked any real hostility.

Ignoring their never-ending banter, she tried to be succinct. "According to our unwelcome guest, Pern Keire had a fondness for war brides."

"Lots of Rodytes took war brides. It would have been more of a shock if he hadn't." Blayne clearly didn't understand the inference, but Odintar did.

"Gerrod claims Pern Keire captured Lierra?" He'd drawn the correct conclusion, but he didn't sound completely convinced.

Blayne scoffed. "Not a chance. Being battle born isn't shameful on Rodymia. If Pern Keire had a son with one of Bilarri's royal daughters, the entire galaxy would have known about it."

"Unless there was a reason they kept it quiet." Odintar rubbed his chin as he gazed into the distance. "The only thing Rodytes like better than brutality is deception. Gerrod could have been part of some grand scheme Pern didn't quite pull off."

"Anything's possible," Blayne agreed. "But this is all speculation."

"It won't be for long." Odintar countered. "Ontarian security has a sample of Pern's DNA. It will be simple enough to prove whether or not he fathered Gerrod. Let's start there."

"How did Ontarian security get a sample of Pern's DNA?" Blayne wanted to know.

"Overlord Lyrik was there when Pern died. Of course he wasn't overlord at the time." Odintar looked at her and smiled. "I'll request the test and we'll take it from there."

Blayne nodded. "I better go update Lor. Even unsubstantiated, this is pretty important."

Odintar waited until they were alone again to ask, "Are you all right?"

"I'm fine. Earth-shattering surprises are my specialty."

He smiled and pulled her into a loose embrace. "If you'd like to see your mom, I can take you to Bilarri tonight."

"It's not fair to bring my mother into this."

He chuckled. "I've always been a dirty fighter."

"I'm aware."

He sighed, his gaze filled with compassion and concern. "I think we both know what the test is going to show. If you're a direct descendant of Pern Keire, everyone from Lor, to Morgan, to Indric will insist that you leave Earth."

Her chin came up. "Then Roxie's coming with me."

"What is your fixation with Roxie?"

"Did you know she's still here, locked in a room somewhere?" She put her hands on her hips. "They're treating her like a prisoner and she's done nothing wrong."

"It's my understanding that she's in protective custody because of Nazerel's cryptic warning. Did Gerrod happen to explain what that's all about?"

"No. He said Roxie is his ticket out of here. That he has no intention of explaining until he's safe on some obscure planet."

"Not a bad strategy."

"So I told him he had to decode the rest of the thumb drive and all of the notebook pages before we'd even consider relocating him."

A pleased smile warmed his expression. "I think you've discovered your true vocation. That was one hell of a negotiation."

"We'll see if any of it means anything." She sighed, blowing a stray strand of hair off her forehead. "I feel like we've come so far and yet we haven't really gotten anywhere."

"That's not true." His arm tightened around her waist drawing their lower bodies into intimate alignment. "You've provided us with possibilities. That's a lot more than we had a few days ago."

"I won't let Roxie become a bargaining chip," Jillian stressed. "She has nothing to do with any of this."

"Actually we don't know that for sure. Sevrin's interest in her couldn't have been coincidental."

"Because you don't believe in coincidences?"

"Yes." He cupped her chin and turned her face up toward his. "I know you feel responsible for Roxie, but they are protecting her."

"By locking her in a cage?" She shoved against his chest and tried to twist free of his embrace.

His arms tightened instead, drawing her closer. "She's going to be moved to the safe house as soon as she calms down."

"Then I'll go help her calm down."

He leaned down and kissed her, using his amazing mouth to melt the indignation from her body. "That's cheating."

He smiled against her lips. "Dirty fighter, remember."

"As soon as I've seen her, the rest of the night is yours. I promise."

He chuckled. "Stubborn to the end."

"I won't be able to relax until I know she's okay."

"I get it, and you win. We'll go check on Roxie." He shifted his arm to her shoulders and they headed off across the gym.

Contentment spread through her in languid waves. She wasn't sure where the emotion originated, but it sure felt good.

"After we've seen Roxie, do you want one final night at home?"

She thought about it for a second then looked into his eyes. "It doesn't matter where we sleep, my love. I'm already home."

Book Five: Unique Ink

Roxie finds herself in the middle of an interplanetary conflict, though she has no idea why she was targeted. She's kidnapped by the Mystic Militia, who claim they're protecting her. Roxie doesn't know what to believe or who she can trust, so she trusts no one. Then her ruggedly handsome interrogator arrives and her determination crumbles.

Elias is ordered to find out what Roxie knows and see if he can figure out why the Shadow Assassins are obsessed with her. He must use every tool at his disposal to unravel Roxie's mysteries. So he flirts and teases, even turns on the Southern charm. The only trouble is their attraction flares into passion the second his lips meet hers. How can he remain objective when all he can think about is touching her, tasting her, and keeping her by his side forever?

More than hearts are on the line as pressures mount and devastating decisions must be made. To finally put an end to the Shadow Assassins, the Mystic Militia must be willing to risk everything.

Chapter One

The front door to Unique Ink swung open and Roxie Latimer turned to greet her visitor. The last few weeks had been turbulent, to say the least. Still, she hoped the stress didn't show. Rather than a customer, however, Jett, one of her employees, ambled into the tattoo shop. She released her pent-up breath and let the forced smile fade.

"Hey." He added his characteristic chin lift to the greeting and Roxie tried to relax.

"Tess needed some time off, so you're stuck with me today." Tess and Jett were technically her employees, but they had all been friends long before Roxie's appearance on a national tattoo competition show allowed her to open Unique Ink. Even though she'd come in second, name recognition and industry buzz convinced a venture capitalist to invest in the endeavor. And Roxie had worked tirelessly to make her dream reality.

"Such a sacrifice." Jett blew her a kiss. "I only have two appointments, so I should be able to handle the walk-ins. What's your schedule like?" Jett was always ready to roll with the changes, though his laid-back attitude and kind heart were a sharp contrast to his appearance. His ink-black hair had been styled with asymmetrical flare, slashing across his forehead and frequently blocking one eye. Not surprisingly, colorful tattoos covered much of his body, even creeping up one side of his face. The subtle facial design drew attention to his expressive green eyes, which he also accented with "guy-liner". Roxie counted on his unflappable demeanor and loyalty, and he'd never let her down.

"If the mystery men have actually left town, my schedule is wide open." For the past nine weeks Roxie had been working for a woman named Sevrin Keire. Though strikingly beautiful and obviously rich, there was something about Sevrin that screamed danger. Roxie had reluctantly agreed to make herself available to Sevrin's "boys" and Sevrin had more than tripled Roxie's usual rates. Sevrin's "boys" were anything but boyish. They were tall, muscular men with strong foreign accents. Roxie, Jet and Tess had spent the following weeks trying to guess their occupation. Bodybuilders, private security, professional athletes? But they kept coming back to the most obvious choice—mercenaries.

As unexpectedly as Sevrin had appeared, she dropped by the night before to inform Roxie that her services were no longer needed. Sevrin was moving her operation to another location, so Roxie had "dodged a bullet". There had been more to the conversation than that, but Roxie refused to think about it now. All her suspicions and fears were irrelevant as long as Sevrin and her "boys" were out of her life forever.

"Are you missing them already?" Jett softened the question with a teasing smile, but he'd been the first one to speak up about the menace they all sensed. He'd been reluctant to leave Roxie alone with any of the men and he'd been thrilled to hear that they were leaving.

"More like the opposite. I've never been so relieved to have a job end."

"I'm right there with you, Rox." He strolled toward the large display case filled with jewelry and souvenirs then paused. "My first appointment isn't until eleven. Why don't I go get us some coffee, or better yet, breakfast?"

"I never say no to coffee and I haven't eaten since yesterday."

"No surprise there. If me and Tess didn't feed you, you'd starve." He retraced his steps, arms loose, stride rolling. "So what sounds good? Breakfast burrito, croissant sandwich, ooy-gooy sticky buns?"

She chuckled at the last suggestion, but before she could make her selection, the front door swung open, drawing their attention to the main entrance. Nazerel, the most dangerous of Sevrin's men, stepped across the threshold. Dread dropped into the pit of Roxie's stomach and all the tension Jett's arrival had eased sprang back into place.

With predatory grace and a purposeful stride, Nazerel stalked toward her. "I would speak with you alone." His hand encircled her upper arm and he guided her toward the back of the shop.

Jett opened his mouth to argue, but Roxie backed him off with a warning look. Though brusque and somewhat abrasive, Nazerel had never been abusive toward her. In fact, he'd been oddly protective.

The front of the store was designed for potential customers. They could look through portfolios and spend time with an artist before deciding on the designs that would grace their bodies for the rest of their lives. Once the decision was made, each customer was taken to the actual work area, which took up the majority of the compact shop. Nazerel brought Roxie into the larger area and drew the curtain across the archway separating the two. Roxie had a desk in the back corner of the room, but there hadn't been enough space to enclose an actual office. This was as close as they could come to privacy inside Unique Ink.

"Are you aware that we are leaving?" He spoke with obvious care, yet his accent was less pronounced than most of his cohorts'.

Was this all he wanted, to say goodbye? That would be a wonderful development, but her life was never that simple. "Sevrin told me yesterday."

"I know you don't trust me, but it's important that you listen to what I'm about to tell you."

He sounded so dire, so filled with conviction, that her heartbeat picked up its pace. "All right."

Before he could present his grand revelation, she heard voices in the front of the store. Jillian, the ex-showgirl Roxie had hired as a receptionist, wasn't scheduled to begin until tomorrow, but Roxie was certain it was Jillian talking with Jett. Anyone who interacted with Nazerel could be endangered by the exposure. Jillian was still recovering from a devastating injury and Roxie refused to add to her misfortune in any way.

Roxie held up her hand, determined to send Jillian away before she even saw Nazerel. "Give me just a minute. I'll be right back. Please, stay here." Roxie opened the privacy curtain and hurried around the display case. She needed to appear friendly, yet insistent, so Jillian wouldn't ask questions. "I thought I recognized that voice."

Jillian smiled in response, but that was as far as the conversation progressed.

Nazerel moved into the archway. "Well, isn't this awkward?"

Jillian's eyes widened with obvious shock, then she quickly composed her expression. "Excuse me?"

Roxie looked at Nazerel then back at Jillian. They knew each other. Despite Jillian's denial, it was obvious they were acquainted.

"Do I know you?" Jillian's innocent act wasn't convincing.

"Oh I think you do." Nazerel brushed past Roxie and rushed toward Jillian. The subtle menace Roxie always sensed became an overt threat.

Shit! Roxie glanced at Jett. He shoved his hand into his pocket, likely reaching for his phone. She wasn't sure they should call the cops. Nazerel hadn't really done anything wrong, yet.

Light burst all around Roxie, momentarily blinding her. Pain stabbed into her head and darkness barreled toward her. Suddenly three men materialized around Nazerel. *What the...* Her thoughts faded and everything went black.

AWARENESS RETURNED to Roxie more gradually than it had left, but the pain lingered. Her head throbbed with agonizing spasms, as if her skull had developed a pulse. She vaguely remembered falling to the floor, so how had she ended up in the armchair across the room?

She forced her eyelids upward, ignoring the increased pressure in her head. No one was near her, so why had she blacked out?

"Hello. How are you feeling?"

She didn't recognize the deep, male voice. "Like someone kicked me in the head." Pushing her hair back from her face, she blinked until her eyes focused. The man was tall and brawny, with the confident bearing of a military commander. If he'd spoken with an accent, she would have presumed he was one of Sevrin's men. "Who are you?"

"Special Agent Elias Bertram." The dark-haired stranger held out his hand.

Rather than shake it, she rubbed her aching temples. "Holy mother of God, my head hurts."

A different man moved into her peripheral vision. Her heart lurched and she sucked in a breath. This was one of the men she'd seen just before she blacked out. If they hadn't been a hallucination, then... She couldn't complete the thought. Even her pain-addled brain knew people didn't just appear out of nowhere.

What the hell is going on?

The second man moved behind her as he said, "If you'll allow me to touch you, I can ease the pressure."

Roxie didn't respond, was in too much pain to care if he meant her further harm. Then his warm fingers pressed against her temples and waves of soothing heat flowed through her mind. "Wow." She blinked again, finally clearing the haze from her vision. The first man stood in front of her, scowling furiously. She didn't care if the healer had crossed some unacceptable line. She could finally think again. "What did you do? The pain is just—gone."

"Pressure points," the healer muttered. "Western doctors scoff at the concept, but they really do work."

He was full of shit, but Roxie wasn't about to confront him in front of Jett. She pushed to her feet, her legs still wobbly. Jett stood back, silently watching through wide, disbelieving eyes. What had they told him while she was unconscious? Had Jett seen the three men just blink into the room? She'd find out what he knew later, when the others weren't around. "Go cancel the rest of the appointments for today. I don't think either of us is fit to work."

"You got it."

She waited until Jett was gone before she spun toward the healer. "What the hell are you?"

"*What* am I?" He laughed, apparently surprised by her hostility. "I'm human. What are you?"

"Humans can't materialize out of thin air or heal with a touch. And it wasn't just you. I saw the others. Don't bother denying it. I know what I saw."

Tension escalated in an uncomfortable surge. The healer glanced at Jillian, and Jillian looked at the soldier. No one seemed to know what to do with a mouthy human. It probably would have been wiser to keep her suspicions to herself. But this was the culmination of months of stress and unanswered questions.

"The weapon Nazerel used on you can cause hallucinations," the healer told her, his angular features suddenly stern. A strange blue glow smoldered in the depths of his dark eyes, reinforcing her conclusion that he wasn't human.

She didn't bring it up, knew he'd deny anything she claimed to have seen. "All right. Let's talk about whatever kicked in my head. Why didn't it work on you?" When the healer couldn't come up with a believable lie, she turned to the soldier and snapped, "I've had it with this bullshit. Who are you people and what are you doing on my planet!"

A rush of energy swirled around her, tingly and warm. Then someone grabbed her from behind. The arms encircling her were long and muscular, obviously male. She gasped and tried to struggle, but the man was incredibly strong.

Before she could reason through where he'd come from or why he was restraining her, the room blurred again. A burst of acceleration propelled her into blackness and then her surroundings reformed, becoming a room she'd never seen before.

The man behind her loosened his grip then stepped back. She spun around and gasped again. This was another one of the men she'd glimpsed before passing out. A hundred questions inundated her mind, creating an unintelligible buzz. Who...why...where the hell was she! She backed up, instinctively lodging herself into the nearest corner.

"I won't hurt you," the man assured, both hands extended, palms up.

She wanted to believe him, needed to believe that she'd stumbled into something good for a change. Keeping him in her peripheral vision, she glanced around the room. With stark gray walls, no windows, and a single door, the room could only be described as utilitarian. Or militant.

The first man she'd seen in her shop had definitely put off soldier vibes. For that matter, so had the healer.

She shuddered then swayed, teetering between laughter and tears. The teleporter took a cautious step forward and she tried to retreat, but there was nowhere left to go. "Just leave me alone!" The demand came out shrill rather than commanding, but she was doing good just to remain on her feet.

What did these people want with her? She'd thought the drama ended when Sevrin said goodbye.

"Roxie, I will not harm you."

"How do you know my name? Why am I..." Another wave of vertigo had her grasping the walls for support.

He lightly touched her shoulder and the rings in his eyes slowly blended into a swirling mass of turquoise. "Do you need to lie down? Teleporting can be hard on the stomach if you're not expecting the rush." Tall, blond and undeniably handsome, he spoke with authority and compassion. And only the barest hint of an accent.

She stared into his gently rotating gaze, terrified yet oddly soothed by the overt proof that her wild conclusion had been correct all along. These men were not human.

At least she wasn't losing her mind.

Twisting away from his touch, she took a deep breath. "Where am I?" It was the logical place to start. There was no furniture in the room, no shelves or storage compartments. The room was just an open space with no apparent purpose. "Why did you bring me here?"

"I'm Commander Lor dar Joon. I'll explain everything as soon as I'm sure you're not going to throw up on me." He smiled, obviously trying to put her at ease.

She appreciated the effort, but she was far from ready to relax her guard. "Are we still on Earth?"

His eyes returned to concentric rings, though they remained a vivid mixture of blue and green. "We're still in Nevada."

"Actually, we're just across the border in Arizona."

Roxie snapped her head toward the doorway. A woman stood there, though Roxie hadn't heard the door open. The newcomer wore dress pants; her simple white blouse pinstriped in dark gray. Her red hair had been pulled back into a severe twist, but the style only accented the woman's flawless skin and sculpted features. Was their race genetically engineered to be physically perfect? This was ridiculous.

"And you are?" Despite the emotions raging through Roxie, she tried to appear calm.

"Director Morgan Hoyt." Special agent, commander, and now director, they were sure as hell fond of titles. "Lor can answer your questions as soon as he explains why it was necessary to bring you here."

Morgan's obvious annoyance allowed Roxie a moment to compose herself. Though Lor emanated authority, Morgan was obviously in charge. And apparently his actions hadn't been authorized. Could any of this work to Roxie's advantage? She still had no idea what they wanted or why Lor had brought her here.

"This is Roxie Latimer," Lor began.

"I know who she is." Morgan was all business. Not even her bright blue eyes held a hint of emotion. "Why did you deviate from the original plan? Where are Jillian and Odintar? For that matter, where is Elias?"

So Jillian was a spy. The news didn't surprise Roxie, but a fresh wave of anger drove her fear a little farther back, allowing her to think more clearly. Was Elias the soldier or the healer? And what happened to Nazerel? He'd been nowhere in sight when she woke up.

As if Lor heard her mental ramblings, he said, "Nazerel was with Roxie when Jillian arrived at the shop."

Roxie listened intently. They were answering her questions. All she needed to do was stand here and keep her mouth shut until she understood the situation. Then she'd strategize.

Morgan's lips pressed into a grim line. "Is he in custody?" She tensed as if preparing for disappointment.

"He insisted that he didn't want to fight and did nothing but defend himself when we attempted to trap him. It was really strange."

They tried to "trap" Nazerel. That had to mean they were adversaries. Roxie tucked the fact away for later consideration. Anyone out to trap Nazerel had to be a better option than Sevrin and her boys.

"So you let him go?" Morgan's expression finally registered anger.

Roxie moved to the side, trying to peer past Morgan. The door to the corridor remained open, but it was unlikely Roxie could make it out of this room. Besides, was it physically possible to outrun someone who could teleport?

"Of course, we didn't let him go," Lor snapped. "He insisted that he'd only come to warn Roxie that she was in danger and then he flashed to safety. As usual, we were unable to track him. He's just too damn fast."

So Nazerel could teleport too. It stood to reason that...wait a second. "*Why* am I in danger?"

Morgan waved away her concern without even turning her head. "Lor will explain in a moment."

She'd been shushed like a child. Crossing her arms over her chest, Roxie glared at Morgan. Who the hell did she think she was? Being director of a military installation didn't give her the right to act like a condescending bitch.

"Was anyone else there?" Morgan continued her interrogation.

Lor glanced at Roxie as he responded. "Jett, one of Roxie's employees. He knows something *odd* happened, but he didn't see us teleport. Roxie not only saw us flash in, she also had direct contact with Nazerel. At the very least, she needs to be questioned. However, I suggest keeping her in protective custody while we investigate Nazerel's warning."

Morgan glanced at Roxie then back at Lor. "Was he specific about the potential threat?"

"He said Sevrin had some nefarious use for Roxie and that she needed to be protected."

This was the first time he'd mentioned Sevrin. It was unlikely that he'd know Nazerel and not know Sevrin, but he'd just confirmed his connection to the real villain. Just the thought of Sevrin gave Roxie the shivers.

Morgan finally faced Roxie, including her in the conversation for the first time. "What did Nazerel say to you? How long had he been in your shop when Jillian arrived?"

The smarter course would have been to cooperate, but Roxie had always struggled with authority. The harder they pushed, the more rebellious she became. And Morgan wasn't just autocratic, she was insulting. "Screw you! You can't be bothered to answer my questions. Why should I answer yours?"

Morgan shook her head as she turned back to Lor. "I don't have time for this and neither do you. Put her in a holding cell and go get Elias. He's good at this sort of thing. Then you and Blayne get back out there and find Nazerel!" Without so much as a backward glance, Morgan stormed out of the room."

Roxie was floored by Morgan's rudeness as well as the implication in her orders. "I'm not allowed to leave?" She dragged her gaze back to Lor, finding him slightly less obnoxious.

"Why would you want to when Elias is about to answer all your questions?" A hint of challenge threaded through Lor's question. A much wiser strategy, but Roxie had already dug in her heels.

"I've committed no crime. If you intend to interrogate me, I want my lawyer present. If not, I demand to be released." Lor reached for Roxie's arm, but she twisted away. "You can't keep me here."

"It's for your own protection."

"Bullshit. Nazerel was just screwing with you. They're on their way out of town. Sevrin told me so herself."

"Sevrin wants us to believe the danger is past so we'll let down our guard." With terrifying speed, he wrapped his arm around her waist and teleported into a room even smaller than the first. This room had a built-in bunk and a bolted-down table and chairs. Obviously the holding cell Morgan had mentioned.

Infuriated by her own helplessness, she shoved him away and rushed across the tiny room. "Why are you treating me like a criminal? I haven't done anything wrong."

"Elias will take you through it step-by-step." He paused and compassion warmed his gaze. "I'm sorry we haven't been more welcoming. Nazerel is extremely dangerous. If there is even the slightest possibility we can pick up his trail, we need to keep trying."

Before she could respond to his apology, Lor flashed out of sight.

Stunned beyond rational thought, Roxie just stood there staring at empty air. Then emotions rushed in, weakening her knees and compressing her chest. She wanted to scream and she needed to cry, but neither reaction would get her out of this cell.

She stumbled to the door and tried to push it open. There wasn't even a handle on this side and it was locked solid as she'd feared. Pounding only hurt her hands, but at least it was an outlet for her anger. If anyone heard her furious yelling, they ignored it. There was a large window beside the door, but some sort of film prevented her from seeing out.

Too exhausted to continue her tantrum, she crossed to the bunk and sat, no longer trusting her legs to support her. Was Jillian an alien or had the woman in Unique Ink only looked like Jillian Taylor? Maybe these creatures could take on other shapes or—she shook away the unknown. What she knew for certain was intimidating enough. They were faster and stronger than humans; they could heal with a touch and teleport.

Rather than wasting energy on useless speculation, she took stock of her environment. Morgan had said they were in Arizona, but that didn't really mean anything. How far was the nearest town? Were there public roads nearby or were they isolated? Could she find a vehicle on the compound or did everyone teleport in and out? She couldn't tell anything by the inside of this cell and she was powerless to change the setting.

A second, smaller door sat adjacent to the bunk. Hopefully it led to a bathroom. If she was going to be stuck here for hours, she'd rather not be at the mercy of her bodily functions. Curious, she stood and approached the doorway. The door slid sideways automatically, revealing a tiny lavatory.

"Thank God for small favors," she muttered under her breath. Still, there was no shower and no food. How long did they intend to keep her imprisoned here? She'd been thinking hours, but it could be days. Months? She shuddered.

Now that the rush of adrenaline had run its course, she felt weak, yet jittery. The cell wasn't even big enough to pace, so she returned to the bunk. She scooted back against the wall and folded her legs in front of her. If they'd treated her with such discourtesy, what had they done to poor Jett? Her phone was in her purse, which was locked in her desk drawer. She had no way to check on her friend without the assistance of her captors. It also meant if she somehow managed to escape, she had no money, no credit cards, not even her ID. What a disaster. With an exasperated sigh, she closed her eyes.

The main door buzzed, popped then swung outward. She opened her eyes in time to watch the soldier from her shop move into the cell. Without searing pain clouding her vision, it was as if she were seeing him for the first time. He was six foot four, at least, with a body perfectly proportioned for such a large frame. Dark green cargo pants and a black T-shirt, his clothing was right in line with his pseudo-military appearance.

"Elias, I presume?"

A lazy smile quirked one corner of his mouth as the door swung shut behind him. "Guilty as charged. I brought water and a protein bar." He held up a plastic bottle and a foil-wrapped bar. "Thought you might be hungry once you calmed down."

"What makes you think I'm calm?"

He tossed her the bar and waited to see if she'd catch it before tossing her the bottle of water as well. After eying her for a moment longer, he crossed to the table and swiveled one of the chairs around to face the bunk. Then he sat, looking particularly oversized in the compact setting. "How much did Lor explain?"

Not yet ready to play nice with anyone, she glared at him. "What did you do with Jett?"

"Jett is your assistant?"

"Employee and friend." She stressed the last word so he'd clearly understand her position. Then she twisted the cap off the water bottle and took a long drink. Cool, soothing moisture spread across her tongue and down her dry throat. She hadn't even realized she was thirsty, but water had never tasted so good. "What will happen to him?"

"He was told Nazerel is an international arms dealer specializing in experimental weapons. You were feeling ill, so we wanted to make sure the weapon Nazerel discharged hadn't caused any lasting damage."

Jett had "been told" Nazerel was an arms dealer, which implied the truth was something else. "Did he believe you?" Jett was fiercely loyal. It was unlikely he'd let things go with a superficial excuse.

"I don't know. I left so they could tell him I was the one who drove you here."

Which they both knew was untrue. She'd been teleported here by Lor dar Something-or-other. "I want to talk to him, make sure he's okay."

"And I'll arrange the call, as soon as you've convinced me you're going to behave yourself."

His tone was patronizing enough to make her hand tense around the protein bar without motivating her to throw the water bottle at his face. "Can everyone from your planet teleport?"

Elias grinned and the gold flecks in his green eyes shimmered. Though short on the sides, his dark hair was long enough on top to form distinct waves. It made him look as if someone had just run their fingers through his hair. He wasn't model perfect like Lor or exotic like the healer. Still, his stark ruggedness appealed to her. He appeared strong, more than capable of protecting her. And whether or not Roxie was willing to admit it out loud, she was in desperate need of protection.

"Sorry to disappoint ya, darlin'. I was born in Austin." His voice took on a subtle twang she hadn't noticed before. Had he intentionally rid himself of the cadence or was he using it now in an attempt to make himself seem less intimidating?

"You're human?" She wasn't sure she believed him. The others had looked human too, at least to begin with. Besides, he hadn't denied being an alien. He'd just claimed to have been born on Earth.

"Don't I look human?" He crossed his arms, stretching his T-shirt even tighter.

What a poser! It would take more than rock-hard muscles to scramble her brain. But then this man had more than his share. "Lor looked human too until his eyes started spinning. And the healer only had a freakish blue light inside his eyes *after* I confronted him."

"The healer's name is Odintar. He and Lor are from different planets within the same star system. Morgan and I work with aliens, but we're both US citizens, just like you."

That brought up all sorts of new questions. What the hell were aliens doing on Earth? Was the government officially involved or was this some sort of private venture profitable enough for the government to ignore?

Not wanting to lose herself in the details, she started with the basics. "How long have they been on Earth?"

"We've been working together for about a month, but they arrived a few weeks before that."

"What are they doing here?"

"Trying to protect you from some extremely dangerous people."

Roxie scoffed then ripped open the protein bar and took a bite. "Humans in general or me in particular?" She paused for a drink of water before adding, "Either way they're not doing a very good job." She'd been terrified for the past nine weeks, intimidated and verbally abused. She'd even been subjected to some sort of alien technology that might well have damaged her brain. She started to tell him about the language infuser, Sevrin had forced Roxie to endure. But she gained nothing by volunteering information. "Is Nazerel some sort of fugitive? Why are you trying to capture him?"

"How long have you known him? Is your relationship strictly professional or—"

"We don't have a 'relationship'. He's a customer. That's all." She studied his features for a moment. Though his eyes were bright and attentive, she could discern nothing but intelligence behind his stoic expression. The man had one hell of a poker face. "Why'd you dodge my question?"

"Did he and his companions just happen upon your shop or was there some sort of formal arrangement?"

Tension wound through Roxie like a massive constrictor. Was he building a case against her? Did they think she was involved with Sevrin's men? "I tattooed them; nothing more." She looked at the door as discomfort surged into fear. "How long are you going to keep me here?"

Elias reached over and touched Roxie's foot. Even dressed in black leather and chains, she looked like a frightened kitten. He wanted to comfort her, calm her, but her agitation worked to his advantage. He needed her to believe he was dangerous, that he'd do anything to find out the answers to his questions. That wasn't far from the truth, but even bastards like him had limits. And harming women was high on a very short list of things he would never do.

"I need to understand how it started." He kept his voice even, yet unemotional. "What brought you together with those men?"

Roxie shrugged. The absent motion made the delicate chains draped from shoulder to waist jingle against her breasts. She was lithe and lean, her gentle curves perfect for her narrow frame. Snug black leather pants showcased her long legs and sleek hips, while a sexy cropped tank top left the artwork on her arms and sides visible.

"Would you like me to undress?" The challenge in her tone snapped his attention back to her face.

"I was distracted by your tattoos. I apologize."

She chuckled, clearly unconvinced by the lame excuse. "Sorry, Tex, but you weren't looking at my tattoos."

He'd already apologized, so he ignored the comment and brought the conversation back on track. "How'd your interaction with Nazerel and his companions begin?"

"It didn't start with Nazerel. Sevrin strolled into my shop one night and offered me an obscene amount of money for an exclusive contract."

Not willing to derail the conversation again, he focused on her powder-blue eyes. "An exclusive contract to do what?"

"I'm a tattoo artist, dumb-ass. What do you think she wanted me to do? Clean their apartments?"

He pushed to his feet and turned toward the door.

"Where are you going?" She swung her legs over the side of the bunk, but didn't stand.

"I'm attempting to be civil. If you're not ready to exchange information, I'll return when you are."

She did stand then, an angry flush coloring her high cheekbones. "If this *were* an exchange, I might not be so bitchy. I've answered your questions, but you've dodged all of mine."

He advanced, backing her against the wall with two long strides. Pressing his hands against the wall, he caged her, surrounding her without actually touching her. "You're in more danger than you can possibly imagine. Even if Sevrin has left Las Vegas, she hasn't lost track of you. Cooperate with us and we'll protect you. Continue to be a pain in the ass and we'll turn you loose. Do you really want to be at Sevrin's mercy again?"

"I'm not afraid of Sevrin." She glared up at him, her expression mutinous.

Damn. She was going to be harder to break than he'd thought, but he was known for his patience. It was one of the things that made him so good at interrogations. "Fine. I'll arrange for your discharge." Before she could react to the dismissal, he walked from the room.

"Wait."

He pretended not to hear her cry and locked the door behind him. He'd let her stew for an hour or two while he found out what was going on with the others. Hopefully, when he returned, she'd be more reasonable.

Her stubborn expression and angry gaze lingered in the back of his mind as he hurried toward his office. He'd expected her to be more frightened, more overwhelmed. It was almost as if today were not the first time she'd been exposed to paranormal abilities. Had the Shadow Assassins been showing off for the feisty tattoo artist? And if they had, what abilities had they revealed? She insisted that her only interaction with them had been professional, but what else would she say? She gained nothing by admitting to more.

As Elias approached his office, he found Bates and Larossa, two of his men speaking with Lor. "Please tell me you caught the bastard."

Lor looked at him then shook his head, displeasure tightening his features. "Nazerel is like smoke. We get close enough to smell him, but there's nothing there to catch."

"Hopefully the new guy will give us something useful," Bates said.

"If he survives," Larossa grumbled.

"What are you talking about? What new guy?" He pushed the door to his office open and Lor followed him inside while Bates and Larossa loitered in the doorway. Neither of the soldiers had worked directly with aliens before and their unease tended to show. He couldn't blame them. The Mystic Militia weren't going out of their way to network with their human counterparts. Master-level Mages were treated with respect and reverence on Ontariese and they expected the same deference on Earth. Only trouble was most humans weren't used to bowing and scraping to anyone.

"Jillian sensed danger as she and Odintar were headed back here," Lor explained. "He flashed her to the source of the disruption and they found Gerrod Reynolds."

Now that was completely unexpected. "Why would Jillian's father be a danger to her?"

Lor shook his head again. "Jillian wasn't in danger, Gerrod was. In fact his throat had been slit and he'd been left to die."

Which explained Larossa's comment. "Was Odintar able to heal him?"

"They're still working on him, so hope for the best. We really need an opportunity to question him."

"Gerrod's still alive," Blayne announced from the hallway. Elias wasn't sure how long the other Mystic had been standing there. His attention had been focused on Lor. "But Jillian just told me Gerrod and Odintar both need energy."

"Are you going?" Lor asked and Blayne nodded. "Then I'll stop by later and transfuse them again."

Blayne stepped farther into the office. Bates and Larossa automatically moved out of his way. They might not be as awestruck as the Mystics would have liked, but his men could sense real power. "Jillian wanted Elias to know that Jett is expecting a video call from Roxie within the next hour or so. He threatened to call the media if he doesn't hear from her."

Elias rolled his eyes. "As if anyone would believe him. I can see the headline now, *Tattoo Artist Kidnapped By Secret Government Operatives.* Details to follow on *TMZ.*"

Blayne hesitated a moment longer. "Jillian promised Jett she'd make it happen."

With a frustrated sigh, Elias rubbed the bridge of his nose. "Roxie isn't being very cooperative at the moment. I doubt I can convince her to do anything."

"You'll figure out something," Blayne said with a cheerful smile. Of the three Mystics currently in residence at the Bunker, he was the most likable. Then Blayne looked at Lor and spoke in Ontarian. Lor nodded and Blayne hurried off down the hall.

The exchange annoyed Elias, but not enough to confront Lor with the rudeness of telling secrets. It was little things like that that made it hard to mesh with the Mystic Militia. "Do you know who tried to take out Gerrod?"

"My money's on Sevrin," Lor told him.

She topped the list of usual suspects, but they needed to be careful not to be overly focused on any one person. "What's her motivation?"

"I'm not sure. All indications were that Gerrod was one of her father's spies. Maybe he knew too much or maybe he tried to blackmail her." He shrugged, then added, "She's the only one on Earth with any connection to Gerrod."

"Except for Jillian." He stopped Lor's immediate objection with an upraised hand. "I'm not accusing her. Sevrin could have set her up to take the blame."

"There are a lot of possibilities and Gerrod is the only one who can confirm the truth. We need to make sure he survives."

"Well, I'll leave that to you and Odintar. I have one seriously pissed-off tattoo artist to deal with."

"Good luck with that." Lor chuckled and turned toward the doorway.

Chapter Two

Nazerel stood on the wide railed deck that extended the entire width of the new Team South house. A large two story overlooking Lake Mead, this house was even more luxurious than the one they'd left behind. The area was more secluded, more easily defended than the previous location. Yet defense didn't seem to be a concern while surrounded by the tranquil beauty of this local. The long narrow lake stretched off into the distance, melding with the horizon. An occasional boat zipped past, but mostly there was vivid blue sky and calm, clear water.

After spending the majority of his life underground, Nazerel was almost overwhelmed by the vastness. It was a promise whispered on the wind. *Freedom.* Hope for a life free from manipulation and deceit. A state of existence he had yet to experience.

When Sevrin told him they were moving operations to a new location, he'd expected a much longer journey. But they hadn't ventured to another state. They'd barely left Las Vegas. Something kept Sevrin tethered to this area and he needed to discover the nature of her anchor. It might be a weakness he could use against her.

And, speaking of weaknesses. He shook his head. His instinctive need to protect Roxie had nearly cost him his life. He'd managed to elude the Mystic Militia and return to his men without anyone being the wiser. Still, it had been much too close. No matter how compelling he found these females, he could not allow compassion to endanger his men. He was their leader. He'd convinced them to risk coming to Earth and now it was his responsibility to see that they received the stable, independent lives they'd been promised.

Someone slid the glass door open and Nazerel glanced over his shoulder. Flynn ambled out onto the deck. Dark circles shadowed his eyes and his clothing was rather wrinkled. Sevrin's sexual demands were taking their toll on his friend. And knowing Flynn subjected himself to the desires of that Rodyte whore because of Nazerel's encouragement left a bad taste in his mouth.

"How are things progressing?" Flynn asked in Rodyte, the language they always used when they were alone. There were a few on Earth who could understand the language—Sevrin and her staff topped the list—but the practice decreased the chances of anything important being overheard by the Mystic Militia.

"The truck is unloaded and everyone has claimed their bedroom." He turned around and lightly leaned against the railing. "You've been assigned a bed, though you haven't needed one lately."

Flynn made a derisive sound as he gazed out across the water. "I've needed nothing *but* a bed lately. That lusty bitch can't get enough."

"Well, she hasn't replaced you yet, so our strategy is working."

Pivoting to face him, Flynn suddenly looked grim. "You might not think so when you hear the latest."

Nazerel tensed. There never seemed to be any good news with Sevrin. She'd lured him and his companions to Earth with the promise of a life lived on their own terms, yet she was the most controlling master they'd ever served. "What now?"

"She took me to the new lab." Flynn's voice filled with frustration as he added, "It's impressive."

"Is it nearby?" Anticipation surged through Nazerel. If they could seize possession of Sevrin's headquarters, they might finally be able to control her. "Is that why she insists on staying in this area?"

Flynn cringed, clearly uncomfortable with what he was about to say. "We're not allowed to know the actual location. She drugged me before we left."

"Why the hell did you allow her to drug you?" Seducing her for information was one thing. Why would Flynn surrender control to that cold-hearted whore?

"I'm not sure 'allow' is the right word. She told me we were going for a ride then shoved a needle in my neck."

Flynn was looking everywhere but at him and a faint flush colored his cheeks. Flynn was lying to him. "You weren't able to flash away from her before the drug kicked in?"

He started to say something then sighed. "She threatened to replace me if I didn't let her do it. Unless I was willing to have debased myself for nothing, I had no other choice."

Nazerel relaxed. He benefited from Flynn's access to Sevrin, so he wasn't about to ridicule the decision. If Flynn lost favor with Sevrin, Nazerel might have to swallow his pride and allow her to— Never! Even the thought of her touch was repellent. "You were already inside the new lab when you woke up?"

"It was worse than that. She'd put this band around my neck. I don't know how it worked, but I was weak as a child and unable to access any of my powers."

"A suppression collar." Nazerel turned back to the railing, too conflicted to maintain a calm expression. This was bad, really bad. If Sevrin now had the ability to render Shadow Assassins helpless, she would be impossible to control. "The elders used to talk about them. Bilarrians developed them decades ago. But I didn't think they worked on hybrids."

"They do now. I've never been that helpless. It was horrible."

"When and why did she take it off?" He turned his head, assessing Flynn's response.

"That's part of a much longer story."

"So get to it," Nazerel snapped. "I'm already tired of this conversation."

"She's established new rules with ridiculous penalties for disobedience."

With a bland chuckle, Nazerel crossed his arms over his chest. Now that he knew Sevrin had the collar, he'd make damn sure she never got close enough to use it. Still, he needed to know what she intended. "What rules?"

"No more females in the team houses."

Nazerel just grinned. Until they claimed their mates, the only females they interacted with were pleasure givers. Pleasure givers were known to be accommodating. The rule was an annoyance, nothing more. "What else?"

"No more unsanctioned hunts."

"What do you mean by unsanctioned? We only hunt those who appear in the notebook, which means they've been sanctioned by Sevrin."

"That's not what she meant. From now on, she will choose one hunter at a time and he will bring his mate back to the old warehouse. He and his mate will be drugged and he will be collared before they're taken to the new facility. Once there, they will be allowed to bond, but only under strict supervision."

It was obvious Flynn was reciting Sevrin's words, issuing her commands. Nazerel could almost hear her voice coming out of Flynn's mouth. Frustration and anger boiled up inside him, but he captured the intensity, storing the energy for his inevitable confrontation with their useless employer. "That's ridiculous and she knows it."

"She claims her men will shoot anyone who violates the new rules."

He glared at Flynn, his aggravation focused on the issue not the man. "They'd have to find us first."

"Guards are already stationed at the new team houses and they've been equipped with tracking devises."

Nazerel scoffed. This became more preposterous by the moment. "It takes a Shadow Assassin to track a Shadow Assassin. Has she sent to Ontariese for reinforcements?"

"She didn't need anything from Ontariese. Our nanites were manufactured on Rodymia."

Dread washed over Nazerel in a slow-moving flood. For the past twenty years Shadow Assassins had been using nanites to boost their natural abilities and allow their bodies to regenerate. The elders had worked closely with Rodyte scientists to perfect the technology. Had the Rodytes knowingly created this weakness and had they created others as well? The possibilities were daunting.

Rather than losing himself in speculation, he needed to focus on one detail at a time. "They can track our nanites?"

Flynn nodded. "She told me she'd prefer to work with us, but she's willing to kill us all and start over with a more cooperative group of recruits."

"Or make examples of a few so the rest will fall in line?"

Flynn nodded, looking defeated and ashamed. "And she meant every word. She's just waiting for someone to defy her so she can demonstrate her power over us."

Nazerel clenched his fists and cursed under his breath. That conniving bitch. "If I'd responded well to threats and intimidation, I'd still be on Ontariese."

"Then you'll really enjoy her final stipulation."

Forcing his fingers to uncurl, he looked at Flynn. "What stipulation?"

"Each hunter must spend one night in her bed before he'll be allowed to hunt. She wants a child, but she's decided that fathering her child is too high an honor for any one man."

Nazerel scoffed. "It doesn't matter how many of us screw her. One of us will have to form a mating bond for her to conceive."

"And once he's bonded with her, there would be no reason for him to hunt." Again Flynn nodded. "I'm well aware and so is Sevrin. She might have claimed she wants a child, but this is simply a way for her to exert her authority over us. Or her scientists have found a way around the limitation. I don't know which. When she told me all this, I was fighting the overwhelming need to strangle her, so I didn't ask a lot of questions."

Much of Sevrin's control was an illusion Nazerel allowed because they were working toward the same goal. But if she continued to push like this, she'd find out that his reputation for ruthlessness was well-deserved. She'd promised that she would find a way to transfer their abilities to their mates and it was past time for her to fulfil that promise. If that claim, like all her other promises, had been nothing more than empty air, then her days were numbered.

"Have you told the others about the new rules?" Nazerel asked.

"Not yet. Most of this we can work around, but their ability to track us is a serious problem."

Nazerel nodded as he milled over the implications. There was no way around it. He'd postponed the inevitable long enough. The Sevrin problem needed to be solved *permanently*. "Why did she free you from the collar? It would have sent a more powerful message if you delivered your dire warnings while helpless."

"I think she only has one. She took it off me so we could use it on someone else."

Something in Flynn's voice, and the ambiguity of his statement, made Nazerel curious. "Who did you use it on?"

"Gerrod Reynolds."

That was so unexpected, Nazerel faced Flynn again. "Why did you collar Gerrod? He's been on Earth for decades and hasn't caused any trouble."

"Sevrin considered him a loose end and she hates loose ends."

"You killed him?" Nazerel was a mercenary. Death was his stock and trade, but he never killed needlessly and never without a damn good reason.

Flynn lowered his gaze and shifted his weight from one foot to the other. "I slit his throat, but he'd already started to teleport by the time she got the collar around his neck. He flashed out of sight, so we're not sure if we finished the job or not."

"There's no honor in such an act." His tone was tight with displeasure. "Why did you agree to do it?"

Flynn's gaze snapped back to his. "Your hands are far from clean, Nazerel. Don't pretend assassination is beneath you."

"I have taken lives during war or to prevent further atrocities. There is a difference between political assassination and pointless murder."

"You have also carried out the sentence on those who have earned the fate." Challenge dripped off every word.

"What had Gerrod Reynolds done to deserve death?"

"He ruthlessly seduced countless females for the express purpose of getting them pregnant. Our infamous notebook is filled with the daughters of Gerrod and this Dirty Dozen."

"Their actions were despicable, but they do not warrant death. Did he rape these women? Use a Mystic compulsion to make them want him? That was not my understanding of how they operated."

"If I'd refused, she would have left me collared and in a cage," Flynn snarled, but regret soldered just beyond the anger in his eyes. "Because I was willing to take the life of an aging reprobate, she now trusts me implicitly."

Despite the frustration raging within him, Nazerel backed off. They'd both known things would become progressively more complicated the deeper she took Flynn into her trust. Still, Shadow Assassins lived by a strict code of conduct. It was the only thing separating them from cold-blooded murderers.

It was obvious Flynn needed reassurance, so Nazerel said, "You did what had to be done. We must focus on the things we can control."

"And fight to regain control over the things we've lost," Flynn stressed.

"Agreed." He paused for a moment as he composed his thoughts. "Where is the collar now?"

Flynn began to fidget again. "Gerrod was still wearing it when he flashed. I'm not sure Sevrin has another."

"We have to find out what happened to him. If he ended up with the Mystic Militia, they could backward engineer the damn thing."

"Sevrin is frantically searching. I'll let you know if she finds out anything."

Nazerel nodded. *And I'll warn the men telepathically before I explain the new rules. Sevrin's guards are doubtlessly watching, waiting for us to react to the new routine. The men must seem suitably outraged without saying anything we don't want the guards to overhear.*

A wise precaution.

"Tell me about this new lab. How much of it were you allowed to see?" They always tried to maintain an audible conversation, hoping it would mask their telepathic exchange.

"It's huge. She said it had been under construction for the past two years. She also received three shiploads of technology and personnel from Rodymia. She's convinced the next attempt at transference will succeed."

And you have no idea where the facility is located?

I don't know how long I was unconscious, so I can't even guess how far we drove. My instincts tell me we hadn't gone far, but I honestly don't know.

Nazerel acknowledged the telepathic information with a subtle nod. "Let your mistress know I'd like to speak with her at her earliest convenience." *If I take this without argument, she'll know we're up to something.*

LYING ON HER BACK ACROSS the narrow bunk, Roxie extended her legs up the wall and considered her shoes. She loved boots with stiletto heels, owned more pairs than she cared to admit. But they were impractical for work so she tended to wear slip-ons or sandals. Today it had been both, a pair of slip-on sandals. Rather than providing her with a long, dangerous spike, the rubber soles and simple thong-style upper were utterly useless as a weapon. She was draped in chains, but they were strictly ornamental. Even if she tripled the strands and swung them like a whip, they wouldn't do any real damage. Could she strangle someone with a pair of pants?

The question made her smile despite the mind-numbing monotony.

"Can a person literally die of boredom?" she whispered to the ceiling.

She'd already counted the tiles twice and paced off the room over and over. There was nothing to look at, nothing to occupy her mind except useless speculation and an ongoing barrage of emotions. Her mental thrill ride started off with paralyzing fear. She'd been sure every sound in the hallway was Elias returning to ring her neck. Lord knows he was big enough to do it without breaking a sweat. But none of these men had harmed her since this nightmare began. In fact, Odintar had taken time out to ease her pain and Lor had been surprisingly diplomatic.

Gradually anger burned off the fear and anxiety required motion. She hadn't done anything wrong. They had no right to lock her up like a criminal! She prowled the tiny room, sitting, pacing, then pounding on the door again and yelling for attention.

No one came.

It took at least an hour for her temper to burn itself out. They obviously didn't give a damn or she wouldn't be locked in a cell. That was when depression and self-pity took over. She'd cried, cursed, then cried some more. Her life was a long series of unfortunate tragedies, one bizarre situation after another, and the only common denominator was *her*.

She'd never tolerated useless emotions, so the woe-is-me phase didn't last long. She needed information and she obviously wasn't going to get it if she continued to provoke her captors. She had no idea what they thought she knew or how long they intend to keep her, but cooperation made more sense than continuing to indulge her rebellious impulses.

The electronic lock popped, drawing her attention to the door. Then she heard the subtle scrape of a mechanical lock as well. Redundant safeguards. How comforting.

She didn't bother getting up. Instead she folded her hands behind her head and crossed her feet at the ankle.

Elias strolled into the cell and rewarded her with a startled expression. "You look—comfortable."

"I'd been standing on my head, but my arms got tired." Even upside down the man was easy on the eyes. Was that part of the strategy? Did they send gorgeous women to interrogate heterosexual men? Or was physical beauty a prerequisite for their organization. She hadn't seen an ugly person yet.

He sat several large foil packets on the table as well as a basic takeout carton. "I've come to barter."

"Really?" She swung her legs down and to the side, rotating her body until she sat on the edge of the bunk more or less facing him. "The only thing I want is out of here. Is that what we're bartering for?"

"One step at a time, Miss Impatience." His tone was almost playful. What happened to the drill sergeant who'd questioned her before? She wasn't sure which Elias she found more unnerving. "How about we barter for dinner?"

"Dinner? What happened to lunch?" She'd attributed the tightness in her stomach to stress rather than hunger. It seemed like he'd been gone for hours, but time always passed slowly when there was nothing to do. "What time is it?"

"A little after four, so we're early for dinner or late for lunch. Take your pick."

She looked at the assortment of packages on the table and then at her captor. "What are my options?"

"Well, these are MREs, standard field rations. They really have to be experienced to be believed. And this..." He motioned toward the takeout container. "Is a flame-broiled hamburger from a local sports bar with lightly seasoned, hand-cut home fries."

She started to say she was vegan, then realized she only punished herself with the claim. "And what do I have to do to earn the burger?"

"Call Jett and let him know you're fine and we're taking good care of you."

She laughed at the absurd suggestion. "But my mother taught me not to lie."

"He's worried about you and the call's already late. There's no reason for him to think the worst when you can—"

"What did he threaten to do? Post a notice on social media that I'd been kidnapped by spooks?" Jett could be fiercely protective when someone he cared about was threatened. It was one of the things she liked most about her unconventional friend.

"Something like that." Elias swiveled one of the chairs and sat, motioning toward the other. "Call him so you can eat while we have a civilized conversation."

The smell of the food was making her mouth water and all her stubbornness had earned her was a five-hour time-out. Besides, Jett was a worrier. If he'd been suspicious of their cover story from the beginning, he'd be frantic by now.

"He has no way of locating you. Even if he calls the most tenacious reporter on the planet, he'll just make himself look foolish."

"He threatened to call the media?" She chuckled. "Go Jett."

"Do you want him to be ridiculed and investigated? Good reporters do background assessments on witnesses before they pursue a lead."

She tensed at the subtle slur. Tattoos were becoming more and more mainstream, but the stereotype managed to linger. "Jett dyes his hair and is covered in tattoos so he must have a criminal record?" She sat down across from him and picked up one of the field ration packets. She'd heard horror stories about them, but she was still tempted to defy this pompous jerk. Sweeping generalizations always pissed her off.

"I don't want to argue with you and I didn't mean to insult your friend." He slid the takeout container closer, torturing her with the appetizing smell. "Make the call."

Elias might have annoyed her with his approach, but he was right. Jett didn't have a hope in hell of finding her and no one would believe him if he tried to go public with the story. She'd already put Jett and Tess in danger with her decision to work for Sevrin. Roxie would not let him pay the price for her willfulness.

"Fine." She huffed. "But this doesn't mean we're friends."

He handed her a compact tablet computer as he came around to her side of the table. "We had to use the satellite network. There are no phone signals down here."

"Down here?" She arched her brow at him, but he just shook his head. Were they underground?

"He's expecting a video call, and I'm expecting you to behave."

"Silly you." She took the tablet from his hand, trying to ignore how intimidating he was at close range. She was tall for a woman, but he seemed to suck all the space out of the room. She woke up the computer with a swipe of her thumb and found the video call programed and ready to launch. "How did you get his number?" Jett wasn't even his real name.

A ghost of a smile lifted one corner of his mouth. "Isn't that what spooks do?"

Probably the internet, she tried to convince herself as she activated the call.

Jett's image came onscreen after the first ring. "Thank God! I don't usually answer blocked numbers, but I thought it might be you."

"A little birdy told me you're being a mother hen, as usual." She hoped her smile was convincing and her hand didn't shake too much. There really was no reason for Jett to be stressed out by her misfortune. And the less he knew about all of this, the safer he'd be.

"Jillian promised she'd make this happen, but the two-hour window came and went and I still hadn't heard from you."

"They had to finish their tests before they could release me from quarantine."

"Quarantine?" Disbelief raised his voice half an octave. "What sort of weapon did he fire on us?"

"They weren't sure. That's why they're being so careful."

"But if it might have been contagious, shouldn't they have quarantined me too?"

She forced herself to snicker. "Feeling left out? You felt fine when you woke up, so I guess they knew you didn't have it." She paused for an elaborate shrug. "I don't know. It was a toxin not a pathogen, so we're both going to be find."

"I've been worried sick." And he looked it. His hair was a spiky mess and his makeup was smeared. Not like Jett at all.

"Well, I've been just plain sick. Nazerel's new toy did a number on my head. As I said, they've ruled out anything contagious, but they want to run more tests. They want to make sure nothing got scrambled in there. Lord knows I don't have any brain cells to spare."

"Yeah right." He finally smiled. "You're easily the smartest person I know. When will they release you for good? Do you need a ride home?"

"I'm not sure. It depends on the tests. And they'll deliver me safe and sound to my front door or they'll be hearing from my lawyer."

"Are you sure you're okay?" His gaze narrowed as he studied her face.

"I'm fine. Really."

"Okay."

"Now stop worrying about me. That's an order." He reluctantly agreed and Roxie ended the call.

"Nicely done." Elias took the tablet back and moved the takeout container in front of her.

She opened the container and inhaled. Her stomach growled so loud it made her blush. "You'd think I hadn't eaten in days not hours."

Elias returned to his side of the table and sat. "Now for the civilized conversation."

After setting aside the top bun, she picked up a ketchup packet. "Does that mean you'll finally answer my questions?" The food was still hot. He'd either microwaved it before he walked in or they weren't as secluded as she'd presumed.

Or he knew someone who could teleport.

She sighed. Elias really was her only hope for understanding any of this. She'd been desperate for answers ever since Sevrin walked into Unique Ink. It had been obvious from the start that something was *off* with Sevrin. It had been equally obvious that Sevrin had zero interest in explaining what was really going on. This was as close to understanding as Roxie had come and she couldn't afford to squander the opportunity.

"How many of the men did you tattoo?" His voice was deep and assertive without seeming confrontational.

"Ten or eleven. I'd have to check my records." She covered the burger with ketchup then replaced the bun. She was hungry, but she was also glad to have something to do with her hands. Something about Elias made her nervous. No, not nervous exactly, more like restless.

So much of her life had been filled with uncertainty and danger that an image had formed in her dreams, a strong, heroic man capable of vanquishing her enemies and protecting her from anything that even tried to upset her. As she grew older, and more lonely, her dream protector became something more, an aggressive lover capable of driving reality away with the force of his desire for her and only her. She never really saw his face, but he had a body just like Elias.

"And you never saw any of them outside the shop." His rumbling voice drew her back to reality.

She froze with the hamburger halfway to her mouth. "I thought we had that much settled. I'm not their girlfriend. They didn't pass me around like a communal toy. I gave them tattoos. That's all."

"Do you have phone numbers for any of them?"

"Half of them didn't bother with names." She quickly took a bite before his questions dried up her appetite.

He rubbed his jaw, obviously lost in thought. His eyes appeared particularly green as he stared through her. He was being almost friendly at the moment and still he was imposing. She dragged her gaze away from his rugged face and tried to concentrate on her food, but his image lingered in the back of her mind.

"You seem convinced that they've left town," he digressed. "Did they give you any idea where they were going?"

"No. And why are you fixated on the men? It was pretty obvious to me that Sevrin is their leader."

He shifted on the metal chair as his gaze moved over her face. "She's more familiar with Earth, so the men depend on her. But it's unlikely that any of them consider her their leader."

"If you say so." She took another bite and closed her eyes as she chewed. Ground beef had never tasted so amazing.

"Do you have any water left? I forgot to grab you a beverage."

She opened her eyes and wiped her mouth with the paper napkin that had been tucked inside the takeout container. "I'd kill for a cup of coffee."

"That won't be necessary." He stood and smiled down at her. "All ya have ta do is keep talkin' ta me." The Texas twang was back and it was a lethal combination with that sexy smile.

The jerk could actually be charming when he wasn't trying to be such a hard-ass. She'd finished the hamburger by the time he returned, but she was happily munching on the fries. He set down a large mug of steaming coffee and a pile of cream and sugar packets. He'd even remembered to grab a stir stick.

For half a second she pictured throwing the coffee in his face. It was as close to a weapon as she was likely to come. She shook away the notion. He'd be pissed off and she'd still be locked inside this room.

He chuckled. "Contemplating mischief?"

"Malicious mischief is more like it, but I talked myself out of it."

"Glad to hear it. We were getting along so well."

If he was willing to indulge her, she had all sorts of questions. "Who are these guys and why are they on Earth?"

"They're called Shadow Assassins. They consider themselves political refugees. We consider them fugitives."

"I had them pegged as foreign mercenaries. I just didn't realize *how* foreign." She added cream and sugar to the coffee then picked up the mug. "Are they wanted for specific crimes, or just being assassins in general?"

He hesitated, his gaze narrowed and bright. "Everything I'm about to tell you is classified. You can't tell Jett or anyone else. If you don't agree to this stipulation, we'll go back to our earlier dynamic."

"One-sided interrogation?"

"Yes."

"Obviously, I'll keep my mouth shut." As with Jett, no one would believe her if she started spreading tales about aliens and the secret government organization trying to apprehend them. She wasn't sure she believed it herself. Well, they were obviously aliens; no human could do what they did. But the rest was still an undefined conflict into which she'd stumbled.

"The Shadow Assassins operated on a planet called Ontariese until six or seven months ago. They were a closed society populated entirely of men. They enslaved their members with a combination of intimidation, logistics, and ritual beliefs."

"Like a cult?"

"More like a private army that had been brainwashed into obedience. The generation who was liberated from the Shadow Maze had all been born there. They knew no other way of life, had nothing with which to compare their Sacred Customs." He emphasized the last phrase with finger quotes.

"They literally lived underground?"

He nodded. "Those who couldn't teleport were prisoners of their own society."

"And those who could teleport? Like Nazerel. Were they allowed to leave whenever they wanted?" She couldn't even imagine what it would have been like to live without sunshine and rain-washed breezes.

"It's complicated and few of the specifics affect the current situation. Let's stay focused on the present."

"Fine by me." She hadn't meant the phrase to sound as snotty as it had sounded. His meandering explanation was just feeding her anxiety.

"Their way of life was no longer tolerated on Ontariese, so a small group of the Shadow Assassins came to Earth. We don't know when they connected with Sevrin or who contacted whom, but they're obviously working together now."

"Tell me about Sevrin." She pushed aside what remained of the fries, more than ready for this topic. Learning that the men were part of some bizarre secret society didn't seem real or particularly relevant. Her interaction with each of them had been superficial. Sevrin, on the other hand, had been terrifying. It would be a relief to know anything about her. "Is she from Ontariese like her men?"

"She's from Rodymia. There are three inhabited planets in their star system, Ontariese, Bilarri and Rodymia. The inhabitants of Rodymia are known as Rodytes and the current planetary ruler is Sevrin's uncle."

The revelation didn't surprise Roxie. Sevrin emanated power like no one Roxie had ever met, except for maybe Nazerel. "Oh my God, does that mean she has diplomatic immunity?"

He shook his head. "That only works when diplomats are in our country with our permission. She's an illegal alien in the truest sense of the word. However, no one is in a hurry to piss off a race of people more technologically advanced than our own. With one transmission to Uncle Quentin, she could summon a Rodyte army. We really don't want it to come to that."

Hungry for overall understanding, she didn't allow herself to pause over the details. She'd analyze the implications once she saw how all the pieces fit together. "You said Sevrin and the Shadow Assassins are working together. What are they trying to accomplish?"

"Shadow Assassins have abilities similar to Lor or Odintar. Sevrin is working on a way of transferring those powers to people who were born without them."

"Seriously?" He inclined his head, obviously expecting her disbelief. "You said she's 'working on a way' to do it. Does that mean she hasn't done it yet?"

"To our knowledge, none of her attempts have been successful—yet."

"Well, that's good at least." Her mind went blank, objecting to the rapid saturation of unbelievable facts. Aliens from two different planets were on Earth trying to create more beings like Lor and Odintar. She shivered. And what would they do when and if they achieved their goal? How would they use those superhuman abilities? "You said the Shadow Assassins already have magic powers. What do they gain by helping Sevrin?"

"They want mates with powers equal to their own, which in turn will increase the chances that their offspring will also be able to manipulate magic. As it is now, only a small percentage of their children end up with abilities."

He spoke of magic powers as if they were nothing special, nothing she should have a problem accepting. She couldn't deny what she'd experienced firsthand, but it was still hard as hell to digest. "The women on Ontariese can't manipulate magic?"

"Some can, but it would have been many years before the Shadow Assassins were allowed to claim a mate."

Claim a mate? She shivered again, yet this time the reaction felt warm and tingly instead of cold and unpleasant. Claiming her was what her imaginary lover did every time she summoned him to her dreams. "Why weren't they allowed to find mates?" She softened the phrase for her comfort, but Nazerel and the others definitely seemed more like the *claiming* type.

"Instead of going to prison, they were given mandatory years of service with the Ontarian military."

"Then Nazerel and his men are deserters? That's a serious crime on Earth."

"It is on Ontariese as well, but leaving the military without permission is a minor infraction compared to their other crimes. Shadow Assassins used to hunt their mates. They'd kidnap a female and take her to the Shadow Maze where she would be held until she had a child. If it was a boy, she was released while the child was kept with his father. If she had—"

"Wait a minute. They would keep women prisoner for a year or more?" She pushed to her feet and moved to the other side of the room. It wasn't much of a separation, but she suddenly felt threatened by the entire situation. "If these women were kidnapped, they didn't willingly participate in the breeding program. Were they raped over and over until..." Her voice broke and she furiously blinked back tears. It was too horrible to even imagine. She'd never been forced to have sex, but she knew what it was like to be helpless, powerless, utterly at the mercy of others. Her entire childhood had been one intolerable situation after another, and her teenage years had been even worse.

"They claim rape is abhorrent to them, that each woman was gradually seduced." She started to object, but he stopped her. "I'm not trying to justify any of this. I'm just passing on information. Personally, I'm right there with you. Even if it was seduction rather than rape, the distinction doesn't justify the rest."

"And after months of imprisonment and abuse, their reward was having their baby stolen from them?" She felt physically ill as if someone had just kicked her in the stomach.

He swiveled his chair to face her but didn't rise. She was glad he didn't try to touch her. She was holding on to her composure by a thread. Any physical contact at this point would have made it impossible to hold back the flood of emotions.

"It was a barbaric practice and it has been stopped on Ontariese." He spoke carefully and an emotionless mask took over his features.

Had they relocated their disgusting operation to Earth? That was the logical conclusion. Still, she was stuck on the specifics. "What happened if she had a girl?"

"Either both would be released or she would remain a prisoner and her captor would try again."

And if she couldn't conceive or she produced girl after girl? How long would they keep her—it didn't matter. It was no longer happening on Ontariese. But what about Earth? "Is this why they're here? Are they kidnapping human females?"

"They've taken it a step further. They're hunting mates and attempting to transfer their powers into the females. We've found six of their failed attempts, but there have probably been more."

Dread knotted her stomach so tightly her legs shook so she returned to the table and sank onto her chair. "What does all of this have to do with me?"

"That's what we're trying to figure out. If you'd been targeted as a mate, they most likely would have made their move already. But I don't believe in coincidence. Sevrin didn't just happen upon your shop. She doesn't do anything without a specific reason." He crossed his arms over his chest, prominently displaying his impressive biceps. "Now is there anything else you can tell me, anything that might help us understand Sevrin's motivation?"

She hadn't felt safe for months and Elias' story compounded her foreboding. Sevrin's interest in her had always felt personal, personal and *creepy*. She might be making the biggest mistake of her life, but she needed to trust someone, someone with a whole lot more power than she possessed. Elias had offered her information. It could all be bullshit, but she didn't think it was. Too much of what he'd said confirmed what she already knew.

"They get off on pain."

His gaze narrowed and he unfolded his arms. "I thought all you did was tattoo them."

"That's what I'm talking about." Why did he persist in putting her in bed with one or more of those muscle-bound lunatics? "Lots of people get a rush while they're under the needle, but it was like a drug to Nazerel and the others. They craved it, *needed* it. I think Sevrin was using it to keep them calm and under control."

"They were ruthlessly trained from birth to be impervious to pain. Maybe one of their strategies is learning how to process pain as pleasure."

That was a trivial fact, interesting yet unlikely to be helpful. He was obviously waiting for something more, something strategic. After a tense pause, she said, "Sevrin didn't trust Nazerel."

"We're aware of the friction, but what led you to that conclusion?" He twisted to the side and stood, anxious energy setting him in motion.

"She wanted me to spy on him for her, see if he was saying anything to his buddies that he wasn't supposed to share." They'd basically switch places. She sat at the table, chair turned sideways so she could watch him prowl about the tiny room.

"And did you?"

"There was a small problem with her wish." His arched eyebrow prompted her to explain. "I didn't speak their language."

His gaze bore into hers, sharp with sudden interest. "Did she have a solution for that complication?"

"Yeah, she took me to a hotel room and hooked me up to this machine. I'd never seen anything like it. The thing made me feel like crap for days afterwards, but it worked. I could suddenly understand all the obnoxious things they'd been saying behind my back."

He shook his head, clearly upset by something she'd just told him. "Language infusers have to be carefully calibrated for each user. She never should have used one in a hotel room."

Language infuser was the exact term Sevrin had used for the brain-scrambling device. Apparently, Roxie had been in more danger than she realized. "I feel fine now. Though unpleasant, the side effects were temporary."

"I'll ask one of the Mystics to scan you, make sure you're really okay." He pushed his hand through his dark hair, making the natural waves more pronounced. "Did you learn anything from Nazerel?"

"I learned that this *planet* was making him paranoid and he was sick and tired of *irrational humans*. The bizarre phrases, as well as the fact that I'd just learned a new language in less than a day, were what convinced me I was in way over my head."

"You're right about that. You stumbled over an interdimensional hornets' nest."

"Lucky me." She swiveled her chair back around so she didn't have to put up with his penetrating stare. "That's honestly all I know. Can I go home now?"

Chapter Three

Severin stood in the middle of a sprawling field of wind turbines. The rhythmic *whoosh* of the massive blades vibrated through her body and made the air sizzle with energy. As wind farms went, this one was small yet strategically located along US 93. She was less than an hour from Las Vegas yet far enough removed from the never-ending action to remain inconspicuous, almost invisible. No more dank warehouses or shabby motels. She'd always found it amusing to hid in plain sight.

Her new headquarters sprawled beneath her feet; its massive need for energy provided by the oddly graceful giants surrounding her. Wind farms had become so common along these barren stretches of highway that no one gave this one a second thought. A small maintenance building was the only overt sign of civilization, so there was nothing here to draw attention.

Construction of the underground complex had blended with assembly of the wind turbines. Large equipment was large equipment to the untrained eye. And human projects were notoriously ineffective, stretching on for years when they should have been completed in a matter of weeks. All of this worked to her advantage and would continue to mask her movements well into the future. Her guards used utility trucks and SUVs stylishly labeled with the Boulder City Energy Solutions logo. And she filtered enough money through the imaginary corporation to make it appear legitimate.

A supply convoy had arrived two weeks before, landing deep in the desert. Her staff had been shuttled from the landing area in sightseeing buses and they were only allowed to leave "the Farm" a few at a time, escorted by one of her guards. She'd assured them they weren't prisoners.

However, interaction with the indigenous population was grounds for immediate *termination*. A smile curved Sevrin's mouth as she pictured their faces. She'd used the word intentionally, leaving them to wonder if she meant she would end their employment or something more nefarious.

The laboratories and medical facilities were equipped with the newest and best Rodymia had to offer. She'd even tried to make the living quarters and common areas comfortable in an attempt to minimize restlessness. Besides, the faster each staff member completed their assigned task, the faster they could return to Rodymia.

"Everything seems to have settled into a routine below." Marat, Sevrin's head of security, walked out of the maintenance building and moved up beside her. Marat meant more to Sevrin than any of her family members. She depended on his wisdom, his steadfast calm. He was part mentor, part parent, and her only confidante.

"What about Orrit and Salidan?" She glanced up at him and paused. Usually she found character and experience etched into his wrinkled features. Today, he just looked tired. She started to ask him what was wrong then shook away the impulse. If she detected any weakness in Marat, he would demand that she replace him. Her safety was his purpose in life and he took the responsibility very seriously. "Have they stopped threatening to sabotage the program?"

"The warning from your uncle settled them down, at least outwardly. No one likes to be scolded by the Crown Stirate of Rodymia." He crossed his brawny arms over his chest and gazed out across the churning field of turbines. "Orrit is the instigator. Salidan follows his lead."

"Are they lovers?"

"I'm not sure. If they are, they're extremely discrete."

She walked toward the maintenance building and Marat fell in step beside her. "How close are their sleeping quarters?"

"Adjacent with one room separating them."

She arched her brow at that. "Close yet distant enough to leave some doubt." She had no problem with staff fraternization. The gods knew there wasn't much else to do on this primitive rock. However, knowing about such relationships could be advantageous when it came time to motivate a reluctant subordinate. In this case, Salidan had a bonded mate and Sevrin doubted the wealthy female would react well if she found out Salidan was offering his body to someone else.

Marat opened the door for her and she stepped inside the blessed coolness of the air-conditioned building. "Why did humans choose to populate an area of their planet that is so inhospitable?" She looked up at Marat and shook her head. "It makes no sense to me."

Marat chuckled. "Much of what humans do makes no sense to me."

A numerical keypad limited access to a room labeled "utility closet". Behind a sliding panel near the back of the long, narrow closet waited a second door, which required a facial scan. Only the élite members of Sevrin's staff had been registered with the security system. Everyone else required an escort into or out of the Farm.

The primary elevator took them to the commons, which was currently empty. Good. Everyone should be hard at work. There was a freight elevator as well, but it was located on the other end of the complex, closer to the storage areas.

"Do you have specific plans for this evening? Anything I need to know about?"

Before she could answer Marat, Flynn rushed into the commons, obviously agitated about something. "It is ridiculous that I must endure these indignities every time I leave this place." Anger tightened his features and made his voice snarl. A secret thrill raced through her body. She liked him best when he was like this, savage and impossible to control.

Always the consummate professional, Marat slipped away without another word.

Flynn advanced, yet she didn't back down. Soon they stood toe-to-toe. He glared down at her and she breathed in his aggression, allowing his strength to soothe her in ways she would never admit. All her life she'd worked to convince those around her she was strong and ruthless, a worthy successor for her infamous father. She didn't want a protector, didn't need to be sheltered. But just once, it would be nice to have someone at her side, someone strong and capable, someone she could depend on and trust. Like Marat, only much younger and more attractive.

"You're *earning* my trust," she reminded him. "That's an ongoing process." He made a dissatisfied sound, but didn't argue. "You were drugged the first time I brought you here. Today you were only blindfolded. My indulgence will increase as your cooperation continues."

He grabbed the back of her neck with one hand and banded her waist with his other arm, drawing her against him with one firm yank. "You know I'll punish you as soon as we're alone. Is that why you continue to provoke me?"

She concealed her arousal with a bored expression. If she let him simmer for the next few hours, their nightly session would be even more intense. "The security measures are necessary. I won't relent. Now what did you learn? How did Nazerel react to the new rules?"

Gradually his fingers loosened and he lowered his arms, taking one step back. "Nazerel wants to see you, explain his concerns face-to-face."

"His 'concerns.'" She laughed, already missing the firm pressure of Flynn's hands and the nearness of his warm body. She shouldn't allow herself to enjoy him so much. Depending on him for her pleasure gave him power over her. But she couldn't help the cravings of her body. Flynn was by far the most entertaining hunter she'd taken to her bed and they'd barely begun to explore the pleasure they could give each other. "He agreed to submit to the new procedures?"

"Of course not. He wants you to come to him."

"Well, the next time I have a reason for visiting Team Southwest I'll—"

"About the name. Nazerel has secured the allegiance of all the former Team West members. They are now members of Team South, so it's really just the new Team South house."

Labels were an incidental detail, yet the principle frustrated Sevrin. Every time she turned around, Nazerel found a way to rub her face in his authority. The men cooperated with her because there was no viable alternative, but they *chose* to follow him. "What about you? You're a member of Team West. In fact, you're the strongest remaining member of Team West. Why did you allow Nazerel to take over your team?"

"The men no longer trust me." His hungry gaze swept over her body as he added, "They know where my allegiance lies."

She scoffed under her breath. If only she were so certain of his allegiance. Like the others, Flynn was manipulating the situation to his advantage in every way he could. He might willingly pleasure her body, but he didn't trust her, sure as hells didn't respect her. "I'll deal with Nazerel. Did you inform the entire house or just him?"

"I told the team leader and he'll tell the men. It's not my place to manage his team."

"Then how do you know he told them anything? He's stubborn enough to ignore the new procedures and continue on as if nothing happened."

"In which case the guards you stationed at the Team South house will start shooting. Nazerel can be irrationally stubborn, but he's not stupid. He will never intentionally endanger his men."

"My men," she snapped. "You are all *my* men."

"Of course, mistress. It was just a figure of speech."

It wasn't and they both knew it. Nazerel was the true leader of the Shadow Assassins. She was just their employer. "I have work to do. I'll see you later." She dismissed him with an impatient wave of her hand.

She'd had enough of stubborn employees and insubordination. She was Rodyte royalty and people would start treating her accordingly or they would find out why the name Keire was whispered with fear and awe. Quentin wasn't as brutal as her father Pern had been. Still, anyone who underestimated a Keire was soon shown the error of their thinking.

Storming through the living quarters, she headed for Orrit's lab with long, purposeful strides. The research wing was on the right, medical facilities on the left, security and technology straight ahead. Four smaller labs surrounded Orrit's work area. Researchers and scientists moved freely between the five rooms, sharing information and assisting each other with complications. The sense of community was tangible. But then, she'd given them a common ground when she sent each a royal summons. They had been dragged away from their own projects, forced to abandon their families. They'd been transported to a distant planet and were basically captives until they'd each accomplished their goals.

And each despised her for her heavy-handed tactics. She didn't care if they grumbled and glared, as long as the produced results.

Orrit paused his holographic simulation as her entrance silenced the room.

"Leave us." She didn't need to say more, the others hustled out the nearest door.

"I'm not quite ready for a full report," Orrit told her as she approached his workstation. With silver sprinkled dark hair and perfect posture, he looked right at home in the orderly environment.

Her temper fizzled and her curiosity engaged as she absorbed the implications of his statement. "There's been progress since your last report?" That had been five days ago. How much could he have accomplished in less than a week?

"Significant." He slipped his hands into the pockets of his light blue lab coat as he glared into her eyes. "You wanted results. I got you results."

A chill teased down her spine and she paused to lick her lips. "Explain."

"My predecessor was on the right track, but her methods were too conservative." That didn't explain the nature of the progress, so she simply waited for him to continue. "Breakthroughs are so named because something usually breaks so that something else can survive."

"Stop being so damn cryptic. What have you done?"

"I've replicated the bonding agent and used it successfully in several live hosts."

Shocked that he would dare such a claim—unless it was true. She moved closer. Dr. Porffer, his predecessor, had been this close before. She'd thought she isolated the hormone complex that allowed Shadow Assassins to make genetic changes in their potential mates, but each time she attempted to use the synthetic version of the complex, the results had been disastrous.

"What sort of live hosts?"

His snicker was filled with derision. "As if you need to ask. I followed the established protocols to the letter. First rats, then primates, and finally humans."

She gasped, unable to suppress the reaction. "You've already tested this on humans. Why wasn't I notified before you began?"

"I wanted to be sure of my results before I reported my findings. Dr. Porffer thought she'd succeeded too." He slipped off his stool and moved around the raised table until nothing remained between them. He didn't approach her, just created a clear path between them. "I want to go home. It's insulting and demoralizing to be forced into servitude. I am a world-renowned geneticist. I deserve better treatment than this."

An apology slid toward her lips, but she stubbornly bit it back. She was *royalty*. It was an honor to be chosen to serve her in any capacity. "How were you able to accomplish this so quickly?"

"All you care about it results. Don't ask the question unless you're prepared for an honest answer."

Something usually breaks so that something else can survive. His words echoed through her mind, feeding her trepidation. How many Shadow Assassins had he butchered as he unlocked the secrets of their unique physiology? "How many?" Did she really want to know?

"Eleven."

She pressed her hand against her throat, barely smothering another gasp. "Where did you get eleven Shadow Assassins? That's more than half of those remaining on Earth." He couldn't have used the hunters. The two remaining suppression collars were securely locked in her private quarters. Without the collar's debilitating effects, the earthbound Shadow Assassins would have teleported away from danger. Orrit had to have snatched his test subjects directly from Ontariese. But when, how...

His smile turned snide and he leaned his hip against the workstation. "You doubt my resourcefulness? You're not the only one with well-placed connections. Salidan's bonded mate might not have royal blood, but her family is every bit as powerful as yours."

"Where did you get them?" Now she was the one glaring.

"They were on a training exercise launched from the City of Tears. I arranged for the fighters to be intercepted. Twenty Shadow Assassins were taken and the four instructors killed. Then their ships was blown up, making it look like an accident. Pieces of the instructors were littered among the debris to make the scene more believable."

"Until they scan the body parts and realize what's missing." It was a paranoid concern. Even if the Ontarians suspected foul play, assassination was a far more likely crime than abduction. Many on Ontariese had reason to hate Shadow Assassins. "You said you captured twenty. Where are the other nine?"

"Four are in a holding cell. The other five are in the infirmary. Dr. Utoff is relatively certain at least two of them will survive."

"Relatively certain? What does that mean? What exactly did your team do to them?"

Rather than reply, Orrit returned to his workstation and scooted his stool out of the way. For one infuriating moment, she though he was ignoring her questions and continuing on with his work. Then he manipulated the three-dimensional display. "Scans were insufficient. We needed direct access to the simplenata gland in their brains and, of course, their reproductive organs."

An image of the infirmary came into view. Tall, impossibly thin Dr. Utoff moved between the beds, checking readings and adjusting levels on various consoles. Five of the six beds were occupied by men. Actually, two looked to be little more than boys. She shifted her weight from one foot to the other, refusing to acknowledge the emotions compressing her chest. Three of the five males had bandages wrapped around their heads and she shuddered to think where else the poor men were bandaged.

"Which does Utoff believe will survive?" She didn't know why she cared. She shouldn't care. They were a means to an end, an end she'd pursued her entire adult life.

"It was impossible to access the simpenata gland without causing significant damage to the surrounding tissue. Utoff is squeamish about euthanasia, so he's basically waiting for those three to die. The other two tolerated the procedures well, but I'm not sure they'll want to live without their reproductive organs. Warrior types are strange about things like that. If they insist on death once they've learned what we've done, I'll dispose of them while Utoff is elsewhere."

Shocked and repelled, she just stared at the image. They'd been systematically mutilated, analyzed and dissected while they were still alive. And these were the lucky ones. Eleven others hadn't even survived the ruthless experimentation. Sevrin shivered as bile rose into the back of her throat.

Her reaction would have infuriated her father. *Keires are stronger than this. Keires have ruled for centuries because of our brutal convictions. Pull it together, girl!* His deep, demanding voice echoed through her memories.

Gradually, cold detachment spread through Sevrin, easing the pressure in her chest and turning her heart back to ice. They were criminals, *assassins*. At least this way their deaths had meaning. "And the human test subjects? How many are there and how have they tolerated the transmutation?"

Orrit made a quick adjustment to the display as he said, "This is the first female injected with the synthetic compound. Her transition began four days ago."

The image of a holding cell appeared, a pale blonde woman curled up on her side across the bunk. She stared across the room, her features devoid of expression. "Is her transformation complete? Is she just depressed or were there complications?"

Orrit shrugged and a lingering spark of guilt pinged Sevrin's soul. How could he be so indifferent to their suffering? Was the man incapable of emotion? "Utoff isn't sure. He's familiar with human physiology, but this procedure has never been done before. Her vital signs are stable, but she's been largely unresponsive for the past two days. Utoff has been unable to determine if it's a psychological response to captivity or if her brain chemistry was adversely affected by the transformation."

But the female was still alive and the mutation appeared to be stable. This was a much better outcome than Dr. Porffer achieved. "And the others?"

"There is only one, so far." He called up the image of a different holding cell. This female sat on the bunk, a tablet computer in her hands, absently scrolling through the pages of an electronic book. "Salidan injected her with nanites before we gave her the compound. The nanites were able to regulate the transition, making it less traumatic and creating a more stable result."

Sevrin had always thought nanites played an important part in the transformation. That was why she'd insisted that Salidan join the team. At first her uncle refused, insisting that he couldn't be without Salidan for even a few weeks. Salidan was brilliant, his work years ahead of any other nanotechnologist in their star system. Besides, Salidan's bonded mate was from the highest echelon of society. Not even the Crown Stirate angered those families without a damn good reason. As a last resort, Sevrin had reminded her uncle that completing this project had been her father's dying wish. It was emotional blackmail, but Quentin finally relented and issued a royal summons to Salidan. Apparently, Sevrin's instincts had been right. It seemed unlikely that Orrit would have progressed this far without Salidan's involvement.

"Both of these females are human-Ontarian hybrids?" she asked.

Orrit nodded as he deactivated his display. "Unfortunately, the male who's DNA we replicated was only marginally gifted, so neither of these females will have significant abilities. We wanted to perfect the process before attempting to incorporate the genetic pattern of any of the hunters."

"I understand." She was torn by the progress. They were closer to her goal than ever before and yet several intimidating obstacles remained. She wanted this so badly, she was almost afraid to hope. "We might have a ready supply of Shadow Assassins, but only a few are truly gifted."

"Yet that is the next step." He slipped his hands back into his pockets and moved to the corner of the table. "With your permission, I'd like to attempt a conversion using Flynn's DNA as a pattern for our formula."

She carefully guarded her expression and kept her tone conversational. "Will he be harmed by the procedure?"

Orrit chuckled. "None of us would dare harm your favorite pet, your highness. All I require is a blood sample and a reasonable amount of his ejaculate."

She nodded, having already revealed too much with her concern. "I'd like the female to be a human-Rodyte hybrid this time. Will that complicate the experiment?"

Again his amusement was obvious, the gleam in his eyes knowing. "It requires a different formula. Luckily, I'm almost finished with the

Rodyte version of the compound. Still, it makes more sense to introduce one new variable at a time. If a human-Ontarian female tolerates Flynn's pattern, I'll then attempt a Rodyte conversion."

"All right." He watched her silently, so she added, "You've done very well. I'm pleased."

Rather than the beaming smile she expected, he acknowledged the praise with a subtle nod and went right back to work.

MORGAN LOOKED UP FROM her laptop as Elias knocked on the doorframe to her office. The door had been open, as per usual, but Morgan had been engrossed in her task. As per usual too. "How's Roxie?" After a few keystrokes, likely to close the program, Morgan lowered the screen and folded her hands on top of the small computer.

Elias crossed to the chairs in front of her desk and sat. He wasn't sure how to answer. There was something about Roxie that bothered him. He was convinced everything she'd told him was true, and yet he hesitated to share what he'd learned. He felt an unmistakable need to protect her, though he couldn't identify the cause of his unease. He'd never lied to Morgan, never intentionally deceived her. So why was he tempted to do so now?

He wanted to smuggle Roxie out of the compound and stash her somewhere safe. Safe? He sighed. If Sevrin Keire sent one of the Shadow Assassins after Roxie, he'd be completely outmatched. It wasn't something a former Army Ranger cared to admit, but he wouldn't let his pride compromise his ability to protect her.

"Did you need something or were you just lonely?" Though Morgan's face remained serene, amusement shone in her bright blue eyes.

Most saw Morgan as cold and unapproachable. Elias knew better, had spent enough time with her to see beyond her professional reserve. Morgan was driven, but she wasn't cold. "Roxie wasn't surprised to learn she'd been tattooing aliens. She'd already figured out as much on her own."

"Had she figured out anything we don't already know?" Her thumb tapped out a rhythm on the laptop.

"Sevrin used a language infuser on her."

Her hands stilled then she slid the laptop aside. "Why?"

"She wanted Roxie to spy on the men and Roxie didn't speak Rodyte."

"Did it work?" She sounded skeptical though her suspicion didn't show on her face. "Was Roxie able to listen in on the men's conversations?"

"Yeah, she was."

"And did she learn anything interesting?"

"They said something about being stuck on this planet and not trusting humans. They didn't know she could hear them, so they stopped being careful about what they said."

"And they didn't say anything more damning than that? Are you sure she told you everything?"

Elias shrugged. "I was surprised she told me anything. She has no reason to trust me."

"Everyone trusts you. You just have one of those faces." She leaned back into her chair, her gaze turning distant and thoughtful. "No wonder Roxie has taken all this in stride. We're not nearly as scary as Sevrin. But it's not like Sevrin to be this careless."

"I agree." Elias scooted to the edge of his seat. "Which is why I can't help wondering if Sevrin had another reason for wanting Roxie to know what's going on."

Morgan's gaze narrowed and her lips thinned as she considered his theory. "What does Sevrin gain by enlightening a human tattoo artist?"

"Free ink?" When she just stared at him without changing her expression, he asked, "What if she's not human?"

"Roxie's not in the notebook. I already checked."

"That just means she wasn't a result of the Dirty Dozen's escapades. She could still be a hybrid."

"So ask Lor to scan her. We need to figure out why Sevrin is so fascinated with Roxie before we can even consider letting her go."

Pushing back his chair, Elias stood, but he didn't immediately leave the office. "Can I at least let her out of the holding cell? She really has been cooperative."

"Only if you shadow her. I can't have her wandering into restricted areas and our little tattoo artist strikes me as the type who would have no problem nosing around."

He agreed with her assessment of Roxie's nature, but hated the implications for him. "I can't babysit her indefinitely. I do have other responsibilities."

"Not anymore." The corners of her mouth twitched as if she was fighting a smile. "Roxie's your only assignment until further notice. Find out everything you can about her, favorite color, childhood friends, hobbies, favorite sexual position. Compile a complete background. No detail is irrelevant. We have to figure out why Sevrin wants her, and Roxie likely doesn't realize what she knows. Understood?"

"Understood." He tried not to sound as frustrated as he felt. He was good at interrogating certain types of prisoners. That didn't mean he enjoyed doing it.

"And try not to make it feel like an interrogation. Just get her talking and see where it leads."

"Got it." Trying to change Morgan's mind was always an exercise in futility, so he turned and left without further argument.

His footsteps dragged as he went in search of Lor. First and foremost, they needed to make sure Sevrin hadn't implanted more than the Rodyte language inside Roxie's head. Then he'd take her to the mess hall or officers' lounge. Roxie wasn't the only one going stir-crazy inside that holding cell.

Lor was in the communal office the Mystic Militia used more like a small lounge. Some of the technology cluttering the small corner desk had been given to them by Morgan, but more of it was obviously Ontarian and he could only guess at its purpose. Elias paused in the doorway, tapping on the open door as he'd done with Morgan.

"What can I do for you?" Lor asked as he looked up from some sort of holographic report.

"Do you have a minute to scan Roxie?"

"What's the nature of her aliment? Odintar might be a better choice."

"There's nothing wrong with her. Sevrin used a language infuser on her and we need to make sure nothing else was transferred during the process. Also, we'd like to know if she's a hybrid."

"Of course." Lor deactivated his display with a wave of his hand and joined Elias in the hallway. "Roxie spent hours alone with the Shadow Assassins, was she able to tell you anything useful?"

"Not really. She'd figured out they weren't human before she encountered you and Odintar, but she kept things strictly professional."

"Or so she claims."

Elias glared at Lor's profile. Why did everyone assume Roxie was sleeping with her customers? Probably because her customers were sex-starved men who didn't take no for an answer. It was hard to believe that none of the Shadow Assassins had at least attempted to seduce Roxie. "She tattooed them, nothing more." Echoing her words made Elias smile. When and why had he become her champion?

Roxie was the most compelling combination of rebellion and vulnerability. She wasn't the most beautiful female he'd ever seen. Morgan's features were closer to the classical standards of beauty, yet Roxie's unconventional appearance intrigued him. Not that her appeal mattered. The demands of this project made anything resembling a social life almost impossible.

He triggered the electronic lock with a palm scan then slipped his key into the deadbolt. No power outage was going to compromise the security of this facility.

Roxie was sitting on the bunk, right side up this time, with her long legs crossed in front of her.

"I am so damn bored! I'm going insane." She noticed Lor and tensed, swinging her legs over the side of the bunk. "Am I going somewhere?"

Lor moved forward, which forced Elias aside. "I am capable of more than teleportation."

"Yeah well, that ability is the only one I'm interested in. If you're not here to take me home, you can leave now."

Lor didn't react to her belligerence, at least not outwardly. "It's possible Sevrin used the language infuser to transfer something other than a language into your mind. If such is the case, wouldn't you like to know?"

She stared at Lor then looked at Elias, her gaze softly pleading. "What do you think she transferred?"

"We don't know that she transferred anything." She'd looked to him for reassurance, so he kept his tone easy and light. "We're just trying to figure out why she's fixated on you."

"This will not harm you in any way," Lor assured her.

She scoffed, throwing him an annoyed glance. "That's what she said too."

Lor clasped his hands behind his back. "I will not enter your mind without permission, but this is in your best interest."

Elias brushed past Lor and sat next to Roxie on the narrow bunk. He tried not to crowd her but the confines of the room made it impossible. "How much do you know about your parents?"

Her brow furrowed and she scooted back far enough to bring her bent knee onto the bunk between them. Okay, maybe he wasn't as much a reassurance as he'd thought. "What do my parents have to do with anything?"

"Were you raised by your biological parents?" Lor asked.

"I don't have to talk to you about this."

Elias leaned back against the wall in a futile attempt at appearing relaxed. "You don't have to talk to us about anything, but you're not going home until we figure out why Sevrin wants you so badly. Answering our questions and allowing this scan could bring you closer to going home."

"Fine." She huffed. "Scan me."

The questions had been meant to secure her permission for the scan, so he allowed the evasion. He motioned Lor forward, but the Mystic just smiled. Elias should have realized a Master-level Mage didn't need to touch someone to scan them.

She is definitely a hybrid, but her origins are murky. I sense Rodyte strongly. The other components are less clear. Lor's gaze narrowed as he pushed deeper or scanned more broadly. "I sense something—" Suddenly he rushed forward and pressed his hands to either side of Roxie's head.

She grabbed his wrists, trying to force his hands away. "Stop it! What are you—" She screamed and Elias jumped up, prepared to drag Lor off her.

The Mystic turned her loose and straightened. "There was a nano-tracker. I disabled it."

Elias whispered a curse under his breath. "But she's been here for hours."

"The signal wasn't strong. It couldn't have penetrated the shields."

"Morgan still needs to know. This is technically a breach in security."

Lor nodded. "I'm heading back in that direction. I can inform her if you prefer."

Elias took one look at Roxie's pale face and wide uncertain eyes and returned Lor's nod. "Please do."

"Wait." She came alive suddenly, scooting to the edge of the bunk. "Did you sense anything else? Was my brain damaged by the infusion or that tracker thing?"

"I sensed no damage and the nano-tracker was the only anomaly." Lor offered her a belated smile. "You're fine."

Elias waited until Lor left to speak again. "Would you like to go for a walk? I'm sure you're sick of this room by now."

"Walks generally lead back to where they started. Are you going to lock me up again as soon as you're finished *walking* me?"

He smiled. Her spirit was much easier to deal with than her depression. At least it was for him. When she turned fearful and uncertain, he wanted to wrap his arms around her and comfort her in completely unprofessional ways. "That's the offer. Take it or leave it."

"Oh, I'll take it." She hopped up off the bunk as if it were electrified. "Anything's better than staying here."

They were in the middle of the dinner hour, so the mess hall would be packed and he couldn't take her outside without revealing clues about their location. Maybe that wasn't such a bad idea. The compound was in the middle of nowhere. It might do her good to realize any escape attempt would be pointless.

He scanned open the door and motioned her out into the hallway. Her steps were quick and purposeful, yet she took in her surroundings with obvious interest. There wasn't really much to see in this section of the complex, well-lit corridors leading to offices and store rooms. All the good stuff was kept in the high-security zones.

She didn't hesitate until she reached the first intersection. Then she glanced up at him and asked, "Where to?"

Left was a more direct route to the main elevators, but the corridor also led past the mess hall. If Roxie caused a scene, Morgan would insist she stay locked up. He turned right, his fingers lightly brushing the small of her back, which was left bare by her cropped tank top. She looked up again as awareness pulsed between them, alive with tension and electricity.

She allowed his touch, neither twisting away from nor pressing into the light contact. "Why did you ask about my parents?" She shifted her gaze back to the hallway ahead of them, but the awareness lingered.

Her skin was soft and warm, beckoning further exploration. He wanted to venture under her shirt, caress her back and shoulders as he pushed the fabric higher. But he resisted temptation, stubbornly keeping his hand at the small of her back. "I think you know why."

"You think I'm an alien."

"No." He paused for a smile. "I think one of your parents was. Tell me about them."

She hesitated, obviously uncomfortable with the subject. "I was raised by my maternal aunt. I know nothing about my father."

He quickly guided her past the living quarters and into the lesser used corridors. Their steps echoed off the walls, making the area seem abandoned. "What happened to your mother?"

"Hit and run. The police told us the driver was likely drunk, but Aunt Shelia never believed them."

Pain rippled through her words and he nearly let the subject drop. But his assignment was to compile a detailed background on Roxie and they had barely begun. "What did your aunt think happened?"

Roxie glanced up at him and then away. "She thought it was deliberate, that Mom was murdered."

Her tone hinted at skepticism. All he saw in her eyes was grief. "Did your mother have enemies, someone who benefited from her death?"

Anxious energy sped her steps, taking her body just out of reach. "I was only six when it happened and Aunt Shelia was a mess. She pulled it together enough to take care of me, but she was never the same."

They reached the secondary elevators and Elias summoned a car. Without physical contact she felt very far away. Still, she was too tense now for Elias to risk touching her again. He kept his questions conversational. They were just two strangers getting to know each other. Hopefully, Roxie wouldn't figure out that she was still being questioned. "What was your aunt like before your mother's death?"

"Fun-loving and happy." She followed him into the elevator, staying just out of reach. "After Mom died, she never smiled and seemed really paranoid. We moved at least once a year and never kept the same phone number. She was convinced someone was after us, that the people who murdered Mom were going to get us too."

They stepped out of the elevator and he hurried her away from the transport hangers. Keys to all of the vehicles were kept under guard, but he wouldn't put it past Roxie to know how to hotwire a car. Unless her appearance and demeanor were a total façade, but that didn't seem likely. "Except for continually moving you around, did she provide for the rest of your needs?"

"I was clothed and fed, but she completely checked out as I became more self-sufficient."

Despite his determination to remain objective, his gut clenched. They'd barely scratched the surface of her past and already he could sense a creeping darkness, a foreshadowing of the horrors to come. "That couldn't have been healthy. Many adolescents require more supervision than children."

Her lips curved into a smile, but regret shadowed her gaze. "I was a regular hell-raiser during my teens, but Aunt Shelia had nothing to do with it. I have no one to blame but myself for all the crap I went through."

Her insistence revealed more than she realized. She obviously felt guilty about the choices she'd made, yet some part of her still longed for her aunt's attention. "Is she still alive?"

She shook her head, but offered no other information.

He peeled back the emotions and reviewed the facts as he led her out a side door of the small above-ground building. Her mother had died under suspicious circumstances and her aunt never again felt safe. "Did your mother and Shelia share both parents?"

"Same mother, different fathers." Even in the shade created by the structure, the desert setting was oppressively hot. Roxie stood beside him and looked around, taking in the endless arid vista with a combination of wonder and dread. "Are there even roads out here?" She crossed her arms over her chest and pressed her back against the side of the building as if she were trying to hide from the heat.

"SUVs are advisable, but there are dirt roads. Did you ever meet any of your grandparents?"

She shot him an annoyed look and shook her head. "Why is my genealogy so fascinating to you?"

"During one of our raids, we recovered a notebook with information on the women the Shadow Assassins are targeting." It was bait. He'd reveal a little to gain a whole lot more.

Her eyes rounded and she turned toward him, her shoulder pressed against the wall. "Am I in the notebook?"

"No, but the women who are have one thing in common."

"They're all part alien?"

"We call them hybrids, and yes, when Lor scanned you just now, he confirmed our suspicion that you're more than human."

"Could he tell what sort of alien..." She shook her head and pushed off the wall. "This is too weird." She walked to the corner of the building and stared out into nothingness. "My mother slept with an alien."

The utter disbelief in her tone made him smile. Considering all they'd thrown at her, she was coping remarkably well. "It's possible she had no idea what he was. As you've seen, they can be pretty damn convincing when they want to appear human."

She turned as he approached, her eyes wide and shimmering. "Was Aunt Sheila right? Have they been chasing me my entire life?"

"I don't know." Very slowly, he placed his hand on her upper arm. She didn't flinch or turn away and his pulse sped up.

"I was so relieved when Sevrin told me they were leaving. I just want this to be over." Gradually, she seemed to melt into him, pressing her forehead against his shoulder while only allowing the merest hint of contact with the rest of his body.

"You're safe now," he whispered, gently stroking her hair. "We'll make sure no one can harm you."

"I found her, you know. She was in the bathtub, water running, but the radio wasn't on. She always turned on the radio when she showered. I know it was staged."

It took him a minute to realize she was talking about Sheila. Her mother had been hit by a car, so she had to be talking about her aunt. "Did you tell the cops?"

Her head shifted back and forth, but she didn't look at him. "I'd just turned fifteen and was decked out in Goth makeup. They didn't believe a word I said."

He wrapped his arm around her waist and slowly pulled her against him. She tensed, shivered, then relaxed into the embrace, and Elias could hardly breathe. She felt so tiny pressed against him, small, yet soft and warm.

The last thing he wanted was to continue his questioning. He wanted to comfort her, drive away the painful memories, not rub her face in them. But this was his mission, his obligation, and it was important that they understand Roxie's connection to the enemy.

He swallowed past the sudden dryness in his throat and forced out the next question. "Where did you go? Did you have any other relatives?"

"Group home," she whispered. "I stayed eleven days then realized I didn't need that sort of bullshit." She kept her face pressed against his throat, but he made out every heart-rending word. "This hallelujah couple ran the place and did their best to maintain order, but most of those kids had been in the system all their lives. They knew nothing but intimidation and violence."

It didn't take a clairvoyant to figure out where this story led. He didn't want to hear it, didn't want to think about Roxie being harmed in any way. But it was obvious she needed to talk and needed someone to listen. That rational was easier than admitting he was still doing his job. "Why did you leave?"

Her arms tightened around him and her breath shuddered out against his skin. "The two oldest boys cornered me in a shed and told me I had to blow them or they'd beat the shit out of me. I opted for the beating, but two days later they came after me again."

She didn't elaborate and his hands clenched into fists. It was too easy to picture a younger, more rebellious Roxie trying to fight off two older boys. He had to work hard to keep his embrace supportive. His anger would only add to her pain. "Did you tell anyone what they'd done?"

"What they *tried* to do." Her voice was stronger now, though her hair concealed her face. "I went sort of crazy the second time and gave even better than I got. I left them both dazed and bleeding on the floor of the garage and didn't look back. I stuffed my things into a backpack, 'borrowed' some money from the hallelujah woman's purse, then hit the road. Aunt Shelia had taught me how to avoid attention and how not to leave a trail."

He eased her back, needing to see her face. "You've been on your own since you were fifteen?"

She blinked back tears though miraculously her cheeks remained dry. He shouldn't be surprised by her composure. She'd had many years to learn how to suppress emotion and focus only on survival. "Life on my own wasn't that much different. Like I said, Aunt Sheila checked out long before she died."

"But where did you stay? What did you do for money?"

"Do you really need to hear it?" She pushed against his chest and twisted out of his arms. "Street kids only have two options."

"Drugs or p-rostitution?" He stumbled over the last word. It was a common enough story. It had just never felt personal before. They weren't speaking in abstracts, describing the unfortunate reality no one could seem to change. This was Roxie's life, what she'd endured, how she'd survived.

"I wasn't about to sell myself, but I had to eat." She stood beside him again, leaning back against the wall. And with each word she retreated deeper into a protective indifference. "I started out as a courier and pretended I didn't know what I was delivering. Then one of the dealers, a guy named Smoke, noticed me. And it wasn't the sort of attention I wanted to attract."

He braced himself for the worst. Stories like this never had happy endings. "What did you do?"

"I was about to take off again. I wasn't willing to whore myself for anyone. But he had a girlfriend named Jodi. She was literally a swimsuit model. I couldn't figure out why he'd want a skinny, foulmouthed, street rat when he had someone like her. One day I got brave and told her that Smoke had been eyeing me for weeks. She laughed and promised me that his interest wasn't sexual."

"Then what did he want?"

"He wanted a street-smart girl with the sort of face and figure that would allow her to stroll into high-class clubs and exclusive parties without raising an eyebrow. Jodi had done the job for a while, but he didn't want her directly involved with the drugs anymore."

"But he had no problem with you being involved?"

She shrugged away his concern. "I was already involved. Besides, I wasn't sleeping with him."

"Expensive nightclubs and private parties sound like a huge step up from the streets."

"No kidding. They cleaned me up and refined my speech until I could pass for a rich party girl. I was still a courier, but now I drove a Mercedes and traveled with a body guard."

The pieces were starting to fit together, so he tried to steer the conversation back toward the present. "How did you go from being a high class courier to owning Unique Ink?"

Chapter Four

The past pulled at Roxie like a silent vacuum. She'd made so many mistakes, so many bad decisions, and yet she'd survived. She'd staggered out of the darkness with her soul mostly intact. Wasn't that an accomplishment to be celebrated?

"I broke the first rule of surviving as part of a drug ring." Why was she telling Elias all of this? He wanted to know about her connection to the Shadow Assassins, not her misspent youth.

"What rule is that?"

"Never use the product." She looked up at him and sighed. How could such an intimidating man be so easy to talk to? He was solid muscle from head to toe, yet his eyes were kind, patient. Maybe he'd slipped something into her coffee that made her talkative. She'd known Jett and Tess for months before she told them about any of this.

"Is that even possible? That would be like working for a rock band and not liking music."

"I never stayed at the parties after the package was delivered and most deliveries were made before the real partying started. I avoided it all whenever possible."

"Then why did you start using?" There was no condemnation in his tone, just calm curiosity.

That was part of the reason she kept talking. Elias didn't judge, didn't make her feel ashamed or foolish. Still, she wasn't completely blind to what he was doing. This wasn't a first date. He didn't want to know her better. He was trying to figure out why Sevrin had targeted her. And Roxie wanted to know too. Maybe an outsider would see something in her past that she was too emotional to understand. "A particularly nasty customer insisted that I sample the goods and I wasn't in a position to refuse. My body guard got me out of there before any real harm was done, but I liked the way the drugs made me feel. I *really* liked it."

"Are we talking cocaine or something worse?"

"The deliveries were usually a mixture of substances, so I tried all sorts of things. I'd seen what crack and meth can do, so I never went near either. My poison of choice was good old-fashioned cocaine. Well, I was pretty fond of ecstasy too." She shook her head and pushed away from the wall. "I don't even know why I'm telling you all this. It has nothing to do with the alien invasion."

He lightly caught her arm and drew her gaze to his. "You can't stop in the middle of the story. The aliens aren't going anywhere." He was so damn appealing with his green-gold eyes and teasing smile. The distinct waves in his dark hair made her want to run her fingers through the soft-looking strands. How could anyone resist his lazy charm? "How'd ya get out? Once you're in that deep, it's harder than hell to make a clean break." When he relaxed and become engrossed in the conversation, his Texas roots crept back into his speech. She'd always thought the accent sort of annoying, but Elias made it sound sexy.

"My break wasn't even close to clean." She eased her arm out of his grasp and stared out across the desert. She felt empty like their surroundings, dry and nearly void of life. "I got swept up in a police raid with a purse full of our best products. I didn't have a criminal record, but I was in the system, so it didn't take them long to figure out who I was. They told me if I provided them with names and locations of all the pivotal players in our network, they'd send me to rehab instead of jail."

"Did you cooperate?"

She glanced at him with a soft smirk, but inside her heart was breaking. "Their interrogator was almost as good as you are. I've always been a sucker for the soft approach. Besides, I was so strung out by then I didn't know what I was doing. They convinced me Smoke would kill me even if I kept my mouth shut. They were probably right. He was a ruthless son of a bitch." She released a long, ragged sigh as an image formed within her mind, an image that frequently haunted her dreams and filled her with bitter regret. She saw silky dark hair, kind brown eyes, and the perfect body of a swimsuit model. "I felt guilty as hell helping the cops. I know drugs destroy lives, but Smoke and Jodi rescued me from the streets. They took better care of me than my family had."

"You were a valuable commodity. Smoke was protecting his investment."

"I know." She fought back a wave of grief, cold and hollow like the echo of an emotion that had long since done its damage. "They picked up Jodi and several of the other curriers the same night they caught me. They promised they'd leak several different stories so Smoke and his bosses wouldn't know who gave them up. I didn't tell them much. I didn't *know* that much. No one was stupid enough to tell me anything important. But I provided the missing pieces to a puzzle they'd been working on for months, maybe years. Before it was over, they'd dismantled one of the largest drug networks in the Southwest." She lapsed into silence, unable to find words capable of explaining what came next.

"Did Smoke or one of the others come after you?" Elias reached out for her again, but she wasn't ready to be touched. Even after all these years the wound was still raw and painful.

She shook her head as her lips began to tremble. "The cover story worked a little too well. Jodi's body was found in an alley a few days later. Her tongue had been cut out."

"I'm sorry." He pressed his hand against the wall beside her shoulder, his body easily within reach.

All she had to do was turn toward him and accept the comfort he offered, but she didn't feel worthy of comfort. With another unconvincing shrug, she concluded, "Jodi had been kind to me, protected me from more abuse and danger, and she paid for my weakness with her life."

"It wasn't weakness to cooperate with the police. They left you no choice."

A sharp, humorless laugh escaped her throat. "Says my current interrogator. Maybe you're the one in danger. Dead bodies tend to pile up wherever I go."

"I'll risk it." He caught a strand of her hair and wrapped it around his finger. How many ways could he find of touching her without actually touching her? And she wanted his touch, ached for the shelter of his strong arms. But she didn't deserve compassion, much less comfort. "Were you still a minor?"

"No such luck. I'd turned eighteen three months before the raid."

He released her hair as his warm gaze moved over her face. "So they sent you to rehab?"

"I told them the punishment had to be more severe or it would seem suspicious. But I ended up with this bleeding-heart judge who felt like the system had failed me."

"I can't imagine why," he flared, his expression suddenly fierce. "The system *did* fail you. You survived the only way you could."

She shrugged again, trying to recapture her protective detachment. Compassion shone in his eyes and it was obvious he wanted to kiss her. She just didn't understand why. They'd known each other for less than a day. How could he possibly have any sort of feelings for her? She was his prisoner. "The judge suspended my two-year sentence with the condition that any infraction, regardless of how minor, would reinstate the sentence. Then I went to an in-house rehab center for ninety days. When I was released from rehab, I was on probation for the remainder of the two years." Succinct and factual, she recited the events like a shopping list. Though unspoken, she hoped the message was clear. She was finished talking about her past.

"When did you become a tattoo artist?"

Fine. She could compromise. This was still technically the past but the events were more recent and more applicable to the current situation. "Drawing had always been an emotional outlet for me, sometimes the only one I had. I'd had more than one teacher tell me I had raw talent. But it was my probation officer who encouraged me to take classes at a community college. The art classes led to private lessons and my interest in tattooing flowed naturally out of my love for art, and my nonconformist personality."

A soft smile curved his lips without parting them. "Didn't you win a TV contest or something?"

She nodded. "I came in second on the show, but it helped me build a fan base and develop name recognition. That made it possible for me to secure financing so I could open Unique Ink."

"Well, no one can deny all you've accomplished. You should be proud of how far you've come."

"I am." Still, it was hard to escape the shadows cast by her past.

He pushed off the wall and motioned toward the door behind him. "Ready to head back inside? It's hot as hell out here."

"Not a chance." She was more than ready to change the subject, however, so she turned and faced him. "You just heard my entire life story. I want to hear yours."

He laughed. "I'm no mystery. I'll tell you anything you want to know, but I'm getting dehydrated out here. Let's find somewhere cooler so we can finish our conversation."

"Cooler" shouldn't be hard to find. He was right. It was hot and miserable outside. They retraced their steps, using the same elevator to return to one of three belowground levels. She hadn't seen much of the complex except hallways and locked doors, but it was much bigger than she'd first thought.

"Does this place have a name?" She did her best to sound casual.

"We call it the Bunker."

"Fitting. And how many people are stationed at the Bunker?"

He chuckled. "I guess I should have qualified my offer. I'll tell you anything you want to know *about me*. Anything else has to be approved by Morgan and she hasn't been in a generous mood lately."

Morgan? It took her mind a second to produce a face to go with the name. When the image formed, she grimaced. The snooty red-haired bitch. Poor Elias. "How long have you worked for Morgan?"

"I've worked for the program for two years. Morgan has been my direct supervisor for the last nine months."

Roxie was more interested in his story than hallways she'd already seen, so they walked much faster now. "Why did you decide to join the military?"

"I come from a long line of military professionals. Dad made it to general before he retired. Mom started out as an Army medic and later became a nurse. She's retired now too. My grandfather was a Navy pilot. Both my brothers are in the military. One's a Navy SEAL the other a Marine. It never occurred to me to pursue any other career path."

She'd labeled him a soldier when she first saw him, so the information didn't surprise her at all. "Which branch did you join?"

"Army. I served for three years then became a Ranger. I'd been a Ranger for six years when, much to my father's chagrin, I was recruited by the FBI. He still refers to it as my demotion."

Many military personnel had a general distrust of government agents. Even she knew that. "How'd you end up chasing aliens?" They turned down a wide corridor she was pretty sure they hadn't used before. New territory was good and anything was preferable to being locked in the holding cell.

"I was working a kidnapping case when I first crossed paths with Morgan." He ushered Roxie inside a large cafeteria. The kitchen staff was tearing down and the subtle disorder of the tables and chairs indicated recent use.

"Where is everyone?"

"The kitchen stops serving at six thirty. Looks like we just missed dinner."

She chuckled at the evasion. "I'm still digesting that hamburger, but you didn't answer my question."

"Some of the staff have gone back to work, the rest are in the living quarters or one of the common areas like the gym."

"Does everyone eat at the same time?" She looked around, trying to gauge the maximize occupancy of the room.

He leaned down and whispered in her ear, "Just because a room seats over a hundred doesn't mean all of the chairs are used."

They helped themselves to fountain drinks then sat at a six-person table near the door, away from the clatter, and curious stares, coming from the kitchen.

"Sorry for the distraction. You were in the FBI, about to meet Morgan." She took a sip of her cola as she waited for his tale to resume.

"Morgan claimed to have been dispatched from a different office, but her involvement didn't make sense to me. I tried to be courteous and respectful, but it was obvious she was trying to take over."

"Morgan trying to take over?" She laughed, savoring the simple pleasure of cool air and a refreshing drink. "I can't even imagine it."

"I know her better than you do. Morgan isn't always such a hard-ass."

Her brow arched as she fiddled with her straw. "I'll have to take your word for it. She's certainly been all business with me."

"Military men will take advantage of any hint of weakness, especially in a female commander."

"Wow, that's not sexist at all."

He leaned back and crossed his arms over his chest, tension creeping into his expression. "It might be sexist, but it's reality. She's had to work really hard to earn the respect of the people she commands."

"Does someone have a crush on his CO?"

He smiled. "Is someone trying to annoy me?"

She returned his smile then paused for a sip of soda before digressing to the original subject. "You were working a kidnapping case."

"All I'd been told was that a seven-year-old girl had been snatched from her school by someone the child knew. Morgan told me she believed the child's father was the culprit and I had nothing that indicated otherwise."

"Did you find the little girl?"

"We did and not a moment too soon. Her father had her in this amazing ship and was just about to take off. The entire thing went down so fast Morgan didn't have time to warn me, so you can imagine my shock when I was faced with an honest to God spaceship."

"Dad was an alien?"

He nodded. "We returned the girl to her mother and deported Dad. Then Morgan and I had a nice long talk. She told me she had an opening and wanted to know if I'd consider working for a black ops organization focused on mitigating conflicts with extraterrestrial life forms. I already had a top level security clearance, so the transfer was simple. As far as the rest of the world is concerned, I still work for the FBI. Occasionally I'm asked about my current assignment, but no one is too surprised when I tell them I can't discuss it."

He made it all sound so common, so ordinary, while Roxie still felt stunned. "How many planets have visited Earth?"

"Generally it's the inhabitants who visit not the planets," he corrected with a playful smile.

She glared at him. "You know what I mean."

"The inhabitants of thirty-two different planets have allowed us to know of their visits. We suspect there have been quite a few more."

Her head shook in automatic denial. He had no reason to lie about the statistic, but her mind still resisted the information. "How long has this been going on?" Sevrin and her boys weren't an isolated incident. All sorts of aliens had been toying with humanity.

"Hundreds, perhaps thousands of years."

"Then why doesn't the public know about this. They/we have a right to know."

"Humans still slaughter each other over lines on a map. Can you imagine how they/we would react if they realized aliens were living among us? Most of the visitors are just curious. They study us for a while and then move on. There have been some creative trade agreements, but for the most part, we don't have much to offer people who have mastered interstellar travel. It would be like us negotiating a treaty with cavemen. We're just not that interesting to them."

"And none of the visitors have been hostile? None have posed a danger to..." Her words trailed away as she answered her own question. "Shadow Assassins pose a significant danger to the general public and still they're kept in the dark."

"It's necessary," he insisted.

"I don't agree with all the secrecy."

"Humans are volatile and unpredictable. This sort of threat would panic the general public and endanger even more lives. The Shadow Assassins are focused on hybrid females. Nothing is gained by including the general public in the conflict."

She wasn't sure she agreed with him, but there was no point in arguing about it. "So did anything I tell you help you figure out why Sevrin wants me?"

He rubbed his chin as he considered the question. "I'm not sure. I don't think she's interested in anything you've done. I think the answer lies in who you are."

"Which brings us back to my parents?" She sighed.

Before he could answer, Morgan came bustling into the room. She was out of breath and tendrils of her upswept hair had come loose to frame her face. "I've searched this entire base for you. Where the hell did you take her?"

"Just outside the transport hangers." He shoved his drink aside and scooted back from the table. "What's the matter?"

Morgan smoothed her hair back from her face and took a deep breath. She glanced at Roxie but continued to converse with Elias. "May I speak with you in the corridor for a moment?"

Roxie bristled. "If this has to do with me, I want to hear it. People need to stop talking about me and start talking to me."

"All right." Morgan rested her hands on the back of the chair directly across from Roxie, but made no move to pull it out. She didn't want to give up the power position of standing while others sat. "Lor assured me that the nano-tracker he disabled wasn't strong enough to transmit through our shields. However, Sevrin would have lost contact with the tracker as soon as Lor teleported you here."

"That's not my fault. It's not as if I asked to be kidnapped."

"I'm not ascribing blame." Morgan paused and her expression turned thoughtful. "The longer you remain here, the more suspicious Sevrin will become."

"What are you thinking?" Elias seemed particularly guarded, as if he wasn't happy with Morgan's interruption.

"Sevrin knows we've had contact with Roxie, that can't be avoided. But with everything that happened immediately after Jillian left Unique Ink, it's likely Sevrin won't conclude that we've had Roxie this entire time."

"What are you talking about?" Afraid Morgan would just ignore her, Roxie looked at Elias for the explanation. "What happened to Jillian after she left my shop?"

"Sevrin tried to murder Jillian's father, but she sensed his peril," Elias told her. "They brought him here and Odintar was barely able to save his life."

"Lor and Blayne were out searching for Nazerel," Morgan muttered to no one in particular.

"So were teams of my men," Elias added.

Morgan's gaze narrowed as she focused on Elias. "Has Nazerel ever seen you? Does he know who you are?"

"There's no reason why he would. I'm a powerless human. I'm not worthy of his notice." The sarcasm in each word made it obvious he didn't agree with the assessment.

"So we send Roxie home with you at her side. She can tell everyone you've been corresponding online for months, but this is the first time you've actually met. She was upset by the dustup at her shop and asked you to fly in from wherever you live and give her some moral support."

"You're talking *about* me again. If you're deciding my next move, don't you think I might want to participate in the planning?"

"Sorry." A smile lifted the corners of Morgan's lips, but her gaze remained hard.

"The story might fool Sevrin," Elias said, "but Jett saw me at Unique Ink."

"Damn," Morgan muttered. "We have to do something. Sevrin will investigate why the nano-tracker stopped working. We need to be there when she does."

Elias shook his head. "She won't come herself. There have been too many close calls lately. She'll send someone to repair the chip or implant a new one."

Roxie pressed her fingertips against her temples and rubbed. They couldn't seem to help themselves. As soon as they started strategizing, she just faded from view.

Morgan shook her head. "I'm not so sure. Sevrin has been unusually hands-on where Roxie is concerned. If we'd realized this connection sooner, we could have utilized it better."

"I'm not a 'connection,'" Roxie snapped. "Just say what you mean. You want to use me as bait to catch the most dangerous person on Earth."

Morgan didn't deny it. "This is an opportunity we don't dare pass up. You could be our way—"

"I am not an opportunity. I'm a person!" She shot to her feet, toppling her chair in her haste. "Can't you see me. I'm standing right here." Elias stood and tried to wrap his arm around her, but Roxie twisted away. "Stop it! You're just like her. All I am to either of you is an opportunity, a worm for your frigging hook." For the first time in years tears trailed down her cheeks. She angrily wiped them away, but knowing they'd driven her to tears only upset her even more. "Put me back in my cage. I want no part of this."

Morgan started to say something, but Elias silenced her with a look. "Come on. I'll take you back."

He held out his hand, but Roxie crossed her arms, stubbornly tucking her hands against her sides. She would not be lulled by his fake compassion. He didn't give a damn about her. He was worse than Morgan. At least Morgan didn't play these cruel games.

They returned to the holding cell and Roxie moved inside, feeling desolate and alone. He knew better than to invade her space, but he lingered in the doorway. "We're not trying to be insensitive, but time is running out. There are almost three hundred names in the notebook. We can't possibly protect them all. Our only hope is to cut off the head of the snake before it strikes again."

"I won't be your sacrificial lamb." Even as she spoke the words her heart rebelled. If she could keep someone else from being abused, or save even one life, wasn't it her responsibility to try? "Go away." He'd dragged her through her past and left her bruised and bleeding. She just wanted to be alone.

"I'd be at your side at all times and the Mystics would be ready to flash in at the first sign of trouble."

"Then why not have a Mystic pose as my lover? Aren't they more capable of protecting me than you are anyway?" It was a cheap shot, but she had to take it. Pain like this demanded company.

His shoulders tensed and his lips thinned. "Unfortunately, all of the Mystics have recently claimed their mates. Sevrin would know it's a setup if she saw one of them with you."

"You'll figure out something. I have faith in your creativity." She crossed to the bunk and lay down, presenting him with her back.

"LET ME TALK TO HER." Jillian paced the Mystic Militia's small office, obviously furious at what she'd just learned. Roxie had been in their custody for two days now and still she refused to relent. Odintar, who was leaning against the front of the desk, didn't look any more at ease with the direction Morgan had chosen than his agitated mate.

Elias shook his head. "No visitors, except me. Morgan wants—"

"I don't give a damn what Morgan wants," Jillian snapped. "Roxie hasn't done anything wrong. It's ridiculous that she's being treated like a criminal. No wonder she won't cooperate with you. You've handled her all wrong."

Elias hadn't begun to "handle" Roxie, but that was the next step in Morgan's plan. She wanted Roxie to realize what was at stake, that her stubbornness was putting others at risk. Most of all, Roxie needed to understand that her services were *required* not requested. Morgan had given him permission to use whatever means necessary—cajoling, intimidation, even seduction—to enlighten their reluctant guest.

"Roxie's the best chance we have, but she's scared," Elias admitted. "I'm going to help her understand that she'll be protected at all times."

"And how are you going to protect her from a Shadow Assassin without allowing us in the house?" Odintar challenged. "I don't think you understand how fast they are, especially Nazerel. He could flash in and take her from you before you realize he's there."

Jillian stilled and her gaze began to smolder. "That's what Morgan wants, isn't it? She isn't baiting a trap; she wants them to take Roxie to their new headquarters. Oh my God, that woman is cold."

He found it hard to defend Morgan when he happened to agree with Jillian. This new strategy revealed just how desperate Morgan had become. It was merciless and reckless, and Roxie deserved better. "We're just using their strategy against them, only our tracking system is more sophisticated."

"Really?" Odintar hadn't moved but his voice grew more aggressive. "What sort of tracking system can't be jammed or removed."

"We'll inject her with an isotope that emits a harmless form of radiation. The radiation can be tracked over long distances. It doesn't transmit any sort of signal, so most shielding is ineffective."

Odintar pushed off the desk and stalked toward him. "So let's say her plan works flawlessly. Nazerel snatches Roxie and flashes her to their new headquarters. What then? If the warnings from Ontariese are accurate, three sizable Rodyte ships activated the hyperspace gates leading to this sector. Sevrin could have an army protecting her by now. We just don't know."

"And we can't gather recon until we find the new facility." Elias' response was just as passionate.

Jillian walked to Odintar's side and joined the prosecution. "And Roxie is just supposed to endure whatever they do to her while we're checking out the situation? How long should she enjoy Sevrin's tender mercies? Two days? A week? Several months?"

"I'm open to suggestions." They were out of options, had been for weeks. "If you oppose this plan, offer us another? We've tried standing around and hoping for a break. We're going to have to make something happen if we ever want this to end."

Jillian looked at Odintar and silently shook her head. "I hate everything about this, but he's right. We have to do something."

"We cannot force this on Roxie or we're no better than they are," Odintar insisted. "If solitude has not cleared her head, then try another strategy, but you must find a way to make her see reason."

Elias laughed. "Have you ever seen two stubborn females locked in a power struggle? Roxie will let the world burn just to spite Morgan. This stopped being rational shortly after it began."

"Let me talk to her." Jillian's tone was softer this time, yet no less insistent. "You're Morgan's right-hand man. Roxie won't respond to you."

Elias sighed. Morgan was being as irrational as Roxie. And Odintar was right; isolation had only reinforced Roxie's stubbornness. "All right. Give me a few minutes to set things up. I'll have to loop the surveillance feed and distract the guards."

ROXIE GLARED AT THE door as she heard the familiar sounds of someone intruding on her solitude. Elias was the only one allowed to see her and she wanted nothing to do with him. He was Morgan's lap dog and whatever appeal he'd possessed had been eclipsed by his willingness to follow irrational orders.

"Hey, stranger."

She'd prepared her best scowl, but Jillian stepped through the doorway rather than Elias. "What are you doing here?"

Jillian smiled. "Does that mean I'm not welcome?"

"That depends. Does Morgan know you're here?"

"She doesn't and Elias is risking dismissal by countermining her direct order."

It was about time he grew a pair. In the past two days, he'd brought her food, had taken her to the women's locker room so she could shower and provided her with a change of clothes. If a charming ensemble that looked like a cross between hospital scrubs and a prisoner's uniform could be called clothes. Still, he seldom bothered to stick around and keep her company, and he'd made it obvious he wasn't open to compromise. She agreed to bait their hook or she would rot in this cell forever.

"Where is he?"

Jillian's smile widened and she took another step into the tiny room. "Should I go get him? I thought you'd be glad to see a familiar face."

"Is your face familiar? Are you even Jillian Taylor?"

"In the flesh. I promise." She moved to the foot of the bunk and sat.

Roxie folded her legs in front of her, giving Jillian a little more room. "How long have you been spying for *them*?"

"If by 'them' you mean aliens, I recently learned that I'm one of them. Like yours, my father wasn't human."

She'd said that as if it were an established fact. "Lor told Elias I was a hybrid. I was under the impression that they needed a blood sample to determine the specifics."

"Blood, hair, saliva, anything that contained DNA."

Her gaze narrowed and she shook her head. "Meaning they've already done the test." Another invasion of her privacy. These people really needed to reevaluate their treatment of prisoners. Even if she'd done something wrong, which she hadn't, they still needed to treat her like a person rather than a reluctant tool.

"It was pretty rude, I agree, but would you like to know what they found out?"

Roxie's instinct was to say no, to disassociate herself with anything associated with Morgan. But such a refusal wouldn't punish anyone but herself. "Sure. Tell me what they learned."

"Your father was a hybrid, half Rodyte and half Bilarrian. Your mother was primarily human, but they detected traces of Bilarrian as well, probably from a grandparent."

Roxie waited for the information to have an impact. Her mother was "primarily" human and her father was a hybrid. Shouldn't the knowledge make her feel somehow different? But they were just words, meaningless words. "All right. Thanks."

They lapsed into silence as Roxie stared across the room. She felt like a stranger in her own life, an onlooker forced to watch a really depressing movie.

"Why did you apply for the receptionist job?" Roxie asked as the silence became oppressive. "You seemed shocked when you first saw Nazerel. Didn't you know he was one of the men I'd been tattooing?"

"I was shocked. Like you, we'd heard they'd left town. I had no idea he'd be there."

"And the job? What were you hoping to learn?"

"Anything new, anything helpful. We knew you'd been tattooing Shadow Assassins. We had no idea you'd been contacted by Sevrin herself." Jillian sighed and pivoted so they basically faced each other. "We're out of options. We've exhausted every lead, explored every clue, and none of it has led us to Sevrin."

"I don't want to sound like a heartless bitch, but Elias said they want to behead the snake before she strikes again. If they use me to get to her, how is that any different than just waiting until she strikes to move in? Either way there will be one more victim."

"Maybe, and maybe the hunters would have gathered six or seven more before we found even one. Would you be okay with that? We're in a lull right now because Sevrin just moved her operation to a new facility. As soon as that facility is operational, they will start up all over again." She waited until Roxie looked into her eyes and then went on. "I've seen the results of their failed experiments. Those innocent women mutated, becoming hideous echoes of humanity. And then they died in agony."

Jillian was pulling at Roxie's heartstrings, using pity in an attempt to control her. "They might have been horribly deformed when you found them, but how could you possibly know if they were in pain when they died?"

"The last three victims were still alive when they were found. Would you like to watch one of the videos?"

"No!" Roxie scrubbed her hands over her face. She'd known this was inevitable ever since she returned to the holding cell. She wasn't the type of person who could look the other way while someone suffered and died. "This is so unfair. Why do I have to be the one to—"

"We didn't choose you. Sevrin did." She reached out and touched Roxie's hand. Their gazes locked, Roxie's hostile, Jillian's warm and compelling. "I thought my life was over when my leg was crushed. Dancing was all I knew, all I cared about. Nothing has ever been more painful, or more frightening, than letting go of my old life. But I had to let go before I could embrace something new and amazing. This fight is important. We need your help and it has to be soon."

"I'm afraid." The admission slipped out between her trembling lips.

"Of course you are, but Elias is strong and competent, and he'll be backed up by the Mystic Militia. You won't be doing this alone."

Roxie covered her face with her hands, knowing the fight was lost. She was paralyzed by fear and uncertainty and yet she knew she would act anyway. She'd put herself in danger, offer herself as a willing sacrifice, so others could escape Sevrin's cruelty.

Warm hands grasped her arms and pulled her up off the bunk. She couldn't say when Jillian left, but Elias stood in her place. "You okay?"

"No." She wrapped her arms around him then pressed even closer as he encircled her with his arms.

"I won't leave your side." He stroked her hair and shifted his body so their contrasting shapes more closely aligned.

She was his assignment, his mission, but it didn't seem to matter to her affection-starved body. He felt wonderful wrapped around her and all she could think of was *more*. She licked her lips then eased back far enough to look into his eyes. "We're going to have to convince everyone we're lovers. How do we sell that when we've never even—"

His head dipped and his mouth covered hers in a bone-melting kiss. Soft yet insistent, his lips guided hers apart and then his tongue teased its way inside her mouth. She clutched his back, enjoying the bunch and flex of his muscles. His taste filled her mouth and his scent became more familiar with each ragged breath.

Her head started spinning and she tried to forget where she was, that they were likely being watched, and this was still a job to him. She sank into the kiss, allowing anger and fear to flow out in a tingling rush of sensation.

"Okay," she sighed when he finally released her, "so that won't be a problem."

He took her by the hand and led her out of the holding cell. "Chemistry is defiantly not a problem, but we need to rehearse our story."

"Where are we going?"

"My quarters are more comfortable. I didn't think you'd mind."

She hesitated, heart thudding wildly in her chest. Just like that, did he expect her to spend the night with him? "We're *pretending* to be lovers."

A sexy smile bowed his lips. "All I'd planned to do was talk, but I'm more than willing to explore this attraction if you think we need more practice."

One kiss had left her weak and tingly. She didn't want to consider how malleable she'd become if they did more than kiss.

He chuckled at her panicked look. "We can go back to the mess hall if you honestly don't trust me to keep my hands to myself."

"I trust you." It was herself she didn't trust. Even while she'd been furious with Elias, she'd been fascinated by him, anxiously awaiting the next time he'd stop by her cell. And she'd used naughty fantasies about him to fill the time while she was alone. She'd imagined them indulging in all sorts of forbidden pleasures—always instigated by him. But they'd been fantasies, harmless indulgences with no consequences or regret. "I just didn't want you to misinterpret my willingness to be alone with you."

"We'll construct our cover story and nothing more."

His quarters were four times the size of the holding cell with a neatly made bed in one corner and a sitting area near the door. Everything was organized and immaculate, in keeping with his military background.

"Lies work best when they're as close to the truth as possible," he began. "It's a lot less to remember."

She watched him move through his private domain, calm and confident, each action controlled. "So you're from Austin."

"Yes, ma'am." He tipped an imaginary hat. "I'm career military, so I move around a lot, but Austin's my home."

"Are you still in the Army?"

He thought for a second then shook his head. "It's unlikely I could get leave on such short notice. Better make me a security consultant. That way I can set my own hours. Lots of ex-cops and former GIs go into private security."

"Okay. Let's see, why don't we say I own a tattoo shop." A smile automatically appeared as she began to relax. She shouldn't be this comfortable with him, but there was something about Elias that made her feel safe. And safety was something Roxie hadn't experienced a lot of in her life.

He sat in one of the upholstered chairs and motioned her toward the other. "Have you ever been married?"

She shook her head as she took her seat. He was right. This was infinitely more comfortable than the holding cell "Have you?"

"I was engaged once. We lived together for a couple of years, but she couldn't take all the secrecy. She broke it off a few weeks before the wedding." His expression didn't change, but his voice grew tight, nearly growling.

"We need a different reason. That doesn't work unless we admit you're with the FBI."

"All right. We'll say it happened while I was still in the Army. She couldn't take all the uncertainty, never knowing where I'd be deployed or how long I'd be gone."

"That makes sense." They might be constructing a factious background, but it was offering her another glimpse into his past. "Did you take the breakup hard?"

"I've never been that angry in my life, but it was the right decision. The marriage would have been a mistake."

Despite his calm expression, she could sense his pain. Right decision or not, his ex-fiancée had hurt him badly. "I'm sorry."

He shrugged and the emotional cloud seemed to dissipate. "It was a long time ago."

"I'm still sorry you had to go through that."

Their gazes locked and awareness escalated, pulsing between them as the silence lengthened. She wanted to touch him, or more specifically, she wanted him to touch her. She wanted him to pull her out of her chair and back into his arms. It was going to be really hard to remember they were just pretending.

He cleared his throat then blinked, severing the invisible tether. "What about you? Any serious relationships?"

She took a deep breath and looked away from his face. Those steady hazel eyes saw too much and penetrated too deeply. "I have trust issues. I tend to expect the worst from people and they seldom disappoint me."

"That's understandable, but sad. And it sounds like you just haven't found the right person yet."

They'd fallen back into a natural comradery. He really was easy to talk to, and wow could he kiss. She'd never been with a man who was so assertive, so confident. It was exciting, yet intimidating. All of her other relationships had developed gradually, simmered for a time then faded away.

This wasn't a relationship! They were *pretending*. "So we met online, flirted for several months, and I called you in a panic after I was released from here. Jett will want to know where this place is. What do I tell him?"

"You had a blinding headache when you arrived and you were blindfolded on the way out."

"He won't like it, but he'll probably believe it. When did you arrive? Wait, my car is still at Unique Ink. How did I go pick you up?"

A secretive smile parted his lips, relaxing his features and making him look younger. "Your car is in one of the transport hangers. I had one of my men go get it last night."

"Good thinking." It must be nice to have "men" at one's beck and call. She envied his authority for only a second before another implication took shape in her mind. He'd *presumed* she would give in and agree to bait their trap. How arrogant. But what other conclusion could he draw? This program had no oversight, no one to hold them accountable for their actions. Or if they did Roxie didn't know about it. Morgan could have kept her locked up indefinitely and no one would have known or cared. She shivered. Power like that invited corruption. It was dangerous. "Did your man leave a note or something? Tess and Jett will think my car was stolen."

He offered her a guilty smile that did little to ease her misgivings. "I might have told him to let himself in so he could snoop around for your purse. I was pretty sure it was in your shop somewhere."

More evidence to prove her point. These people broke laws without a second thought. Just like Smoke and Jodi. "It was in my desk drawer."

"I know." He reached in his pocket and pulled out her phone, which had been in her purse. "And I might have sent a couple of texts to Jett and Tess, letting them know you had a surprise for them."

He'd done it so her friends wouldn't worry, and to pave the way for their deception. Did his good intentions excuse a criminal act? "Ever heard of breaking and entering?"

"That only counts if you get caught."

She tried to smile but it came out more like a grimace. Ever since her arrest—and Jodi's death—Roxie had played by the rules. She'd worked hard to remain focused and productive. Besides, if Roxie screwed up even once, broke any law for any reason, she'd go to jail. And Jodi's death would have been meaningless as well as tragic.

Needing a distraction from her thoughts, she pressed the power button on her phone. She wasn't getting a signal now, which wasn't surprising. They were three stories underground. She scrolled through her missed calls and text messages. His presumption was still annoying, but she was relieved to see how skillfully he'd defused the situation. "I'm glad you're on my side." She looked at him so he'd realize she meant it as she added, "You're too comfortable breaking the law."

Someone knocked on the door, postponing his reply. He crossed to the door and pulled it open, momentarily blocking Roxie's view. "What's going on?"

"Is Roxie with you?" Morgan asked, her voice sounding oddly tense.

He swung the door all the way open and motioned toward Roxie.

Without moving from the doorway, Morgan looked at her and said, "Gerrod, Jillian's father, promised us information in exchange for a new identity."

Morgan was talking to her instead of talking about her. This was an improvement. "Why did he need a new identity?"

"Because Sevrin tried to kill him," Elias reminded her.

"One of the things he promised to explain was Sevrin's connection to you." Morgan's expression remained grim.

"Can you trust him?"

"At this point, he has no reason to lie."

Tension coiled around Roxie's chest, making it hard to breath. "What did he say? Why is Sevrin obsessed with me?"

Chapter Five

Forcing herself not to squirm, Sevrin closed her eyes and savored the warmth of Flynn's strong hands as they moved over her body. This was what she craved, what her treacherous body needed. Yet each moment of surrender amplified the echoes from her past. Her father's voice insisted that control equaled power and compromise was for the weak. Anything she wanted, she better be ready to take and she must always be willing to make sacrifices.

"You seem distracted." Flynn fisted the back of her hair and tilted her face up. "Who are you thinking about?"

She opened her eyes and fought back a smile. Flynn was a handsome devil, with symmetrical features and a body shaped by genetic engineering and decades of discipline. But underneath his superficial glares and whispered commands, there was something almost insecure about him. He was like a guard dog that had been beaten once too often. He was just as likely to curl into a protective ball with his tail tucked between his legs as to attack.

Rather than admit that the ghost of her father was tormenting her again, she brought up the first believable subject that popped into her mind. "I was wondering what Roxie Latimer was doing tonight. Are you jealous?"

"I'm jealous of anything that intrudes on our time together. But why are you so obsessed with that human?" Flynn buried his face in the bend of Sevrin's neck, his teeth lightly scraping. "And if she's so important, why did you leave her behind?"

Flynn had Sevrin pressed against the wall in her bedroom. She was finally surrounded by an apartment worthy of royalty. Her quarters at the Farm were spacious and well-appointed, providing her with a level of comfort she hadn't enjoyed since leaving Rodymia. The furniture was sleekly modern, the decorating tasteful, and her bed was large enough to accommodate two, perhaps even three people.

The thought made her smile. She could just imagine how Flynn would react if she invited someone else to participate in one of their sessions. He was delightfully possessive and willing to demonstrate his displeasure. He'd already made her strip down to her underwear, but he seemed to be in no hurry to get her naked. "Roxie is right where I need here, for now. She only thinks she's been left behind."

Without releasing her hair, he used his other hand to unfasten her bra. "Are you sure she's where you think she is?"

She tensed, splaying her fingers against his chest. "What are you talking about?"

He swallowed with obvious difficulty and glanced away from her face. "I haven't seen her for the past two days."

"What?" She shoved him back then hissed as he inadvertently pulled her hair. His fingers released a millisecond later and her bra slipped down her arms. Unconcerned with her nudity, she didn't bother catching the undergarment as it sailed toward the floor. If the frustration twisting his expression was any indication, he hadn't intended to tell her even now. "She hasn't been at work for two days?"

"It was easier to keep track of her when I could enter the store. Her car was there to begin with, so I thought she was just laying low after all of the excitement the other day. But her car isn't at her apartment either. I'm not sure where she is."

"And you didn't think this was important enough to mention?" She put her hands on her hips and glared up at him. He absently cupped one of her breasts, but she slapped his hand away. With blinding speed, he spun her around and dragged her arms behind her back. Sevrin tugged against his restraining fingers as his free hand moved boldly over breasts. "Let. Go."

"Don't want to." He caught one of her nipples between his thumb and forefinger and squeezed. She gasped then slammed the back of her head into his chest. He chuckled, but didn't release her. "I think you misbehave, so I'll have no choice but to spank you."

"I am not in the mood for our games. This is important." She made her voice snarl, but her core melted and her inner muscles fluttered, desperate for the demanding fullness he was sure to give her. "Now let go of me."

He tensed for a moment then pushed on with reckless indifference. "I need this and so do you." With her hands still locked at the small of her back, he propelled her toward the bed. "You can stop being stubborn and enjoy it or grit your teeth until it's over. I honestly don't care which you choose." After kicking her feet apart, he bent her over the bed and dragged her panties down around her knees. Then he slowly pushed his hand between her thighs, testing the level of her arousal. "Yeah," he chuckled. "You're not into this at all." His fingers slid easily over her desire-soaked folds, each touch echoing his mocking tone.

She renewed her resistance, needing the strength of his hands as much as the arousing caress of his fingers. "If you can't control yourself, then get it over with."

He laughed again and drove two fingers deep into her aching core. "You've never seen me lose control, princess. Trust me, you'd remember."

Already the rhythmic tension of an orgasm gathered around his fingers. She sucked in a breath and forced her muscles to relax. She needed him to command her pleasure, but she wasn't willing to reveal how readily her body obeyed. "Roxie is incredibly important. We cannot lose track of her."

He shifted his fingers to her clit, leaving her empty and aching. "I thought you tagged her when you used the language infuser on her."

A strangled moan escaped her throat as he slowly tugged on the puffy little bundle of nerves. Damn, he was good at this. Maybe too good. "The tracker is malfunctioning." She tensed as she heard her own words. The device error had seemed like a minor annoyance, something that required attention, yet hadn't triggered her protective instincts. But paired with Flynn's observations, the malfunction was much more suspicious. Unique Ink was Roxie's life. She was never inattentive to her business. "I thought we'd kept the Ontarians too busy to worry about an insignificant human. Maybe I was wrong."

Flynn's hand came down hard on her naked ass cheek. Sevrin yelped then groaned as tingling heat spread through her lower body.

"Pay attention," he snapped.

"But we—" He spanked her again and pleasure burst with shocking intensity, crawling across her nerve endings until her entire body seemed to pulse. She trembled, helpless to do more than gasp as the spasms went on and on.

He released her hands, and half a second later, his cock drove into her still clenching body. A fresh wave of sensation crashed over her and she cried out. She'd never been with anyone who could make her come so fast or so hard. He grasped her hips with both hands and filled her with strong, steady thrusts.

"Again." He growled the word into her ear then bit her lobe hard enough to make her curse. "Let me feel you come."

She fought the sensations this time, determined to make him work for it. When she didn't immediately obey, he eased one of his hands between her thighs and fingered her clit again. She tossed her head, intentionally whipping his face with her hair. The wilder and more aggressive he became, the more she liked it.

Suddenly he pulled out then lifted her off her feet and tossed her onto the bed. She rolled to her back and tried to kick him as he joined her on the bed. He yanked her legs apart and bent her knees to her chest.

"Beg me." His dark gaze drilled into hers as he held her legs open.

"Fu—"

He cut off her words with a punishing kiss and rubbed against her, dragging his shaft over her clit without entering her hungry body. Her inner muscles clenched, intensifying the emptiness inside her. She bucked, trying to align their bodies so he would have no option but to fill her again.

She pulled his hair and he paused long enough to trap her hands above her head. Gods she loved it when he held her down and pounded into her like he would die without her.

"Beg me." He whispered the command against her lips as his hips continued their sensual movements.

"No. You're already much too arrogant."

Pulling back far enough so he could see her body spread out beneath him, he took his cock in his free hand and positioned it over her clit. "You love my arrogance. Now beg me or I'll leave you like this, wet and empty, desperate for another taste of this." He pushed just inside, giving her a teasing hint of fullness.

She bucked wildly, tossing her head as anger and frustration surged through her. "In me. Please." The plea slipped out without her permission. She hadn't meant to give in, at least not this easily!

He filled her slowly this time, forcing her to feel how tightly she stretched to accommodate his thick length. He pushed deeper and deeper, not stopping until his pelvis pressed against hers. "Now isn't that better?" He brushed her hair back from her face, his gaze warm and caressing. Despite his outward aggression, his expression was surprisingly tender.

She needed to find out what had happened to Roxie. If the Mystic Militia had gotten their hands on her, it would spell disaster for Sevrin. She was about to voice her concerns when Flynn decided to move. He pulled nearly out just as slowly as he pushed in. She drew her legs up along his sides, resting her heels on his muscular back. He covered both her hands with his, interlacing their fingers. They stared into each other's eyes, sharing emotions neither dared to acknowledge. Then he moved faster, sliding over and into her, claiming her body and forcing rational thoughts from her mind.

TOO ANXIOUS TO REMAIN seated, Roxie stood up. This nightmare was supposed to have ended when Sevrin left town. Roxie wanted it to be over more than anything. Still, understanding Sevrin's motivation should make the situation more tolerable. Wasn't information supposed to be empowering? Then why was her heart racing and her mouth so dry she could barely swallow?

"Has Elias explained who Sevrin is?" Morgan asked, still loitering in the doorway to Elias' living quarters.

"Her uncle is a ruler on their planet." Rodymia. Their planet was called Rodymia.

"He isn't *a* ruler, he's the Crown Stirate, the ultimate authority for the entire planet."

"What does her pedigree have to do with me?"

"Why don't you come in and sit down. You're making me nervous." Elias closed the door behind Morgan then leaned his shoulder against it as she joined Roxie. There were only two chairs in the grouping, and the bed was on the other side of the room, which left Elias nowhere to sit.

Roxie sank back onto her chair but Morgan hesitated. "I'd love to break this to you gently, but we're rapidly running out of time." She motioned Elias toward his chair and positioned herself so she could see them both. "I have a lot to explain, so please keep your questions to a minimum."

Though annoyed by the request, Roxie only nodded.

"According to Gerrod," Morgan began, "your mother was a war bride. Do you know what that means?"

Roxie shook her head. If Elias mentioned it, she didn't remember what he'd said. He'd told her so many things in the past two days, much of it had blurred.

"Bilarri and Rodymia have been at war for centuries. Hostilities ebb and flow, but the war has never officially ended." When Roxie said nothing, Morgan went on. "Rodyte warriors capture Bilarrian females and force them to bear their children. The children are then termed battle born."

"It sounds like the Shadow Assassins."

"The Shadow Assassins were founded by a powerful Rodyte warrior," Elias told her. "Many of their practices are similar."

"Let's stay focused." Morgan clasped her hands behind her back, as she often did during briefings, likely to maximize her height and make her shoulders look broader. "The people on Bilarri can manipulate magic."

"And those on Rodymia can't. I know. Elias told me."

"What else did you tell her?" Morgan asked Elias. "I don't want to repeat what you've already covered."

"Start with Pern," Elias suggested.

Morgan nodded. "Pern Keire was the first ruler with balls enough to be honest about what he wanted. He was openly hostile toward anyone with paranormal abilities, while he frantically worked to restore such powers to his people."

"Who is Pern Keire?"

"Sevrin's father," Elias clarified. "He's dead now and his younger brother Quentin is on the throne."

Roxie nodded, not wanting to slow down the process.

"Sevrin was not his only child, but she was by far his favorite," Morgan continued. "She was born to his royal consort, the Rodyte version of a queen."

"And who gave birth to the rest of his children?" Every question she asked postponed the specifics of her situation, but this seemed important.

"Before Pern bonded with his consort, he captured five war brides. Gerrod is Pern's eldest battle-born son."

A knot formed in the pit of Roxie's stomach and a continuous stream of questions flooded her mind. Miraculously, she remained silent, needing to understand how the surreal events affected her.

"Pern wanted to restore magic to his people and he didn't care who he destroyed along the way." Morgan paused for a moment, likely to organize her thoughts. When she resumed, her voice was stronger, more authoritative. "We're not sure who made the discovery or even if the phenomenon is naturally occurring, but human physiology is unusually receptive to alien DNA."

Roxie swallowed past a sudden lump in her throat. "Do I want to know what that means?"

"It means humans are one of the few species able to breed with Ontarians, Rodytes and Bilarrians." Morgan hurried on before Roxie could distract her. "Pern wasn't just fond of claiming war brides for himself, he encouraged his warriors to target Bilarrian females with powerful abilities. A great number of the battle-born daughters were born with abilities, but very few of the sons seemed to be able to manipulate magic. Rodymia is a patriarchal, warrior culture so this was unacceptable to Pern. He'd begun searching for other methods of empowering male offspring when he learned about Ontarian hybrids being born of human mothers."

"But humans can't manipulate magic. How would his discovery help him?" Roxie fiddled with the drawstring on her borrowed pants, unable to stop the nervous motion.

"He wasn't sure it would, but he was the type of person to explore any and all possibilities. He sent his eldest son with a small contingent of men and they hijacked the Ontarian program."

"What sort of program?" Roxie braced for another flood of information. Even the simplest question seemed to result in a twenty-minute answer.

"The details aren't nearly as important as what Pern learned."

Even Elias looked confused by Morgan's evasive response. "You're talking about the Dirty Dozen, correct?"

"Correct. According to Gerrod, they had a purpose far more nefarious than knocking up coeds."

"Knocking up coeds?" Roxie felt her jaw drop and snapped it shut. "Twelve Rodyte warriors went around intentionally impregnating human females?"

"Gerrod started with twelve Ontarian rebels. They were the ones known as the Dirty Dozen. However, Gerrod's primary motivation for forming the group was to shield the movements of his real team, his Rodyte team. And there were a whole lot more than twelve of them."

Roxie was stunned. Elias claimed that humans held little interest for the visiting aliens, but each word Morgan uttered proved him wrong. Human technology might be primitive compared to other planets, but humans themselves had attracted all sorts of unsavory attention. "Don't Rodytes have to be bonded to produce children? Is the bond that easy to turn off and on?"

"Not at all," Morgan assured her. "But a stubborn person can get good at anything if the motivation is powerful enough."

"What possible motivation could there be for 'knocking up coeds'?" Roxie shuddered. The more she learned about the Rodytes, the less she liked them.

With obvious reluctance Morgan explained, "Originally Pern was just testing the compatibility of human females. As I said, there aren't that many species able to reproduce with Rodytes. But Gerrod is a battle-born hybrid. His mother was an exceptionally gifted Bilarrian. Gerrod's abilities are scattered at best, but each of his female offspring was not just gifted, they were extremely powerful."

"All that affects Jillian not Roxie." Elias crossed one leg over the other, his foot lightly bouncing.

That was right—Gerrod was Jillian's father. The one Sevrin had tried to murder!

"I'd agree, if that's where the story ended. But it doesn't. Pern was never content to let progress unfold naturally. He took a group of Gerrod's children back to Rodymia, so his best scientists could figure out if it was a predictable pattern or a genetic anomaly."

A sudden chill made Roxie shiver. Talk about ominous. This story sounded worse by the minute. "What did the scientists learn and were the children harmed by their experiments?"

It took a moment for Morgan to find the least provocative phrasing. "Gerrod didn't mention the wellbeing of his children, so I presume we don't want to know. And I'm not a geneticist, so I only understood a fraction of what he rattled off next."

"Well, you better dumb it down even more if you expect me to understand any of it," Roxie cautioned. "Science was my least favorite subject."

Morgan released her hands and allowed her stance to relax just a little. "It wasn't an anomaly. It was a consistent pattern. The mutation takes place in two stages and it's triggered by coding contained on the X chromosome. The first time the coding appears an aptitude for magic is created, but a second X chromosome must be present for the person to utilize the gift. Anytime the Y chromosome is present, the child's abilities remain dormant."

"That's why the girls could use their magic and the boys couldn't?" Morgan nodded and Roxie sighed. All this conversation was doing was making her feel stupid. "I still don't see what any of this has to do with me."

"Be patient a moment longer. We're almost to the part that directly pertains to you." After Roxie's reluctant nod, Morgan continued. "Because battle-born sons are seldom born with powers, they're considered inferior."

"That's so hypocritical," Roxie muttered, unable to silence her indignation. "Their fathers don't have powers."

"The battle-born exist for the express purpose of changing that fact and the vast majority of battle-born sons failed. They're good for menial labor or they're trained as frontline soldiers. They're not considered shameful, but they are expendable." Morgan's bitter tone mad it obvious she didn't agree with the attitude. She was just explaining how the Rodytes thought.

"Are there any good parts to this story?"

"The secret Pern uncovered was a second chance, a way for them to claim a higher place in society," Morgan told her. "And by this time there were thousands of them. Though the men were basically powerless themselves, they were capable of creating empowered daughters. That would give them worth again, a purpose."

Roxie was so confused, she couldn't even think of a logical question. There had to be a reason Morgan was telling her all of this, but Roxie still didn't understand.

"Pern was never content to play by the rules. He'd found an unexpected advantage and he intended to exploit it to the fullest. He had his scientists program a retrovirus that could be injected as part of the bonding process. It increased fertility in human females and greatly increased her chances of producing female offspring."

Roxie swallowed, her throat suddenly tight. The random facts were finally starting to feel personal. Morgan had already told her that her mother was a war bride. "Was this done to my mother?"

"Yes. You're one of the daughters that resulted from this experiment."

"But the experiment failed," Roxie insisted. "I don't have abilities."

"We'll find out if that's true in a moment. I wasn't finished explaining the program. War is expensive, so is space exploration and scientific research. Pern indulged liberally in all three. So when he was ready to test his hypothesis, he didn't have enough money to fund another trip to Earth."

"I don't like that sound of that." Elias uncrossed his legs and his gaze grew even more intense. "Where'd he get the money?"

"He approached the fifteen most powerful families on Rodymia and told them he could provide a mate for the male of their choice and guarantee her ability to manipulate magic, all they had to do was fund the expedition."

"Okay, hold on." Roxie scooted to the edge of her chair. "If Rodytes are patriarchal, why would Pern pursue research that empowered females?"

"Because nothing else provided consistent results. Claiming war brides on Bilarri was a necessary step, but the offspring weren't always empowered. Pern had unlocked the code. He found the perfect combination of ingredients that *always* resulted in an empowered child."

"But that child was female," Roxie pointed out. She needed that fact to be significant, to make her less desirable, yet the regret in Morgan's eyes didn't give her hope.

"Having each of his strongest warriors bound to an empowered female would still make Rodymia stronger than it had ever been before."

"There are more like Roxie?" Elias tensed. "Are they listed in the notebook? How do we find them?"

Elias had already accepted Morgan's story as fact and moved on to strategy, but Roxie was still struggling with the details. "There's a Rodyte warrior out there who considers me his property?"

"Rodytes don't own their mates, so the analogy is inaccurate."

Now Morgan wanted to mince words? Roxie had to resist the urge to fly across the room and strangle her. "Fine. He doesn't want to own me; he just wants to claim me as his mate and force me to pop out a bunch of magical baby girls. And Sevrin is going to make damn sure he knows where to find me."

"It's not just you," Morgan reminded, though the fact did little to slow Roxie's thundering heart. "The fifteen strongest, most politically connected Rodytes will soon come to Earth, expecting to collect their mates from Sevrin."

"The fifteen are incidental. When word gets out that battle-born sons can produce empowered daughters simply by bonding with human females..." Elias just shook his head. "This is only the beginning. Earth won't know what hit them."

"Which is why this situation must be contained ASAP. Gerrod insists that Sevrin is the only one who knows how well the experiment worked and Sevrin is in serious trouble. Pern died suddenly. He didn't have time to fill her in on the details of this program. She's frantically searching through files and interviewing contacts, but Roxie is the only daughter Sevrin has been able to locate."

"Lucky me." Over and over Roxie had tried to imagine why Sevrin had targeted her. A prearranged marriage to an alien warrior never entered the equation.

"You *are* damn lucky," Morgan snapped. "If our paths hadn't crossed, you'd be at the mercy of the Rodytes right now."

She knew Morgan was right, but she was too upset to apologize. Ever since these people barged into her life, situations had gone from bad to worse. Nausea twisted her stomach as she realized—if what Morgan said was true—her bad luck had begun before her birth.

"As of right now, Sevrin hasn't told Quentin the details about any of this. All he knows is that Pern was conducting some sort of breeding experiment involving battle-born sons and human females. She doesn't want to admit that she doesn't know how to find the empowered brides."

"Control Sevrin and we control the message?" Cunning sharpened Elias' gaze, made him look dangerous.

"Exactly. We can use Sevrin's likeness to convince Quentin the experiment failed, that Pern's hypothesis was wrong. But that will only be an option if the real Sevrin can't contradict our message."

"It's a serious Hail Mary pass," Elias grumbled.

"It's the only play we have left. Quentin is being pressured by the families. He has to tell them something. Why not use that pressure to our advantage?"

Roxie shook her head. She might not know much about alien politics, but she understood proud men. "He's not going to admit that he failed. No ruler would."

"He didn't fail. Sevrin did. And when her body is found, he'll claim that he made her pay for bringing shame on his family. Win-win situation."

"Unless you're Sevrin." Roxie knew Sevrin was ruthless and corrupt, but that didn't keep a spark a pity from erupting.

"This is all according to Gerrod." Elias scrubbed his jaw, clearly looking for flaws in the story. "We thought he was a harmless refugee hiding from his past and suddenly he's Pern's right-hand man."

"That's what he needed everyone to think," Morgan explained. "He was hiding in plain sight while he carried out his father's orders. Even Sevrin thinks he's just one of their father's many henchmen."

"Maybe she found out who he really is. That could be why she tried to kill him." Roxie shivered. She'd thought her life had moved beyond associations with people ruthless enough to kill for power or profit.

"It's possible, maybe even probable. We just don't know for sure."

Elias shook his head. Apparently Morgan had yet to win him over completely. "How do we know we can trust him?"

"We don't need to trust him," Morgan insisted, "as long as we can verify his information."

"Then what tangible proof do we have that any of this is true?"

"As you know, Gerrod had a thumb drive hidden in his shoe. He never went anywhere without it. He finally unlocked the coded entries and showed me a bunch of messages between Quentin and Sevrin and between the families and Quentin. I have no idea how Gerrod got ahold of them, but they looked authentic to me. The families want to know when their investment will be rewarded. If Sevrin jerks them around for too long, it's more than possible that they'll head this way and hunt for their brides themselves. Don't forget this is the culture that gave the Shadow Assassins their love for hunting mates."

Finally understanding the scope of her peril, Roxie crossed her arms over her stomach. "What the hell are we going to do?"

"The objective hasn't changed," Morgan insisted. "We have to find Sevrin. But there are a couple of details that need to be sorted before we set our trap."

"Like whether or not I have latent abilities?"

"Yes. I'd much rather send a novice Mystic into danger than someone who has no way to defend herself."

"I thought that's what I was for," Elias objected.

"You are. And human to human, you will never lose. Unfortunately, we're not dealing with humans. If Roxie can learn how to raise a shield or open a lock with her mind, it's worth delaying her return for a day or two."

"I have to call Tess and Jett. They need to hear my voice. Text messages are too easy to fake." The glare she shot Elias earned her a soft chuckle from him. "If you let me talk to them, I'll cooperate."

Morgan nodded. "I'll tell Lor what's going on and he can decide how to proceed. This is out of my realm of expertise. As soon as one of the Mystics has scanned you, Elias can take you topside so you can make your calls."

"Sounds good." Compromise. They were starting to work together rather than butting heads and it was infinitely more productive.

"We're going to conference at o-six-hundred to discuss options. Obviously, I expect you both there." Morgan looked from Elias to Roxie and back. "I'll see you in the morning."

Chapter Six

After letting Morgan out of his apartment, Elias returned to Roxie. She sat on the edge of the chair with her hands tucked between her legs. Her face was pale, eyes wide, nearly unblinking. "You look dazed."

She came back to life with a sudden burst of energy. "I can't just sit here. Can we go find Lor?"

Easily understanding her anxiousness, Elias took a step back so she could stand. "Lor's likely in his office, but let me call and make sure."

"Let's just go there. I need to move. The walls are closing in on me."

She started for the door so he followed, reaching around her to pull open the door. "That way." He motioned to the right and they started walking.

They didn't speak and she was so distracted that she nearly collided with two different people. He finally took her by the hand and adjusted his pace so he walked at her side. His semi-rude behavior drew several annoyed looks from the people they passed, but it was better than letting her smack into someone.

"Are you okay?" He knew the answer. He was just hoping to draw her out of her stupor. "That was a lot to take in all at once."

"I haven't been okay since Sevrin strolled into my store." She glanced up at him then shook her head as she continued down the corridor. "I'm not a coward and I'm not going to fall apart on you. I just can't understand how all of this could be true when I knew nothing about it."

"You were still very young when your mother died. It's likely she would have told you." Roxie had fought all of her battles alone, unaware of the forces shaping her life. It was a wonder she'd survived. Yet Roxie hadn't just survived, she'd blazed a trail through the destruction and built a life of which anyone would be proud.

She looked at him again, her gaze more focused. "Suddenly Aunt Shelia doesn't seem so crazy. She might not have known the nature of the danger, but she knew something was wrong. Maybe if I'd listened to her, both of our lives could have been different."

He paused and turned her to face him, his hands lingering on her arms. "Her death was not your fault. Neither was Jodi's. You have to stop blaming yourself for things you had no control over."

Her initial response was a tense nod then she shrugged off his hands and squared her shoulders. "I'm not trying to be melodramatic and I did play a part in Jodi's death. But that's not the point. If I'd been old enough to sense the truth behind Shelia's paranoia, if I'd taken her warming seriously, my aunt might still be alive."

"Or whoever staged her suicide might have gotten you too." Unless Shelia's death had actually been a suicide. From what little he knew about her, it seemed just as likely that she had just neglected to turn on the radio because she knew she wouldn't be singing anymore.

Roxie thought for a moment then sighed. "You're right. Speculation is a waste of time. We need facts and Lor is a good place to start." With that settled, at least in her mind, she turned and continued down the hallway.

Elias watched the sway of her hips and the stubborn tilt of her head. Even in a utility uniform the woman managed to look appealing.

Lor and Blayne were engaged in a terse conversation when Elias and Roxie arrived. Lor sat in the desk chair, but at some point he'd turned around and faced his friend. Elias tapped on the open door, drawing the other two's attention. "Can we interrupt for a minute or should we come back?"

"We were just venting." Lor motioned them forward. "Come in."

Elias ushered Roxie into the office/lounge. They were halfway across the compact room when he noticed Roxie staring at Blayne. Her expression was hesitant yet curious, so he disregarded the unexpected surge of possessiveness twisting through his being. "That's Blayne, one of the other Mystics. He and Lor are married to sisters." Why had he felt it necessary to establish the fact that Blayne was unavailable? Jealousy wasn't usually one of his problems.

Roxie offered the Mystic a quick smile, but didn't hold out her hand. It hadn't taken Elias long to realize Roxie didn't like to be touched, especially by people she didn't know. And his quick trip through her past made her reaction tragically understandable.

"It's nice to meet you." Blayne returned her smile and Elias felt another annoying surge of jealousy. Blayne had responded to the crisis at Unique Ink along with the other Mystics, but Roxie must have blacked out before she saw him.

"Did Morgan step on your toes again?" Elias asked Lor. It was a safe bet. Lor and Morgan had been politely butting heads ever since her project networked with the Mystic Militia. Neither leader was used to having their decisions questioned and the collaboration required compromise on both sides.

"Actually my mood has nothing to do with Morgan, for a change." Lor rubbed the back of his neck as Elias and Roxie sat down. "King Indric found out about Gerrod and sent three of his private guards to 'escort' Jillian to Bilarri. Just like that," he snapped his fingers, "I'm out one sixth of my team."

Roxie leaned closer and whispered, "Who is King Indric?"

Before Elias could reply, Lor provided the explanation. "He's one of four regional kings on Bilarri. His sister was the war bride who gave birth to Gerrod, which makes her Jillian's grandmother. King Indric never knew who captured his sister. She claimed that she never learned his name."

"Why would she lie? Was she protecting her captor?" Roxie made it sound like the worst sort of betrayal.

Elias shook his head. "She was protecting her people. The hostilities between Bilarri and Rodymia had deescalated at that point. The war continues to this day, but there hasn't been a full-blown battle in years. She knew if Indric found out that Pern Keire had been her captor, Indric would rally all of Bilarri on her behalf. Hundreds, maybe thousands, would have lost their lives over something that couldn't be changed."

"Is that going to happen now? Will King Indric call his forces to war now that he knows who abused his sister?"

"It's doubtful," Lor told her. "Pern is dead, as is King Indric's sister. King Indric was simply protecting his progeny."

"And of course Odintar went with her," Blayne grumbled. "So we've lost our best healer."

"Enough about our problems." Lor waved away the gloom and managed to smile. "What can we do for you?"

Roxie looked exhausted and was obviously still on edge, so Elias dove right to the heart of the matter. "When you scanned Roxie, did you sense any latent abilities?"

"I was focused on the language infusion. What you're requesting requires a more invasive scan." He looked at Roxie as he said, "The scan won't harm you, but it might be uncomfortable."

"It's important." She produced a wan smile. "I'm not afraid of a little pain."

The comment sent a jolt of pity through Elias. She'd dealt with way too much pain in her young life. He wanted to surround her, protect her from anything that might hurt her again. Starting with Lor. Elias knew the scan was necessary, but he didn't want any of the Mystics near Roxie, physically or metaphysically.

"I'm going to go see if our mates are finished with training." Blayne smiled at Roxie again. "It was nice meeting you. Hope the scan reveals what you want it to show."

After Blayne left, Lor persisted, "Are you sure you want to do this? You seem hesitant?"

"I'm just tired." Her weary tone reinforced her claim. "It's been a really long day."

"All right. Then close your eyes and try not to resist me." Lor bowed his head and silence descended.

Much to Elias' surprise, Roxie reached over and took his hand as she closed her eyes. This wasn't the first time she'd turned to him for support and it pleased him immensely. Protecting her was his primary focus and earning her trust would be an integral part of his success.

But it wasn't professional responsibility that sped his pulse each time his fingers encountered her skin. Roxie attracted him, intrigued him. He wanted to be near her. Hell, he wanted to be inside her, surrounded by her heat as he caressed her entire body with his.

He brushed the back of her hand with his thumb and her fingers tensed against his. She squirmed in her chair, her features tight with concentration and uncertainty. He didn't speak, didn't want to distract her, but he wanted her to remember she wasn't alone.

The silence lengthened and her discomfort became more apparent. He covered their joined hands with his other hand and gave her a little squeeze. He desperately wanted to pull her into his lap and wrap both arms around her, but he drove back the impulse through sheer force of will.

"Almost done," Lor told her. "Take a deep breath. Now another."

She leaned closer, resting her head against the side of his shoulder. He couldn't wrap his arm around her because she still clutched his right hand, so he settled for caressing her forearm with his left hand. Her light, clean scent filled his nose, making him hungry for another taste of her mouth. Kissing her had been an impulse, an unwise impulse apparently. He'd thought of little else since their mouths separated. She'd responded far more enthusiastically than he'd thought she would, which fueled his already errant imagination.

Her hand tightened around his and a ragged hiss escaped her lips. Elias looked at Lor, ready to make him back off, but the Mystic raised his head.

"I sense no latent abilities of any kind." He waited for Roxie to open her eyes before he added, "She has trace amounts of Mystic energy, as all hybrids do, but not all hybrids can manipulate magic. I hope this isn't too much of a disappointment."

"Actually I'm relieved." She might have been able to convince Lor with her sincere-looking smile, but Elias didn't miss how quickly she glanced away. "Let's get going." She pulled her hand out from between his and stood. "Thanks for your help."

Elias hurried after her, knowing she wasn't nearly as calm as she appeared.

"What does this mean?" she asked as soon as they were alone in the hallway. Not that anyone was ever really alone in the Bunker. Every square foot of the complex was under continual surveillance. Except for the living quarters. With his hand on the small of her back, he led her back in that direction.

"I'm not sure what it means. Either Pern's hypothesis was wrong or there's something unique about your DNA that prevented the conversion."

"Either way, I'm dead." Her voice sounded flat, hopeless.

He stopped and spun her toward him. "Not a chance. We will protect you. *I* will protect you."

"I know you mean it, but protecting me is certainly not Morgan's priority. I'm a means to an end, an acceptable loss applied toward the greater good."

It was hard to argue with her when everything she said was true. Morgan had been particularly ruthless where Roxie was concerned. "Nothing is going to happen to you."

After twisting out of his hold, she walked even faster. "You don't know that. No one does." She led him straight to the freight elevators without missing a turn. Obviously, she'd been paying more attention to her surroundings than he'd thought. Like most doors in the secure levels, the elevator required a palm scan to access, so knowing where things were didn't help her all that much. Still, he was impressed by her ongoing attempts to control the situation. Most civilians would have given up long before now.

"Even outside, the signal sucks," he warned as the elevator took them topside. "We'll be lucky if we can get a call to connect."

"How do you guys communicate with the outside world? What about Ontariese? Can 'ET phone home'?"

"We're playing cat and mouse with the Shadow Assassins. We don't want them to know where we are any more than they want us to find them. The Mystics can communicate with other planets, but for the moment they're limiting their transmissions to absolute emergencies. Same with our transmissions. Every call we place, be it cell phone, satellite uplink, or two-way radio, runs the risk of revealing our location."

"Is that your way of talking me out of this?"

They stepped out into the purple twilight as she dug her cell phone out of her pocket. "Not at all. I'm just warning you that you might have to be content with texts."

She held the phone up, likely looking for a signal. "Two bars. I'll give it a go." She activated the call and raised the phone to her ear. "Hey, Tess, can you hear... Yeah I know the connection sucks... I'm fine, I promise... I know, but... I'll explain everything... Damn." She looked at the screen. "It's gone." She glanced at him and asked, "Will a text go through?"

"Go ahead and enter it. If the phone finds a stray signal, it usually sends the message."

She quickly entered several messages then returned the phone to her pocket. "Hopefully she heard me well enough to know I'm still alive."

"She'll see you tomorrow and you can explain... Well, you can't tell her much more than our cover story, but at least she won't be worried anymore."

She was quiet and brooding as he took her back to his quarters. He'd hoped talking with one of her friends, though extremely briefly, would lighten her mood. The opposite seemed to have happened. He scanned open the door and she hurried inside.

"Are the corridors monitored?" she asked.

He fought back a smile, impressed by her instincts. "They are, but what made you ask?"

"Your demeanor changes whenever we're in the hallways. You tense up and your speech becomes more formal."

"Really?"

"But this room isn't monitored. You're relaxed here, more yourself."

He let the smile for when the impulse came again. "After a few short days, you know me well enough to spot the real me?"

"Nothing about these days has been short." She moved away from the door but didn't return to the sitting area. It was as if she wasn't sure where she wanted to go or what she wanted to do. "I feel like I've been locked up for months, not days, and you've been assessing me the entire time."

"I'm sorry about that. It's never fun to be under the microscope." Her agitation was palpable. She was like a cat brushing against his legs, begging to be petted, reassured. Who was he trying to fool? Her need for comfort was real, but he'd been fighting the urge to touch her since the first moment he saw her in a helpless heap on the floor of her shop.

"It's your job." She heaved a weary sigh and strolled toward the workstation, which also took her closer to his bed. He doubted that the maneuver was intentional, but his body hardened all the same. "I know your interest isn't personal."

"Then you don't know me as well as you think you do."

Her gaze shot to his and lingered for a long, tense moment. She nervously licked her lips then looked away. "I don't think I can deal with the holding cell right now. Would you please ask Morgan to assign me my own room?"

"I know what she'll say." She dragged her gaze back to his and arched her brow. "It's the holding cell or here. I'm not allowed to let you out of my sight."

"She can't lock me inside a room with an actual bed?"

"Security protocols don't work that way. Living quarters are tuned to the occupant. The doors lock automatically, but the occupant needs to be able to come and go as they please." It wasn't an outright lie, more like an exaggeration. Security routines would have to be reprogrammed, but Morgan could make it happen. The details didn't matter. Roxie needed to trust him and they didn't have time to build that trust through more conventional means.

Roxie looked at the bed then her anxious gaze swept the room. "You don't even have a couch. Am I supposed to curl up in one of the chairs?"

"No. You're supposed to curl up in my arms and trust that I won't do more than protect you. We'll be posing as lovers. You need to stop flinching away from my touch."

"I don't flinch away from your touch."

He closed the distance between them in less than a second and framed her face with his hands. She immediately drew back so he let her go, despite the very real urge to tighten his grip. "You do."

"I don't mean to." She brought her hands together in front of her, creating an obstacle between them.

"I know, but that doesn't change your instinctive reaction."

She crossed her arms over her chest, looking lost and alone. "And you think sleeping with you will change instincts developed over decades?"

"The more I touch you, the more comfortable you'll become with being touched." He stepped closer, not quite recapturing the ground he'd lost. "As long as you enjoy the way I touch you."

Her lips trembled as she asked, "Did Morgan tell you to seduce me?"

He lightly grasped one of her wrists, easing her arm down. "I don't think any power on Earth could keep me from seducing you. You fascinate me. And you're not indifferent. I've seen the way you look at me."

"You're an attractive man. Of course, I've looked at you. That doesn't mean I'm ready to surrender." Despite her objection, she lowered her other arm, though she kept her hands at her sides.

He didn't rush her, just let the tension build. As long as she didn't push him away, he could be as patient as she needed him to be. "This isn't a battle, darlin'. We're not at war."

"Well, it isn't a romance either. I'm your assignment."

She was already more than that. He'd accepted that this connection had nothing to do with his assignment, but Roxie wasn't ready to hear it. "Then think of it as a negotiation. I'll never take more than I'm offered, but you can't blame me for needing to ask." He placed his hand on her waist and waited for her to accept or reject the featherlight touch.

Again, she didn't pull away. "I don't want to have sex tonight. My emotions are too...tangled."

He slid his hand to the small of her back and slowly drew her toward him. "I never said anything about having sex. I know you're confused and I would never take advantage of you like that."

"Then what are you proposing?"

"I just want to touch you, kiss you, comfort you. The rest can wait until you're ready for more."

Roxie chuckled, her hardened nipples inadvertently teasing his chest. Damn his confidence. She usually hated arrogant men. So why was Elias the exception? He definitely qualified as arrogant, and still she was drawn to him. "You're presuming I'll eventually be ready to have sex with you."

Rather than argue with her, he pulled her firmly against his chest then grasped the back of her neck with his other hand. He covered her mouth with his and staked his claim with overt purpose. She gasped and tensed, her hands clutching his upper arms.

She was just about to push him away and demand that he return her to the holding cell when he eased back and let her breathe. He didn't release her entirely though. His lips caressed hers, sliding and pressing as his tongue teased. Gradually she relaxed into his embrace and tilted her head to a better angle. His long fingers splayed against the back of her head, holding her still while his tongue sank deeper. He pushed his taste into her mouth as their breaths mingled. She felt dizzy, almost drunk with the sudden rush of desire.

"Share my bed." He whispered the words against her parted lips then kissed her deeply again.

"I don't want—"

He cut her off with another kiss. "I know and we won't. I just want to touch you, feel you arch against me and gasp my name."

"Gasp your name while you're doing what exactly?" She turned her head when he tried to kiss her again. "This is a negotiation, remember. I want the terms spelled out."

With a sexy chuckle, he nipped the side of her neck. Hot tingles erupted deep in her body and she squirmed against him. "I agree not to pressure you for sex tonight if you'll allow me to touch your naked body in any way I want."

"With your hands?" she persisted.

He looked up and grinned. "I'm good with my hands, but I'm even better with my mouth."

She groaned at the thought then shivered. "Which is why your mouth will not wander below my waist."

He closed his eyes for a moment then growled. "Ah, honey, you're heartless."

"No, heartless would be pretending I don't want this at all."

His thick lashes lifted and his hazel eyes stared into hers. "When we do this for real—and we will—you'll be as desperate for me as I am for you."

Her body was there already, but he was right. Her mind was filled with uncertainly and her emotions were raw. If they made love tonight, she'd never be sure if she'd wanted him or just wanted an escape from the worst day of her life.

He stepped back and undressed with frantic speed as she fiddled with the drawstring on her pants. He tugged off his boots and socks then peeled his shirt off over his head, leaving him bare to the waist. She watched him as she kicked her sandals aside, captivated by the stark symmetry of his amazing body. Even through his clothes it had been obvious he was in good shape, but her imagination hadn't done him justice. Every muscle was highly defined, sculpted to human perfection.

"Do you need some help?" He'd been about to unfasten his pants when he asked the question.

She shook her head. "I'm just enjoying the view."

He chuckled and stripped away his pants, leaving only tan boxer-briefs. He flexed his arms and struck a body builder pose. She laughed then looked away. "Your turn," he urged.

She wasn't ashamed of her body, exactly. She'd just never been with someone who looked like Elias. Her legs were long, her hips narrow, and her breasts were small. Did he like skinny women or did he prefer someone shaped like Morgan? Most men liked curves on a woman. Maybe she should—

His warm fingers brushed the side of her face, drawing her gaze back to his. "I want to see your tattoos."

The heat in his gaze combined with his encouraging smile and her apprehension melted. She pulled her shirt off and tossed it aside. He had the drawstring untied and her pants halfway to her knees before she disentangled her arms from the sleeves. She wasn't wearing anything under the borrowed uniform even though her original clothing had been returned to her freshly laundered and neatly folded.

"Well, this is a naughty surprise." His gaze dropped as he cupped one of her breasts.

"I wanted to keep my clothes clean for when I'm released."

"It wasn't a criticism. I think clothes as a whole are overrated." He pulled her lower body against his as he bent to her breasts, forcing her to arch her back. His lips fastened on to one nipple and she gasped as he drew her deeply into his mouth.

This was happening too fast and she wanted too much. Desire made her vulnerable. "This is a bad idea." He switched to the other side, ignoring her protest.

And then he was touching her. His hands slid over her body without rhyme or reason. Well, he had an obvious reason, driving her insane, but there was no pattern, no predicting where he'd touch her next. His lips trailed after his hands until she stood trembling in front of him.

"Wow," he murmured as his lips drifted over her shoulder and onto her back. He stood beside her now, one arm wrapped around her waist in front while the other moved freely over her back, hips and butt. "Did the same person do all of these?"

She shook her head, not trusting her voice.

"This is obviously the same artist." He touched the intricate floral piece that ran down the right side of her back and then spiraled around her right thigh. "It's amazing."

His fingers traced the female warrior dominating the left side of her back. She was one of Roxie's favorites, sexy yet fierce. "Is this how you see yourself?"

She looked back at him then shook her head. "She's not me. She's my guardian spirit, someone to watch my back."

He pressed a kiss to her temple and just held her for a second. "You've never had that before, have you? I forget how lucky I am to be part of a team."

The observation cut deeply. He was right. She'd been alone her entire life, struggling through each crisis, each challenge, with no one to count on, no one to look to for support. "It made me strong."

He turned her toward him, his gaze searching her. "It made you suspicious."

"It kept me alive."

"It makes me sad." He kissed her slowly, tenderly, stirring emotions she wasn't ready to feel.

She responded to the gentleness for only a moment before fear forced her to react. Reaching between their bodies, she squeezed his cock, wanting passion to burn away the pain. He felt thick and long beneath her palm, and her groan was as loud as his. "Aren't you going to get naked?"

"Not unless you change the rules." He guided her hand to his hip. "And none of that. You can't touch me below the waist unless you're ready to renegotiate our deal."

"But that's not fair. You get to touch me anywhere you want."

He swept her up in his arms with a predatory grin. "I never said it would be fair, just mutually agreed upon." He placed her in the middle of his bed then stretched out on his side. "Tell me about the phoenix. It's really well done."

He meant the tattoo on her left shoulder. "I've had her for a long time. She's one of the only early ones I don't regret."

"You don't like all of your tattoos? Then why did you get them?" He slipped his arm beneath her neck and rested his hand on her chest. His fingers nestled between her breasts.

"Tastes change and I learned what a really good tattoo looks like. How long have you had yours?" She reached up and traced the intricate black and gray pattern banding his upper arm. "It's really different, geometric, yet whimsical. Whoever did it was good."

"That's high praise coming from you."

Her gaze returned to his and they just stared at each other for a moment. Then she whispered, "I'm scared."

He lifted his hand from between her breasts. "About this?"

"No." She guided his hand to her breast and held it there. "I need this. I'm scared about tomorrow."

"Fear isn't always a bad thing. We just have to work with it rather than letting it control us."

"That's easy for you to say. You've been at this a lot longer than I have."

"Which is why I won't leave your side. Even if I have to handcuff myself to you, I won't let you face this alone."

It was a sweet sentiment, but she knew it wasn't that simple. There was a very real chance one of the Shadow Assassins would teleport her to Sevrin's new facility and Elias would be left behind. "I know I'm not just bait. Morgan wants them to take me. Does she have a way to track me once they do?"

He looked away, clearly tormented by the possibilities. "Yes, but I don't want to talk about this now. We have a few precious hours before reality intrudes again. Can't we just focus on each other?" His hand shifted to the underside of her breast, his thumb stroking her nipple.

More than ready to escape reality, she pulled his face down to hers and let her troubled thoughts just fade away. Elias was here now, warm and commanding, and she needed to be overwhelmed by pleasure rather than uncertainty. She opened to the first touch of his tongue as desire curled through her body.

He worked her nipples into hard little peaks as his tongue explored her mouth. She returned the kiss without hesitation, her tongue stroking just as boldly. She touched his shoulder and chest then squeezed his arm, unable to reach more of his hard body.

Emotion surged to the surface with staggering intensity. She needed more than these teasing touches. She needed him over her, inside her, driving reality away with each forceful thrust. A whimper slipped out between their sliding lips and she murmured. "More. Please."

He eased one of his legs between her thighs then pulled her up onto her side, pressing their bodies together from neck to knee. His fingers tangle in her hair and his free hand grabbed her ass, sliding her up his thigh then back down. Understanding what he had in mind, she began to rock her hips. Her mound pressed against him and slid over him, creating friction against her clit. She groaned and moved faster, pressing harder.

Their kiss turned desperate as tension gathered low in her belly. He held her head steady as her body arched and churned against his. Despite the need pulsing inside her, she became aware of his stillness, his complete focus on her pleasure.

She tried to reach down between them, but he caught her wrist and moved it away from his crotch. She tore their mouths apart. "I don't want to do this alone."

"You're *not* alone." His tone was harsh, his features tense. "Let me do this for you. I need you to trust me with your pleasure." His hand returned to her butt, squeezing firmly as he urged her back into the rocking motion. She closed her eyes, prepared to concentrate on the friction. "No. Look at me. Share this with me. Trust me."

The last phrase morphed from a plea into a silken command. She shifted her hips, searching for the angle that created the most sensation. The flecks in his eyes gleamed like polished gold, bright and mesmerizing.

Pleasure intensified with each rotation. His mouth returned to hers, his tongue taking on the rhythm of her hips. She felt suspended above the bed as if her mind were separate from the feelings pulsing through her body. Close. She was so damn close.

His long fingers pushed between her thighs, teasing her folds from behind. He wasn't even touching her clit, but it didn't seem to matter. Her core clenched hard, grasping a fullness that wasn't there. Then everything flew apart, propelled from deep inside her.

She cried out against his mouth, shuddering as spasm after powerful spasm tore through her. His mouth slowed and gentled as she flowed through the pleasure and gradually returned to reality.

She couldn't remember closing her eyes, but her lids felt heavy as she raised them. He rolled her onto her back and urged her legs apart then knelt between her thighs. She stared up at him in stunned confusion. Why did he look so...hungry?

He found both her wrists and pulled her arms above her head. She just watched him, still tingly and relaxed from her amazing orgasm.

"Don't move your hands."

She was so sleepy she could hardly move at all, so she didn't argue. He caressed his way down the underside of her upraised arms then peppered kisses over her features. His lips teased hers then moved on before she could deepen the kiss.

"What are you doing?" She began to squirm as he nipped his way down the side of her neck. "I'm not sure how you could have missed it, but I just came really hard. Now it's your turn."

He lifted his head and grinned at her. "I'm not finished with you yet."

Excitement tingled down her spine at his uncompromising tone. "Is that so?"

He palmed the underside of her breast and sucked hard on her nipple. "You're going to come for me again." He switched to the other side. "And again." His gaze bore into hers with possessive passion as his hand skimmed over her abdomen and pushed between her thighs. "And again."

MORGAN DRAGGED HER gaze away from yet another useless report and rubbed her eyes. There hadn't been any new information from any of her sources for weeks and she'd been building her network of contacts for almost a decade. Roxie really was their only hope and she was innocent of any wrong doing. Collateral damage was almost unavoidable in a situation this complex, but that didn't make the potential sacrifice any easier.

Someone knocked on her office door, drawing her attention away from her laptop, and her troubled thoughts. "It's open." She quickly closed the report. It was a semi-paranoid habit, but so much of what she dealt with was classified. She couldn't afford to let her guard down for even an instant. Too many lives were counting on her.

Lor eased the door inward but didn't actually enter her domain. She still wasn't sure if it was politeness or intimidation that kept his manner so formal. He had no reason to feel threatened by her. He had powers at his command that she could barely understand, much less hope to emulate. "Have you spoken with Elias since I scanned Roxie?"

"No." She pushed back from her desk and stood. If he wouldn't come to her, she'd go to him. She was tired of shouting across the room. "What did your scan reveal?"

"I'm not sure why, but Roxie has no latent abilities."

She froze, shocked by the news. "Really? Are you sure? Her DNA scans confirmed that she's a hybrid."

"I'm sure." He relaxed enough to lean his shoulder against the doorframe as his gaze turned speculative. "I spent the last hour speaking with two of your geneticists. They confirm what Gerrod told you. The combination Pern discovered should consistently produce empowered females."

Confirmation was always nice, but that didn't jive with what Lor had just discovered. "Then why didn't it work with Roxie?"

"Roxie's father didn't follow Pern's formula."

"In what way?"

"All of the females Gerrod bred with were one hundred percent human. Roxie's mother already possessed alien DNA, which disrupted the mutation."

Morgan rubbed her temples, no longer able to ignore the throbbing "I'm so tired, I'm not even sure if this is good news or bad."

"For our purposes, I think it's moot. All of the Shadow Assassins on Earth are hunters. It's unlikely they possess the skill needed to detect this weakness. They'll probably conclude that her abilities are still latent and proceed as if nothing were wrong."

"There were a few too many qualifiers in there for my comfort." Morgan sighed. "I was really hoping we could arm her with some sort of ability before we sent her into the lion's den. I'm not sure how to ensure her safety, yet I'm even more convinced that we have no other choice."

"Elias indicated that you have a way to track her."

"I do. It's an isotope we came across in our dealings with another group of visitors. As long as they keep her on Earth—and Sevrin wouldn't have built a new headquarters if she intended to return to Rodymia—I can track Roxie. But knowing where she is doesn't keep her safe. I need to look her in the eyes and explain how I'm going to do that."

"That's not your job. It's mine. The Shadow Assassins are my responsibility. I've sent for reinforcements and requested a larger team. The new personnel should be here by morning. If you can keep track of Roxie, I can ensure her safety."

Morgan hesitated. She hated having to rely on others for any element of her success, but Lor was right. She didn't have the tools needed to take on the Shadow Assassins and he did. "I know your right. It's just not comfortable admitting that there is something I can't do."

"I wouldn't know." He softened the boast with a smile then pushed off the doorframe. "Go get some sleep. You look exhausted."

She chuckled, pleased that they had bonded to the point where he would tell her. "Right back at you, buddy. I'll see you in the morning."

She returned to her desk and turned her laptop toward her. As if the infernal machine knew she was about to turn it off, it pinged, indicating a new email just hit her inbox. It was well past midnight. Who would email her at this ungodly hour?

Curiosity trumped fatigue and she launched the program.

The new message was from Flynn. Good thing she'd checked. His messages had been erratic since he started sleeping with Sevrin, but he never risked a message unless it was important.

As was his habit, his information was succinct and urgent:

Put Roxie back! Sevrin intends to check on her in the morning. More details to follow as situation allows.

"Shit." She rushed across the office and ran after Lor.

He turned around as he heard her call his name. "What's wrong?"

"We're out of time. We have to move Roxie now."

Chapter Seven

Elias watched his fingers sink into the heat of Roxie's snug passage. He was working on her third orgasm and her scent was driving him crazy. If he didn't taste her soon, he wasn't sure he could control the other desires pounding through his body. Hoping to distract her with the shuttle of his fingers, he slowly lowered his head between her thighs.

She grabbed his hair with both hands and tugged him away from his target. "You're violating the terms of our agreement." She laughed at his startled expression. "If I can't touch you, you can't lick me."

Unable to deprive himself completely, he withdrew his fingers and raised them to his mouth. His gaze stared into hers as he savored her salty-sharp taste. "Then let's renegotiate. I really want to put my mouth on you."

A frantic pounding on his door preempted her reply, then Morgan's voice called from the corridor. "Elias! Open up. It's important!"

He scrambled off the bed and struggled into his jeans as he rushed across the room. "What's wrong?" He only opened the door far enough so they could see each other.

"Roxie better be in there with you. I just came from her holding cell."

"She is. What's wrong?"

"Sevrin plans to check on Roxie first thing in the morning. We have to get her in place now."

"How can she possibly know that?" Roxie asked from beside the bed. She'd pulled on her shirt and was tying the drawstring on her uniform pants. Close enough to decent. He let the door swing inward and went to his closet for a clean T-shirt.

"We managed to recruit one of the Shadow Assassins," Elias told her. "He's been feeding us information for months, but his value exploded when Sevrin let him into her bed."

"Sevrin's lover is working for you?" She looked at Morgan as Elias finished dressing. "Does Lor know about this?"

"He does now." Morgan stepped into the room and closed the door behind her. "I wasn't intentionally keeping it from him. The detail just never came up."

"Yeah right. Did Lor buy that line of bullshit?"

Morgan actually laughed. "Not any better than you did." The light moment passed as quickly as it had formed and Morgan was all business again. "Lor will be here in a minute. He had to send a message to Ontariese requesting reinforcements ASAP. We were hoping to have everyone briefed before we sent you home, but that's not possible now. We'll have to do things in stages."

"Elias said you'll be able to track me even if they teleport me to their new lab."

Like Morgan, Roxie seldom beat around the bush. Elias hoped they'd eventually find other commonalities. The tension between them made it uncomfortable for everyone.

"With your permission, we'll inject you with an isotope that transmits a harmless form of radiation. The radiation lingers in the air for several hours, so it can be detected over very long distances."

"Like from another planet?" Roxie crossed her arms over her chest, her emotions already shutting down.

Elias moved up beside her and took her hand. "They're not going to take you to another planet. Half of Rodymia just came here."

"And we're not going to send you into the fight without any sort of weapon." Morgan pulled a slender metal band out of her pocket. It rolled in on itself, creating concentric rings. "This is a suppression collar. It prevents a Shadow Assassin from accessing their powers. They're still strong and fast, but it will prevent one from teleporting you long enough for Lor's men to arrive."

"Is it still functional?" Elias took it from her and looked it over. "Didn't they cut if off Gerrod?"

"They did, but that wasn't the problem. It needed to be reprogramed. These things are 'tuned' to an owner's DNA. Anyone can activate it, but only the owner can activate the release mechanism."

Elias reluctantly handed it to Roxie. He was thrilled that she'd have some form of weapon at her disposal, but she'd have to be within arm's reach of the Shadow Assassin to use this one.

"Who owns this one?" Roxie slowly unrolled the band, as she turned it this way and that.

"Lor and I co-own it, thought it would be safer that way." Morgan held out her arm. "Hold tightly to the end and snap it against my forearm." Holding the end firmly between her thumb and forefinger, Roxie snapped the device against Morgan. The curved band expanded, rolling smoothly outward until it encircled Morgan's arm. "And the harder you snap it, the faster it unrolls." Morgan pressed her thumb against the seam and spoke a word Elias didn't recognize. The locking mechanism clicked, hissed, and then released. "When you're ready to use it, don't hesitate. It's the only one we have." She handed the device back to Roxie.

Before Roxie could respond, someone knocked on the door. Elias reluctantly left her side and opened the door for Lor.

"I'll have two new Mystics within the hour and an additional four by morning," Lor told them.

Morgan nodded. "Good. We need all of the help we can get."

Elias returned to Roxie's side and placed his hand at the small of her back. They faced each other in a messy circle in the middle of Elias' living area. Judging from their disheveled clothing and the purple smudges under their eyes, neither Morgan nor Lor had been to bed yet. A conference room would have been more comfortable, but everyone was too focused on strategy to relocate.

"Did Lor tell you about my lack of abilities?" Roxie asked Morgan.

"Yes and my geneticists think the transformation wasn't triggered because your mother already had alien DNA. All of the empowered daughters were born to full-blooded humans."

"Good to know," Elias muttered though he wasn't sure how, or if, it affected the current situation.

"Will the Rodytes be able to tell that I don't have abilities?" Roxie asked. "Can they scan me like Lor did?"

She'd posed the question to Morgan, but Lor answered. "Their skills are different than mine. All of the Shadow Assassins on Earth functioned as hunters. If any of them had sweeper skills, we'd be in trouble, but I just confirmed that they do not."

"Wasn't Nazerel eligible for both programs?" Morgan sounded as if she were reluctant to bring it up.

"He was, but he was never trained as a sweeper. I just spoke with Varrik about this very thing."

"Who is Varrik?" Roxie wanted to know.

"He was the alpha sweeper," Lor told her. "Likely the most powerful of all Shadow Assassins."

"He's the one who helped them liberate the Shadow Maze, so most consider him a traitor," Elias added.

"We need to get moving," Morgan reminded. "Have you two worked out the details of your cover story?"

"We have," Elias assured.

"Then the next step is being seen together. Don't wait around for Sevrin. She might not want you to know she's there. Take him to your shop, introduce him to your friends, act like you're in a new relationship and can't keep your hands off each other." She glanced at the rumpled bed and smiled. "Somehow, I don't think that will be too difficult."

Lor took a step forward angling his body more fully toward Elias and Roxie. "I'll have my team in place within the hour. Most of the time you won't see us, but you'll have backup at all times. If you're willing to permit it, I'd like to form a telepathic link so we can speak to you directly. I also had another thought."

"I'm listening," Roxie said.

"Now that you've been intimate, I can create a proximity bond."

She looked around, obviously panicked. "Elias said this room wasn't monitored. How do you know..."

Lor just smiled. "Lucky guess."

Elias moved his hand from her back and interlaced their fingers. "Basic powers of observation. The room is *not* monitored. What's a proximity bond?"

"It's a metaphysical link that tethers you together. Where one goes the other will follow."

"Even if I'm teleported?" No one could have missed the hope in Roxie's tone.

"Yes," Lor assured with another smile. "But emotions and thoughts can escape across the link so it's not wise to create such a bond unless the couple shares some level of intimacy."

"I'm game," Elias said without hesitation. If Roxie didn't have to face this alone, any emotional sharing would be worth it. Besides it might be interesting if she could feel the full impact of his attraction to her. It would obliterate her fear that he still considered her an assignment.

"Having to go through this alone was my biggest fear," she admitted. "I'd welcome the bond."

"You were never going to be alone," Lor stressed. "We just had to work out the logistics."

"I hate to rush you," Morgan said, "but we don't have a lot of time. We have to get you two in place before Sevrin arrives."

"Wait a minute." Suspicion and anger suddenly animated her delicate features. "If Sevrin's lover is your spy, why do you even need me? Can't he tell you where the new lab is located?"

Morgan shook her head. "Nothing is ever simple when Sevrin is involved. Flynn is either drugged or blindfolded when he's taken to the complex. He doesn't know the exact location. We know it takes less than an hour to reach, so our search area has shrunk considerably. But that still leaves a lot of ground to cover."

"Are you sure you can trust Flynn. He's kind of an asshole."

The description made Morgan smile. "He's been playing up his ruthlessness to attract Sevrin's attention."

"And Nazerel's," Roxie countered. "Those two are thick as thieves."

"That's by design, as well. I promise you. He's one of the good guys."

Roxie waved away the subject. "It makes no difference to me, except it sounds like I'm still needed."

"Definitely." Morgan's expression grew serious and she moved directly in front of Roxie. "We're doing everything we can to mitigate the danger, but you're still taking a huge risk. I'm aware of all you're risking and appreciate your willingness to help us."

Roxie smiled. "Careful, ma'am. You're going to ruin your reputation as a hard-ass."

Morgan chuckled. "Well, we can't have that." She motioned Lor forward and moved out of the way. "Get busy, Master dar Joon. We haven't got all day."

"Or all night as it were," Lor muttered. "Frist things first, I'll anchor a telepathic link with each of you and then I'll form the proximity bond."

Elias had been working with the Mystics for almost two months now and they still managed to amaze him. Lor was skilled and powerful, and Elias barely felt it when Lor anchored the first link.

Can you hear me? Elias nodded and Lor smiled. *The link is interactive. You can respond silently.*

That will come in handy. Will Roxie and I be able to talk mind-to-mind?

Only when the link is already open. The connection must be activated by a Mystic.

Lor moved closer to Roxie and asked, "Are you ready?"

"I should be used to this by now." She sighed, but her fingers tightened against Elias' hand. "Go ahead."

For a moment Elias sensed nothing and then his connection with Lor tingled and expanded. Like an operator searching for a radio signal, his mind filled with white noise then Lor's thoughts cut through the static.

Is my signal clear? Lor looked at Roxie and she nodded. *Try to respond. We need to be able to hear you as well.*

We? She turned her head sharply and looked up at Elias. *Can he hear my thoughts too?*

Lor chuckled, but his expression remained patient. *Only after a Mystic has opened the link. But you need to be careful what you say. Anyone skilled with telepathic links can access this connection. If I shield it any more securely, you wouldn't be able to hear me.*

She accepted the limitation with obvious disappointment. *Okay. I can hear you fine.*

Can you hear me? Elias asked.

Loud and clear.

And that's all there is to it. Lor smiled at Roxie. *Now that wasn't so bad, was it?*

She blinked a couple of times then shook her head. "No, but you're not finished."

"The proximity bond is only a little more complicated, still nothing to fear." Lor held out his hand, palm up. "Place your hands on mine. You must be touching each other as well as me." Elias put his free hand on top of Lor's and Roxie followed his example. "Roxie, your hand must touch mine as well as his."

"Sorry." She curved her fingers until her palm pressed against his hand and her fingertips rested on Lor's.

"Now try to relax and accept the new sensations. It will feel strange, but it shouldn't be painful."

Roxie closed her eyes, but Elias watched her. He could still feel her silken skin as he slid his hands over her body. A faint hint of her taste lingered on his tongue, teasing him, making him hungry for more. With a frustrated sigh, he dragged his gaze away. His distraction endangered them both. He needed to resist these feelings and focus on her safety. At least until the danger had passed.

It was just easier said than done.

As if to mock his determination, emotions flowed into his mind and cascaded through his body, pulsing desire and urgent anticipation. He wasn't the only one remembering their love play and Roxie's imagination was just as detailed as his. Elias shivered and finally closed his eyes.

"That should do it." Lor's voice sounded strained as if he was trying not to laugh. "The next few days should be interesting for you two."

"How far apart can we get?" Roxie asked.

Elias opened his eyes and arched his brow. "Trying to escape me already?"

"Actually I was wondering if I could still use the bathroom alone. If you must know."

She was lying. He could see a clear image of them together in a steamy shower and he was more than open to the idea.

"The bond will keep you within ten feet of each other. That should give you enough of a separation for bodily functions and the occasional moment of privacy."

"Why don't you see if it works?" Morgan suggested.

Roxie rushed toward the bathroom and Elias felt a shockingly strong pull as she hit the proximity limit. He was literally dragged across the floor until they were within ten feet of each other again. "Okay, this is going to be strange."

"Better strange than separated." Roxie looked at him, a complex tangle of emotions making her blue eyes shine. "And I think you should have this." She held out the suppression collar. "If he's focused on me, you'll have a better chance of actually getting that thing around his neck."

He wasn't sure he agreed with her, but he accepted the device. She was obviously overwhelmed and he would do everything in his power to make her feel safe. "Whatever you need, I'm there."

She smiled. "I appreciate you doing this for me."

He started to say it was his job, but the words felt dishonest now. She was more than his assignment and he couldn't pretend otherwise. "We'll get through this together."

SEVRIN STOOD IN THE parking lot outside Roxie's apartment building, feeling like a desperate voyeur. "Are you sure she's in there?"

Flynn shrugged. "That's where she lives." He pointed to the corner unit on the second floor. "Whether or not she's in there is anyone's guess." He scraped at the pavement with the toe of his boot, obviously restless and annoyed. "I could slip in behind an invisibility shield, but every time I use my abilities I risk detection. A wise woman once told me that."

Her only response was a smirk. She'd issued the warning because the hunters had been using their abilities indiscriminately. People on

Ontariese were used to Mystics flashing into sight and walking through walls. Earth was different. Humans stopped and stared when anything out of the ordinary happened. And worse, they whipped out their phones and started recording.

"Why don't you go up there and knock on the door," he suggested.

"Maybe I will." The sarcastic retort sprang automatically to her lips, but the idea took root within her mind. If the Mystic Militia had gotten to Roxie, Sevrin needed to know about it now. She could not allow Lor and his team of busybodies to realize Roxie's true value. Sevrin had suffered too many setbacks already. She had no choice but to press onward. "If they tagged her, will you be able to sense it?"

Flynn stopped fidgeting and looked at her. "My abilities don't work that way."

"Your father was a sweeper. Didn't you inherit any of his abilities?" Flynn frequently bragged about all of the things his father had been able to do. Only Varrik, the alpha sweeper, had been more skilled, at least according to Flynn's stories.

"My aptitudes more closely aligned with hunter training."

She glared up at him. "That didn't answer the question. Can you sense Mystic energy or not?"

"I can, but Roxie is a hybrid. Mystic energy will resonate from her even if her abilities are latent. It's unlikely I will be able to sort through the specifics with any reliability."

"We know Lor and at least two of his men were in her shop. I need to know what happened after Nazerel left."

"And you think she's going to tell you?" His scoff, though quiet, made her palm itch for contact with his lean cheek. She tolerated insubordination from no one. "She's terrified of you."

"Exactly," she snapped. "And I want to make damn sure she stays that way."

"She'll tell the Mystic Militia you're still in town. Right now, they have no idea where you are."

"Maybe, and maybe not. There was no way to completely shield the arrival of the supply convoy. We avoided human detection, but any Ontarian ship would have been able to identify where the transports landed. If Lor is as clever as they say, he knows we're still in the area. I'm not quite ready for Roxie, but from this point on, I need to know her exact location." With her decision made, Sevrin smoothed down her narrow skirt and started across the parking lot.

It was still early, yet already the sun glared across a cloudless sky. Rodymia was hot compared to Ontariese and Bilarri, but the air was soft and moist, and trees were plentiful. It was far superior to this barren wasteland. She took the nearest staircase to the second floor then strode to Roxie's front door. The complex was clean and well-maintained, yet far from luxurious. There was no doorbell, so she raised the metal knocker and rapped several times. When no one responded, she had Flynn pound with the heel of his hand.

"What do you want?" Roxie called without opening the door.

"I just want to speak with you. Open the door."

"I can hear you just fine like this."

Sevrin looked around to make sure no one was about then moved closer to Flynn. "Flash me inside."

"Say please." He leaned down and nipped the side of her throat.

"We don't have time for this." She smacked his shoulder. "Flash me inside."

His arm encircled her waist and he yanked her hard against him. An instant later, they stood in the front room of Roxie's apartment.

"How did he..."

Roxie's shock was almost believable. "Don't pretend you've never seen someone teleport before. I know for a fact you have."

Instantly Roxie dropped her little-girl-lost act. "Fine." She crossed her arms over her chest. "I did everything you asked me to do. What do you want now?"

"Where did they take you after Nazerel left your shop?" Sevrin watched Roxie carefully, waiting for a twitch or guilty glance, any sign of deception.

"They all went after Nazerel. I never left my shop."

Roxie remained composed and sounded sincere, but Sevrin knew better. "You're lying. After an inadvertent exposure, you would have been debriefed. Where did they take you and what did they do?"

"This is between you and them," Roxie insisted. "I want nothing to do with it!"

Sevrin crossed her arms under her breasts, pleased by the flicker of fear in Roxie's gaze. She was a latent hybrid, unaware of her true worth. She should be frightened. "Answer a few simple questions and I'll be on my way."

The bedroom door inched open and Flynn sprang into action. He flew across the room and kicked the door inward, driving the unseen observer back. But rather than retreat, the dark-haired man attacked in an admirable—though foolish—attempt at bravery. The stranger slammed his shoulder into Flynn's stomach, wrapped his arms around his hips and drove Flynn to the floor, flat on his back. Momentum carried the stranger down as well. Flynn gasped in a breath then his hands glowed as he prepared to launch energy pulses at the other male.

"Don't kill him," Sevrin commanded, her voice sharp and urgent. "I want to speak with him."

Flynn's fingers curled and the glow slowly dimmed. "Get off me, *human*." He snarled the last word, making it sound extremely unpleasant.

The human climbed off Flynn, and Sevrin had her first good look at him. He was tall and muscular, with short yet wavy hair. His sharp green gaze settled on her for just a moment before he looked at Roxie. "Are you okay?"

"I'm fine. You should have stayed out of sight."

Roxie was trying to protect this mass of muscle? How sweet. "Who are you?" She moved closer, wanting a better look at his eyes. Was he truly human or an Ontarian in disguise?

"He has nothing to do with this." Roxie reached for her upper arm, but Flynn intercepted her attempt, moving her hand well out of range. Roxie jerked her arm out of Flynn's grasp and insinuated herself between Sevrin and Elias.

The human wrapped his arm around her waist and kissed the top of her head. "I can take care of myself, darlin'. You don't need to worry about me."

There was a slight accent to his speech that Sevrin found intriguing. Was he Roxie's lover or something more interesting? "I wasn't aware you had a significant other," she prompted. "Why have I never seen him before?"

"This is the first time we've actually been together."

"Let me guess," Sevrin muttered. "You met online."

Roxie's gaze sharpened as she shot back. "Recent events prompted his visit."

It was an explanation and yet so much was left undefined. "Which events do you mean and from where does your handsome suitor hale?"

"That would be Austin, Texas, ma'am." He held out his hand with an unassuming smile. He was like a large canine, ever eager to please his master. She wasn't sure if she was amused or disgusted by his friendliness. It was foolish for anyone to be that trusting.

After a quick handshake, Sevrin focused on Roxie again. "What happened after Nazerel left?"

Roxie licked her lips, clearly uncomfortable with the subject. "The weapon he discharged gave me a terrible headache."

Sevrin fought back a smile. So that was how they explained her sudden unconsciousness. The Mystics hadn't admitted to using a mental compulsion; Nazerel had discharged some mysterious weapon. "Go on."

"They wanted to make sure—"

"Who are 'they'? How many people did you see?"

"I just saw Jillian and her boyfriend."

Did Roxie really think she was stupid? "If you only saw two, who went after Nazerel?"

"Jillian mentioned the others. I never saw them."

Possible, but not probable. Roxie's caginess could be the result of fear, but she could also know a whole lot more than she was pretending. "I interrupted you. What were you going to say?"

"They wanted to make sure Nazerel hadn't harmed me, so they insisted I come with them."

That was interesting. "Where did they take you?"

"I'm not sure. I was blinded by the headache on the way there and they blindfolded me when they drove me home."

"And when was this?"

"Five or six hours later." Roxie shrugged, looking more uncomfortable by the minute. "I don't know exactly. The entire day is sort of blurry."

Had they taken her to their ship? No, that would have created more problems than it solved. "To what sort of facility were you taken?"

"It was a small clinic or doctor's office in a building all by itself. There wasn't much around it either. I have no idea how they stay in business."

"How long did it take to get there? Could you tell what direction they drove?" She paused for a challenging smile. "Did they drive you there or choose a faster means of travel?"

"Like a helicopter?" the human suggested in an attempt to be helpful. Too bad he didn't have a cunning mind to go with that handsome face. It might have been amusing to provoke Flynn with the possibility of competition.

"We were in a SUV, nothing more elaborate." Roxie licked her lips again and snuggled back into her companion's embrace. "They gave me something for the pain, so I was pretty groggy on the way there."

"And on the way back? How long were you in the SUV?"

Roxie shrugged again. "I've never been good at gauging time, especially when I can't see what's going on around me. Maybe an hour and a half."

"Who did you see while you were at this clinic? Describe them for me."

The Texan had a calming effect on Roxie. Her voice grew stronger, her expression more composed as she leaned back into his embrace. "Jillian stayed with me. She felt really bad about everything that had happened. I saw a doctor and a nurse. The doctor was a balding man in his fifties. The nurse was maybe thirty-five, blonde, a little on the heavy side. Neither of them were anything special. Why do you ask?"

Why indeed. Had the Ontarians taken her to a human doctor or had Roxie agreed to keep their secrets? Sevrin could usually sense it when someone lied to her. Roxie just seemed nervous and impatient. "How did your boyfriend become involved?"

"He *isn't* involved. That's the point."

He caught her gaze over the top of Roxie's head. "She called me in hysterics, ma'am. Asked if I could fly in for a few days. I wasn't about to tell her no."

"You flew in from Texas?" Why would he drop everything and come to the rescue of someone he'd not yet met? Humans were so strange.

"Yes, ma'am. We kept saying we should meet in person. This gave me a hard enough push to make it happen."

"When did you get in?"

"Around three yesterday morning," Roxie told her. "We've been here ever since." She made a bland gesture toward the bedroom.

That explained the sexual tension sizzling between them, but Sevrin lingered a moment longer. Flynn had said Roxie's car wasn't at her apartment when he'd checked the day before. He might have been lying about checking. Sevrin had been angry with him at the time. It was hard to believe Roxie knew nothing more than she was saying. It was just too convenient. Or Roxie had been carefully insulated against information that could harm her. But why would the Mystic Militia care about the fate of a latent hybrid? Something here just didn't add up.

After a long, strained pause, Roxie said, "I thought you left town."

"I did." She motioned toward Flynn. "He *drove* me back so I could speak with you. Flynn drives really fast."

"Well, I'm sorry you wasted the trip. I don't know any more than I did the last time you saw me."

"Somehow I doubt that, but I'm willing to let it go for now. Just remember how fast Flynn can have me here if I ever find out you've betrayed me."

"I haven't betrayed you." Roxie calmly met her gaze, almost daring her to doubt the claim. "I don't know what's going on between you and Jillian's friends. More importantly, I don't care. Your fight has nothing to do with me, so leave me out of it."

Sevrin stared at Roxie for another moment then motioned Flynn toward the door. They opened the barrier this time rather than flashing through it.

"What did you sense in there?" She waited until they were well away from the apartment to ask.

"I felt pulses of Mystic energy, but that's not unusual with a hybrid. I also sensed a link between them, but that's not unusual for a couple who recently became lovers."

"It wasn't a mating bond, was it?"

"No. A mating bond is significantly stronger. I'm not even sure this one was formed intentionally. Does Roxie even know she's a hybrid?"

"I certainly haven't told her. And if what she told me is true, the others have no reason to tell her either. Could you tell if she was lying or not?"

He shook his head. "My powers don't work like that."

She sighed. She had no reason to doubt him. Still, something didn't feel right. She couldn't define her discomfort, but she'd learned long ago to trust her instincts.

They reached a small weedy clearing between two of the three apartment buildings. She carefully checked to make sure they weren't observed then stepped into Flynn's embrace. "Take me to the Team South house. It's time I had it out with Nazerel."

"WHY DIDN'T YOU FLASH in here?" Roxie shouted at Blayne. She was so angry she was shaking. When the Mystics failed to intervene during Sevrin's visit, Roxie had presumed something had gone horribly wrong. But moments after Sevrin's departure, Blayne and his two new friends casually knocked on the front door. "Sevrin was right there! All you had to do was grab her."

"You were never in any danger." Though compassion shone in Blayne's silver-blue eyes, his tone remained resolute. "Capturing Sevrin is no longer our primary objective."

"What are you talking about?" Elias flared, every bit as pissed off as Roxie.

The Mystic glanced at his silent companions before he explained. The other two Mystics stayed well back, allowing Blayne to take the brunt of their hostility. "Early this morning Morgan received a detailed update from Flynn. The situation is much worse than we thought. Sevrin has six females in varying stages of transformation. This has become a rescue mission."

"I don't understand what you're talking about." Roxie took a deep breath, trying to calm down enough to recall everything she'd learned in the past few days.

"Sevrin has been trying to transfer Mystic abilities into someone born without them for decades. The Shadow Assassins were part of that process. We thought she'd given up when she found out about the battle-born daughters. Apparently, we were wrong."

"Apparently," Elias grumbled. "What makes you think she's still at it?"

Blayne visibly braced for their reaction as he said, "She's not just 'at it'; she has succeeded. There are six human females at her lab that now exhibit Mystic abilities."

"That sucks, but what does it have to do with why you didn't help us?" Roxie crossed her arms, her hands still tightly clenched. "This could have been over. It *should have* been over!"

"Flynn can't lead us to the lab," Blayne reminded. "If he could, none of this would be necessary."

"I know that, dumb-ass." It was all she could do not to slap the serene expression off his face. "Sevrin sure as hell can."

"It would have taken days, perhaps weeks of Mystic interrogation to unlock Sevrin's mind. She has trained for years to resist such probing. By that time the captives would have been slaughtered, along with any nonessential personnel, and all evidence of the research destroyed. Rodytes are ruthless. Our only hope is a fast, clean, surprise attack on the actual lab."

Dread dropped like a brick into the pit of Roxie's stomach. "Meaning there is no longer any other option; she has to take me there?"

"She has to take *us* there." Elias slipped his arm around her waist and pulled her against his side. "You're not going anywhere without me."

"Do you still have the suppression collar?" Blayne asked Elias.

"I do."

"Thank you for not using it. It's much better if they don't realize we have one."

Roxie tensed and looked up at him. "Did Blayne tell you not to use it?"

"He didn't have to. It would have been wasted on Flynn. Besides, by the time we were wrestling, it was obvious the Mystics weren't going to interfere."

"Why was it obvious to you?" She twisted out of his light embrace and moved several paces away. "It surprised the hell out of me."

"Sevrin was just doing recon. This wasn't an attack."

Roxie turned back to Blayne, emotions still seething inside her. "Go. Away! If you can't bother to show up when I need you, you sure as hell aren't going to hang around when I don't."

Blayne motioned to the other Mystics and all three flashed out of sight.

An exasperated cry tore from Roxie's throat. "I really need to hit someone!"

Elias ambled toward her, all calm, composed, alpha male. She wanted to kick him in the shins just to change his expression. "Go ahead. I can take it."

She shot him a disdainful look. "It would probably just hurt my fist." He reached for her hand, but she snatched it away, not yet ready to accept the comfort waiting in his warm embrace. "Do you think she bought it?"

He lifted one broad shoulder in a lazy shrug. "I don't know how much of your story Sevrin believed, but she wasn't suspicious enough to confront you and you're still safe. We couldn't ask for more."

"Yes we can!" She planted her hands on her hips and glared up at him. "I want this finished. I want all of the aliens out of my life and I want..." Her breath shuddered out and she furiously blinked back tears. That evil bitch would not make her cry! She wouldn't allow it. "I'm going to take a shower. If I don't cool off, I'm going to punch a hole through the wall."

"Or," he stepped even closer, his gaze beginning to smolder, "we can work off your frustration and take a shower together when we're done."

"I won't perform for Blayne and his cronies."

"I'm sure they're nearby, but they know you're upset. They'll give us a little space."

She stared into his eyes as their proximity bond vibrated with excess energy. She couldn't deal with a gentle seduction right now. Fast and frantic makeup sex was more in line with the emotions surging through her. With a silent prayer that he'd understand what she was doing, she drew back her hand. She paused for a heartbeat, making her intention obvious, then swung fast and hard, her open palm angled toward his face.

He caught her wrist a millisecond before her palm connected with his cheek. "I'm not the enemy." His tone was dark and smoky, filled with sensual promise.

"No, you're my jailor, my shadow, my guard." The words sprang automatically to her lips, fueled by lingering resentment and insecurity. She yanked against his fingers, reveling in the strength so obvious in the simple hold. "Why won't you leave me alone?"

"I can't." He leaned down and whispered, "I won't."

She shoved against his chest with her free hand, but he felt solid, grounded, unmovable. Excitement tingled through her, awakening her senses as heat trailed in the wake of the other sensations. Rocking up onto the balls of her feet, she twisted his T-shirt around her hand. "What do you want from me?"

"You know what I want." He released her wrist and wrapped both arms around her, pressing her tightly against his body. "I've made my desires clear. The question is, what do you want from me?"

"Nothing." She wiggled and twisted, rubbing against his hard body until they were both breathless. God it felt good, but her temper was still churning. "You're an arrogant jerk! I don't even like you." She threw her weight back, knowing he'd catch her, keep her safe within his arms.

He chuckled, both hands moving down to grasp her butt. "Your pride's sayin' one thing, honey, while your body's sayin' another. Which should I believe?"

"Believe whatever you like." She arched away, turning her head sharply to one side. "You don't care what I say."

Effortlessly reading her silent signals, he fisted the back of her hair and turned her head back around. "No more teasing, no more games."

His mouth covered hers, urging her lips apart for the bold thrust of his tongue.

She moaned into his mouth, retuning the kiss with equal urgency. Her body came alive with a sudden jolt, anger fueling her desire. Her skin felt tight and hot, her nipples tingled and her core clenched hard enough to warrant another moan. She'd never needed a man like she needed Elias.

Her arms wrapped around his broad back and her hips started rolling. She rubbed against him like an affectionate cat. Suddenly, he stilled and clasped her hips with both hands. He tore his mouth away and looked deep into her eyes.

"Can you feel that?" He rubbed against her, leaving her no chance of misunderstanding his meaning. She licked her lips and nodded. "Then you know exactly what I want from you, what I need more than breath right now."

The hunger in his gaze hypnotized her and triggered an ache deep inside. Before she could think of another objection, he picked her up and carried her into her bedroom. "You better not stop this time," she whispered against his throat. "I need this too badly."

"You're not leaving this bed until I run out of condoms." He bent his head and kissed her, the touch soft and tender this time. "Unfortunately, that's not much of a threat. I only have two." He tossed her onto the bed where she landed with a little bounce.

Roxie laughed, joy bubbling up inside her. "I think we can survive long enough to buy more." His playfulness was even sexier than his growling intensity and she responded to it just as readily.

"We don't actually need them, you know. Of course, you only have my word on that." He sat on the side of the bed so he could pull off his boots and socks.

"What do you mean? I'm not on the Pill."

"You don't need to be." He looked back at her then tucked his socks down inside one of his boots. "Hybrids can't conceive without a mating bond and you're immune to the vast majority of human diseases."

Her pulse raced as he waited for her reply. His expectation was obvious, the hope shimmering in his eyes. She wanted to trust him, but there had been so many stories about aliens intentionally impregnating Earth's females.

Elias wasn't an alien.

But you don't really know him that well.

Her inner voice won out in the end. If she didn't protect herself, no one would. "I..." She swallowed hard and tried again. "I'd be more comfortable if you used a condom."

"I understand." His expression didn't change, though he quickly looked away and disappointment sparked across their link.

Her heart sank and she reached out for him, not wanting the closeness they were building to slip away. He stood before her fingers made contact and hurriedly stripped off his shirt.

The bunch and flex of his muscles momentarily scattered her thoughts. She'd seen pictures and videos of people who were toned like this, but she'd never had the opportunity to touch one until she met Elias. He took off his jeans, pausing to dig the condoms out of his wallet before he let the garment fall to the floor. Dressed in nothing but his underwear, he turned back toward the bed. "If you're not ready for this, we can—"

"I'm ready." She knelt on the bed and pulled off her tank top. "I'm more than ready. But all the talk about war brides and knocking up coeds has made me a little paranoid."

He tossed the condoms on the bed then pulled her toward the edge. With her kneeling on the mattress and him standing beside the bed, they were nearly the same height. "We'll never do anything you're not comfortable with and I'll never lie to you."

She lightly rested her hands on his shoulders, stubbornly meeting his gaze. "Never is a really long time. Let's start with today."

"Deal."

Flashing his sexy grin, he swept her legs out from under her. She landed on her back with a gasp as he attacked the laces at the front of her black leather pants. She'd kicked off her sandals by the front door, a long-standing habit, so he was able to peel the supple fabric down her legs.

He caught her foot with one hand and raised her ankle to his lips. Tingles danced up her thigh and heat erupted in her core. He'd wanted to taste her the night before and she'd stopped him, hoping to slow the consuming fire devouring them both. The heat in his gaze made it obvious the need had returned. Or maybe it never left, maybe he'd been thinking about this ever since Morgan pounded on his door.

His lips brushed her ankle as his fingers blazed a trail up her calf. She tried not to squirm, to enjoy the light caress, but her body had other ideas. She felt tense and overstimulated and he'd barely begun to touch her. How would she survive once they really got going?

"Please," she whispered, helplessly arching toward him.

"Relax," he murmured, his lips caressing her skin. "I've got you."

She clutched the bedding as his mouth explored her knee, finding sensitive patches she hadn't realized were there. He took his time, frequently gazing into her eyes as his tongue stroked over her tingling skin.

It took him an eternity to reach her panties and still he wanted to tease. His fingertips skimmed along each edge, barely touching her skin. Anticipation crept closer to desperation and her thighs began to shake. She felt like a rubber band stretched to the breaking point, vibrating at that moment just before it snapped.

"You're killing me," she lamented, but his shoulders were firmly wedged between her legs now and she couldn't do more than whisper protests.

Finally, he caught the sides of her panties and eased the garment down. She held her breath, tense and hyper-aware of everything about him. She felt the heat of his skin against hers and the gentle brush of his fingertips. His gaze burned into her flesh as she was revealed to him inch by inch. Even her lungs seemed determined to echo the rhythm of his breathing.

"Oh God…" He tossed her panties aside and buried his face between her thighs.

His tongue found her clit and the rubber band snapped. She cried out, coming in deep spasms that radiated out from her abdomen. His low chuckle assured her that he knew what just happened, and yet he didn't stop. His lips slid against her folds and his tongue wandered from her clit only to return to the knot of nerves again and again.

The sensations had barely begun to recede when a fresh wave of pleasure flowed in behind it. Roxie rubbed against his mouth, helpless to resist the intoxicating aftershocks. It felt so good and yet it only made her desperate for what he'd denied her the night before.

She reached down and pushed her fingers into his hair, pulling gently until he raised his gaze. "Please. I need you inside me, *now*."

In a blur of motion, he dragged off his underwear then grabbed a condom off the corner or the bed. He opened the package with his teeth and rolled the barrier down his shaft as he positioned himself at her entrance. His hands grasped her hips and their gazes locked, then he entered her in one long, steady thrust. Her eyelids drooped as fullness overwhelmed the other sensations. This wasn't her first time, not even close, but nothing had ever felt so...significant before.

He pulled his hips back just as slowly then drove forward much faster. She gasped and drew her legs up along his sides. His hands moved up to her waist and he pulled her entire body even closer to the edge of the bed. He still stood on the floor, but arched over her now, his mouth latching on to one nipple.

Sensations zinged from her breast to her clit then rippled up along the walls surrounding him. She'd never been this aroused before, hadn't realized her body was capable of all these sensations. Her entire body seemed attuned to his. He drove into her over and over, each thrust pushing the pleasure higher.

He kissed his way to the base of her neck, but couldn't reach her mouth. With a frustrated growl, he wrapped both arms around her and pulled her up off the bed. He spun around and sat down then arranged her legs so she straddled his hips. They were still connected, but just barely.

His fingers tangled in her hair and he brought her mouth to his. "Ride me." He whispered the command half a second before his tongue thrust into her mouth.

She clutched his shoulders, lost in the wild possession of his tongue, but gradually realized the rest of his body had stilled. He wanted her to "ride him", she remembered through a haze of passion. Adjusting the position of her knees, she lowered herself onto his cock. He moaned into her mouth and his hands grasped her hips, steadying her without taking over.

Following his example, she pulled up slowly then drove down fast and hard, taking him deep into her body as they moaned in unison. One of his hands moved back to her hair, shifting her head to a different angle. His lips caressed and his tongue slid as she gradually found a similar rhythm.

Needing to feel all of him, not just the parts moving inside her, she stroked over his chest and onto his shoulders, down his arms then up his sides. Every inch of him was lean and tightly muscled, strong and capable. And every inch of his amazing body, every ounce of strength, every beat of his noble heart would protect and comfort her. Rather than looking for ways to manipulate and abuse her, he would take care of her. She shivered as the realization sent unexpected emotions crashing over her.

The smooth motion of her hips became stilted and then she stopped, tearing her mouth away from his. She turned her face to the side, not wanting him to see the tears gathering in her eyes. Her heart thundered in her chest and conflicting emotions twisted and pulled, making her feel anxious and afraid. He would never hurt her. She had no doubt about that. But could he really care for her, want more for her and from her than a stolen moment of physical release?

"What's this?" His voice was low and patient, though their link still pulsed with unfulfilled desire. He brushed the hair back from her face, but she wouldn't look at him. "Do we need to stop?"

"No." She tightened her inner muscles and buried her face against his neck. "Just give me a minute."

"Take all the time you need." He held her, his hands caressing her shoulders and back. He didn't ask questions or whisper platitudes. He surrounded her with warmth and caring, protecting her from her own insecurities.

Finally, she composed herself enough to lift her head. She pushed her fingers into his hair and stared into his eyes as she moved over and against him again. His expression was open and honest, hungry yet compassionate. She moved faster, taking him deeper, and desire burned brighter with each firm stroke.

His hands returned to her hips, helping now, yet still allowing her to set the pace. "Kiss me," he urged.

Without slowing the rolling motion of her pelvis, she pressed her lips against his and pushed her tongue into his mouth. He sucked her deeper, his fingers digging into her hips. Emotions, hot and consuming, streamed into her mind. Afraid of the sudden deluge, she resisted at first. But individual feelings curled through her, identifying themselves as they passed. Affection, respect, and a protective sort of longing that could only belong to Elias. Sensing his personality in the unfamiliar emotions, she gradually surrendered to the intensity.

His emotions fueled hers and the kiss became wilder, more demanding. He thrust up into her, no longer able to remain passive. The combined movements doubled the impact, sending bursts of sensation all through her body. She gasped and arched, her inner muscles hugging him tightly.

Then he drove his full length into her and held her snuggly in place as he shuddered violently. Pleasure surged across their link, detonating a fresh cycle of rhythmic pulses. She shook with the force of her climax, lost to anything but the pleasure ricocheting between them.

He collapsed back across the bed, taking her with him. Her muscles gradually relaxed as she sprawled across his chest. He was still buried inside her and she couldn't find the strength to crawl off him or roll to her side. This just felt too good.

"You okay?" His hand swept down her back and squeezed her butt with intimate familiarity.

"Why wouldn't I be?" It was a foolish evasion. She knew exactly what he was asking about.

"Why'd you freeze up in the middle?" He hesitated over the description as if he couldn't find exactly the right words to define what she's done.

Not surprising. She wasn't sure what had brought on her "freeze up". "I'm not afraid of you."

"I'm glad. The last thing I want to inspire in you is fear." He touched her face. "Will you please look at me?"

Slowly, she pushed against his chest and raised her face until their gazes locked. "Everyone I've ever known wanted something from me." He started to say something, but she shook her head. "I want to believe this is different, that it has nothing to do with your job, but I can't forget how we met."

"Earning your trust is an ongoing process. I understand that." He stroked the side of her face then brushed his thumb over her lower lip. "And nothing I *say* is going to change your mind. You need actions, tangible proof that what I say is true."

"I need time." She sighed and nipped his thumb. "But I'm trying."

"I know and I'll do my best not to rush you."

He wasn't entirely to blame for the whirlwind pace, but everything was happening much too fast. "We should go see Jett and Tess. I'm afraid the half-connected call might have made them even more suspicious." Reluctantly, she separated their bodies and crawled off the bed.

"We're going to take a shower first." He rubbed his bristly chin. "And I need to shave. Then let's grab something to eat on the way. I'm starving."

She glanced at him and longing clutched her heart, making her insides feel empty. Even sex tousled and scruffy, the man was gorgeous.

She shook away the now familiar ache and focused on one of the many questions lingering within her mind. "Something has been bothering me."

Rolling smoothly off the side of the bed, he ambled over to her and pulled her into a light embrace. "Something I can help with, I hope."

"I'm not sure. Morgan said Rodyte hybrids can't conceive without a mating bond. If I can't manipulate magic, how will I form one?"

His lips thinned and his jaw tensed, then he offered her a tight smile. "I don't know." He sighed and lowered his arms to his sides. "The obvious answer is you'll need to mate with someone who can manipulate magic, but there are probably other ways. Lor linked us with the proximity bond and neither of us can manipulate magic. Don't panic." He smiled at her, a slow, sexy smile this time. "I just used us as an example. I haven't forgotten that we just met."

She nodded, but Elias had misunderstood her expression. She hadn't panicked at the thought of bonding with him. Just the opposite in fact. Earth was her home and their uninvited guests had brought nothing but trouble into her life. She might have alien blood, but in her heart she would always be human. If mating with a Mystic was the only way she could have children, then she would adopt a human child.

"Let's go take a shower." She took him by the hand and led him toward her bathroom, turning her head so he wouldn't see the uncertainty lingering in her eyes.

Chapter Eight

Morgan paused in the corridor outside the conference room and took a deep breath. The second wave of Lor's reinforcements arrived a few minutes before and he asked that she join their briefing before they headed out to the field. Her team still outnumbered the Mystic Militia twenty to one, and her people were much more familiar with the setting. Still, that didn't keep a knot of tension from forming every time she witnessed the Mystics' extraordinary abilities. It was daunting to think what such people could do if their ambitions drove them toward conquest rather than cooperation.

Never one to avoid conflict, Morgan squared her shoulders and walked confidently into the room. "Good afternoon, gentlemen." She glanced around the table to make sure she didn't need to amend the greeting. As she'd presumed all of the new arrivals were male. Ontariese was still struggling with a disproportionately male population, so it had been a fair assumption.

Lor sat in her usual place at the head of the table, so she slipped onto the chair at the other end.

"This is Director Morgan Hoyt, leader of the human task force and our gracious hostess." Lor's tone stopped just short of condescension and four sets of curious eyes shifted toward her. Each man was dressed in jeans and a casual shirt. Their gently swirling gazes had been concealed behind contact lenses, making them appear human. The other two new Mystics were already in the field with Blayne. Their briefing had been on the fly, so Morgan hadn't been involved. "Have you heard from Elias? Has Sevrin made contact with them yet?"

Morgan swallowed before she spoke, making sure her voice was calm and authoritative. "She walked right up to the door like the big bad wolf and demanded that Roxie let her in."

"Is she a shapeshifter?" One of the Mystics asked, clearly baffled by her reference.

"Figure of speech." Fighting back a smile, she waved away his confusion. "When Roxie didn't oblige, Sevrin had Flynn teleport them inside."

"Is she usually so bold?" another Mystic asked.

"She's a Rodyte princess," the original speaker muttered. "Of course she's irrationally bold." Though the war raged between Bilarri and Rodymia, the people of Ontariese had long since chosen the Bilarrian side.

"I presume Roxie wasn't harmed or we wouldn't be sitting here." Lor brought the conversation back on track.

Morgan folded her hands on the table and kept her gaze focused on Lor. Though she couldn't help wondering about the new Mystics' abilities, she didn't let it distract her. Their biggest challenge had been containing people who could teleport. Could the new Mystics solve that problem? "Sevrin bought the cover story or at least decided not to push her luck. Once again Flynn's information proved accurate. Sevrin just wanted to make sure Roxie was easily accessible when the time comes."

"When the time comes for what?" the chatty Mystic asked. There was one in every group, the self-appointed leader and spokesperson. If the facilitator could control that one person, he controlled the entire room.

Lor didn't seem annoyed by the questions, so Morgan didn't interfere. She generally asked people to wait until she finished her explanation before they voiced concerns or asked for clarifications, but this wasn't her briefing.

"Sevrin has to verify that Roxie is healthy and capable of producing offspring," Lor replied. "Does that make sense, Bentar?"

"Each prominent family was not simply promised a mate. They were promised an *empowered* female capable of producing empowered offspring," Bentar persisted. "The élite families might have accepted Pern at his word, but they will demand proof from Sevrin."

"Or they'll bring someone who can determine the validity of her claims, like a Bilarrian slave or a rogue Mystic," one of the others agreed.

"Which is why we attack, and attack aggressively, the moment Sevrin snatches Roxie," Lor stressed. "Sevrin cannot be allowed to send word to her uncle that the first bride is ready. Pern's final program must follow him to the grave or this could spark an interplanetary war."

Bentar scooted closer to the table, clearly unsatisfied with the answers so far. "How do you know she hasn't already sent word to the Crown Stirate? These noble sons of Rodymia could have arrived with the supply convoy."

"We know they haven't the same way we know about the supply convoy," Morgan interjected. "Flynn isn't able to provide us with all of the information we need, but the information he has supplied has been accurate."

Bentar accepted her statement with a serene incline of his head. It was hard to judge the reactions of people who never changed their expression.

"Have there been any new developments?" Lor asked her.

"Not since this morning's bombshell."

"Which was?" Bentar wanted to know.

"Six captives in need of rescue and Sevrin's reported success with human transformation. It's what I explained just before Morgan arrived. The urgency of our mission has escalated and we have no choice now but locating the lab before we raid the Team South house." Morgan detected tension in Lor's silky tone. Apparently Bentar's persistence was finally starting to annoy his commander.

"This informant provided the location of the Team South house?"

"He did, and we've already confirmed that it's right where he said it would be." Lor paused to rub the back of his neck.

"How many of these team houses are there?" There seemed to be no end to Bentar's curiosity.

"Originally four. Team North is already in custody. Teams South and West combined, and it's their house to which Flynn just gave us the address. Flynn doesn't know the exact location of the Team East house." Lor rattled off the facts with a minimum of elaboration, likely hoping to discourage follow-up questions.

Before Bentar could speak again, Morgan addressed the room at large. "We've been tracking phantom energy spikes for several weeks now. The spikes stopped while the hunters were moving to their new locations. They tried to make it seem like they'd left town and scattered to the wind, but the spikes have started up again and they're still relatively close. The move was smoke and mirrors. They might be in new buildings, but they're still within a hundred-mile radius of Las Vegas."

"Our largest challenge has been capturing men who can teleport through most containment fields." Lor returned to Morgan's earlier point.

Not surprisingly, Bentar had a question. "Odintar was not able to contain them? How is that possible?"

"As I said, Odintar was recently injected with their nanites, but the hunters have had them since birth. Their physiology is in perfect harmony with the nanites, so they simply function better."

This brought up a question Morgan had been eager to ask. "I know you asked Jillian's guards about better weapons or a compact containment system. Were they able to help?"

"Who is Jillian?" Bentar asked.

"One of the hybrids we encountered in our search for Nazerel," Lor explained. "It turned out that she was a direct descendant of King Indric, so he provided her with a safety contingent."

Bentar nodded his approval. "If anyone can help us deal with Rodyte technology, it's the Bilarrians."

"And were they able to help?" Morgan brought the subject back to the original point.

"Yes and no." Lor spread his hands with a frustrated shrug. "Bilarrian weapons are better than ours, but incapacitating the hunters is only half the problem. We have to be able to keep them once we catch them."

His discouragement worried her. "I thought the holding cells at the new safe house had solved that problem. Elias told me you had tested them for us."

"Blayne couldn't teleport out, but Odintar could. It took him several tries and a massive amount of energy, but that won't bother the Shadow Assassins."

"So we're stuck transporting them to Ontariese?" This was not what she'd wanted to hear. Each time they opened an interdimensional portal they risked discovery and triggered a mountain of paperwork for her.

"Perhaps not. King Indric sent over the prototype of a mobile containment field generator. When I asked for assistance six weeks ago, this prototype was still in development. He can't guarantee it will work, but it's definitely worth a try."

"How is it used?"

Thank you, Bentar. She'd been just about to pose the question herself.

"It creates a field large enough to encase an entire house. As long as it's turned on before the hunters realize we're there, no one will be able to flash out. Theoretically, anyway."

"How long can it be sustained onsite?" Morgan asked, beating Bentar to the punchline.

"Not long. Here's the tricky part. Each hunter will need to be incapacitated and then moved to the safe house. With a steady source of energy, we should be able to use the prototype to augment the holding cells. Even Nazerel shouldn't be able to escape."

"Shoulds and shouldn'ts make me uncomfortable," Bentar grumbled. "Are there no better options?"

"If there were, we would have used them long ago," Lor concluded. "We have two primary objectives. We must be prepared at any moment to respond to Roxie's capture. Following her to the lab is our only hope of rescuing the captives and recovering the details of Sevrin's research."

"And two?" Bentar asked.

"We raid the Team South house, trapping as many hunters inside as possible. If we can accomplish those two objectives—and it will likely happen simultaneously—it will provide us with what we need to locate the Team East house and finally conclude this mission."

"Are you sure?" Morgan didn't want to rain on his parade, but she wasn't willing to ignore a hole in his strategy. "Flynn indicated that the teams operate autonomously. Team South members aren't going to be able to tell you how to find Team East. And it was my understanding that Sevrin has been conditioned to resist Mystic interrogation."

"She has." Lor paused dramatically. "But her guards have not. Flynn's report indicated that Sevrin is always accompanied by one or more of her guards. One of them will know the location of the Team East house."

She couldn't argue with his logic, but it sounded like a lot to take on all at once. Unfortunately, they'd run out of alternatives. The time for action was now and their move had to be all or nothing.

"In the meantime, we start searching for the other brides. We know Pern contracted with fifteen families, but we don't know how many hybrids he created. It could be considerably more than fifteen. Sevrin is alone in her search. She can't involve others without admitting that her father didn't trust her with the location of the females. At the moment, this is our only advantage and we must exploit it to the fullest. Assimilate the background information. Speak with anyone who might have known the war brides. Someone had to have delivered the babies. Learn the identity of the physicians or healers and find out what became of the infants. Were they adopted or did they become wards of the state?"

"I think we should contact the Symposium," Bentar suggested. "Surely the Wisdom of the Ages contains some of this information."

"It's worth a try, though the Symposium's information on humans is not nearly as extensive as it is on the life forms in our star system."

Bentar nodded then said, "I will contact them anyway."

"Are there any other questions?" Lor asked, looking pointedly at the other new arrivals.

"How is Roxie being monitored?" Bentar asked.

"She was injected with a radioactive isotope," Morgan told him. "This form of radiation is harmless, but it's so light it lingers in the air long after the person has left the area."

"And you are able to track this radiation with human technology?" Bentar sounded skeptical.

"I didn't say that." She smiled at the argumentative Mystic. "The system didn't originate on Earth. But don't bother asking. Where we acquired the technology is irrelevant."

"Does everyone understand their assignments?" When no one indicated otherwise, Lor said, "Dismissed."

ELIAS LOOKED AROUND Unique Ink with new interest. Now that he knew Roxie better, he easily picked out aspects of her personality reflected in the decorating and arrangement of the tattoo shop. It was organized with a natural flow that maximized the limited space. Though at a glance the shop was rebellious and edgy, an underlying practicality was evident as well.

Roxie had timed their arrival for the late-afternoon lull, hoping to find her employees between customers. Her instincts had served them well. Jett and Tess sat on the sofa in the front of the shop, enjoying chai lattes.

"Roxie!" Tess set down her paper cup and ran to Roxie, hugging her tightly. "We have been worried sick about you." She pushed Roxie to arm's length and looked her over. "No bumps and bruises? You're really okay?"

"I'm fine." She laughed and gave Tess another quick hug before stepping back. "And relieved to see my shop is still standing."

"You'll never have to worry about that," Tess assured. "We love this place as much as you do."

Jett set his drink aside with more deliberation then sauntered toward them. "Welcome back, *Special Agent* Bertram." His tone was anything but respectful. "Odd that the regional office of the FBI has no record of you."

Doing his best to hide his amusement, Elias glanced at Roxie's indignant employee. "My home office is in Virginia. I gave you a business card when we first met. Did you call that number?"

"As if that would prove anything." He cocked his head and narrowed his liner-accented eyes. His lips parted as if he'd say more, but Roxie cut him off.

"Give it up, Jett. As you can see, no harm was done." Her expression remained bland, but Elias didn't miss the mischievous sparkle in her eyes. "Special Agent Bertram took good care of me."

"But where have you been for the past three days?" Tess looked at Elias, uncertainty widening her eyes. "We were starting to wonder if someone else had your phone."

"That's why I called last night, or at least tried to. I know the connection was really bad."

"You didn't answer her question," Jett pointed out.

"My reaction to the experimental weapon was more serious than they originally thought. It took a bit longer to stabilize my condition than anyone expected, but I'm back now. Everything's okay."

"What about Nazerel and that woman?" Jett slipped his hands into his back pockets, puffing out his narrow chest. "What if they come back?"

"That's why I'm here." Elias met Jett's gaze but kept his tone conversational. Jett needed to understand that he wouldn't back down, yet he didn't want to provoke a fight either. A pissing contest at this point was counterproductive and pointless. "It's doubtful that either will return, but we aren't willing to take chances with any of you. Until all of the culprits are in custody, I'm Roxie's shadow."

"But no one can know who he is," Roxie stressed. "As far as the rest of the world knows, Elias and I have been talking online for the past few months. I was upset by the bizarre attack and asked if he'd fly in for a few days."

"He's staying at your apartment?" Disapproval sharpened Jett's already hostile tone. Was this friendly protectiveness or did his feelings run deeper for his lovely employer? It was easy to understand why Jett would be attracted to Roxie, but Elias had originally thought Jett was gay. "Why is that necessary?"

"It's hard to protect her if I'm not with her." Elias took a step toward Jett and let his tone growl. He'd tried being civil and Jett had grown more belligerent. The fastest way to shut down a yapper was to establish dominance. "Relax. I won't let anything happen to her."

A tense moment passed as they stared each other down, then Jett's shoulders lowered and he looked at Roxie. "Are *you* okay with this?"

Tess rolled her eyes. "Any straight woman on the planet would be okay with having him as a bodyguard." She moved closer to Elias and motioned toward the tattoo peeking out from the bottom of his sleeve. "Can I see the rest? It's unusual."

Happy for the distraction, Elias pulled up his T-shirt sleeve, revealing the majority of the geometric design.

"Nice and clean," Tess muttered. "Really unique."

"I've seen similar designs before," Jett grumbled, earning a reproachful chuckle from both of the women. Then he moved in for a closer look. "But this is really well done."

Tess walked her fingers up Elias' chest and smiled flirtatiously. "Have any more ink hidden under there?"

"He's not taking his shirt off," Roxie snapped, though laughter quivered through her voice.

"But you already know the answer, don't you?" Jett moved back and folded his arms, looking petulant rather than mean.

"That's none of our business," Tess insisted, then she looked at Roxie and amended, "But you'll tell me all the details later, right?"

Roxie laughed at their antics. "You're both impossible." Then, before the conversation could spiral completely out of control, Roxie casually changed the subject. "How does the rest of the day look?" She crossed to the display case and opened the appointment book, which lay near the cash register.

"I'm booked solid," Tess told Roxie as she moved up beside her. "But Jett only has one appointment. Walk-ins have been sort of slow. We'll be fine if you want to be somewhere else." She glanced over her shoulder and smiled at Elias. "I know I would."

"I think she's trying to get rid of us," Elias said in a stage whisper.

"Not Roxie. Just you." Jett went to the other side of the display case so he faced the other three. His demeanor was still faintly adversarial. "Your cover story is irrelevant to our customers. Anyone can tell at a glance that you're law enforcement. You'll make people nervous. Drive customers away."

"But I didn't even wear my bulletproof vest." He clasped both hands to his chest. "I'm hurt."

Tess turned around and leaned back against the display case. "If this was really an online romance and you'd just met for the first time, she'd want to be anywhere but here."

Roxie turned as well, smiling at Elias. "It's an ambush."

"We're thrilled that our fears were unfounded," Tess told Roxie, "but you should go play tourist for a couple of days. After all, Elias just got here. Right?"

"And he can't stay indefinitely." Now Jett sounded hopeful.

"I've never been to Las Vegas before," Elias played along. "I'd love to see the Strip." He had no objection to spending more time with Roxie. But was it safe for them to stroll around town? Would they be protected by the crowds or was it needlessly reckless? He was honestly not sure. Conventional wisdom said that the risk of discovery would decrease the chances that they would harm or attempt to kidnap Roxie, but nothing about these people was conventional.

"You win." Roxie held up her hands. "I'll entertain Elias. You two get back to work."

"Yes, boss." Jett finally smiled, but a hint of longing shadowed his gaze. "We'll see you in a couple of days."

Elias led Roxie back out into the Nevada sunshine. Dusk had yet to cast its cooling haze across the barren vista so the air was oppressive. They hurried to Roxie's car and she set the vehicle in motion, hoping to aid the air conditioner in its never-ending battle against the heat.

"Where to?" she asked as she maneuvered the car into the flow of traffic.

"I've seen the Strip a million times," he confessed. "Let's just go for a ride."

She kept her gaze focused straight ahead but her lips parted in a gentle smile. "I thought we already did that. Twice."

He'd meant a leisurely time spent in her car, but more of what they'd done that morning sounded even more appealing. "Doesn't mean we can't do it again. And Again."

"We need to stay in character, reinforce our roles." Color blossomed across her cheeks as she glanced at him. "Do you think I'm shameless?"

He laughed softly and reached over to touch her bare thigh. "You'll never be as shameless as me." She'd worn a short, flirty skirt today, making the game even more fun. He pushed his hand between her thighs as he freed himself from the seat belt so he could kiss her neck. She squirmed and laughed, trying to push his hand away while still maintaining control of the car. "Both hands on the wheel."

"You unfastened your seat belt," she objected with another laugh, but obeyed the throaty command.

His fingers brushed against her panties, which were already damp. "Don't mind me. Just keep driving."

"Elias." The word was part warning, part plea.

He pushed her left leg over, not wanting to disturb the foot responsible for acceleration—and braking. The insides of her thighs were smooth and warm. He teased the sensitive skin with the tips of his fingers, fascinated by the silky texture. "Can you come without closing your eyes?"

"No." She wiggled as his touch grew bolder, skimming over her mound before returning to her thighs. "You need to stop."

"You need to relax and accept the pleasure."

She shivered, her hands shifting on the steering wheel. "We're almost there. Just wait until we..."

As if to mock her assertion, the traffic light she approached turned red. He laughed and eased his fingers beneath the edge of her panties. He'd only intended to tease her, fuel their anticipation. But there was no one on either side of them and she was *so* warm.

"You're wicked." His finger gently parted her folds and she moaned, arching back against the headrest.

"And you love it." Aided by her slick moisture, he easily found her clit. Each circular stroke of his finger drew the tension in her body tighter. He could see it in her face and feel the intensity pulse across their telepathic connection. Her lips parted and her hips rocked, increasing the pressure of his touch. She was close, so—

A horn blast behind them shattered the mood and she shoved his hand away. "I can't believe you did that." She laughed as she drove through the intersection and hurried on toward their destination.

"You started it." He straightened in his seat and refastened his seat belt. "I'm glad your apartment is nearby."

They arrived a few minutes later but didn't make it to her apartment. Elias pushed her up against the wall on the railed walkway and kissed her with all the hunger she unleashed in him. She wrapped her leg around his thigh and clutched his shoulders, returning the kiss with equal urgency. They were both breathless and frantic by the time he pulled away.

"I want you inside me." She whispered the words then ducked under his arm and ran for her door.

He was half a second behind her, hands flattened on the door as she fumbled with the key. "Let me." He took the key out of her shaking hand and slipped it into the lock. She turned the knob and the door swung inward, drawing him off balance.

His weight nearly toppled her as they stumbled across the landing. He grabbed her keys, kicked the door closed, then rotated the lock before pouncing on her. "Thank God you wore a skirt."

She wrapped her arms around his neck and held on tight as he urged her to the floor on her back. Their mouths met and locked, breaths mingling. And the bedroom was simply too far away. She tugged his shirt up around his armpits, but could go no higher because he wouldn't raise his arms. Her skirt bunched around her hips as he reached beneath and pulled off her panties. He didn't bother with her boots or any of his clothes. He frantically unzipped his pants and filled her snug core with one desperate thrust. Then he froze over her, eyes open wide.

"We didn't stop for condoms." His heart was beating so fast he could hardly speak. He hadn't meant for this to happen, figured she would need some time to process the rapid-fire changes. But her thoughts immediately turned to sex and he'd been more than happy to follow along.

She wrapped her legs around his waist and squeezed him inside and out. "Look into my eyes and tell me we don't need them. I'll be able to feel the deception if you're lying to me."

He moved one hand to the side of her face and met her gaze. "You don't need a Mystic link for that, darlin'. I'll never lie to you." He pulled his hips back then pushed deep again, never loosing contact with her eyes. "We don't need protection." He thrust again and she arched to meet him. "I want nothing between us. I need to feel *all* of you."

Her inner muscles rippled and he was lost. He rocked back onto his knees and grasped her hips, taking her with deep, forceful strokes. Bending her knees even tighter, she drew her legs up along his sides. He watched her flushed face, amazed by the trust he saw in her gaze. She was open and welcoming, eager, yet surrendered to sensations she didn't fully understand.

He could feel her pleasure as well as his own and the combination was exhilarating. He draped her legs over his arms and rolled her hips up, giving him even deeper access. Her heat surrounded him, desire and affection swirling through his mind. Unable to resist the intensity, even though he knew it would end much too soon, he threw back his head and arched, making each drive longer and harder.

She gasped suddenly, her body bucking beneath him. Pleasure barreled across their link, punching into him with staggering force. He groaned and drove deep as her core rippled around his entire length. The rhythmic tightening snapped what little remained of his control. He let go, shuddering violently as he came in deep, pulsing spasms.

Humiliated by his lack of control, he separated their bodies and helped her up from the living room floor. "Well, that was a pathetic attempt on my part. You probably have rug burns on your ass."

She laughed merrily as she retrieved her discarded panties. "I started it, remember? And you weren't the only one in a hurry."

He caught her arm and pulled her close. "Will you give me another chance?"

She smiled up at him, not nearly as upset as he was. "I think I can be persuaded. Are you up for a challenge?"

"Definitely."

"Then let's see if we can both fit in my bathtub."

SEVRIN WALKED DOWN the corridor of her underground Farm, enjoying the rhythmic ring of her boot heels on the gleaming white floor. The sixth transformation had begun and the female was still alive. Better yet, the first female—or actually the first to survive—had begun to demonstrate hints of the donor's Mystic abilities. Just when she thought all was lost, a flicker of hope sparked within the ashes. If the unexpected progress, supplied by Orrit's ruthlessness, continued along this trajectory, her future might actually begin to untangle.

"We're so close, Father," she whispered to the ever-present ghost who shaped so many of her decisions. Learning of her father's secret project had been both crushing and exhilarating. She had been demoralized by the unavoidable fact that he hadn't trusted her with the details, yet the opportunity to establish personal relationships with the most powerful families on Rodymia was invaluable. Unlike her father, who had always ruled through fear and intimidation, her uncle was ridiculously popular. Her only hope of influencing him was to create a network of backers so powerful he would be incapable of ignoring their collective will.

She shook away the far-flung aspirations. Her long-term goals could only be achieved one step at a time. And each step she'd taken lately had been solid and shockingly progressive. Even if Roxie was the only product of her father's program that she located, it wouldn't matter. Her father had promised the families empowered females capable of producing empowered offspring, and thanks to Orrit, she was now in a position to fulfil that obligation. Her customers didn't need to know the means by which she accomplished her goals.

Pausing outside the holding cell containing the newest female, Sevrin studied her through the mirrored observation window. The other females had reacted to their captivity with tearful hysterics or sullen devastation. This woman was different. After an initial period of fear and anger, she had become composed and shrewdly observant. Orrit said she'd made some startlingly accurate guesses about what was being done to her, even though he conducted each procedure in stoic silence.

The woman was a bit older than the others, perhaps nearing thirty. She sat on the narrow bed, her legs folded in front of her. A tablet computer like the one she held had been given to each of the test subjects. Each device had been loaded with videos, books and games, while access to the internet had been disabled. Keep their minds occupied seemed to make them less combative.

Curious enough to make contact, Sevrin scanned open the door. The woman looked up, but didn't speak. Sevrin waited until the door clicked shut behind her before she broke the tense silence. "How are you feeling?"

"Like a caged animal. How would you feel?"

So much for casual pleasantries. "Life as you knew it ended the night you were chosen for this program. You can live in miserable servitude, resenting the changes which have been thrust upon you or you can embrace the unexpected and flourish in your new environment."

"Or I can spend the rest of my life trying to escape." There was no anger in her tone just the calm assurance of an established goal.

"Trying is the operative word in that alternative. Once it has been established that your transformation is stable, you will be taken to another planet. Have you factored that into your escape plans?"

"It's impossible." She set the tablet down and unfolded her legs, scooting to the edge of the bed. "I can't leave Earth. I have two children, and I'm raising them alone."

Ah, it all made sense now, the reason for her maturity and caution. She had to survive this ordeal so she could return to her children. "Why have you not mentioned children before now?"

"It was pretty obvious that no one else gave a damn. The guards are drones; they just follow orders. The scientist was only interested in my 'mutations' and that skinny-ass doctor never once looked into my eyes."

Her assessment of each was accurate. Orrit was right. This one was special. "What makes you think I give a damn about your children?"

"You're the first one to bother talking to me instead of whispering about me." Her leaf-green eyes met Sevrin's gaze with calm curiosity. "The others answer to you, don't they?"

"They do. As do you. What happened to the father of your offspring?"

The human tensed and lowered her gaze. "He's no longer part of my life."

An all too frequent happening with these humans. "Who ended the relationship?" Sevrin wasn't sure why she cared, but the feisty human intrigued her.

"I did."

Sevrin wasn't surprised. "Why?"

"He was a cheating bastard who contributed nothing to the relationship but frustration and pain. I don't have the time or energy for deadweight, so I cut him loose." She folded her hands in her lap and looked back into Sevrin's eyes. "Why all the questions?"

"What if your children were allowed to go with you? Is there anything else holding you here?"

The woman's brow crinkled as she worried her lower lip. "Would they have to go through...whatever it is you're doing to me?"

"No."

"And releasing me is not an option?"

"Correct."

Unshed tears made the human's eyes shimmer, but she stubbornly blinked them back. "Then I would much rather have my children with me. Without them I will never survive."

Unlike many cultures, Rodytes had always been more concerned with fertility than virginity. It could work to Sevrin's advantage to have a female who was undoubtedly fertile. Her hybrid children would obviously take precedence over her human offspring, but there were many males who would tolerate another man's offspring if their mother was empowered.

"If you survive the transformation, I will ensure that your children are sent along with you to Rodymia."

After a long pause, the human looked at her again. "Why would you do that for me? I'm obviously at your mercy."

Sevrin smiled. "You answered your own question."

"Will you explain what's going on, what's being done to me and why?"

Sevrin thought about the options then decided to compromise. "If you're still alive three days from now, I'll return and provide a detailed explanation."

The woman nodded but had nothing more to say.

"She's interesting, isn't she?" Orrit was waiting for her in the corridor. "Her name is Emily."

Sevrin made a noncommittal sound. Why Orrit thought she would care about a captive's name, Sevrin had no idea. Like all the others, Emily was a commodity, something to be bartered for power and wealth.

"Everyone is drawn to her," Orrit rambled on. "I was thinking perhaps the other test subjects would be as well."

"To what end?" He fell into step beside her as Sevrin headed back toward her office.

"I believe her positive attitude has helped produce some of the most stable results we've achieved so far. If she can calm the others, help them become more cooperative, it would benefit everyone."

She looked at him, not quite sure if he was serious or not. "There are risks inherent in allowing them to interact. Do you believe the benefits would outweigh the risks?"

"There is only one way to find out. Subject four has been particularly combative. She has to be restrained or sedated, sometimes both, just to draw blood."

Sevrin stopped walking and turned toward him. "Do you know what happened to Emily's children? Before we start negotiating with her, we need to know if we can give her what she wants."

"Good point. I'll speak to the extraction team leader and find out the details of her capture."

"Let me know what you learn and I'll let you know what I decide about recruiting her as an in-house mentor."

Orrit nodded and walked back the way they'd come. Her praise at his miraculous progress had defused his resentment, at least to some extent. He still made it painfully clear that his primary motivation was returning to Rodymia as quickly as possible, but he wasn't quite so hateful.

Thoughts of Emily had her so distracted that she cried out when a large, warm hand came down on her shoulder. She whipped her head toward the intruder, ready to berate them for touching her, but Flynn flashed his sexy smile and her annoyance melted.

"Don't' scare me like that."

He chuckled. "I called out to you twice. What has you so distracted?"

"Progress. Whenever things are going this well, I brace for impact."

"Being prepared is always wise, but don't let fear spoil all you've accomplished." He hesitantly touched her arm, knowing he wasn't allowed such liberties in public. "You work too hard."

"And all that hard work is starting to pay off." She raised one hand to the back of her neck and rubbed at the knot of tension. "What time is it?"

"Time for me to rub you down with hot oil and—"

"I think we should go get Roxie first. I can't shake the feeling that something is wrong with that situation and I've learned to trust my instincts when they're this persistent."

Flynn's steps lagged and tension filled his voice. "I thought you wanted to locate the others before you messed with Roxie. It could still take months to find them all. Do you want Roxie in captivity for that long?"

"I'm not sure I need to bother with the search. Orrit can provide me with brides for the families. Why do I need to drive myself crazy chasing shadows?"

"All right." Flynn fidgeted, obviously uncomfortable with her decision. "Are you sure you want to do this tonight. It's been a long day already. Why not let me help you relax and we'll collect her first thing in the morning?"

She chuckled and started walking again. "We'll compromise. You can give me that massage, we'll enjoy ourselves for an hour or two, and then you'll go get Roxie."

Chapter Nine

Content for the first time in months, Roxie relaxed in Elias' warm embrace. Her back was pressed against his chest and his long legs framed her body, leaving minimal room for the bath water. It didn't matter. He used the hand sprayer to keep their upper bodies warm and his free hand frequently sneaked up from her waist to caress her breasts.

"This was a really good idea," he whispered into her damp hair.

"I'm glad you approve."

She closed her eyes and concentrated on the silken flow of the water over her skin. She didn't want to think, wanted just to be present and enjoy the peaceful moment. There was no telling when life would allow them another. Tension bled from her muscles and her breathing slowed, but her mind refused to cooperate.

A lifetime of doubt and mistrust scratched at her contentment. How could Elias care for her? They'd known each other for less than a week, even if they had been together for the vast majority of that time. Their relationship was still so new.

"What's goin' on inside that pretty head of yours?" As it often did when he was relaxed or extremely distracted, his Texas twang crept back into his speech. "You're gettin' all squirmy again." He set the hand sprayer back in its bracket and turned off the water.

"I've never been intimate with someone this soon after meeting them," she confessed. "It's all happening so damn fast."

"I'm right there with you." He gave her a little squeeze. "I haven't had a serious relationship in years because they take more time and energy than I have to offer."

376

"Is this a 'serious' relationship? Is it a relationship at all? I don't understand what's happening to us."

"I think it's the link."

She leaned forward and craned her neck so she could look back at him. "You weren't attracted to me before Lor formed the link?"

"That's not what I meant and you know it." His steady gaze challenged her to deny it. "I was attracted to you the moment I spotted you in an unconscious heap on the floor of Unique Ink. There was something about you that drew me. I'd never felt like that before."

"Not even with your fiancée?" Like the coward she was, she turned back around before she saw the answer in his eyes.

"I loved Lori, but our lives were incompatible. It's so far in the past, it feels like another lifetime. What I feel for you is similar yet completely different, unique."

Her heart missed a beat and she pressed her hand over her upper chest. "You can't love me," she whispered. "You barely know me."

"Even without the link, that's not true." He smoothed her hair back from her face and pressed a kiss against her temple. "I know you, Roxie. I feel like I've always known you. The connection fuels the fire. It reinforces what we naturally feel, but the flames were burning before Lor formed the link. Are you going to try to deny that you love me too? Don't forget the link works both ways."

"I can't love you. I'm not ready."

He chuckled, relaxing against the sloped end of the bathtub. "I'm a patient man. I can wait until you're ready to admit what's already there." She tried to follow his example and let her troubled thoughts fade into the shadows. One of his arms held her snugly against his chest as the other hand glided over her damp breasts. "Stop brooding or I'm going to give you something else to think about." He caught one of her nipples and slowly rolled it between his thumb and forefinger.

"We should both be thinking about the captives and Sevrin's ambitions for—"

"Absolutely not." He pinched her nipple hard enough to make her gasp. "That's the last thing we should be thinking about. She checked in to make sure you were still where you're supposed to be. Unless something drastic changes, she has no reason to return. You need to relax and refuel. Neither of us is going to be any good to anyone if we're emotionally exhausted."

She sighed and covered his hand with hers. "I know you're right, but it feels selfish to indulge our desire when others are in jeopardy."

"This is a lull, the calm before the storm. We'll be battling gale-force winds and frantically boarding up windows soon enough. Relax. That's an order."

She finally surrendered with a dreamy smile.

"Tell me about Tess and Jett. How long have you known them? How did you meet?" His hand resumed its gentle exploration of her breasts.

"I met Tess at one of my art classes and she introduced me to Jett. He was already working as a tattoo artist and I ended up apprenticing with the owner of that shop."

"Has Jett always had the hots for you?"

She laughed and arched into the palm of his hand. "I suppose. He had a boyfriend when I met him, so I totally missed the signals. But he's had girlfriends too. I know he's attracted to me. Unfortunately, he's not my type at all."

"You have a type?" His hand migrated down along her abdomen with slow yet deliberate intent.

"Let's see, I like tall, ruggedly handsome men, who know what they want and aren't afraid to go after it." She arched her neck and looked up at him. "Sound familiar?"

Rotating her torso toward him, he shifted her neck into the bend of his elbow. Then his wandering hand cupped the side of her face. "I don't know how all this will play out. It could take a long time to resolve this conflict, but I want you in my life." He bent his head and sealed his mouth over hers. Their lips pressed, gradually opening as his tongue teased its way inside.

Their connection dilated, filling her mind with warmth and affection, and drawing out responding emotions in her. It wasn't rational. No one fell in love this quickly, but she couldn't deny what she felt. Elias loved her and she loved him.

For a long time they sat there, lost in the kiss, and the freedom of accepting the inevitable. Then he eased her back and traced her lips with his thumb. "Stand up." A slow, sexy smile bowed his lips and made the gold flecks in his gaze shimmer. "I'm ready for my second chance."

She stood, ignoring her reflection in the hazy mirror as she reached for a towel.

"No." He caught her wrist and shook his head. "I'm not ready to get out."

"Then why..." She shivered as the sudden heat in his gaze told her what he had in mind. His right hand glided down her side and came to rest on her hip as his left hand urged her closer. She'd experimented with positions before, but this one was new.

His gaze shifted to her body as he lifted one of her legs and draped it over his shoulder. She steadied herself against the wall and closed her eyes, concentrating on the sensations. He was gentle, at first, using his tongue with careful strokes and teasing flicks. She gasped and moaned, accepting each sensation without anticipating what he'd do next.

Moisture gathered on her eyelashes and she blinked it away, unsure where the moisture had come from. Was it condensation from their marathon bath, or was she overwhelmed by the pleasure he found in such a selfless act. He took his time, arousing her slowly as she greedily basked in his attention.

Her eyelids drifted open and her gaze was drawn back to the mirror. She looked pale and thin, all arms and legs, in sharp contrast to his golden perfection. Before her dissatisfaction with her physical form could defuse her building arousal, she noticed his blissful expression and the gentleness with which he touched her. His hands flowed over her meager curves as if she were fashioned especially for him. He found her beautiful, desirable, perfect. At least perfect for him.

He slowly pushed his tongue right into the core of her body and Roxie dropped her head back, their reflection forgotten. His desire burned hotter now and his mouth became more demanding. His fingers dug into her flesh as his lips slid against her folds, his tongue surging into her again and again.

She rocked against him and rotated her hips, searching for the perfect combination of motion and pressure. Electric bursts of sensation jolted through her, making her gasp and shake. Suddenly his lips closed around her clit and he sucked with focused care. The signals coalesced, drew tight, then burst free, showering her with tingling pleasure.

Roxie returned to her body gradually. Her leg slipped down from his shoulder as her other leg buckled. She ended up straddling his thighs, her face on a level with his. He kissed her, pushing the taste of her pleasure into her mouth. Her core twitched with little aftershocks as their tongues tangled and slid.

"Not. Enough. Room." He only forced one word out at a time, unable to be without her kiss long enough to form the entire sentence.

She reached back and triggered the drain then pushed back onto her trembling legs. "We can move to the bedroom, but I am going to return the favor before we go crazy again."

He chuckled, a deep rumbly sound. "We'll see."

After climbing from the tub, she held a towel out toward him then found another one for herself. Her hair would be a tangled mess unless she took time to comb it out, but she didn't care. He'd watched her come over and over. Finally, it was his turn to lose control.

They were more or less dry by the time they crossed to the bed. Determined to have her way, she urged him to sit on the edge of the bed. Then she knelt between his legs and wrapped her hand around his shaft. "I've wanted to do this since the first time you kissed me."

He put his hands on the bed and moved his legs father apart. "I'm all yours."

"Yes you are." She let the claim resonate as she took him in her mouth. Their gazes held until the angle made it impossible, then she focused on pleasuring him. He remained passive longer than she expected, letting her explore him as thoroughly as he'd explored her.

Her lips formed a snug ring as she slid her mouth up and down his cock. She cupped his balls in her other hand, fascinated by the weight and the heat of his body. He grew harder and thicker as she worked him and the emotions surging across their link left her dizzy and restless. She wanted to feel him moving inside her, stretching her to capacity as his big body pressed her down into the bed. But she didn't want to stop until she shattered his control. She needed his willing surrender.

With a predatory growl, he lifted her, freeing his cock from her mouth. "If you want to watch me come, you'll have to keep your eyes open." He tossed her to the middle of the bed and knelt between her legs. Then he caught the underside of her knees and opened her wide.

Roxie pushed his hands away and held her legs for him, offering her body in blatant invitation. "Please," she whispered.

"I mean to." He positioned himself at her entrance then arched over her, capturing her gaze with his. Then he pushed inward slowly, filling her inch by wonderful inch. She stared into his eyes as heat and hunger blazed within her mind. He paused for half a second with his entire length buried inside her then kissed her with aching tenderness. "No matter what happens in the next few days, I'll be with you, part of you."

Before she could respond to the claim, his mouth returned to hers in a breath-stealing, mind-numbing kiss. He rocked into her, steady thrusts that rubbed her in all the right places. Desperately needing to touch him, she released her legs. Then her hands wandered over his straining muscles, grasping and squeezing as he claimed her body and heart.

Nothing had ever felt so perfect, nothing so intense. She lifted into each of his downward thrusts, compounding the impact. His rhythm sped as his need escalated. He tore his mouth from hers, unable to maintain the kiss as his thrusts grew more forceful.

She watched his face, awed by the consuming desire he felt for her. And her emotions were just as demanding. She reached for him with her arms and legs, her soul flowing across their link to meld with his. They breathed as one, moved as one, their beings completely in tune.

"Now."

His harsh command combined with the burst of pleasure flooding across their link. Sensations detonated deep inside her, stealing her breath with their shocking intensity. She arched off the bed, taking everything he had to give. Their hearts beat as one and their spasms of pleasure synchronized. They clung to each other, shuddering over and over as they flowed through the stages of release.

Roxie recovered first and waited for passion's haze to leave his eyes. "That was...well worth the wait."

He rolled to his side, taking her with him. Then he pulled her leg high onto his hip and pressed their bodies back together. "I never want to leave this bed, or the warmth of your body."

She wiggled closer, tucking her head under his chin. "You'll hear no arguments from me. We can order pizza and Chinese. There's even a deli that delivers. Of course one of us will have to answer the door."

He chuckled, his fingers gently rubbing her back. "Sounds like you're hungry."

"Getting there, but I'm not ready for you to move. It feels too good to have you there, where you belong."

Tilting her face up, he kissed her slowly, tenderly. "I'm not going anywhere." Suddenly he nipped her lower lip and laughed. "Couldn't even if I wanted to. We're tethered together."

He rolled again, bringing her on top of him. She folded her legs and settled her weight on her knees. They kissed and kissed, their hands moving freely over each other. She felt him gradually harden inside her and tightened her inner muscles, encouraging the response. He slipped his hands between their bodies and teased her nipples so she squeezed his cock again and again.

"Are you trying to kill me?" He grasped her hips and arched into her core.

"No." She pushed against his chest, sitting up so she could move more freely. "I closed my eyes before. I still want to watch you come."

He laughed as he bucked up into her. "Good luck with that."

LONG HOURS LATER ROXIE was jarred from a contented sleep by Elias' sudden movements. He rolled out of bed and fired an energy pulse at the shadowy intruder.

"I'm on your side, asshole!" Flynn flipped on the light after twisting to narrowly avoid the blast. "We don't have much time and I need to...

For gods' sake, put your pants on." He snatched Elias' jeans off the floor by the bathroom door and threw them to him. His impatient gaze switched to Roxie and one corner of his mouth twitched. "Now you are more than welcome to stay just like that."

She scrambled out of bed and donned Elias' T-shirt then wiggled into her panties. "Why are you here?"

"You know why I'm here." He looked at Elias again and asked, "Can you get a message to Lor before I take her to Sevrin."

"Tell us where the lab is and there's no reason for either of you to go back," Elias countered, looking flushed and furious.

"I don't know where it is and she's never going to tell me, so the Mystics better be ready for this."

"Where are you taking her?" Elias demanded.

"To the Team South house. She won't be there long, so I hope someone is already in position over there."

Tell him we're ready. Lor's voice eased into her mind.

She started to convey the message, but Flynn waved his hand dismissively. "I heard. Now come here."

Despite all the preparations and the unseen support, fear rushed through Roxie and she couldn't move. She knew Elias would be teleported with her and she knew everything possible was being done to make sure they came out of this alive, but her feet were glued to the carpet and her heart pumped away at twice its normal speed.

"I'm not going to hurt you." When she remained immobile, he made an impatient sound and went to her. His arms encircled her and her gaze flew to Elias.

Elias mouthed the words "I love you" as everything around her blurred. For a moment his shape blended with the twisting colors, then the proximity bond kicked in and he was pulled back into focus.

"What the—" Flynn looked over his shoulder then growled deep in his throat. "That was stupid. Lor just got his pet human killed."

They materialized in the living room of a large, luxurious house. Roxie stumbled back as Flynn released her, but her attention shifted immediately to Nazerel. He stood several paces away, surrounded by his team of hunters. They were all tall, lean and lethal, and each one of them was staring at her.

"Too bad she didn't sleep naked," someone muttered, his appreciative gaze moving over her bare legs.

Then Elias materialized and the hunters sprang into action. They pounced on Elias like a pack of wolves desperate for a long denied meal. Nazerel watched the attack with dispassionate amusement, obviously more interested in Roxie than Elias.

"Don't hurt him," Sevrin shouted, but the men didn't seem to notice.

"Enough!" Nazerel's order was immediately obeyed. The hunters released Elias as if he'd been electrified, leaving him panting and bloodied on the floor. Elias climbed back to his feet and wiped his split lip on the back of his hand. Rather than address the human, Nazerel looked at Flynn with obvious scorn. "You didn't notice you had another passenger?"

"I noticed. There was just nothing I could do about it. They're tied together by some sort of link." Flynn moved to Sevrin's side, ignoring everyone else. "We're going to have to take him with us. I can't sever the bond."

"Let me try." Nazerel took a step toward Roxie and instantly Elias stood in front of her. Already bruises were forming on his shoulders and back, but he was ready for more punishment, ready to risk any danger, in an effort to protect her. Though foolish, his determination was humbling and sweet. "I can end your life without touching you, human. Now move aside."

"Leave him alone," Sevrin snapped. "We don't have time for this."

"It will just take a minute." Nazerel reached for Elias.

Rather than recoil, Elias lunged, driving Nazerel back a step. Then Elias whipped the suppression collar out of his pocket and snapped it against the side of Nazerel's neck. The band unwound, neatly coiling around Nazerel's throat until the ends connected with a foreboding click.

"What the fuck is this thing?" Nazerel tugged at the offending band as his gaze murdered Elias.

"Oh dear." The humor in Sevrin's tone brought Nazerel whirling toward her.

"This isn't funny!"

"I disagree, but we don't have time to argue the point."

"Get it off me." He clawed at the band, leaving welts on his own flesh. "Now!"

With an exasperated sigh, Sevrin motioned Flynn toward Roxie. "Start breaking her fingers until the human releases the collar."

Elias shielded her again, arms outstretched. "I'm not the owner and neither is Roxie. We can't unlock it."

"Then who can?" Nazerel shouted, calming enough to resume his tug-of-war with the band.

"Quite a conundrum," Sevrin muttered. "Unfortunately, I don't have time to explore it right now. Come." She motioned toward Elias and Roxie.

"They aren't leaving until I find out who can take this thing off me." Nazerel blocked their path to the front door.

"Nazerel, we've got company," one of his men cautioned.

"Shit!" He spun on his heel and rushed to the front window where his man had spotted the possible intruders. "Two cargo vans and an SUV. Yeah, that's subtle."

Sevrin's semi-amused expression faded and she looked at Flynn. "You said she wasn't bugged. How the hell did they find us so fast?"

"I have no idea." He motioned toward Elias. "He must have signaled them somehow. I haven't scanned him."

"Scan him now!" Her agitated gaze shifted from Elias to Roxie and back as she waited for Flynn's diagnosis. "Well?"

"Nothing," he insisted. "They're both clean."

"Then how do you explain our visitors?" Nazerel challenged.

"Persistent recon," Flynn shot back. "They've been shadowing you for months."

"And there's a lot more than six people out there," Nazerel snarled, then he glared at Sevrin. "Why didn't you warn us that Lor had sent for reinforcements?"

"I don't think he has," Sevrin insisted. "I think he hired some locals somewhere along the way." She motioned toward Elias. "Case in point. He might be screwing Roxie, but he's obviously military."

"I'm not concerned with humans, military or otherwise," Nazerel sneered. Even collared and surrounded by a larger force, he was impossibly arrogant.

"Glad to hear it. Distract them and make damn sure I'm not followed." Sevrin grasped Roxie's arm and headed across the room, Elias close behind.

Flynn started to follow Sevrin, but Nazerel fisted the back of his shirt. "We're about to defend our home. Are you a member of Team South or not?"

Jerking his shirt out of Nazerel's grasp, Flynn glanced at Sevrin then said, "I am."

"Good. Grab a weapon."

Sevrin took Roxie through the house and out a side door. Two of the men joined them as Sevrin hurried along the side of the house. Roxie didn't think they were Shadow Assassins, more like Sevrin's guards. They'd stood apart from the hunters, a group unto themselves.

"Where are you taking us? What's this about?" Roxie felt obligated to ask. A complete lack of interest would have seemed strange.

"You'll find out soon enough."

"I didn't tell them anything. Why did you send Flynn after me?"

Sevrin ignored her questions until they reached a dark SUV, not unlike the one waiting to confront the hunters. She pulled open the side door and motioned toward the interior. "Get in. Boys in the way back." She held Roxie out of the way as one of her men urged Elias into the third-row seat and then climbed in behind him. "Now you."

Reluctantly, Roxie climbed in and sat on the bench seat in the middle of the SUV. Sevrin's other guard rounded the front of the vehicle and slipped in behind the steering wheel. Then Sevrin joined Roxie on the middle seat. Sevrin pulled the door closed and motioned for the driver to get moving.

The front door to the team house opened and five of the hunters filed out. They were little more than silhouettes in the surrounding darkness, so Roxie wasn't sure if Nazerel or Flynn was among them. She half expected gunfire or pulse blasts to follow, but they simply positioned themselves around the unwanted vehicles and made it impossible for them to move.

Roxie had no way of knowing if the confrontation turned physical. The SUV she was in turned a corner and she could no longer see what was going on in front of the Team South house.

"What do you want with me," Roxie tried again. If she weren't fully aware of what was going on behind the scenes, she would be terrified right now. Of course, knowing that Sevrin wouldn't kill her, but intended to barter her to a Rodyte warrior was only slightly less traumatizing.

Before Sevrin could respond, Elias grasped the arm of the man guarding him. "What is that?"

The sharp question drew Roxie's attention to the object in the guard's hand. It was a long, slender cylinder, and he had his thumb angled over one end, likely covering some sort of trigger. The guard twisted, Elias countered, and the wrestling match was on. Elias punched the man squarely in the face, but the guard remained focused on his task. Ignoring Elias' violent struggles, the guard forced his hand close enough to Elias' body to use whatever was in his hand. Roxie heard a soft click and Elias gasped, jerking back violently.

"What the hell was in that thing?" He shoved the guard away with both hands and one of his feet. The man slammed into the opposite wall of the SUV.

"It's just a sedative," Sevrin told him. "It was meant for Flynn, but it shouldn't hurt you. Relax. If you fight it, you'll throw up and then go under anyway." Sevrin turned back to Roxie, her gaze gleaming in the shadowy interior of the SUV. "Care to explain how your online lover, who supposedly knows nothing about any of this, came to be linked to you by a Mystic bond?"

"They were afraid you'd come back for me." Roxie smirked at her. "Can't imagine why."

"But why saddle you with a human?"

"They're running short of Mystics right now." Elias was already starting to sound drugged. He blinked repeatedly and still couldn't keep his eyelids from drooping. "Send sex-starved Mystics to guard human females and they have a way of ending up with mates."

Sevrin looked out the window without outwardly reacting to his statements. They'd left the subdivision while Roxie was watching Elias struggle with the guard, but she had no idea which direction they traveled. They were on a well-maintained two-lane street. There were no sidewalks or traffic signals, so it was likely a lesser-used state highway.

"Any hint of a tail?" Sevrin looked at the guard beside Elias.

"No, mistress. All's clear as far as I can see."

Roxie glanced around again. The guard was right. They had the road to themselves. When Roxie shifted her gaze back to Sevrin she was holding an injector like the guard had used on Elias.

"Your turn."

There was no point in resisting. The sooner they arrived at Sevrin's secret lab, the sooner this nightmare would be over. Roxie braced for the sting then waited silently for oblivion to overtake her.

"I DON'T LIKE THIS," Sevrin muttered as Roxie slumped against the window. "See if anyone will answer the radio. I need an update before we head home."

The driver picked up the two-way radio that had been nestled in one of the cup holders. "TSH come in. This is mobile 3 requesting an update."

"Little busy right now," someone said with obvious impatience. The microphone picked up shouts and muffled crashes along with the hunter's voice.

Sevrin leaned forward and snatched the radio out of the driver's hand. "How many Mystics are at your location?" She was usually careful not to say anything over the radio that might draw unwanted attention, but she was too anxious right now to worry about codenames.

"All of them," the speaker snapped.

"Give me a number."

"Four from the MM, five locals. TSH out."

Four from the Mystic Militia and five humans. That was interesting. She was under the impression that Lor only had two other Mystics in his annoying little troupe. Nazerel was right. Lor must have received backup from Ontariese. *Damn it.*

"Shall I divert, mistress?"

They weren't being followed and Flynn had insisted neither of her passengers was bugged. Even if Lor had more personnel now, they were all engaged at the Team South house. She was being paranoid.

"No." She motioned him onward. "I have too much to do back at the Farm. Carry on."

Chapter Ten

Roxie woke up far less gently than she'd fallen asleep. Pain gripped her muscles, catapulting her from darkness into glaring light. She screamed and sprang up in bed, shaking with confusion and fear. For a muddled moment she'd thought she was in bed, struggling free of a nightmare. No such luck. This nightmare was her life.

"Sorry about the rude awakening." Sevrin stood beside the hospital-style bed on which Roxie sat, one of her wrists secured to the side rail by a padded restraint. A sheet had been draped over her bare legs and the restraint had an electronic lock rather than a buckle. "You were taking forever. So I had Dr. Utoff help you. The cramps will pass in a moment. Take some deep breaths."

"Where am I?" She tugged against the restraint. "Why am I locked to this bed? Where's Elias?" Shit! She shouldn't have said his name. Her thigh muscles continued to tense and her head was throbbing so badly she could hardly think.

An extremely thin, dour-faced man stood a step back from Sevrin, watching Roxie closely. He didn't speak. There were five other beds identical to the one on which Roxie sat, but none of them were occupied. The room looked like an urgent care clinic or an emergency room in a really small hospital.

Forcing herself to think, she looked at the equipment surrounding her bed. With strange symbols and three-dimensional displays, it was obvious that the devices hadn't originated on Earth. They had defiantly arrived at Sevrin's new lab.

"Hey." Sevrin snapped her fingers impatiently. "Focus. Who in the five hells are you and what did you do with the battle-born female?"

"I don't know what you're talking about." She closed her eyes and rubbed her temples, buying herself a second or two to puzzle through the question.

"You're not latent. You have no Mystic abilities of any kind, which means you cannot be the female I've been searching for since my father died. What did you do with the other hybrid?" By the time Sevrin worked her way through the explanation, she was shouting.

Slowly, Roxie opened her eyes. Would Sevrin's inaccurate conclusion defuse the situation or render Roxie expendable? A hostage with no value was usually dead. She hadn't prepared a lie and her head hurt too much for creativity. "I only know I'm a hybrid because the others told me. I know nothing about anyone else. What led you to me in the first place?"

"Faulty assumptions, apparently." Sevrin's gaze lingered on Roxie for a moment longer and then she dismissed the entire incident with a casual shrug. She turned to the tall, thin man hovering at the room's perimeter. "Have her moved to one of the holding cells as soon as her head clears. I'll take care of her later."

Roxie refused to think about what that meant. Lor and the other Mystics should be here any moment with a small army of Morgan's soldiers. They might be here already. She didn't know how long she'd been unconscious. Knowing it would be better if they found her in this unsecured room than in a holding cell, she lay back and pressed her hands to the sides of her head, moaning softly. Besides, it wasn't like she had an option until she found a way to free herself from the restraint.

She could still see the thin man out of the corner of her eye. He hesitated a moment, as if deciding what to do, then moved to the workstation tucked in one corner of the room and sat down. Apparently, he was going to wait a little while longer for her head to clear.

Rolling to her side, she took a better look at the locking mechanism on the cuff. It was smooth, with no writing of any kind, no keyhole or release trigger. How the hell did it open?

Are you alone in the room? Lor's welcome voice pushed into her mind.

No. Sevrin made the doctor stay and monitor me. I don't think he's armed, but I'm tethered to the bed.

We'll be there momentarily. Try not to react to our arrival.

Got it.

Elias had to be in an adjoining room, she could feel the subtle pull of their proximity bond and his smoldering frustration. Good. He was awake and aware. That would make things much easier than dragging around an unconscious body.

Roxie's job had been to lead them to the lab. Now that they'd found it, she wasn't sure what to do. She closed her eyes, fighting back a staggering rush of emotions. She could fall apart later, rage against the injustice and cry for a week. Right now she needed to remain clearheaded and calm.

The thin man's startled gasp drew Roxie's attention away from her troubled thoughts. She sat up in time to see Lor lowering the thin man's now unconscious body to the floor. Two Mystics she'd yet to meet flashed into the room a moment later.

"Can you walk?" Lor asked in a calm yet urgent tone.

"Yes, if you can get me out of this." She raised her hand, displaying the restraint.

Lor rushed to her side and quickly examined the securement. "Hold *very* still."

Roxie rested her hand on top of the side rail and didn't so much as breathe. Orange-red light erupted in Lor's palm, making his entire hand glow. Then he formed a fist and condensed the energy into a tiny, ultra-bright flame. The flame spiraled down his index finger and burned into the padded part of the cuff. Roxie's instinct was to pull away, but she kept her hand in place, watching in rapt amazement as Lor burned a perfect line from top to bottom. He pulled the cuff apart and Roxie pulled her hand free and rubbed her wrist. Her skin was untouched by a fire hot enough to burn through metal.

"That was..." She looked at him with unblinking awe. "You can control fire."

He just smiled and motioned toward the door, a gentle reminder that the crisis was far from over. "Let's go."

Shaking away her amazement, she scooted to the end of the bed and hopped down. "Elias has to be nearby."

"He's our next stop," Lor assured her. "Reinforcements are still ten to fifteen minutes away. We need to prepare as well as we can without alerting them to our presence."

Lor's companions dragged the thin man into a storeroom and closed the door. Hopefully he'd remain unconscious until after the others arrived.

"Were you able to flash inside without setting off an alarm?"

Lor nodded as he moved to the doorway and checked the corridor. "We were, but the soldiers won't have the same luxury. We'll have to move fast once the others arrive."

"This access point is live," one of the new Mystics said as he manipulated the three-dimensional display beside the bed Roxie had just vacated. "I'm inside their primary defenses. Let's see if I can assess some sort of floor plan."

Lor stepped past Roxie and looked at the display. "I am so glad you volunteered for this."

"Few Mystics are literate in Rodyte. I suspected the skill might be useful."

The other newcomer approached Roxie with compassion in his eyes. "Are you sure you're unharmed? This must be terrifying for you."

"It hasn't been fun, but I'm fine. Really." She produced an anemic smile before looking around. If they had a few minutes to kill, maybe she could find something to cover her legs. She pulled open cupboards and cabinets, but found nothing useful. Then her gaze landed on the door to the storeroom. "Do you think the doctor's still out?"

The friendly Mystic joined her as she crossed to the storeroom door. "I hear no movement." He stepped past her and eased the door open.

Thin man lay exactly as Lor had left him, unconscious yet breathing steadily. Roxie spotted a stack of neatly folded scrubs, or the Rodyte equivalent of scrubs. She grabbed one of the light blue garments and shook it out, delighted when she saw it was a uniform bottom with a drawstring waist. She moved back into the main room and pulled the pants on while the Mystic secured the storeroom. Shoes, or better yet boots, would have been nice too, but she was glad to be less exposed.

By the time she finished dressing, the other new Mystic had located a three-dimensional floor plan. Everyone gathered around the diagram as he explained, "This is the infirmary. I believe that's where we are. Elias is most likely in the exam room on the other side of that wall." He pointed to the wall on Roxie's right.

"Are these the holding cells?" Lor pointed to a double row of similarly shaped rooms.

"I believe so."

"Let's head that direction after we collect Elias," Lor advised. "Freeing the captives will be a good use of our time if we can do so without revealing our position. Once the fighting starts, it's going to be chaotic."

"Understood," the other two Mystics said in turn.

"And pass the floor plan to the others. Everything will run more smoothly if we know where things are."

"Already done." The Rodyte-speaking Mystic assured.

Lor looked at her and paused for a reassuring smile. "You did really well. Ready for a little more excitement."

His tone was playful rather than condescending, so Roxie nodded. "Can you guarantee 'a little more excitement' is all we'll see?"

"Sorry. Mystics try to speak only truth."

Lor led their small group into the hallway after checking to make sure it was clear. Roxie stood anxiously between the two newcomers as Lor flashed inside the locked exam room and returned with Elias.

Still shirtless, Elias swept her into a quick hug as soon as Lor released him. "Are you okay?" He kept her face between his palms as he quickly looked her over.

"I'm fine."

"This way," Lor urged.

They reached a corridor adjacent to the holding cells without incident, but the entire area was well guarded. Roxie could feel ripples of energy flowing around her, but she couldn't hear what Lor and the other Mystics were saying. They must be using a different frequency than the one created by her telepathic link to Lor. Or he was shielding the conversation in some way. She still wasn't sure how it all worked.

Lor's intense turquoise gaze shifted toward her and their link vibrated as his voice sounded inside her mind. *The others have arrived. Stay down as much as possible.*

It was a diplomatic way of telling her and Elias to keep out of their way. She had no problem with the order, but Elias tensed beside her, clearly insulted by the dictate. The Rodyte-speaking Mystic shifted quickly to the other side of the hall and Elias moved closer to her. He held a pulse pistol in his right hand, but she had no idea where he'd gotten it. From one of the Mystics probably. Nothing else made sense.

"Stay behind me," Elias said softly and Roxie couldn't help but smile. He hadn't liked being told to stay back, yet he had no problem reinforcing Lor's position. It didn't seem quite fair.

Yeah well, she wasn't an Army Ranger nor had she received training from the FBI. Immediately regretting the moment of brutal honesty, she looked around to see if anyone had overheard her pessimistic thought. Everyone else was anxiously waiting for Lor to determine it was time to begin. She needed to get her head in the game and keep it there.

Setting things in motion with a sharp hand gesture, Lor flashed from his position at the intersecting corridors and materialized behind the largest of four guards. The other two Mystics followed his lead, teleporting to their targets to maximize the element of surprise. Lor had engaged the last guard by the time his companions flashed into position and all three worked with focused precision, incapacitating the guards before anyone had time to trigger an alarm. They moved with a fluid grace Roxie found mesmerizing and incredibly efficient.

Elias rushed down the now secure corridor and stopped in front of the door to the first holding cell. He fired a quick blast into the scanner panel. Sparks erupted and the circuitry hissed. Elias tucked the pistol into the back of his pants and flattened his palms on the smooth metal, heaving the uncooperative door aside.

A frightened young woman rushed out of the cell and started to throw herself into his arms. When she saw his state of undress, her eyes rounded and she shied away.

Roxie hurried forward, her welcoming smile meant to ease the captive's fear. "We've come to get you out of here."

The captive rushed toward Roxie then clung to her arm as they followed Elias toward the next holding cell.

The Mystics worked to free captives as well and soon they were surrounded by a small crowd of terrified females. Flynn had warned of six test subjects, but they found a total of eight, several so ill they had to be assisted by others just to walk.

The Rodyte-speaking Mystic was about to open last holding cell when he motioned to Lor instead. "Commander, there are four men in this cell. Are they captives or Shadow Assassins?"

"Why would she have them locked up?" the friendly Mystic asked.

"Leave them for now. It's more important that we get these women out of here." Then he seemed to reconsider. "Do they all look healthy and unharmed?"

"Yes, just angry that I'm not opening the door."

"Tell them we'll return for them in a few minutes and to be quiet until we do."

Once again speaking in Rodyte, the Mystic quickly explained what was going on. Roxie couldn't hear what the male captives said in return, but the Mystic lingered by the door way a few minutes longer.

"Who sent you?" one of the female captives asked. She seemed less agitated than the others. "How did you know we were here?"

"What's your name?" Roxie asked, careful to keep her tone light.

"Emily."

"I'm Roxie and we'll answer all your questions as soon as we're in a safe location."

Emily nodded then went to help one of the sick ones as they started down the corridor.

Suddenly Lor spun toward Elias and said, "One of the other teams is in trouble. Can you get the women out of here?"

"Of course. Go."

"Two rights then a left," Lor told him. "If you see the elevators, you've gone too far."

"Got it."

Without further ado, the three Mystics flashed out of sight.

The captives gasped at the abrupt departure then looked to Elias for instructions. The pulse pistol was back in his right hand and determination hardened his expression. "I'll lead, Roxie bring up the rear."

Roxie nodded, happy to follow any directive that took her out of this place as quickly as possible. Elias stayed close to the wall and halted the line at each intersection or open doorway. They came to a lab with the lights on. No one was in sight, but Elias wasn't taking any chances. He motioned for the women to crouch beneath the level of the windows and keep moving. Roxie urged them along as quickly as possible.

They reached the final corner and Elias had just deemed it safe when a shrill alarm echoed down the corridors. "We have to hurry," he warned, forced to yell above the pulsing alarm. "Intruder protocols often lock down the entire building."

He rounded the final corner and someone ordered him to stop in Rodyte. Several resounding blasts followed, but Roxie couldn't see who'd discharged their weapon. Crying out and huddling together, the frightened women pressed against the wall, staying out of sight of the guard or guards who had engaged Elias. Roxie hurried past her terrified companions and peered around the corner. One of the guards was sprawled on the floor, likely the victim of one of the blasts. Elias was trying to physically subdue the final guard, but Rodytes were fast and brutal.

The fallen guard's rifle lay on the floor not far from where Roxie stood. Unwilling to stand there helplessly while Elias fought for his life, she reached down and picked up the rifle. Surprisingly light yet well balanced, the weapon seemed pretty straight forward. She'd shot all sorts of guns during her youth, so she knew better than attempting to fire it until she knew what she was doing. With the barrel pointed at the floor, she depressed what she thought was the trigger. A thin red light drew a perfect line from the barrel to the floor. Laser targeting. Cool. That made things easier. She hoped the thing was set on stun, but she sure as hell wasn't' going to mess with the settings. The soldier was about to get whatever his companion had intended for them.

With the rifle braced firmly against her shoulder, she identified her target with the laser and then smoothly pulled the trigger. A shimmering stream of energy, or maybe plasma, arced from the gun and blasted straight through the guard's thigh. He screamed, shuddered violently, then collapsed, losing his hold on Elias.

Elias glanced at her with pleased surprise shining in his eyes, but she wasn't able to bask in his approval. Severin flew around the corner behind him, gun aimed at Elias' head. Without conscious thought or hesitation, Roxie activated the laser and targeted Severin's hand. Roxie's shot flew fast and true, but the stream passed through Severin's hand and drilled into the middle of her chest.

The world slowed and Roxie's perception narrowed to Severin's reaction. Severin's eyes flew open wide as disbelief and pain contorted her features. Her pistol slipped from her mangled hand and her knees buckled. She clutched her chest with both hands, making it hard to tell if the blood rapidly saturating her blouse was coming from her chest or her shredded fingers.

Elias was suddenly beside Roxie and he slipped his arm around her waist.

"I didn't mean to kill her."

"She's not dead yet," Elias pointed out. "Let me see if I can get her some help." He closed his eyes and called out to Lor. The Mystic would only be able to hear him if he'd left the link open, but it was worth a try.

The distinct ringing of boot heels grew closer and closer. Roxie looked down the corridor to their left and saw nothing, but when she turned and looked behind her, uniformed soldiers moved into view, approaching at a brisk run.

She started to shoulder the rifle, but Elias shook his head. "They're mine."

As the soldiers reached them, Roxie realized that the kind-eyed Mystic had been running inside the formation. She didn't know if he'd been there for protection or stealth, but she was glad to see him.

"Are you a healer?" she asked as the soldiers parted, allowing him to leave formation.

"Among other things." He smoothed down his pants and straightened his shirt before continuing. "Who needs my help."

She pointed toward Sevrin who had collapsed onto her side. "It would be a really good thing if that one didn't die just yet."

"She deserves to die," one of the captives sneered. "That's the leader. She's the one behind everything that's going on."

"We're aware of her atrocities and she will be held accountable for everything she's done," Elias assured them. "But she needs to be questioned at length before we can determine the full extent of her crimes."

That seemed to satisfy the captives. They lapsed back into anxious silence.

"Let's get you out of here," Roxie suggested, needing to be away from the bloody scene herself.

One of the soldiers stepped forward and explained, "We're here to escort the captives to the safe house."

"I don't want to go anywhere but home," Emily argued. "My children have no idea where I am."

"You'll be allowed to speak with them or someone will be dispatched to bring them to you," the team leader told her. "But we need to move now. The transport is waiting."

The captives walked off with the soldiers, leaving Elias and Roxie alone in the hallway with Sevrin and the Mystic. He knelt at Sevrin's side, head bowed in concentration. His hands hovered just above her body, moving in slow, sweeping waves from her shoulders to her waist and back. His palms glowed with yellow-orange light and Sevrin writhed and moaned.

Sevrin's hand was no longer bleeding, but three of her fingers and most of her thumb were now misshapen stumps. The Mystic paid much more attention to her chest wound, working tirelessly and not letting anything distract him.

Roxie slipped her arm through the strap and swung the rifle onto her shoulder. She suspected fighting was still going on in other parts of the complex, but this hallway was quiet as a tomb.

Lor returned about twenty minutes later. The Mystic was still working on Sevrin. "Will she survive?" Lor asked Roxie.

She shrugged. "He hasn't said a word since he began chanting."

Lor nodded then slowly approached the kneeling Mystic. Lor placed his hand on the Mystic's shoulder and the Mystic jerked as if Lor has shocked him. "Take all you need, Brother. You're exhausted."

It sounded as if Lor was feeding the other Mystic. Roxie couldn't help wondering what else these men could do.

"All of their gifts require a tremendous amount of energy, but a sustained healing like this is particularly difficult," Elias explained.

"Is the fighting over? Are we safe now?"

Lor looked at her without moving from his comrade's side. "The complex is secure. We've begun evacuating the employees. Most were brought here against their will and are anxious to return to Rodymia."

"What happened to the men we found?" Roxie asked.

"They are Shadow Assassins, but they were brought here without their permission. Apparently, there were twenty of them when they arrived."

Roxie suspected she didn't want to know the answer to the next logical question, but her curious nature wouldn't be denied. "What happened to the other sixteen?"

"Sevrin's research team literally tore them apart."

She wasn't surprised, but she was still revolted. She'd sensed Sevrin's evil, but this was the first time she'd come face-to-face with victims of her cruelty.

After a long, tense silence, Elias asked, "What happened at the Team South house? Is Nazerel finally in custody? I collared him for you. Surely he wasn't hard to bag?"

Clearly less comfortable with this subject, Lor lifted his hand from the Mystic's shoulder and moved over to Elias and Roxie. "As soon as we piled out of the vehicles, the hunters ran back inside, which was exactly what we needed them to do. We turned on the field generator and their entire house became a prison."

"Then why aren't you pleased?" Roxie asked. "All of your objectives have been met. There will be a ton of follow-up needed, but basically your mission here is finished."

"One last objective remains," Lor admitted as he scrubbed his chin with his fingertips. "Somehow during the hostilities, Nazerel took Morgan hostage and teleported through the containment field. He was the only one strong enough to do it, but he—"

"Nazerel has Morgan?" Elias' face paled. "This is unthinkable. Does he know she can free him from the collar?"

"She won't," Lor predicted. "She knows if she does he'll be at full strength again in a matter of minutes. Her only hope is to pretend she can't do it and find a way to turn the table on him."

"Easier said than done," Elias snapped. "Each of us has tried to turn the tables on Nazerel since this thing began and all of us have failed."

"If anyone can do it, it's Morgan. She has weapons at her disposal the rest of us do not."

"If you're talking about the fact that she's a woman, it's irrelevant." Elias growled, clearly upset by the knowledge that his friend was in so much danger. "She is first and foremost a soldier, and a damn good one."

"My point exactly. Her face and figure will be horribly distracting to Nazerel. Morgan is a remarkably beautiful woman and Nazerel has been without female companionship for a very long time."

"You're not making me feel any better here!" Elias raked his hair with one hand and took a deep breath before he went on. "We treat her with respect and honor. Nazerel has no such restraints."

"Morgan is shrewd and competent. As you said, disguised within her desirable form is the heart and mind of a warrior. Nazerel won't know what hit him."

Elias lapsed into thoughtful silence for a moment. Sparks of frustration and fear zinged across their connection, giving Roxie a hint of the emotional tumult waging inside him. "I hope to hell you're right."

Beside Sevrin, the Mystic struggled to his feet, looking dazed and shaky. "I've done all I can, Master dar Joon."

Lor rushed to his side and steadied his comrade. "Will she survive?"

"It's doubtful. I've stabilized her for now, but she needs to be scanned immediately. She will not regain consciousness."

"I understand and thank you."

The Mystic inclined his head and walked, rather shakily, down the corridor.

"I hate to bring this up." Lor bent and scooped Sevrin up in his arms. "But you're Morgan's second-in-command."

"Which means I'm acting director until she returns." Elias nodded then took another deep breath.

"What are you going to do with her?" Roxie's curious nature surged again.

"Take her to Varrik," Lor replied.

"Varrik?" The name sounded familiar, but her mind refused to provide any more information.

"The alpha sweeper," Elias reminded. "Manipulating memories is what he does best."

"I shouldn't be long," Lor told them. "We're going to be shuffling personnel for hours. They have everyone up in hanger bay 2. Blayne is trying to get things organized." Without further explanation, Lor flashed out of sight, Sevrin still cradled in his arms.

Elias released a long, weary sigh as he looked at Roxie. "Technically, your part in this battle is finished. If you'd rather not stick around, I can find someone to drive you home."

"Not a chance." She shifted the rifle farther back on her shoulder then wrapped both arms around his lean waist. "I'd just pace my apartment worrying about you."

He tilted her head up and smiled into her eyes. "I welcome the company. This endless night will pass a little faster with you by my side."

"There's no place on Earth I'd rather be."

He chuckled as he bent to kiss her. "What about on Ontariese or Bilarri?"

"There is no place in the universe I'd rather be than in your arms." She closed the last inch and brought their mouths together for a long, passionate kiss.

Epilogue

Roxie sat at the conference table feeling awkward and out of place. Everyone here was a trained operative, many with supernatural abilities. She was the lone civilian, an outsider. This wasn't her world, but she wanted to understand it, because of Elias.

Elias sat at the head of the table looking authoritative and fierce. He wore black pants and a camo T-shirt that outlined every ripple and curve of his incredible torso. In any other room he would draw attention, but here he was one of many. He belonged.

Many people lived their entire lives without finding a place where they truly fit in. She'd found her home at Unique Ink and Elias was part of this world. A world most humans didn't even know existed. Roxie felt honored to have been allowed inside, but she honestly hoped she would never need to be directly involved again. She was an artist by nature and preferred to hold nothing more violent than a tattoo machine.

"The raid on the lab was an unqualified success," Elias began. "All eight captives have been taken to a medical facility for observation and transitional support. Each woman was traumatized as well as genetically modified. Their recovery will take time. The one named Emily became quite a resource once her children were brought to her."

Lor slipped into the silence as Elias paused. "The four Shadow Assassins that Sevrin captured rather than recruited were returned to the City of Tears. Everyone is grieving for the sixteen who were lost. Shadow Assassins do not fear death, but knowing *how* they died is hard for them to accept. Still, knowing that Sevrin paid the ultimate cost for her brutality is helping them heal.

"Sevrin's guards became shockingly cooperative as soon as they learned of her death. It wasn't even necessary for Varrik to read their minds. They told us everything we wanted to know. The Team East house was raided this morning. The containment field generator worked even better the second time around."

"All of the hunters, with the exception of Nazerel, have been returned to Ontariese," Elias resumed as Lor fell silent. "The Overlord has appointed Lor to oversee the tribunal that will decide the fate of each hunter based on his level of involvement.

"Everything in both the team houses is being assessed and analyzed. If it holds no importance, it will be sold or destroyed. Anything of importance will be entered into evidence and become part of the trial."

"I don't envy you that nightmare," Blayne told Lor. "I'd much rather catch criminals than suffer through endless months of trials."

"It's a necessary evil," Lor countered. "After all, we're not Rodytes." Blayne just smiled, so Lor continued with the summary. "All of the research we found at the lab, as well as the lead geneticist, have been taken to Ontariese. Crown Stirate Quentin has been notified of his niece's death. He was surprisingly reasonable, though he insisted that Sevrin acted entirely on her own. He went so far as to claim he'd been about to launch a full-scale investigation into her actions after several of his best scientists mysteriously disappeared."

The ridiculous claim made Roxie chuckle. Plausible deniability at its finest.

"You find this amusing?" Lor looked at her, his gaze slightly narrowed.

"Of course not. I find the Crown Stirate's attempt to duck any of the blame amusing in a pathetic sort of way. Does he honestly expect you to believe he didn't know what Sevrin was up to and hadn't been supporting her every step of the way?"

"What we know and what we can prove are two different things," Elias told her.

"We don't want to start a war with the Rodytes," Lor pointed out. "Sevrin was the most to blame and she paid for her ruthlessness with her life."

Roxie wanted to be quiet and let the briefing run its course. Everyone else seemed content to accept the information as it was given out. Her mind didn't work that way. She was plagued by questions that demanded immediate answers. "What about the fifteen Rodyte families? Will they still come to Earth and search for their battle-born brides?"

"They were told the program was a scam, that Pern took their money and never intended to follow through with his end of the bargain." Lor paused, almost as if he was waiting for her next question.

She didn't disappoint him. "And they'll believe that without proof? They're a hell of a lot more trusting than I'd be."

Lor had reached for his water glass so Elias responded. "It's in Quentin's best interest to be convincing. All of his subjects know he and his older brother were frequently at odds. He'll blame it all on Pern. The families have no reason to doubt the story and no real recourse even if they have suspicions. We really are down to the cleanup and evaluation stages of this mission."

"With one glaring exception," Lor reminded. "Nazerel's capture."

"And Morgan's rescue," Elias stressed.

"Aren't they one and the same?" Blayne asked with a hesitant smile.

"Are there any new strategies?" one of the soldiers asked. Roxie was pretty sure his name was Dekker, but she'd been introduced to so many people in the past few days it had all begun to blur.

"Just one," Lor said with an enigmatic smile. "It takes a Shadow Assassin to find a Shadow Assassin, so I've arranged a clash of alphas." Lor tapped the audiocom tucked inside his ear and said, "We're ready now. Send them in."

Everyone turned and watched as the conference room doors swung open. A man strode into the room as if he owned the world, a stunningly beautiful woman at his side. The man's dark hair, which was pulled straight back from his face, was streaked with subtle threads of blue and bright blue rings blazed within his dark eyes. From the fierce expression on his angular features to the impressive width of his shoulders, everything about him screamed Rodyte warrior.

Like the male, the female made no attempt to hide her alien origins. Vivid purple eyes dominated her delicate features. Not only was the color unusual, but her irises flowed in a gently swirling pattern. That meant she was Ontarian. Was she the warrior's mate?

As if he'd heard her question, Lor introduced the visitors. "This is Varrik and Echo dar Aune, soul-bonded mates. Varrik was the alpha sweeper and there is no one alive who knows more about the Shadow Assassins than him."

"Excuse my rudeness, sir, but why wasn't this man included in the team from day one?" the outspoken soldier asked.

"It's a fair question, Dekker," Lor said, but he let Varrik answer for himself.

Varrik stood beside Lor at the foot of the table, his hands clasped behind his back. "I was asked to lead this expedition, but the unrest on the City of Tears was still too volatile. You've been chasing fifteen of our best hunters. I was dealing with a massive lifestyle transition for thousands, but Nazerel must be stopped."

"And you think you can do by yourself what all of us could not?" The question came from the generally good-natured Blayne.

"I can, but it's not a reflection on you. Nazerel is the First Son of South. I am the First Son of North. We were reared together, taught by the same mentors, subjected to the same disciplines. More was expected of First Sons than any of the other Shadow Assassins. I know how he thinks, what he relies upon and his weaknesses."

"I wasn't aware he had any," Dekker grumbled.

"He has weaknesses and I will exploit each one."

When no one had any immediate objections, Lor motioned toward the female. "Echo isn't here as moral support for her mate. She is a fully trained member of Ontarian Covert Operations with abilities that will greatly assist Varrik."

Talk about a power couple. The woman's gaze swept the room, pausing for a moment on Roxie. Her purple gaze drew Roxie in and made her feel slightly dizzy. Roxie had no idea what powers Echo commanded, but there was a calm assurance in her demeanor that Roxie found enviable.

Everyone scooted over and chairs were provided for Varrik and Echo. The briefing progressed with more enthusiasm, but Roxie's thoughts began to wander. She couldn't wait to return to Unique Ink, to the creative, peaceful environment where the most challenging decision was which design would look best on which area of the body. She helped people memorialize loved ones, process loss, and celebrate important events in their lives. She was ready to go home.

By the time the briefing ended, Roxie was unable to hide her restlessness. Everyone was crowded around Varrik and Echo, trying to learn more about the impressive couple. She loitered near the doorway, not wanting to interrupt, yet unwilling to leave without speaking with Elias.

He noticed her standing all alone a few minutes later and joined her by the door. "Are you all right?"

"I'm fine. I just don't belong here." She stopped him when he started to object. "I want to go home. I've neglected my responsibilities long enough."

"Give me a minute to wrap things up and I'll drive you—"

"You're acting director, love. You can't just leave." She placed her hands on his shoulders and moved closer. "I'm not breaking up with you. I just need to go to work."

He leaned down and kissed her, their lips lingering even as he pulled away. "And when my workday's done, shall I come to you or will you return to me?"

"I know my apartment is small, but I'd like to keep you all to myself, for a while anyway."

"Done." He kissed her again then pressed his forehead against hers. "I miss you already."

Lor approached and Elias eased her back though his hand remained on her waist. The Mystic smiled at them. "I need to dissolve the proximity bond if she's ready to leave."

"I'd forgotten all about it," Roxie admitted. Sharing emotions with Elias had become second nature. It would feel strange to have her mind to herself again.

Lor's knowing gaze moved from her face to Elias and back. "Mating bonds can be formed in stages. I wasn't sure if you knew about that."

"What do you mean?" Elias wrapped his right hand around her waist so he could face Lor.

"Some couples want the intimacy of sharing thoughts and feelings without the risk of immediate offspring. This seldom happens on Ontariese, but the connection is easily formed."

She looked into Elias' eyes and tried to gauge his reaction. "Are you interested in that sort of—"

"Absolutely. I'm not ready for kids right now, but the rest sounds amazing."

"Very well. Then I'll convert the existing link rather than removing it." He held out his hand. "A physical connection makes this easier."

Roxie placed her hand on Lor's and Elias covered her hand with his, curving his fingers downward so they touched Lor as well. Energy tingled through Roxie's palm, flowing down her fingers and up her arm. Instinctively she closed her eyes and followed the sparkling trail within her mind. She felt the proximity bond expand and transform, becoming something deeper.

Once I withdraw, the link will remain, allowing you access to each other's thoughts and feelings. After you've become comfortable navigating the connection, I'll teach you how to shield it.

It doesn't feel that different, Roxie told Lor.

Intimacy of any kind will strengthen the connection. It will feel very different before long.

And when we're ready for the final step?

Elias' question made Roxie look at him. Was he really thinking about children, about building a future together with her?

Lor slipped out of the link and pulled his hand out from under hers. "When you're both ready for a true mating bond, just let me know." Then he glided off across the room to rejoin the crowd surrounding Varrik and Echo.

"I'm not trying to pressure you, darlin'," Elias promised with a sexy smile. "I'm willing to wait as long as it takes, but I can't pretend I don't want it all. And I want it with you."

Thanks to the newly formed link she could feel his sincerity and the depths of his commitment. Rather than frightening, she found it liberating. She was free to embrace her attraction to him because his devotion to her was even stronger.

She started to kiss him again then thought better of it. "If I don't go now, I'll never leave. You're just too damn tempting."

With a warm chuckle, he bent down and brushed his lips over hers. "Until tonight." It wasn't really a kiss, more like a promise of all the wonderful things to come.

Book Six: Rebel Heat!

Desperate to escape the suppression collar that has robbed him of his Mystic abilities, Nazerel kidnaps Morgan, director of the human taskforce helping the Mystic Militia. She sabotages him at every turn, determined to escape before he regains his powers.

Locked in a battle of wills, they use every weapon at their disposal as each tries to outwit the other. Heightened emotions unleash a passion neither invited, nor can they control. They are enemies and yet they hunger for each other with an all-consuming need.

Don't miss this exciting conclusion to the *Shadow Assassins* series.

Chapter One

"Why are they just sitting there?" Flynn muttered as he peeked between the horizontal blinds.

Nazerel moved closer to the front windows of the Team South house and peered out into the hazy light. Dawn had just begun its ascent and much of the scene was still lost in shadow. An SUV and two panel vans were parked in a conspicuous cluster on the street of the quiet residential neighborhood. Increased pressure and successive raids by the Mystic Militia had prompted Sevrin to relocate her base of operations, as well as the two remaining team houses, to less obvious locations outside Las Vegas. Yet Nazerel and his men had not even unpacked and already their enemy was literally at their front door.

Sevrin. Just the female's name sent frustration coursing through Nazerel. She was the primary reason he and his fellow Shadow Assassins were on Earth. With far-reaching connections and fantastic promises, she'd lured them to a planet most of his men had never heard of before. But her promises had proved false and her connections far less advantageous than she'd led them to believe. Sevrin was self-serving and ruthless. For a time their goals had aligned, so Nazerel went along with her demands. Such was no longer the case. He was tired of being her puppet, even if his obedience was largely feigned. It was time for Nazerel to secure the freedom he'd promised his men, and Sevrin stood in his way.

"Look," Flynn, a fellow Shadow Assassin, motioned toward the SUV.

Two black-clad figures slipped out of the vehicle and crept toward the house, staying low and deep in the shadows. "They're headed to the backyard." Nazerel turned and projected his voice to his men scattered throughout the house. "Hold your positions. They'll try to keep this fast and quiet. They don't want to end up on the nightly news—again. Make them come to us." Turning back to Flynn, he added, "I'm going to check out the lawn creepers."

"Maybe we should just get the hell out of here. Tell everyone to flash—"

"Shadow Assassins don't retreat," Nazerel snapped. Flynn's brow arched in silent challenge. There had been many occasions when retreat was the only viable option and they both knew it. "We sure as hell don't give up without a fight. You've spent too much time inside Sevrin. She's made you weak." Before Flynn could respond to the slur, Nazerel turned around and headed toward the sliding glass door that led to the backyard. One of the others shifted closer to the exit, covering Nazerel without exposing his own position.

Flynn continued his surveillance of the front yard, appearing sullen and restless. Nazerel couldn't blame his friend for being discontent. Nothing had gone as planned since they left Ontariese. And tonight was no exception.

Sevrin had showed up with Flynn and her bodyguards about an hour ago, waking up the entire house without explanation. She owned the place and was their primary employer, so they weren't really in a position to object to her predawn visit. Flynn teleported out a short time later then returned with Roxie Latimer in his arms. Nazerel had done everything in his power, including endangering himself, to warn the foolish human that Sevrin was obsessed with her. Roxie's human lover flashed into sight a moment later, drawn to their location by a Mystic bond. Nazerel's men fell on the human like a pack of wolves, but Sevrin intervened, refusing to allow their unexpected visitor to be seriously harmed.

Nazerel touched the slender band encircling his neck and a fresh rush of fury surged through his system. That helpless human, unable to teleport on his own—unable to manipulate magic of any kind—had slapped a dreaded suppression collar around Nazerel's throat before Nazerel had any indication that he was a threat.

Now Nazerel was as powerless as the worthless human.

Sevrin and her entourage departed a short time later with Roxie and her companion in tow. Nazerel still didn't understand why Sevrin was so fixated on the human, but it was no longer his concern. His warnings had gone unheeded by Roxie and those claiming to protect her, so her fate was beyond his control.

Forcing the distractions from his mind, Nazerel visually swept the backyard. No sign of the creepers. They must not have come this far. He followed their example and stayed to the shadows, moving as stealthily as possible. At the corner of the house he paused and peered into the darkness of the side yard. Here the hazy light was mostly blocked by the house. His nanites seemed sluggish and ineffective as they adjusted his vision. The collar must be interfering with their operation as well as his Mystic abilities.

There was nothing he could do to rectify the limitation, so he ignored it. Crouching low to the ground, he studied the area. Fences were not allowed in this neighborhood; a fact Nazerel had greeted with fierce objections. But Sevrin insisted there would be no need for security, that the Mystic Militia thought they had left Nevada for good. Yet here they were. A strike team waited in vehicles on the street and these two black-clothed figures kneeling in the grass. Even their heads were covered, making them blend with the shadows. They spoke in urgent whispers as they franticly worked to assemble some sort a device.

About the size of a female's purse, they placed the device in the rock bed bordering the grass then activated a three-dimensional control panel. Was it a bomb? The technology seemed too sophisticated to have originated on Earth. Nazerel dismissed the possibilities. The Mystic Militia were unrelenting, not bloodthirsty.

He shifted his weight and something beneath his foot snapped.

The invaders jerked their heads in his direction. The smaller one motioned toward him and issued a command, setting the larger one in motion. The smaller one was in charge? How odd.

Nazerel needed to warn his men that a device was in play then make damn sure these two didn't turn it on. Instinctively, he reached for the common telepathic link all Shadow Assassins shared, but no sooner had he located the connection within his mind than he hit an impenetrable block. *Shit*! He'd almost forgotten about the collar.

For a split second he considered retreat. He was powerless, even somewhat weakened. But the creepers might activate the device before he could dispatch someone else. His opponent reached him in the next instant, making the debate irrelevant. The creeper gripped a pulse pistol firmly in one hand and a glimmer of hope penetrated Nazerel's pessimism. Most Mystics didn't bother with conventional weapons. Could this be one of Lor's human underlings?

The soldier moved closer, squinting into the darkness in an attempt to separate Nazerel's shape from the shadows. A Mystic would have increased the intensity of his vision or illuminated the area with an energy pulse. This was no Mystic.

Nazerel charged the soldier, batting the weapon out of his hand before the man could counter the blow. After the briefest pause to recover from the unexpected advance, the soldier punched Nazerel several times in quick succession. Nazerel blocked one blow, but the second and third landed with resounding force. His ears rang and pain pulsed through his head. Simple physical contact had never hurt this much before. His nanites again. Damn the collar!

The soldier took advantage of his distraction and swept Nazerel's legs out from under him with a perfectly executed spin kick. Nazerel landed hard on his back and the soldier followed him down, straddling his legs as he ruthlessly punched Nazerel's ribs and belly.

Anger flared within Nazerel and he felt a surge of strength tighten his muscles. He used the intensity without letting the emotion cloud his thinking. He bucked and twisted, easily dislodging the soldier. Before the man could right his awkward position, Nazerel swung his arm, catching the side of his opponent's head with his forearm. The soldier groaned, wobbled, then fell sideways into the grass.

Nazerel scrambled to his feet. The smaller one was still there, working with even more urgency. "Now!" Fear made the soldier's voice oddly high. "Move in now!"

The second command was clearer, less frantic—and far more *feminine*.

Rather than attacking with his full strength, Nazerel pounced on the woman. She went over sideways, but he quickly wrestled her to her back and pinned her arms to the grass on either side of her head. She jerked against his restraining hands, bucking and twisting like a wild animal. Huge, luminous eyes stared up at him in murderous outrage, but the rest of her face was obscured by the knit cap also covering her head.

Time paused and everything went silent as he stared into those shimmering eyes. As if in a trance, he shifted her wrists into one hand and pulled the cap off her head. Her hair had been pulled away from her face and bound at the nape of her neck. His nanites amplified the meager light, revealing features so perfect, so delicate they seemed unreal. Could a human woman be this beautif—

The toe of a boot kicked the back of his head as the woman beneath him lurched violently. Pain and humiliation jerked him out of his stupor and sent another rush of strength through his system. He moved farther back on her thighs, preventing her from repeating the agile maneuver.

"Disable that thing!" He jerked his head toward the device that was vibrating and sparking. Streamers of energy crept across the walls of the house like flickering spiders weaving a luminous web. The phenomenon was even more apparent across the angles of the roof. Was it some sort of shield? Or a *containment field*.

Shouts and pulses erupted inside the house. There was only one window on this side, but Nazerel could hear stomping feet and the unmistakable thuds and crashes of a violent struggle.

"Turn it off!" He yanked her to a sitting position, still straddling her legs. She didn't respond with either word or deed, so he reached for the device himself. His fingers encountered a transparent field that sent fire up his arm. Jerking his hand back, he glared at his captive.

"What is that thing?"

No response.

Fisting the front of her jacket, he dragged her to her feet. She grabbed his wrist with both hands and tugged against his hold. He spotted a large rock in the landscaping and picked it up. She stomped on his instep and he instinctively turned toward her, rock still in hand. Her hands flew upward, covering her face and he just shook his head. If he bashed in her head, any hope he had of turning off the device went with her. Not that he would actually kill a female, but she didn't know that.

He bent to one knee and slammed the rock against the device. The shielding gleamed at the point of impact and his arm vibrated so forcefully that his hand went numb. The rock slipped from his tingling fingers and his captive chuckled. He shook his arm and glared at her.

"So it's self-shielding," he muttered.

With the female fighting him every step of the way, he retrieved the rock and moved to the window. He threw the rock at the window and it bounced off. He pounded on the window with the rock, but each impact only vibrated more painfully through his arm and shoulder.

The rock slipped from his hand again and the woman jerked out of his grasp. He abandoned his attempts to break in and ran after the woman. She didn't make it far. Even without the assistance of his nanites, his legs were more powerful than hers. He wrapped his arms around her hips and tackled her to the grass.

She quickly rolled to her back, writhing in obvious desperation as he situated himself astride her. He captured her wrists, once again pinning them to the grass on either side of her head. "You're a wild one." If he couldn't disable the machine or break through the energy field, she would have to turn it off.

Which meant he had to control her.

Carefully shifting both her wrists into one hand, he scooted back onto her upper thighs. She continued her silent mutiny as he felt along her belt for the delightful metal restraints human enforcers sometimes carried. Instead he found long, ridged plastic strips that served the same purpose. Her eyes widened when she spotted the strips in his hand and her struggles returned even more violently.

Morgan tried to kick or bring her leg up between Nazerel's thighs, but his knees squeezed hard, halting the ascent of her shin before it reached its destination. She jerked against his hands and twisted, desperately trying to dislodge his grip. Damn, the man was strong.

"Stop it," he snapped. "I don't want to hurt you, but I will."

She believed him. At least the part about him being willing to hurt her. Moonlight cast eerie shadows across his angular features and blue rings erupted within the darkness of his gaze. According to Odintar, one of the Mystic Militia, that meant a Rodyte hybrid was pissed off or extremely turned on. Either possibility meant disaster for her.

He flipped her over and drew her arms behind her back. She wiggled and bucked, but he hardly seemed to notice. Within seconds her hands were firmly secured at the small of her back with one of her own zip ties. Why was he bothering to restrain her? Wouldn't it be easier to teleport... She turned her head sharply, twisting her torso as she looked back at him. He scrubbed his face with one hand and she saw that his neck was now encircled by a metal band.

Hot damn, they did it. Roxie and Elias collared the most dangerous male on planet Earth. Excitement surged through Morgan, renewing her purpose and curving her lips into a subtle smile.

"You find something amusing about being bound and helpless?" His voice growled with annoyance.

Continuing in silence was wiser, but Morgan was suddenly feeling much more secure. "I was just admiring your jewelry."

In an instant his hand gripped her throat, squeezing just hard enough to illustrate his restrained strength. "Don't fool yourself, *female*. I don't need Mystic abilities to control you."

The ease with which he'd done so thus far proved it was no idle boast. Even collared, his strength far exceeded hers. But he'd said he could "control" not kill her, which should give her time to escape. She calmly met his gaze, silently waiting for his next move.

"Tell me how to power down the device." He sounded composed and lethal now.

She said nothing, nor did she move. He was an alpha hunter. There was no thrill in the chase once the prey stopped running.

Using his grip on her throat to steady rather than hurt, he turned her over and pushed her down into the grass. Her bound arms arched her back and he effortlessly immobilized her legs. She spotted Dekker still slumped in the grass where Nazerel had left him. Was Dekker unconscious or dead? Her chest tightened at the possibility, but she couldn't allow compassion to distract her right now. Nazerel was too unpredictable.

He slowly unzipped her jacket and ran his hands over her torso with far more thoroughness than necessary. She stared up at the sky, trying to ignore the tension gathering in her belly. Surely he wouldn't rape her while the battle raged inside. Everyone claimed Shadow Assassins found rape detestable.

His warm fingers traced the outer curve of her breasts and her breath shuddered out. His touch was gentle, strangely curious as if he'd never touch a woman before. The possibility muddled her thinking and made her squirm. Her nipples tingled and she closed her eyes. This had to be fear and adrenaline or the early morning wind. She *did not* find his touch arousing.

He slipped his hand under her tank top and her eyes flew open. One corner of his mouth quirked as he ran his fingertips between her breasts, first one side and then the other. His expression challenged her to object or admit she was enjoying his overly careful search.

"Are you trying to find weapons or determine my bra size?" Rather than cutting, her voice sounded breathless and uncertain.

His gaze locked with hers and his thumb brushed over her nipple. "Which would you prefer?"

When she just glared at him, he moved on, going through each compartment on her utility belt. He stashed the things he deemed useful into the pockets of his black cargo pants and tossed the rest aside. He tucked her pulse pistol into the back of his pants and put her compact 9mm in the seam pocket of his pants. Finally, he unbuckled the belt and examined the inside surface. When he found nothing interesting there, he left the belt open across the grass to either side of her body.

"Last chance." He placed his hands on either side of her head then leaned down until their noses almost touched. "Turn it off and I'll leave you here, unconscious yet unharmed. Continue to defy me and I will show you no mercy."

She scrambled for a believable lie then miraculously he provided one.

He angled his head, whispering into her ear, "It has been a very long time since I had a female alone and at my mercy. The pleasure givers share their bodies freely with anyone who can meet their price. I find you much more arousing. Surrender now or it will be my pleasure to break you in very slowly."

A violent shiver passed through her entire body. Without pausing to analyze the cause, she met his gaze and let her lips tremble. "Please. I don't want...that." She glanced away, afraid he'd detect her deception. She could do nothing flat on her back, especially with her hands bound behind her. "I'll do what you want." Her voice broke and she prayed that he'd think she was terrified. "I'll turn it off."

He grasped her chin and turned her head back around. For a long, tense moment he searched her gaze. The blue rings gradually subsided, leaving a darkness even blacker than the night. He pushed off the ground and climbed to his feet, then used her unzipped jacket to drag her up as well. "Do not provoke me."

It was sound advice. Unfortunately, there was too much at state for her to listen. She let her shoulders slump as if she were beaten. With obvious reluctance, his fingers eased up on her jacket.

"I can't turn it off with my hands tied behind my back."

She'd managed to sound pathetic but he still laughed. "I'll be your hands. Tell me how to disable it."

Pivoting slightly to the side, she took a step back and gave him another moment to relax his guard. Then she centered her weight over her left foot and took a deep breath. She jump kicked him squarely in the gut then took off running. His loud grunt echoed in her ears. She saw a blur of motion, but didn't look back.

She raced toward the street and the waiting SUV, chaotic thoughts buzzing through her mind. She couldn't join the fight as long as the containment field was active, yet it needed to be turned off soon so the Mystics could teleport the Shadow Assassins to the safe house. But she couldn't risk deactivating it until she knew for sure all the Shadow Assassins were unconscious. At least locked inside the Suburban, she'd be less vulnerable. First and foremost, she had to free herself from the zip tie. If worse came to worst, she'd drive across the lawn and use the vehicle to knock Nazerel on his ass.

She was almost across the street when something collided with her back, propelling her forward. She nearly lost her balance then was slammed into the side of the Suburban. Keeping her tightly pressed against the passenger door, Nazerel opened the door to the backseat then forced her inside. She kicked and twisted, banging her head in the process, all to no avail. She ended up on her stomach across the bench seat, hands still firmly bound at the small of her back.

Nazerel climbed into the vehicle, awkwardly kneeling on the floor as he slammed the door shut behind them. Then he held her down with one hand and thoroughly searched her pockets with the other. He had to be looking for the keys. He'd already disarmed her.

She squirmed and twisted, trying to slow his progress. She did not want to be alone in some secluded place with this monster! "You're going to run away from a fight?" So much for not provoking him. "I thought Shadow Assassins never retreated?"

"If you must know, I'm going to ram this vehicle through the shield." A triumphant smile parted his lips as he drew the keys from her pocket.

"You'll kill us both." She shifted to her side, but couldn't sit until he moved out of her way. "It's not a bluff. Driving into the containment field will be like hitting a brick wall. Neither of us will survive, but your men will still be trapped inside."

He glared at her. "Then tell me how to turn it off."

"You know I can't." They glared at each other in silence for a moment. Defiance escalated his aggression, so she smoothly changed tactics. "It has to end, Nazerel. Sevrin is never going to give you what she promised. Negotiate with Lor. It's the only hope your men have."

His gaze narrowed, but he didn't move. It was an educated guess. They'd been told by numerous sources that Nazerel and Sevrin were butting heads, but she didn't know the specific points of contention.

"Morgan, where are you?" Dekker sounded dazed and strangely far away. He'd broken protocol and used her real name. She looked down and muttered a curse. Her earpiece was caught in a strand of hair that had come loose during her wrestling match with Nazerel.

Following the direction of her glance, Nazerel snatched the earpiece out of her hair and raised it toward to his face. "Morgan is busy right now. You'll have to carry on without her." He grabbed her jacket and searched the pockets—the only ones he'd yet to search—easily locating the small transceiver. Then he opened the door and threw her com unit out into the street, ignoring Dekker's frantic response.

Morgan cringed. Not only had he rid her of her only means of communicating with her team, he'd stripped her of their ability to track her. Each com unit was equipped with a GPS chip and hers would now reflect her location as the street in front of the Team South house.

At least with Dekker awake and responsive, the rest of the mission wasn't in jeopardy. She could focus on escaping or incapacitating Nazerel.

"Hello, Morgan." He looked at her with new interest. "Would that be Morgan Hoyt, leader of the human taskforce assisting the Mystic Militia?" He chuckled. "No wonder I couldn't find you. I'd been looking for a man."

Morgan carefully blanked her expression. She hadn't realized Sevrin knew anything about the taskforce, much less who was in charge. It had to be a recent discovery if she hadn't even figured out that Morgan was female. "Morgan Hoyt is my boss. It's an unfortunate, and confusing, coincidence."

"Sure it is." He sat back on his heels and looked at the team house. The fighting appeared to be over, but the occasional sparkle of energy streams indicated that the field was still active. This had to be killing him. Nazerel was a man of action, a hands-on leader who ran headlong into danger.

Hearing her own thoughts, she shook her head. That made him sound admirable and Nazerel was anything but. Hadn't his threat to "break you in very slowly" revealed his true nature?

He took a deep breath and apparently made up his mind. Without explaining what he intended, he lowered the armrest at the end of the seat and lifted her feet to the padded rail. Then he quickly bound her ankles with a zip tie. Releasing her was obviously not on his agenda.

"This is a really bad idea," she blurted.

"What is?" He didn't even glance at her face.

"Anything that requires me being trussed up like a turkey."

"I don't know what a turkey is, so I'll take your word for it." He pushed her down onto her stomach and bent her knees, then used two looped zip ties to secure her bound feet to the slim metal pole protruding from the bottom of the headrest. There was a good bit of slack in the makeshift restraint, yet it kept her from rolling to her back or kicking out a window. "Remain quiet or I will gag you with my socks and, believe me, you don't want that."

The hint of humor surprised her. She hadn't realized Rodytes could be playful. Odintar was certainly grim and serious all the time. She watched Nazerel turn and twist his big body with surprising agility as he climbed into the front seat and slipped in behind the wheel. When had a Shadow Assassin learned how to drive?

He started the engine and the door locks activated with a resounding *snap*. "Was that a malfunction?" He adjusted the rearview mirror so he could see her without turning around.

She tried hard not to smile. "Someone just shot out the tires."

His brows arched, but he didn't reply. It took him a moment to figure out the controls, but they were soon on their way.

"Where are you taking me?"

"I told you not to provoke me." Their gazes locked in the mirror for one intense moment then he turned his attention back to the road. "You should have listened."

The cryptic statement echoed through her mind as each moment took her farther away from safety. Dekker knew she was missing, but he didn't know Nazerel was collared. Dekker would presume Nazerel had teleported her away from the scene, which meant the missing SUV would likely go unnoticed until her team was ready to move to the second location, Sevrin's lab. Morgan was on her own, at least for the time being. The obstacles were daunting, but she was miles away from giving up. She was no match for him physically, so their battleground must be mental and emotional.

Nazerel was ruthless and driven. He also had a soft spot for beautiful women. His determination to warn Roxie Latimer proved that he could be protective. He'd been provoking Morgan with his overly thorough search, yet he was obviously attracted to her. Those were the qualities Morgan needed to exploit if she hoped to survive her captivity.

He'd only driven for ten or fifteen minutes when he suddenly stopped. She raised her head and tried to look around, but her position didn't allow her to see much. There didn't seem to be any buildings, just a narrow swath of dark blue sky.

"Remain quiet or you will be punished." He got out so fast she didn't have time to scream.

Was he leaving her here? Then why was the engine still running?

A car horn blared and then she could hear a second engine. The horn beeped again, more tentatively this time.

She tugged and twisted, trying to assess the situation. What the hell was he doing? She wasn't worried about being "punished", but she didn't want to endanger the motorist by revealing that he had an unwilling passenger.

Someone shouted and then there was a long nearly silent pause. All she could hear was the engine and the frantic beating of her heart.

The door by her feet opened and Nazerel sliced the zip tie connecting her to the seat with *her* pocket knife. He dragged her across the seat like a bundle of lumber then draped her over his shoulder. Her breath whooshed out as her belly connected with solid muscle. She tried to scream, but she couldn't draw enough air into her lungs.

If Nazerel switched vehicles, it would be much harder for her team to find her. Arching wildly, she caught a quick glimpse of the situation. The Suburban was more or less pulled over to the side of the road and a dark-colored sedan had stopped at an awkward angle. Had he stood in the middle of the street and forced the poor driver to stop?

Where was the driver?

Dread knotted her stomach and she tried even harder to look around. Each step he took drove his shoulder into her abdomen, making it difficult to breathe and impossible to see clearly. He opened the back door of the car and tossed her onto the seat. She quickly bent her knees, keeping the door from smacking her feet as he slammed it shut behind her. Then he hurried around to the other side of the car and slid onto the driver's seat.

"What did you do with the driver?" Accusation sliced through her tone.

"I snapped her neck and tossed her body in a ditch, of course." He paused long enough to adjust the mirror so she could see his glare then set the car in motion. "She's unconscious, yet otherwise unharmed. I even moved her well off to the side of the road so no one will run her over."

He was the criminal, so why did she feel guilty for thinking the worst of him?

She was no longer bound to the seat, so she was able to squirm onto her side. From there she wiggled toward the edge of the seat then threw her weight sideways as she tightened her abdominal muscles. It was awkward as hell, but she was finally sitting. More of her shoulder-length hair had come free from the tidy bun. She blew a strand out of her eyes and looked around. There was nothing to see, open road and miles and miles of empty desert.

"Disappointed?"

It was impossible to miss the mockery in his tone. The jerk was laughing at her. "Where are we going?"

"I'm not sure yet."

What did that mean? Had he not decided on a destination or was he waiting for someone else to provide one? If he was waiting for Sevrin to direct him, he might have a long wait. If phase two went off as planned, Sevrin should be in custody shortly.

She wiggled around a bit more, leaning against the door until she found a relatively comfortable position.

"I'm sorry it's so late." The strange statement drew her attention back to Nazerel and she found him driving with one hand as he held what looked like a cell phone with the other. It hadn't taken him long to adjust to life on Earth. "All right. I'm sorry it's so *early*. This can't wait for a more appropriate hour."

The other person spoke again, but Morgan couldn't make out what they were saying.

"I understand."

Nazerel nodded as the other person continued.

"All of that is acceptable, but I have additional requirements." After a short pause, Nazerel continued in a language Morgan didn't understand.

She tensed. He had to be talking about her. What else could he mean and why switch languages? Would he leave her with someone else while he made the ransom demands? Did he even know how to contact her people without giving himself away? He'd managed to stay a step ahead of everyone ever since he arrived on Earth. She could not underestimate him. That would be lethal.

Nazerel chuckled then muttered, "Something like that. I appreciate your help." Then he set down the phone.

How long could he hope to outrun the authorities in a stolen car? His fast thinking might have bought him an hour or two, but that was all.

Instead of criticizing his strategy, she asked, "What do you hope to accomplish by kidnapping me?"

"I'll offer your safe return in exchange for being released from this collar."

"Can't you just cut it off?" If he damaged the collar in any way, it released an electric charge that made a Taser seem tame, but she wasn't sure if he knew that.

"I would be incapacitated or killed depending on the model." His dark gaze clashed with hers in the mirror then he looked back at the road. "I likely know more about this device than you do. My father was Rodyte after all."

His father was Rodyte. Did that mean he didn't think of himself as Rodyte? Interesting.

They lapsed into silence again as he drove on through the early morning haze. The dossier she had on Nazerel hadn't contained many images, but the few she did have hadn't begun to capture the intensity of his presence. She'd expected him to be large and muscular, all the Shadow Assassins were, but there was a strength of character in his features that the images hadn't reflected and the collar couldn't suppress.

She was doing it again, granting him nobility when he deserved scorn.

"They can't turn you lose, and it's pretty obvious you don't want to kill me, so I'm afraid this is a waste of time."

"What I want to do and what I'm willing to do are often different things." Conviction rang through his tone and a shiver tingled down Morgan's spine.

Maybe she better leave well enough alone. At least for now. Unless she was ready to die, there wasn't much she could do to sabotage him at highway speeds. "If I promise to behave, will you release my hands or at least tie them in front of me? This is killing my back."

His gaze narrowed as he considered his options then he shook his head. "Not yet. And you need to lie back down or I'll have to blindfold you."

"With your socks?"

An unexpected smile flashed across his features and then vanished. She's barely registered the transformation before it disappeared, but the image lingered in her mind. His dark eyes shimmered and his harsh, angular features softened, well as much as anything about Nazerel could be described as soft. He looked years younger and infinitely more attractive. Attractive? Had she just thought of Nazerel as attractive? The awkward position must be cutting off the oxygen to her brain.

"I mean it. Lie down." He looked in the mirror to make sure she obeyed. "I'll secure you more comfortably when we switch vehicles."

So that was what the call had been about. He'd arranged for an untainted vehicle. Damn. That would make them even harder to find. But who had Nazerel called? All of her information indicated that Sevrin was the one with all the human contacts; that the Shadow Assassins were basically at her mercy. Either Morgan's information was wrong or phase two of their plan had failed. Unfortunately, the only one who knew for sure was Nazerel and he wasn't likely to tell her.

Left with no other option but to endure the discomfort and uncertainty, she stared at the back of his seat and concentrated on not throwing up.

Chapter Two

The sun had risen well above the horizon by the time Nazerel reached the exchange point. Not much of a destination really, just an emergency pull-over lane on the side of the highway. Phil Mortsen had already arrived and the compact SUV in which he sat looked perfect for what Nazerel had in mind.

"Why'd we stop?"

He unfastened his seat belt and looked at Morgan. She'd been asleep for over an hour and still sounded groggy. Exhaustion and boredom were a potent combination. "Stay down and keep quiet. If you obey, for once, I'll allow you to sit up after the exchange."

She looked as if she'd argue then released a loud sigh and returned her head to the seat of their borrowed car. Though she was no longer bound to the seat, her arms and legs were restrained, so she shouldn't be able to cause too much trouble. With lingering reluctance, Nazerel left her alone in the car and went to speak with Phil.

Phil swung his door open and unfolded his tall, thin body from inside the SUV. With medium brown hair and common brown eyes, Phil went out of his way to appear ordinary, forgettable, and mistakably human. The Bilarrian trader had been recommended to Nazerel by a trusted friend before he left Ontariese. Phil was known for locating the unusual, arranging the impossible, and the exorbitant prices he charged for his miracles. All of that had been well and good, but what convinced Nazerel to contact Phil had been his reputation for keeping secrets.

Sevrin had been careless in many ways because of her belief that he was utterly dependent upon her. Such had never been the case. Nazerel had carefully crafted plan B long before he accepted her invitation to join her on Earth. He had hoped Sevrin would live up to her promises, had proceeded as if he believed every word she told him, but in secret he nurtured a few strategic contacts and Phil was one of them. It hadn't taken long for Nazerel to realize the precautions had been wise. Sevrin was a lying, self-serving bitch who wanted to exploit the unique physiology of Shadow Assassins.

"Greetings First Son of South," Phil said with a friendly smile.

"I'm Nazerel Southmor now and we're beyond such formality." They shook hands and Nazerel returned his smile.

"The provisions you ordered are packed in the vehicle and your special order is in here." He held out his hand, a plastic bag dangling from his fingers by the handles.

Nazerel accepted the bag and quickly looked through its contents. He took out the mist dispenser and asked, "How long will the sedative last?"

"Depends on the size of the person."

"Athletic human female."

"Around eight hours."

Something behind Nazerel caught Phil's attention, so Nazerel turned around to see what had distracted him. Morgan's shiny red hair was clearly visible between the two front seats. She had one shoulder braced against the back of the seat as she looked around. He better make this quick. His feisty prisoner was getting restless.

He turned back to Phil, continuing on as if neither of them had seen anything unusual. "Eight hours?" Phil nodded. That should give him plenty of time to reach his destination and set up camp before Morgan became a problem again. "And there are no side effects?"

"It's harmless and effective. We've used it on Bilarri for decades." He motioned toward the bag. "I loaded one of the sedative cartridges for you, but there are several other varieties included as well, analgesic, antibiotic, antitoxin." He shrugged. "I wasn't sure how long you planned to be tromping around in the woods."

"Not long enough to need any of that, but I appreciate the thought."

"All right then. Obviously your transfer of funds was successful or I wouldn't be here."

The sizable fortune Nazerel had brought with him from Ontariese was another advantage of which Sevrin was unaware. He had guarded every word and expression to make sure no one realized he could sever their arrangement at any moment and just walk away. Not even his men knew. He hadn't been willing to risk Sevrin finding out about his deception. It would have been utter folly to follow her to a strange planet without any means of providing for his needs and the needs of his men.

"Disposal of the car was included," Phil told him. "Is there anything else I can get for you?"

"Everything seems to be in order for now, but how are plans for off-world transportation going?"

"Things were much easier when you could open a portal yourself. Any hope that you'll free yourself from the collar before you're ready to depart?"

"It's my top priority, but you better make arrangements for either situation."

"Of course. It's more complicated without your abilities, but I've arranged this sort of thing before. It shouldn't take more than a day or two. Do you have a final head count yet?"

"I don't. Is that important?"

"Not really. Smugglers prefer smaller groups, but I can accomplish most anything."

Nazerel smiled. "I noticed."

"I'll contact you when everything is in place."

"Wonderful and I appreciate the fast delivery on this. I look forward to doing business with you again." Nazerel motioned toward the car. "Give me a minute to move my belongings."

Phil flashed a conspirator's smile. "Would you like me to assist you with that?"

"No need."

Nazerel slipped his arm through the handles on the bag as he returned to the car. He opened the door by Morgan's head. She looked up at him and he pressed the button on the top of the mister. She gasped as the cloud of mist hit her face, which was the intention of the design.

Her eyes blinked and she sputtered, but the drug became more effective with each indignant breath.

Scooping her up in his arms like a child, Nazerel pulled her from the car and walked to the passenger side of the SUV. Phil had opened the door for him but then quickly turned away. His customers expected discretion and Phil never failed to provide. Nazerel set Morgan down on the seat then straightened. "We're good. You don't need to stick around."

Phil needed no other prompting. "Until next time." He climbed into the stolen car and drove away.

Anxious to resume his voyage, Nazerel freed Morgan's wrists and drew her hands in front of her. It was unlikely she'd regain consciousness, but he wasn't taking any chances. He took out the velvet-lined cuffs and couldn't help but smile. These would be much easier on her skin than the plastic strips, but she would likely find them even more provoking. He enjoyed annoying her. Her soft ivory skin flushed and her sky-blue eyes gleamed when she was angry. It made him hunger for the feel of her arching beneath him, rubbing her soft curves against his chest.

But such distractions needed to wait until they were in a safer location. He buckled the cuffs around her wrists then secured the buckles with a tiny padlock. A small length of chain connected the cuffs and it could be fastened with a matching padlock. Instead of bothering with the third lock, he wove the seat belt through her arms further restricting her movements. Last he located the lever for the seat back and adjusted the angle until she rested more comfortably.

With his passenger once again secured, he moved to the driver's side and climbed in behind the wheel. He took his phone out of his pocket and launched the security program for the Team South house. He'd already checked the camera feeds twice, but he couldn't stop hoping the images would change. Room after room scrolled across his screen, each one the same. Overturned furniture and blast marks on walls, but each room was empty. The only thing that gave him hope was the complete lack of blood. It was unlikely anyone had died in the battle, but were his men fugitives, scattered to the wind, or prisoners of the Mystic Militia?

He could do nothing to assist his men if he was caught. So escape must be his top priority. Freeing himself from the suppression collar was equally important, like it or not, that was where his prisoner became useful.

With a six-hour drive ahead of him, there was no reason to delay. He sighed at the thought. How did humans tolerate the excruciating pace of automobile travel? He plugged his phone into the power adapter and then connected it to the radio. Flynn had introduced him to a genre of music called Grunge. Nazerel found many things about humans strange, but he was fascinated by their music. Something about the distorted guitars and angst-filled voices struck a common chord within his soul. He found his longest playlist and set it on shuffle. Hopefully that would help fill the empty hours.

MORGAN WOKE UP SLOWLY, drifting back to consciousness as if she were trudging through mud. She was no longer moving. In fact she was flat on her back on something relatively soft. Her legs were no longer bent and her arms were extended above her head. There was no way she was still in a car.

She tried to move her arms, but her body felt weighted, sluggish. Or she was bound! Her eyes flew open and fear cleared her mind. She tugged against whatever was holding her hands. The bite of the zip tie was gone, but the new bindings held her firmly. She twisted her head, hoping to unravel the mystery. Her hair had come loose from its neat bun and now spread across her arms, covering her hands. She drew up her knees, thrilled to discover her legs weren't tied down. But the next revelation was even more upsetting. She wore only her bra and panties. The bastard had even removed her boots and socks. Was he simply trying to discourage her from running away or had his motives been more licentious?

Refusing to panic, she looked around. She was in a mid-size camping tent and her bed was several unzipped sleeping bags. There was a cooler near the entrance and two large crates loaded with supplies. Where the hell was she? Her throat tightened and her mouth dried up as her heartbeat echoed in her ears. It looked as if he intended to keep her here for quite some time, but where was here?

She closed her eyes and held perfectly still, forcing on audible clues. The buzzing of insects reached her first then the distant call of a bird. There were no city sounds, no engines or car horns. They were definitely secluded, but she couldn't tell more without seeing outside.

The tent smelled a bit stale and she detected something else as well. Smoke, faint and pleasant, like the telltale scent of a campfire. How long had she been out? More importantly, was Nazerel arrogant enough to use a public campground? She opened her eyes and turned her head toward the zippered opening that served as a door. There was one easy way to find out.

She took a deep breath and screamed as loud as she could. When no one immediately responded she screamed again.

Mocking her with each lazy movement, Nazerel made his way inside the tent. He even took time to lower the zipper before he turned to face her again. "I was beginning to wonder if you'd ever wake up."

The smug bastard looked amused not concerned. "Where the hell are we and why am I still tied up?" Not to mention nearly naked!

"Our location isn't important—though screaming is obviously a waste of breath—and you're still bound because you defy me at every turn."

"I'm your prisoner. Of course, I defy you. Humans don't do well in captivity."

He actually smiled. The jerk. "I think with the right master you'll do just fine in captivity."

She gasped at his boast, which was probably what he wanted. "You're not my master. You're not *my* anything."

"Perhaps not, but you're my prisoner until I see fit to release you."

It was a little hard to argue with that while she was flat on her back and tied up to boot. She couldn't hope to best him in a physical confrontation, she had to think, strategize. "I need some water."

His head tilted and his brow arched. "Ask me nicely."

Her mouth was so dry she could hardly speak. Defying him now only punished herself, but she was seriously tempted. "May I please have some water?"

Sauntering over to the plastic crates, he rummaged around for a moment and found a bottle of water. He twisted off the top and took a leisurely drink before approaching the makeshift bed. "If you kick me, I'll restrain your legs. If you spit on me at any time for any reason, you forfeit the rest of your clothes." He bent to one knee beside her and slipped his arm under her shoulders. Lifting her slightly, he brought the bottle to her lips and let her drink her fill.

The time for anger was past. She couldn't escape him as long as she was bound and virtually naked. Despite her very real need to "defy him at every turn", it was more important to earn his trust and find, or create, an opportunity to get the hell away from him. "So what will it take for you to 'see fit to release' me?"

He just stared at her for a moment, his arm warm and solid against her back. "I told you what I wanted before we left." After lowering her to the bedding, he stood and returned the half-empty bottle to the crate. "Your freedom for mine."

She shook her head despite her pounding heart. "They will never—"

"Cut the bullshit, Morgan." His expression turned fierce as he faced her. "You're director of the taskforce, which means you *own* this collar." She felt her eyes widen and quickly relaxed her lids. "Yes, I know how it works. Anyone can close the collar, but only the owner can open it. There is no 'they' involved in this negotiation. It's between you and me. Release me from the collar and I'll release you from my tender care."

She'd known Nazerel was smart, but she hadn't expected him to put the pieces together this quickly. "Lor owns the collar and he will never release you." The statement was true. Bilarrian scientists had provided her team with the coding needed to establish co-ownership. Lor *was* the collar's owner, but then so was she.

"I think you're lying."

"I don't care what you think. How did you find out about the taskforce? My contact said Sevrin didn't know."

One of his brows arched and she didn't think he'd answer, then he said, "I stopped depending on Sevrin for reliable intel shortly after we arrived on Earth. Who's your contact?"

"It doesn't matter and you can browbeat me all night. I can't unlock the collar."

"There's another option."

Thank God. She did not want Nazerel focused on her personally. "I'm listening."

His gaze moved over her body with insolent interest as he stalked toward her. "My power spikes whenever I'm feeling strong emotions, like anger." He looked directly into her eyes. "Or lust." He knelt beside the sleeping bags and placed his hand on her belly. He just let it rest there, a warm weight against her tense abdomen. "It might take days, even weeks, but I'll keep trying. Once I find the perfect combination of desire and rage, I'll access my power long enough to disable the collar."

"I don't respond well to threats." She twisted around and kicked him in the shoulder.

He laughed. "It's not a threat and your response isn't necessary." He grabbed her ankle when she tried to kick him again. "But you will respond."

He couldn't be serious. *Please God, let this be a bluff.* "Shadow Assassins detest rape. Everyone insists their captives aren't abused."

"I have no intention of raping you." He moved closer. His knees pressed against her side as his fingers lightly caressed her skin. "I'm going to look at your amazing body and touch you in progressively more intimate ways until my senses are on fire. Then I'll use the intensity to burn through the collar's circuitry." He slid his hand just under one of her breasts and pushed his thumb between, still on top of her bra. "Or you can admit you own the collar and avoid all those unwanted touches."

"I don't own the collar and your definition of rape must be different than mine. Any *unwanted* touching falls within my definition of rape."

"Really?" His fingertips skimmed across her skin, circling her navel and tracing the waistband of her panties until she began to squirm. "Do you feel defiled?"

"Not yet, so stop now."

He laughed and the blue rings flickered to life within his dark eyes. "Let me know when I've crossed the line." He retraced his path then avoided her breasts entirely and explored her upraised arms.

"This isn't funny." Morgan turned her head, unable to think with his penetrating stare boring into hers. Everything about him was brutal, so how could he touch her so gently. He found a particularly sensitive spot near her elbow and she shivered.

"Are you ticklish?" He teased the sensitive bend with ruthless patience until she was wriggling helplessly.

It didn't tickle, exactly. It sent strange tingles down her arm and lower, much lower, to places she refused to think about. Her nipples were getting hard and her skin felt tight and prickly. She couldn't let him do this to her. She would not be turned on by his sick game. Rolling away from him, she brought her knees up toward her chest and pressed her thighs together. "Leave me alone."

"I don't want to."

She could see him moving in her peripheral vision. Oh God, he was taking off his shirt. Was that all he was taking off? Panic sliced through her and she looked over her shoulder. Big mistake. He knelt on the edge of the sleeping bags bare to the waist, a golden-skinned sculpture of masculine symmetry. She whipped her head back around, but it was too late. His image was seared into her brain. She found his features harshly intriguing, so full of determination and pride, but his torso was a work of art, perfectly proportioned and harshly defined. Even his eclectic collection of tattoos only added to his savage beauty.

Despite her fear and determination to remain unaffected by his seduction, her body came alive, melting and aching for the pleasures she continually denied herself. It wasn't that she didn't like sex, she did, quite a lot actually, but her life made intimate relationships almost impossible.

This wasn't the beginning of an "intimate relationship", this was cruel manipulation. So he had an amazing body. That didn't mean she was powerless against him. Elias was well-built too and she didn't go into heat every time she saw him without his shirt. She was just tired and stressed beyond belief.

Nazerel lay down behind her and slipped one arm beneath her neck. Then he pulled her toward him, which angled her upraised arms away from her head. It also took the slack out of the restraints so she couldn't slam her elbow into his face, she realized. The man didn't miss much. He pressed against her back and wrapped his other arm around her waist. He did nothing else for a long time, just lay there and let the heat of his body surround her.

She could finally see her hands. Wide leather cuffs with silver buckles and miniature padlocks now encircled her wrists. A length of chain connected the cuffs and he'd passed the chain behind one of the tent poles. The pole wasn't secured with stakes and rope. He'd somehow driven it directly into the ground, providing a much sturdier anchor for her confinement. But the chain simply passed behind the pole. It wasn't locked down like the cuffs. If she could unfasten the chain without him realizing what she was doing, she could easily free herself.

Slowly easing her hands together, she reached for the chain's simple clasp. He grabbed her wrist and pulled her hands apart. "You won't like how I bind you if you free yourself now."

Indignation rushed through her, making her want to scream. Was she just supposed to lie here and accept whatever he chose to do to her? She'd been trained by the FBI. Surrender was not in her nature.

She closed her eyes and concentrated on filling her lungs, keeping each breath slow and even. But his scent became more familiar with each inhalation. Rich and earthy with an intriguing hint of spice, he smelled wonderful.

"When was the last time a man held you in his arms?" His voice was barely a whisper, his tone oddly rough.

Her eyes flew open as a possibility unfurled within her mind. "Last night. My *husband* loves to cuddle. I'm called away so often, we have to make the most of every minute we have together."

His chuckle ruffled her hair, his breath warm against her skin. "If you were with a man last night, cuddling was all you did. I would be able to smell him if it were otherwise."

"I showered this morning, thank you very much." She tried to wiggle away from him, but he simply tightened his arm.

"It can take many days for a male's scent to leave a female completely. That's why pleasure givers never satisfy. It's hard to loose myself in passion when all I smell are other males."

If she could shift his focus yet keep him talking, maybe he'd give up on seducing her. Anything was better than giving in without a fight. "What about Roxie? She's not a pleasure giver. You've been very protective of her."

He brushed her hair away from her neck, which also exposed her face and ear. "Why does everyone want to put me in bed with Roxie?"

"You've clearly spent a lot of time with her. You're covered in tattoos."

His face pressed against her neck and he inhaled deeply. "Gods, you smell good." He slowly swept his hand down her neck then up her extended arm. "Do you taste as good as you smell?" His lips brushed the sensitive spot just below her ear then he touched her skin with the tip of his tongue.

Her treacherous heart leapt in her chest and tingles skittered off to all sorts of unacceptable places. She had to stop this *now*. "Flynn is my contact."

He tensed, his arm tightening around her. "What are you talking about?"

"Varrik gave us profiles on all of you guys. Elias determined that Flynn was the most likely to flip, so we recruited him."

"Who is Elias?"

"You met him this morning. He was with Roxie when Flynn brought her to the team house. That was all part of our plan by the way. I'm pretty sure he's the one who collared you."

Disentangling his arm from hers, he sat up and rolled her onto her back. Then he swung one of his legs across hers to keep her from kicking him. He propped himself up with one arm and rested his other hand on his thigh, which was still covered with black cargo pants. Thank God.

"I've known Flynn my entire life. He has many faults, but he is not a traitor."

She licked her lips. This was a dangerous distraction. If she pissed him off too badly, she just might give him what he needed to free himself from the collar, yet failing to make the conversation interesting would likely result in their returning to their earlier activity.

"Is Varrik a traitor?"

"Yes," he snarled the word, clearly demonstrating his dislike for the man. "Varrik is the worst kind of traitor. He was a First Son, like me, and still he chose to abandon the Sacred Customs for a female."

"Varrik wanted a lot more than a beautiful woman. He wanted to liberate your people, to free them from the world below and—"

"You know nothing about the world below!" He leapt to his feet and raked his hair with his fingers, menace radiating off him in tangible waves. "I know what you're doing."

"I'm trying to understand your point of view."

He scoffed. "You're trying to keep my hands off you, but all you've done is postponed the inevitable." He dropped to his knees, straddling one of her legs. She braced for an attack, accepting that her risk had failed, but all he did was free her arms from the tent pole. "I'm no longer in the mood for lust. Let's focus on anger." He pushed off the floor and stood up, moving to the other side of the tent.

She drew her arms down, groaning as her muscles protested the new position. Her wrists were still locked within the cuffs, but the length of chain between the two gave her a reasonable range of motion. "Where did you get these or why did you think you would need them? Did you plan on taking a hostage all along?"

"I planned nothing that happened this morning," he snapped. "You attacked us!"

"Then when...that's right. You called your outfitter and told him you had additional requirements then you started speaking in Rodyte."

"We were speaking Bilarrian." He paced what little space there was in the middle of the tent, clearly distressed by the implications of what she'd said. His features were tight and the telltale rings in his eyes had begun to glow. "What did you promise Flynn? He wouldn't have sold us out for money."

She sat, rolling her shoulders and stretching her back before she reached over and retrieved his discarded shirt. If he was determined to parade around half-naked, then she was going to make use of the garment. She folded her legs in front of her and then draped the T-shirt over the front of her body, leaving the bottom to pool between her legs. It was as close to decent as she was likely to come until he returned her own clothes.

"You're right, it wasn't about money with Flynn," she began. "He'd figured out that Sevrin was full of shit, but returning to Ontariese wasn't really an option. We offered him an opportunity to take responsibility for his mistakes and start to rebuild his future."

"By betraying the rest of us?" His hands fisted at his sides and the rings in his eyes blazed like blue fire. "That's a coward's way out. He knew I had other plans. I would have given him other options."

There was a lot more she could say, a lot more she wanted to say, but it was smarter to back off right now, give him a minute to calm down. "How did you pay for all this?" She motioned to their surroundings. "I was under the impression that the council's funds were seized when the Shadow Maze was liberated."

A secretive smile curved his lips, but the rings in his eyes continued to burn. "High Queen Charlotte only knows what Varrik told her, and Varrik doesn't know everything."

"Then you didn't get the money from Sevrin?"

He scoffed again, but sadness dampened the sound this time. "Sevrin made us beg for everything. We were honestly better off in the City of Tears. Roxie was the only luxury Sevrin allowed. Why do you think she was so popular?"

"Roxie told Elias that you get off on the pain."

His gaze locked with hers and a smile finally parted his lips. "What else did Roxie tell you?"

She could almost see the tension flow out of him. Roxie was the first name she'd mentioned that had a soothing effect on him. "She told us Sevrin was the real villain not the Shadow Assassins."

"Lor should have known that without having to be told." He turned his back on her and grabbed the open bottle of water out of the crate. He drained it then tossed her a new one. "Are you hungry?" he asked without looking at her.

"Starving actually. What time is it?" If she could figure out how long she'd been unconscious, she'd have a better idea how far they'd traveled.

"It's almost dark. I better locate a light source."

He rummaged through the first crate with no luck, so he unloaded the second. Morgan watched him set the lantern aside without realizing he'd found what he was looking for and debated what to do. If she doomed him to darkness, she doomed herself as well. She struggled up from the makeshift bed while keeping his T-shirt pressed to her chest.

"That's called a lantern. When the middle part is ignited it emits light." She pointed at the lantern with her foot.

He turned around and his gaze swept her from head to toe. "I didn't give you permission to cover yourself."

"Tough shit." She softened the phrase with a mischievous smile. "It's getting cold as well as dark." She was hoping to keep him off-balance with her semi-flirtatious rebellion. "And even slaves have to eat."

Without warning, he fisted the back of her hair and snatched the T-shirt out of her hands. He held it out of reach and made her watch it sail to the floor. Then he wrapped his other arm around her waist and pulled her firmly against his body. Finally, with obvious restraint, he pulled her head back until their gazes locked. "Then you admit you're my slave?"

"That is not what—"

He silenced her protest with his mouth. The kiss was hard and demanding, yet slow, advancing by degrees until she found herself responding, despite her intention to resist him. His tongue teased her lips, caressing and tracing without venturing between. Smart man. If he dared to invade her mouth, she'd bite him hard enough that he'd need stitches.

Suddenly he shifted her head to the bend of his elbow and eased his hand between their bodies. She felt his fingers moving against her breasts, but he wasn't really caressing her. The cuffs, she realized. He unhooked the tether connecting the cuffs, so she could separate her arms.

With an impatient growl, he moved her hands out of his way and crushed her breasts into his chest. "You're so soft." He sounded drugged as he whispered the words against her lips and then he kissed her again.

His hand moved up and down her back, occasionally dropping a bit lower. But he didn't squeeze her ass or fondle her breasts. It was almost frustrating. He obviously wanted her, so why was he being so...careful?

Because Shadow Assassins didn't rape their captives. They meticulously seduced them until they were willing participants in their own degradation. Understanding helped clear her head and refocus her purpose. She needed to earn his trust, convince him to let down his guard long enough for her to escape.

And two could play at this game. She wrapped her arms around him and touched him even more aggressively than he was touching her. His skin felt oddly soft in comparison to the flesh beneath. His back wasn't just dramatically tapered, it was corded with defined muscles. She rubbed against him, easing her legs apart until she straddled his thigh.

Her participation made him bolder. His tongue swept over her lower lip, brushing against her teeth before retreating again. She returned the caress and he groaned, his fist returning to her hair. He dragged his mouth away from hers and stared deep into her eyes. "I want to kiss you, really kiss you."

"I know." She allowed herself to smile. "Feed me first and I'll consider it."

His gaze narrowed and his nostrils flared, then he released her with a sigh. "Even slaves have to eat."

And round one goes to Morgan. Thank God he couldn't read her mind. Thoughts like that would likely land her flat on her back again. Taking advantage of her momentary freedom, she snatched his T-shirt off the floor and put it on.

He took a step toward her, but she held up both hands. She even lowered her gaze. "May I please wear your shirt? I really am cold." He said nothing so she glanced up at him.

"What game are you playing?"

The question was probably rhetorical, but she answered anyway. "No game. I was just cold." He obviously didn't believe her, but he didn't press the issue.

Rather than continue their power struggle, he turned around and motioned to the mess he'd made earlier. "Do you see something with which to ignite the lantern?"

Hoping the question wasn't just a ploy to reel her in, she moved up beside him. The tent had gone from gloomy to dim while they made out, so she didn't have much time to solve the problem. She didn't see a box of matches or a grill starter, so she moved to the first crate, the one he hadn't unloaded. It took a few minutes, but she found a lighter sliding around in the bottom of the crate. Good thing the bottom was solid.

She lit the lantern then hung it from the hook attached to the center support pole of the tent. "Be careful not to brain yourself on this."

"Brain myself?" He looked at the position of the lantern and nodded. "I'll never master human vernacular."

She tossed the lighter back into the crate then thought of something that didn't make sense. "Did you make a fire earlier? I thought I smelled smoke."

"I was bored," he admitted with a hesitant smile. "It was about to gather more wood when you woke up, so I just let it burn itself out."

"But how did you light a fire without matches or a lighter?"

The hesitant smile turned into a cheeky grin. "I'd do well on *Survivor*."

"You watched a lot of TV, I take it?"

"There was little else for us to do. We worked out and sparred with each other. We occasionally reinforced Sevrin's guards, but mostly we just tried not to go insane from the monotony of it all."

She had no idea what to say to that, so she motioned toward the cooler. "Can I just help myself?"

"Go on. I ate while you were sleeping."

She opened the cooler and selected a sandwich from the surprising selection of food. The cooler must be battery powered. There was no ice inside, but everything was cold. She took out a cola as well as the sandwich and paused before closing the lid. "Do you want a drink or something?"

"Did he pack any beer?"

She had to dig a bit, but she found a six-pack and tore off a can. "There are only six, so make it last." She closed the cooler then handed him the beer, moving out of reach before he could stop her. Not that he intended to stop her. She just wasn't taking any chances.

The stupid cuffs were still buckled around her wrists, the connecting chain dangling from one side. She could easily take them off, but she didn't feel like asking permission and being rid of them wasn't worth the fight she'd start if she took them off without asking him first.

So she picked up her meager meal and looked around for a place to sit down. If the outfitter had given Nazerel chairs, he'd chosen not to unpack them. Instead, she pulled the cooler away from the wall and sat down, shivering as her bare legs connected with the smooth metal. He watched her silently, leisurely sipping his beer.

The attack had begun at dawn, but they'd sat in the vehicles for almost an hour waiting for Sevrin to take off with Roxie and Elias. It had been vital that Sevrin lead Lor back to her lab before the rest of them moved in on the Team South house. So it could have been as late as eight o'clock before Nazerel drove away with her. Then it had been at least hour before they made the final vehicle switch. Much to her mortification, she'd fallen asleep in the stolen car, so she couldn't be sure of the intervals. Still, that left roughly nine hours before she woke up here. The problem was she had no idea how many of those hours he'd been driving and how many he'd been setting up the campsite and building campfires. He'd been here long enough to get bored.

"What are you thinking about? You look perplexed." He'd taken off his boots and was sitting cross-legged in the middle of the bed, the bed he obviously intended for them to share.

She saw no reason to lie, so she said, "I was trying to figure out how far you drove while I was out."

"There aren't many pine trees in Las Vegas."

"You haven't let me go outside. We could be in a parking lot for all I know."

"Close your eyes. Can't you smell them?"

She closed her eyes and inhaled slowly, analyzing each scent that registered in her mind. She was closer to the door now, and less drug-addled. He was right. She could defiantly smell pine trees, damp earth—and Nazerel! Had he imprinted her with his scent or something? Why was his smell still so clear?

Ignoring the disquieting phenomenon, she opened her eyes and unwrapped her sandwich. "Are we still in Nevada?"

He arched his brow and took a sip of his beer. "Maybe."

There were numerous places he could have reached in eight or nine hours, but Utah looked very different than California. She glanced at the zippered exit, wondering if he'd stop her if she poked her head outside.

"It's dark. You're not going to be able to see much more than what I just told you. We're in a mountainous location surrounded by pine trees."

"Yes, but are the mountains gray or red?" Gray meant they'd traveled north or northwest, either staying in Nevada or crossing over into California. Red meant east into New Mexico or northeast into Utah. She'd know more when she could see their surroundings.

He patted the sleeping bag beside him. "Come here."

"I'm comfy right here. Thanks anyway." Despite her growling stomach, she'd yet to take a bite of her sandwich.

His expression remained relaxed, but his tone sharpened. "Are you that anxious to feel me on top of you again? I enjoyed our wrestling match in the grass. Are you ready for another?"

Heat cascaded through her body as his taunt reminded her of how strong he was and how effortlessly he'd controlled her. "Why can't I stay here?" She tried not to sound like a petulant child.

"Because I told you to join me."

Another crossroad. If she gave in too easily, he'd realize she was pretending. Yet angering him could give him access to his power. "I worked very hard to become a leader because I'm not very good at following orders."

He didn't argue. He just stood up and crossed the tent then scooped her up in his arms. Without bothering to set down his beer, he returned to the bed and sat back down. "I wanted you beside me. Apparently, you wanted to be on my lap instead." He lowered her into the limited space between his thighs and crossed his ankles, surrounding her with his strong legs. His arm remained at her back, ensuring that she stayed right where he'd placed her.

It was actually more comfortable than the cooler had been, so she decided not to fight with him. She arched her legs over his and used his other thigh as lumbar support then finally took a bite of her sandwich.

He leaned in and whispered, "Have you decided yet?"

She turned her head and looked into his eyes. Their faces were much too close together like this. She could see the blue rings in his eyes even though they weren't illuminated. "Decided what?"

"If you're going to let me kiss you after you finish eating."

Her gaze dropped to his mouth and she was suddenly fighting off the irrational urge to nibble on his lower lip. "Are you sure that thing is working?"

His brows flew nearly to his hairline and then he burst out laughing. "Give me your hand and I'll let you feel how well it's working."

Heat washed over her face and she slapped at his chest, barely touching him. "I meant the collar, you jackass."

"Why do you ask about the collar?"

There was no way she was going to admit she wanted to kiss him so badly she'd wondered if he'd used some sort of compulsion. "Never mind." She quickly took another bite and then a long drink of soda.

"Tell me what you meant or kiss me. I'll let you choose."

She glanced at him then studied her sandwich as if it were the most fascinating thing she'd ever seen. She could kiss him, really kiss him, or admit that she wanted the kiss as badly as he did? That wasn't much of a choice. Reluctantly kissing him made more sense. She couldn't let him know he was wearing her down already. She had more pride than that.

"I'll kiss you, when I'm finished eating." She stressed the caveat as he began to lower his head.

"Eat quickly."

So, of course, she nibbled at the sandwich, taking as long as she possibly could. Time to cool his jets even more. "Tell me about Varrik. Why do you hate him so much? Was it just his betrayal, or is there something personal between you two?"

Chapter Three

Varrik stepped out of the transport conduit with Echo at his side. The destination coordinates Lor had provided led to a small, barren room within the human complex known as the Bunker. Lor rushed forward, his smile warm and welcoming. Lor shook Varrik's hand then gave Echo a quick hug. Lor and Echo had known each other their entire lives, so the familiarity didn't bother Varrik. Besides he trusted his life mate, knew she loved him unconditionally and would never stray from his side.

"I appreciate your coming so quickly," Lor said. "I know things are still hectic in the City of Tears. You will be missed."

"There is still much to do at home, but Nazerel is dangerous. This couldn't wait."

Lor indicated the archway to Varrik's right with a sweeping gesture. It was odd to see Lor in paramilitary clothing. On Ontariese the Mystics wore light gray robes.

Varrik reached for Echo's hand and she interlaced their fingers. Even after nine lunar cycles his heart reacted to her simplest touch. He hadn't expected to find a life mate when he kidnapped a princess, but he was grateful for every moment they had together.

The archway led to a tiled corridor that was devoid of decoration. Though well-lit and spacious, the windowless hallway made Varrik restless. He was unusually sensitive to underground settings after having spent the majority of his life in the Shadow Maze.

"Were your raids successful?" Echo asked.

"Very much so." Lor smiled. "We captured Team South this morning and followed Sevrin back to her lab. We'll hit Team East as soon as we're able to regroup, though we have people watching them now. It doesn't appear that they have any idea the others have been captured. We're still processing everyone who was apprehended in the first two raids. There were quite a few civilians at the lab."

"Where are you taking them?" Echo wanted to know.

"The Bilarrians lent us a containment field generator, so the high-interest targets are being kept at a safe house for questioning. Everyone else has been, or will soon be, taken back to Ontariese."

Varrik nodded. "Congratulations. This mission became much more complicated than any of us anticipated."

"No kidding," Echo reinforced with a faint smile. "Lor was sent to round up a handful of refugees and ended up in the middle of a Rodyte plot that went back two generations."

Lor waved away the praise as he directed them down another corridor. "Sevrin Keire is dead, and all that remains of the refugees is Nazerel."

Varrik tried not to react to the name, but their mutual history was long and turbulent. "If he is still on this planet, I will find him in a matter of days. If he has managed to leave Earth, I will still find him. It will just take a bit longer."

Lor stopped beside a privacy panel much like the others they'd passed. They'd only been walking for a minute or two, but the corridors seemed to go on forever. Varrik would love to see a diagram of the complex. It appeared vast.

"This apartment has been assigned for your use," Lor told them. "The work station is voice activated and you've been given access to human and Ontarian databases. There's an overview of the events that have transpired since my arrival on Earth as well as a report detailing Sevrin's research. There will be a briefing after the Team East raid. I'd like to introduce you to everyone then. Will that work for you?"

"That will be fine," Varrik assured him.

"Good." Lor entered a code into the palm scanner beside the privacy panel. "As soon as this scans you and Echo, the room will belong to you. No one else will be able to open the door, except in an emergency of course."

Echo gave Lor another quick hug as Varrik scanned his palm.

"It's always good to see you," she told her friend. "When do we get to meet your mate?"

"Tori's abilities allow her to discern truth from lies so she has been helping with the interrogations. We'd planned a quick dinner tonight, as soon as we can both break away for a few minutes. It will have to be informal and fast, but why don't you join us?"

Echo looked at Varrik and he nodded. They would begin the search for Nazerel in earnest as soon as they figured out where he might have gone. Even with their combined powers, they couldn't scan the entire planet for one man.

"Obviously, if we find a clue to Nazerel's location, we'll have to reschedule. Otherwise, we'd love to," Echo told Lor.

"I'll let you know about a time as soon as Tori and I work it out."

Lor departed and Echo scanned her palm before following Varrik into the apartment. The compact space was well organized and functional, if a bit utilitarian. He didn't mind the simplicity, but he wanted nothing but the best for Echo. "It's unlikely we'll spend an entire night here. Still, it's nice to know we have somewhere to crash if we need a couple of hours sleep. I want this finished as quickly as possible."

"I agree, but where do we start?"

"We need a deeper understanding of the situation. I've kept up with the basic events, but Lor's right, things have been hectic. We must work smart as well as fast."

Echo came up behind him and wrapped her arms around his waist. "Tell me about Nazerel. You've only mentioned him in passing. Who is he?"

Dreading her reaction to the explanation, Varrik dove to the heart of the matter. "Nazerel is the only son of Elder South."

A long pause followed and then Echo moved around to face him. "Elder South, as in the man we confronted on the Rodyte ship, the man who tortured Aila and was an all-around dirtbag?"

"That's the one." The words tasted bitter and filled Varrik with regret. "Nazerel and I were once close friends. As you can imagine, he despises me now."

"We had no choice. If we hadn't—"

Varrik shook his head. It was an excuse they relied on too often. "There are always choices." She started to argue but he stopped her with a lingering kiss. "Past details have no bearing on this situation. Nazerel must be caught."

"What makes him so much harder to catch than the others?" She remained in his embrace, hands lightly resting on his chest.

"There were four alpha hunters, one for each tribe. Nazerel was by far the strongest. He is cunning and ruthless, not a pleasant combination. And much of his bitterness stems from my actions. I'm the person best suited to finding him, but if he learns I've agreed to the hunt, this will become personal."

She stepped back, out of his embrace, her delicate features now tense with concern. "But Lor's message said Nazerel had been collared. Doesn't that mean he has no powers right now?"

"He is collared, which is why we must catch him as soon as possible. If he finds a way to release his abilities, it will be virtually impossible for anyone to find him, and that includes us."

"Then we better get busy." She plastered on a cheerful smile, yet worry lingered in her gaze. "I'll read the information on Sevrin's research and you read Lor's overview, then we can memory share. That will bring us both up to speed more quickly."

"An excellent idea."

NAZEREL STUDIED MORGAN'S profile as she nibbled on her sandwich. She was stalling and they both knew it. Even with her gaze averted, her eyes were incredibly blue. And her hair was just as bright, blending all the colors of autumn into one shiny mass. Unable to resist the impulse to see her hair spilling over her smooth white shoulders, he'd freed the long strands while she slept. He'd been tempted to do all sorts of things while she slept, but honor kept him from indulging his baser instincts. Only the truly corrupt took advantage of the helpless.

He knew her body was just as appealing as her lovely face, but he kept his gaze squarely focused on her features. If he let himself think about the curves so delightfully displayed by her undergarments, he would abandon his determination to seduce her slowly and ravage her instead. He was equally adept at either tactic, yet he knew Morgan would respond better to a gradual seduction.

"Tell me about Varrik," she said again without shifting her gaze from what little remained of her sandwich.

Her stubbornness challenged him, but he was intrigued by her spirit. He'd never met anyone quite like Morgan. Even bound and helpless, she'd dared to defy him. "Why are you so interested in Varrik? He has a mate."

She ignored the jibe and finally looked at him. "I always try to understand both sides of an issue. All of the information I have on the Shadow Assassins came from Varrik or people like him, people who resent the Customs. Tell me the other side of the story. I want to understand your world."

He caught a lock of her hair and curled it around his finger, avoiding her gaze for a change. "My world is gone. There is no reason for anyone to understand it now."

"I disagree. The past shapes us, it helps define who we are and the choices we make in the present." She was allowing his touch, which in itself was suspicious, but her tone was coxing, almost seductive.

Pushing his fingers into her hair, he turned her face up and teased the corner of her mouth with his thumb. "You're finished eating, now kiss me."

"Not until you tell me about the world below. Were you and Varrik always enemies?"

His pride demanded that he kiss her into submission. Captives did not direct their masters. It was the other way around. But ever since the Shadow Maze was "liberated" he'd waited for the opportunity to speak, to offer a different perspective on the situation. The tribunal had met, conducted its inquiry and announced its decision, and still he waited for anyone to show an interest in his side of the story.

"Varrik and I are both First Sons." Why was he indulging her? Her interest wasn't genuine. She was trying to distract him.

"What exactly is a 'First Son'?"

"The chosen heir of a council member. It's usually the council member's first-born son, but with Tribe North it became complicated. Varrik's brother was still a child when their father died, so their uncle became Elder North. Then North's only son didn't survive infancy and Varrik's brother died, so Varrik became North's heir. I am, or rather was, First Son of South."

"Then positions on the council were hereditary not elected?"

The world below was far more structured than most people understood. Everyone thought of the Shadow Assassins as mindless killers, but theirs had been a complex society rich in unique culture and traditions. "When a councilman died or, less frequently, stepped down, his First Son took his place. At that time, and only at that time, the transition could be challenged by any member of his tribe. But challengers fought to the death, so few challenges were ever issued." He paused, his mind a muddle of troubling memories. It all seemed like another lifetime, as if the events had happened to someone else. "Varrik and I were born within the same season cycle, so we trained together. Any son of an elder was held to a higher standard, so the training was often...harsh."

"Did you help each other or were you hostile from the start?"

"We were rivals, very competitive until the summer when our abilities were assessed."

"Why did that change things?"

"I was assigned to the hunters and Varrik was assigned to the sweepers. It changed the dynamic between us. We were no longer in direct competition, so there was no reason for our hostilities. We became friends, close friends." They'd been more than just friends. They'd been constant companions and confidantes. Varrik was the closest thing Nazerel had ever had to a brother. And when Varrik lost his brother, Nazerel had been the only one Varrik trusted enough to show his grief, the only one who'd been able to help him deal with the devastating loss.

"Go on." Her expression was open and curious, but he understood her true motivation. The longer she kept him talking, the longer she postponed their inevitable showdown.

Unwilling to indulge her without a cost, he ran his fingers down her neck and onto her upper chest. She sucked in a breath and her breasts swelled well above the lacy cups of her bra. He swallowed hard, no longer sure who he punished with this strategy. "Varrik fought his destiny, denied his abilities, even tried to hide them from his uncle. I, on the other hand, accepted the path chosen for me and dedicated myself to becoming the best hunter the world below had ever seen."

She reached for his wrist then stopped herself and lowered her hand to her lap. Already her nipples were starting to peak. She was not nearly as indifferent to his touch as she would have him believe. "When and why did it go wrong?"

Resentment and pain rushed to the surface. Who could blame him for being bitter? He'd been betrayed by his best friend. He lowered his hands to his knees. Even touching her wasn't enough of an incentive for him to offer the details of those events. "Surely you know about Varrik and Echo. You seem to know everything else."

"I know what Varrik put in his report. I want to hear your side of the story."

His side of the story. The reoccurring phrase made him seethe. No one gave a damn about his side of the story. Varrik sure as hell hadn't cared about how his decisions affected those around him. "Varrik fell in love with his captive and all hell broke loose," he snapped. "He sold us out for a female. Then he killed my father, after his mate had stripped the location of the Shadow Maze from his mind."

She stilled and her gaze locked with his. "I'm sorry. That must have been devastating." She even sounded sincere. Apparently Varrik hadn't bothered recording his cowardly actions in his precious report.

"My father was ruthless, harsh and sometimes violent. He was a product of the world below, but he didn't deserve to die." Almost of their own volition, his hands returned to her soft skin. He ran his hands down her arms, soothing himself with her texture and warmth. "He was loyal to the Customs, loyal to his tribe. And Varrik murdered him."

"May I ask another question?"

He shook his head, shocked that she'd bothered asking. "Will you drop the subject if I answer?"

"Yes." She glanced at him then away, but their gazes connected long enough for him to see the pity smoldering in hers. He tensed. He would never accept her surrender if it was born of pity. "How could Varrik not know the location of the Shadow Maze?"

Nazerel sighed. He didn't want to talk about the past. The present held plenty of challenges and the past could not be changed. But he understood her confusion, so he explained, "We locked on to a beacon when we teleported in. Only the elders knew the exact location of the maze."

"Then Varrik told High Queen Charlotte how to find the maze. That's how they managed to liberate it after all those years." She stared past him, her tone speculative.

"Except not everyone wanted to be 'liberated,'" he stressed. "Varrik had no right to make that decision for all of us. Not all of us were discontent. Many would have chosen to stay if they had been given a choice." She fell silent as he continued to stroke her arms, his thumbs occasionally brushing the outer curve of her breasts. She didn't need to speak. He knew all the arguments. Their lifestyle was barbaric and abusive to women. Progress demanded that they adapt. "What? No more questions?"

"How many Shadow Assassins were there?" she blurted.

He laughed. "I suppose I asked for that." But he'd lost interest in the conversation so he resumed their sensual game. "Around four thousand. I'm not sure of the exact count."

"Was finding mates your only job or did you have other responsibilities?"

"What happened to dropping the subject?" He really didn't want to talk at all. If she pushed too hard, he'd stop indulging her.

"I agreed to stop asking about Varrik. This is completely different."

Technically, she was correct and this topic wasn't nearly as painful. "Hunting mates was one task among many." He traced her collar bone and the hollow beneath. Her skin was even softer here than on her arms.

She grew restless beneath his touch and still she didn't try to stop him. "What were some of the other tasks? Take me through your typical day."

Intrigued by her willingness to allow his exploration, he drew her bra strap down her arm. The top edge of her bra rolled downward, exposing another inch of her creamy flesh. "We are mercenaries. We did what any other soldier does. We trained, we gathered intel, we prepared for missions and fought wars."

"But the Great Conflict was over before you were born. What wars are you talking about?"

Most Ontarians believed the Shadow Assassins wandered around in their maze frustrated and idle because the Great Conflict had ended. It was a ridiculous notion, one that had obviously been passed on to Morgan. "The House of Joon was not our only employer. In fact, they were not our primary employer. The Shadow Maze was our base of operations, but we frequently left Ontariese." He pulled down her other bra strap and she quickly righted the first. That was more like it. He preferred Morgan when she was feisty. "If you won't offer me your mouth, I'll find something else to kiss."

Her gaze flew to his, anxious and smoldering with heat she was trying to hide. "When did you meet Sevrin? Did she approach you or was it the other way around?"

"Offer me your mouth or you forfeit your bra. You have two seconds to choose."

Anger sparked to life within her expressive eyes. "You're a bully. You know that, don't you?"

"I've been called worse." Two seconds elapsed and she wasn't kissing him, so he reached for the fasteners at the back of her bra.

She twisted away from his hand then rolled to her knees. After a rebellious pause, she swung her leg over his and straddled his thighs. "My mouth is all I'm offering." She whispered the words as she leaned in and pressed her lips to his.

Her scent reached him first, warm, clean, lightly floral, and incredibly arousing. He buried his fingers in her hair, knowing it was the only way to keep his hands from wandering at will. Her soft lips parted for the first brush of his tongue and Nazerel was lost. He kissed her deeply, wildly as hunger unfurled inside him. He wanted her beneath him, arching into each thrust as he filled her completely. She was *human*—and his enemy. Why was she unleashing these urges in him?

He moved his head to a better angle and kissed her again. At first she submitted to the onslaught, allowing him to take what he desired. But little by little she awakened in his arms. Her lips moved and then her tongue dueled with his.

Desire, hot and demanding, tore through him. His cock hardened with enough pressure to make him groan and he wrapped his arm around her, pulling her tight against his body.

"Enough." She broke away suddenly now flushed and panting. "I think I more than paid for my sandwich."

She tried to crawl off his lap, but he grasped her hips, not yet ready to let her go. "I thought you wanted to hear about Sevrin." Passion clogged his throat, making his voice sound thick.

"Your ears stop working if I sit next to you?" For the first time since he met her, he saw fear in her eyes. Why had their kisses frightened her when all of his threats and intimidation had not? He lifted his hands and let her shift to his side. She didn't stop there. She scurried to the top of the bed and slipped her legs in between the two sleeping bags as she leaned back against the tent pole.

I won't hurt you. The words formed within his mind, but he bit them back before they escaped. Fear was useful. She would surrender sooner if she were afraid of him, so why did he find the reaction so unsettling?

"Sevrin," she prompted. "Did she approach you?"

"We corresponded through an agent in the beginning and then directly after Sevrin had deemed me worthy of trust. We actually met for the first time on Earth."

"That didn't really answer the question." Her gaze darted to him and then away. He'd never seen her so rattled. "Who started the correspondence?"

Her reaction to their kiss was far more interesting than the conversation. Nazerel crawled toward her, his hands on either side of her legs. "Why are you so upset?"

"I'm not upset," she snapped, her voice higher than usual.

"Your skin is still flushed and you won't look at me. You're either feeling guilty or you're terrified and neither reaction makes sense."

As if to prove him wrong, she glared into his eyes. "Did they teach you how to do this?"

"How to do what?"

"How to systematically unravel a woman? Was seduction 101 part of your training?"

A slow, predatory smile spread across his lips. "Is it working?"

"I'm serious. Did someone teach you how to deal with your captives? There's a structure to what you're doing."

He sat back on his heels and debated what to tell her. She seemed honestly curious now, if a bit defensive. "I'm an alpha hunter, sweetheart. I was the teacher, not the student."

Her eyes widened as understanding burned away her fear. She pressed her lips into a tight, disapproving line then gradually regained her composure. "You taught the other hunters, but someone had to teach you. No one is born knowing the psychology of mind control."

"Mind control." He laughed. "Kissing me made you want sex, so I must be brainwashing you. That's a bit drastic, don't you think?"

"Do you deny that there's a psychology to what you're doing?"

Before he answered he moved off her and folded his legs in front of him. The position uncomfortable now thanks to the erection he still sported. "You're a field operative, likely working for or with the FBI. Were you taught how to read body language and facial expressions?"

"Of course."

"The techniques are similar. All I've done is watched you and adjusted my approach according to your reactions. When your skin flushes and your respiration speeds, I know it's time to push harder. When you grow still and defensive, it's better to back off and wait until you calm down."

"Can we talk about something else? This subject is annoying."

"You're the one who wants to talk." He reached for her hand, but she snatched it away. "I'd much rather continue our exploration."

Rather than rising to the bait, she scooted over, putting even more space between them. "Sevrin first contacted you?"

"Yes."

"And why did you ally with her? What did she offer you?"

He waved away the question. "She's a lying whore who broke every promise she made us. The details are irrelevant."

"Lor and his team followed Sevrin back to her lab when she left the Team South house this morning. By now everyone is either dead or in custody. They'll have learned the location of the Team East house as well. It's over, Nazerel. You realize that, don't you?"

"That's only true if every aspect of your plan went off without complication. Neither of us knows how much of that agenda was accomplished." He sounded calm, almost indifferent, but his pulse leapt and his throat burned with anger and frustration. He'd finally decided to break all ties with Sevrin and move on. His men deserved a better life than they'd found on Earth. But his plans had yet to solidify. Was it possible that the entire situation had unraveled while the collar made him powerless to stop it?

"Is there cell reception up here? With one phone call I can find out what happened this morning."

"No reception." That was true, but he had a Rodyte comlink. It looked very much like a cell phone, but the device was far more sophisticated than human technology. He just wasn't ready to admit the fact to her. "You had an eight-hour nap, but I'm exhausted. Do you need to pee before I secure you for the night?" Her cheeks darkened as she nodded. Why were females so squeamish about bodily functions? Everyone had to pee from time to time. It was an unavoidable fact of life. "Reconnect your cuffs. I'll go get your boots." He tugged on his boots and left the tent.

He could see her silhouette though the wall of the tent, so he paused and pulled his comlink out of his pocket. Thank the gods he hadn't given this frequency to Flynn or the Mystic Militia would be able to track him. Sevrin could probably track the signal, but she had no idea that he had the device. Not willing to risk an off-world call, he input Darrian Eastman's code. All the Team East alpha had to do was respond to the call and he'd disprove Morgan's claim. The signal connected but no one responded. *Shit*. Nazerel reentered the code, but again no one activated the other end of the call.

So the Team East house had been raided or they'd abandoned it when they learned of the raid on Team South. That didn't mean everyone was in custody. The Mystic Militia had yet to conduct a raid without losing at least one person. Shadow Assassins had protocols in place for when anyone became separated from their team, so he connected to the designated voice mail box. There were no messages. Unbelievable. There were other possible explanations, but this was discouraging to say the least.

He paused long enough to take care of his own bodily functions before he unlocked the SUV and grabbed her boots off the backseat. Morgan was wily. He didn't dare take his attention off her for even a moment.

"Did you forget where you hid them?" She was standing near the door now and she'd refastened her wrist cuffs as instructed. So she could follow orders when it struck her fancy.

"Something like that," he grumbled and dropped her boots in front of her.

"Your mood sure got dark all of a sudden. Are you sure there's no cell service up here?"

He arched his brow at that. "Were you spying on me?"

"You were standing ten feet from the tent. It didn't take much spying."

"There really isn't any cell coverage. The device I was using was Rodyte and it's more like a two-way radio. It won't do you any good." That was bullshit, but he wasn't ready to indulge her further.

"No one answered on the other end?"

"No." She didn't need to know more. "Come on."

"Can I have my pants too? The underbrush will scratch up my legs."

He was obviously being too easy on her. He shouldn't allow her to argue at all. Rather than answer her question, he bent and threw her over his shoulder.

"Nazerel!" she half-shrieked so he smacked her upturned ass.

He ducked through the opening and carried her into the woods. She was right. The underbrush was thick and coarse. It would have been hell on her legs. But she hadn't known that for sure. She was just being argumentative. He found a relatively clear spot and set her down. "Get on with it." He even turned his back, though he could still see her in his peripheral vision.

"You expect me to squat down and pee while you're standing right there?" She sounded horrified.

"Yes." His tone brook no refusal.

He stared off into the darkness unable to make sense of the implications swarming his mind. He needed to get off this godforsaken planet, but he couldn't leave until he knew the fate of his men. If they were all in custody as Morgan said, then it was only a matter of time before they were returned to the City of Tears. Their service to the Ontarian military had been mandatory and it had been sentenced instead of prison time, which meant his men were likely headed to prison.

Morgan touched his arm and he startled.

"Are you all right?" Her voice was soft and coaxing.

"No. Are you finished?"

"Yes."

Rather than throw her over his shoulder again, he picked her up in his arms. His fingers splayed against the firm flesh of her leg and then registered the icy temperature. "Your legs are freezing."

"Tends to happen when one goes traipsing through the woods half naked."

Feeling guilty now, he hurried back to the tent and set her down beside the bed. "Get under the covers."

"Yes, sir." She mocked him with a salute.

"That's yes, *master*."

"In your dreams." She'd whispered the phrase just loud enough for him to hear.

He picked up her boots, even though she hadn't worn them. "I'll be right back."

"Take your time."

After locking her boots back in the SUV. He tried Darrian's code again. No answer. He switched to cell phone emulation mode and called Sevrin. The call went straight to voice mail. Gods be damned! That told him nothing. She could be in serious trouble or she could just be ignoring him out of spite. Sevrin was often irrational.

He heaved a frustrated sigh then walked back to the tent. It wasn't fair to take this out on Morgan, but his anger allowed him to refocus on why he'd brought her here in the first place. If he was the only one left, then seeing to the welfare of his men became his sole responsibility. It was more important than ever that he find a way to rid himself of the debilitating collar.

When Nazerel reentered the tent, he looked like a man on a mission. His lips were pressed into a grim line and his gaze was narrowed yet bright.

"You don't look happy." Rather than crawling into bed as she'd been told, Morgan sat near the bottom of the sleeping bag and folded the top half over her legs. It allowed her body to rebuild heat without looking as if she were blithely waiting to be seduced.

After zipping them in, he took down the lantern and set it on top of the cooler. Next he tugged off his boots and socks. She watched each movement with tense uncertainty. Was he just preparing for bed or had his mission changed in the past hour? Not really changed, more like regressed. She'd managed to avoid this confrontation by engaging his mind. Obviously, her stall tactics had stopped working.

He reached for his fly and Morgan panicked. She jumped up and quickly unfastened the chain connecting her cuffs. She grasped the loose end of the chain, creating a makeshift weapon. It was possible he was just getting ready to sleep, yet his dark mood made that seem improbable.

His lips curved into a humorless smile and challenge lifted his eyebrows as he lowered the zipper on his pants. She quickly averted her gaze, but he stepped back into her field of vision as he set his folded pants on top of one of the crates. He was wearing gray boxer briefs that left very little to the imagination. Still, she'd been somewhat desensitized to his esthetic appeal by staring at his chest for the past two hours.

He turned off the lantern, plunging them into darkness. She blinked, impatiently waiting for her eyes to adjust. Even with moonlight penetrating the walls of the tent, he was little more than a menacing silhouette.

For a long tense moment he stood there in silence while her heartbeat thundered in her ears. Then he lunged across the tent and grasped her wrist. She swung the chain at his face, but he easily deflected the blow with his forearm then caught that wrist as well. Damn he was fast. Fast and strong. She was in serious trouble.

Drawing her hand to his neck, he pressed her fingers against the cool metal collar. "Unlock it or I'm going to stop being nice." His tone was flat and serious, convincing her he meant every word.

"I can't. You know I can't." She brought up her knee. He twisted away. She stomped on his instep. He barely noticed. Tugging against his hands, she tried in vain to break his restraining hold on her arms. She kicked and kneed him, throwing her weight one way and then the other. When none of it did any good, she slammed her head into his chest then sharply raised it, hoping to catch his chin.

"Are you finished?" The bastard sounded amused and he wasn't even out of breath.

With a growl of utter frustration, she vowed, "Never."

He spun her around and yanked the T-shirt off over her head. Then he unfastened her bra with a deft flick of his fingers. She gasped, instinctively clutching the loosened fabric to her breasts. "Don't do this. *Please,* Nazerel. You don't have to do this." She was beyond pride, beyond strategy, and more frightened than she'd ever been in her life. His kisses and gentle touches had already proven that he could make her feel, make her want things she dare not want with this man.

After snatching her bra out of her clutching fingers, he tossed it aside and then lifted her into his arms. He placed her in the middle of the sleeping bag, making it seem effortless despite her continued struggles. He straddled her hips as he pulled her arms over her head. She clawed at his hands and twisted wildly. He simply ignored her efforts and focused on his task. When he wrapped the chain around the tent pole this time, he secured it with a tiny padlock identical to the ones attached to the cuffs. *Shit*. Where had that come from? Her last hope had been to wait until he fell asleep and then free herself from the tent pole. She'd already tried to yank the pole from the ground. It felt like he'd driven it into solid rock.

His face was directly above her now and he looked seriously pissed. This was the Nazerel she'd expected to see ever since he tackled her to the grass beside the Team South house, ruthless and oblivious to everything except his goal. Instead he'd been rational and reasonable, even charming at times. Then he hadn't been able to contact his people, which brought out this darker side. He realized his situation was desperate, and desperate people did horrible things.

"It doesn't matter what you do to me," she tried again. "I cannot unlock the collar."

"So you say. But you're right, it doesn't matter. It's time for my other strategy."

Lust. He intended to work himself into a sexual frenzy and then channel the energy into the collar. And she was the fuel for his bonfire.

Pushing off the floor, he sat up while still straddling her hips. "You can stop this at any time. Remember that. You are in control." His gaze lowered to her breasts and the blue rings in his eyes ignited.

She closed her eyes and tried to empty her mind, tried to calm her body. Tension coiled through her chest and lodged in her stomach. She was in control? What a joke. She was restrained and at his mercy, and worst of all a dull ache had already erupted in her core. Her logical mind might scream against the injustice, but her body was more than willing to play.

Pull it together, Director Hoyt. You can resist him. You must.

Her only alternative was to release him from the collar and that would restore his abilities. He'd be able to read minds, teleport and who knew what else. No one seemed to have an accurate list of his abilities. They just knew he was more powerful than the other Shadow Assassins, which meant he was much too dangerous to unleash on Earth. She couldn't endanger others because she was afraid of the things he'd make her feel.

His warm hand covered her breast, squeezed gently, then shifted so her nipple was framed by his thumb and forefinger. As before, her body responded immediately to his simplest touch. Her nipple tingled as it hardened. His thumb circled the bud, encouraging the reaction. She concentrated on breathing, trying in vain not to feel the firm support of his fingers or the tentative brush of his lips.

"Your body is fashioned for pleasure." He paused to draw on her nipple before he added, "You're wasted in the military." Then he sucked in earnest, pulling heat into her breast and launching tingles lower. He switched his mouth to the other side, but kept the sensations swirling with the firm pressure of his fingers.

And it felt good. Why did everything this bastard did feel so damn good?

Each ragged breath made her beasts quiver and he seemed fascinated by the subtle motion. He stroked her skin, exploring her curves with one hand while he aroused her with his lips, tongue, and teeth. She clenched her hands and turned her head to the side, fighting every tingle, every unwanted burst of sensation.

"So lovely." He murmured the words in between slow, deep sucks and her back arched helplessly.

She felt as if he were drawing her soul to the surface so he could feed on her energy. Some species could take energy directly from other beings. But even if such a thing were among his abilities, he was collared, unable to access that part of his nature.

He scooted down her body, straddling her knees and then her calves. His lips released her nipple and she opened her eyes, curious to see what he'd do next. She wasn't foolish enough to think he was finished. So why was he moving away? She hadn't begged for mercy. Perhaps his hunter's spirit couldn't stay excited when there was no struggle, no chase. The hopeful thought lasted only a moment and then he caught the sides of her panties and pulled them to her knees.

She instinctively drew up her legs and tried to kick him. The impulse only made it easier for him to rid her of her final garment. He pushed her legs apart and knelt between them, opening her body to his heated gaze.

"I want to be inside you so badly I can hardly breathe." His voice was so tight he sounded strangled by the confession. "But release me now and I'll return your clothes instead."

The power struggle was already lost. He'd issued an ultimatum to which she could never surrender. Each of his skillful caresses only compounded her shame, her failure. She wanted it over as quickly as possible. "I'm not a cringing virgin. You're not going to terrify me with threats of sex. Do your worst or leave me alone. I want to get some sleep."

He arched over her, supporting himself on one forearm as he pressed his other hand to the side of her face. "You misunderstand my intention. This won't be over quickly. I will arouse you with my fingers and my mouth. I will know your taste as well as the softness of every part of your delightful body. It will take hours before I am finally ready to thrust inside you and *do my worst.*"

Her heart fluttered in her chest, but she honestly couldn't tell if it was fear or anticipation. "But you need to build your lust not mine."

His thumb traced her lower lip as his penetrating gaze stared into hers. "There is nothing more arousing than watching a woman come and knowing I'm responsible for her pleasure."

Dread washed over her, momentarily cooling her wayward body. It was easy to justify simple surrender. Fighting him had accomplished nothing. Her goal now had to be survival and escape, which meant she had to make it through tonight without physical damage. A sprained ankle or broken wrist would greatly hinder her escape. But how did she justify wanting him, craving each and every pleasure he'd mentioned?

He lowered his head and kissed one corner of her mouth and then the other. His breath warmed her cool skin and rekindled sensations she thought she'd banished. Her lips trembled as her pulse ramped up to an even faster rhythm. She felt restless and needy, almost drugged.

His body shifted, his hips pressing into hers as his chest lightly grazed her beaded nipples. He rested on both forearms now, his hands framing her face. His image filled her vision and his scent drifted through her nose, sinking deeper with each anxious breath. He brushed his lips back and forth over hers, teasing her, awakening her responses.

"I know this isn't what you want," he whispered against her lips. "But I also know you're wet and this isn't the first time my touch has aroused you."

Before she could protest or argue, he sealed his mouth over hers. His lips pressed then slid, caressing as he urged her mouth open. She clenched her hands and remained perfectly still. Allowing this because she had no other choice was a legitimate strategy. Losing herself in these sensations was...weak.

She jerked her head to the side, panting harshly. "I can't stop you from touching me, but I don't want to kiss you."

He turned her head back around as challenge hardened his expression. "Why? You enjoyed kissing me before."

"This is war." She stared past him, refusing to meet his gaze. "It's a twisted sort of battle. I can't enjoy anything about it."

A warm chuckle rumbled through his chest. "You keep telling yourself that, *morautu*."

Then his mouth was on hers again and his tongue swept back and forth, easing farther inward with each pass. *Bite him. Prove that you mean what you say. Make him listen.*

He advanced slowly, completely focused on the kiss. His fingers stroked the side of her face as his sensual assault on her mouth progressed. She couldn't bring herself to bite him, so she tried to remain passive, utterly uninvolved in what he was doing. But his tongue stroked over hers then curled around it, the invitation unmistakable. She was already defeated. Why couldn't that be enough?

"Kiss me, Morgan," he whispered. "I want your tongue in my mouth."

Temptation shivered down her spine, making her skin feel hot and her nipples tingle. Her social life was nonexistent. Most of the men she met were her subordinates and she worked too hard at earning their respect to muck things up with sex. This was going to happen, one way or the other. Why shouldn't she scratch a long-neglected itch?

She'd never met anyone who aroused her as effortlessly as Nazerel. He'd barely begun and already her body was wet and pulsing. "I shouldn't."

"You will." He kissed her with fierce determination for one overwhelming moment then eased back, obviously waiting for her to obey his tantalizing command.

Cursing herself for a coward, she tentatively touched his tongue with hers. She couldn't explain why she wanted him, why she *needed* the pleasures he offered, but she was tired of fighting, tired of always being alone.

She eased her tongue into his mouth then groaned as his lips closed around her and gently sucked. Desire cascaded through her body then coalesced between her thighs. She wanted him inside her. She wanted to feel his strong, hard body moving over and into hers. The thought made her wilder, more demanding. She dueled with his tongue and breathed in his breath, drunk on his scent and ravenous for more of his taste.

Always she was expected to be strong, detached and in control. Everyone looked to her for the tough decisions. If she hesitated, people died. She'd been isolated by her authority for the past fifteen years. She deserved this moment of madness, a few hours of pleasure that no one needed to know about. She would revel in the forbidden and then concentrate all her energy on escape.

His mouth tore away from hers and his passion-muddled gaze searched her face. "You feel it too, don't you? The pull, the connection?"

She shook her head. She wasn't sure what he meant, but she didn't like the sound of those words. A pull toward what? And what sort of connection? "I don't know what you're talking about." But she did. Despite her denials, her body understood. Nazerel was different than any man who'd ever touched her. Maybe it was just his alien DNA, but she didn't think so. This felt familiar, somehow preordained.

He didn't argue with her. Instead he kissed his way down her body, lingering over her breasts again before continuing his descent. She braced for the next phase in his seduction. He'd warned her of what he intended to do. Touch her and *taste* her. She waited for bitter dread to wash over her, clearing her head and cooling her ardor, but all she felt was the persistent ache of anticipation.

Chapter Four

Energy sizzled through Nazerel as he kissed his way across Morgan's silken belly. Her body was a feast for the senses. He'd never encountered a female more pleasing to the eyes, or hands, or mouth. His torso worked like a wedge, pushing her legs wider as he neared his destination.

He caught the back of her knees and spread her thighs even wider. She tensed and her thighs trembled. She didn't want to want this, but she obviously did. He understood the contradiction all too well. He'd hoped to use lust to burn through the barriers created by the suppression collar. That was still his goal. However, touching her, kissing her, had unleashed so much more than physical desire. He felt protective and possessive, ravenous and restless, almost as if— No, he would not complicate this with useless speculation. She was an enjoyable means to a desperately needed end.

His body ached for the soft heat of hers and he had to build on that hunger, intensify the need until it consumed everything around it.

Shifting one of her legs to his shoulder, he spread out on his stomach so he could use his hands as well as his mouth. His chest was on the sleeping bags, but his legs rested on the cold tent floor. It didn't matter. He had to touch her as well as taste her and he couldn't do so if he was holding himself up.

He pushed one hand beneath her, pleased at how well her firm ass cheek fit the palm of his hand. She squirmed away from the intimate touch, which only brought her sex closer to his face. Her scent was intoxicating, clean, yet faintly musky, clearly excited. Rather than hold her open with his fingers, he gently parted her with his tongue. She moaned, tensed for a moment, then melted into the kiss.

Her folds were slick with arousal, so he ventured deeper, pushing right into the core of her desire. Soft, wet heat enveloped his tongue, and he never wanted to leave. He closed his eyes and imagined this same snug passage grasping his cock, caressing him with firm ripples as he drove them both toward completion.

The temptation was nearly more than he could bear. He had never been with a female who belonged to him and him alone. He'd just been granted permission to hunt for his own mate when Varrik kidnapped the royal twins, leading to the chain of events that had ended their way of life. Another injustice for which Varrik must pay.

Forcing the memories aside, he raised his head and looked at his lovely captive. Her back was slightly arched, breasts thrust out, and the uncertainty in her eyes was unmistakable. "You don't like that?" He'd be shocked if that were true. Most women couldn't get enough of this particular pleasure.

"What will you do if you succeed in freeing yourself from the collar?"

The collar. He'd all but forgotten why he was doing this. "If your mind is clear enough to worry about the future, I'm not trying hard enough." He draped her other leg over his shoulder as well and lowered his mouth to her creamy slit. She gasped as his tongue stabbed into her again and again. They both knew what he simulated and that it only foreshadowed the joining they both craved. Still, she was right. This wasn't about sex, wasn't about pleasure.

With both her legs resting on his back, he slid his hands up her sides and cupped her breasts. Silky-soft yet wonderfully firm, the abundant mounds more than filled his palms. He couldn't seem to stop touching them. Even so, he needed to focus inward, so he licked his way to her clit and began a slow orbit.

Energy arced between them, sizzling with potency and promise. He could clearly sense the metaphysical barrier blocking his access to his Mystic energy. Being able to sense the barrier was an improvement over half an hour ago. So he carefully sucked on Morgan's clit, bringing her to a sudden, intense orgasm. She cried out and rocked her hips, pressing herself against him.

Capturing the rush of energy in his mouth, he carefully absorbed the molecules, not quite ready to use them. He reluctantly abandoned one of her breasts and eased his hand between her legs. She seemed dazed by the powerful release. Her eyes were still unfocused.

Part of him wanted to hold her, bring her back to reality slowly then give her what she really wanted, what they both wanted. But there was so much more at stake than their pleasure. If his men were in custody, and he had little doubt they were, he had very little time to intervene on their behalf and even fewer resources at his disposal. And the only way to change that was to rid himself of the collar.

Her eyelashes fluttered and she looked at him, all flushed and rosy. "Ready for more?" Before she could reply, he pushed two of his fingers into her wet passage.

She moaned and wiggled just enough to set her breasts in motion. Gods below, she was beautiful, and responsive. He shuttled his fingers in and out, watching her face closely. She licked her lips and tossed her head. Her restless movements sent her legs sliding down his arms, which forced her to bend her knees and rotate her legs out. She was sprawled before him now, completely open and accessible.

Instinctively he reached for her mind and for half a second he could sense her, the burning desire, threaded through with guilt and frustration. Then the emotions were gone and all he could sense was the steady rise in her energy.

He bent his head and found her clit with the tip of his tongue, then matched his oral caresses to the rhythm of his fingers. He closed his eyes and summoned his nanites. Their response was sluggish but accurate to the command he'd issued. They absorbed the energy he'd siphoned from Morgan a few minutes before.

She came again and he channeled her energy directly into his nanites now that they were awake and responding. Rather than give her time to recover, however, he drove her on toward a higher peak.

"I don't think I can..." She gasped as he sucked on her clit. "It's too soon."

He avoided the over-sensitive nub long enough for her body to reset. Then he went right back to arousing her.

You're using her. This is cruel. A pang of guilt accompanied the thought, but he couldn't stop. This was his only chance and lives were literally at stake. He was still relatively certain she owned the collar, but she was too stubborn to free him. So this was the only way, his only hope.

He flicked his tongue over her clit and she cried out, not in pleasure but in pain. Damn it. He was pushing her too hard, expecting too much, too soon.

Rather than abandon his plan entirely, he slowed the motion of his hand and curved his fingers so they dragged the front wall of her passage. She shivered and then whimpered. "That's not fair. Most of my lovers haven't been able to—"

With his fingers still buried deep inside her, he lunged upward and silenced her with his mouth. "You have no other lovers." He kissed her again, less frantic, yet still seriously possessive. Then he hovered over her, his gaze boring into hers. "Look at me, *morautu.*"

After a moment, she did. Her gaze was cautious, though still passion bright.

"Who is touching you?" He filled her with his fingers as he waited for her response.

"You are."

"And who am I?"

"Nazerel." She licked her lips then added in barely a whisper, "My enemy."

He didn't correct her. It was a fact. They were on opposite sides of this conflict. He just didn't give a damn right now.

Her arousal gradually built, so he increased the speed of his fingers. She moaned and started to close her eyes. "No. Look at me. Share your pleasure with me. Hold nothing back."

Their gazes locked and her energy spiraled around his fingers, sending zings of sensation all through his body. His neglected cock bucked against the floor as if sensing her energy and wanting more. He groaned and struggled to keep his own eyes open. He was so close to release. One firm squeeze would launch him over the edge.

She cried out suddenly and arched her back, her hips coming up off the bedding. Her inner muscles contracted around his fingers in rhythmic pulses. He was so captivated by the beauty of her surrender that he nearly forgot to capture the surge of energy. His nanites were ready however. He pulled the molecules through his skin and they siphoned the power with ravenous intensity until they vibrated with excess energy.

Would it be enough? It had to be. There was no other option.

Destroy the collar. Free me!

His nanites rushed through his bloodstream, ready—and finally able—to do his bidding. He eased his fingers out of Morgan and moved to her side. He felt dizzy and unfocused as nanites from all over his body hurried to assist with the attack. Sharp stings erupted all around his neck as the nanites burst through his skin. He'd expected that, but *damn* it hurt without their assistance defusing the pain.

"You're bleeding." He had no idea how Morgan had accomplished it, but she was sitting at the top of the sleeping bags, her hands still bound to the tent pole.

"Necessary." Heat sliced through his flesh as the collar seared his skin. He screamed, unable to suppress the reaction. Pain stabbed into his brain and flowed down his back. Were they freeing him or killing him? He gasped then gagged as the stench of burning flesh filled his nose. *His* burning flesh.

One final protective instinct flashed through the blinding agony. He couldn't leave Morgan helpless and bound. Crawling across the tent, he frantically reached for his pants. Balling them up, he threw them toward her and then promptly passed out.

Stretching out her arms and legs, Morgan barely reached the pants Nazerel had thrown in her general direction. His aim had been off and the garment had flown past her, colliding with the far wall of the tent. He lay in a graceless heap near the cooler and the smell of burning flesh lingered in the air. Was he still breathing or had his final bid for freedom cost him his life?

She couldn't find out while she was chained to the tent pole, so she pulled the pants toward her with her feet, then rolled to her side and drew her knees to her chest so she could reach the pants with her hands.

It took some serious contorting, but she was soon rummaging through the pockets of his pants.

Her initial search came up empty. Still, she didn't give up. It was possible Nazerel had been delirious. He'd certainly been in enough pain. But he'd seemed intent on getting the pants to her. There had to be a reason he wanted her to have them.

She looked at him again, trying to determine if he was breathing. He lay twisted on his side, his back toward her. From this angle it was impossible to tell if he was alive or dead. If she didn't find a way to free herself, they would both be dead in a matter of days. No one could survive without water and she couldn't reach their supply from here.

With renewed purpose, she meticulously checked the pockets again. Nothing. Okay, so it wasn't an obvious pocket. She paused to roll her neck and shoulders. Even hugging the tent wall so she could sit, this was an awkward position in which to search. Still, she refused to give up. She felt along the waistband and down the side seams. Finally, she rolled up the hem and felt for any telltale hardness. Her fingers passed over the tiny key so quickly she almost missed it. But she looked closer and found the slit into which the key had been slipped.

"Thank God." She unlocked the chain, but left the cuffs in place as she rushed across the tent toward Nazerel. Without moving him, she held her hand in front of his face and waited for the faint brush of his breath to warm her fingers. He exhaled and so did she. At least he was still breathing.

She grabbed the T-shirt off the floor and wiggled into it then pulled on her panties. Her bra could wait until she figured out her next move. It was unlikely Nazerel had injured his spine as he fell. The man was solid muscle. So she dragged him onto the sleeping bags, covered him to mid-chest, then relit the lantern. She needed to find the keys to the SUV and get the hell out of here, but she didn't want Nazerel to die of exposure before she could summon a team of Mystics.

But had Nazerel's powers returned?

If he was only stunned, he could flash himself to safety long before she could figure out where she was and contact Lor. Yet if she left Nazerel here without learning the severity of his condition, he could die before she returned. What a mess.

One thing was certain. She was not going to put herself at his mercy again, not if she could help it. She unlocked the cuffs and adjusted the buckles so they'd fit his larger wrists, then she approached him cautiously. He hadn't moved since she dragged him onto the sleeping bags. In fact, she could barely see the rise and fall of his chest.

She knelt at his side and waited for him to react to her nearness. He didn't move, didn't make a sound. One of his arms was already over his head, because she'd used it to drag him across the floor. She fastened one cuff around his raised wrist then positioned his other arm and encircled it with the other cuff. After locking both cuffs, she wrapped the chain around the tent pole then locked it down as well. If his abilities returned, he'd be able to flash himself out of the restraints, but she wasn't convinced that he'd succeeded.

Curious enough to investigate, she took the key and carefully placed it on top of the cooler. Then she returned to Nazerel and touched the collar, gently shifting it upward. The skin beneath was blistered and raw. That had to hurt. She pulled on either side of the metal band, but it was still securely fastened around his neck.

The collar contained an emergency beckon. It should have been activated by the power surge, but she could also trigger it manually, except the control panel was on the inside of the band. But did she dare take it off him? She rocked his shoulder. His head lolled to one side, but he didn't stir, didn't make a sound. She poked him in the ribs several times, but again there was no reaction.

It would only take a moment to trigger the alarm and then refasten the collar. It really was her best option. She hadn't heard any sign of civilization the entire time they'd been here, not a plane or car, not a motor of any kind. Even if she found the keys to the SUV, it could take hours for her to find a clue to their location.

Seeing no other choice, she pressed her thumb against the latch and spoke the Bilarrian phrase Lor had taught her. The collar hissed then parted beneath her thumb. Very carefully, she eased the band away from his neck. Several layers of skin peeled off in the process. She cringed and swallowed then turned her attention to the inside of the band.

Something hit her, knocking her over backward half on and half off of the sleeping bag. The band was snatched out of her hand and she stared up into Nazerel's murderous face.

"You lying bitch!"

Shocked beyond words, it took her a second to comprehend what had just happened. "You tricked me." Hearing the words only added humiliation to her surprise. He'd played upon her sympathies and masterfully anticipated her moves. Not to mention endured the pain of the collar's removal without so much as flinching.

She didn't have to ask if he had access to his powers now. The nasty burn on his neck healed right before her eyes.

None too gently, he dragged her to her feet and turned her so she faced away from him. "Give me the key."

She ignored him. Her chances of escape had just dwindled dramatically. There was no reason left to cooperate. He held her in place with one arm while he paused to look around. It only took him a few seconds to spot the key on top of the cooler. He shoved her to her knees on the sleeping bags then yanked the restraint system free of the tent pole. After opening all three of the locks, he set the key aside. Then she was flat on her back again with Nazerel straddling her hips. He returned the cuffs to her wrists and locked them together without the relative freedom of the chain. Instead, he wrapped the chain around her waist and locked the cuffs to the chain, restricting her movement even more.

Through it all she cursed her strategic misstep. She'd done the one thing she'd sworn she'd never do. She underestimated Nazerel's ruthlessness and his dedication to this endeavor. He did nothing without a reason. He hadn't been concerned about her wellbeing. He'd needed her free so she could release the collar. But how had he known about the emergency beckon? The Bilarrian team had added the feature along with co-ownership.

He pulled on his pants, tucked the key to the restraints into one of his front pockets, and then stormed from the tent, the collar clasped firmly in one hand. She saw a flash of light and knew he'd teleported somewhere, but would he come back? Why bother restraining her if he meant to escape? He'd only been wearing pants, no shirt or boots. No, he was coming back.

She sat up then rolled to her knees so she could climb to her feet. Not being able to move her arms was a serious hindrance, but this was immanently more comfortable than having her hands tied behind her back. She had no idea how long he'd be gone, so she had no time to waste. She searched for the keys to the SUV and/or his Rodyte communicator. Nazerel told her it was basically a two-way radio, but she didn't believe him. The Rodytes were one of the most technologically advanced races she'd encountered. They wouldn't manufacture something as limiting as a two-way radio.

After looking through the crates and inside the cooler, she spotted his boots near the doorway. It was as good a hiding place as anything else. She picked up his first boot and turned it upside down over the cooler. The SUV keys came tumbling out. She quickly overturned the second boot and was rewarded with the communicator, which looked very similar to a cell phone. No one would think twice if they saw him using it on a public street.

Her clothing was in the SUV, but she needed to put some distance between them before she bothered dressing. She ducked through the open entrance and slammed into Nazerel.

"You're free. You have no reason to keep me now."

He ignored her plea, grasped her upper arms and pushed her back inside the tent. "I don't like liars."

"I didn't lie. Lor *is* the owner of the collar."

He shot her a disbelieving glare. "Then how were you able to unlock it?"

"I'm also the owner. The Bilarrians made some improvements when they helped us reset the programing."

He left her standing in the middle of the tent as he found a clean shirt and clean socks.

"All I've tried to do is escape," she pointed out. "You would have done the same."

He pulled on the socks, donned the shirt and tugged on his boots all without saying a word. Then he held out his hand expectantly.

"Leave me here."

"Give me the keys and the comlink," he snapped. "I'm finished playing with you."

Hope fluttered through her being. Did that mean he'd do as she asked? The anger in his gaze promised something much more dangerous.

She tossed him the keys then held out the communicator. Another wrestling match held zero appeal.

After tucking the keys into his front pocket, he activated the comlink and spoke in rapid Rodyte, or Bilarrian, she hadn't heard either often enough to distinguish one from the other.

"Thank you, again. I'll see you shortly." He put the comlink away and grabbed her arm. "Come on."

"Where are we going?" When he said nothing she dug in her heels. "There is no reason for you to take me with you. I insist you leave me here."

"No." He dragged her outside, ignoring her frantic tugging against his grip. He shoved her up against the SUV as he unlocked the vehicle and grabbed her pants off the backseat. "Get dressed." He dropped her boots in front of her and handed her the pants.

If she refused, he'd likely drag her around half naked, and being barefoot was a definite disadvantage. Despite her very real need to rebel, she did as she was told.

If the beckon had activated, someone should have been here by now. But any chance of assistance she had would be abolished if he teleported her away from this location. "Nazerel, you need to listen to me. Right now you're in trouble with the Ontarians. If you let me go, I'll make sure the humans stay out of it. If you harm me, I no longer have that option. Do you really want to be a fugitive on two different planets?"

"I've been a fugitive my entire life. Why should that change now?"

Without further argument, he pulled her into his arms and teleported off the mountain.

VARRIK WALKED AROUND the campsite, his empathic receptors wide open. He could detect Nazerel's energy, but the pattern was faint, barely discernable. Elias hadn't been sure the momentary blip his people detected had been a legitimate signal. Still, it had been worth checking out.

Scanning together, Varrik and Echo had located the lake, but there had been no sign of Nazerel. Worse, they weren't even sure the energy pulse the humans detected had anything to do with the fugitives. Still, they had no other leads, so they searched in concentric circles, scanning outward from the lake. It had been time-consuming and tedious, but their patience paid off.

"They were definitely here." He looked at Echo and allowed his disappointment to show. Façades were pointless with Echo. Their life bond allowed her to sense his emotions and hear every thought he didn't shield. "But they've been gone for at least six hours, probably more."

"There was nothing personal in the tent, just generic camping supplies. Even the clothing looked new. Most of the garments still had sales tags on them."

"Then it stands to reason that Nazerel didn't assemble this himself. He must have purchased everything from a supplier."

"Or suppliers."

He nodded. A different person could have supplied each component, but each person Nazerel involved in his escape was a potential liability. Having one supplier assemble the entire package was a wiser choice.

"What about the vehicle?" Echo asked. "Is it registered?"

"It's locked. I haven't searched it yet." He approached the vehicle cautiously. "Why did they leave it behind?"

She bent and tilted her head so she could see beneath it. "He could have set some sort of trap, but it's more likely that they just didn't need it anymore."

"My thoughts exactly." Their biggest advantage had been the collar suppressing Nazerel's abilities. If he had already regained access to his power, their job just became exponentially harder.

They quickly searched the vehicle to make sure it posed no danger, then he smashed the driver's window with an energy pulse. There were more camping supplies in the rear compartment, but again nothing personal.

"It's registered to a rental company," Echo told him. "Lor and Elias are both running the information through their databases."

She must have contacted Lor telepathically and asked him to pass the information on to Elias. Echo appeared fragile and feminine to those who didn't know her well. It made her all the more dangerous. She was a trained operative who had been involved in countless covert operations long before Varrik met her. He'd thought he kidnaped a helpless princess, but found himself dealing with a female warrior. He was still captivated by the contrast.

"There are some female garments on the backseat. They don't appear damaged." Sometimes the smallest detail would end up being the most significant, so he tried to notice everything.

"There was a bra in the tent as well." She tensed, suddenly looking uncomfortable. "I know the Sacred Customs forbid rape, but how do we know Nazerel still honors the ancient ways?"

"We don't. All we can do is process each clue as quickly as possible. The sooner we find them, the less risk there is that circumstances will escalate beyond his control."

The rotation in her eyes slowed for a moment then her voice appeared in his mind.

Go on Lor. I just brought Varrik in as well. We can both hear you.

The rental company was real, but the customer was phony. The only real piece of information given was the credit card. It was a corporate card belonging to a failed auto dealership. We're running down the authorized users now.

If the dealership went out of business, why was the card still active? Echo beat him to the question.

We're not sure. Give us a few more minutes to dig. The layers of misinformation are multiplying quickly.

Understood.

She pinched off the connection, yet lingered in his mind, surrounding herself with his energy. The telepathic caress made Varrik smile. "Keep that up and you'll find yourself on your back in that tent with your mate deep inside you."

She laughed, her cheeks bright pink. "That's not much of a threat."

They continued to search the campsite, but they both knew they were wasting time. Without some idea of where Nazerel went, he could be anywhere on Earth. Or even much farther away by now. Varrik tried not to let frustration take over. He'd expected disappointments. He knew Nazerel too well to think this would be easy. Still, he hadn't expected to be shut down this quickly after the search began.

Chapter Five

Nazerel sat on the bed beside Morgan, watching her sleep. The hotel room Phil had provided was shabby, but clean. The Bilarrian trader promised to have Nazerel's order ready by six o'clock the following morning. Nazerel was frustrated by the delay, but his request hadn't been simple. Needing time to fill the order was a reasonable stipulation. When he told Phil the campsite had been compromised, the Bilarrian suggested that he take Morgan to one of Phil's preregistered hotel rooms so they could get some sleep. Phil even gave them a backpack with clean clothes and toiletries. The layover had been a good idea. Nazerel didn't require as much sleep as humans, but he'd already been up for almost twenty-four hours when this adventure began.

Exhaustion dragged him into a fitful slumber shortly after they arrived at the hotel, yet troubled thoughts soon had him brooding again. He needed to know exactly what had become of his men. If they were still on Earth, he might be able to free them. If they'd already been dragged back to Ontariese, he would have to be much more creative with his assistance.

Morgan murmured something in her sleep then shifted her bound hands to a different position. He'd unlocked her hands from the leash around her waist though he'd left the cuffs in place. Then he'd reinforced her natural need for sleep with a light compulsion before surrendering to oblivion himself.

She was more challenging than any adversary he'd faced thus far. Not physically, of course. But mentally, she was agile and strategic, using every weapon at her disposal with surprising skill. She'd negotiated, interrogated, bartered, and deceived. And through it all she never lost sight of her real motivation—escape.

When he regained consciousness on the floor of the tent, he'd decided to play his final card. Compassion. Could Morgan face her enemy helpless and in need of care and just walk away? He'd accurately predicted her actions. She had removed the collar, but not to tend his burn as he'd assumed. She'd been in the process of trigging some sort of signal rather than easing his pain.

He was relatively certain he'd stopped her before the signal had been activated. Still, he wasn't willing to risk capture on a hunch. So he threw the collar in a lake many miles from the campsite then returned for Morgan. Abandoning the campsite had been frustrating, but it was the safest course. Finally, he'd contacted Phil, letting him know that plans had changed again.

Phil wasn't the only one who needed to know his plans had changed. He took out his comlink and entered Garin's personal identification code. He waited until Garin entered the corresponding code securing the connection then kept his message short and to the point.

Everything has unraveled. I need to arrive tomorrow morning.

After a short pause, Garin responded, *You're always welcome. Knock before you enter.*

I have a reluctant guest. Is that a problem?

How reluctant?

There was no point in lying. She'd arrive in restraints. *Very.*

He could almost hear Garin's sigh. This wasn't the first time his decisions had created problems for his cousin. *Is she dangerous?*

Only a Rodyte would presume his guest was female. *Not to you or your crew. She's human. No Mystic abilities.*

Then she is entirely your responsibility.

Understood.

See you tomorrow.

The connection terminated and Nazerel slipped the comlink back into his pocket. Morgan complicated his plans considerably. So why was he even considering taking her with him? Releasing his own heavy sigh, he reached out and caught a lock of her hair. The colorful strands curled around his finger, making his chest ache. Kissing her, touching her, tasting her had been blissful torture. Each of her sighs, each shiver of pleasure, had been surrendered begrudgingly. Her body had been unable to resist his skill, yet her heart remained unaffected.

Her heart? What in the five hells was wrong with him. Why would he care about her heart? She was the enemy. She'd looked into his eyes and lied without flinching. He would never be able to trust her.

Then why not leave her here?

He dropped the curl and looked away from her lovely face. He should have left her at the campsite. He should lock her in this room tomorrow morning and go collect the package from Phil. Nazerel could be off this planet before she freed herself from the restraints. It was the smart thing to do.

And yet even the thought of being separate from her was intolerable.

She rolled to her back, her hands resting just below her breasts. He'd been with more females than he cared to remember. His father had been very indulgent when it came to carnal pleasures. Shadow Assassins were allowed so few indulgences. South had provided his son, and himself, with an ever changing selection of pleasure givers. Young ones who had been sold to his father by their families, mature ones eager to teach him all the different ways to arouse a female. Thin ones and voluptuous ones, sometimes more than one, Nazerel had experienced it all.

So what was it about this female that he found so fascinating? Yes, she was physically pleasing, but he'd had sex with beautiful females before and they hadn't left him desperate for more. Maybe that was the answer. He hadn't actually had sex with Morgan. Their intimacies had been rudely interrupted by excruciating pain.

Morautu. The Rodyte word echoed through his mind, mocking any other conclusion. How could Morgan be his mate? It didn't make sense, yet he'd never felt like this before. Permanent mates weren't allowed in the world below. Even so, the concept had secretly fascinated Nazerel for years. He'd never been with a woman who wanted only him, shared herself with only him and the thought was more than appeling.

"What time is it?" she asked without opening her eyes.

"Six thirty."

Her lids slowly opened and their gazes locked. Hers filled with purpose, though her expression remained calm. "Now that you've had time to reflect, do you agree that it's time we part ways?"

He laughed. She sounded as if she were speaking with an errant child. "I have no intention of releasing you until I'm well away from this wretched planet."

Her brows drew together and mouth tensed. "Then you'll leave me with Phil tomorrow when you—"

"So one of the Mystics can scramble his mind? Is that how you treat your friends?"

Rolling to her side, she used her elbow to leverage herself from the mattress. "I'll create more problems than I solve. I promise you that."

She was doubtlessly right. He just didn't care. He'd never met a female like Morgan before and he had no intention of being parted from her. "Give me the number for Elias' phone," he ordered as he pulled the comlink back out of his pocket.

"Why?"

"I want to find out what happened to my men and your lieutenant is going to tell me."

She shook her head, eyes blazing defiance. "He won't tell you anything."

"Don't you want him to know that you're still alive, that he should continue searching?"

That got her attention. Her sensual lips pressed into a grim line and she averted her gaze as she did so often when she was deep in thought. "Put him on speaker. I want to hear both sides of the conversation."

He laughed. "Will you ever figure out who is master and who is the slave?"

"It's doubtful."

"I can reach into your mind and take the number, but it has been many years since I used those skills. It will hurt like fire and likely cause damage. What do you gain by refusing this simple request?"

His lie must have been believable. She scooted back, nearly off the bed, before she spoke again. "It wasn't a request. It was an order."

He didn't have time for her obstinacy. "Will you please tell me Elias' number, so I can inform him that you're still alive?"

With obvious reluctance she told him the number. He didn't really care if she heard what Elias said, but he wasn't willing to reward her insubordination, so he didn't activate the speaker.

The call connected and Elias snapped, "Who is this? How did you get this number?"

"I'll confirm that your boss still lives if you accurately detail the condition of my team members."

"Nazerel." He made the name sound profane. "Your team has been obliterated. So has Team East. All of the hunters are in custody and Sevrin is dead. *It's over*. Release Morgan now and you might come out of this alive."

Infuriated by the human's arrogance, he lashed out in the only way he could. "Sorry, I have other plans for Morgan."

"Let me speak with her. You said you'd provide proof of life."

Morgan held out her hand expectantly. She could obviously hear enough of what Elias said to guess at the rest.

Your team has been obliterated. It's over. The hateful words echoed through his mind like the resonant clang of a gong.

Stunned by grief and frustration, Nazerel ignored her persistent gestures. "It took some convincing, but she freed me from the collar. We're on our way off this useless rock."

"Well, Varrik is hot on your trail, so you better watch your back."

Varrik. Of course they'd send for Varrik. It took a Shadow Assassin to find a Shadow Assassin. That had been their trouble all along. Anger pushed through his regret and fury made him reckless. "Morgan's still a little sore after last night, but she's alive. I'm developing quite a taste for human pussy."

Morgan gasped and tried to grab the comlink out of his hand.

Elias cursed profusely then shouted, "Let me talk to her!"

"Elias, I think we're still in—"

He cut off the call. Elias had likely heard Morgan's indignant yell, but Nazerel could take no more of the human's venom. Elias had said Team South was "obliterated" yet Nazerel refused to believe they were dead. The Mystic Militia didn't work that way. They had done their best to capture each hunter and take them back to Ontariese. His men would have fought ferociously, but the Mystics would have incapacitated not murdered them. As long as they drew breath, there was still hope.

"Just when I think you can't stoop any lower, you prove me wrong."

He ignored the disappointment in her eyes and the frustration gnawing at his belly. He wasn't surprised by anything Elias had told him. Morgan had basically said the same thing last night. And both reports substantiated the clues he'd dug up on his own. Still, having the defeat confirmed made it real. His entire team was in enemy hands, beyond his reach, if not beyond his influence.

And he was surprised it had taken Varrik this long to join the hunt. The traitor had been the obvious choice from the beginning.

Grasping her bound wrists, he pulled her to the edge of the bed and unfastened the chain from around her waist.

"You're vile," she sneered. "Worse than my reports indicated."

"Why do you sound surprised? I'm a Shadow Assassin, worst of the worst. Everyone knows I'm a murderous animal."

She tugged against his hold, fear flickering through her anger. "There is no reason for you to take me with you."

"You're female. Do I need any other reason?"

"Yes," she cried. "Why needlessly endanger yourself? This makes no sense."

"It's like I told Elias. I've developed a taste for human—"

"Don't you dare say it again." She raised both hands as if she would backhand him, cuffs and all.

Rather than react to the provocation, he shoved her to her back and quickly unzipped her pants.

"What are you doing?" She grabbed his hands, fingernails digging into his skin.

"Calm down." He pushed her hands aside and grabbed the sides of her pants. "I'm just discouraging you from running away." She kicked and wiggled, but he pulled off her pants then snatched off her socks. He'd made her take off her boots shortly after they arrived. He grabbed her bound wrists and pulled her back up to a seated position. "Do I need to take the T-shirt too?"

"No."

He searched her gaze then realized the futility of the action. He hadn't been able to tell she was lying the night before. Why did he think he could now? Gathering up her garments and boots, he stuffed everything in the wardrobe. Then he unplugged the phone and placed it in the wardrobe as well. Finally, he wrapped the chain around the handles and secured the chain with the tiny padlock. She could probably pry off the hinges if she had enough time, but this would definitely slow her down. Unless she chose to take off half-naked, hands bound and barefoot as well, which was still a possibility. He wouldn't put anything past Morgan.

She sat on the edge of the bed, watching him through narrowed eyes. "Do you believe me now?" When she finally spoke her tone was calm and collected. "The fight is over. Your side lost."

"I'm hungry."

Pressing her legs together, she pulled the T-shirt down over her knees.

He chuckled. "I was thinking pizza, but if you'd rather continue what I started in the tent, I'm more than happy to oblige."

"There was no reason for you to say that to Elias. Now he'll think... It was just cruel."

"I'm feeling cruel at the moment, so don't provoke me." He crossed to the desk and found a laminated flyer for a pizza delivery shop. "Do you care what I put on it?"

"Onions tear up my stomach and I'm not a fan of anchovies."

He placed the order then slipped his comlink back into his pocket. The situation wasn't nearly as hopeless as Morgan presumed. He'd made arrangements for his escape even before he came to Earth. Only a fool would blindly trust a complete stranger. And Nazerel was no fool. The hardest part was that most of his men didn't realize he hadn't deserted them. A few had shipped out with him often enough to know he never left anything to chance. The others would just have to believe the worst until his actions proved them wrong.

"What is Phil buying for you?" She'd moved from the bed to one of the chairs arranged around a small round table.

It didn't matter where she sat. One look at those long, toned legs and his mind carried them back to the bed. She tried to make herself less attractive, but her efforts were futile. The woman was pleasure personified. So why had no one claimed her? Perhaps she had been claimed at one point, but her mate died. That would explain her resistance to being touched and touching in return.

She'd rebel against a direct question on such a personal subject, so he answered her question instead. "Phil is buying me an insurance policy of sorts. How long have you been chasing aliens?"

"Wasn't that in my dossier? You said you'd learned all about Morgan Hoyt. You just didn't realize I was female."

"I know you started as a profiler for the FBI, but there weren't a lot of details about your taskforce."

Her brows arched and a smile teased the corners of her utterly kissable mouth. "That's because it doesn't officially exist. I'm surprised you found mention of it at all. I have people in my IT department who routinely scrubs that sort of information."

"What drew you to criminal investigation? It's an odd occupation for a female."

"Maybe on Ontariese. Earth is more open-minded."

He joined her at the table. His primary reason for the conversation was to keep his mind off how badly he wanted her, but he was also curious. Though lacking many details, the information he'd dug up on Morgan Hoyt had made him picture a middle-aged man with military bearing and a no-nonsense attitude. It was hard to believe this delicate female had earned such power and authority. "Ignore my sexist attitude. Why did you become an investigator?"

"Why do you care? You've made it obvious that females only had one purpose in the world below."

"That's not true." He grinned. "They had two. We had pleasure givers as well as mates."

"That's not funny."

"Then stop dodging the question. I told you everything you wanted to know about me. Now it's your turn to share."

She rested her hands on the table and fiddled with her fingernails. "My mother is a workaholic and my father was a drunk. It gave me a rather warped perspective of life. Mom was never around because she always had some late-night meeting or out-of-town conference she couldn't afford to miss. It didn't take long to realize she was simply avoiding her husband." There was no emotion in her tone. She sounded hollow, alone.

"Why did she remain bonded to such a man?"

One of her shoulders lifted in an unconvincing shrug. "She was a good Catholic girl, so she didn't have a choice."

"I don't understand the reference. Is Catholic a race or a religion?"

"It's a religion with lots of unbendable rules. Devout Catholics, especially of my mother's generation, find divorce unthinkable. Besides, Dad wasn't abusive. He was just useless."

"Did you have siblings?"

She shook her head. "The Catholic religion also frowns on birth control, but Mom quickly realized she had two dependents, not one, and she was solely responsible for both. Her ambition grew out of a sense of responsibility, but it was an escape as well. She was embarrassed and exasperated by her husband, so she made a life for herself apart from him. They might have lived under the same roof, but they weren't a real couple."

"I want to know about you, not your parents." Their gazes locked and he was shocked to realize how much he meant the statement. He really did what to know more about her, to understand the forces that drove her, had made her so strong.

Both her shoulders lifted this time and still her indifference was unconvincing. "My story isn't unusual or particularly interesting."

"Let me be the judge of that."

Her tongue touched her bottom lip and she lowered her gaze. "I was what's known as a latchkey kid. I'd let myself in to our house after school and ignore my father who was usually passed out on the couch when he wasn't at one of his favorite bars. Then I'd spend the next four or five hours in my bedroom alone entertaining myself. I was fed and clothed. I always had what I needed and most of the things I wanted. My childhood wasn't that bad."

"Weren't you lonely? Isolation like that had to be hard on a child." His childhood had been filled with challenges and cruel discipline. Still, he'd been surrounded by people who cared for and supported him.

"It was horribly lonely, but it also made me self-sufficient and unafraid."

Thinking of her as a neglected child only made him angry at her parents. He wanted to find them and shake some sense into them, yet that wasn't the purpose for this conversation. "How did your isolation ignite an interest in investigation?"

"It was a gradual progression. I was eleven when I was picked up by the police for the first time. Shoplifting. Luckily, the shop owner only wanted to scare me, so he didn't press charges. My mother was horrified and immediately sent me to therapy. The councilor helped me understand that the actions of my parents didn't need to define my life."

"That's a lesson many people never learn."

She nodded. "I understood what she meant, but it took many years for me to implement the concept."

"Then your misbehavior continued?"

"Of course. I was desperate for attention and determined to get it anyway I could."

It was easy to see where her story led. It was a fundamental law of nature. Without energy, or in this case direction, any situation deteriorated into chaos. "Your mother continued to ignore you and delegate your care to others?"

"When my 'antics'—her favorite word for my misbehavior—became more outrageous, Mom sent me to a boarding school."

"I've read about such places. From Lowood in *Jane Eyre* to Harry Potter's Hogwarts, few of them are pleasant."

She smiled, her gaze returning to his face. "Don't believe everything you read or see on TV. Boarding school was the best thing that ever happened to me. With the help of a really good guidance counselor, I was able to explore my aptitudes and interests. I originally thought I wanted to be a lawyer, but I found criminals more interesting than the laws that protect them."

"Human laws protect the criminals? Shouldn't laws protect the victims and punish the criminals?"

"Oh, they should, but too often people manipulate the system or the system is just so convoluted that it's ineffective. Anyway, I realized my personality required something more hands-on than being a lawyer so I investigated other options."

A firm knock at the door interrupted their conversation. Morgan looked toward the door, a cunning gleam in her eyes. "You will not move and you will remain silent." He reinforced the directive with a powerful compulsion and paused to see if it took hold. Her eyes widened and subtle twitches indicated her attempts to move. "I will release you in a moment."

He answered the door, paid for the pizza and a two-liter bottle of cola. He kept the door angled, blocking the young man's view of Morgan. After the delivery person departed, Nazerel locked the door and returned to the table. Only then did he release her from the compulsion.

She sprang back to life with a gasp, knocking her chair over as she jumped to her feet. "What the hell... How did you do that?"

"Let's eat while it's hot." He placed the box in the middle of the table and divided the stack of paper napkins. The delivery person hadn't provided disposable plates, so they would have to eat over the box. "If you want ice for your drink, I'll have to compel you again."

"Only the sweepers can use compulsions. How were you able to paralyze me?"

A true sweeper, like Varrik, would have compelled away her desire to escape. Nazerel had never achieved that level of control. Still, she didn't need to know his limitations.

There was a stack of glasses by the ice bucket. He grabbed two and brought them to the table. "I had aptitudes for both disciplines. I was just better at hunting."

"But you said you hadn't used those skills in years."

He looked into her eyes and smiled. "I lied."

Morgan stared at him, shocked beyond words. Everyone had hinted that Nazerel was no ordinary Shadow Assassin. She was just starting to understand what they meant. He'd been difficult enough while the collar suppressed his abilities, now her hope of escaping him was threatening to desert her entirely.

No. She would not give up or give in to his magnetic personality. As long as she was alive, she would keep fighting.

"Are you going to join me or shall I begin?" He raised the lid on the pizza box and let the aroma fill the air.

Her stomach growled and her mouth watered. They had their days and nights switched around, but it had been at least nine hours since she'd eaten anything. To escape she would need mental sharpness and physical strength, and both of those required energy. Satisfied with the rationalization, she righted her chair and sat back down.

"Dig in. He didn't bring plates, so we'll be dining bachelor style."

She picked up a slice of pizza and took a bite. The crust was a little tough, but there was plenty of cheese and inviting flavors. "No one just figures out how to control their power." She paused for a quick drink of cola. "Who taught you how to form compulsions?"

"My compulsions are strong, but they don't last very long. That's why I became a hunter."

"Good to know, but that's not what I asked. Who trained you?"

"Can't you guess?" He devoured one piece and reached for another before he clarified. "Varrik taught me how to use my sweeper abilities and I taught him how to use his hunter abilities. We did so in secret to begin with, but once the elders realized what we were doing, they decided cross training wasn't such a bad idea."

"How many Shadow Assassins are able to use compulsions?" Controlling minds was so dangerous, even if it was for a short period of time.

"I'm the only Shadow Assassin left on Earth, so why does it matter?"

He was right. She needed to focus on Nazerel. He was her objective, her target, her enemy. So why did she keep forgetting. Her wrists were restrained and he'd taken off her pants and still she found herself fascinated by him rather than repulsed.

"How long have you been with the alien taskforce?" Nazerel asked in between bites.

So they were back to quid pro quo. He'd answered her questions, so it was time for her to answer his. "I'm one of the original members, so fifteen years. I've been director for the past six."

"You don't seem old enough to have so many responsibilities."

She paused with her slice of pizza halfway to her mouth. "Thank you, I think."

"How did you come so far so quickly?" His tone was conversational, his expression calm.

This was way too close to comfortable. It felt like a date, a slightly kinky date, but a date. Could Stockholm syndrome kick in this fast? Or was he influencing her, making her feel... She'd love to blame it all on him, but she'd felt this connection, this irrational attraction even before his powers were restored.

"You really don't like to talk about yourself, do you? It's most people's favorite subject."

She fought back a smile. At least he hadn't said, it was most females' favorite subject. She didn't see any harm in answering his question, but she kept it succinct and factual. "I've always been self-motivated and driven. I graduated from college at sixteen and was contracted by the FBI a few months later. I was restricted to desk work until I turned twenty-three, but by then I was working for the taskforce and we tend to bend all sorts of rules. After all, we don't really exist."

"Then you're in your early thirties?"

"Why is my age important? How old are you?"

"I'm older than I look. Between my Rodyte heritage and my nanites' ability to regenerate flesh, I could live for hundreds of years."

"Lucky you." She took another bite of pizza and tried not to brood, but human existence had never felt so limited before. She couldn't paralyze people with her mind or teleport. She didn't have nanites to regenerate her flesh and—she could nurture a growing life inside her body and give birth to the next generation. That was something he would never be able to do, even if he lived for a thousand years. Maybe she wasn't so useless after all.

"Did something I say upset you? You seem annoyed."

She laughed. "I'm sitting here in my underwear eating with restrained hands. Why would I be annoyed?"

"Stop trying to run away and I'll unlock the cuffs."

She wiped her mouth with a napkin and picked up her glass. "You have your powers back. Why do you need me?"

"Maybe I intend to trade you for my men."

If only it were that simple. "Why didn't you make that offer to Elias rather than being obnoxious?"

He smiled, clearly entertained by the memory. "Why did my boast bother you? Are you ashamed of the things I did to you or that you enjoyed them so much?"

Ignoring the taunt, she pushed back her chair and stood. "I'm going to take a shower. Can I have my other outfit?"

He shook his head. "We'll both dress in fresh clothes before we depart. You can sleep in that."

Depart for where? And she'd just awaken from a long nap. It was unlikely she'd fall asleep again. Unless he compelled her. She shivered. Knowing he could make her do whatever he wanted was terrifying, so she refused to think about it.

Rather than ask for a clarification, she said, "At least give me the toiletries. I'd like to brush my teeth."

"Fine." He motioned toward the backpack Phil had given him. "Help yourself."

She rummaged through the contents and found what she'd need in the bathroom then held up both hands. "Can you unlock me, please? I don't want to get the cuffs wet."

He'd checked the bathroom for escape routes and possible weapons when they arrived, so there was no reason for him to refuse. There wasn't even a window in the small space. Still, his hesitation was proof positive that he didn't trust her. Why should he? She'd given him nothing but trouble since he forced her into the Suburban and she didn't intend to become sweet and docile now.

Dragging the key out of his pocket, he unlocked the cuffs then quickly worked the buckles, freeing her from the restraints. "They go back on as soon as you're finished."

"Whatever." She hurried into the bathroom and closed the door, unable to hide her frustration or her growing desperation. Out of habit she locked the door then shook her head. What good were locked doors when her adversary could teleport through walls? She could pound on the bathroom wall and scream her head off, but it wouldn't do any good. Nazerel would flash them to a new location before anyone who heard her screams could dial 9-1-1. Never before had she faced an opponent who had this many advantages.

Nazerel knocked on the door, startling her out of her gloomy thoughts. "Get going. I'd like a shower too while there's still time."

She glared at the door. The mystery package wouldn't be ready until morning. What was his problem? She turned on the water at the sink rather than the shower then freed her toothbrush from the rigid packaging.

After giving her teeth a good scrubbing, she closed the shower curtain and turned on the water. The bathtub was small, but the curtain rod bowed outward, keeping the enclosure from feeling claustrophobic. She gave the water a few minutes to warm up then climbed into the bathtub. With her back to the spray, she tilted her head and let the water saturate her hair.

She couldn't fight her way out of this situation. Nazerel was faster, stronger, and much more powerful than she. Still, her other options were nearly nonexistent. Nazerel had teleported her from Phil's shop to the hotel room, so she had no idea where they were. Still, if she could get the communication device away from Nazerel, maybe she could figure out how he'd called Elias. Did the Rodyte version of a phone have a redial function?

With a sigh of frustration, she picked up the miniature bottle of shampoo and poured a good amount into her palm. Nazerel was so different from the man portrayed in his dossier. He was ruthless, no one could deny his focus, but he wasn't bloodthirsty or cruel. Well, he had moments of cruelty. What he'd said to Elias had certainly been mean-spirited. But she'd heard enough of what Elias said to understand the reaction. Elias had rubbed Nazerel's face in his failure and Nazerel lashed out. If the situation were reversed, Elias might have done the same or worse.

Oh dear God, she was defending Nazerel like a besotted schoolgirl.

She raised her hands to her hair and closed her eyes as she worked the shampoo into a fragrant lather. Nazerel's treatment of Elias might be debatable, but there was no excuse for what Nazerel had done the night before. He'd mercilessly seduced her, used her passionate nature against her in the most humiliating way.

Lather slid over her breasts and belly like a whisper-soft touch. Her nipples peaked and her core ached as images rolled through her mind. His kiss had been consuming, intoxicating. Just thinking about it made her head spin. He'd looked into her eyes and made it clear that one word from her would have ended the session. So why had she remained silent? Why hadn't she tried to negotiate, to calm him down and shift his focus away from her body? She'd been trapped by her own stubbornness as much as by his agenda.

She was doing it again, justifying his deplorable behavior. He wasn't a hapless victim of circumstance. He was the leader of the Shadow Assassins, one of the most ruthless groups of mercenaries she'd ever heard about.

Which brought up another contradiction, Nazerel's ongoing focus on his men. Heartless murderers weren't generally loyal to their subordinates.

A familiar scrubbing sound interrupted her troubled thoughts. It sounded like someone brushing their teeth. She opened her eyes and tried to detect Nazerel's tall form through the curtain, but the rubbery material barely let any light through much less a silhouette. She eased one side back an inch and cringed. He stood in front of the sink, naked to the waist, casually brushing his teeth. Unbelievable!

She started to bolt then realized he stood between her and the door. He'd catch her and push her up against the wall. And she'd be naked while he was still partially dressed, an advantage he obviously enjoyed.

Maybe he'd finish cleaning his teeth then return to the outer room. He hadn't announced his presence. Maybe he was just tired of pizza breath. And maybe she'd win the lottery tomorrow. She sighed. He was about to join her in the shower. There was no other reason he'd be in here now. All she could do was decide how to react when he did. The ends of her hair were still sudsy, so she stepped back under the spray and closed her eyes.

A strange current washed over her naked body. Her nipples tingled and goose bumps broke out on her arms. That was fast. Had he taken time to undress? She cleared the water from her face with a quick swipe of her fingers then opened her eyes. Nazerel stood in front of her, stark naked, a miniature bar of soap resting on his palm.

"You forgot the soap." He punctuated the observation with a sexy smile.

He was obviously hoping for a reaction, so she calmly took the soap from his hand and turned around. "Thanks, but I'm not quite finished. Give me another five minutes and the shower's yours." Despite her wildly pounding heart and the need spiraling through her body, she sounded casual, as if showering with her captor were an everyday occurrence.

Moving up behind her, he pressed his chest against her back and wrapped his arms around her waist. "I have a better idea." He snatched the soap out of her grasp and spun the tiny bar between his hands. With his arms still wrapped around her, he set the soap aside and began to lather her arms and shoulders. "I'll make sure you're nice and clean."

"Like hell you will!" She turned around and shoved against his chest. "Enough with these games. I'm your hostage not your pet. Stop trying to seduce me."

His slick fingers slid across her shoulder and down her back while his other arm banded her waist. "Am I to believe you felt nothing when we kissed last night? Were you pretending to enjoy my touch?"

"I was staying alive." She arched, using his chest as leverage, but the action only drove her pelvis into his. Each of her agitated movements emphasized the conspicuous hardness rapidly forming against her belly. So she stilled and glared up at him. "Let go of me."

"I'm not human." His tone was deep and filled with meaning.

"I'm aware."

"I sense things, smell things, *taste* things no human can understand."

She closed her eyes and balled her hands into fists. If this was where he told her she "tasted" like his mate, she was going to scream. "I don't care what you think you know. I want out of this shower."

"Kiss me and I'll let you go." Challenge rippled through his voice and one of his hands slid down until his palm cupped her behind.

Her body stirred as memories of the pleasure he'd given her the night before surged to the surface again. His hands caressing, his lips sucking, and his tongue... Gritting her teeth against the temptation, she took two slow breaths. "I don't want to have sex with you." She opened her eyes and met his smoldering gaze. "Has no one ever told you no before?"

"You claim that you don't want me. I think you do. Prove me wrong. Kiss me so deeply my head spins then shrug it off and walk away."

How could she resist such a challenge? The fastest way to shut up a bully was to confront them. And after last night it would feel damn good to put this jerk in his place. She slid her hands up to his shoulders and rocked to the balls of her feet. He bent his head, ready to take over, but she nipped his bottom lip.

"I'm kissing you, remember?"

"Then kiss me."

The growling roughness of his voice sent shivers through her body and still she refused to be rushed. She pressed her lips to his, hers barely parted. Then she moved her head back and forth and caressed his lips with hers. His hand fisted in the back of her hair, but he didn't pull, didn't try to control her.

Empowered by his restraint, she traced the seam of his lips with the tip of her tongue. His cock bucked against her belly and she smiled. He tasted of mint, his breath hot and humid. She continued to tease his mouth while her hands began to wander. His body felt as incredible as it looked, every bulge and ridge of muscle covered with hot silky skin.

She pushed her tongue all the way into his mouth and inhaled his appreciative moan. His tongue slid against hers and his response grew more demanding. Before she lost herself in the need he ignited so effortlessly, she tore her mouth away from his and stepped back.

He caught her wrist, his gaze narrowed, the rings glowing.

"I'm not leaving," she assured him and his expression turned quizzical. She reached over and grabbed the soap, quickly lathering up her hands. "I want to touch you, like you touched me. Are you brave enough to let me?"

"If you mean to leave me wanting..."

She closed her slick fingers around his rock-hard cock and he didn't finish the warning. "Did you leave me wanting?" Her hand slid up and down, her thumb brushing across the sensitive tip at the top of each stroke.

He grasped the back of her neck and drew her to his side so he could kiss her without interfering with the motion of her hand. She didn't want to kiss him, wanted to remain in complete control while he lost himself to the demands of his body. But his mouth was warm, his kiss coaxing rather than demanding, and she couldn't make herself pull away.

She savored the tenderness threaded through his passion, amazed by the patience it revealed. His hips began to rock, driving his shaft with more force between the circle of her fingers. Her body ached, craving the fullness she stroked with her hand.

"Oh gods." His head dropped back and tension rippled down his body. She tightened her hand as his cock bucked against her fingers. His hand covered hers and tripled the speed of her stroking. Pearly fluid jetted from him with each frantic motion. He shuddered and came, then groaned and came some more.

She watched his face as well as his body, fascinated by the agony of his surrender. He'd lost control, submitted to her touch just as quickly as she'd succumb to his. She felt dizzy and empty, yet giddy as she realized what she'd just done. She hadn't needed restraints or compulsions. With nothing more Mystic than her kiss and her touch, she'd commanded the mighty Nazerel.

Before he could recover from the rush, she threw back the curtain, snatched a towel off the rack and rushed into the outer room.

Chapter Six

B racing his hands on his knees, Nazerel fought to catch his breath after the powerful release he'd just enjoyed. That crafty little vixen had not only taken control of his game, she'd turned it back on him. He'd challenged Morgan to make his head spin. Well, she'd done that and a whole lot more. Still, he didn't dare leave her unsupervised. She'd left the bathroom without grabbing her T-shirt, but there was still an outfit in the backpack. Luckily, her boots were locked in the wardrobe.

He quickly washed then turned off the water and stepped out of the bathtub. He wrapped the remaining towel around his hips as he opened the bathroom door. Morgan had borrowed his T-shirt again and stood at the window carefully peeking out between the blinds.

"If you keep stealing my clothes, I'll have no choice but to go around naked."

She turned from the window with a sigh. "You just like being naked. It has nothing to do with me."

"I enjoy being naked, but it has everything to do with you."

She rolled her eyes then motioned toward the window. "It's starting to get dark outside. Any chance we can go for a walk? I'm going stir-crazy in here."

He smiled, amused by her transparent ploy. As long as she stayed bound and contained within this room, her chances of escape were basically nonexistent. "I might be persuaded to change our surroundings." The longer they lingered in one place, the greater the chances were that Varrik would stumble upon some clue to their location.

Without explaining what he had in mind, Nazerel dressed. He put on the T-shirt he'd intended for the following morning, not wanting to fight with her about the one she was wearing. Then he unlocked the wardrobe and tossed Morgan the rest of her clothes. She dressed without argument while he packed up the rest of the room.

He held up the cuffs and motioned her over.

"Is that really necessary?" she grumbled.

"You tell me? If you could put me back in the collar, would you?"

Her gaze narrowed and she tilted her head. "Do you still have it?"

He laughed. "It wasn't hard to figure out you'd triggered some sort of homing signal. I threw it in a lake about fifty miles from the campsite." A sudden gleam in her eyes revealed that she'd tucked the fact away for future use. "Do you ever stop strategizing?"

She arched her brow in silent challenge then whispered, "Do you?"

Rather than fuel their budding argument, he crossed the room and buckled her into the cuffs. He attacked the locks as well, but allowed her the relative freedom of the connecting chain. Finally, he pulled the bedding off the bed.

"Why do we need blankets? Aren't we just going for a walk?"

"You'll see." He draped the bedding around her shoulders and put on the backpack. On impulse, he grabbed the half-full bottle of cola and tucked it into the limited space remaining in the backpack. Then he pulled her into a firm embrace and teleported out of the hotel room. She gasped and clutched his shoulders, clinging to his body as well as the cuffs allowed. He wasn't sure where he was going, so he scanned far ahead. He needed something secluded, yet not so inhospitable that it would make their night miserable.

It was easier to travel along familiar paths, so he found himself in the Toiyabe National Forest, the same general area as the campsite. Though this location was much more secluded. There were no hiking trails or dirt roads, just trees, mountains and the sky. He materialized and continued to hold her as she acclimated to their new setting.

Her arms relaxed and her hands slid down from his shoulders to his chest. She looked around, eyes wide, legs still shaking. "Where are we?"

Ignoring the question, he motioned toward the western sky. "I thought we'd watch the sun go down. Nothing cures stir-craziness faster than fresh mountain air."

She seemed almost reluctant to let go of him and her hesitancy made him want to pull her back into his arms. Rather than satisfying his passions, what she'd done in the shower only made him want to continue their sexual exploration. No other female had inflamed his senses so fast or so well.

As if sensing the direction of his thoughts, she stepped back and turned around. "Wow. Now that's what I call a view."

He agreed wholeheartedly. The mountain on which they stood rested at one end of a broad valley. Other peaks and canyons undulated off into the distance, creating a jagged foreground for the expansive sky. The sun hovered on the horizon, stubbornly fighting for its last few minutes of supremacy.

Morgan shook out the bedspread then sat down, wrapping the blanket and the sheet around her shoulders. She hadn't offered him the protection of the bedding, but at least she'd left room for him on the bedspread. He slipped off the backpack and sat down beside her.

She watched the sunset and he watched her. How could such strength and such fragility reside in the same person? She was so tiny compared to him and yet she was fierce and unafraid. "What happened to your mate?"

He didn't realize he spoke the question out loud until she turned her head and looked at him. But the pain in her gaze confirmed his suspicions. She hadn't been ignored by the men of Earth. She'd been claimed and then lost her mate.

"I thought we already established that there isn't a man in my life." She turned back around and gazed out across the serene valley.

"But there once was. What happened to him?"

She drew her legs up and flipped the chain over her knees so she could wrap her arms around her legs. The blankets slipped off her shoulders, but she made no move to retrieve them. "I don't want to talk about it."

He scooted closer and wrapped the bedding around them both. "Is he still alive?"

"Yes. At least, I presume he's still alive. We haven't had contact since he left the taskforce."

A certain catch in her tone sent protective anger rushing to the surface. "Was he your mentor? Did this man take advantage of you?"

"What part of 'I don't want to talk about it' was unclear?"

He wanted to wrap his arm around her, or better yet pull her onto his lap, but he did neither. He sat beside her, acutely aware of her small warm body so close to his. He turned his face toward the horizon and silently watched the sunset. Gold gave way to orange then the bottoms of the clouds turned bright pink.

When he'd offered her glimpses into his past, she'd reciprocated. If the strategy had worked once, perhaps it would work again. "As I said, I've never had a female who was mine and mine alone. But there was this one pleasure giver who was special to me."

"What was her name?" Morgan's voice was barely above a whisper and she didn't turn her head.

"Rinatta. Her father sold her to the elders so he could feed his other six children. She was young and terrified, so my father gave her to me."

Morgan did look at him then and disapproval shadowed her confusion. "Why would your father give you a girl who was utterly terrified?"

"Because I was patient and willing to—"

"Break her in very slowly?"

She was echoing the taunt he'd used when he first met her, hoping to make him feel guilty. Rather than backing down from her displeasure, he pressed onward. "The elders had very different means of motivating people to do their will. Starvation, isolation, cold, and pain were my father's favorite strategies. I saw *300* and it made me curious about the Spartans. Their training methods were similar to ours. Like Sparta, there was no place for weakness or cowardice in the world below. If you didn't grow hard and ruthless, you died."

"So you made Rinatta hard and ruthless?"

He sighed. If she insisted on twisting each word he uttered, he would do better to remain silent. Reaching back, he pulled the backpack to him and retrieved the two-litter bottle. He took a swig, wishing it were something a whole lot stronger than cola.

She lightly touched his arm, drawing his attention. "I'm sorry. My world is very different from yours. It's hard to accept that things like you describe happened in this day and age. You mentioned the Spartans, and I understand the similarities. But the Spartans existed hundreds of years ago."

He handed her the bottle and watched as her lips pressed against the place where his had been moments before. "This land enjoys a freedom that I have yet to experience. I understand that. But such is not the case all over your world. There are still many nations who are barbarous and warlike. Some even kidnap women—and children—to sell for the pleasure of others."

"You're right." She looked into his eyes as she added, "And those humans are just as wrong as the Shadow Assassins."

They lapsed into silence as they passed the bottle back and forth. The sunset faded and the temperature dropped with staggering speed. He eased closer to her and she didn't object, so he wrapped his arm around her shoulders.

"Tell me about Rinatta. I promise I won't interrupt."

Her request surprised and pleased him. He'd thought the opportunity lost. Choosing his words carefully, he spun his tale. "First of all, I want you to know that I wanted to free her."

She tucked her shoulder into his armpit and pressed against his side. "Why didn't you?"

All he could see was the top of her head, but her willingness to touch him was more important anyway. "If she'd belonged to my father alone, I would have. But she belonged to all four of the elders. They'd shared equally in her cost."

"Why did that make a difference?"

"They would have demanded my life if I released her without their permission and they made sure Rinatta knew it."

She tensed, her head shaking back and forth. "That's wrong on so many levels. I don't know where to start my objections."

"The elders were master manipulators. On that Varrik and I agree."

"I don't think the elders were the only ones," she muttered under her breath as she set the empty bottle aside. "I know I'm going to regret this, but continue the story. I'd like to know what happened to the poor girl."

"I'll spare you the details of her training, but—"

She pushed back and her gaze locked with his. "She wasn't the first one you'd 'trained' was she? That's why your father gave her to you. You didn't just teach the men how to deal with reluctant females. You also taught females how to submit to... No wonder I was putty in your hands. You've been doing this for years, maybe decades."

He couldn't deny her charge. He'd been the primary trainer for all things sexual and Rinatta had played an active role in that development. Still, the story was more provocative to her than he'd realized. "I think we should change the subject."

"Not a chance. I'm curious now. Why did you think your seduction of a virgin would appeal to me?"

Her sharp tone rekindled his determination. She had drawn so many false assumptions about the world below. He felt obligated to enlighten her. "Once Rinatta realized there was no possibility of her returning to the world above, she not only accepted her new life, she reveled in it."

"She was to be the sexual play thing for four old men. How could she possibly have any other reaction?" She pulled her side of the blanket closer about her and averted her gaze.

"You obviously never met Rinatta. She was shrewd and intensely determined to control her own destiny." Morgan reminded him of the feisty little pleasure giver, but Nazerel wisely kept the observation to himself. "She told me that she wanted to be so captivating, so passionate and so skilled that the first man who actually took her would kill to keep her from the others."

"You never actually..." She glanced at him then away. "Then how did you teach her... Never mind. I really don't want to hear the specifics."

Hadn't their interaction in the tent taught her how many pleasures could be found without actual penetration? Perhaps she needed another demonstration. Desire wrapped around him, speeding his heart and hardening his cock. They still had all night to kill and nothing much to do.

"So did it work? Was she so desirable that the first elder who took her fought off the others?"

Fine. So they'd talk for a little while longer. "Tribe North was prime, so Elder North was Rinatta's first lover."

"Why was Tribe North prime and what exactly did that mean?"

"Vade, the founder was the original Elder North so his vote basically counted as two. That practice kept many votes from ending in a tie, so every Elder North that followed was considered slightly above the other elders."

"Okay, got it. Now back to Rinatta. Did her plan work?" She sounded impatient, as if she wanted the conversation over so they could move on to more important things. Like giving each other pleasure?

Well, he might be projecting his desires just a bit, but she did sound anxious. "North paid off the other elders, but the result was the same. She was North's consort for seven years and many whispered that she was responsible for many of his decisions. She also made sure the other pleasure givers were not abused and did her best to help the mates accept their fate."

"You already know how I feel about that subject, so I'll spare you another tirade. I'm still curious about one thing though."

"Only one?" He nudged her with his shoulder, hoping to lighten her mood.

"You said Rinatta was special to you. You brought her up hoping I would tell you about my serious relationship."

He was afraid the circumstances of Rinatta's arrival had eclipsed that fact. "North was the first male to share her bed, but he never touched her heart. I was her true lover."

"Couldn't North smell you on her? You've made a big deal about how easy it is to smell other males."

"We have a device similar to your condom. I made damn sure my scent never touched her in any way."

After a long pause, she asked, "What would have happened...I guess a better question is, did Elder North ever find out?"

"We risked death each time we touched, but it didn't seem to matter. And, no, he never found out."

She finally looked at him, her gaze luminous in the gathering moonlight. "Then what happened to her? I presume you'd be with her still if that were an option."

He thought about that for a moment. Would he be with Rinatta if they had both been liberated from the Shadow Maze? "I'm not sure. My affection for her changed over time, but it broke my heart when North set her free."

"Why did North let her go?"

"According to the Sacred Customs pleasure givers had to be offered their freedom after one season cycle had passed. Some stayed much longer, but the offer had to be made each year."

"So why did Rinatta choose to leave you? Had her love burned out?"

He shook his head and gazed off into the night. "Just the opposite actually. We had a close call, a really close call. It forced us both to admit that we might not be so lucky the next time. Besides, North had grown bored with her. Staying would have meant she made herself available to the other elders. Neither of us wanted that. So I encouraged her to accept her freedom and asked Varrik to cleanse her mind of every memory we'd created."

"Why? If she truly loved you, she would have wanted to remember."

"Varrik agreed with you. Rinatta begged him to leave her memory intact, except for the specifics of her captivity of course. I checked on her two or three times a year to make sure she was doing well. The last time I saw her, she was holding an infant and her heart was filled with love. I accepted her happiness and never went back." He glanced at her and was shocked to see tears shimmering in her eyes. "Why are you crying?"

"I'm not." She stubbornly swiped her cheek with the back of her hand and looked away from him.

"So back to the beginning of this rambling conversation. When I asked about your mate, I saw something familiar in your eyes. It made me wonder if your love might have been forbidden like Rinatta's and mine. That's why I asked if he was your mentor."

"He wasn't my mentor, but he was quite a bit older than me." She didn't look at him, so he remained quiet, hoping she'd say more. "We both knew better. Fraternizing with other agents was against the rules. We weren't risking death, but it definitely made the relationship more interesting." She glanced at him with a wistful smile. "Don't we always want what we can't have?"

"How long were you together?" He risked the question after she slipped into silence for several minutes.

"We were lovers, off and on, for three years."

Another long pause followed, so he prompted her again. "Why did you stop seeing him?"

"I received a promotion he thought he deserved and things got ugly fast. He started the rumor that I'd slept with our boss to secure the promotion."

"And you couldn't defend yourself against the allegation without admitting why he was being so vindictive?"

"Exactly. Those who knew me well knew the rumor was bullshit, but it made things extremely awkward. I'm a staunch supporter of the no office romance policy now."

"I'm sure you are, but knowing your lover valued his occupation more than your affection had to have caused you pain." He shouldn't care about the specifics. Why did he keep asking about her past?

"I think it bruised my ego more than my heart. It had been obvious from the start that he was superficial and self-absorbed. That's why I never put more energy into the relationship. It was a flirtation, nothing more."

"How long ago did he leave the taskforce?"

"He applied for a transfer three days after my promotion was announced. That was seven, no, eight years ago."

"And there has been no one special in the past eight years?" How was that possible? Morgan was intelligent, confidant, not to mention the most desirable woman he'd ever seen. Human males should be trampling each other in their haste to claim her.

"It's not like I've gone out of my way to avoid relationships. The taskforce keeps me extremely busy and I move around a lot. The people I interact with on a regular basis are all coworkers, most are my subordinates. I'm rather isolated."

"I understand isolation better than most."

She looked at him and smiled, yet sadness still shadowed her gaze. "I suppose you do."

For a long tense moment they just stared at each other. He wanted to touch her, wanted to find the subject or phrase that would shatter her misconceptions and make her receptive to the attraction pulsing between them. His blunder in the shower was infuriating. Yes he recognized her scent and even more so her taste, but she was worlds away from ready to accept what he sensed. They were enemies. How could they possibly be mates?

"Why did you come to Earth?" She whispered the question as if she were afraid of breaking the spell.

"You know why."

"I know what the report says, what Lor and the others have told me. I want to hear it from you. What brought you to Earth? What were you hoping to accomplish?"

He sighed and dragged his gaze away from hers. He'd told her enough already and there was so much he was forbidden to say. If she didn't believe that he was trying to find a new start for his men, then no amount of detail would change her mind.

Her small, cold hand touched his arm and he shivered. "I really want to know. What made you put your trust in Sevrin?"

"I never trusted Sevrin," he snapped then clenched his teeth. "The Overlord reluctantly took us into the ranks of his soldiers, but most of us are part Rodyte. Ontarians will never trust Rodytes, never really accept them."

"Go on. What did you do?"

"I started looking for somewhere else to take my tribe, somewhere we could really call home."

"What's wrong with Rodymia? You said most of your men are at least part Rodyte."

"At the moment Rodymia is ruled by Sevrin's kin. Need I say more?"

"I suppose not."

"If that changes, I might reconsider. Rodymia is the obvious choice in many ways."

He would be happy to share his thoughts and explain his actions if her interest were real. But others were protected by the secrets he kept and he couldn't help thinking she was playing an angle, trying to manipulate him in some way. Still, he was tired of lies, so he told her a stripped-down version of the truth constructed around several significant omissions. "Sevrin's promises were wild and wonderful. I knew Rodytes had been manipulating DNA for centuries, so I needed to find out how much of what she told us was true. I warned the other alpha hunters not to trust her and to verify everything she said."

"They didn't listen to your warnings?"

"They wanted it to be real badly enough that they turned a blind eye to everything else. It didn't matter that we were Sevrin's prisoners and that their females were dying."

"Why didn't you stop it?" She kept accusation from showing on her face, but it sharpened her tone. "If you knew about the victims, why let it go on?"

"I was gathering evidence against her just like Lor. I was about to turn everything over to him when Sevrin announced we were moving."

"That would have been a good time to turn yourself in," she pointed out.

"No it wasn't. I'd convinced Flynn to spy on her for me." He scoffed then shook his head. "Apparently, I wasn't the only one who took advantage of Flynn's weaknesses."

"None of that explains why you didn't shut her down."

"I wasn't in a position to 'shut her down', but I was determined to get myself into that position. I pissed her off hoping she'd punish my entire team. I needed them not to hunt, but I couldn't explain why my attitude had suddenly changed or it would have made Sevrin even more suspicious."

"Did it work? Did she forbid your team from hunting?"

She was firing off questions like a seasoned interrogator, not giving him time to concoct lies. "Yes. And during the move no one hunted, so no one was in danger. The lull gave me time to try to find her new headquarters."

"Did you find it?" Now her tone was tinged with challenge.

"No. Which was why I didn't turn myself in. We were your only link to Sevrin. If the Mystic Militia rounded up all the Shadow Assassins, Lor would have abolished any hope he had of finding Sevrin. And Sevrin was the real villain whether anyone on Ontariese wants to admit it or not."

"They're not as oblivious as you presume. But it doesn't change the fact that Shadow Assassins kidnapped human females and those females ended up dead."

"I agree. Those particular hunters must be punished, but none of them are on my team."

"No one on Team South hunted the entire time you were here on Earth?" Her disbelief was obvious.

"I knew you wouldn't believe me. This was a waste of breath."

Morgan stared at Nazerel's stubborn profile, not sure what he expected her to say. She wanted to believe him. God knew his story was compelling, but it also seemed a bit convenient. He didn't trust people in authority, for obvious reasons. If half of what Varrik reported about the elders was true, it was a wonder Nazerel trusted anyone. So it wasn't farfetched to believe that he'd try to go after Sevrin himself. The events supported his claim. Or his claim had been carefully crafted around the chain of events.

She sighed and drew her legs up closer to her chest. "Are we staying here all night? It's already pretty cold?"

His gaze narrowed, the expression part glare, part speculation. "Do not move."

She felt the terrifying weight settle over her muscles and then he flashed out of sight. Each breath was a tremendous effort and she couldn't even blink her eyes. Suddenly, the sensation passed and strength flowed back into her body.

Holy shit. This was her chance to escape, meager though it might be. She scrambled to her feet and threw off the blanket—and Nazerel returned.

"I must really be tired if the compulsion wore off that quickly." He moved the blankets out of the way and spread one of the sleeping bags he had bundled in his arms.

"You went to the campsite?"

He just smiled and continued to make their bed. He spread the sheet, the blanket, and finally the second sleeping bag. "This should keep us warm and snugly until morning."

She was too cold and too frustrated to argue with him. Sitting on the edge of the makeshift bed, she pulled off her boots then crawled between the layers.

A few minutes later he crawled in behind her and pressed himself against her back. One of his arms slipped beneath her neck and the other encircled her waist. "Would you like me to put you to sleep? It could be a long night."

"No," she stressed. "Stay out of my head."

He buried his face in her hair and inhaled.

I sense things, smell things, taste *things no human can understand.* The memory made her shiver and sent restless longing ricocheting through her body. Surely he hadn't meant what it sounded like he meant.

"Cold?" He pulled her tighter against him, amplifying the heat coming off his big body.

"What did you mean?" She hadn't meant to ask, but the question just slipped out.

He chuckled. "You'll have to be a little more specific."

"In the shower." Anxiety tightened her throat and kept her from blurting anything else.

"You know what I meant." He brushed her hair back and kissed the side of her neck. "I think you might even suspect I'm right. You're just not ready to admit it."

She rolled to her back and stared up at him, but the angle of the moon cast his face into deep shadow. All she could see was a faint blue glow coming from his eyes. "I'm attracted to you. As ridiculous as that is, I admit it. But that doesn't mean—"

He pressed his index finger to her lips, stemming her flow of words. "You're not ready. I accept that. You don't need to say any more."

She turned her head, dislodging his finger. "I will *never* be ready. Do you accept that?"

"I accept that you believe that at this point in time."

"You're impossible." She rolled back to her side and tried to ignore him. It was the only viable option when he was in this mood.

"There are significant advantages for a human when they bond with a Rodyte, especially a Shadow Assassin."

His tone was so light, so conversational that it made her smile. "Is that so?"

"Would you like to hear what they are?"

"Do I have a choice?"

He leaned in and whispered in her ear. "You can ignore me."

She chuckled, amazed by how easily he changed gears. "We both know how well I do that."

"Once the female's physiology transforms, making her more compatible with the male, she also becomes compatible with his nanites."

"How does that transformation take place? Does it happen with all Rodytes or just Shadow Assassins?" He'd piqued her curiosity. That was for sure. They were talking about the elusive ability that had originally drawn Sevrin's attention.

"The transformation is more dramatic with us, but it happens with every Rodyte."

"But how? What triggers the transformation?"

"Can't you guess?" He rocked his hips, subtlety rubbing against her. "Each time the couple mates, they become more compatible, more unified."

His lips brushed her neck, sending shivers down her spine. She swallowed hard and tried not to squirm. "And the nanites? What would they allow the females to do?"

"Nanites are what heals my injuries and eradicates illness. They would make you stronger and faster, healthier than—"

"We're not talking about me," she pointed out in a breathy rush. "We're speaking in generalities."

His arm slid up under her breasts, but he ignored her reminder. "You would live much longer than an ordinary human, as would our children."

Their children? She wanted to laugh, but the image formed, clear and tempting within her mind. Sweet round faces with auburn hair and blue-ringed eyes. Why was it so easy to picture a future at his side?

Because he was a master seducer! He literally taught others how to wear down the emotional defenses of their captive mates. Her mind tripped over the last phrase as she waited for a rush of righteous indignation. The thought once filled her with disgust and sympathy for the victims, yet all she felt now was discontent. She wanted, needed, something she refused to name.

"I'm not going to mate with you just so I can live for two hundred years."

"I wasn't suggesting you should. I just thought you should know."

She didn't respond, had no idea what he wanted her to say. Instead, she shoved the troubling thoughts to the back of her mind and closed her eyes. She tried to relax. A cold breeze caressed her cheek, but her body was cocooned in warmth. Their bed was surprisingly comfortable and his strong arms held her securely. The rest of the world had never felt so far away. It was just her and Nazerel, no conflict, no danger. She felt safe—which was utterly irrational!

Her eyes flew open and she stared into the darkness. How in God's creation could her enemy make her feel safe?

His tall form contoured to her back from neck to knees. He was just lying there, his breath teasing her hair. He wasn't touching her or trying to arouse her and yet her body ached for his. She pressed her bound wrists against her chest, as her nipples tingled for no apparent reason. She wanted him to kiss her, to hold her down and make her feel all the things she'd felt in the tent. But that was even more irrational than feeling safe in his arms.

She was the queen of hopeless relationships. That was all this was. In the back of her mind she knew nothing meaningful could come from this, so her body went haywire.

"Your pulse is erratic." His breath was warm on her neck and the arm at her waist slid up until it encountered her elbows. "What's the matter?"

"You're making me crazy and you know it."

"I'm just lying here holding you."

He was right. She was the one who couldn't stop wiggling, rubbing against him and... "Are you doing this intentionally?"

"Doing what?"

She pressed her lips together, refusing to speak the words.

"Do you ache, sweet Morgan?" He moved his arm down to her hips and realigned their bodies so she could feel how hard he'd gotten. "I'm not ashamed to say it. I need you. I want to be inside you more than anything."

She shook her head and tried to wiggle away as her body responded with a painful clench. "I can't."

"I know it's too soon for what I want, but there is no reason for you to be miserable. Let me touch you. I'll ease the ache. If you relax, then I'll be able to relax as well."

"No." She glared at him over her shoulder. "I don't need you to touch me. I need to be away from you." She even managed to sound determined rather than desperate, and still he chuckled.

"If you say so."

"Take me home. No one will expect that. I can't tell them where you're going because I don't know."

"That's not going to happen."

"I can't take any more of this," she cried. "Just let me go."

His arm tightened around her and his breath escaped in a long sigh. "I can't, *morautu*. You know I can't."

"Why?" She tried to turn back around, but his arm tightened, keeping her in place. "I don't understand why you're being so stubborn."

"Yes you do." He pressed another kiss to the side of her neck.

If he meant to take her off-world, she was doomed. She could not allow that to happen. "Once you get your 'insurance policy' from Phil, you won't need a hostage anymore. I am your hostage, Nazerel. That's all I am."

"Go to sleep." A hint of impatience crept into his tone.

She lay perfectly still, afraid to provoke him, yet not even close to falling asleep. How had she ended up in this hopeless situation? She reviewed each decision, each move she'd made, trying to figure out what she'd done wrong. There were no glaring errors. She was simply outmatched and she'd been out maneuvered every step of the way.

Maybe if he fell asleep, she could slip away and and...and what? She didn't have a flashlight much less a vehicle and Nazerel could hear her heartbeat. Tears of frustration gathered in her eyes and she furiously blinked them away. She couldn't give up. She *would not* give up. There had to be something she could do, some tactic she'd yet to try.

His hand stroked up her arm and then his lips brushed against her ear. "Go to sleep." When he whispered the words this time they were laced with gentle compulsion.

PHIL WAS WAITING FOR them in his tiny storefront bright and early the following morning. Disguised as a gritty pawn shop, the store was really just a cover for his interstellar trading, which had made him an extremely wealthy man. "This was not easy to come by, especially in the timeframe you gave me to do it."

"But you have what I need?" Nazerel asked hopefully.

"I do." He took a deep breath then blurted, "But my fee has doubled. I took significant risks and—"

"Done." He triggered the transfer with his comlink.

Phil confirmed the transfer then handed him a memory stick. "This contains everything you requested. I also transmitted the information directly to your device. Please verify it before you leave. I always strive for complete satisfaction."

Nazerel's comlink chimed and he navigated to the file that had just downloaded. He scrolled through the lengthy report, stopping every so often to verify the content, then nodded. "It looks good. Did you keep a copy?"

"No. I want no part in any of that." He sounded sincere, but Nazerel wasn't sure he believed him. This information was extremely valuable and Phil was first and foremost a businessman. But any threat at this point would be bluster. Nazerel wasn't sticking around long enough to enforce anything other than goodbye.

"As usual, it has been nice doing business with you."

"Likewise." For the first time since they met, Phil looked uncomfortable.

"I require a bit of privacy. May we exit through the back?"

"Of course."

He grasped Morgan's upper arm and dragged her through the shop. They emerged through the rear exit and found themselves in a tiny parking lot nestled between several buildings. Complete seclusion would have been better, but Nazerel was still regaining his strength after attempting to burn through the collar. This would have to do.

"Don't do this." She twisted her arm as she jerked against his hold. "There is no reason for you to take me with you. It makes no sense."

He yanked her to him, her back pressed against his chest as he pulled energy into his body with his other hand. The ground vibrated and clouds rolled across the sky, making the area dark and hazy. Morgan went wild, thrashing and kicking like a trapped animal. He tightened his arm around her waist, but otherwise ignored her. Ontarian Mystics called this Summoning the Storm. He didn't care what it was called as long as it brought him to his destination.

Multiple streaks of lightning flashed at exactly the same time. Wind gusted, rocking them forward then back. He raised his free hand and a slit formed directly in front of him. The opening widened as if someone were peeling back layers of space, creating a void in between the twin distortions. Inside the void bursts of color and light danced and darted against the darkness.

Morgan screamed, clawing at his forearm as her body trembled.

"Time to go," he shouted over the roaring wind. Then he wrapped both arms around her and leapt into the interdimensional portal.

Chapter Seven

A mental ping warned Varrik of Lor's telepathic approach. Rather than wait for Varrik to network with Echo, Lor simply sent his signal to them both. *We have a name. No guarantee that he's important, but he's gone way out of his way to conceal his identity. Oh and he just appeared fourteen years ago. There's no record of him at all before that.*

What's his name and where can we find him. Varrik was anxious to get moving. They had already wasted far too much time searching the deserted campsite for clues.

He goes by several, but the most documented is Phillip Mortsen. He runs a pawn shop in the seedy part of downtown Las Vegas. He rattled off an address.

Got it, Echo assured. Her memory was infallible, so Varrik believed her.

Go get him.

Varrik wasn't sure if Lor meant Phillip Mortsen or Nazerel, but it didn't matter. Hopefully one would lead to the other.

Teleporting to a place one had never visited before was tricky. Varrik had studied maps and images of Las Vegas and the state of Nevada, so he knew how to find the "seedy part of downtown". The exact location of the pawn shop, however, was more challenging. Echo had many skills. Teleporting just wasn't one of them. So she snuggled against his chest and he flashed them to the heart of downtown Las Vegas.

The continual bustle of Fremont Street was several blocks away, yet Echo motioned in the opposite direction. "It's four blocks over and two up."

She must have imprinted a city map on her memory. He was pretty sure this was her first visit to Earth. "Have you ever been here before?"

"I've been to Earth before, but this is my first time in Las Vegas."

Apparently, he shouldn't assume anything about his enigmatic mate. "How many times have you been to Earth?"

"This makes trip number four."

The area grew more neglected with each block they passed. Obviously the urban renewal efforts hadn't spread this far from the casinos, which were the lifeblood of this city. He moved closer to Echo, his hand finding its way to the small of her back.

She looked up at him and smiled. *I can take care of myself, love.*

He knew she was a competent fighter. Still no power in the universe could keep him from protecting his mate. Not even her stubbornness.

The pawn shop was cluttered and dingy, much like the neighborhood surrounding it. Varrik was loath to touch anything and anxious to finish their inquiries and move on.

It's designed to make people restless and uncomfortable, Echo cautioned. *This isn't a legitimate business.*

"Are you looking for anything in particular?" The proprietor or employee sat on a wooden stool behind a glass-topped display case. He was on the slim side of average with brown hair and brown eyes. He was neither handsome nor homely. Basically forgettable, which in itself made Varrik suspicious.

"Are you Phillip Mortsen?" Echo asked with a friendly smile.

"You can call me whatever you like." He returned her smile, but didn't answer the question.

Keep him talking, Varrik urged as he positioned himself to prevent their target from fleeing. If the man had something to hide and he could teleport, it was highly probable that he would have flashed to safety already.

"I'm interested in novelties, things I wouldn't find anywhere else."

The man glanced at Varrik for one assessing moment then returned his full attention to Echo. "I'm not sure anything I have can't be found anywhere else, but I've got lots of unusual items."

"Show me your favorite," she suggested.

Varrik eased into the man's mind with the lightest touch he could manage. His shields were much too dense to be inherent and the pattern was well organized, obviously a practiced skill. This was no innocent human. He pushed harder and the man snapped his head toward Varrik.

"What do you want?" All pretense of ignorance was gone and faint light glowed behind the contacts covering his eyes.

"Are you Phillip Mortsen?"

"Phil," he stressed. "Only my mother calls me Phillip."

"Well, Phil, you sold camping equipment to a very dangerous man. The campsite has been abandoned. Do you know where he went?"

Phil shrugged. "My interest in the transaction ended the moment his funds hit my account. I'm a business man. I have no interest in anything else."

"Lower your shields so I can verify your statement." Varrik moved closer, his gaze locked with Phil's. "If you cooperate, I will scan no deeper than that one transaction."

Slipping off the stool, Phil faced him, shoulders squared, head slightly titled. "What gives you the right to scan me at all? I've done nothing wrong."

"To operate a business on foreign soil you must have a government sponsor. Who is sponsoring you?" Phil reached under the counter and Varrik grabbed his wrist. "Slowly."

"You asked to see my charter." He pulled a laminated document out from one of the shelves behind the counter and placed it in front of Varrik. "Now show me your credentials."

Varrik pulled out his badge and flipped it open. "I'm on special assignment for the Ontarian Overlord."

"Good for you. I'm Bilarrian, so you have no jurisdiction over me."

"You did business with an Ontarian criminal. That gives me jurisdiction and the authority to scan your memories."

Phil rolled his eyes and made an impatient sound. "Then get it over with and get out of my shop."

Varrik eased back into Phil's mind and found his primary shields lowered. To a less skilled investigator, it would have appeared that Phil was cooperating fully. Varrik, however, was no ordinary investigator.

He'd spent decades learning how to manipulate memories. "You can show me the past two days or my mate will touch you and take the memories from you. We're only interested in your interaction with our target, but she will have access to every image, every thought, contained within those two days. The choice is yours."

"I've broken no laws. Both transactions were within the parameters of my charter." Phil's worried gaze shifted from Varrik to Echo and back.

"*Both* transactions?" Echo moved closer to Varrik. "What else did you sell our mutual acquaintance besides camping equipment?"

"I don't honestly know what it was. Some sort of scientific study. The whole thing was way above my head."

"And where did you get this 'scientific study'?" Varrik suspected he knew the subject of the study, but he had no idea how a Bilarrian trader would have gotten his hands on it.

"Our mutual acquaintance gave me a name, told me this other person owed him a debt of honor, but our mutual acquaintance couldn't contact him directly. I was basically a messenger. All I did was facilitate the exchange."

Varrik looked at Echo for a moment, but her expression was unreadable. *Do you believe him or do you need to touch him?*

I'm not sure yet.

Every time she absorbed a memory, it remained perfectly clear within her mind forever, so she only used her gift when there was no other choice. He turned back to Phil and asked, "Do you have a copy of the study?"

"No. I prefer to deal in merchandise. Information might pay better, but it always leads to trouble. I've stayed in business this long because I avoid trouble. Or at least I try to."

"But you had to have seen what you gave him. What was the study about?"

He swallowed hard then scrubbed the lower half of his face with one shaking hand. "I knew that man was trouble. Should have listened to my conscience rather than my wallet."

"What did you see?" Echo's tone coxed rather than demanded and Phil immediately looked at her.

"Genetics. There were diagrams with the DNA spiral and phrases like 'transition', 'controlled mutation' and 'empowered offspring'. That's honestly all I know."

Varrik wasn't surprised. Sevrin's research was the only scientific study conducted on Earth that would interest Nazerel. "Show me this other man's face and we'll be on our way."

Phil crossed his arms over his narrow chest, looking persecuted. "If anyone finds out I gave up one of my customers, I'll be finished on this planet—or dead. There are a lot of people who depend on the services I provide."

"No one needs to know." When Varrik eased back into Phil's mind all of his barriers were gone. He quickly located the pertinent memories and absorbed the necessary information. "I'd like to remove the memory of our visit so there will be nothing to incriminate you. Do you agree?"

"Only if you take it all. Wipe my memory of the last two days. I want no part in any of this."

It was a common request. Once people realized they were involved in something dangerous, they often wanted to turn back time. "I must implant a believable reason for the lost days or your natural curiosity won't leave the implant alone. Do you ever overindulge in alcohol or drugs?"

"Make it an illness. I've been sober for the past nine years."

"As you wish." Varrik meticulously erased the events involving Nazerel then constructed faint memories of a burning fever and long delirium. Erasing memories was a straight forward withdrawal of energy, while constructing them required a higher level of proficiency. Echo helped him return Phil to his stool and then they hurried from the shop. Phil would emerge from his trance in a few minutes feeling dazed and tired, but remembering nothing of their visit or his interaction with Nazerel.

"What did Phil show you? Who did Nazerel have Phil contact?" She slipped her hand into his as they walked briskly down the street.

"That's the problem with spies. If you find a motivation powerful enough to convince them to turn, it's likely someone else can find a similar motivation."

"Is that a convoluted way of saying Nazerel shamed Flynn into helping him?"

"Basically." He pulled her into a dank alleyway several blocks from Phil's shop. "We need to update Lor and find out exactly what Flynn gave Phil." She wrapped her arms around his back and pressed against his chest. He located the telepathic beckon pulsing in the transport deck of the Bunker. Short jumps were almost instantaneous and required little energy. Opening an interdimensional portal, on the other hand, could tire a Mystic for days afterwards.

They were greeted by an armed guard, but the soldier immediately lowered his weapon when he recognized the unannounced visitors.

"Where is Lor?" Varrik asked. "It's important."

"He's in his office, sir."

Rather than humiliate himself by asking directions from a human, Varrik pinged Lor's mind and requested the information telepathically. *We have news. Show me the way to your current location.*

Lor complied without slowing him down with questions. Varrik took Echo by the hand and hurried through the corridors. Elias was with Lor when they reached the small room that served as a command center/lounge. A cluttered desk and office chair had been arranged in the far corner, while an unmatched collection of furniture clustered around a vending machine and beverage station.

"What have you learned?" Lor appeared fully engaged though he remained seated on one of the couches.

Varrik glanced at Elias who sat in an adjacent chair. "What did you promise Flynn in exchange for his cooperation?"

Elias and Lor exchanged "oh shit" expressions before Elias said, "Basic amnesty. He helped us catch the others and his charges were dropped."

"Were there any conditions put upon the exchange? Any situation that would void the deal?"

"Just spill it, Varrik," Lor advised. "What have you learned?"

"Nazerel is out of the collar and Flynn gave him some sort of report. We need to find out exactly what the report contained. Where is Flynn right now?"

Lor scooted to the edge of his seat, looking progressively more uncomfortable. "He's locked in his quarters. His charges were dropped, but that doesn't mean we trust him. I'll summon him immediately."

"No," Elias cut in. "Have him escorted here by someone who can keep him from flashing. If he suspects we know he's been passing information to Nazerel, he'll take off."

Lor nodded then glanced off into the distance, likely making the arrangements Elias had suggested. His attention returned to Varrik as he asked, "Is Nazerel still on Earth?"

"We're not sure," Varrik admitted.

"Where would he go?" Echo mused. "He can't return to Ontariese and he has no living relatives left. He's a stranger in a—"

"He has relatives on Rodymia," Varrik corrected. "In fact most of the Shadow Assassins do."

"Do you?" The challenge in Lor's tone was unmistakable.

"I'm a direct descendant of the founder, so my father was born in the Shadow Maze. That's not true for most of the others. Their fathers, or occasionally their grandfathers, chose to leave their lives in the world above and become part of the world below. Many left brothers and sisters behind when they made their decision, which left relatives scattered across the face of Rodymia."

"Have many of them remained in contact with those family members?" Lor was clearly displeased with the revelation. "Why is this the first I've heard of Rodyte relatives? Was this taken into consideration by the Overlord and High Queen Charlotte?"

"Most Shadow Assassins didn't hold allegiance to any nation. We existed separate from the world above, so your laws and your leaders held no meaning for us."

"Our laws held no meaning?" Lor's tone took on a dangerous edge. "Disagreeing with our laws does not make you exempt from them."

"I was simply explaining the way Nazerel thinks. Most Shadow Assassins connect the Rodytes too closely with the elders and the elders were corrupt and cruel."

"But Nazerel is the exception?" Lor persisted.

Before Varrik could explain, Flynn was brought into the room between two Mystics. One of the Mystics grasped Flynn in two places, apparently keeping him from flashing out of sight.

"What is this about?" Flynn's indignation would have been more believable if his gaze hadn't been filled with fear.

Varrik crossed the room and looked deeply into Flynn's eyes. "We know you gave or sold Nazerel a detailed report. We also know it had to do with genetics and 'empowered offspring'. Now tell me what else was in the report and where you found the information."

For a long time Flynn just stared back at Varrik. He hated having to involve Echo in these situations, but they needed to know what Nazerel had planned. He raised his hand toward his mate without taking his gaze off Flynn.

"You're a traitor and I'm a coward," Flynn sneered. "Nazerel is the only one who has been loyal to the men through all of this. He has put himself on the line over and over. I will tell you nothing that endangers him."

"You don't have to tell me anything. I'll find out for myself." Without warning, he pressed his palms against the sides of Flynn's head. His mental touch was not gentle as it had been with Phil. He shoved into the traitor's mind and demanded answers. Flynn screamed and tried to shake him off, but the other Mystics held him firmly.

Echo's warm hand touched Varrik's shoulder. "Let me."

The two words held a wealth of meaning. He was furious and acting on anger never led to good decisions. He would likely damage as much of the information as he extracted until he calmed down. Bowing to the wisdom of her approach, he eased back and let her touch the side of Flynn's face.

When she finally stepped back from Flynn, she looked pale and her hands were shaking.

"Are you all right?" He wrapped his arm around her waist and helped her into one of the mismatched chairs.

"I'm fine. It always makes me shaky for a minute or two. It will pass."

"What did you see?" Lor wanted to know. He motioned to the Mystics and they dragged Flynn out of the room.

"Nazerel has all of Sevrin's research. Not just the summation you gave us, but her actual documentation."

"That can't be good." Elias pushed to his feet. "But Nazerel's not a scientist. What good does it do him?"

"I'm not sure what he has planned," Varrik admitted. "But there is only one place information like that has any real value."

"Rodymia," Lor, Elias and Echo all said at once.

Varrik nodded, but his expression remained grim. "It looks like Nazerel is going home."

NAZEREL'S ARM GRADUALLY released Morgan and she sank to her knees. Vertigo blurred her surroundings and softened the reality of what she had just experienced. Her stomach rebelled against the brutal acceleration and the ringing in her ears was starting to recede. She inhaled slowly, hoping the extra oxygen would clear her head. She'd heard descriptions of interdimensional travel, even seen a video of a Mystic Summoning the Storm, but nothing prepared her for the bone-jarring thrust of the conduit or the immense pulses of energy.

She heard voices, deep male voices speaking in a language she didn't understand. Nazerel grasped her forearm and pulled her to her feet as he said something to the two guards who still had their weapons trained on the intruders, namely Nazerel and her.

Finger-combing her hair back from her face, she caught her first unobstructed view of her surroundings. The textured floor flowed into matte gray walls without seams or separation. Faint colors, purple, blue and gold marbled through the metallic surface, keeping the area from looking like a prison. The wall to her left appeared to be some sort of control panel, but there was no furniture in the room, no obvious purpose other than a reception and perhaps departure area.

Her attention shifted to the guards when the room held little of interest. They were both wearing dark blue armor that seemed rigid one moment and supple the next. It followed every bend and curve of their muscular bodies or it had been sculpted to make them appear more impressive. Their weapons were sleek daggers with sharp-looking edges and controls were inset in the hilts. Could they launch projectiles or an energy stream from the blade? How the hell would they aim them? She'd never seen anything like them.

Nazerel motioned toward her and the lead guard nodded.

"What's going on? Where are we?"

"Silence," Nazerel snapped. Then in a sharp, impatient tone he added, "I'll explain everything when we're alone. Now lower your gaze."

She paused for another assessing glance at the guards, before following Nazerel's directive. Both guards had short dark hair, and blue-ringed dark eyes. The one who spoke most often also had cobalt strands threaded through his hair. Both had sharp, angular features and semi-hostile expressions.

The less-talkative guard motioned them onward while the apparent leader remained in the strange room. Nazerel's hand lingered on her arm as they followed the guard down one passageway after another. The corridors were rounded, making them feel more like tunnels than hallways and many of the walls had ladders leading to other levels. There were no windows, no natural light. Was this an underground complex like the Bunker?

Or were they on a spaceship?

The possibility dropped like a stone into the pit of Morgan's stomach. It wasn't as if her people had more hope of finding her on an alien planet than on a movable spaceship. Still, somehow the idea was even more daunting. If the guards' blue-ringed eyes and angular features were any indication, Nazerel was exploring his Rodyte heritage.

After indicating a doorway with a sharp jerk of his head, the guard strode back the way they'd come. Nazerel opened the door with a command in the same staccato language he'd been speaking with the guard.

She waited until the door closed behind them to speak. The room was small, the furniture built into the walls. It reminded her of the holding cells in the Bunker, an ultramodern prison cell. "Where are we? And why are we here?"

"We're docked at Space Station 438. And this is where I need to be."

She scowled at him, much too anxious to appreciate his sense of humor. "Spaceships dock at space stations. Are we on a spaceship?"

"This is the *Fotrastal*, which roughly translates to *Undaunted*. Welcome aboard." He looked around the room with obvious distaste. "Once the commander finds out we've arrived, I suspect he'll move us to more comfortable accommodations. The guard was being an ass."

"Are we in Rodyte space?"

He shrugged. "I think SS 438 is considered neutral, but the crew is Rodyte and I think that's what you're really asking."

"Why do you 'need to be' on the *Undaunted*?" It was unlikely he'd explain, but she had to try again.

He clasped his hands behind his back and stared past her. "I promised my men a better life, freedom and a chance at a future of which they could be proud. I haven't given up on that promise."

The answer surprised her. His men were in custody on Ontariese, likely headed to prison. How did he intend to change their situation from a Rodyte spaceship?

Before she could ask for a clarification, a buzzer sounded in the small room. Nazerel looked toward the door and spoke another Rodyte word. The door slid open and a robot rolled in. It was waist high and designed for function rather than form. A variety of appendages could be extended from the barrel-shaped body. It held a rimmed tray on which rested two small cylinders. It picked up one of the cylinders and held it out toward Nazerel as it spoke several words in Rodyte.

"What is that?" She was too curious to pretend indifference.

"Standard inoculation. It will protect you against alien microbes and suppress any you carry that might infect the crew."

He motioned her toward him, but she hesitated. "Is it safe for humans?"

"This formula is specifically engineered for humans." When she still hesitated, he went on, "You can't interact with any of the crew until you've been vaccinated. Do you really want to stay locked in this room indefinitely?"

Indefinitely? How long did he intend to keep her? There had to be a reason he brought her along. Beyond the fact that she was female. He'd only said that to rattle her cage. At least she prayed that had been his reason for being so hateful. "Is the other one for you?"

"I was vaccinated as a child." He picked up the other injector and dismissed the robot. "This one contains translator nanites. I thought you might want to understand what's being said around you."

He was going to inject her with alien technology? Dread washed over her in icy waves, but the alternative was worse. She could trust that he wouldn't harm her or she could remain locked away and be unable to understand anyone but him. Not a pleasant choice.

"I don't like this." Still, she crossed to him.

"I know." He pulled up the sleeve of her T-shirt and injected her with the vaccine. Then he turned her around and injected the translator nanites near the base of her skull. She'd barely felt the first injection, but the second stung like fire. She rubbed the area, hoping to disperse the pain. He walked across the room and tossed the injectors into a compartment near a different door than the one through which they'd entered. After waiting until she recovered, he asked, "Can you understand me?"

Her ears registered the alien words, yet her mind provided their meaning. "That's really weird. Will it allow me to speak Rodyte as well?"

"No. You'll need a language infusion at some point. This is a temporary workaround."

"Then no one on board will understand what I say?"

"Translator nanites are mandatory for members of the Rodyte military. You speak your language and they speak theirs. The nanites provide translations for both of you. But you can't issue voice commands or read Rodyte, which means you won't be able to operate most of the equipment."

"It's still pretty amazing."

The buzzer sounded again and when Nazerel called out, Morgan understood that the word meant "enter".

The door slid open and their visitor bounded into the room.

"Nazerel!" With unmistakable familiarity, the man surrounded Nazerel with a back-pounding bear hug. "Garin told me you were coming, but I didn't believe him. How in the five hells are you?"

They spoke in rapid Rodyte, yet Morgan easily followed along.

"Honestly, I've been better. But it's always great to see you." He returned the newcomer's hug then stepped back so he could more easily meet his gaze. Nazerel toped six feet by several inches and he still had to tilt his head back to look at his visitor. "Zilor, this is Morgan. Morgan, meet Zilor Nox, my cousin."

Zilor was a handsome devil with wavy dark hair that flowed past his shoulders and a beaming smile. Unlike the other Rodytes she'd seen, the rings in his dark eyes were a glittery shade of silver. He wore black pants and a formfitting shirt, primarily black with wide blue stripes down each side.

"It's nice to meet you, Morgan." Then without missing a beat, he asked, "Why are you in restraints?"

"Escape is no longer an issue." Nazerel decided with an unapologetic shrug. "I suppose I can release her."

"I'm glad, but why was escape an issue before."

Never one to ignore a possible opportunity, she moved closer to Zilor. "I'm his hostage. If you return me to Earth, I can see that you're well compensated by the US government."

Zilor chuckled, clearly unimpressed by her plea. "Sorry, doll. You'll have to take that up with Garin and I seriously doubt he'll intervene."

"Who is Garin?"

"*Pferitor* Garin Nox, commander of this ship and Zilor's oldest brother," Nazerel explained. "The closest human parallel would be a four star general. Garin's the reason I'm here."

Morgan sighed. If Garin and Zilor were brothers, then Nazerel was the commander's cousin. Zilor's friendliness had given her false hope. No one on board a Rodyte ship would give a damn about the plight of a human female. Rodytes might be technologically superior to humans, but their attitudes about females were primitive.

As if to prove her point, Zilor turned back to Nazerel and continued conversing as if she hadn't just told him she was here against her will.

"Garin has been in negotiations for the past three days. He hates dealing with temperamental diplomats, but he's good at it. Which is why Stirate Quinten trusts him with these situations."

"Any idea when he'll have time for me?"

"He'll *make* time for you, but it will probably be later tonight." He motioned to the room and shook his head. "Who put you in this closet? You need to be up on the officers' deck."

"May I have my own room?"

Zilor looked at her as if she'd just asked him to strangle a kitten. "And leave you unprotected? Garin would have my head."

"But Nazerel isn't protecting me." She held up her bound wrists as evidence. "I need protection from him."

Zilor laughed and slapped Nazerel on the back. "You have far to go with this one, brother."

"I'm well aware."

She seethed as they walked through the ship, but even her anger couldn't keep her from noticing how many men they passed or how far they traveled. They took an elevator from deck three to deck sixteen. The corridors were wider here, less claustrophobic, yet the crewmen still eyed her with obvious displeasure.

"Are females not allowed on board? Why is everyone glaring at me?"

She'd looked at Nazerel when she posed the questions, but Zilor answered, "It's your outfit. It's disrespectful for a female to appear in public in masculine garments."

She waited until he looked away to roll her eyes. What utter bullshit.

Zilor showed them to an apartment easily twice the size of the first. This one had a sitting area as well as a large bed. A bank of built-in cabinets extended the length of the far wall and a compact kitchenette was tucked into one corner, a workstation in another.

"The bathroom is through there." Zilor pointed out a door to the right of the kitchen area. "You'll have to register with security before you can use the data terminal, but I'll officially assign you the room. Once the room is assigned the door only responds to the resident. That will help keep your 'guest' safe. Everything else should function normally. Do you need anything else?"

"I need to speak with your brother," Nazerel grumbled.

"He's aware and he'll summon you as soon as he's available."

"Any chance of borrowing some clothes for Morgan? We don't want to agitate the crew every time we leave the cabin."

Zilor looked at Morgan intently for a moment. "I'll see what I can do."

"I appreciate it."

With a distracted wave, Zilor left the cabin.

"So what exactly is considered acceptable clothing for a female?" Morgan hadn't meant to sound so bitchy, but her patience had worn out hours before. "I'm not going to be wrapped up like a mummy."

"I'm not sure what a mummy is, but I don't think you'll object to Rodyte garments. I saw females on Earth wearing similar clothing."

"What's their objection to what I'm wearing now?"

"Pants are for males. Females wear skirts and dresses."

"Seriously? Females aren't allowed to wear pants?" Actually, she should have expected this. Everything she'd read indicated that their treatment of females was archaic. It was more surprising that they allowed females to cover themselves at all.

"Rodytes celebrate the differences between males and females rather than trying to meld the two into one as you've done on Earth." He shook his head then shuddered. "I've never seen so many effeminate males and masculine females. At times it was hard to tell one from the other."

She couldn't help but smile. "There are certain cities where that's more of a challenge than others. Las Vegas is definitely one of them."

"Well, there is no such confusion on Rodymia."

He sounded so superior, she had to challenge him. "There are no homosexuals on all of Rodymia?"

"What does sexual orientation have to do with anything?"

Now she was confused. Rather than delve deeper into an issue that had no bearing on her current situation, she waved it away. "Never mind." She held up her bound wrists. "Will you please unlock these cuffs, so I can take them off?"

"Do you promise to behave yourself?"

"Of course not," she shot back automatically.

"Then the cuffs stay locked."

"We're on an alien spaceship. What do you expect me to do?"

He moved toward her, his expression suddenly serious. "Zilor has a sense of humor. Garin does not. I expect you to be respectful and obedient. If I don't control you, Garin will. He cannot allow anyone to interfere with the smooth operation of this ship. Do you understand?"

"I don't understand why you dragged me along. I'm a liability, not an asset."

"You have details I didn't have time to confirm and a perspective that will be important once we start building a strategy."

"A strategy for what?" She was thrilled to hear him admit she had a purpose other than warming his bed, but she didn't understand what he was hoping to accomplish.

"I'll explain it all tonight." He pulled the key out of his pocket and released the locks. "If I can't convince Garin to join my cause, the rest is moot." He deftly unbuckled the straps and freed her from the cuffs. "If you embarrass me or cause any sort of disruption, I'll strip you naked and chain you to the bed. There are seven thousand male warriors on this ship. Zilor wasn't exaggerating. You must be protected."

She rubbed her wrists as she sank deeper into depression. She was a stranger in an alien dimension. She had no money, no form of identification. She could barely speak the language. Even if she managed to escape Nazerel and find her way off the ship, what would she do then? She had no way to contact Earth and it was highly doubtful anyone would help her. She'd been in some challenging situations before, but she'd never been this helpless.

He tossed the restraints on the bed and moved to the bare expanse of wall between the desk and kitchenette. "Display exterior view." The wall shimmered then transformed becoming a stunning image right out of a high-budget sci-fi movie. A small section of the space station filled most of the screen while the wedge of hull visible in the sharply angled view indicated the massive size of the *Undaunted*. And beyond the sharp angles and gleaming lights of both structures stretched the vast blackness of space.

She was in outer space. Even faced with visual proof of her situation, it was hard to believe.

Moving up beside him, she felt mesmerized by the grandeur of the surreal setting. "Have you been on this ship before? You seem pretty familiar with everything."

"The *Undaunted* has been in service for less than a year, but I've been on Garin's other ships." He stared at the display and offered no more information.

She didn't want to care about his past, tried to be as indifferent to him as he was to her. But she was curious by nature and so many things about Nazerel didn't fit his profile. "You were allowed to come and go as you pleased? But Varrik said—"

"Varrik was a sweeper. He had no reason to leave the Shadow Maze. And his uncle was controlling and cruel. North forced restrictions on his tribe that my father disregarded. No one in Tribe South was a prisoner. No one was forced to participate in a life they despised. Varrik told the high queen what she needed to hear so she would consider him a victim of circumstance."

"You're inferring that he lied, that his stories weren't accurate."

Leaning his shoulder against the wall, he pivoted toward her. "His stories were more or less accurate within Tribe North. But each tribe was led by a different elder."

"If this is true, why did no one speak up? Why didn't you?"

"We weren't given the opportunity to object. The queen's forces barged in and 'freed' us from centuries of tradition. No one asked us if we needed or even wanted to be rescued. They rounded us up like livestock and transported us to the City of Tears."

"Why didn't you teleport to safety if you were so opposed to being rescued?"

"And desert my men?" The idea was clearly abhorrent to him.

She'd read through Varrik's report, or rather skimmed the information. The details hadn't seemed important at the time. "Your traditions terrorized females and separated mothers from their children. Surely you see the cruelty of such practices."

"Our way of life was different from the norm. That doesn't mean it was evil. I did a lot of reading while I was on your planet. The Spartan culture wasn't the only one I found intriguing. Stories about the American West were particularly interesting."

She wasn't surprised that he'd felt an affinity for Native Americans. Parallels between the two cultures were easy to draw. In fact, she'd used the analogy herself a time or two. Still, she wanted to hear his conclusions so she could better understand his perspective. "In what way?"

"Native Americans were considered soulless savages and many of their traditions were ridiculed. They were feared and despised by those who did not understand them. And when others thought they knew what was best—and coveted their land—they were forced to abandon everything that made them unique and adopt the mannerisms of their enemies. Their way of life was not evil. It was just different. The Great Spirit was no less real to them than the God of the missionaries determined to 'save' them."

It was hard to argue when she agreed with most everything he'd said. "Freedom is important to you."

"Of course."

"What about your captives. I threw the first punch, so to speak, so you could argue that I deserve everything I'm getting. That's not true of the other female captives. They've done nothing other than be born female and their freedom was stolen along with their children. How would you react if your offspring was stolen from you?"

He clasped his hands behind his back and stared at the display again. "It was necessary."

"No, it wasn't. Forcing your will on your captives is just as wrong as having Varrik's decision forced on you. You can't complain about something of which you're also guilty. It's hypocritical."

He accepted the criticism with a stiff nod. "Still, we could have changed without abandoning everything we were. We were never given that option."

She couldn't argue with that, so she said nothing. He had some valid points and his willingness to debate made her even more curious to find out what he intended for that evening.

Chapter Eight

"**R**odymia is much smaller than Earth, but it is more densely populated. If that's where Nazerel has gone, how do we even start to find him?" Lor shook his head as a sigh of frustration escaped his mouth.

The office/lounge felt smaller than it had moments before. Varrik moved behind Echo's chair and rested his hands on her shoulders. The position was both protective and comforting. "He won't be on Rodymia." Varrik waited until Lor looked at him to continue. "He'll be on whatever ship Garin Nox is commanding."

"Who is Garin Nox?" Elias' long stride made pacing the room difficult. He was only able to take three steps before he pivoted and headed back in the other direction.

"Nazerel's cousin," Varrik explained. "Elder South was born Vortar Nox, youngest son of a very powerful Rodyte family. Rather than live in the shadow of his older brother and accept whatever scraps life left for him, Vortar joined the Shadow Assassins. He quickly rose through the ranks until he challenged the First Son of South during the transition festival and became Elder South. Garin Nox is the eldest son of South's brother, which makes him Nazerel's cousin according to human genealogy. Last I heard, Garin was about to be named *pferitor*, or general. I don't know his current assignment."

"Nazerel is cousins with a Rodyte general?" Elias sounded doubtful, yet the dread in his expression made it obvious he believed every word. "Why didn't he go straight to Rodymia when he decided to leave the City of Tears?"

"Sevrin promised him a mate with Mystic abilities. Someone like Echo. Wouldn't that have tempted you?" Varrik shifted his weight from one foot to the other. He was a man of action, debates and endless conversations always made him restless.

"How often did Nazerel sneak away from the Shadow Maze to visit his cousins?" Lor grumbled.

"There was no sneaking involved. South encouraged the visits. And the answer to your question is a couple of times a year. There are three Nox sons. As I said, Garin is the oldest."

Without explanation, Lor stood and walked over to his workstation. He didn't bother to sit down. With a few hand gestures he found what he needed. "General Garin Nox is assigned to the *Undaunted*."

"Damn." Varrik rubbed Echo's shoulders as much to calm himself as to comfort her. "I didn't realize it had been commissioned. It had yet to launch last I heard."

"What is the *Undaunted*?" Elias wanted to know.

"The Rodyte version of an aircraft carrier," Lor told him. "I saw some early specs of the ship. It's enormous." Lor returned to the seating area, but didn't sit down. Elias followed him, stepping to his side as Lor continued. "If that's where Nazerel has gone, it's time to involve High Queen Charlotte. We can't start a war with the Rodytes over one man."

"One man, his human hostage, and all of Sevrin's research," Elias reminded. "If this general gives the documentation to Quinten, he could easily pick up where Sevrin left off."

"Overlord Lyrik is a better choice than High Queen Charlotte," Varrik decided. "A military man will respond best to another military man."

Lor shook his head with sudden vehemence. "Not in this case. Overlord Lyrik can't go anywhere near Rodymia."

"And why is that?" Varrik didn't understand Lor's reaction.

"Lyrik killed Pern, or at least Quinton holds Lyrik responsible for his brother's death. It was actually an incorporeal entity that ended Pern's life, but—"

"Sounds like a story for another day," Elias suggested.

"Fine. But I don't think a diplomatic approach is the right strategy." Varrik shifted his hands to the back of Echo's chair.

"I doubt the Rodytes want a war over one man either," Echo mused. "I think we should find the *Undaunted*, figure out where the general is, flash to his location and explain that all we want is Nazerel and his hostage. There is no reason for the Rodytes to be involved."

"Garin will hand over Morgan and keep Nazerel," Lor predicted.

"Is that an acceptable outcome?" Elias looked at Varrik, but Lor responded first.

"No. Nazerel was the driving force behind this rebellion. He must stand trial or the others will become even more belligerent. The only way to permanently end this rebellion is to capture Nazerel."

"What about the report. We can't just leave that information with the Rodytes," Elias insisted.

"You're right," Varrik said. "Recovering the report is as important as rescuing Morgan."

"I didn't say that. Nothing is more important that rescuing Morgan."

"Let's focus on Morgan." Lor grew even more agitated. "I'm not sure we can do anything about the report. Thanks to Flynn, that ship has sailed. We could demand that they return the report or even steal it back from them, but we have no way of knowing who has seen it or how many copies exist. Besides it's more than likely Sevrin was forwarding updates to her uncle every time she made any sort of progress."

"We won't know what is or isn't possible until we assess the situation," Echo stressed. "Which means our first step is locating the *Undaunted*."

"HOW IS THIS LESS OFFENSIVE than my pants," Morgan cried as she looked at her reflection in the portion of the wall Nazerel had just transformed into a mirror.

"I told you it wasn't about modesty. It's about respect. Your pants might have covered more skin, but now you're unmistakably female."

"Yeah, a little too unmistakably." She tugged on the neckline of the dress, but the stiff material wouldn't budge. The fabric was gorgeous, a shiny midnight blue with a muted geometric pattern. It was the style she found objectionable.

"Truth be told, the only females on board are pleasure givers."

She scoffed as she tried to find an angle from which she didn't look like a trollop. "That explains a lot." A robot had delivered three dresses an hour ago. This was the least revealing of the three. The strapless bodice molded to her torso like a corset then the skirt flared dramatically to just below her knees. Her breasts swelled boldly into view and her waist looked incredibly small. If she weren't on a ship with thousands of men, she might not have felt so self-conscious.

"I think you look lovely."

Her gaze snapped to Nazerel's, sure he was mocking her. But his expression was unreadable, except for the obvious hunger in his eyes. She acknowledged the compliment with a tight smile as he moved up behind her.

"You should wear your hair up." He gathered the thick mass and held it near the back of her head. "Your neck and shoulders are breathtaking."

She eased to the side and shook her head, freeing her hair from between his fingers. "I'm not trying to steal anyone's breath."

He lowered his arms and closed his hands into fists. "You don't have to try and I think you know it. You're a very beautiful woman."

She knew that look, the literal burning deep in his eyes. "Nazerel." The warning sounded more like a sigh as he pulled her into his arms. "Zilor could be here any minute and I—"

His mouth silenced her, lips firm and demanding. He pressed her against him, his arms much more gentle than his mouth. His tongue caressed her lips as it eased deeper and deeper. She tried to resist him, wanted to remain passive until he gave up and turned her loose. But this was Nazerel. He never gave up and he never surrendered.

Gradually she relaxed into the security of his embrace. She stroked his tongue with hers and wrapped her arms around his back. He'd changed into a uniform similar to Zilor's. The pants were neatly tailored, but the shirt's clingy material outlined every bulge and ripple of Nazerel's torso. Her hands moved over the impressive terrain with hungry appreciation.

"I was unable to put myself to sleep," he whispered then kissed her again. "All night I lay there, surrounded by your smell, aching for the warmth of your body."

She was saved from responding by Zilor's arrival. Nazerel called out a greeting without releasing her. Their visitor hurried into the room and a knowing smile parted his lips, making him appear even more rakish. "Well done, Nazerel." He assessed her appearance with a less that polite sweep of his gaze. "She would look beautiful no matter what she wears, but this is much more respectable."

She shook her head and wiggled out of Nazerel's arms. "The Rodyte definition of respectable is confusing."

Zilor started to explain, but Nazerel stopped him. "She understands. She just doesn't agree."

"I see."

"Do I have time to fix my hair? I wasn't quite ready." She wasn't even wearing shoes. Not that anyone was looking that far down.

"Of course," Zilor assured her with another charming smile.

"Garin isn't typically patient, so don't dawdle."

She started to point out that he was the one who had slowed down her preparations, but didn't want to argue in front of Zilor. Nazerel's demeanor changed whenever his cousin was around. Nazerel became more assertive, more intolerant, more Rodyte.

Not wanting an audience, she grabbed the bag of toiletries they'd gotten from Phil and went into the bathroom. Or the Rodyte version of a bathroom. She'd needed a guided tour from Nazerel before she understood how everything worked. There were no fixed objects in the perfectly square space. Various appliances could be flipped, rolled or pulled into view depending on what the user needed. She pulled out the counter then touched the wall directly in front of her and uttered the word Nazerel had taught her. The surface above the counter became reflective.

Nazerel was right, her hair would look best up, but she wouldn't give him the satisfaction of following his advice. She combed out the tangles, then French braided it at an angle so the end rested over one shoulder. The simple style confined her hair and left her shoulders bare. She seldom bothered with makeup, but the dress called for a different look. She darkened her lashes with mascara and smoothed on a subtle lipstick.

She walked into the outer room and slipped her feet into the black flats also provided by the robot. "This is as good as it gets."

Zilor looked at Nazerel as if she'd said something outrageous. "Is your female blind?" Nazerel must have responded telepathically, because Zilor said, "I see."

"We better get moving," Nazerel suggested. "Garin hates being made to wait."

Nazerel walked at her side, his hand pressed against the small of her back. Zilor walked in front of them and it didn't take long for Morgan to suspect he was warning everyone off with some sort of signal. Those who couldn't duck into an adjoining corridor plastered themselves against the wall and turned their heads. No one made eye contact with her or Nazerel.

"Why is he doing that?" She glanced at Nazerel, though he didn't seem surprised by the crew's odd behavior.

"Having an unclaimed female on board is never a good idea. Zilor is just making sure everyone behaves."

"But how do they know I'm not..." Scent. They would smell her mate if she had been claimed. But all they smelled was female, so she was fair game. She shivered. It was all so animal.

Zilor turned down a short corridor that only led to one doorway. "You should address him as General Nox, not Garin. We use his given name because we're family."

"I understand."

"This is his private quarters, but he expects protocol to be followed at all times."

"Don't speak to him until he first speaks to you," Nazerel warned. "And even then it's best if you only answer his questions."

"O-kay." And she thought human protocols were needlessly formal. Apparently Rodyte generals were treated like English royalty. "Can I look at him or should I fold my hands in my lap and keep my gaze lowered?"

"Once he acknowledges you, you're free to look at him," Zilor told her. "If he chooses not to speak with you, then you basically don't exist."

"In that dress." Nazerel chuckled. "He'll want to know all about her."

Zilor didn't seem amused by the thought. "Which is why you should have claimed her before you brought her here. You are far too trusting of our familial ties."

"Meaning she's not safe with you?" Nazerel moved directly in front of him, chest puffed out, eyes instantly blazing.

Before Zilor could answer the challenge the door slid open and Morgan forgot to breathe. A man stood there, his shoulders nearly spanning the doorway. Though similar to Zilor's uniform, this man's shirt was accented with gold. He wasn't as tall as his younger brother and his features weren't as perfect, but he emanated authority without saying a word. His hair was short, his dark gaze sharp, the blue rings clearly visible though at the moment they weren't glowing.

He glanced at the two men who looked like they were about to come to blows then held out his hand to Morgan. "I'm General Nox. Nazerel never told me your name."

"It's Morgan." She placed her hand on his palm and his fingers closed into a firm yet painless grip.

"Welcome aboard the *Undaunted*." He pulled her across the threshold and into his private domain. But then the entire ship was his domain.

Unwilling to smile and pretend she wasn't bothered by the fact that she'd arrived in chains, she licked her lips and chose her words carefully. "I appreciate the welcome, sir, but I've been brought here against my will."

He paused and faced her, his expression unreadable. "I thought humans were fascinated by the unknown in general and aliens in particular. Have you ever been off-world before?"

"No, but—"

"You would squander the opportunity to experience things few on your planet will ever imagine simply because you were reluctant to begin the journey? That seems wasteful to me."

Though politely worded, the message was clear. He didn't give a damn that she was a prisoner. "I understand, General Nox. I'll endeavor to make the most of *each* opportunity." Hopefully, her message was just as clear. She had no intention of casually accepting her captivity.

He continued across the room, drawing her with him. "Morgan is an unusual name for a female, even on Earth."

Did he really know enough about Earth to make that assessment? "I'm aware." And she was tired of hearing about it.

One corner of his mouth turned up in the subtlest hint of a smile. "Now I've annoyed you." His gaze barely left her face even as they reached the table. "That wasn't my intention."

He seated her in the first chair on the near side of the rectangular table then took his place at the head, which put Morgan on his right. Her back was to much of the room, so she'd only gotten an overall impression of understated elegance and the Rodyte obsession with gray and black. There was a siting area to her right and a large desk to her left. The general's bedroom must be behind one of two doors adjacent to the dining area.

"When Rodyte children come of age they're encouraged to choose their adult name, something more suited to their personality and aspirations. Do humans have a similar custom?"

Garin shook out his napkin and spread it on his lap, so Morgan did the same. Still, it all felt a bit absurd. "There are many cultures on Earth. I'm from America and we don't have that sort of custom. We're stuck with the names our parents choose for us. I hated my name when I was a child, but it has become an asset in recent years."

"Really?" His gaze drifted no lower than her mouth and still he made her feel more vulnerable than Zilor had with his open appraisal. "Please explain."

"I chose a profession dominated by men. Often people judge my actions while under the impression that I'm male. It tends to lead to a fairer assessment."

Zilor sat down across from her and Nazerel took the chair to her right. Zilor had been worried that Garin would ignore her. The general's unwavering attention was even more disconcerting.

"Why did you choose a profession dominated by men?" He motioned to the young crewman standing stiffly by a beverage station. The crewman came alive and circled the table, filling the men's glasses with a murky blue liquid. When he reached her, however, he switched hands and filled her glass with a ruby-red drink. "It's Bilarrian blood wine. Most females find the taste pleasant."

She let the chauvinistic comment slide and motioned to his glass. "And what are you drinking?"

"It's called *g'haut*. There is no human equivalent."

"Is it harmful to humans?" She offered him her most angelic smile.

Garin chuckled and Nazerel began to fidget beside her. "It's really strong," Nazerel warned.

Drinking her coworkers—most of them men—under the table had become a matter of pride down through the years. Men were convinced that anyone who couldn't stand up to pee and devour massive quantities of alcohol was inferior. Even though she considered the attitude infantile, she loved proving the idiots wrong. "If General Nox has no objections, I'd like to at least try it."

Garin signaled the drink steward with a stiff nod and the young man presented her with a small amount of the blue beverage. Bracing herself for the worst, she tossed back half of the serving. She swallowed fast enough to prevent herself from gasping, but her chest burned and her stomach cramped as the liquor sank like liquid fire through her body.

"Would you like some more?" Garin was grinning now, and the smile softened his features, made him look more approachable.

She forced herself to inhale slowly even though her lungs were screaming for air. "No thank you." Blinking back the excess moisture from her eyes, she admitted, "I was just curious."

"I think you will find the blood wine more enjoyable."

She picked up the original glass and hesitated again. It really did look like blood.

Zilor winked at her. "The name refers to the color. There's no blood in it."

The taste was fruity like human wine, yet there was also a spicy heat. Still, it was far less abrasive than the *g'haut*. "It's delicious."

"It's still very potent, so sip it." The tension in Nazerel's jaw revealed his displeasure with Garin's fixation.

"Your occupation," Garin prompted.

"She's Morgan Hoyt director of the human taskforce assisting the Mystic Militia," Nazerel answered for her. "I explained about the taskforce in my last message. But as Morgan indicated, I thought she was male at the time."

"That wasn't the question." Impatience narrowed Garin's gaze, but he merely glanced at Nazerel then returned his attention to Morgan. "What made a woman like you join the FBI?"

Rather than starting a fight by asking him to define "a woman like you", she smoothly shifted the focus of the conversation. "Actually they recruited me, so you'd have to ask them about motivation. I am curious, however, how do you know about the FBI? Have you been to Earth?"

Though his smile failed to part his lips the expression was almost mischievous. "You would be horrified if you knew how many Rodytes had been to Earth." His penetrating gaze lingered for another moment, then he took a deep breath and looked at Nazerel. "So, is this another visit or are you finally home to stay?"

"That depends on you."

"Well, I want to hear all about your adventures on Earth, but not until we've eaten."

Summoned by the simple statement or some silent signal, a parade of young men filed into the room. They all wore a variation of the adult uniforms, black pants and fitted shirts, though the shirts were solid gray rather than color blocked like the men's. Not only was Morgan surprised by their silent efficiency, she was shocked by how young some of them were. "Are these boys members of the crew?" Afraid of insulting Garin she looked at Nazerel for the answer.

"In a manner of speaking," Zilor replied. "Most are battle born sons who have been discarded by their fathers. It's the military or a factory. They're not allowed into battle. If that's what you're worried about."

That was part of it, but she had many other questions. Were they educated? Who took care of them? Were they ever allowed to be children or were they treated like servants? She wisely kept her concerns to herself and focused on the food.

Though none of the dishes looked familiar, many were surprisingly tasty. There was an ornate knife and a combo utensil that looked like a fancy spork. Short prongs extended from the end of the spoon, which was turned sideways for use. Nazerel warned her each time something was particularly spicy. Zilor kept the conversation moving, which allowed her a few minutes to look at the brothers more closely. Their coloring and sculpted physics were similar, but that was true with every man she'd seen on board this ship. Garin's eyes were ringed in blue, while Zilor's were silver. And now that she could see them side by side, Zilor's features were much more angular, more exotic. Garin's jawline was imperiously square, yet his cheekbones weren't nearly as sharp.

"You've barely touched your food," Garin pointed out. "If our fare doesn't agree with you, I can have them bring whatever you like."

"No. This is delicious. I'm just distracted." She speared a piece of some sort of meat with the eating utensil, but the bite didn't make it to her mouth.

"Females are frequently distracted by Zilor's pretty face, but you've been staring at me as well. Tell me why."

It wasn't a request. She set down her spork. Nazerel reached over and lightly squeezed her leg, the warning unmistakable. "I didn't mean to offend. I'm curious by nature and it frequently gets me into trouble."

One of Garin's dark brows arched and his tense expression softened. "What were you wondering? I'm not easily offended."

Nazerel squeezed again. Apparently, he disagreed.

Entertained by the undercurrent, Morgan chose honesty over caution. "There's a resemblance between you and Zilor, yet not as much as I'd first thought. I was wondering if you shared both parents."

All of a sudden Zilor looked extremely uncomfortable. Garin must have assured him telepathically. After a tense nod in the general's direction, Zilor relaxed.

"The specifics of family connections are considered quite personal," Garin explained. "You're foreign, so I'll make an exception. But in the future avoid such questions."

"I apologize."

"We were born to the same father of different females," Garin told her.

"Garin was born to Father's *morautu*, his chosen mate," Zilor clarified. "Both Bandar and I were born to war brides." His brow creased and he glanced at Nazerel before asking, "Do you know what that means?"

"I do. You and Bandar are battle born." Her reply eased the tension twisting through the room, so she let the topic drop. Zilor had said brides plural, which indicated that he and Bandar had different mothers as well. She'd ask Nazerel later if her assumption was correct rather than continue the awkward conversation. "Thank you for indulging me. I really didn't mean to insult you."

So *morautu* meant chosen mate. Nazerel was right. She wasn't ready to think about all that might mean if she explored the concept.

They lapsed into silence as the boys cleared the table of everything but their glasses. Soon only the drink steward remained. Garin relaxed against the back of his chair and placed his hands on the padded armrests. He looked like an indolent king presiding over his court and finally his assessing gaze shifted to Nazerel. "So, what finally lured you away from the tender mercies of Ontariese?" No one could have missed the sarcasm in his tone. "I'd just about given up on ever having you among the members of my crew." A rhythmic tone drew Garin's attention toward the door. "You're late."

"It was unavoidable." The would-be visitor sounded even more impatient than Garin.

"Admission authorized."

The door slid open and Bandar stalked into the room. At least Morgan presumed the man was Bandar. He had the same dark, wavy hair as Zilor though his had been pulled back and bound at the nape of his neck. His firm jaw and square chin were nearly identical to Garin's, but Bandar's eyes were ringed in gold, the effect mesmerizing.

"Quadrant leader Lizten has finally seen the error of..." Bandar's gaze landed on Morgan and his steps slowed considerable. He skirted the table and sat beside Zilor, but he never completed his thought.

"Morgan meet my brother Bandar. Bandar this is Morgan Hoyt. She arrived with Nazerel." Garin paused for a drink before he looked at Bandar. "Update me later. We don't need to bore our guests with business."

Guests? Everyone was being polite and attentive, which only made their hypocrisy even more frustrating. This wasn't a social call. She was Nazerel's prisoner!

The drink steward placed a glass of *g'haut* in front of Bandar then hurried back to his station. Garin didn't ask his brother if he wanted anything to eat. Apparently, if someone was late for dinner on this ship, he went without.

"Nazerel was just about to update us on the developments since our last correspondence." He motioned toward Nazerel then resumed his relaxed pose. "Proceed."

Morgan sat silently steaming. Garin's politeness had made it obvious from the start that he wouldn't help her, but referring to her as a guest brought her frustration back to the surface. Enlisting the general's assistance had been the only reason she'd gone along with any of this. She was tempted to stand up and storm from the room, if the door would open and if she could find her way back to Nazerel's quarters. All the ifs kept her from indulging the impulse.

"I'm glad you're here, Bandar." Nazerel offered his cousin a quick smile. "This concerns all of us. In fact it concerns almost every man on this ship." He pulled in a deep breath before he began the explanation. "Shadow Assassins and battle born sons face the same long-term challenges. We're both considered inferior and are treated with distain by the societies responsible for our existence."

"I don't have all night, Nazerel. Get to the point. Did the bitch succeed or not?"

The bitch? Did he mean Sevrin? Of course he did. But how had a Rodyte general learned of experiments Sevrin was conducting on Earth? The Shadow Assassins had come from Ontariese.

Dread spread through Morgan with paralyzing force.

"According to Flynn much was accomplished in the past few weeks. Unfortunately, I recently learned that Flynn was a less reliable source than I'd first presumed." Nazerel shot her a sidelong glance, the brief connection filled with meaning.

"Why do you doubt what Flynn told you?" Zilor had seemed easygoing, almost playful since Morgan met him, but he was all business now.

"He was working with the Mystic Militia."

Suddenly everything snapped into place. Nazerel had never been a helpless victim of circumstance. He was General Nox's spy. Significance pressed her back into her chair. When Garin spoke of correspondence, he'd meant frequent and ongoing. Nazerel had kept his powerful cousin informed about everything that transpired on Earth. But why? Was this a roundabout way for Quinton to find out what Sevrin was doing or was this arrangement independent from the royals?

She wanted to grill Nazerel with questions and clearly demonstrate her indignation, but she remained silent and still, watching, listening for all the inferences woven through their words.

"According to Flynn, Sevrin's team succeeded in transferring Shadow Assassin abilities into several female hosts. All of the females were human, but many didn't survive the transformation. Technically her experiments were successful, but I believe the risks outweigh the gains. We need to focus our efforts in a different direction."

Morgan's fingernails bit into her palms. He spoke so dismissively, as if the victims were no more important than cultures in a petri dish. She'd sweat and bled in her efforts to end Sevrin's evil and he checked it off like any other item on an agenda.

"The alternative I'm about to suggest is safer, easier and much more reliable."

"Were you able to secure a copy of Sevrin's research?" Garin asked. "Even if we don't pursue that avenue, much can be learned from her progress."

"'Pursue that avenue'?" Morgan's control snapped. Pretending she was a willing guest was one thing. She was not going to sit here like a good little girl and listen to this. Rather than attack Garin directly, she turned nearly sideways in her chair and went after Nazerel. "You told me you were trying to stop Sevrin. You claimed you only allowed the murders to go on so you could find her lab and *shut her down*. What the hell is this?"

"Is she necessary for this conversation?" Garin's voice cracked like a whip and Moran risked a quick look at him. He sat forward in his chair, hands flat on the table, gaze cold yet blazing. This was General Nox, not cousin Garin.

"Actually, she is," Nazerel insisted. "Flynn has been compromised, so I need her to confirm any information given to us by him. That includes the final cache of data he sold me right before I left Earth."

"I'm not going to tell you anything," she sneered, not caring how disrespectful she sounded. "You dragged me here in chains. There is no way in hell I'm cooperating with any of you."

"Your cooperation isn't required." Nazerel's Rodyte heritage took over his personality whenever he was surrounded by other Rodytes. "I can access the information in your mind without your permission. It's less painful and much less damaging if you allow the scan, but I can force my way into your mind."

"This is your 'insurance policy', isn't it? You sold out every female on Earth so you didn't have to spend five years in an Ontarian detention center." She pushed back her chair and stood, glaring down at Nazerel. "You're worse than Sevrin. At least she came at us head-on. You're deceitful and duplicitous. Worse, you're a coward!"

Nazerel stood, the motion slow and menacing. He grabbed her upper arm then looked at Garin. "I'll return momentarily."

"That's fine, but she remains in your quarters until you've claimed her. I will not have a rebellious female inciting the crew. Is that understood?"

"Yes, sir."

"I'm serious, Nazerel. If you don't take care of this problem, I will give her to someone strong enough to tame her."

"I understand."

Chapter Nine

N o sooner had the door to Nazerel's quarter's closed behind them than Morgan flew at him. Unencumbered by restraints for the first time in days, she kicked and punched with remarkable strength and agility—for a human. Nazerel did little more than deflect her blows and avoid her kicks, hoping she would tire herself out. But she kept on. Calling him vile names and shouting accusations that were mostly true, at least from her perspective.

Finally tired of her tantrum, he caught her wrist and spun her around then jerked her tight against him, her back to his chest. "Calm. Down." He wrapped her tightly in his arms, ever mindful of her head. He didn't care if she slammed back into his chest, but one lucky impact with his chin could render him unconscious. "My intention is to negotiate with your planet not steal their females."

"I don't believe you." Her voice was muffled and tight as if she forced the words out between clenched teeth.

"It doesn't matter what you believe. Like it or not, this situation is beyond your control." Oh she didn't like that at all. She arched and twisted, then stomped on his foot. Her soft-soled flats were no match for his boots, so the attempt was merely annoying.

"Let go of me."

He wasn't fooled by her calm tone. She was still furious. "Do you know about the deal Pern made with the fifteen elite families?"

She heaved an exaggerated sigh as she wiggled one of her arms free. "That was thirty years ago and Pern is dead. What difference does it make now?"

"I'll explain, but I need to know if what you believe is anything close to the truth." She dug her fingernails into his wrist and tugged one of his arms away from her body. Needing to gage her reactions to his information, he allowed her to escape his embrace and turn around. "What were you told about those events?"

"The fifteen most powerful families on Rodymia funded Pern's last trip to Earth, so he promised them first pick of the empowered females."

"There were other stipulations, but that's the gist of it. Garin Nox is one of the men who was promised an empowered bride."

"Good for him. What does that have to do with anything?"

Nazerel tensed. Garin was right. Morgan's defiance was out of control. He'd been so enamored with her beauty and fiery personality that he'd allowed her belligerence. Most Rodyte males craved a spirted mate, but Morgan wasn't just spirited, she was disrespectful and rude. Like it or not, he needed to tame her and his leniency so far would make the process even more challenging.

His purpose for returning to Rodymia, however, must take precedence over his personal affairs. "During Pern's reign, the Nox family was the most powerful family on Rodymia. They're still rich and influential, but Quinton doesn't trust them. He will always see them as his brother's henchmen regardless of their actions over the past fifteen years."

"I'm still not seeing a connection." Her defiance had eased somewhat. Now she merely sounded impatient.

"Sevrin assured the elite families that she would uphold the conditions of her father's contract with them. Garin, and the others, only want what they were promised but Sevrin kept putting them off."

"They were promised the *victims* of Sevrin's experiments. If it weren't for the elite families' money, Pern wouldn't have been able to continue his research. You speak of these events as if they were harmless medical procedures. They weren't. People died and the elite families are partially to blame."

"I'm well aware of the victims. Many Shadow Assassins died too. Garin never would have made the deal with Pern, and his primary motivation for demanding his bride is to protect her from abuse."

"What about the other fourteen? Who will protect them?"

"He will."

Morgan laughed, the sound humorless and bitter. "And you gave him Sevrin's research for the same reason? To protect human females? Garin Nox must be the most philanthropic *general* the universe has ever known."

"I haven't given him anything and I'm not sure I will. Information is a form of power. The data is part of a much larger negotiation. I'm not sure when, how or *if* I'll use it."

"I don't believe you." She was shaking with suppressed rage, ready to explode into another fit of violence. Part of him wanted to encourage the reaction. She obviously needed the release and a period of vulnerability often followed such bursts of energy. He could use that openness to begin her training. It would allow him beyond her emotional barriers and—no. He was through manipulating her. Their battle of wills would be a fair fight and now was not the time to begin such a lengthy confrontation.

"This conversation is pointless. You need to calm down." He turned and headed for the door. One of her shoes thunked against the wall slightly to his left. The second one smacked the middle of his back half a second later. He started to turn around. Maybe he had time after all.

But the Nox brothers were waiting and the Shadow Assassins depended on him. He wasn't here to claim a mate. He was here to secure a future for his people. With a frustrated sigh, he hurried from the cabin without even looking back. She was too angry to listen to reason right now. She needed to calm down before he had any hope of making her understand.

He hurried back to Garin's quarters, knowing the general wouldn't wait indefinitely. The three brothers had moved to the sitting area, but they appeared relaxed and attentive.

"Sorry about the outburst. Morgan can be volatile." He crossed the room and chose a chair that allowed him to see the others without craning his neck.

"Fiery females have always intrigued me," Bandar said with a distant smile. "Do you intend to claim her or is she open to suitors?"

"I intend to claim her, likely tonight." All Bandar had done was pose a simple question and still Nazerel wanted to strangle him. It was never good to be so distracted by anything.

Garin's glass was nearly empty, but he waved away the drink steward. "Was Sevrin unable to locate the original females as I suspected or is she simply playing games with me?"

There was no easy way to broach the subject, so Nazerel just spit it out. "Sevrin is dead. She was killed by the Mystic Militia when they raided her lab two, or has it been three, days ago."

Setting his glass aside, Garin scooted to the edge of his seat. "And all of Pern's contracts become null and void with the death of his only heir."

Nazerel nodded. Garin didn't seem overly upset, but it was hard to tell with Garin. He had mastered his expressions long ago. Pern had other offspring, but Sevrin was the only one he had honored with a legal claim. All the others were simply battle born, unable to inherit his titles or fulfill his contracts.

"Does Quinton know?" Bandar's expressions were easier to read, though he often seemed grim and angry.

"The Ontarians will wait until they're good and ready before they inform Quinton, but he has spies everywhere."

"Unfortunately for him, most of them actually work for me." It wasn't an idle boast. Quinton wasn't well liked. None of the Keires had been, which made it easy for Garin to flip Quinton's informants. The problem with double agents was they notoriously flipped back whenever things became too dangerous.

"If he doesn't know about Sevrin already, it's just a matter of time before he learns."

"How much of Sevrin's research did she share with her uncle? Their relationship has always been strained."

Nazerel paused before he answered. Garin's interest in the data was understandable. It was also dangerous. If anyone had the moral fortitude to control something so powerful, it was Garin. Still, ultimate power corrupted ultimately. Nazerel didn't want to cause the downward spiral of one of the few honorable men he'd ever known. "According to Flynn she was playing the same game with Quinton that she was playing with you, excuses and evasions. She'd hint at developments that never happened, while she promised astonishing breakthroughs were just around the corner."

"Sevrin isn't or *wasn't* a scientist," Bandar pointed out. "What happed to her research team? They're the ones with the actual knowledge."

"Everyone was taken to Ontariese. If the Mystics are smart, they'll scan everyone for details and then scrub their minds of the memories."

Bandar waved away the possibility. "Ontarian Mystics are too squeamish for such a ruthless course of action. They'll give them a stern warning or make them sign a contract." He scoffed at the idea and shook his head. "Any chance we can intercept them before they're returned to Rodymia."

"Normally, I'd agree with you, but there's a new player on the Ontarian team."

"Varrik." Garin nodded. "No Shadow Assassin will settle for a diplomatic resolution."

"And he is now life bonded with the high queen's daughter," Nazerel reminded.

"A development, I still find hard to believe." Garin shook away the speculation then summarized. Keeping things clean and simple was what Garin did best. "So containment is our objective in regard to the research. If the Ontarians are foolish enough to release any of the scientists with their memories intact, we'll intercept them. Despite the very real temptation, such secrets are better left alone."

Relief washed over Nazerel. He needed Garin's power and influence, but he really hadn't wanted to keep Sevrin's research in play. It was time to move the conversation on toward other discoveries. "Flynn also provided me with copies of various messages."

"What sort of messages?" Garin's voice took on a growly undertone though Nazerel wasn't sure what caused the displeasure.

"The sort that confirm Quinton's duplicity. Even if Sevrin had managed to locate the empowered females—which I don't believe she did—they had no intention of turning them over as promised."

Despite the subtle tensing of his jaw, Garin appeared remarkably calm. "The entire situation became irrelevant the moment Sevrin died." No Rodyte accepted betrayal with such indifference. He had to be furious. Yet he was disciplined enough to know other things were more important right now. "You mentioned an alternative."

"Pern refused to divulge the specifics of his plan to even his closest allies. Your father assumed it was because they would object to the means by which Pern was producing empowered brides. The truth is much more interesting."

"Go on," Bandar urged. "Zilor hasn't said a world. Obviously, we're captivated."

Zilor punched Bandar in the arm and Bandar responded with a semi-playful push. It was easy to picture the two as boys, wrestling and chasing each other with enough enthusiasm to shake the house. Nazerel had always envied the closeness of the Nox brothers. Each challenge they faced, and there had been many, they faced together.

"Pern didn't genetically engineer empowered hybrids as he led everyone to believe." Suddenly three sets of eyes stared at Nazerel with rapt interest. "He stumbled upon a naturally occurring genetic anomaly."

"What sort of anomaly and how often does it occur?" Never one to mince words, Garin cut right to the heart of the matter.

"Every time a battle born male breeds with a human female their female offspring will possess magic abilities. They're usually similar to the father's, but there have been throwbacks to previous generations."

Zilor shook his head, clearly confused by the statement. "Battle born males don't have abilities. That's the problem."

"That's what you were taught, what they want you to believe, but it's not true. Battle born males can't access their abilities, but they possess them. Apparently the genetic anomaly requires two xx chromosomes to manifest. Whenever a y chromosome is present, the abilities remain dormant."

"Then only female offspring will be empowered?" Garin rubbed his chin as speculation narrowed his eyes.

"Yes, but it's consistent. Every single girl born to a battle born male and a human female will be able to manipulate magic."

"But this only happens when battle born males impregnate *human* females?" Bandar wanted to know.

Nazerel nodded. "It's a very specific equation. Human female plus Rodyte/Bilarrian hybrid male equals empowered female offspring. If even one of the constants changes in any way, the equation fails."

"Did the messages indicate if Quinton ever intended to tell us about this anomaly?" Bandar's eyes glinted dangerously. Of the three brothers, he was having the strongest reaction to the information. That wasn't surprising. Garin wasn't battle born and nothing bothered Zilor.

"I'm not sure Quinton knows about it. Pern was the one who identified the pattern and Sevrin understood the value of the information. I think she intended on using it against Quinton. All of the messages between Sevrin and Quinton dealt with genetic manipulation. I'm relatively sure Sevrin didn't share her secret with Quinton before the Mystic Militia ended her life."

"But the Ontarians know?" Zilor mused.

"They have many more reasons not to tell Quinton than to tell him," Nazerel pointed out.

"As do we." Bandar was still glowering.

"I agree," Garin stressed. "I'm not sure what, if anything, we should do with the information, but Quinton must never find out."

That really fired up Bandar. He slammed his empty glass down on the end table and shot to his feet. "You might not know what to do with this information, but I sure as damnation do! We've been treated like failures our entire lives. We are discarded by our families and forsaken by our government regardless of who sits on the throne. We're good enough for manual labor or to fight their endless wars, but beyond those roles we're unworthy. This changes everything. Within one generation, we can restore magic to the Rodyte people."

Well used to his brother's passionate outbursts, Garin remained seated. "What do you propose we do? Fly the *Undaunted* to Earth and demand that they turn over their females?"

"Of course not." Apparently Bandar had released enough of his ire to think again. "We could barter technology—"

"For eight hundred thousand females?" Zilor shook his head, but his smile was wistful. "That's how many we'd need. There are over a million battle born sons. Maybe half of those are still children, but you're still talking five or six hundred thousand females. No society is going to willingly give up that many of their citizens."

"But there are over seven *billion* humans," Bandar persisted. "Half a million would hardly be missed."

Garin shook his head, dismissing the subject outright. "A mass exit of the battle born would leave Rodymia defenseless. Even if we were welcomed with open arms by the humans, Quinton would have no choice but to pursue. I won't be responsible for starting a war between Rodymia and Earth." Bandar started to object, but Garin silenced him with an upraised hand. Instead he looked at Nazerel and asked, "If the equation only works with Rodyte/Bilarrian hybrids, how does this help the Shadow Assassins?"

Nazerel sighed as Garin pointed him back toward his own moral dilemma. "It doesn't. I'm faced with a difficult choice as well. We, the Shadow Assassins, can subtly blend with the population of Earth and live as humans or we can perfect Sevrin's formula and transform our females into mates worthy of our seed. She hadn't even begun on the Rodyte formula, but the Ontarian formula was basically finished."

"And that's where I come in?" A calculative smile spread across Garin's mouth without parting his lips. "You want my scientists to perfect the formula, but you're worried that I won't stop there."

"No, sir." He used the title intentionally, making sure Garin understood that he was negotiation with General Nox not asking a favor of his cousin. "I trust you implicitly. I'm concerned that a secret this powerful would slip beyond your control regardless of the procedures you put in place to prevent it."

"We have two choices," Garin said. "And both are dependent upon what Quinton already knows. If Sevrin kept him informed every step of the way, then it's a race to the finish line. We lose nothing by participating in the competition and it will allow us some control over how the formula is used. However, if Quinton knows little or nothing, which is more likely, then we must ensure that it stays that way. Unfortunately, that requires that we leave the formula untouched and destroy all evidence of Sevrin's research."

"I understand and I agree. Obviously, I'm horribly tempted by the possibility of transforming my mate into a being of power. But I've also seen where such ambitions lead. If Sevrin's secrets followed her to the grave, I am more than willing to leave them there."

"But what about the genetic anomaly? We haven't decided what to do about that."

Garin glared at Bandar as he pushed to his feet. "The decision has been made. You just don't agree with it and I will not argue the point. You're dismissed."

Bandar's back straightened and he squared his shoulders, but his gaze remained defiant. "As you say, *sir.*" Without another word he rushed from the room.

"At the risk of starting a fight." Zilor paused for a quick smile. "I agree with Bandar. A mass exodus isn't the answer, but we need to think about other ways to take advantage of this opportunity. Producing empowered daughters would prove beyond doubt that we are not expendable."

"I am not battle born, but the vast majority of this crew is. Anything that concerns this crew concerns me. I've just begun to analyze the possibilities. This thing is far from over."

Zilor shook his head as his smile broadened. "And you couldn't say that to Bandar?"

"Bandar was arguing with me. He knows better."

"Everyone knows better than arguing with you." Zilor stood and looked at Nazerel. "Do you need help with Morgan? Taming the wild ones is my specialty."

"In your dreams," Nazerel shot back.

"Very likely." Zilor chuckled and headed for the door." Enjoy yourself."

After Zilor left, Garin shifted his chair toward Nazerel. "This is quite a tangle you've brought to my door."

"I know, but there is no one else in the universe I trust with something this important. As Bandar said, this could change everything for the battle born. They have been taken for granted for far too long."

"I'll see what I can do to defuse the situation with Overlord Lyrik. I don't know him well, but we've interacted a time or two." Garin crossed his legs and leaned into the back of his chair, looking more relaxed than he had all evening.

"I appreciate any assistance you can give me. As you said, I've dug quite a hole for myself."

"But I put the shovel in your hands. The overlord needs to understand that you were acting on my behest and your actions were sanctioned by the crown."

Nazerel didn't argue. Garin had technically dispatched him to Earth, but Nazerel had been desperate for any excuse to escape the City of Tears. "They'll demand some form of retribution and I'm prepared to pay. Still, they need to understand that Varrik is one voice among many, yet his was the only one they heard."

"Then you're going to turn yourself in?" Garin didn't sound pleased by the idea.

"I can't improve the situation for my people unless I take responsibility for the choices I made. There is no future for them on Ontariese. Not only are they feared and reviled, but there aren't enough females for the Ontarian males. My men have no hope of claiming mates. They must be given other options."

"Speaking of claiming mates." A lazy smile finally parted Garin's lips and he picked up his nearly empty glass of *g'haut*. "What is Morgan's story? I know she's your prisoner, but her feelings for you are not entirely hostile." Garin had never admitted that he was empathic, at least not to Nazerel. Still, what the general sensed about others was often too specific, and too accurate, to have been conjecture.

"Morgan led the raid on my team, though I didn't know who she was when I grabbed her. I only intended to use her long enough to escape, but things got complicated fast."

Amusement lightened Garin's tone as he said, "No doubt. I know you don't want my advice, but I'm going to give it to you anyway. She's obviously proud and she's used to authority. A woman like that isn't going to allow herself to surrender to an enemy. Ignore everything she says, or better yet gag her, and then scan her emotions. Emotions don't lie. If she feels nothing but fear and anger, I'll help you protect her. But if she desires you, as I suspect, claim her tonight. She will be much safer if your scent is all over her."

Nazerel knew Garin meant well, but he found the advice insulting. He would never force himself on an unwilling female for any reason, so the option was unnecessary. As for seducing Morgan, he already knew she desired him. He also knew she was worlds away from admitting the fact even to herself, so tonight was going to require serious creativity. "If she remains unclaimed by morning, I will accept your assistance. But I haven't given up hope for tonight."

MORGAN PACED NAZEREL'S cabin, her bare feet soundless despite her agitation. He'd been gone at least an hour, likely closer to two. But time was hard to gage in her current state of mind. Nazerel was with the Nox brothers right now, planning the invasion of Earth. She'd frequently thought information on the Shadow Assassins had to be exaggerated. How could such barbaric attitudes still exist in this modern age? Then she'd met a few Rodytes.

If you don't take care of this problem, I will give her to someone strong enough to tame her. The general's hateful ultimatum still echoed through her mind. If Garin had only said it to rile her, then he was the best actor she'd ever encountered. No, he'd been deadly serious about what he expected from Nazerel. What he expected from her.

She'd never been this angry and had never had so little control over her circumstances. Regardless of how furious Nazerel made her, she was utterly dependent on him, which scared the hell out of her. All of her skills and training meant nothing on an alien spaceship filled with sex-starved males.

"Shit!" she cried, unable to suppress her frustration. She needed to focus, to decide on her next move. Yet screaming and smashing every object in the room was much more appealing. None of it would do any good, of course. But it might make her feel better. She was trapped and helpless. She couldn't even take off this ridiculous dress. None of the cabinets would open without the proper voice command so she had nothing else to put on.

She couldn't believe how gullible she'd been. Nazerel's unexpected charm and superficial sincerity had convinced her he wasn't the villain she'd originally believed. Then they'd arrived on the *Undaunted* and she'd seen behind his mask. He was every bit as ruthless as everyone claimed. Not only had he given Sevrin's research to a man with the resources to continue her work, but he'd probably told the Rodytes about the genetic anomaly.

Pausing for a moment, she felt a spark of hope flicker in the back of her mind. All Nazerel had said was he had an alternative that was safer and more dependable than the transformation formula. Was it possible Nazerel didn't know about the genetic anomaly?

But Flynn knew, which meant Nazerel likely knew. She sighed. Flynn was a double-dealing jerk who'd played each side against the other. His only true allegiance was to himself.

The door hissed then slid open and Nazerel walked in, dangerously handsome and composed. He carried a metallic decanter and two glasses. Were they going to toast the subjugation of Earth or just the mass kidnapping of human females?

"If you were waiting for me to calm down, you need to come back," she warned him. "I'm still pissed."

Pausing near the door until the portal closed behind him, he then crossed to the table near the kitchenette and set down the glasses and the decanter. "I understand why you're angry, but you don't have all the facts."

"Really?" She dragged the elastic band off the end of her hair and quickly unwove the braid. "You paid Flynn for Sevrin's research then gave it to a Rodyte general who obviously has the means to pick up where Sevrin left off."

"Garin doesn't have the research and I won't give it to him unless we find out that Quinton has it as well."

The revelation took a bit of the wind out of her sails, but only a bit. She dragged her fingers through her hair as she glared at him.

She needed to stay angry, needed to distance herself from the savage attraction drawing her to him. "Why the stipulation?"

"If Quinton controls the formula, he literally decides who accesses magic and who is left depending on technology. That's too much power for any one person."

"And if Sevrin didn't keep Quinton in the loop, what will you do with the data?" *Think. Focus on facts and implications.* She couldn't allow herself to notice how well the austere uniform suited him or how accurately the top outlined his chest and abdomen.

"I'll destroy it," he said emphatically. "Both Garin and I think that's what will happen. We'll contain the fallout and make sure no one opens Pandora's Box."

His easy use of human vernacular always surprised her. How much had he known about Earth before Sevrin stranded him in a house with nothing to do but surf the internet and watch TV? There were still holes in his understanding, but he'd assimilated a remarkable amount in a few short months. "Even if I agree with the strategy, that's not all you did. Was it? You also promised them an even better alternative. Care to explain what the hell that meant?"

"I know about the genetic anomaly."

Damn it! For half a second she'd allowed herself to hope he'd meant something else, something that didn't involve human females. "You told the Rodytes that empowered children are waiting for them on Earth. All they have to do is claim a human female and all of their daughters will be extraordinary?"

Tension rippled across his shoulders though his voice remained calm. "So think of it from the female perspective. Human females can make each of their daughters stronger, healthier and more intelligent by breeding with battle born males. Have you forgotten what I told you on the mountain? Bonding with a Rodyte will more than double the life expectancy of a human female, as well as making her stronger and healthier during those extra years. Why wouldn't you tell your friends, spread it all over the internet, maybe call a press conference?"

"It's not the same," she cried.

"It's exactly the same."

"You've dangled my species in front of your cousins like a pirate's treasure. You've made my world more vulnerable than Sevrin ever did. And I don't even understand what you gain by betraying us like this. The equation doesn't work for you." Her voice had grown shrill, so she took a deep breath and tried to rein in her emotions. This was beyond disastrous. "You've offered them the answer to their prayers, a way to rise above their mediocrity. Who could resist such a promise?"

"A promise is all it is, *morautu*. Two thirds of the Rodyte military is made up of battle born soldiers. If they all ran off to Earth, Rodymia would be defenseless. No one—including Garin Nox—will allow that to happen."

His assurance was much less distracting than the name he kept calling her. Each time he uttered the word his voice became soft and caressing.

"Then why are you here?" she asked instead. "What do you gain by sharing all of this with General Nox?"

He poured blood wine into both the glasses and handed her one. "I'm just completing my mission."

"What mission?" She took the glass from his outstretched hand, unable to resist the temptation. Maybe the wine would help settle her nerves and make her feel less jittery.

"When Sevrin originally contacted me, I had no idea what she wanted and she wouldn't specify. Garin, the entire Nox family, has been in political limbo ever since Pern died. Quinton doesn't trust them, yet Sevrin isn't strong enough to restore the power they once commanded."

"So Garin told you to spy on Sevrin?" He nodded, but didn't elaborate. "Isn't she supposed to be an ally of the Nox family?"

"Exactly. She's *supposed* to be their ally, yet she'd grown secretive and scattered." He paused then sighed. "As with everything, it's more complicated than just Sevrin and Garin."

Despite her lingering anger, she allowed herself to smile. "Well, try to summarize."

"Sevrin had been playing games with Quinton too. So Quinton talked to Garin, asked if he knew anyone who could get close to Sevrin, maybe find out what she was really doing on Earth."

"This was after Garin had already decided to send you?"

"Just before I was scheduled to leave. Garin let Quinton think it was a huge imposition, an 'I will but you'll owe me' sort of thing. Royal promises are a handy thing to stash away for a rainy day."

"So Quinton thinks you're spying for him, but you're actually working for Garin."

"That's the ultra-simplified version of events."

She had to admit it was clever and she could appreciate a sound strategy. Sound strategy? She tensed. Is that what this was to Nazerel? He was filling her mind with intriguing information as he waited for her emotions to subside. And eroding her anger left her open to his appeal.

She knew where this night was headed. It was basically inevitable. Still, she couldn't let him win this easily. She avoided his gaze, knew the power of those night-black eyes. Yet his fingers looked long and strong against the narrow glass. His muscular arms were easily capable of holding her down while he kissed her senseless. His mouth would taste sweet and spicy from the wine. She licked her lips, barely able to remember what they were talking about.

Nazerel's mission. The fact that Nazerel was a spy didn't excuse what he'd done, or more accurately, what he'd allowed others to do. "Why didn't Garin pull you once you found out what Sevrin's project was about?"

A harsh sort of laugh escaped his throat and he took a long drink of wine. "Do you honestly think Sevrin trusted me with the details? She claimed she could transfer Shadow Assassin abilities into human females. I thought she was full of shit, but I had to stick around long enough to find out how many of her claims were true and why she needed Shadow Assassins to accomplish her goals. Why didn't she use Bilarrians or Ontarian Mystics?"

He had a right to protect his people, but not at the cost of hers. "It couldn't have taken you long to find out the answers to those questions. Why did you let it go on, and on?"

"Again you're overestimating the relationship I had with Sevrin. Flynn was my primary source of information and, thanks to you, I'm not sure I can trust anything he told me."

They were arguing in circles and the issues were becoming more and more transparent. This wasn't a real conversation. It was a stall tactic. Even so, she couldn't seem to stop. "Sevrin is dead and your men are back on Ontariese, so what is General Nox's interest in all this?"

"Garin thought Sevrin had lost track of the empowered females her father had promised the elite families and her new project was a desperate attempt at fulfilling the contract."

"Was he right?" Her taskforce had managed to learn most of what Sevrin had done, but no one understood why the ruthless bitch did anything.

"That might have been how this started, but that wasn't where it led. We're pretty sure Sevrin's true aspiration was to overthrow Quinton with the help of her empowered army."

"And rule as Rodymia's first empowered queen?"

"Crown Stirate, but yes. She wanted it all."

What Sevrin wanted was irrelevant now. All of her scheming failed and she'd died at the hands of her enemies. Morgan might have a clearer picture of Nazerel's role, but she wasn't sure the Ontarians would consider any of this justification for what Nazerel had done. Still, his words rang true.

"So you've reported in with your handler," she concluded, "what now?"

"That depends on you."

"Really." She took several sips of wine then prompted, "How does any of this depend on me?"

He closed the distance between them and took her nearly empty glass from her hand. After setting both glasses aside, he placed his hands on her shoulders. "You're too smart not to understand what comes next. The only question is how is it going to happen?"

She tried to disguise her nervous laugh as a cough, but that only made her sound strangled. "Do I get to choose a position?"

"You can stay locked in this room until I'm ready to return you to Earth or—"

"When will you return me to Earth? If we leave now, I won't press charges."

He ignored the interruption and completed the ultimatum. "Or we can finish what we started in the tent."

She was about to tell him she was fine with confinement, but he didn't give her the chance. He pulled her into his arms and silenced her with his mouth. Yet the kiss was filled with longing not demand. His arms held her securely against his chest as his lips moved over hers.

Her pride required that she resist. He'd just exposed human females to an unprecedented threat and now he expected her to fall into bed with him. Her mind registered the irony, yet her body didn't give a damn. He was fierce and determined, more exciting than any man she'd ever known. She wanted him, had longed from this moment ever since their first kiss.

Tugging his shirt out from inside his pants, she slipped her hands under the clingy fabric. His back was warm and broad, the muscles flexing beneath her touch. He eased his tongue into her mouth and she pressed even closer. The spicy/sweet taste of blood wine lingered in his mouth, making the kiss even more intoxicating. She curled her tongue around his and dug her fingernails into his back, wanting him closer. Needing...just needing.

He framed her face with his hands as he slowly pulled away. Their gazes locked and his breath warmed her parted lips. "You can pretend Garin gave us no choice, but I've wanted this since I first saw your face."

Not ready to speak the words, she pushed to the balls of her feet and pressed her mouth to his. He accepted her silent assent with a passionate growl then continued kissing her. She tugged his shirt up until it bunched beneath his arms. He tore his mouth from hers long enough to rid himself of the shirt then went right back to kissing her. They clung to each other, hearts pounding, breaths mingling as they exhaled in harsh pants.

"This is crazy," she whispered more to herself than to him. "I should hate you."

"But you don't." It was a statement not a question.

"I can't want you. It's disloyal."

He stroked her lower lip with the pad of his thumb as he gazed deep into her eyes. "Disloyal to whom? There is no male in your life."

"To my team, my gender, my *planet*," she cried. "You're more dangerous than Sevrin by far."

"Not to you, never to you." Apparently tired of her arguments, he swept her up in his arms and carried her to the bed.

Garin had given her the perfect excuse for allowing this to happen, yet Morgan tried not to lie to herself. She wasn't reluctantly allowing Nazerel to "claim" her so the other seven thousand males would leave her alone. She was allowing herself to surrender because she needed this release. She needed to be selfish and irresponsible, and Nazerel attracted her like metal to a magnet.

His chest was warm, his neck even warmer. She curled into the security of his embrace and let go of her inhibitions. She was surrounded by people who depended on her strength and composure, her logic and strategies. Was it really so surprising that she wanted to revel in mindless passion for one night?

But was this only for one night?

He set her down beside the bed and reached back to release the fastenings on her dress. His expression was intense, hungry. She grabbed his upper arms. "This is just sex, right? You're not going to form any sort of bond?"

His fingers splayed against her back and his gaze bore into hers. "Forcing a bond into an unwilling mind is dangerous and it corrupts the connection. Even if that weren't true, I would never do that to any female, much less one I—" He stopped himself from finishing the thought and glanced away from her face. "This is just sex."

Chapter Ten

"This is just sex." The lie tasted foul in Nazerel's mouth, but he knew Morgan wasn't ready for any other answer. Their attraction was unexpected and inconvenient, yet trying to resist the forces drawing them together was pointless. He'd had sex often enough to know that this was something different, something deeper than just a physical joining.

She slowly let go of his arms and lowered her hands to her sides. "What does *morautu* mean?"

Taking advantage of her distraction, he unfastened the back of her dress. "What do you think it means?"

"Zilor said Garin's mother was a *morautu,* a chosen mate. But you make it sound more like honey or sweetheart."

"And that upsets you?" The word was an endearment, but nothing so generic as sweetheart. The meaning was specific and intensely intimate. When she was ready to hear the explanation he'd tell her exactly what it meant, but not until she was ready.

A millisecond before the dress slipped away from her body, she pressed the front against her breasts. "I didn't say it upset me. It just seems odd to be called sweetheart by my enemy."

He caught her wrists and pulled her hands away from her chest. The dress slid to her hips, exposing her breasts. His breath caught in his throat and his already hard cock jerked in appreciation of the sight. "We're not enemies tonight." He looked into her eyes then at her breasts, not willing to pretend he didn't find her amazing. "We're two consenting adults who need a few hours away from reality."

She wiggled and the dress pooled around her ankles, baring the rest of her body. Surprise spiraled through his system, lust half a step behind. She wasn't wearing undergarments of any kind.

"Apparently pleasure givers aren't big on underwear." Her cheeks flamed, the flush spreading onto her upper chest.

She'd sat there all evening, surrounded by Rodyte warriors, wearing nothing but that alluring dress. Nazerel could have slipped his hand up under her skirt and touched her naked flesh. None would have been the wiser. Until her scent filled the cabin and drove them all into a lustful rage. He would have been forced to fight off his cousins and claim her right there on the dining room table. A dark smile curved his lips. The scene appealed to the most savage part of his nature. It was fortunate for her that he hadn't known until now.

"I'm certainly not complaining." He wrapped one arm around her waist and cradled the back of her head with his other hand. "You were stunning in that dress, but you're even more beautiful without it." He lowered his head before she could reply.

Her lips parted for his and he pushed his tongue deep into her mouth, savoring the heat and softness. She caressed his arms and back as she sensually rubbed against him. He could smell her arousal, knew she was wet and ready for him. But, if she had her way, this would be their only night together. He intended to take his time and savor every moment she was naked and willing in his arms.

He urged her backward. The bunk's edge connected with her knees and she automatically sat. Her hands trailed down his chest and came to rest on his hips. Her gaze traveled even lower. She licked her lips and desire clasped Nazerel's body like a punishing fist. Ever since she touched him in the shower he'd been tormented by the image of her on her knees, naked and eager as he slid in and out of her mouth.

She reached for his pants, her fingers lightly brushing the bulge barely contained within. He hissed and caught her wrists. "I want you too badly for that, at least right now." He moved her hands to each side and slightly behind her then knelt on the floor. He eased her legs apart, making room for him between her knees.

"What about me?" She tried to bring her legs back together, but he moved closer and pushed her legs even farther apart. "I want you just as badly."

"Do you? That's hard to believe." Challenge rang through his words and he slid his hand up her leg. He teased her inner thigh, his touch creeping higher and higher.

She tensed, her muscles quivering beneath his fingertips. Her skin was silky and warm, then suddenly slick as her body proved her claim. She was so wet that moisture had spilled from her core and dampened her inner thighs.

His lids drooped as his fingers reached her folds. "So soft," he whispered. "And *so* wet." He caressed her, allowing his middle finger to sink between the petal-soft folds. She held perfectly still except for the rapid rise and fall of her chest. He avoided her clit, knew she was already close to orgasm. "How long have you been like this?"

Rather than answer with words, she took his face between her hands and kissed him. Her lips moved with wild passion, her tongue boldly seeking his. He wrapped his free hand around the back of her neck and pushed a second finger into her snug passage. When he filled her as well as his fingers could, he found her clit with his thumb and caressed her with a soft, circular motion.

She moaned into his mouth, her hips rocking against his hand. Her scent was making him dizzy, making him ravenous for her taste. He wanted to bury his face between her thighs and coat his tongue with her cream. He wanted to anchor a link inside her mind so they could share thoughts and feelings. The physical joining became so much more intense when both parties could experience all the pleasure. But he'd promised not to touch her mind, to keep this strictly physical.

Her mouth tore away from his and she cried out as release claimed her. She clutched his shoulders and arched her back, her inner muscles rippling around his fingers. He mirrored the rhythm of her body with his thumb, prolonging each spasm until she was panting and dazed.

"Lie back."

She happily obliged and he paused to enjoy the view. Her colorful hair spread out around her like a sunset, accenting the beauty of her face.

One arm curved above her head, the other rested across her abdomen, just below her breasts. Her waist dipped dramatically then flared into rounded hips. Long and sleekly muscled, her legs sprawled, allowing his hand to nestle between her thighs.

Unable to resist the temptation, he slid his fingers in and out, imagining the clingy heat surrounding his aching cock. Soon, but not quite yet. Once he joined their bodies, he knew he'd lose control. His only hope of prolonging these pleasures was to wait as long as possible to enter her.

His gaze returned to her breasts and lingered. The tips had tightened into deep pink knots, the vivid color a stark contrast to the full ivory mounds. He'd never seen a woman more perfectly suited to his fantasies. It was as if she'd materialized out of his mind and spread herself across his bed.

"Gods, Morgan." He curved his fingers around one breast and stroked the nipple with his thumb. "You're so beautiful."

She shifted restlessly, the subtle undulation of her hips pulling her body nearly off his fingers. He'd been so distracted by her breasts that he'd almost forgotten his fingers were still inside her. Slowly he pulled his hand back and then thrust into her with enough force to jostle her breasts. She raised her other arm over her head, the submissive position thrilling him.

He watched her face as he filled her with his fingers. Her eyes were closed, her lips parted, her cheeks deeply flushed. He curved his fingers, dragging the front wall of her passage until he found the spot that made her gasp. She lifted into each stroke, increasing the impact and depth. But when the faint flutters of her orgasm started, he pulled his hand out from between her legs and brought his fingers to his mouth.

Her eyes opened and she whimpered as she watched him lick her cream from his skin. "I was almost there." She sounded breathless and needy.

"I know." He lifted one of her legs and draped it over his shoulder. "You already came once. I don't want you to get sleepy on me."

She laughed as he shifted her other leg over his shoulder as well. "I seriously doubt that will ever happen with you."

Emboldened by the praise, he inhaled deeply, absorbing her scent as he lowered his mouth to her slit. She tensed, shivered, then relaxed, accepting the caress of his lips and tongue. Exotic, yet strangely familiar, her taste spiked his hunger. The more of her he had, the more he wanted. It was a delightful contradiction.

She cried out suddenly and pulsed against his lips, but he couldn't make himself stop. She might not be ready to consider the possibility, but she was his. And he was hers.

He slid his hands up her sides and covered her breasts, needing to touch as much of her as possible. His lips moved against her folds and his tongue gently teased her clit. She shook beneath him, her head tossing back and forth, as he patiently aroused her again.

"Please." She gasped. "I can't take any more."

He lifted his head and she whimpered. "You could, and I'd make sure you enjoyed it. But I'm not sure I can right now." After pausing to squeeze her breasts one last time, he eased his hands down her sides and lowered her legs from his shoulders. She watched every move he made, eyes wide and shining. He stood and unfastened his pants, then pushed them to his knees. But when he started to position himself to take her, she sat up and grabbed his wrist.

"I want to see you, touch you before we..."

Her fingers closed around his shaft and Nazerel groaned. "Next time." He moved her hand aside then angled himself toward her entrance. "I need *this* now." He pushed inside her with one smooth stroke.

She arched, taking him deeper as her inner walls rippled around him. "Yes. Oh God, yes."

He wrapped his arms around her as she wrapped her legs around him. Their mouths found each other and everything else faded away. She clung to him desperately as he crawled onto the bed and then carefully lowered her back to the bunk. Then he braced his weight on his knees and his forearms so he could move his hips.

She unhooked her ankles and pulled her legs up high on his sides. He slid in and out of her core, his strokes rhythmic and deep. He'd longed for this, dreamed of it, and still his imaginings were a pale shadow of reality. Her breasts cushioned his chest and her legs squeezed his sides as her core grasped his shaft with greedy hunger.

He thrust faster, needing more. Her body was perfect, but the joining was incomplete. He wanted to feel what she was feeling, know beyond doubt that he was pleasing her as completely as she pleased him. Tearing his mouth away from hers, he gazed deep into her eyes. Her pupils were huge, her lids drooping. She arched and twisted, eagerly taking his entire length.

It wasn't enough, but he knew she would surrender nothing more.

He pulled out and flipped her over, pulling her hips up until she folded her legs beneath her.

"What's wrong? Why did you—"

He thrust back in, stealing her breath. His hands clasped her hips as he pounded out a demanding rhythm. She lowered her shoulders and moved her knees farther apart, providing more resistance for each stroke. It felt amazing, physical perfection, so he didn't want her to see the disappointment in his eyes.

She remained tense and resigned beneath him, willing yet distant. Unable to tolerate the compromise, he slowly adjusted the angle of his penetration until she gasped and shivered with each thrust.

He felt savage yet confined, frustrated while still running wild. The contrast drove him harder, made him more aggressive. He wrapped her hair around his hand and drew her head to the side. "Come for me. I want to feel you tighten around my cock."

"I'm not sure...I can." Before she could complete the sentence, her body obeyed his command.

Thrilled by her surrender. He pulled her up and pressed her tightly against his body. Her back contoured to his front, her head still sharply twisted to the side. He kissed her deeply, his hand still tangled in her hair. His other hand wandered over her body, pausing to pinch her nipples or tease her clit before moving on again.

Restless and breathless, she reached back and clasped his hips.

He banded her waist, keeping himself buried deep inside her. "I can't come if I can't sense you. It's like you're not really here."

She froze, her hands still clutching his hips. "Then how did you come in the shower?"

"I was so shocked that you wanted to touch me that it was basically spontaneous. I won't anchor the connection, but I need to feel all of you."

Morgan dragged his arm away from her waist and crawled forward, separating their bodies in the process. He pulled her hair several times before he managed to disentangle his fingers. Then she turned around and sat, her legs drawn up to her chest. "I don't want you in my mind."

"Why are you so afraid of mental connections?" He continued to kneel and made no effort to cover his massive erection.

"I'm human. What goes on in my mind is private, personal."

He chuckled and motioned toward her. "What we've done so far is more personal than what I'm asking of you now. Or were you only pretending to enjoy my touch, my kiss?"

A heated shiver ran down her body as he stressed the last word. "No one is that good at pretending."

"Then there is no reason for your fear." He held out his hand, the rings in his eyes glowing like sapphires. "Share yourself with me and I'll share myself with you."

"Just for tonight? You promise there will be no lasting link."

His disappointment was obvious, but he whispered, "Just for tonight." She placed her hand on his and his fingers closed around her wrist. "Come here."

Before she could obey, he pulled her to him and separated her legs. He sat back on his heels as he wrapped her legs around his waist. She couldn't reach the bed, could only relax and let him take her. His gaze drilled into hers as his broad tip pressed against the entrance to her body.

"Open for me." He whispered the words against her mouth then his lips sealed over hers. *Accept me into your mind and body.* Then he slowly lowered her onto his cock as his energy pushed into her mind.

She shifted against him, taking his body deeper as she shied away from his mental touch. It felt strange, intrusive, yet undeniably intimate. It was like losing her virginity all over again. She'd been scanned before, had even heard thoughts Mystics pushed into her mind. This was completely different. Nazerel flowed around her and cascaded through her, igniting sensations where their bodies joined.

A moan escaped her throat as he pulled her up, nearly off his shaft, only to lower her again, filling her completely. The intensity of his desire burned away the last of her hesitation. He shared himself with her, an obvious invitation for her to do the same. But he took nothing from her. He waited for her, needing to share her emotions, yet unwilling to take anything without her permission.

Sensations erupted all over her body. Her nipples rubbed against his chest and his thickness caressed her clit. She started there, offering him the physical sensations they created rather than the resulting emotions.

His hands clutched her hips and he moved her faster, sliding her body up and down as their tongues swirled around each other. *More. Show me more.*

His thoughts were so close to begging that she couldn't resist. She allowed her emotions to flow into his mind, sharing her loneliness and the bone-deep ache she felt each time he touched her.

He tore his mouth from hers and wrapped her firmly in his arms. "Never again," he whispered. "You will never feel abandoned again."

Abandoned? It wasn't a word she would have used to describe her isolation, but it was unavoidably accurate. Because of her ambition, she'd shut out anyone willing to protect or nurture her. Her brutal self-reliance might have been the reason they all gave up and left her on her own, but that didn't change the fact that they left. No one had loved her enough to combat her stubbornness. No one had been strong enough to make her see that she didn't need to face life's challenges all alone.

He carefully lowered her to the bed, keeping their pelvises locked together. His hands framed her face and he started to kiss her, but she turned away. "Tell me what it means, what it means for you and me."

Drawing his hips back, he momentarily separated their bodies then thrust home again. "You're not ready to hear it." His disappointment rippled across their connection, but tenderness soothed the emotional sting.

She turned back to him, looking deep into his eyes as she enjoyed his demanding rhythm. She'd felt this connection, this pull almost from the moment they met. Then each kiss, each touch, had intensified the attraction. This wasn't infatuation or even lust, but she was terrified to give it a name.

"Tell me anyway." She shifted her hips, taking him deeper.

He pushed his entire length inside her then paused to stroke the side of her face. "It means chosen mate. Mate of my heart and my mind. You are not only the one my body craves, but the one I *choose* to love."

"But you've been calling me that for days, almost from the start."

Rather than argue with her, he pulled back and drove deep again. Only this time he filled her mind as completely as he filled her body. Desire, fascination, tenderness and regret twisted through her mind like an emotional kaleidoscope. His heightened senses made it impossible for him to avoid the truth. He'd recognized his mate as soon as he saw her. Then her scent, the texture of her skin and the taste of her desire confirmed what he'd already suspected. His enemy was also his mate.

"Don't fight it." He caught the back of her knees and rolled her hips up, allowing him to thrust more aggressively. "We didn't ask for this, but there is no way we can escape it."

He hit that sweet spot deep inside her and a cry of pleasure barreled past her objections. She refused to accept what he'd said, but she no longer denied it either. She concentrated on the thick slide of his body in and out of hers and shut out anything resembling thought.

Hooking one of her legs over his elbow, he freed his other hand to roam while maintaining the angle of her hips. She closed her eyes, unable to bear the stark hunger in his gaze. It didn't help. The intensity of his need surged into her mind with each forceful thrust of his hips. It was empowering to be so desired, yet frightening too.

He pressed her nipples between his thumbs and fingers, drawing her attention back to the physical. He only lingered for a moment before descending along her ribs. She squirmed away from the ticklish sensations, but again he didn't stay long. And then his hand eased between their bodies and his thumb covered her clit.

"Look at me, *morautu*."

Mate. He'd called her mate. No, not just mate, *chosen mate*, the one he would select above all others. "Don't," she whispered, but she opened her eyes.

He released her leg and caught both her hands, intertwining their fingers. Then he pressed them against the bunk to either side of her head. "You are my *morautu*." He thrust deeply, an obvious claim. "Nothing and no one can change that fact."

The heat of his gaze burned into her as tangibly as his thickness filled her body. She was surrounded by him and filled with him, and nothing had ever felt so perfect. She drew her knees up along his sides and opened her mind, allowing him deeper than he'd gone before.

He cried out and thrust even faster. His fingers closed around her hands and his mouth swooped down, angling over her lips. She opened to him, greeting his tongue with a sensual swirl. All the while his hips kept up their frantic pounding. He staked his claim on her body as his energy blazed through her mind. And she was just as aggressive, bucking and twisting, her fingernails digging into his hands.

Morgan felt consumed, yet instantaneously reborn. She reveled in his frenzy as she abandoned herself to her own desire. She was beyond thought, beyond regret. She was on fire and Nazerel was the fuel that kept her flames burning. Nothing else existed; nothing else mattered.

Suddenly she arched clear off the bed and screamed into his open mouth. Pleasure tore through her body and blasted into his. The violent throbs shook him, triggering his release before washing over her again. Her inner muscles rippled around him as pulse after pulse gripped her core.

She recovered slowly, regaining her senses gradually. He'd released her hands, but was still inside her, still surprisingly hard. He held himself off her with his knees and one elbow while his free hand caressed her face.

"Are you all right? I thought you blacked out there for a minute."

He sounded almost smug, so she punched him in the shoulder. "That was no better than average."

"Liar." He leaned down and brushed his lips over hers. "I'm not taking credit for it, but that was extraordinary."

"If you say so."

He chuckled. "The link is still open, Morgan. You can't lie to me."

"Well, I'm not going to feed your ego either, so change the subject."

"All right." With obvious reluctance, he separated their bodies and sat up. "What would you like to talk about?"

"Dissolve the link then we'll talk." Frustration and pain blasted into her mind for just a moment then the connection went dead. She understood the frustration, but why had her insistence on privacy caused him pain? "Thank you."

He nodded once then scooted off the bed and reached for his clothes.

"Aren't you going to clean up first? I thought we could take a shower."

"No shower for either of us. We need to make as strong a statement as possible."

Mortified by what he'd just suggested, she crawled off the bed and stood facing him. "You expect me to put on that dress and walk around the ship reeking of sex?"

"Yes. Once it's been established that you've been claimed, we'll come back and take a shower."

"I can't." She covered herself as best she could with her hands. "I won't."

"Suit yourself, but the utility room is locked and you're not leaving this cabin until we establish my claim." Then his expression softened and he took a step toward her. "I know you noticed the way my cousins reacted to you. Do you really want the entire crew undressing you with their eyes?"

"But they'll know what we were just doing," she cried.

"That's the point. Rodytes are extremely territorial. Another male's scent makes a female unattractive, even one as beautiful as you."

Seeing no other option, she reluctantly gave in. "Then let's get this over with so we can both relax."

They dressed in awkward silence. She felt his gaze on her frequently, but she wasn't ready to share her thoughts, wasn't sure she could express the myriad feelings assailing her mind. He opened the utility room for her, then loitered in the doorway to make sure she didn't do more than run a comb through her hair and splash water on her face.

Once she'd repaired her appearance, he took her by the hand and led her from the cabin. When they encountered a crewmember, Nazerel slipped his arm around her waist and pulled her closer to his side. Morgan could tell the exact moment Nazerel's scent reached the other man. He averted his gaze and hurried past without acknowledging Morgan in any way.

They took an elevator up two levels then followed a corridor to a large observation deck. The area was enclosed by curved panels that created a transparent quarter dome. A huge wedge of star-dotted sky arched overhead while triple rows of smaller ships spread out before her. The ships were sleek and angular, not unlike human fighter jets. Crewmen moved among the ships without spacesuits or any form of breathing apparatus, yet the area didn't appear to be enclosed.

"Why aren't they all dead or being sucked out into space?" She glanced at Nazerel and found him watching her, his expression intense yet unreadable.

"The launch decks are surrounded by energy barriers. It keeps the oxygen in while allowing the fighters to depart without delay."

"'Launch decks'? How many are there?"

"Eight."

"And each deck has," she quickly counted the ships, "thirty fighters?"

"Taking an inventory?" He pivoted toward her and reached for her hand.

"As if it matters." She shook her head, overwhelmed by the scope of her surroundings. "Our most sophisticated ship seems like a toy compared to this."

"The actual hanger is below the launch deck and stores several hundred fighters. Good thing we're on the same side." He pulled her toward him and placed his hands on her hips.

"Are we?" Not wanting to forfeit the comfort of his touch, she wrapped her arms around his neck. Her body had barely stopped tingling and already the fantasy was fading. "How long will we stay that way once your cousins start hunting human females?"

Nazerel sighed, clearly frustrated by her stubbornness. "Your government negotiated with Ontarians, more than once. Why would they refuse to negotiate with Rodytes?"

She didn't want to fight, but their break from reality was over. He'd brought her here against her will in a rash attempt to avoid capture. All of his talk of chosen mates and an hour of spectacular sex didn't change the basic facts. He was a fugitive and it was her job to apprehend him. "Will the Rodytes negotiate or will they fly this behemoth to Earth and take what they want? We have no way to stop them. When the positions are this disparate, there is very little motivation to negotiate."

He pushed her away and crossed his arms over his chest. "You're determined to cast us as villains before we've even chosen a course of action. Don't judge my entire race by the actions of one woman."

"It's hard not to when you want the same thing. Sevrin was trying to genetically engineer what the battle born can accomplish naturally. You said two-thirds of the Rodyte military is battle born. How many males is that? Thousands? Hundreds of thousands? Earth is not going to give up that many females without a fight."

"Are you sure?" His tone was cold and cutting as he added, "They assisted Sevrin, and she was one of many."

"What are you talking about? We did everything in our power to stop Sevrin."

"Your taskforce creates deniability, but the truth is more troubling. Sevrin's project wasn't 'officially' sanctioned. Those sorts of projects never are. But the US government not only knew what she was doing, they allowed her ships to land in the desert and provided her with various supplies and personnel crucial to her success."

She could barely concentrate through the ringing in her ears. "You know this or you suspect?"

"You tell me. How reliable is Flynn? The data he sold me contains numerous messages between Sevrin and various government officials."

Feeling like she'd been punched in the stomach, she took a step back and looked out into space. "This is unbelievable. I busted my ass trying to find that woman and she was being aided by my own government?"

He touched her arm, his fingers warm and strong against her skin. "We've all been betrayed. My people were enslaved by the elders, the battle born were forsaken by the elite, and your government is corrupt and self-serving. It's past time for change, significant, even radical change."

She shivered and he wrapped his arm around her shoulders, slowly drawing her toward his chest. "I need to see the messages."

"I welcome your insight," he assured. "If Flynn was having fun at my expense, I need to know."

"And if my taskforce is a cover for government corruption, I need to know."

VARRIK HELD ECHO AGAINST his chest as he meticulously scanned their surroundings. When they combined their powers, they were able to shield themselves so well they were undetectable to most security systems. Still, they'd never tested their abilities on a Rodyte space station before. Rather than risking the environmental upheaval of an interplanetary jump, he'd teleported from Earth to Ontariese and from Ontariese to a ship not far from Space Station 438. The final jump had been short and stealthy, leaving plenty of energy for their combined shields.

"I think it's clear." Echo eased away from him without leaving the circle of his embrace.

He ran his hand down the back of her hair as tenderness flooded his heart. "Maybe I was just enjoying having you in my arms."

"As I was enjoying being there."

"But," he smiled and kissed her forehead. "We have a job to do."

She pivoted to his side as they crossed the storeroom into which he'd teleported them. They were near the large commerce hub in the center of the space station, yet isolated enough to avoid detection. He scanned the corridor then slowly opened the door and confirmed that the hallway was empty.

The hallway led to the outer ring of the commerce hub, but most of the shops weren't currently open. The lack of activity wasn't surprising, however. It was almost two o'clock in the morning. They'd studied a diagram of the station, so they had a general idea of where they needed to go. They walked briskly through the area, not making eye contact with anyone. Arrival gates were located to the left of the hub, departures to the right. Maintenance bays and long-term docking were one level down and directly below the commerce hub.

The *Undaunted* had just undergone some minor repairs and was expected to depart in a day or two. They found the stairs leading to the lower levels but paused to scan ahead before they descended.

"Is security always so lax?" Echo asked as they started down the stairs. "Why are there no guards or surveillance bots?"

They'd prepared documentation to account for their presence on the space station. Echo had even worn an ankle-length skirt in deference to Rodyte customs. Still, it seemed odd that they'd encountered no check points or scanner stations. "Perhaps we just haven't entered a high security zone yet."

As if in response to their confusion, there was a check point at the entrance to Sublevel 1. Echo lagged a step behind and pulled the hood of her lavender jacket up to shadow her face. Varrik pulled the documents out of his pocket and confidently approached the guard.

"What is your business on SS 438?" The guard examined their papers then looked up as he waited for Varrik's answer.

"My brother is stationed aboard the *Undaunted.*"

"The female belongs to you?"

"Absolutely." He moved closer to the guard without changing his expression. He needed to accent his claim without starting a fight.

"Keep her close. General Nox has been stingy with shore leave, so everyone who disembarks is ready for trouble."

"I appreciate the warning."

The guard passed his scanner wand over the documents. "You're cleared for a ten-hour stay. If you need more time, you'll have to report to a security station and be reauthorized."

"I understand."

He handed the documents back to Varrik and triggered the gate in front of them. "Enjoy your stay."

They didn't need to ask direction to the *Undaunted*. The massive ship filled the observation windows at the end of the concourse directly in front of them.

Echo's hand slipped out of his as she moved closer to the windows. She bent sharply to the left and looked up along the side of the ship. "I can't see the top." She straightened and shook her head. "You told me it was big, but damn. I've never seen anything like it."

"It's the largest ship the Rodytes have ever built and they've built some mammoth ships."

Moving back from the windows, she turned to face him. "If this is the most sophisticated ship the Rodytes have ever built, what are our chances of flashing on board without being detected?"

"Slim to none, but it doesn't matter. I have something else in mind." He lowered her hood and unfastened the clasp at the back of her hair.

"What are you doing? Someone might recognize me." She snatched the clasp from him, but he continued on as if she hadn't objected.

"There's no reason to start a fight when a little deception will work even better." He fluffed her hair and arranged it around her shoulders. "Perfect. Now put on your best princess face. We're going to use your family to our advantage for a change. Pretend you're E'Lanna. Come on." He led her to the uniformed sentries who were guarding the airlock.

"Halt." One of the guards stepped forward and extended his arm, palm out. "Only authorized personnel allowed."

"Well, then you need to get authorization," Varrik countered. "This is *Princess* E'Lanna dar Aune of Ontariese and she would like a tour of this magnificent ship. In fact, contact General Nox. She expects a guided tour of his new vessel."

The guard started to object, but his companion stopped him.

"Do you have proof of her identity?" the second guard asked.

"Scan her face. Her image is in countless data streams all over this star system."

Echo raised her chin and stared past the guards as if they were beneath her notice. Varrik had seen the expression before, but never on Echo's face. She looked just like her twin sister E'Lanna.

The second guard approached with obvious hesitation. "May I scan you, Highness?"

"If you must. Though I don't know why our word isn't good enough." She sniffed and raised her chin even higher.

Moments after the scanner beam passed across her face the guard showed his display to his partner. "Our apologies, Highness. Give us a moment to contact General Nox."

She shooed them away with an indolent wave of her hand. "Do you think he'll respond personally?" she asked once the guards were out of earshot.

"Would you? It's the middle of the night." Varrik smiled as her haughtiness melted away. "He'll send an underling to bring us to him and then the real fun begins. He won't be pleased that we tricked our way onto his ship, but it's less provocative than attempting to teleport through his shields."

"I agree. This was a better choice."

Twenty minutes passed before their escort arrived and as Varrik predicted, he was not General Nox but one of his brothers. The young man walked up to Echo and bowed from the waist, his silver-ringed gaze politely remaining on her face.

"It's an honor to meet you, Princess dar Aun. I'm Zilor Nox."

"Aren't you a sight for sore eyes?" She smiled flirtatiously.

"If you'd given us some sort of warning, we could have arranged a reception."

"I don't need anything fancy." She waved away the concept and motioned toward the ship. "This was an impulse, nothing more." She looped her arm through his and pressed in close. "Of course, your brother's reputation is almost as impressive as the ship's. Please tell me he hasn't refused to see me."

"And insult someone so enchanting?" He patted her hand as they started for the airlock. "Never."

Varrik fell instep behind them, though Zilor hadn't even glanced his way. He watched carefully and listened for any deception in Zilor's tone. This had been almost too easy.

They passed through the airlock and turned to the right—and they were swarmed by armed guards. Varrik was taken to the floor while Echo was shoved against the wall.

"Watch their hands," Zilor shouted. "They can both command magic."

Varrik could have flashed to safety, but only if he were willing to abandon his mate.

Go. Echo urged. *The negotiation might go better if—*
Never!

She responded with a wave of warmth as Varrik was dragged back to his feet. They'd wrapped something around both his hands then secured his wrists behind his back. Echo was similarly restrained, though her hands had been bound in front of her. Foolish Rodytes perceived her as less of a threat because she was female. In many ways her powers were more impressive than his.

"Sorry about the precautions," Zilor said with a lazy smile. "You must admit your visit is a bit unusual."

"It's insulting to be met with such discourtesy." Echo tossed her head, managing to look regal despite the restraints. "I have nothing more to say to you."

Zilor laughed. "Fine by me, but that attitude isn't going to get you anywhere with General Nox. He demands respect from even uninvited guests."

"Release me at once. I've changed my mind. I have no interest in this vessel or its obnoxious commander."

"Too late, princess." Zilor took her by the arm and led her along the corridor. Two guards preceded him and two fell in behind Varrik. "You've earned yourself a visit with a very grumpy general."

Varrik wasn't surprised when they were led to the brig rather than a reception hall or office. Echo sputtered and objected, insisting that she be released. Varrik had hoped for a less aggressive approach, but he'd suspected this was more in keeping with Rodyte hospitality. Still, if they'd ignored protocols entirely, they would have been met with even more hostility.

Zilor guided Echo into a holding cell and Varrik started to push past him and join her in the tiny room. "Sorry. One visitor per cell." He grabbed Varrik's upper arm and pulled him out of the room.

"I must be with my mistress!" He jerked out of Zilor's hand and made it past the doorway before he was yanked back by two of the guards. "I am responsible for her safety."

"Not going to happen." Zilor motioned to the cell across the room and the guards deposited Varrik inside. "You can see her, so you'll know she's in no danger."

"If she's in no danger, why are you treating her like a criminal?" Varrik challenged. *Damn it*! He couldn't teleport her out of here if he couldn't touch her. This was not what he had in mind.

"You must really think we're fools, *Varrik*. Settle in. No one's in a hurry to listen to more of your lies."

Chapter Eleven

"**D**id you get any sleep at all?"

Morgan looked up from the holo-display and offered Nazerel a halfhearted smile. "Off and on."

"That's where you were sitting when I drifted off last night." He swung his long legs over the side of the bunk and stood, toned muscles rippling with each motion. He had donned a pair of snug black shorts that were generally worn beneath his uniform after he showered the night before. "Did you sleep sitting up?"

He was right. She hadn't moved from the workstation in the past four and a half hours and she had the backache to prove it. When they'd returned from the observation deck, she made a beeline for the shower. But as soon as her body was scrubbed clean and covered by a soft nightgown, she'd demanded to see the data he'd received from Flynn.

Nazerel's cryptic warning about government conspiracies had been a much needed distraction from more personal conflicts. She'd done her best to concentrate on the information and ignore her aching heart, but once Nazerel fell asleep her composure crumbled. She returned to the utility room and indulged in a good long cry. As if dragging her to an alien world hadn't been devastating enough, Nazerel shattered her emotions. Maybe that hadn't been his intent, but the result was undeniable.

She couldn't be his "chosen mate". She'd worked too hard to establish herself as a respected authority on all things alien. So how had an alien slipped beneath her defenses? She didn't want to care for him, wasn't ready to consider all the changes he would bring into her life. And yet the emotions he inspired were much too powerful to deny.

She was in love with Nazerel.

And she had no idea how it had happened.

Rather than hint at the emotional upheaval that had shaped her night, she motioned toward the display. "I've been through everything twice and, from what I can tell, Flynn didn't tamper with the information." She paused to rub her neck as she glanced at Nazerel. "Why did he agree to help us in the first place if he still felt loyalty for you?"

"Flynn is a pleaser. He doesn't mean to be disloyal, but he craves acceptance and affirmation from whomever he's with at the time."

"I wonder if Elias and Lor have figured out that Flynn can't be trusted?" She powered down the terminal and pushed back from the desk.

"They should be fine. There's no one left to betray." Nazerel moved behind her before she could stand and slipped his hands under her hair. His long, strong fingers massaged her knotted muscles and Morgan groaned in ecstasy. "Feel good?"

"You have no idea." She closed her eyes and surrendered to the simple pleasure of his touch.

"You make that same sound when you—"

"Shut up." She slapped back at him, but didn't move away from his magical hands. "And keep rubbing."

He chuckled and moved the massage down onto her upper back. "Most of the messages were ambiguous. Were you able to figure out the identity of Sevrin's contacts?"

"I'm pretty sure there are three different people, though two don't identify themselves at all. I'm almost sure the one who calls himself Ranger is my ex-boss. He was an Army Ranger and one of his brothers is a Texas Ranger. He's always been obsessed with the title."

"And the others?"

"Unfortunately, they could be anyone. One uses law enforcement terms, but he or she could also be military. The third sounds like a lawyer or more likely a politician. There just isn't enough specific information to verify their identities."

He continued to work the tension from her muscles for a moment in silence. His voice was low and cautious when he finally spoke. "Then you don't have enough to expose their treachery?"

"Not even close." She opened her eyes and swiveled around in the chair, dislodging one of his hands. "Even if I had something concrete, I can't expose these bastards without exposing the secrets I've sworn to protect."

Challenge arched his brow. "Why are you protecting secrets? Shouldn't you be protecting people instead?"

"I don't know." She shrugged off his other hand and stood. "Maybe the people of Earth deserve to know about our many visitors. Maybe I've been fighting on the wrong side of this conflict all along. I honestly don't know anymore."

"I understand both sides of the argument." Nazerel didn't try to stop her as she brushed past him and started pacing the room. "It's human nature to fear the unknown and frightened people can be dangerous. Still, that excuse is frequently used as a means of controlling the unaware. If Rodyte males can offer human females a different sort of life than they've known on Earth, don't the females have the right to choose?"

"But it has to *be* a choice. No more hunting brides or holding mates captive. The females have to volunteer or... I don't know what I'm saying. I'm probably going to resign as soon as you return me to Earth, so I'm not going to be in a position to make stipulations."

"Why would you resign?"

"They're masking their corruption with the hard work of my taskforce. I won't be used like that. And I'll encourage all of my people to do the same."

"There is another option, you know." She looked at him and he smiled, that slow, sexy smile that never failed to melt her insides. "You can work with us, help us understand how human females think and which strategies will be more effective."

Her heart lodged in her throat and she could hardly swallow. "I have to go back, Nazerel. We both know I have to go back."

He stalked toward her, his gaze locked with hers. "You don't have to do anything." He grasped her upper arms and pulled her toward him. "Stay with me. Be my *morautu*."

She adamantly shook her head, but her hands found their way to his chest and then his shoulders. Hot, hard and addictive, just like the night before. She couldn't make herself stop touching him. "This is insane."

He pulled her into his arms then urged her back against the wall. "This is inevitable."

His mouth sealed over hers, the kiss deep and demanding. She clutched his back and moved her feet apart, making room for his knee between her thighs. The firm muscle connected with her mound and she gasped. Then he dragged the nightgown over her head, separating their mouths only long enough to rid her of the simple garment.

She tugged his shorts down then, unwilling to stop kissing him, she let him do the rest. Soon they were rubbing against each other skin on skin, mouths fused, and breaths mingling. He stroked her breasts with one hand and cupped her ass with the other, controlling the undulation of her hips.

"Open for me." He whispered the words against her damp lips. "Last night was hell. I don't ever want to be without you again."

She tore her mouth away from his and shook her head as the import of his words rocked her. "I'm not ready for that," she cried. "I don't know that I'll ever be ready for that sort of commitment."

He closed his eyes and heaved a frustrated sigh. "The link will ease your doubts. There can be no deception in that kind of communication. You don't have to believe what I tell you because you'll feel what I feel."

She raised her hand and touched his cheek with her fingertips. "Can't you form a temporary link like you did before? I agree that it makes things better, but I still need my own space."

"I can teach you how to shield your mind from me." He moved his hands to the wall on either side of her head. "You are my mate. I'm not sure I can take you again without bonding with you."

"I need you to try." She waited until he looked into her eyes to add, "I'm not ready."

"All right. I'll sever the link when we're finished, even if it kills me."

"Thank you." Emboldened by his willingness to compromise, she grabbed his arms and spun him around, reversing their positions. "Now, I think there's another promise you need to fulfill."

"Is that so?" He brushed her hair back from her face and bent for a lingering kiss. "What did I promise you this time?"

She ran her hands down his sides then steadied herself against his hips as she sank to her knees. "You promised to let me enjoy you the way you've been enjoying me." She had no way of knowing if he'd meant to object because she grasped his shaft with one hand and circled his broad tip with her tongue.

He groaned and leaned his head back against the wall as his eyes drifted shut. She stroked him with her hand as she teased him with her mouth. He was silky soft against her tongue and fingers, yet incredibly hard as well. Fascinated by the contrast, she sucked him deep into her mouth and explored him with her tongue.

His fingers pushed into her hair, clasping yet not restraining. He pulled his hips back, drawing nearly out of her mouth before sliding inward again. She tipped her head back and let him set the pace, thrilled that he allowed her to play at all.

Keeping her lips tight around him, she savored the warm slid of him over and against her tongue. His scent grew stronger as did his taste. She swirled her tongue over his tip, encouraging the response of his body. She wanted to know him as intimately as he'd known her. She wanted to watch him lose control and know she was the one who'd taken him there.

He moved faster, his grip on her hair growing tighter. "I need to stop." He panted harshly, but kept right on pumping into her mouth. "Pull back or I'm going to..."

She sucked him deep and kept him there as he shuddered and groaned. The tilt of her head allowed her to watch his face contort with pleasure. He looked wild, savage, captivating. She swallowed and licked, drawing every last shiver from his body before she finally released him from her mouth.

He pulled her up and kissed her deeply, undeterred by his taste in her mouth. In fact, it seemed to arouse him, make him more demanding. "Just like my scent makes you unattractive to other males, my scent, and my taste, makes you even more attractive to me." Then he pulled her head back and looked into her eyes. "Now open for me."

His autocratic tone sent a shiver down her spine. If anyone else used that tone with her she'd immediately rebel, but hearing sensual commands from Nazerel did irrational things to her body. She parted her lips for the bold thrust of his tongue, yet knew that was not what he meant. She closed her eyes and waited for the surge of his energy.

Rather than thrusting inward as he had before, he eased into her mind then expanded the connection gradually. *The path has already been established, so it requires less pressure.*

It was so strange to have him answer a question she hadn't actually posed. He felt her confusion or curiosity and easily identified the source.

He swept her up in his arms and carried her to the bed, but instead of lying down, he sat and arranged her astride his legs. His hands moved boldly over her body as their kisses went on and on. Pleasuring him had left her restless and achy and still he seemed determined to play. She reached down between their bodies, but he caught her wrist and chuckled low in his throat.

Not yet, morautu. *It's my turn to watch you come.*

Then his fingers found her clit and the intensity made her arch, ripping her mouth away from his.

"That's right." He continued the rhythmic caress with his hand as he bent and caught one of her nipples with his lips.

She rocked her hips, increasing the pressure of his fingers. Her core tightened and the ache turned into a painful emptiness. "Please. I need you inside me."

"Then come." He caught her clit between his thumb and forefinger and carefully pulled on the sensitive knot. She cried out sharply as sensations blasted through her body.

Somehow he kept the spasms going with one hand and positioned his cock with the other. All Morgan knew was one minute her body was clenching in on itself and the next she was squeezing his considerable thickness.

Digging her nails into his shoulders, she let out a savage cry. She felt wild and dizzy. She lifted her hips then slammed them back down, wanting him deeper, wanting as much as he had to give. He grasped her hips, creating a smoother rhythm without repressing the force of her need.

She'd never felt this wild, this *feral*. She wanted to bite and claw, yet she needed him to hold her down and contain the frenzy. Unable to resist the instinct, she raked his back with her nails.

He gasped, shock and lust erupting in his eyes and blazing through his mind. Wrapping his arms around her, he rolled onto the bed and swept her beneath him. Then he caught both her hands and pinned them to the bunk on either side of her head.

With his gaze boring into hers, he filled her over and over. She drew up her legs and took him deeper into her body and her mind. But the fire burned hotter and the frenzy only increased. She dug her heels into the bed and bucked into each of his thrusts.

He entwined their fingers and squeezed her hands. Then his mouth was on hers again, commanding and calming her. His physical strength soothed her, made her feel secure. And the power of his being allowed her to slow the raging impulses and savor the pleasure ricocheting back and forth across their link.

It became a dance, a rhythmic blending of bodies, souls and minds. She surrendered to the intensity, and tenderness flowed out of him like a river, a silky caress that surrounded her and strengthened their bond.

Now. His hips pumped frantically his lips hovering over hers. *Let me feel you come around my cock.*

The graphic command left her no choice. Her body arched and her core rippled, triggering his release. They clung to each other, shuddering and groaning as the world spun away. They hung together in velvety silence for one endless moment then plummeted back to reality.

"Wow." She shivered then laughed as tingling aftershocks sparked through her body.

"A little better than average?"

She laughed again and eased one of her hands out from under his. "Does your ego really need to hear it?" She brushed his hair back from his face. "We are amazing together. It's not you or me. It's *us.*"

He grinned, clearly thrilled by the conclusion. "I'm glad you're finally starting to understand."

A buzzer sounded and Nazerel looked toward the workstation. "Answer call, audio only."

"Sorry to interrupt your training session." No one could have missed the amusement in Zilor's tone. "But Garin has a surprise for you."

"What sort of surprise?"

"Report to Garin's quarters and he'll explain. We missed you at breakfast."

The connection went dead before Nazerel could respond.

"What did he mean by 'training session'?" When Nazerel only grinned she had her answer. "They think you're 'training' me?"

He gave her a quick kiss then rolled away and scooted off the bunk. "Does it matter what they think? We know the truth."

"We do?" She scrambled off the bed and raced for her discarded nightgown. "Which truth is that?"

"We're training each other."

He disappeared into the utility room before she could object or agree. She slipped the nightgown back on with a sigh. Did it really matter what anyone else thought as long as they were content with the arrangement? Content? Was she content with Nazerel? She wasn't even sure she liked him. How could he possibly make her content?

But she was warm and sleepy, utterly at peace for the first time in years, maybe decades.

She closed her eyes and reached for his mind.

Yes, my love? He made the endearment sound playful.

If you promise not to enter my mind without letting me know you're there, we'll try this for a while.

Happiness, bright and effervescent, preceded his thought. *Are you sure?*

Yes. But I don't offer my trust often or easily. No spying on me.

The door to the utility room slid open and he stood there in a freshly pressed uniform, hair still damp from his lightning-fast shower. "If I approach your mind, you'll know I'm there and you'll have time to shut the door if you don't want me to enter."

"Or I will if I knew how to shut a telepathic door."

"I'll teach you. As soon as I return, we'll resume our training session." He punctuated the promise with a wink that sent heat curling through her body.

NAZEREL WAS HALFWAY to Garin's cabin when the computer rerouted him to the brig. The distinctly female voice told him of the change and a lighted indicator on the wall guided him toward the new destination. His gut knotted and his breathing hitched as he neared the detention level. What sort of surprise would Garin have stashed in the brig? Ontarians was the obvious answer, but how in the five hells would Mystics have found him this quickly? Everyone who knew of his connection to the Nox family was either dead or incarcerated.

Except for Varrik.

Dread intensified the weight in his stomach. His former best friend had already betrayed him once. Why should this possibility surprise him? His worst fears were realized a few minutes later when a guard ushered him into the open area between the containment cells. Garin stood there, hands clasped behind his back.

"Surprise." He motioned toward Varrik with a sardonic smile. "Decide what you want done with him or I'll shove him out the nearest airlock. I really don't have time for this shit."

"Yes, sir."

Garin moved toward Echo, who was in an adjacent cell. "You're coming with me, so your mate doesn't feel obligated to perform." He disabled the force field with a terse command and motioned Echo out.

"Where are you taking her?" Varrik demanded.

"Wherever I please," Garin snapped. "This is my ship. You are the intruders."

Varrik's gaze screamed objections, but he wisely held his tongue. Garin had already explained why he was removing Echo and that was more consideration than Varrik deserved.

Nazerel waited until the door slid closed behind Garin and Echo before he spoke to his one-time friend. "I'm not going back to Ontariese, at least not yet."

"Running away is a coward's solution. You're not a coward."

Nazerel shook his head and fought back a smile. Varrik knew him too well. Any other accusation would have fallen on deaf ears, but no one called Nazerel a coward. He glanced at the guard standing beside the door. "Wait outside. I'll call you if I need assistance."

With only an acknowledging nod, the guard stepped out into the corridor and joined the guard already stationed there.

After the door closed again, Nazerel turned back to Varrik. "I'm not running away. I retreated so I could regroup and form a better strategy."

"A better strategy for what? It's over, Nazerel. Sevrin is dead and you must take responsibility for your actions."

"Which actions do you find so objectionable? Leaving the City of Tears without permission or communicating with the *evil* Rodytes?"

"Rodyte blood flows through my veins too. You can't pretend I'm a bigot. And you can't pretend no one was hurt by your presence on Earth. Yes, we know Sevrin's experiments were to blame for the actual deaths, but how did those females end up in Sevrin's lab? And a male had to have triggered each transformation. That wasn't something Sevrin could have done alone."

"No one on Team South hunted while we were on Earth. Ask Flynn. Ask anyone."

Varrik paused, clearly confused by the claim. His stance remained tense and watchful, but his gaze softened. "What are you talking about? We were told there was a rotation that ensured each team had the opportunity to hunt."

"Team South members were excluded from the rotation."

"Why? Who excluded them?"

"Sevrin. I wouldn't lick her boots, or anything else she wanted licked, so she lashed out at my team. She was hoping my men would turn on me, but the injustice only made them more suspicious of her and more loyal to me."

After a long, strained silence, Varrik asked, "Can you give me the names of each man who hunted and what happened to the female or females he caught?"

"Don't confuse me with Flynn. Investigating this mess is your job, not mine."

Varrik accepted the statement with a stiff nod. "You still violated your contract with the Overlord."

"A contract I neither negotiated nor signed," Nazerel sneered. This conversation was so overdue it was pointless. "It was never my desire to be part of the world above, but you dismantled our world so you could remain with your mate. I accept that. I don't agree with it, but I understand the consuming need to keep one's mate at one's side."

Varrik had the audacity to laugh. He ran a hand through his hair as he shook his head. "Let me guess, Morgan? Does she know she's your mate or does she still consider herself your prisoner?"

"We're talking about me, not Morgan." He couldn't let thoughts of Morgan soften his heart or overshadow his resentment. Varrik had escaped this reckoning for much too long and this setting was likely as advantageous as Nazerel was ever going to receive.

"Hate me for dismantling our world if you must, but at least be honest with yourself. Our world needed to be dismantled. The Sacred Customs were tools used by the elders to control their tribes. Our men deserve more than a life of mindless subjugation."

"Maybe that's all the Customs were to you, but to me they were much, much more."

After heaving a sigh of exasperation, Varrik squared his shoulders. "We can spend the next year debating the merits of the Sacred Customs and it will change nothing. The world below is gone."

"Thanks to you," he gritted out between clenched teeth.

"And it should not be reborn," Varrik stressed.

He relaxed his jaw enough to speak clearly. "I agree."

That seemed to surprise Varrik. He took a step closer to the containment field. "I didn't set out to kill South. Your father left me no other choice."

Nazerel clenched his fists, needing a physical outlet for the sudden flash of anger. Varrik hadn't "set out to kill" Nazerel's father, but Varrik hadn't denied being the cause of South's death. "You accused Elder North and Elder South of betraying our people. It's curious that North—your uncle—is still alive while you had 'no other choice' but to kill my father, the only person who could have disproved your accusations."

"Why was he on the Rodyte ship if he remained loyal to our world?" Tension deepened Varrik's voice, adding a menacing growl to his tone.

Moving closer to Varrik's cell, Nazerel found the command to lower the containment field on the tip of his tongue. The Sacred Customs not only allowed murder to be avenged, they demanded a life for a life. But this was Garin's ship. When Varrik breathed his last, it would have to be at Garin's command. "My father was captured by the Rodytes just like you and Echo."

"And yet we found him in a comfortable cabin while we had been locked up and restrained."

Nazerel had heard it all before. He'd watched the vidfiles of the tribunal and read the transcripts, searching for any inconsistency that would exonerate his father or at least cast doubt on Varrik's story. He'd found none. The entire performance had been a carefully constructed lie, or Varrik had been telling the truth. For the first time, Nazerel allowed himself to admit that he wasn't sure which alternative was accurate.

"I have only your word for any of this," Nazerel snapped.

"For most of our lives, that would have been enough."

The reminder only irritated the raw patches in Nazerel's soul. Their past closeness was the primary reason Varrik's betrayal hurt so badly. "And then you met Echo."

"Why would I lie? Why would Echo? She had nothing to gain by spreading falsehoods and everything to lose. Lying during a tribunal is a serious crime."

"You needed the location of the Shadow Maze and you murdered my father to get it!" Varrik had no intention of changing his story. This was an exasperating waste of time.

"Scan me. Look into my mind and learn the truth." It was part challenge, part plea.

Nazerel glared at him. "I know the true scope of your powers. You can easily manipulate memories."

"And you're skilled enough to sense that sort of manipulation. Go on. Let's end this once and for all. Or aren't you interested in the truth?" The plea faded from his demeanor until only challenge remained.

Not sure why he was prolonging this futile conversation, Nazerel said, "This better not be some sort of trick. We still have Echo." It was an idle threat and likely Varrik knew it. Still, Nazerel felt compelled to say something.

Even with his nanites boosting his natural abilities, Nazerel wasn't able to penetrate the containment field, so he issued the command, decreasing the strength by twenty-five percent.

Varrik flashed through the barrier and grabbed Nazerel by the throat. "Never threaten my mate. I will not tolerate—"

Nazerel punched him in the face, snapping his head sharply to the side. Then he dragged Varrik's hand away from his throat and propelled him backward with a burst of energy. "Get back in that cell! You're not in a position to demand anything."

Varrik's only response was a fast, uppercut that Nazerel barely dodged. Another energy pulse sent Varrik stumbling backward, but he recovered quickly and charged Nazerel.

This confrontation had been brewing for months and now both men were fully engaged. Their nanites augmented their strength and speed, but they'd known each other their entire lives. Their arms and legs flew so fast their bodies blurred, yet few of their blows connected. They ducked and waved, twisted and lunged in a dizzying, semi-violent dance.

Nazerel faked with his left then put the full power of his body behind his right fist. Anticipating the first punch, Varrik jerked to the right and his nose collided with Nazerel's knuckles. Blood gushed from both nostrils, coating Varrik's face and Nazerel's hand in a torrent of red. With an enraged cry, Varrik kicked Nazerel's legs out from under him then followed him down to the floor. Varrik drew back his arm, but before he could land even one punch, he was dragged off Nazerel by three guards who must have been drawn by the commotion. A forth stood a short distance away with his pulse pistol aimed at Varrik's head.

"Don't kill him," Nazerel ordered. "I've just begun to question him."

"Why is he out of his cell?" the one with the gun wanted to know.

The rings in Varrik's eyes erupted with blue fire. Understanding the significance of the change, Nazerel scrambled to his feet and caught Varrik's attention. "Don't hurt them. Your quarrel is with me."

"I don't have a 'quarrel' with anyone. You threw the first punch," Varrik snapped, his hands tightly fisted.

"You grabbed me by the throat."

"You threatened my mate!"

They were nose to nose again, the guards struggling to hold back Varrik.

"Do you want him back in the cell or not?" one of the guards holding Varrik asked.

Varrik could have sent them all flying with a surge of kinetic energy, but his anger was entirely focused on Nazerel.

"Not yet," Varrik told them. "He has something he must do first."

All four guards looked at Nazerel for guidance.

"He's right." Nazerel wiped his bloody knuckles on his pant leg. "Release him and return to your stations."

"Are you sure, sir? He still seems hostile." The guard with the gun asked again.

"We were blowing off steam, nothing more. If either of us had meant to cause real damage, you'd be loading us onto hover carts bound for the infirmary. Now go."

"Yes, sir." All of the guards returned to their positions in the hallway.

Varrik wiped his nose on his sleeve, creating a red smear across his face in the process. "I can escape at any time. You realize that, don't you?"

"Only if you leave Echo behind."

"Echo is the High Queen's daughter. One call from Charlotte, and Echo would be released." Nazerel started to argue, but Varrik stopped him with a muttered curse. "My point is I don't want this to be adversarial. I agreed to hunt you because I didn't trust anyone else to bring you back alive. I know how exasperating you can be."

"And you are the epitome of patience."

"Are you going to scan me or not?" Varrik pinched the bridge of his nose as one side started bleeding again. "I'm losing interest in this exercise."

Nazerel deactivated the containment field and motioned toward the small sink inside the cell. "Clean yourself up then I'll scan you."

With obvious reluctance, Varrik walked back into the cell.

Nazerel used the time to calm his spirit. It was impossible to assess another's emotions while his were out of control. Varrik washed his face, pushed a piece of tissue into the stubborn nostril and then stood in the middle of the cell, arms folded over his chest. He stared at Nazerel without expression then a tiny opening formed in his mental shields.

Already dreading what he'd find, Nazerel slipped through the opening. He'd either learn that his bitterness toward his former best friend was justified or he'd see that his father was a traitor. Neither possibility held any appeal. Still, Nazerel needed to know the truth. Varrik drew him into the past, leading him to the night in question. But once they arrived at the scene, Varrik eased back, allowing Nazerel to explore on his own.

The scene was as Varrik had described, a small yet comfortable cabin, definitely not the location one generally found a prisoner. South turned around as Echo and Varrik entered. "Are we rescued?" The question might have been believable if it weren't for the panic in his eyes.

"To require rescuing, one has to be in danger. Are you in danger?" Echo moved slowly forward.

South held up both hands. "Don't come near me." South sounded genuinely terrified, but Nazerel recognized the subtle cunning in his father's expression.

Echo took another step toward South, and Nazerel felt a powerful surge of energy. She paled, swaying as South stabbed into her mind. At this point Nazerel could still argue that South was protecting himself from their attack, but the dynamic shifted rapidly.

Varrik steadied Echo as he forced his way into the power struggle. Nazerel ignored the protectiveness and anger blasting from Varrik and sank deeper into South's being.

He'd never seen his father like this, never sensed his mind without the filter of a son's devotion. Rage, bitterness and desperation spun like an emotional hurricane. How could South teach others to honor and revere customs he despised? The hypocrisy stung, tearing at everything Nazerel believed to be true, yet he'd come too far to turn back now. He scanned deeper, searching for motivations, anything that would explain his father's actions. All he felt was South's determination to escape the life he hated and live in comfort away from the world below.

Not wanting to experience his father's death, Nazerel severed the connection and scrambled back from the cell. It was all true. Everything Varrik had told the tribunal was confirmed by his memories. South had betrayed his tribe and forced Varrik to kill him rather than take responsibility for his cowardly choices.

Nazerel commanded the containment field back to full strength. Then, not wanting Varrik to see the torment in his eyes, he turned around. "You were right. I admit it. Are you happy now?"

"None of this makes me happy. I didn't want to kill him. I—"

"Had no other choice. Yes, I know." Composed enough to face him again, Nazerel shot him a sidelong glare. "The past cannot be changed. We both need to focus on the future."

Varrik scrubbed his hand over his jaw, clearly conflicted. "If this isn't about avoiding punishment, then why are you here? What can General Nox offer you other than a place to hide?"

"It's not in my best interest to explain."

Varrik searched his gaze, a sadly familiar half-smile curving his lips. "You're still the most stubborn man I've even known."

"Except for yourself, don't you mean?"

"Damn it, Nazerel. Tell me what you've got planned. It might not be too late to save you."

His vehemence seemed genuine. Still, Nazerel wasn't impressed. "That's part of the problem. I don't, nor have I ever, needed rescuing. If you behave yourself for the next few days, I might let you watch my plans unfold. It should be very entertaining."

FRESHLY SHOWERED AND adorned in a relatively modest dress, Morgan wandered around the cabin she shared with Nazerel. The door buzzer made her jump then she heard someone trigger the door from outside. Hadn't Zilor said the doors could only be opened by the occupant?

Before her imagination could run away with her, Garin stepped into the room but he went no farther. "I apologize for the intrusion. I wasn't sure if Nazerel taught you the proper command to trigger the door."

"He hasn't gotten around to it yet, but how were you able to open it from out there?"

His grin was unexpected and charming. "It's my ship. I can open any door."

"Of course you can."

He turned to the side and motioned someone forward. The newcomer was female and dressed in an ankle-length skirt, but she wasn't Rodyte. Her gently swirling purple eyes identified her homeworld as Ontariese. She'd pulled her golden-brown hair back into a messy ponytail and her features were delicate, yet striking.

"Echo dar Aune, meet Morgan Hoyt."

Echo crossed the room with regal grace, her right hand extended. "I feel like I know you already."

"And why is that?" Morgan automatically shook her hand, though she was curious to know why this stranger knew her name. Wait a minute. Echo. Wasn't that the name of Varrik's captive princess?

"Enjoy your visit," Garin cut in. "I'll return for you when, and if, your mates ever come to a consensus." Without further ado, the general left.

"You're Nazerel's *mate*?"

She couldn't tell if the catch in Echo's voice had been disbelief or amusement. "So he tells me. And you're the princess who inspired Varrik to abandon the world below."

"Guilty as charged, though there was more to it than just me."

"Why don't we sit down?" She motioned toward the seating area beyond the bed. "If Nazerel and Varrik are trying to agree on anything, you're going to be here a while."

Echo nodded and followed her across the room. "This is rather awkward, but I feel obligated to ask. Were you brought here against your will?"

"'Will' is a curious thing." Morgan sat facing Echo and tried not to laugh. Echo, of all people, should understand how quickly captor could become something very different. "Nazerel didn't ask if I wanted to make this trip, but even before we left Earth I'm not sure I was entirely unwilling. These Rodyte men can be very persuasive."

Echo didn't bother holding back her smile. "You don't have to explain that to me."

"I pride myself in my self-sufficiency. I'm a very independent woman, so it's absurd that I might have fallen this fast and this hard."

"And yet, you can't stop thinking about him and any future without him would be incomplete?"

"Not just incomplete, unthinkable." Morgan sighed. She had very few female friends, yet pouring her heart out to Echo felt natural. "Is the general watching us? Seeing if I'll divulge my deepest secrets to a fellow captive?"

Echo snickered. "Are there any of your deepest secrets Nazerel hasn't already learned?"

"Probably not." She pressed back into the sofa. "How did you find us so quickly?"

"Once Varrik realized Nazerel had left Earth, he knew where Nazerel would go."

"Which is why Lor sent him after us. Varrik knows Nazerel better than anyone."

"Lor sent us after Nazerel. We're supposed to *rescue* you. As far as everyone is concerned you're Nazerel's hostage. You don't have to be part of his prosecution, but there is no benefit from you sharing the blame."

Understanding spread through Morgan reinforcing her calm. "Who had this conversation with you when you were 'rescued' from Varrik?"

Echo's smile returned and a guilty flush colored her cheeks. "My mother. Gods was that awkward. She was convinced Varrik was evil incarnate and nothing I said was going to change her mind."

"Then spare us both the awkwardness. Nazerel is no longer my captor and I won't testify against him. Do I need to be more specific?"

"I think being introduced as his mate told me all I needed to know."

"I'm glad." Echo might seem friendly and easygoing, but they were still on opposite sides of the conflict. Morgan refused to say anything that would incriminate Nazerel, so she chose the next subject carefully. "Your mother is High Queen of Ontariese, isn't she?"

"She is."

"Has she learned to accept Varrik?"

"I'm not sure 'accept' is the right word. She tolerates him because she knows how much I love him. Now my father," she shook her head. "It's all Papa can do to *pretend* to be civil to Varrik. Mostly they avoid each other."

They could bore each other with small talk for the next few hours or Morgan could take advantage of this unexpected opportunity. Echo was Varrik's mate. She had to know more about his past than what he'd put in the official reports. "Can I ask a really rude question? If you don't want to answer I'll understand."

"I'm curious by nature." Echo relaxed enough to scoot back in her chair and cross her legs. "I'll have to at least hear the question now."

"Nazerel blames you and Varrik for his father's death. What really happened on the Rodyte ship? How did Elder South die?"

It took Echo a moment to answer and when she did her voice was soft and sad, hinting at deep regret. "Nazerel is right. We are responsible for South's death."

That wasn't the answer Morgan had expected. And Echo had offered no caveat, no explanation. Had she miscalculated Echo's basic nature? "Nazerel thinks you murdered South so you could learn the location of the Shadow Maze. Was there more to it than that?"

"Of course there was more to it. South was part of a much larger conspiracy that threatened my sister's life. North was determined to take over the Shadow Maze and South was desperate to escape before Varrik brought the Ontarian military down on all their heads. South sold fifty hunters to the Rodytes in exchange for a secure and comfortable life on Rodymia."

"Does Nazerel know about this?"

"He knows, but he doesn't believe his father was capable of that sort of treachery." Her legs uncrossed and she scooted back to the edge of her seat. "I saw a side of South I suspect he never showed his son. South reveled in cruelty. He was utterly ruthless." She tucked a strand of her hair behind her ear and released a deep sigh. "Even so, regardless of the circumstances, Varrik ended the life of Nazerel's father. I'm not sure any friendship could recover from that."

"This isn't about friendship, it's about justice."

Echo's brow furrowed and she tilted her head to one side. "I'm not sure what you mean."

"Varrik feels his actions were justified by the needs of Tribe North. Nazerel sees it very differently. He feels like Varrik's love for you robbed Tribe South of any choice they might have had when leaving the world below."

"If they had been given the option of coming to Rodymia, would their lives have been any different?" Echo motioned to the ship around them. "This environment is not all that different from the City of Tears. Rodyte soldiers are still expected to obey orders and adhere to very strict rules."

"I don't think Rodymia is Nazerel's final destination."

After a thoughtful pause, Echo asked, "Earth?"

Morgan just smiled. She'd probably said too much already, but Echo was incredibly engaging.

"Why Earth? What can Tribe South find on that primitive planet that they can't find in this star system?"

"Compatible females." The answer was so obvious, Morgan was sure Echo was playing dumb to confirm her own suspicions. "There aren't enough women on Ontariese for the men you've got now. How would an ex-Shadow Assassin ever convince an Ontarian woman to mate with him? And from what little I've learned about Rodymia, they have a strict social structure, a sort of caste system. Nazerel keeps referring to his cousins as part of the elite, but he never refers to himself the same way."

"Even if the Shadow Assassins would fare better on Earth, why would humans allow them to immigrate?"

Morgan smiled. That was a question she might have asked a week ago. "I don't think they plan on asking permission. In fact, Earth might end up with a larger illegal alien problem than they ever thought possible."

Confusion drew Echo's brows together as she asked, "Shouldn't you sound more upset by the possibility?"

"I feel sorry for the public and I'll do everything I can to protect human females. But the government deserves everything they're about to get and a whole lot more."

Chapter Twelve

N azerel was halfway back to his cabin when the computer rerouted
him again.

"General Nox would like to speak with you," the computer informed
him. "Please follow the path indicator."

Too wound up to appreciate the assistance, he grumbled, "I know the
way."

"Very good. If you change your mind, I'm always available."

The illuminated indicator blinked out and Nazerel strode on alone,
feeling slightly guilty for grumping at the computer. The ship was
massive, but the basic layout was similar to other Rodyte ships. Besides,
Nazerel was used to navigating the twisting corridors of the Shadow
Maze so he always paid close attention to where he was going and where
he had been.

Hanging over his head like a storm cloud, the truth about his father
simmered and churned. He'd known his father was ruthless, perhaps
even cruel. Yet he'd always believed South honored the Sacred Customs
that he honestly believed the things he taught so passionately. They were
the principles on which Nazerel had built his life. They formed his basic
character, so where did this leave him?

But there had been no deception in Varrik's memories. Like all the
other elders, South had been corrupt and self-serving. Which meant the
Sacred Customs were pointless lies and Nazerel was a fool, fighting for an
ideal that never existed or had been horribly twisted long before he was
born.

None of it mattered anymore. The Shadow Maze was an empty shell
and his brothers were semi-willing prisoners of the Ontarian Overlord.

He released the past with a frustrated sigh. He'd meant what he said to Varrik. The past could not be changed and they both needed to focus on the future. His people deserved better than years of servitude and frustration on a planet with a shortage of females. Life in the Rodyte military wouldn't be a better option if it weren't for what he'd learned on Earth. It was only a matter of time before the battle born made their move, and he meant for the Shadow Assassins to be part of the coming battle.

His thoughts were still troubled and chaotic when he reached Garin's quarters. The proximity sensor activated as he neared the door and he heard the computer announce his arrival to the occupant or occupants of the cabin. The door slid open and Nazerel walked inside. Garin was alone and seated behind the desk in the far corner of the L-shaped room. He motioned Nazerel over as he closed the report he'd been perusing.

"Did you make any progress with Varrik? I heard fists were flying at one point."

Needing a moment longer to organize his thoughts, Nazerel asked, "How did he end up in your brig?"

"I'm not sure what they intended, but they told my guards Echo was an Ontarian princess named E'Lanna and she wanted a tour of my ship." He held up his hand and stopped Nazerel's objecting. "Yes, I know that's her sister and they really are princesses, but why does that entitle her to a tour of this ship? Our people are not currently at war, but neither are we allies. Her social station is irrelevant."

"I'm sure it was just a ploy so they could speak with you. Varrik would have pointed out that I was a fleeing fugitive and there was no reason for you to start a war with Ontariese over the rebellious actions of one man."

"I thought he knew we are related by blood."

"He does."

"Then he knows nothing about Rodytes." He folded his hands behind his head and leaned back in his chair. "I would never turn you over to an enemy and if Varrik came here representing the Ontarian Overlord, he is my enemy."

Nazerel sat in one of the two chairs arranged in front of Garin's desk. "If it were just me, I'd suggest you throw him off the ship, banish him from Rodyte space, and be done with it. Unfortunately, there are one thousand men at the City of Tears that—"

"One thousand? I thought there were *four* thousand Shadow Assassins."

"I'm only responsible for those descended from South. The other tribes must make their own..." Garin often brought insight and wisdom with just a few words. His ability to see the big picture was what made him such a good commander and an even more valuable friend. "You're right. We were all part of the world below, all betrayed by the elders. All four thousand should have the same opportunities."

Garin lowered his arms, but his posture remained relaxed. "I'm glad you feel that way, because I just received permission from the crown to offer any Shadow Assassin political asylum in exchange for military service. It's the same deal they received from the Ontarians, with one important difference. They will be Rodyte citizens when their service is complete rather than barely tolerated on Ontariese. The rest is up to you. When and how do you want to retake control of *your* men?"

The emphasis was meant to motivate him and it worked. He was the last true leader of the Shadow Assassins. It was his responsibility to guide them into a better life, to help them claim a future in which they could be proud and free. "There are two separate situations that must be addressed. I will use the one they wish to discuss to segue into the larger issue."

"Your recent adventures on Earth will allow you to address the liberation of the Shadow Maze?"

"Exactly. This is likely the only opportunity I'll get to speak with the overlord, so I must make the most of it."

"We can easily explain your involvement with Sevrin. I have official documents that will exonerate your actions on Earth."

Nazerel nodded. "And my situation will protect Team South. I'm not sure what, if anything, I can do to protect the other hunters."

"They knew what they were doing when they followed you to Earth."

"But they followed me under false pretenses."

Garin shook his head. "Not really. You weren't able to tell them your true motivation, but they knew what they were doing and the possible ramifications from their choices."

Nazerel didn't argue, but he still felt responsible for the events that followed. He'd convinced the other alpha hunters to accept Sevrin's offer. If he hadn't fueled their discontent and frustration, it was likely they would have eventually accepted the situation on Ontariese.

"What else do you need to strengthen your defense?"

"Are you willing to testify on my behalf?"

Garin suddenly scowled at him. "I'm insulted that you even thought to ask. You are my blood. Would I testify for Bandar or Zilor?"

"Of course. But—"

"Do I love you any less?"

"I apologize, and I don't doubt your loyalty. What I should have said is, are you able to testify on my behalf? I know the demands of your new command are significant."

"I can't fly the *Undaunted* over to Ontariese, if that's what you mean. But I can sure as the five hells schedule a time to attend a video conference. The tribunal might not even require my testimony once they've read the official documents."

"You've never met Lor dar Joon. He'll have questions for you, lots and lots of questions."

"I look forward to his interrogation." Garin's smile seemed rather predatory. "I always welcome a good challenge."

"The easiest way to bring this all to a close is to turn myself in to Varrik."

"I don't trust the Ontarians. I'd like to hold on to the females until after your appearance before the Tribunal. If there is any hint of manipulation on their part, it will give us some leverage."

"I understand your caution, but the Ontarians wouldn't see that as protection, they'd see it as a threat. Lor is as arrogant as they come, but he seems fair and honorable."

Garin stared at him thoughtfully for a long moment, then released a tense sigh. "I don't like it, but ultimately it's your decision." He entered several commands into his computer. "I just sent copies of the documents to the workstation in your cabin. Look them over before you leave to make sure you have everything you need."

"Once my men request asylum, will you have any control over their assignments?"

Garin waved away Nazerel's concern. "I can't assign them all to the *Undaunted*, but I can use my influence to make sure they're assigned to battle born commanders rather than elitist pigs who needlessly risk the lives of their battle born soldiers."

"Which brings us back to what I learned on Earth. Have you decided what to do about the battle born situation?"

"The 'battle born situation'?" Garin chuckled and pushed back from his desk. "Now you sound like Bandar. The situation with the battle born has been escalating for decades and it's not going to be resolved overnight. You brought an intriguing possibility to my attention. However, I'm not prepared to commit high treason so my brothers can claim empowered mates."

Claiming empowered mates was more of a bonus than the crux of the issue, but Nazerel knew Garin understood the situation even better than he did. Battle born sons had been disregarded and abused ever since it became apparent that they would never develop the ability to manipulate magic. While their female counterparts were treasured and exalted, battle born sons had been...forsaken, to borrow Bandar's favorite word to describe the situation."

Before Nazerel could comment, the general went on, "One of my spies in the capital was able to secure a copy of Sevrin's research data. There is no longer any doubt that Quinton was and is directly involved. I'd like a copy of what Flynn gave you to compare against the information I secured myself."

That had been their agreement. If Quinton had the data already, Nazerel would share it with Garin to help balance the Rodyte power equation. Garin had made the decision even easier by securing a copy of the research himself.

Nazerel nodded. "I'll send it to you as soon as I return to my cabin."

Garin nodded then came out from behind the desk. His expression softened and he placed his hand on Nazerel's shoulder. "You've given me a lot to think about and my brothers will guarantee that I continue to think about it, but let's solve one problem at a time."

"I didn't set out to complicate your life when I accepted this mission. Is there anything I can do to help you unravel this mess?"

"You've helped quite enough already." Garin laughed then motioned him toward the door. "Take what's left of today to study the documents, solidify your defense and figure out what in creation you're going to do with Morgan. Then tomorrow morning I'll release Varrik—and his mate. The sooner we solve your problems, the sooner we can begin on the 'battle born situation.'"

BY THE TIME THE GUARDS escorted Echo back to the brig, Morgan felt like they knew each other remarkably well. Though Echo was cautious when it came to specifics about Varrik, she was surprisingly candid about her own history. And Echo's openness encouraged Morgan to be honest about her past. Soon they were chatting away as if they'd known each other for years and time passed quickly.

Echo had only been gone a few minutes when Nazerel returned to the cabin. He looked downright gloomy and his mood was as unapproachable as Echo's had been welcoming. After acknowledging Morgan with a distracted lift of his chin, he crossed to the perimeter wall and asked for an external view from the top deck of the ship. Staring out into space always seemed to calm him, yet it also drew him inward and made him less willing to share whatever upset him.

"Are you all right?" Morgan pressed herself against his back and wrapped her arms around his waist. "If you don't talk to me, I'll have to use our link to read your mind."

She'd been hoping to lighten his mood with her playful threat. Instead, he sounded depressed and distant. "Varrik is in the brig. That was Garin's surprise."

"So I gathered when he brought Echo here and told us you and Varrik were trying to work things out."

Nazerel scoffed softly, but his body began to relax and he folded his arms over hers. "I'm not sure our conversation qualifies as reconciliation, but we were able to establish some basic facts."

"Such as?"

He turned around and pulled her into his arms. "Garin has been compiling the documents needed for my defense. Rather than trying to answer all of your questions, why don't we go over the documents together and I'll take you through it step-by-step?"

"All right." If he was building a defense, did that mean he intended to turn himself in? He was safe here, protected by the influence of his family. Why would he turn himself in?

The answer was so obvious, she didn't bother asking the question. He'd sacrifice himself for his people. And not just the team of hunters he'd led while on Earth. He felt responsible for all of the men in his tribe, perhaps every former Shadow Assassin.

He motioned her toward the small table near the kitchenette and they sat side by side rather than facing each other. Then he used a datapad, an ultra-thin tablet-style computer capable of projecting three-dimensional images, to display the documents. To her surprise, the information detailed events that began long before Nazerel came to Earth, but she quickly realized it was all connected. The speed with which Nazerel moved through the facts made it obvious he wasn't in the mood to elaborate.

"How much of this is true?"

He paused and looked at her. "All of it, but I'm not surprised that you asked. The tribunal is going to find everything suspiciously convenient and I'm not sure what I can do about it."

"Can anyone substantiate what's in these documents?"

He powered down the datapad with a sigh. "Garin can and will, but he's my cousin. It's possible the members of the tribunal will dismiss his testimony as biased."

"Maybe." She motioned toward the datapad. "But that presentation is pretty hard to ignore. How much of this did you share with Varrik?"

"Not much. I already knew I was going to turn myself in, so I didn't see the point in going through it all more than once. He'll take me back to Ontariese and I'll explain everything to the tribunal. Varrik can hear it then. Besides, we had other issues to discuss."

"Like the death of your father?" She hated to bring it up, but she could think of nothing else painful enough to sour his disposition.

"Primarily."

When he said nothing more, she prompted, "And were you able to agree on what happened?"

"You just spent the past hour or more with Echo. Didn't she tell you all about it?"

She reached over and slipped her hand into his. "I don't care what Echo believes. Do you still feel that they murdered your father?"

"Varrik ended my father's life. That fact was never in dispute. But South was false just like the other elders. Worse, he was a coward who was running away from the fight. He left his entire tribe behind without a second thought. He was not a worthy leader."

She knew Nazerel was shielding their connection, but occasional bursts of grief and anger bled through. Despite his calm expression, the emotions were as raw and aching as if the tragedy had just taken place.

Before she could find the words needed to comfort him, he gently squeezed her hand. "Am I a fool to expect fair treatment from the Ontarians? They despise Shadow Assassins."

Glad for an easier subject, she happily followed his lead. "They resent Shadow Assassins and they're afraid of Rodytes, but they will listen to what you have to say. This is the first mission I've worked with Lor, but I've known High Queen Charlotte for years. All of the procedures she's instituted during her reign have been fair and impartial. Besides, I'll be there to make sure this is not a witch hunt. If it starts to look like they're out to get you, I'll help you escape."

He offered her a warm smile that burned through the shadows in his eyes. "I'm hoping it won't come to that, but it's nice to know I'll have at least one friend at the City of Tears."

"You said Garin was going to testify. Doesn't that mean you'll have two friends?"

Nazerel pushed back from the table and stood. "Garin can't leave his ship. He'll testify by vidcom."

"Of course. Even on Earth that's likely how it would happen."

He pulled her to her feet and into a loose embrace. "How about a nice hot bath? Creation knows I need to relax."

"Where is this mysterious bathtub and will others be there or just us?" She didn't have a swimsuit and she wasn't getting naked in front of any male except Nazerel.

Rather than explain, he led her into the utility room. "This is only an option in certain cabins. We just happen to be in one of the best."

He issued a verbal command and a good portion of the floor smoothly lowered and reshaped. Soon they stood on the wide rim of a deep, spa-style bathtub. One side created a molded recliner while the other formed a simple bench. "Is this all right? There are several other styles, but I'd have to go look up the commands."

"This is lovely." Then with a cheeky grin she added, "As long as I get to use the recliner."

He laughed as he pulled off his shirt. "We'll figure it out as we go along. Now get undressed." Another command activated the water, which streamed from multiple outlets all over the surface of the tub.

The water only reached his calves when he lowered himself into the tub. She took longer to undress, so the water was knee-deep by the time she joined him. They stood facing each other as they waited for the tub to fill. She wrapped her arms around his neck and he caressed her back, his touch light and still distracted.

"Before we leave tomorrow, I'll need to sever our link."

"Why?" She'd resisted the connection every step of the way, so why did the thought of losing access to his emotions upset her now?

His hand drifted up to the back of her head as he gazed into her eyes. "If the Mystics sense our bond, they'll accuse me of controlling you."

"You don't need a telepathic link to bend me to your will." She whispered the words against his lips, hoping to lure him away from thoughts about tomorrow. "All you need is your incredible mouth."

Her lips pressed against his, warming them, encouraging him, but he wasn't quite ready to abandon their conversation. "They'll question you. Likely have Elias do it. You trust him and you'll tell him things you wouldn't admit to a stranger."

It was obvious he wasn't going to relax until this was settled, so she rested her hands on his shoulders and gave them an affectionate squeeze. "They can interrogate me all they like. I won't say anything that incriminates you. In fact, if you like, I'll tell them that I helped you escape."

"Absolutely not. If Elias senses that you're lying to him, they'll have Varrik scan your memories. Tell them the truth."

"I won't testify against you," she said emphatically.

"And I won't allow you to be punished for something you didn't do." He buried his hand in her hair and claimed her mouth in a passionate kiss. "You're my hostage. You've done nothing wrong. I'll make sure they know that." He kissed her again, preventing her immediate reply.

His mouth was warm, his breath intoxicating and she no longer wanted to argue. She wanted to touch him and be touched by him. She wanted to savor whatever time they had left. The future was too uncertain for them to waste any more time.

He pulled her down into the water and she melted into his embrace. They kissed and touched and kissed some more, neither in a hurry to escalate their passion. He relaxed against the recliner and she straddled his hips, sometimes arching above him, but more often pressing against him skin-to-skin.

"What did you think of Echo?" His lips brushed against her neck as he spoke.

"I'm sprawled on top of you naked and you're thinking about Echo? Should I be jealous?"

He cupped both her breasts and nipped the side of her throat. "I'm trying to think about anything except how badly I want to be inside you."

"We've got all night." She reached down between their bodies and guided him to her entrance. "We'll go slowly next time." His entire body tensed as she lowered herself onto his cock. She closed her eyes and savored the sweet fullness as it pressed deeper and deeper into her core. "Better?"

"Not yet." He grabbed her hips and pushed her up then pulled her back down. Creating a rocking motion, he maximized the slide of her body over his. "Now *this* is better."

She braced herself against his shoulders and pushed up, giving him access to her aching breasts. They couldn't kiss in this position, but everything else felt so perfect that it didn't matter. His lips fastened onto one nipple as he teased the other with his fingers, then he switched sides. All the while she rode him, reveling in the control he seldom allowed her.

His mind opened, filling her with longing and tenderness. Desire was obvious in his gaze, but the affection always surprised her. Outwardly Nazerel was gruff and unyielding, which made his warmth even more precious.

Wanting him to understand how much his caring meant to her, she pushed her emotions into his mind, revealing her love without hesitation or reserve. He moaned and bucked, trusting up into her with possessive urgency. She responded just as aggressively.

"Next time..." His fingers dug into her hips and tension rippled across his torso. "I'll make it last." He threw his head back and arched beneath her, filling her completely.

She watched him, feeling him inside her mind and body. His overwhelming need thrilled her even though her arousal had just begun to build. He came in shuddering waves. She felt him jerk deep inside her and a fresh rush of love flooded her mind. He wrapped his arms around her and pressed her against his wildly beating heart.

"That was downright pathetic," he muttered as she collapsed across his chest.

Knowing he couldn't see her face, she allowed herself to smile. "I started it and, as I said, we've got all night."

Nazerel brushed the damp hair back from Morgan's face and she pushed herself up again, not all the way vertical, like she'd been before, but far enough so they could see each other. She was so damn beautiful it almost hurt to look at her. With her cheeks flushed and her breasts bare, she looked like a fertility goddess, ripe and ready for more. He'd be more than happy to oblige her as soon as he caught his breath, but the future still loomed in the distance, threatening to consume them.

"I want you to tell the Tribunal the truth, but perspective is a curious thing. I suppose I should at least hear your version of the events."

Her inner muscles clamped down on his length, encouraging his recovery. "You want to talk about this *now*?"

He laughed, sliding his hands from her hips to her breasts and back. "Indulge me and I'll make it worth your while."

She sat up, balancing her weight on her legs. "All right. You grabbed me during the raid, not knowing who I was. It had been your intention to release me, but Dekker said my name over the radio so you realized I could likely release you from the collar."

"I still can't believe how long you held out. You are one incredibly stubborn female." His hands drifted up her sides and over her breasts, his gaze leading the way.

"You're not the first to tell me that and it's doubtful you'll be the last." Suddenly restless, she crawled off his lap and moved to the bench across from him.

He'd obviously upset her and that hadn't been his intention. Still, he needed to know what she would say before he tried to recapture the romantic mood. "What happened after I figured out who you are?"

"It became a battle of wills, which I eventually lost. You didn't want to bring me with you, but by that point I knew too much to leave behind." She droned on as if she were reciting a shopping list.

"Did you try to escape?"

She shot him an annoyed look before sinking deeper into the water. "Repeatedly, but I knew I was screwed once you disabled the collar."

Their connection had existed even with his powers suppressed, but reminding her of the fact would only irritate her further. He didn't want to spend their last few hours together angry with each other. However, this was important. She needed to understand what she'd be facing when they returned. Her friends would expect her to be relieved and joyful that she'd finally been rescued.

"Elias will try to convince you that I've brainwashed you." He caught her gaze before he went on. "He'll say I used a combination of physical and emotional techniques to make you feel things that aren't real."

"What I feel for you is none of their business."

Nazerel shrugged then finger-combed his hair back from his face. "I doubt Elias will agree. He might even insist that you need to be deprogramed."

She straightened, her breasts bobbing just below the water's surface. "Then I'll tell him I've learned that the government I work for is corrupt and duplicitous. Where I go and with whom I choose to spend my time is now irrelevant because I have no interest in continuing to be their puppet."

He finally smiled and held out his hand. "You don't have to convince me, love. Just be aware that they aren't going to smile and wish you well."

Her expression remained tense, yet she returned to his side of the tub and allowed him to pull her down on top of him. She tried to return to her seated position, but he had something else in mind. He helped her spread out with her back pressed against his front and her head pillowed on his shoulder.

"My questions got you all wound up. Now I'm going to have to help you relax."

"Good luck with that." She shifted restlessly against him, her ass undulating against his rapidly hardening cock. "This position isn't conducive to relaxation."

"Nonsense." He drew her arms up. "Grab ahold of my shoulders or lock your fingers behind my neck." She grabbed his shoulders. He ran his hands down the underside of her arms, slowly, moving over her flesh like the water surrounding them. "Close your eyes and stop thinking about anything but the way my hands feel, the heat of my body." *And how much I love you.*

Her sharply indrawn breath assured him she'd heard the declaration. Words of love had gone unspoken between them, yet the emotion was there each time they touched. He cupped one of her breasts and wrapped his other arm around her waist. She remained tense for a moment longer, but gradually relaxed and let her body flow into the contours of his.

"That's right. I've got you." He gently circled her nipple until it pebbled against his thumb. "You're safe with me." She started to lower her arms, but he growled a warning. "Let go and I'll stop touching you."

"But I want to touch you too."

"No." He splayed his fingers across her belly then slowly pushed his hand downward. "You will accept what I give you." His middle finger eased between her folds. "Surrender yourself to me."

"This is torture," she whispered, trapped between his skillful finger and the demanding hardness of his cock.

"Hardly." He nipped her neck then slid her up along his body so his fingers could reach farther between her thighs. "You're going to come around my fingers." He pushed his two middle fingers into her core and rubbed her mound against the heel of his hand. "Then you're going to stand up and straddle my face so I can lick your sweet pussy."

His words had the desired effect. She moaned as her hips rocked, sliding her body along his fingers and grinding her clit against his hand. He shifted his arm to just below her breasts, allowing him greater control over her movements. She rode his fingers with single-minded purpose as her head tossed against his shoulder.

"Now." He increased the pressure of his hand. "Come for me now."

Her inner muscles gripped his fingers as release throbbed through her body. He prolonged the spasms with the motion of his hand while he drank in her pleasure.

When the shudders finally stopped, she sat up and reached between his legs.

"No you don't." He caught her wrist and moved her hand back to his shoulder. "I'm not finished with you yet." He slid down along the lounger until his head was just out of the water. Then he urged her up and around. "Put your knees on my shoulders and brace yourself against the edge of the tub."

"I'll break my neck or drown you—or both," she cried.

"I'll help you." He pulled her closer and then closer still, guiding her up along the length of his body. Soon she was more or less kneeling on his chest and only her calves remained in the water. "Almost there." He caught the backs of her knees and pulled her legs apart.

She gasped then laughed as he stubbornly urged her onward. "Can't we just..." She was laughing too hard to complete the question.

Maneuvering one knee onto his shoulder and then placing the other, he soon had her straddling his face. She braced herself against the wall rather than the edge of the tub, but he finally had her where he wanted her.

His scent was still distinct on her flesh, but her taste was clean and evocative. He traced her slit until she began to rock against his mouth, then he became more demanding. His lips gently sucked and his tongue explored every crease and crevice.

You're so sweet. I never tire of your taste.

She responded with a surge of affection, but was unable to form specific words.

Thrilled by her obvious arousal, he focused in on her clit, rolling the sensitive nub between his lips and flicking it with his tongue. She jerked and moaned with each caress and he knew she wouldn't last much longer.

He'd meant to make her come again before he took her, but his need was simply too great. Moving with nanite-augmented speed, he slid out from under her, spun toward her then surged into her rippling passage from behind.

She cried out as the sudden fullness pushed her over the edge and her knees slid down to rest on the seat of the lounger. He adjusted the angles of their bodies, bending her forward and pulling her hips up. She grasped the rim of the tub and braced for his next thrust.

"There is nothing better than feeling you come around my cock."

She tightened her inner muscles and matched his next stroke. "Except for when you come too."

Unable to argue with that, he grasped her hip with one hand and her shoulder with the other, keeping his thrusts deep and strong. His primal nature was fully roused, yet his earlier release gave him more control than he'd thought possible.

He showered her with affection as he passionately claimed her body. Their spirits meshed as their bodies melded, creating a joining more intimate than most humans would ever know.

"You are my *morautu*," he whispered into her ear. "My chosen mate. I will protect you with my last breath and dedicate my life to making you happy."

"I love you too." He hadn't expected the words, but they thrilled him to the marrow of his bones. And better yet, she wasn't finished. "I want to spend each day at your side and each night in your bed. I want to grow old with you. Share my entire life with you."

He was so consumed with emotion that he had to see her face. Momentarily separating their bodies, he spun her around then lifted her to the rim of the tub above the bench. He knelt on the bench and she wrapped her legs around his hips, drawing her back into her waiting heat.

They moaned in unison, their mouths finding each other as their bodies resumed passion's dance. He steadied her hips as he thrust between her thighs. She wrapped her arms around his neck and kissed him with incendiary hunger.

Her urgency made him more demanding, made him wild. He caught the back of one of her knees and raised her leg up and out, allowing him to reach even deeper into her body. The angle finally aligned his cock with the sweet spot deep inside her body. She tore her mouth from his and cried out sharply, her inner muscles clenching rhythmically.

Even knowing she'd just come, he couldn't stop. He filled her again and again, hitting her G-spot at the apex of each stroke. She came again, head thrown back and eyes tightly closed. She surrendered completely, nearly limp in his arms as he drove them to one final peak.

With her leg still draped over his arm, he grabbed her ass and thrust his entire length deep into her body. He crushed her to his chest and reclaimed her mouth as their bodies pulsed as one. Pleasure and emotion rolled across their link, completing them as nothing else could.

For a long time they just clung to each other, unable to speak, barely remembering to breathe. Then his lips moved against hers, the kiss slow and tender.

"No matter what happens tomorrow, know that—"

She cut off his words with her mouth and saturated his mind with affection. "Nothing can keep us apart. Nothing. We'll face this together and then live our lives as we were meant to live, *together.*"

He wanted it just as much as she did, but he was a realist. The Ontarians would want their pound of flesh, as would the humans. They had one last battle to fight before they could claim their future. At least, as she said, they would fight the battle together.

Chapter Thirteen

C ity of Tears
 Three weeks later
Morgan sat in the observer gallery of the meeting hall in which the tribunal would soon convene. As Nazerel had predicted, they'd been ripped from each other's arms moments after arriving on Ontariese. Even Varrik had seemed embarrassed by the aggressive actions, but Lor had overseen their arrival personally and he had no intention of losing his prisoner yet again.

The hall was long and narrow with a dramatically arched ceiling supported by exposed timbers. The beams had been intricately carved and highly polished, which seemed odd for a room that hosted military meetings. In fact many of the buildings within the City of Tears seemed needlessly ornate. When Morgan asked Echo about the contradiction, she explained that the City of Tears had once been a leisure colony. Then the Great Conflict made military instillations more important than high-end vacation destinations, so the facility had been repurposed.

"You doing okay?"

Morgan looked up as Echo slipped into the chair beside her. They had the observation gallery to themselves though the main floor was filled to capacity. Only military personnel were allowed on the main floor, which was why she was sitting in the balcony.

"Never better," she grumbled.

"Never mind the dark circles under your eyes and the worry lines etched into your brow?" She placed her arm around Morgan and gave her a squeeze. "This will all be over soon."

Every molecule Morgan possessed hoped that Echo was right. The past three weeks had been the longest and most miserable of her life. She'd endured endless hours of questioning, not just by Elias, but by Lor dar Joon. Nazerel had informed Lor that he didn't require representation, but he would only state his case for the entire tribunal. Exasperated by the brushoff, Lor had focused on her, but she'd been just as frustrating as Nazerel. She calmly answered each of his questions. He just didn't like her answers.

Elias had been a bit more understanding, however, he was still convinced that Nazerel had influenced or compelled her into loving him. It had all be tiresome and predictable.

Silence rolled across the assembly as the members of the tribunal entered from a door to one side of the dais on which they would sit. Each person who addressed them would stand at the podium facing the platform while they could see the speaker as well as the audience. They obviously understood the advantage of power positions.

Most tribunals were officiated by a three-member panel. Only those cases involving a possible death sentence required the full five members. This morning's panel would be made up of Lor, Elias and Overlord Lyrik. Morgan had heard many things about Overlord Lyrik but this was the first time she had seen him. He was younger than she'd imagined, and infinitely more attractive. Overlord had brought to mind a bushy beard, grizzled hair and battle-scared face. Lyrik's hair was long, but golden blonde and he'd pulled the strands back into a thick braid. He also had a beard, yet it was closely clipped and accented his strong jawline. His exact eye color was lost to the distance separating them, but they were light, likely blue or green.

Lyrik sat in the middle, his chair slightly larger than the other two. Lor sat on his right and Elias on Lyrik's left. Lor wore the traditional gray robs of an Ontarian Mystic. Elias had donned a business suit and the overlord wore a forest-green tunic with an intricate gold design. His black pants had been tucked into shiny black boots and a wide belt accented his lean waist. He looked like a Viking jarl about to preside over the yearly "thing".

A melodious chime called the meeting to order and then Nazerel was brought into the hall. Morgan scooted to the edge of her chair, half afraid he'd arrive in chains. He was flanked by armed guards, but to her relief, his hands and legs were unencumbered. He was well groomed and dressed in a suit not unlike the one Elias wore. His head turned sharply to one side then the other. Was he looking for her? Their gazes locked and she blew him a kiss. He smiled and then she spotted the suppression collar around his neck. *Damn.* No wonder they hadn't bothered with restraints.

Dread swept through her as she thought of all he must have suffered during the past three weeks. Confinement, humiliation, endless hours of tedium. It was unlikely he'd been harmed physically. Ontarians preferred head games. She hadn't been a prisoner and Echo had done her best to be good company. Still, Morgan missed Nazerel so badly, her heart literally ached.

"It's my understanding that you'll be representing yourself during these proceedings," Lyrik began. Nazerel stood at the podium, so his back was to Morgan. "Is this correct?"

"It is." Nazerel's voice was calm and strong. He squared his stance and clasped his hands behind his back. Without their link or being able to see his expression, it was hard to tell if he was being respectful or defiant.

She knew he was well-prepared and confident of the outcome, but Morgan missed the insight and instant communication provided by their link. She wanted to know what was going on below the surface and be able to calm him if he grew too angry or encourage him if things looked particularly grim. Mostly, she just wanted to remind him that he wasn't alone. Their link had only been active for a few days, so why did she miss it so badly?

Echo reached over and grabbed her hand. Their immediate connection had deepened over the past few weeks. Despite Varrik's misgivings, Echo was proving to be a real and trusted friend.

"Why have you refused representation?" Lyrik wanted to know.

"I have official documents verifying the facts in this case. I will also have live testimony to further substantiate my claims. Unless there are specific procedures of which I am unaware, I believe I'm capable of presenting this evidence for your consideration."

"Aden Kantar is the prosecutor on this case." Lyrik motioned toward the first row directly behind the podium and the prosecutor stood. He was of medium height and build with short brown hair.

Morgan couldn't see much more than the back of his head, so she turned to Echo. "Who is he? Why was he chosen for this case?"

"He's been around for years and he's highly respected. This is a military tribunal, so Overlord Lyrik would have appointed the prosecutor."

"Do you know Kantar personally?"

Echo shook her head. "Just by reputation."

"Mr. Kantar will detail the offenses of which you are accused," Lyrik told Nazerel. "Then he'll present the evidence upon which the charges were compiled. Once he's finished, you will be allowed to present your defense."

"I understand," Nazerel assured him.

"We reserve the right to request clarification on any information presented and to cross-examine your witnesses. Do you understand that as well?"

"I do."

"Then let's begin." Lyrik motioned to Kantar and the prosecutor moved up to the podium as the guards seated Nazerel in the defendant's box which was offset on the right.

"Nazerel, First son of South, you are accused of desertion, illegally teleporting to the world commonly known as Earth, entering into a treasonous alliance with Princess Sevrin Keire of Rodymia, and assisting in the kidnapping of human females for the purpose of genetic experimentation resulting in death."

"Do you understand these charges?" Lyrik asked.

"I do."

The overlord accepted the acknowledgement with a nod and then motioned to Elias. "The US government is bringing charges against you as well. You will be transported to Earth for those proceedings as soon as this tribunal has concluded."

"Even if I'm acquitted?"

Lyrik tensed at the challenge in Nazerel's tone. "If you are acquitted, Elias has been authorized to determine which, if any of their charges still apply."

"Thank you for the clarification." Even though his tone was meek, Morgan didn't believe the subservience. And, if Lyrik's hostile expression was any indication, neither did the overlord.

"Mr. Kantar will now present the evidence collected by the Mystic Militia supporting the charges."

Morgan leaned over and asked, "Is it Nazerel's responsibility to prove the charges are wrong or does the prosecutor have to prove that he's guilty?"

"Burdon of proof lies with the prosecution, just like in America," Echo whispered in return. "Our version of an arraignment, however, is more purposeful and efficient."

"In what way?"

"The judge who presides over the pre-trial hearing is already familiar with the evidence. So if the accused pleads guilty, they're immediately sentenced. Only those out to prove their innocence move on to the actual trial. Tribunals are a bit more streamlined, but by being here Nazerel is declaring that he is not guilty of these crimes."

Morgan looked at Echo in thoughtful silence for a moment. "Do you share your mother's fascination with the law?" High Queen Charlotte had just finished law school on Earth when she met her life mate and learned that she wasn't even human.

"I do." Echo listened to the presentation for a few moments then elaborated, "It's not just Ontarian's system of justice with me. I've studied the judicial systems on hundreds of planets and I find..." A security drone paused as it swept the perimeter of the room. Echo motioned toward the hovering device. "That's a warning. If we don't hush up, we'll be escorted from the room."

"Seriously?" Morgan glared at the inanimate librarian and fought back the urge to flip it off.

"I'll bore you with my conclusions later."

Morgan sank back in her seat and rubbed the bridge of her nose as the prosecutor began to explain each of the charges against Nazerel. She'd been involved, either directly or indirectly, in most of the events so he didn't say anything she didn't already know.

Kantar's approach was factual, clear—and agonizingly detailed. It took twenty-six days for Kantar to present all the facts. He used visual aids and called sixteen witnesses, all of whom testified via vidcom. Morgan felt like she was watching an excruciating reality television show rather than attending an actual trial. Charts, video clips and computer simulations helped move the case along and still Morgan felt as if Nazerel's turn would never arrive.

"That is all the information I have, sir," Kantar concluded late afternoon on the twenty-sixth day. He'd remained grim and focused through each and every day of the laborious presentation.

"Thank you, Mr. Kantar." The prosecutor took his seat then Lyrik turned to Nazerel. "You declined to cross-examine any of the prosecution's witnesses. Once I've moved on you will lose that opportunity. Are you sure you have no questions for any of these people?"

"There is no reason to prolong this, sir," Nazerel said. "They stated the facts as they saw them. I'm simply privy to information of which none of those people were aware."

"All right. Let the record state that the prosecution has completed their case and the defense will begin tomorrow morning."

"Tomorrow morning?" Morgan leaned back into her chair with a groan. Would this dreadful thing never end?

"Sir, my presentation will take less than an hour," Nazerel informed the overlord. "Would it be possible to continue?"

"Less than an hour?" Lyrik looked as if couldn't decide whether to laugh or berate the upstart defendant. He thought for a moment then said, "You have until five thirty, then I adjourn whether you're finished or not. Begin."

Nazerel stood, straightened his jacket, then moved up to the podium. His ever-present guards shadowed him step for step. Morgan knew what came next. She'd seen the documents and understood how they interacted with the events already described, in painful detail. The only real question was would what Nazerel was about to reveal justify his involvement or would the panel still consider him a criminal?

Using a small, hand-held trigger, Nazerel activated the holo-projector, suspending an image directly in front of the panel. The projector also created a mirror image for the audience to see. "This is my certificate of citizenship from the Rodyte Empire. Please note the date, which is many years before any of the other events took place."

Murmurs rippled through the crowd, but Morgan wasn't sure if they were surprised or angry. She'd expected the crowd to thin as the days wore on. Who were all of these men anyway? Law buffs like Echo or did they all know females who'd been captured by the Shadow Assassins. They didn't seem hostile enough for that, so there was another possibility. Were these the men Nazerel was so determined to offer a better life?

"How did a Rodyte citizen become a Shadow Assassin?" Elias' angry voice drew her attention back to the platform. The question was technically out of order. Only the prosecutor and the overlord were allowed to question the defendant directly. Still, Nazerel explained.

"Actually, it was the other way around. I was born in the Shadow Maze, but my uncle insisted on registering my citizenship. It was always his hope that I would leave the Shadow Assassins. Unfortunately, he died before my father, so my uncle's hope was never realized."

"This will run more smoothly if we save our questions until he has completed his presentation," Lyrik reminded.

"I'm sorry," Elias said, though he still looked suspicious.

"Continue." Lyrik prompted Nazerel with a smooth hand gesture.

"For you to fully understand what happened on Earth, I need to take you back a bit farther."

"How much farther?" Lyrik asked.

"To the night the Shadow Maze was liberated."

Lyrik grasped the armrests of his chair, both his thumbs tapping impatiently. "We're all well acquainted with those events."

"Two things happened that night that directly pertain to my defense."

"Get to the point or this is going to take considerably longer than an hour."

It was only taking so long because Lyrik kept interrupting him. Morgan crossed her legs and then uncrossed them, all the while fighting the impulse to climb down from the gallery and shake the overlord.

"I'll do my best, sir." Nazerel sounded almost sincere. "On the night in question, Varrik and Lor, along with two females and forty-six Shadow Assassins were teleported onto a Rodyte ship. Everyone was rescued and the Shadow Maze was liberated, but one important question remains. Who commissioned the capture of the Shadow Assassins and for what purpose?"

"The Rodyte captain was interrogated at length," Lyrik responded. "He claims that he was hired by the Crown Stirate, but Quinten denies any involvement in the incident whatsoever."

"Stirate Quinten was telling the truth. He had nothing to do with the acquisition, but he was nearly sure he knew who had made the arrangements in his name."

"Sevrin, his niece?" the overlord didn't sound surprised. "We had similar suspicions but we were unable to confirm which of the two had been guilty."

Conversational exchanges like this weren't allowed in an American courtroom, but this wasn't America. Apparently, Ontarian tribunals were less encumbered by rigid procedures.

The image in front of the panel changed as Nazerel moved on. "This is a copy of the correspondence between Stirate Quinton and General Garin Nox. For the sake of transparency, I'll note that General Nox is also my cousin."

Lyrik nodded. "We're all aware of the relationship. Continue."

"When Stirate Quinton's usual sources failed to verify who had arranged the mass kidnapping, he remembered that a member of the Nox family had become a Shadow Assassin. He contacted General Nox and asked if the Nox family had remained in contact with that family member."

Lyrik stroked his beard thoughtfully as he asked, "The Nox family member was your father, Elder South?"

"Correct."

"And had they remained in contact?" Something in the overlord's expression made Morgan wonder if he already knew the answer and was trying to catch Nazerel in a lie. Maybe she was just being paranoid.

"The Nox family had corresponded with my father and later with me. Unlike the majority of the Shadow Assassins, I had freedom to come and go as I pleased. I made frequent trips to Rodymia and spent time with all three of my cousins."

"Was your father aware if these visits?" Lor asked.

"He encouraged them."

"What did the striate want your cousin to do?" Lyrik brought the conversation back on track.

"He wanted the general to recruit a spy from within the ranks of the Shadow Assassins. If Sevrin had attempted to capture fifty Shadow Assassins—as the striate believed—then it stood to reason that she would try again."

The panel grew silent as they scrolled through the entire correspondence which went on for several screens. "The participants use codenames," Elias pointed out. "Do you have anything proving that this conversation took place between General Nox and Stirate Quinton?"

The image changed again. "This is an official statement from Stirate Quinton confirming that I am an operative in the employ of the Rodyte Empire. It also confirms that my assignment was to investigate Sevrin's interest in genetic transmutation in general and the Shadow Assassins in particular." He paused, giving them a moment to read the statement.

"When and how did you connect with Sevrin?" Lyrik wanted to know.

"She contacted me through a messenger until she was convinced that I was a rebellious malcontent who would be easy to manipulate."

"She had no idea about your connection to the Nox family?" A flush crept up along Lor's throat and deepened across his cheeks. His painstakingly constructed case was disintegrating right before his eyes and he didn't like it one bit.

Nazerel shook his head. "If she knew, she never mentioned it to me. She knew I was the alpha hunter from Tribe South and that the other alphas would listen to what I had to say. She didn't seem to care about anything else."

Lor scooted to the edge of his seat, clearly uncomfortable with the direction the information was taking. "You would have us believe that it was an elaborate ploy? You only went along with Sevrin's evil plans because you were trying to catch her in the act?"

"I was operating undercover, which meant I was forced to make certain decisions."

"Like how many humans to sacrifice while you attempted to complete your mission?" Lor's voice rose with each word until he was shouting.

Lyrik reached over and placed his hand on the younger man's arm, silently signaling him to calm down.

"I created a rift between Sevrin and myself, knowing it would give me a reason to disobey her orders. No one under my command harmed any female, human or otherwise. Team South members were never allowed to hunt."

The overlord looked at Lor, clearly shocked by the claim. "Is this true?"

"It depends on your definition of the word hunt." The overlord didn't want him to shout, so Lor snarled instead. "Nazerel stalked Tori and Angie. He followed Angie to another state. And the only reason she wasn't captured was because one of my Mystics was there to protect her."

Nazerel actually chuckled, which enraged Lor even more. "Either I was playing a role or I am the most incompetent hunter in the universe. I used so many excuses not to capture females that Sevrin was starting to wonder if I preferred the company of men."

"There were numerous times you could have ended the pretense before more victims were taken." Though his voice remained even, anger lifted Lor nearly out of his chair. "Do you place no value on human lives?"

"Shortly after you raided the Team North house, I felt that I had gathered enough information to make a case against Sevrin stick. She is a princess after all. She would not have been easy to prosecute on Rodymia."

"No, Rodytes tend to find more direct means of dealing with dissidents," Lyrik muttered.

"As do some Ontarians. Isn't that what you did with Pern Keire?" Nazerel shot back. "Many on Rodymia would like to know how their crown stirate died."

The overlord shot to his feet and stalked to the edge of the dais. "Are you threatening me, boy?"

Silence rolled across the hall, tense and electric. Morgan couldn't move, couldn't believe what she'd just heard. Had Nazerel just accused the overlord of murder or was this a horrifying dream?

Nazerel cleared his throat and rolled his shoulders. "I retract the question and apologize for my disrespect."

Lyrik glared at him for a moment longer then slowly returned to his seat.

"If you had enough evidence to prosecute Sevrin after the Team North raid," Lor digressed. "Why didn't you make your move?"

"That's when I learned about the new lab. The facility was reported to be state-of-the-art, allowing anyone to step in and carry on even if I arrested Sevrin. I knew I couldn't reveal my true purpose until the lab had been located."

Lor couldn't argue with that. It was the same reason he'd remained on Earth for so long.

The device in Nazerel's hand must have vibrated or made a subtle noise. He flipped it over and looked at the display on the opposite side from the trigger. "My witness is ready to testify."

"Your witness?" Lor's smile was tinged with mockery. "Don't you mean your first witness?"

"I only have one." He said it with such certainty that it implied he only *needed* one.

"Proceed," the overlord urged.

The document projection blinked out and a holographic image of Garin Nox materialized in its place. Even from the back the man looked intimidating with his broad shoulders and aggressive stance.

"Good evening, gentlemen." He inclined his head to complete the greeting, voice deep and authoritative. "I'm General Garin Nox and I'd like to verify that Nazerel, First Son of South, has been in my employ for most of the past year. He was working undercover at the request of Stirate Quinton for the purpose of investigating his niece, Sevrin Keire. Therefore, any misconduct on the part of Nazerel must be reported to me and will be dealt with through proper *Rodyte* channels."

"That is unacceptable," Lor snapped, his voice growing loud again. "Nazerel, like all Shadow Assassins, is half Ontarian. He is not immune to Ontarian laws. Besides, diplomatic immunity can only be established if the ambassador, or agent, is working with the permission of the Ontarian Joint Council. I assure you High Queen Charlotte knew nothing about any of this."

"I understand that," Garin assured, "but you're forgetting that this mission took place on Earth."

Elias perked up at that. "Our taskforce knew nothing about this either."

"Perhaps not, but your government did." Garin paused for a moment as if to let the implication sink in. "Nazerel has a statement issued by a top official with Homeland Security confirming that the mission was authorized."

Elias looked at Morgan, his what-the-hell expression unmistakable. She offered him a shaky smile, knowing the uncomfortable revelations had just begun. They'd been duped, used, manipulated by the very government to which they had both dedicated their lives. It was depressing, and humiliating.

"Do you have any questions for me?" Garin asked after a long pause. "My schedule, as always, is hectic."

"I think we have a much clearer picture of the situation," the overlord admitted with obvious reluctance.

"Then I expect this to be resolved as quickly as possible. You have detained my agent for nearly two lunar cycles already and that is ridiculous."

"I understand your concern for your *cousin* and I'll do my best to resolve this quickly." Not even General Nox could browbeat the overlord.

"Hold on," Lor suddenly came back to life. "This might explain Nazerel's activities on Earth, but it doesn't change his original sentence.

He is a member of the Ontarian military who deserted his position. That in itself is a serious crime."

"To join a foreign military, a citizen of Rodymia must first relinquish their citizenship." Garin's voice ground out each word. He was obviously losing patience with the tribunal. "Nazerel's citizenship is still intact, which makes his enlistment null and void, not to mention against interstellar laws that prohibit the pressed service of unwilling participants. Any other questions can be submitted in writing." Garin ended the transmission.

"We will take a short recess." Lyrik motioned the other two toward the antechamber without further explanation.

"What does that mean?" Morgan turned to Echo, feeling exasperated and utterly helpless. "Is this good or bad?"

Nazerel was led back to the defendant's box and allowed to sit.

"If everything Nazerel said is true, it's very good. Lyrik will com Mother and verify that there is nothing more he can do to detain Nazerel."

The casual "Mother" made Morgan smile. She'd been so wrapped up in the trial she'd forgotten that Echo's parents were the two most powerful people on Ontariese, the high queen and head master of the Mystics. "And what will your mother tell him?"

"If the documents are genuine, Lyrik will have no choice but to dismiss the charges and let Nazerel go. In situations like this, it's unfortunate that the defense doesn't present their case first."

Hope surged through Morgan firmly lodging in her heart. *It's almost over, my love. I swear, it's almost over.*

Nazerel had severed their link before they left the *Undaunted*, but something made him turn and look at her. She stood and gripped the railing, no longer unable to sit still.

He mouthed the words "I love you" then turned back around.

Nearly an hour elapsed before the panel returned. All three of the men were grim faced, but none more so than Lor. Morgan wasn't sure why he felt that Nazerel's exoneration was some sort of personal affront, but his resentment was obvious.

"We've confirmed your claims and authorizations through independent channels and it appears that we have a massive misunderstanding." Lyrik's professional mask was firmly in place, so Morgan couldn't tell if he was frustrated or relieved by the outcome.

"Before you pass judgment," Nazerel interjected. "I have one other thing I would like to say."

"I'm about to dismiss all charges. What more could you possibly need to say?"

"I have one final document that I'd like you to consider. It doesn't directly pertain to my situation, but it is closely connected."

Lyrik rubbed his forehead as he said, "This entire proceeding has been irregular, so I'll allow it."

Nazerel triggered the last image and moved to stand beside it. "This is an official offer of political asylum to any member of the Shadow Assassins. The same document has been transmitted to each member of the Joint Council. Stirate Quinton will extend Rodyte citizenship to any former Shadow Assassin who transfers to the Rodyte military and then completes his original sentence without incident."

"Why would Quinton do such a thing?" Lyrik jumped off the dais and approached the image as if a closer view would make the concept clearer. "What does he have to gain by this little stunt?"

Nazerel clasped his hands behind his back again, likely to keep himself from punching the enraged overlord. "It's not a stunt, I assure you. As Lor pointed out, most of the Shadow Assassins are half Rodyte and half Ontarian. When our way of life was abolished, we should have been given a choice between the two worlds that created us. We were not."

"You were given a choice." Lyrik's voice dropped to a menacing growl. "Each Shadow Assassin was allowed to prove his worth and loyalty through service to the military or he could choose to be punished for his crimes."

Nazerel took a step closer and faced off with the overlord. "Which crimes are those?" Morgan held her breath, afraid to watch, yet unable to look away. If Nazerel threw a punch the delicate balance would be shattered and he'd find himself in a detention cell facing insubordination and assault charges. "I was at the original tribunal when it was determined that the soldiers were living life according to the only code of conduct they had ever known. The elders were responsible for the 'crimes' and it was my understanding that they have been punished."

"May I speak, sir?"

Nazerel whipped his head around at the familiar voice. Morgan released her pent-up breath, barely able to believe Varrik had risen to Nazerel's defense. Of course, she had yet to hear what Varrik wanted to say. This might not be a good thing after all.

"Why not," Lyrik emphasized the choice with an elaborate shrug and made his way back to the dais. "Half of the star system has weighed in on this mess."

Varrik moved forward, standing beside Nazerel at the podium. "Nazerel is right."

Echo sucked in her breath so loudly Morgan looked at her. "Are you all right?" she whispered.

"I never thought I'd see this day," Echo whispered back with a cautious smile.

"When the Shadow Maze was liberated decisions were made quickly," Varrik began.

"Four thousand men were waiting on the outcome of those decisions," Lyrik reminded as he returned to his seat. "Things had to move quickly."

"Ontariese is ruled by a Joint Council for a reason," Varrik continued. "Regardless of how wise and well-meaning Queen Charlotte is, she cannot rule as well as a multi-person council. I alone represented the Shadow Assassins. That was not the way it should have been. There were four tribes. All four tribes should have given you input on how they wanted their futures to unfold. Nazerel is not the only one with family members on Rodymia, or Rodyte citizenship for that matter. Many will jump at the opportunity to go home."

"I haven't decided if such an opportunity will be offered." Lyrik folded his arms over his chest and scowled at Varrik. Then he turned back to Nazerel. "Are you quite finished?"

"I am, sir." Nazerel glanced over his shoulder and Morgan caught a glimpse of his smile. "I have nothing more to say in my defense."

"Then this tribunal dismisses all charges. As far as Ontariese is concerned, you are free to go."

The hall erupted in joyous cheers, catching Morgan by surprise. She'd never been sure why so many soldiers had been interested in this case. Now she knew they weren't random soldiers. They were former Shadow Assassins, here to support Nazerel.

"Quiet!" Immediately the ruckus crowd stilled and Lyrik motioned toward Elias. "Does Earth concur with this ruling or would you like to request extradition?"

Extradition? Dread washed over Morgan in a chilling wave. Surely Elias wasn't going to put them through this entire nightmare all over again?

Resentment formed every syllable as Elias muttered, "Earth concurs with your findings. However, I would like to speak with Nazerel before he takes off."

"Then this tribunal is officially adjourned." Lyrik motioned to Lor. "Release him from the suppression collar then report to my office. We have some vid-coms to make."

Lor used the stairs to exit the dais and approached Nazerel at a leisurely pace. He spoke in a calm, quiet voice, Morgan could barely make out. "I have nothing against you personally, but I find this all suspiciously convenient."

Nazerel waited until he released the collar to reply. "I understand your frustration, but every word I spoke was true."

"You've forced us into another corner with this asylum nonsense. I will do my best to prevent it from happening."

"I understand."

Without another word, Lor walked from the room.

"What is Lor's problem?" Morgan asked Echo as they made their way down the stairs leading to the main floor of the meeting hall. "He has acted like this entire thing was a personal attack."

"Lor's uncle was working with the elders and everyone knows it. Since Lor became the head of the House of Joon he has worked tirelessly to repair his family's reputation. Hunting down Nazerel and the other renegade hunters was part of that restoration. This makes it look like Nazerel won, which means Lor lost. He can't help but take this personally."

As they reached the center aisle, Elias came striding toward Nazerel with burning purpose in his gaze.

"Shit." Morgan rushed toward the front of the room. By the time she reached the presentation area, her mate and her best friend stood toe-to-toe speaking in hostile whispers.

"I have never forced myself on any female," Nazerel was saying, which gave her a pretty good idea of how the conversation had begun.

"There are many types of force. I'm not saying you held her down and raped her. I think you compelled her to—"

"He was still collared when we spent our first night together." Morgan intentionally led Elias to the wrong conclusion, but the statement was technically true. "He has forced nothing on me. Well, not since he forced me to abandon my team during a fight."

"I don't care how many times you claim otherwise," Elias argued. "You were his prisoner."

"*Were*, as in I am not his prisoner any longer. You don't have to like it, but I will not testify against him"

Rather than continue a pointless debate, Elias turned back to Nazerel. "Every hunter who captured a human female will pay for his part in her death. Your mission does not excuse their actions."

"I agree."

Elias just stared at Nazerel. Apparently, Elias had expected an argument. After another tense moment, he looked at Morgan again. "Were you briefed by Homeland Security? I understand if you weren't allowed to tell me."

"It's ugly, Elias. The taskforce is basically a front behind which they negotiate with aliens and not necessarily to the good of the general public. Not only did they know about Nazerel, but they were helping Sevrin with her experiments."

"What the hell are you talking about?" Elias raked a hand through his hair, completely disrupting the messy style.

"Flynn has copies of emails proving that Sevrin had backers within the US Government. They allowed us to chase after her shadow while they were helping to cover her tracks. They're using us and I have no intention of allowing it to continue."

"Actually, I meant to speak with you about that," Nazerel cut in. "Garin thinks it could be a serious benefit if we have contacts on the inside and access to certain information when—and if—he decides to bring the battle born to Earth."

"Wait a minute." Elias turned toward Nazerel, instantly hostile again. "Why would a Rodyte general 'bring the battle born to Earth'?"

"Long story." Morgan placed a soothing hand on his forearm as she looked at Nazerel. "Are you suggesting we return to the Bunker and pretend nothing is wrong?"

"For now. It would give you the opportunity to do some digging. You told me you don't have enough to expose the culprits, but at least now you know where to look for more evidence."

"True," she mused. "I really don't like the idea of just walking away."

"So what's with this political asylum shit?" Elias asked Nazerel. "Do you really think the Joint Council will reconsider their original ruling?"

Nazerel nodded toward Echo who was politely loitering a few feet away. "Why don't we ask someone who is well acquainted with the High Queen?"

Elias smiled at Echo then moved over so she could join their informal circle.

"Any guesses how your mother will rule?" Morgan asked her new friend.

"Varrik's argument was compelling and Mother loves nothing better than a good debate. As long as the former Shadow Assassins are still required to fulfill the original terms of their sentences, I think the Joint Council will allow the choice."

"Besides the last thing Ontariese needs is another four thousand single males?" Nazerel punctuated the question with a charming smile.

"Well, there is that." Echo returned his smile.

Nazerel stilled and Morgan followed the direction of his suddenly guarded stare. Varrik stood in nearly the same place his mate had been a few moments before. Without saying a word he held out his hand toward Echo.

"Thank you," Nazerel broke the tense silence. "Your testimony was unexpected and invaluable."

Varrik nodded and Morgan thought that would end it. Then Varrik sighed. "I know things can never be as they were, but our mates seem to enjoy each other's company. I'd like for us to be part of your new life—as soon as you figure out what and where that is."

"I'll do anything for Morgan." Nazerel smiled and his gaze filled with warmth.

"I'll com you," Echo promised and gave Morgan a quick hug. Then Varrik took Echo's hand and flashed her from the room.

"So, what's left undone?" Elias heaved a sigh as if a significant weight had been lifted from his shoulders. "I'm not sure what we'll do without the Mystic Militia to boss us around."

Morgan smiled. "I think we should enjoy the lull and take advantage of the relative peace for as long as it lasts. We'll use the time to figure out who our real enemies are."

"Sounds good to me." He bent and kissed her on the cheek. "I better make sure the overlord is finished with me." Then to Nazerel he said, "Congratulations."

The next hour passed in a blur of greetings and smiles. Nazerel introduced her to soldier after soldier, each seemed amazed by what he'd accomplished and most said they would take advantage of the opportunity if the Joint Council allowed the Rodyte option. Morgan tried to be patient. Nazerel had worked long and hard to find a compromise that would empower his men. The leadership role might not be official, but it was obvious that these men thought of Nazerel as their leader.

The crowd finally cleared and Nazerel pulled Morgan into his arms, flashing her from the room before anyone else could waylay him. She gasped then laughed as their surroundings came back into focus. They stood on a hilltop overlooking the City of Tears. A spectacular sunset stretched across the far horizon, the layers of purple and blue so different from the orange, red and gold of Earth.

"A little warning would have been nice." Her beaming smile contradicted the criticism.

"Sorry. I had to get out of that place." He paused for a long lingering kiss. "I couldn't wait another minute to do that." He kissed her again. "I missed you."

"I missed you too." She rocked to the balls of her feet and brought his mouth back down to hers. Their lips slid and their tongues stroked as Nazerel slipped into her mind. She opened for him, welcoming him with warmth and joy. He pushed deeper then carefully anchored the link.

Never again will you be without me. He reinforced the vow with the heat of his devotion.

Welcome home. The word triggered a thought and she slowly pulled back until their lips separated. With her hands on his shoulders and her heart fluttering in her chest, she looked into his eyes. "Can you come back to Earth with me or does Garin need you on the *Undaunted*?"

"Garin has much to do before he'll be ready for my assistance. Before he'll be ready for *our* assistance." He amended with a smile. "And we will serve the cause best back on Earth. Now, do I need to say it again?" He pulled her more snugly against his body. "You will never be without me again." And then, just in case she had any lingering doubts, he kissed her with all the love overflowing his heart.

IF YOU ENJOYED THIS BOOK, PLEASE LEAVE A REVIEW

Spinoff series!

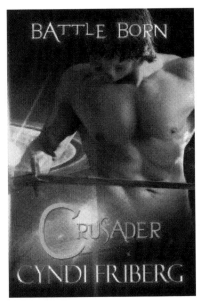

ASHLEY COMES HOME AFTER a long day and finds a spaceman searching her apartment. Before she can call for help, or run like hell, the intruder stabs her and leaves her for dead.

Willing to risk everything for the chance at a better life, Bandar, a battle born soldier, travels to Earth. His superiors believe a geneticist name Daniel Kane holds the key to freedom for Bandar's people, but first they have to find him. Bandar's search leads to Daniel's daughter, Ashley, just in time to save her life. Bandar is so captivated by the fragile human that his need to protect and possess her threatens his mission.

Ashley awakens miraculously healed and filled with questions. Bandar is gorgeous and heroic, but she knows he's full of crap. This isn't the first time she's run across aliens and now she knows it won't be the last. She agrees to help him unravel the secrets surrounding her father's work. Ashley has always believed her father was murdered and now she has a chance to learn the truth. But it's hard to trust Bandar when the brush of his fingers makes her entire body tingle. Their volatile attraction could fulfill her wildest fantasies or open the door for planetary invasion.

Don't miss out!

Visit the website below and you can sign up to receive emails whenever Cyndi Friberg publishes a new book. There's no charge and no obligation.

https://books2read.com/r/B-A-XGQD-LHNCB

BOOKS 2 READ

Connecting independent readers to independent writers.

Printed in Great Britain
by Amazon